uR

D0801668

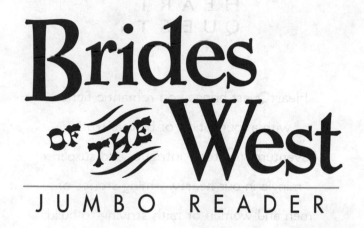

Brides
OF THE West

JUMBO READER

Includes

FAITH · JUNE · HOPE
Lori Copeland

HEART
QUEST™

HeartQuest brings you romantic fiction

with a foundation of biblical truth.

Adventure, mystery, intrigue, and suspense

mingle in our heartwarming stories of

men and women of faith striving to build

a love that will last a lifetime.

May HeartQuest books sweep you

into the arms of God, who longs for you

and pursues you always.

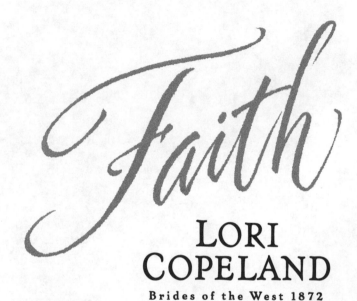

Faith

LORI COPELAND

Brides of the West 1872

CUMBERLAND COUNTY PUBLIC LIBRARY
& INFORMATION CENTER
HOPE MILLS BRANCH LIBRARY
3411 GOLFVIEW DRIVE
HOPE MILLS NC 28348-9998

HEART
QUEST™

Romance fiction from
Tyndale House Publishers, Inc.
WHEATON, ILLINOIS

Visit Tyndale's exciting Web site at www.tyndale.com

Copyright © 1998 by Lori Copeland. All rights reserved.

Cover illustration copyright © 1998 by Michael Dudash. All rights reserved.

Author photo copyright © 1994 by Sothern Studio. All rights reserved.

Scripture quotations are taken from the *Holy Bible*, King James Version.

Editor: Diane Eble

Designer: Catherine Bergstrom

3 in 1 ISBN: 0-7394-0809-7

Printed in the United States of America

*In loving memory
of Tonya Sue Garnsey
and Myrt Petersen.
Your memory lives on
in our hearts.*

Prologue

"You're what?" The tip of Thalia Grayson's cane hit the floor with a whack. Riveting blue eyes pinned Faith Marie Kallahan to the carpet like a sinner on Judgment Day.

Faith swallowed, took a deep breath, and confronted her auntie's wrath with steeled determination. "I'm sorry, Aunt Thalia, but it's done. We took a vote; we're going to be mail-order brides. There's nothing you can say to change our minds."

Thalia's eyes pivoted to Faith's sisters, Hope and June. "Don't tell me you go along with this nonsense."

June nervously twisted a handkerchief around her forefinger. "We've prayed diligently about it."

"Well, I never!" Thalia blustered. The pint-sized figure could turn into thunder and lightning when agitated. Faith didn't relish the coming storm.

A cold wind banged shutters and rattled dead branches of weathered oaks outside the window. Snow lay in dirty patches along leaning fence posts. March wasn't a pretty sight in Michigan.

Faith took a tentative step toward her aunt, hoping to temper her wrath. She knew the news came as a shock, but Aunt Thalia was old, and she couldn't bear the financial burden of three extra mouths to feed. "Aunt Thalia, I know the news is unsettling, but it's the only solution."

Thalia's hand came up to cover her heart. "Marry complete strangers? Thomas's children—mail-order brides? Have you lost your minds? Faith, your papa always said you were rowdier than any two boys put together!

Mail-order brides." Thalia shuddered. "How can you break your auntie's heart like this?"

"Faith. The size of a mustard seed. We are embarking upon this journey with faith that God answers his children's needs." Faith hugged her auntie's stooped frame. "Isn't it wonderful!"

"No, it's not wonderful! It's a terrible idea!"

Faith sighed. Yes, Papa had said she made Belle Starr, the lady outlaw, look like a choir girl, but her tomboyish ways had never hurt anyone. She might favor bib overalls rather than dresses, but the last thing on earth she wanted was to worry or upset anybody—especially Aunt Thalia.

Hope rose from the settee and moved to the hall mirror, fussing with her hair. "Aunt Thalia, it isn't so bad, really. We chose our mates carefully."

"Answering ads like common—" Thalia fanned herself with a hanky. "And just how did you decide who would get what man?"

Hope smiled. "By age, Auntie. Faith answered the first promising response. Then I took the next, then June."

"We've prayed about it, Auntie. Really we did," Faith said.

Opening the magazine in her lap, June read aloud from the classified section they'd answered: *Wanted: Women with religious upbringing, high morals, and a strong sense of adventure, willing to marry decent, God-fearing men. Applicants may apply by mail. Must allow at least two months for an answer.*

Smiling, she closed the publication. "Shortly after Papa's death we decided to answer the ad."

Thalia turned toward the window and made a sound like a horse blowing air between its lips. "Father, have mercy on us all. Thomas would roll over in his grave if he knew what you're planning."

More proud than ashamed for solving what once seemed an impossible situation, Faith calmly met her sisters' expectant gazes. They had agreed. Becoming mail-order brides was the only reasonable way to handle their circumstances. Aunt Thalia was approaching seventy. Although her health was stable, her financial condition wasn't. Her meager funds were needed for her own welfare.

Papa's untimely death had shocked the small community. Thomas Kallahan had pastored the Cold Water Community Church for twenty-six years. While in the midst of a blistering "hellfire and damnation" sermon one Sunday morning three months earlier, Thomas had keeled over dead.

The impassioned minister dead, at the age of forty-two. The community could scarcely believe it.

Mary Kallahan had died giving birth to June sixteen years earlier. With Thomas gone, Hope, Faith, and June—the youngest, so named because Thomas had felt anything but charitable toward the baby at birth—had no one but Aunt Thalia.

Aside from his deep, consistent faith, Thomas had left his daughters with nothing.

Faith had taught school in the small community while Hope and June had taken in sewing and accepted odd jobs. Each had a small nest egg they had earned, but their combined funds could not support a household on a continual basis. For now, they lived with Thomas's elderly sister, Thalia, aware that the arrangement was temporary. Faith had reasoned that they were grown women; they should be starting their own families.

At nineteen, Faith was the oldest. Hope was seventeen; June, sixteen. It was high time the girls found suitable husbands, an unenviable task for any woman in a small community where men were either married, too young, or too senile to be considered matrimonial prospects.

Kneeling beside Thalia's chair, Faith tried to calm her. "We'll be fine, Aunt Thalia. Why—" she glanced at Hope for support—"God truly must be smiling down upon us, for all three of us found a husband within a month."

Hope brightened. "Three fine gentlemen have asked for our hands in marriage."

"Rubbish." Thalia sat up straighter, adjusting her spectacles. "You've agreed to go off with three strangers! Three men you know nothing about! What has Thomas raised? A gaggle of hooligans?"

"They're not complete strangers," June pointed out. "All three gentlemen have sent letters of introduction."

"Hrummph. Self introductions? I hardly think they would write and introduce themselves as thieves and misfits. There's no telling what you're getting into." Her weathered features firmed. "I cannot permit this to happen. As long as there's a breath left in me, I will see to my brother's children. Families bear the responsibility to care for one another. The Lord says those who won't care for their own relatives are worse than unbelievers."

Stroking her aunt's veined hand, Faith smiled. "We know you would care for us, Aunt Thalia, truly. And it would be ideal if there were three young gentlemen in Cold Water in need of wives, but you know there isn't an eligible man within fifty miles." The good Lord knew Papa had tried hard enough to get his daughters married.

Thalia's lips thinned to a narrow line. Her blue eyes burned with conviction. "Edsel Martin lost his wife a few months back. Edsel's a good man. Hardworking. Deacon in the church."

"Sixty years old," June muttered under her breath.

"Merely a pup," Thalia scoffed. "Lots of good years left in Edsel."

Edsel made Faith's skin crawl. She'd never seen him wear anything other than faded overalls and a soiled shirt to cover his enormous belly. His pea-soup-colored eyes cut right through a person. She shuddered. The corners of his mouth were always stained with tobacco spittle.

Edsel was looking for a wife all right, and she only needed to be breathing to meet his criteria.

Faith was plain worn out avoiding Edsel's invitations. The past two Sunday mornings, he'd been insistent that she accompany him home for dinner. She knew full well she'd end up cooking it, but she went, cooked, cleaned his kitchen, then hung his wash, even though it was the Sabbath. And Edsel a deacon! It wasn't the kind of "courting" she'd expected.

Edsel might be a "good man," but Faith wanted a young, strong husband to work beside. She could chop wood, plow a field, or build a fence as well as any man. What she didn't do well were womanly things: cooking, cleaning, tending house. She'd attracted a fair share of criticism because of it, but she was a tomboy at heart and just once she'd like to find a man who valued her help—her ability to seed a field or shoe a horse as good or better than any man.

A gust of wind rattled the three-story house, sending a shower of sparks spiraling up the chimney. Faith shivered, rubbing warmth into her arms. Aunt Thalia's parlor was always cold. Bare tree branches rapped the windowpane; frigid air seeped through the cracks.

Hope left the mirror to kneel beside Faith at Thalia's feet. Arranging the old woman's shawl more securely around her shoulders, Faith said softly, "When I get settled, I'll send for you, Aunt Thalia. You can come live with me."

"Hrummph." Thalia looked away. "Best not be making such promises until you know how your new husband feels about that."

"Oh, I can tell by his letter he is most kind." Frosty shadows lengthened into icy, gray twilight as Faith shared her future husband's promises of a good life and a bright future when they married. "He said he would always look after me, I would want for nothing, and he promised to be a wonderful papa to our children."

Hoarfrost covered the windowpanes as darkness enveloped the drafty old Victorian house. Patches of ice formed on the wooden steps. A pewter-colored sky promised heavy snow by dawn as the women knelt and held hands, praying for their future—a future none could accurately predict.

"Father," Faith prayed, "be with each of us as we embark upon our journeys. Stay our paths and keep us from harm. We pray that we will be obedient wives and loving mothers. Thank you for answering our prayers in a time when we were most needy of your wisdom and guidance. Watch over Aunt Thalia, guard her health, and be with her in her times of loneliness. May we always be mindful that thy will be done, not ours." With bowed heads and reverent hearts, they continued to pray, silently.

Finally, June rose and lit the lantern. Mellow light filtered from the coal-oil lamp, forming a warm, symmetrical pattern on the frozen ground outside the parlor window.

Tonight was Faith's turn to fix supper. She disappeared into the kitchen while June and Hope kept Thalia company in the parlor.

Pumping water into the porcelain coffeepot, Faith listened to Hope's infectious laughter as she thumbed through the family album, regaling Thalia with stories of happier times.

Beautiful Hope.

Faith the tomboy.

June the caregiver.

Frowning, Faith measured coffee into the pot and thought about the decision to marry and leave Cold Water. She ignored the tight knot curled in the pit of her stomach. Weeks of prayer and thought had gone into her decision. She had prayed for God's wisdom, and he had sent her an answer. Nicholas Shepherd's letter gave her hope. Nicholas needed a wife, and she needed a husband. She hoped the union would develop into one of loving devotion, but she would settle for a home with a godly man. During prayer she had felt God's guidance for her to embark upon this marriage.

The idea of leaving Cold Water saddened her. Aunt Thalia wouldn't enjoy good health forever. Who would care for Thalia when she was gone? And who was this man she was about to marry—this Nicholas Shepherd? She really knew nothing about him other than that he lived with his mother in Deliverance, Texas, a small community outside San Antonio, and that he penned a neat, concise letter.

Sighing, she pushed a stray lock of hair off her cheek. Not much to base a future on. Through correspondence she'd learned Nicholas was in his midthirties and a hard worker. She was nineteen, but the difference in their ages didn't bother her; she found older men more interesting. And she was a hard worker. She smiled, warming to the idea of a husband who would always treat her well, who would not allow her to want for anything, and who promised to be a wonderful papa to her children. What more could a woman ask?

She would work hard to be an obedient wife to Nicholas Shepherd. The Lord instructed wives to obey their husbands, and that she would. It bothered her not a whit that Nicholas's mother would share their home. Mother Shepherd could see to household duties, duties Faith abhorred, while Faith worked beside her husband in the fields. The smell of sunshine and new clover was far more enticing than the stench of cooking cabbage and a tub full of dirty laundry.

Laying slices of ham in a cold skillet, Faith sobered, realizing how very much she would miss her sisters. Hope would travel to Kentucky, June to Seattle. She herself would reside in Texas.

Worlds apart.

The thought of June, the youngest sibling, brought a smile to her face. June was impulsive, awkward at times, but with a heart as big as a ten-gallon bucket. Unlike Hope, June wasn't blessed with beauty; she was plain, a wallflower, some said, but with patience a saint would envy. June possessed a sweet, inner light superior to her sisters'. June was the caretaker, the maternal one. Faith prayed daily that June's husband would be a man who would value June's heart of gold and would never break her spirit.

Faith asked the Lord for patience for Hope's soon-to-be husband. He would need plenty of it. The family beauty was shamelessly spoiled. Hope assumed the world revolved around her wants and wishes. Hope's husband would need to be blessed with a wagonload of fortitude to contend with his new bride.

Nicholas Shepherd would need a hefty dose of patience himself. Those who knew Faith said she could be cheerful to a fault, but she knew she had to work hard at times to accept God's will. It wasn't always what she expected, and she didn't always understand it.

The sisters would exchange newsy letters and Christmas cards, but Faith didn't want to think about how long it would be before they saw each other again.

Sighing, she realized the new lives they each faced were fraught with trials and tribulations, but God had always fulfilled his promise to watch over them. He had upheld them through Mama's death, overseen June's raising, and filled times of uncertainty with hope of a brighter tomorrow. When Papa died, they'd felt God's all-caring presence. He was there to hear their cries of anguish and see them through the ordeal of burial. Faith had no less faith that he would continue to care for them now.

Faith.

Papa had always said that faith would see them through whatever trials they encountered.

Besides—she shuddered as she turned a slice of ham—anything the future held had to be more appealing than Edsel Martin.

Chapter One

Deliverance, Texas
Late 1800s

 S HE'S late." Liza Shepherd slipped a pinch of snuff into the corner of her mouth, then fanned herself with a scented hanky.

Nicholas checked his pocket watch a fourth time, flipping it closed. Mother was right. His bride-to-be was late. Any other day the stage would be on time. He poked a finger into his perspiration-soaked collar, silently cursing the heat. He'd wasted half a day's work on Miss Kallahan, time he could ill afford. Fence was down in the north forty, and ninety acres of hay lay waiting to fall beneath the scythe before rain fell. He glanced toward the bend in the road, his brows drawn in a deep frown. Where *was* she?

Calm down, Nicholas. Work does not come before family

obligations. Why did he constantly have to remind himself of that?

A hot Texas sun scorched the top of his Stetson. Fire ants scurried across the parched soil as the town band unpacked their instruments. Tubas and drums sounded in disjointed harmony. He wished the town wouldn't make such a fuss over Miss Kallahan. You'd think he was the first man ever to send for a mail-order bride—which he wasn't. Layman Snow sent for one a year ago, and everything between the newlyweds was working out fine.

Horses tied at hitching posts lazily swatted flies from their broad, sweaty rumps as the hullabaloo heightened.

High noon, and Deliverance was teeming with people.

Men and women gathered on the porch of Oren Stokes's general store. The men craned their necks while womenfolk gossiped among themselves. A few loners discussed weather and crops, but all ears were tuned for the stage's arrival.

Nicholas ignored the curious looks sent his direction. Interest was normal. A man his age about to take a wife fifteen years his junior? Who wouldn't gawk? Running a finger inside the rim of his perspiration-soaked collar, he craned to see above the crowd. What was keeping that stage? It would be dark before he finished chores. He stiffened when he heard Molly Anderson's anxious whispers to Etta Larkin.

"What is Nicholas thinking—taking a wife now?"

"Why, I can't imagine. He owns everything in sight and has enough money to burn a wet mule. What does he want with a wife?"

"I hear he wants another woman in the house to keep Liza company."

"With the mood Liza's in lately, she'll run the poor girl off before sunset."

"Such a pity—the Shepherds got no one to leave all that money to."

"No, nary a kin left."

Nicholas turned a deaf ear to the town gossips. What he did, or thought, was his business, and he intended to keep it that way.

A smile played at the corners of his mouth when he thought about what he'd done. Placing an ad for a mail-order bride wasn't something he'd ordinarily consider. But these were not ordinary times. In the past two years since his father had died, he and Mama had been at loose ends.

Eighteen years ago he'd thought love was necessary to marry. Now the mere thought of romance at his age made him laugh. He'd lost his chance at love when he failed to marry Rachel.

Looking back, he realized Rachel had been his one chance at marital happiness. But at the time, he wasn't sure he was in love with her. What was love supposed to feel like? He'd certainly been fond of her, and she'd gotten along well with Mama—something not many could claim, especially these days. Rachel was a gentle woman, and in hindsight he knew he should have married her. He had come to realize that there was more to a satisfying union than love. Mama and Papa's marriage had taught him that love of God, trust, the ability to get along, mutual respect—those were the important elements in a marriage. Abe Shepherd had loved Liza, but even more, he had respected her. Nicholas knew he could have built that kind of relationship with Rachel if he had acted before it was too late.

Well, water over the dam. Rachel had married Joe Lanner, and Nicholas had finally faced up to the knowledge that love had passed him by. He would turn thirty-five in January, and he had no heir. There was no blood kin to carry on the Shepherd name. No one to leave Shepherd land and resources to.

Mama thought he'd lost his mind when he sent for a mail-order bride, and maybe he had.

He smiled as he recalled her tirade when he told her what he'd done—"Why on God's green earth would you want to complicate our lives by marryin' a stranger?"

Why indeed? he thought. God had blessed him mightily. He could stand at the top of Shepherd's Mountain, and for as far as the eye could see there was nothing but Shepherd land.

Shepherd cattle.

Shepherd pastures.

Shepherd outbuildings.

Some even said the moon belonged to Shepherd—Shepherd's Moon, the town called it, because of the way it rose over the tops of his trees, beautiful, noble in God's glory. God had been good to him, better than he deserved. He owned all he wanted and more, yet at times he felt as poor as a pauper.

The emptiness gnawed at him, a misery that no abundance of material possessions could assuage. Where was the love he should have known? Rachel had walked through his life, then walked out of it. Had he been so busy acquiring material wealth that he let the one missing ingredient in his life, the love of a woman, slip past him? The question haunted him because he knew the answer: He had let Rachel walk away and marry a man who, rumor had it, now drank and mistreated her. He should have seen it coming—Joe was not a godly man. But he'd done nothing to stop her, and now he had to watch her suffer for his mistake.

There were other women in the town who would have given anything to marry Nicholas Shepherd, but he had never loved any of them. Then, after his father died and Mama became so unlike herself—so moody, so irritable, so stingy—he didn't think anyone would put up with her. At the same time, he wondered if what she needed more than anything was another woman around to talk with, get her mind off her grief. He began to think that maybe he should marry—not for love, but for other reasons. To have someone to keep Mama company, help her around the house. Mama wouldn't think of hiring help, though they could afford it. But maybe a daughter-in-law would be a different matter.

Then there was the matter of an heir. What good was all his fortune if he had no one to leave it to? Perhaps a daughter-in-law, and eventually grandchildren, would help Mama and make all his hard work mean something. He had amassed a fortune, and it would be a shame if no blood kin were able to enjoy it.

He had been praying over the matter when he'd come across the ad in the journal for a mail-order bride, and the thought intrigued him. The answer to his problem, and his prayers, suddenly seemed crystal clear: He would send for a mail-order bride. Much like ordering a seed catalogue, but with more pleasant results. He would, in essence, purchase a decent, Christian woman to marry with no emotional strings attached.

This marriage between Miss Kallahan and him would not be the covenant of love that his parents had had; this was a compromise. He needed a wife, and according to Miss Kallahan's letters, she was seeking a husband. He had prayed that God would send him a righteous woman to be his helpmate. To fill his lonely hours. Someone who would be a comfortable companion. Love didn't figure into the picture. When Miss Kallahan accepted his proposal, he accepted that God had chosen the proper woman to meet his needs.

Admittedly, he'd grown set in his ways; having a wife underfoot would take some getting used to. He valued peace and quiet. What his new bride did with her time would be up to her; he would make no demands on her other than that she help Mama around the house, if

Mama would permit it. And he did like the thought of children—eventually—although he wasn't marrying a brood mare.

Mama didn't seem to care about anything anymore. She still grieved for Papa, though he'd been dead almost two years now. Nicholas's fervent hope was that having another woman in the house, someone Mama could talk and relate to, would improve her disposition, although he wasn't going to kid himself. He couldn't count on Mama's taking to another woman in the house. But as long as Faith understood her role, the two women should make do with the situation.

Removing his hat, he ran his hand through his hair. What was keeping the stage?

"Brother Shepherd!" Nicholas turned to see Reverend Hicks striding toward him. The tall, painfully thin man always looked as if he hadn't eaten a square meal in days. His ruddy complexion and twinkling blue eyes were the only things that saved him from austerity. Vera, a large woman of considerable girth, was trying to keep up with her husband's long-legged strides.

"Mercy, Amos, slow down! You'd think we were going to a fire!"

Reverend paused before Nicholas, his ruddy face breaking into a congenial smile. Turning sixty had failed to dent the pastor's youthfulness. "Stage hasn't gotten here yet?"

"Not yet." Nicholas glanced toward the bend in the road. "Seems to be running late this morning."

The Reverend turned to address Liza. "Good morning, Liza!" He reached for a snowy white handkerchief and mopped his forehead. "Beast of a day, isn't it?"

Liza snorted, fanning herself harder. "No one respects time anymore. You'd think all a body had to do was stand in the heat and wait for a stage whose driver has no concept of time."

Reverend stuffed the handkerchief back in his pocket. "Well, you never know what sort of trouble the stage might have run into."

Vera caught Liza's hand warmly and Nicholas stepped back. The woman was a town icon, midwife and friend to all. When trouble reared its ugly head, Vera was the first to declare battle.

"We missed you at Bible study this morning. Law, a body could burn up in this heat! Why don't we step out of the sun? I could use a cool drink from the rain barrel."

"No, thank you. Don't need to be filling up on water this close to dinnertime." Liza's hands tightened around her black parasol as she fixed her eyes on the road. "Go ahead—spoil your dinner if you like. And I read my Bible at home, thank you. Don't need to be eatin' any of Lahoma's sugary cakes and drinkin' all that scalding black coffee to study the Word."

"Well, of course not—" The Reverend cleared his throat. "I've been meaning to stop by your place all week, Liza. We haven't received your gift for the new steeple, and I thought perhaps—"

Scornful eyes stopped him straightway. "We've given our tenth, Reverend."

A rosy flush crept up the Reverend's throat, further reddening his healthy complexion. "Now, Liza, the Lord surely does appreciate your obedience, but that old steeple is in bad need of replacement—"

Liza looked away. "No need for you to thank me. The Good Book says a tenth of our earnings." Liza turned back to face the Reverend. "One tenth. That's what we give, Reverend."

Reverend smiled. "And a blessed tenth it is, too. But the steeple, Liza. The steeple is an added expense, and we sorely need donations—"

"There's nothing *wrong* with the old steeple, Amos! Why do you insist on replacing it?"

"Because it's old, Liza." Pleasantries faded from the Reverend's voice as he lifted his hand to shade his eyes against the sun. His gaze focused on the bell tower. "The tower is rickety. It's no longer safe—one good windstorm and it'll come down."

"Nonsense." Liza dabbed her neck with her handkerchief. "The steeple will stand for another seventy years." Her brows bunched in tight knots. "Money doesn't grow on trees, Reverend. If the Lord wanted a new steeple, he'd provide the means to get it."

The Reverend's eyes sent a mute plea in Nicholas's direction.

"Mama, Reverend Hicks is right; the tower is old. I see no reason—"

"And that's precisely why *I* handle the money in this family," Liza snapped. She glowered toward the general store, then back to Vera. "Perhaps a small sip of water won't taint my appetite." She shot a withering look toward the road. "A body could melt in this sun!"

An expectant buzz went up and the waiting crowd turned to see a donkey round the bend in the road. The animal advanced toward Deliverance at a leisurely gait. Nicholas shaded his eyes, trying to identify the rider.

"Oh, for heaven's sake. It's just that old hermit Jeremiah," Liza muttered. "What's that pest doing here?"

Nicholas watched the approaching animal. Jeremiah Montgomery had arrived in Deliverance some years back, but the old man had kept to himself, living in a small shanty just outside of town. He came for supplies once a month and stayed the day, talking to old-timers who whittled the time away on the side porch of the general store. He appeared to be an educated man, but when asked about his past, he would quietly change the subject. The citizens of Deliverance were not a curious lot. They allowed the hermit his privacy and soon ceased to ask questions. Jeremiah neither incited trouble nor settled it. He appeared to be a peaceful man.

"Who's that he's got with him?" Vera asked, standing on tiptoe.

The animal picked its way slowly down the road, its hooves kicking up limpid puffs of dust as it gradually covered the distance. The crowd edged forward, trying for a better look.

"Why—it looks like a woman," Reverend said.

As the burro drew closer, Nicholas spotted a small form dressed in gingham and wearing a straw bonnet, riding behind Jeremiah. A woman. His heart sank. A *woman*. A woman stranger in Deliverance meant only one thing. His smile receded. His bride-to-be was arriving by *mule*.

Nicholas stepped out, grasping the animal's bridle as it approached. "Whoa, Jenny!" His eyes centered on the childlike waif riding behind the hermit. She was young— much younger than he'd expected. A knot gripped his midsection. A tomboy to boot. Straddling that mule, wearing men's boots. The young girl met his anxious gaze, smiling. Her perky hat was askew, the pins from the mass of raven hair strung somewhere along the road.

"You must be Nicholas Shepherd."

"Yes, ma'am." His eyes took in the thick layers of dust obliterating her gingham gown. The only thing that saved the girl from being plain was her remarkable violet-colored eyes.

Jeremiah slid off the back of the mule, offering a hand of greeting to Nicholas. Nicholas winced at the stench of wood smoke and donkey sweat. A riotous array of matted salt-and-pepper hair crowned the old man's head. When he smiled, deep dimples appeared in his cheeks. Doe-colored eyes twinkled back at him as Nicholas accepted

Jeremiah's hand and shook it. "Seems I have something that belongs to you."

Nicholas traced the hermit's gaze as he turned to smile at his passenger.

Offering a timid smile, she adjusted her hat. "Sorry about my appearance, Mr. Shepherd. The stage encountered a bit of trouble."

"Lost a wheel, it did, and tipped over!" The hermit knocked dust off his battered hat. "Driver suffered a broken leg. Fortunate I came along when I did, or this poor little mite would've scorched in the blistering sun."

Nicholas reached up to lift his bride from the saddle. For a split moment, something stirred inside him, something long dormant. His eyes met hers. His reaction surprised and annoyed him. The hermit cleared his throat, prompting Nicholas to set the woman lightly on her feet. He finally found his voice. "Where are the other passengers?"

"Sitting alongside the road. Stubborn as old Jenny, they are. I informed them Jenny could carry two more but they told me to be on my way." Jeremiah laughed, knocking dirt off his worn britches. "They'll be waiting a while. The stage sheared an axle."

"I'll send Ben and Doc to help."

"They're going to need more than a blacksmith and a doctor." Jeremiah took a deep breath, batting his chest. Dust flew. "You better send a big wagon to haul them all to town."

The Reverend caught up, followed by a breathless Liza and Vera. "Welcome to Deliverance!" Reverend effusively pumped the young woman's hand, grinning.

Faith smiled and returned the greeting. The band broke into a spirited piece as the crowd gathered round, vying for introductions. The donkey shied, loping to the side to distance itself from the commotion.

"Nicholas, introduce your bride!" someone shouted.

"Yeah, Nicholas! What's her name?" others chorused.

Reaching for the young lady's hand, Nicholas leaned closer, his mind temporarily blank. "Sorry. Your last name is . . . ?"

She leaned closer and he caught a whiff of donkey. "Kallahan."

Clearing his throat, he called for order. "Quiet down, please."

Tubas and drums fell silent as the crowd looked on expectantly.

"Ladies and gentlemen." Nicholas cleared his throat again. He wasn't good at this sort of thing, and the sooner it was over the better. "I'd like you to meet the woman who's consented to be my wife, Miss Faith . . . ?"

"Kallahan."

"Yes . . . Miss Faith Kallahan."

Sporadic clapping broke out. A couple of single, heart-broken young women turned into their mothers' arms for comfort.

Faith nodded above the boisterous clapping. "Thank you—thank you all very much. It is a pleasure to be here!"

"Anything you ever need, you just let me know," Oren Stokes's wife called.

"Same for me, dearie," the mayor's wife seconded as other friendly voices chimed in.

"Quilting bee every Saturday!"

"Bible study at Lahoma Wilson's Thursday mornings!"

Liza stepped forward, openly assessing her new daughter-in-law-to-be. "Well, at least you're not skin and bone." She cupped her hands at Faith's hips and measured for width. "Should be able to deliver a healthy child."

"Yes, ma'am," Faith said, then grinned. "My hips are

nice and wide, I'm in excellent health, and I can work like a man."

Women in the crowd tittered as Nicholas frowned. What had God sent? A wife or a hired hand?

"Liza!" Vera stepped up, putting her arm around Faith's shoulder. "You'll scare the poor thing to death with such talk. Let the young couple get to know each other before you start talking children."

Children had fit into the equation, of course, but in an abstract way. Now he was looking at the woman who would be the mother of his children.

"Pshaw." Liza batted Vera's hands aside. "Miss Kallahan knows what's expected from a wife."

When Nicholas saw Faith's cheeks turn scarlet, he said, "Mama, Miss Kallahan is tired from her long trip."

"Yes, I would imagine." Liza frowned at Jeremiah, who was hanging around watching the activity. She shooed him away. "Go along, now. Don't need the likes of you smelling up the place."

Jeremiah tipped his hat, then raised his eyes a fraction to wink at her. Liza whirled and marched toward the Shepherd buggy, nose in the air. "Hurry along, Nicholas. It's an hour past our dinnertime."

The crowd dispersed, and Faith reached out to touch Jeremiah's sleeve. "Thank you for the ride. I would have sweltered if not for your kindness."

The old man smiled. "My honor, Miss Kallahan." Reaching for her hand, he placed a genteel kiss upon the back of it. "Thank *you* for accepting kindness from a rather shaggy Samaritan."

Nicholas put his hand on the small of her back and ushered her toward the waiting buggy.

As he hurried Faith toward the buggy, his mind turned from the personal to business. Twelve-thirty. It would be past dark before chores were done.

Nicholas lifted Faith into the wagon, and she murmured thanks. Ordinarily, she would climb aboard unassisted. She wasn't helpless, and she didn't want Nicholas fawning over her. She hoped he wasn't a fawner. But she was relieved to see her husband-to-be was a pleasant-looking man. Not wildly handsome, but he had a strong chin and a muscular build. He looked quite healthy. As he worked to stow her luggage in the wagon bed, she settled on the wooden bench, her gaze focusing on the way his hair lay in gentle golden waves against his collar.

His letter had said he was of English and Swedish origin, and his features evidenced that. Bold blue eyes, once-fair skin deeply tanned by the sun. Only the faint hint of gray at his temples indicated he was older than she was; otherwise, he had youngish features. He was a man of means; she could see that by the cut of his clothes. Denims crisply ironed, shirt cut from the finest material. His hands were large, his nails clean and clipped short. He was exceptionally neat about himself. When he lifted her from the back of Jeremiah's mule, she detected the faint hint of soap and bay-rum aftershave.

She whirled when she heard a noisy thump! Nicholas was frozen in place, staring at the ground as if a coiled rattler were about to strike.

Scooting to the edge of the bench, Faith peered over the wagon's side, softly gasping when she saw the contents of her valise spilled onto the ground. White unmentionables stood out like new-fallen snow on the parched soil. Her hand flew up to cover her mouth. "Oh, my . . ."

Liza whacked the side of the wagon with the tip of her cane. "Pick them up, Nicholas, and let's be on our way." She climbed aboard and wedged her small frame in the middle of the seat, pushing Faith to the outside. "A body could perish from hunger waiting on the likes of you."

Nicholas gathered the scattered garments and hurriedly stuffed them into the valise. Climbing aboard, he picked up the reins and set the team into motion.

As the wagon wheels hummed along the countryside, Faith drank in the new sights. She'd lived in Michigan her entire life; Texas was a whole new world! She remembered how she'd craned her neck out the stagecoach window so long the other passengers had started to tease her. Gone were the cherry and apple orchards, gently rolling hills, and small clear lakes of Michigan. She still spotted an occasional white birch or maple, and there were pines and oaks, but the scenery had changed.

With each passing day on her trip, the landscape had grown more verdant and lush. The closer they drew to San Antonio, the more the countryside transformed. They passed beautiful Spanish missions with tall bell towers, low adobe dwellings covered with vines of ivy, and bushes of vibrant colored bougainvillea. At night the cicadas sang her to sleep with their harmonious *sczhwee-sczee*. Ticks were plentiful, and roaches grew as big as horseflies!

The elderly gentleman seated across from her had leaned forward, pointing. "Over there is mesquite and— look there! There's an armadillo!"

Faith shrank back, deciding that was one critter she'd leave alone.

"It's beautiful land," the gentleman said. "You will surely be happy here, young lady."

Faith frowned, keeping an eye on the animal scurrying across the road. She would if those armadillos kept their distance.

Deliverance gradually faded, and the wagon bounced along a rutted, winding trail. Faith suspected her new family wasn't a talkative lot. Liza sat rigidly beside her on the bench, staring straight ahead, occasionally mumbling under her breath that "it was an hour past her dinnertime." The tall, muscular Swede kept silent, his large hands effortlessly controlling the team.

Faith decided it would take time for the Shepherds to warm to her. She hoped they would be friendlier once they got to know her. Still, the silence unnerved her. She and her sisters had chatted endlessly, talking for hours on end about nothing. Generally she was easy to get along with and took to most anyone, but the Shepherds were going to be a test, she could feel it.

Please, Lord, don't allow my tongue to spite my good sense.

She might not be in love with Nicholas Shepherd, but she had her mind made up to make this marriage work. Once she set her mind to something, she wasn't easily swayed. Besides, she *had* to make the marriage work. She couldn't burden Aunt Thalia any longer, and she sure wasn't going to marry Edsel Martin without a hearty fight. She would work to make Nicholas a good wife, to rear his children properly, and be the best helpmate he could ask for.

She glanced at Liza from the corner of her eye. Now *she* would need a bit more time to adjust to.

Her gaze focused on the passing scenery, delighted with the fields of blue flowers bobbing their heads in the bright sunshine. The colorful array of wildflowers nestled against the backdrop of green meadows dazzled the eye.

She sat up, pointing, excited as a child. "What are those?"

Nicholas briefly glanced in the direction she pointed. "Bluebonnets."

"And those?"

"Black-eyed Susans."

"They're so pretty! Do they bloom year round?"

"Not all year."

The wagon rolled through a small creek and up a hill. Rows upon rows of fences and cattle dotted lush, grassy meadows.

"Just look at all those cattle!" Faith slid forward on the bench. She had never seen so many animals in one place at the same time. "There must be thousands!"

"Close to two thousand," Nicholas conceded.

"Two thousand," she silently mouthed, thunderstruck by the opulent display. Why, Papa had owned one old cow—and that was for milking purposes only. She'd never seen such wealth, much less dreamed of being a part of it.

Nicholas glanced at her. "Shepherd cattle roam a good deal of this area. Do you like animals?"

"I love them—except I've never had any for my own. Papa was so busy with his congregation and trying to rear three daughters properly that he said he had all the mouths he cared to feed, thank you. I remember once Mr. Kratchet's old tabby cat had kittens. They were so cute, and I fell head over heels in love with one. It was the runt, and sickly, but I wanted it so badly."

Sighing, she folded her hands on her lap, recalling the traumatic moment. "But Papa said *no,* no use wasting good food on something that wasn't going to live any-way." Tears welled to her eyes. "I cried myself to sleep that night. I vowed when I grew up, I'd have all the sick kittens I wanted. Mama said, 'Be merciful to all things, Faith'—did I tell you Mama died giving birth to my youngest sister, June—did I mention that in my letter? Well, she did. Faith, Hope, and June—"

Liza turned to give her a sour look.

"June," Faith repeated, her smile temporarily wavering. "Papa was kinda mad at June when she was born. He took his anger out on that poor baby because he thought she'd killed Mama, but later he admitted the devil had made him think those crazy thoughts. It certainly wasn't the work of the Lord. Lots of women die in childbirth, and it's not necessarily God's doing—but by the time Papa got over his hurt, it was too late to call the baby

Charity, like he'd planned to do in the first place. By then, everybody knew June as 'June' and it didn't feel right to call her anything else. Now Mama always said—" Liza's iron grip on her knee stopped her.

She paused, her eyes frozen on the steel-like grip.

"Do you prattle like this *all* of the time?"

"Do you chew snuff all the time?" Faith blurted without thinking. She had never once seen a woman chew snuff. She was fascinated. Perhaps Liza would teach her how—no, Papa would know. And the good Lord.

"Hold your tongue, young lady!" Liza returned to staring at the road.

Faith blushed. "Sorry." She watched the passing scenery, aware she was starting out on shaky footing with her soon-to-be mother-in-law. She vowed to be silent for the remainder of the trip, but she couldn't help casting an occasional bewildered look in Liza's direction. *Mercy!*

What did it hurt to talk about some poor kitten she hadn't gotten in the first place?

Chapter Two

FAITH shifted in the uncomfortable high-back
chair, keeping a close eye on the mantel clock. Minutes
ticked slowly by. Two, two-thirty, three o'clock. Nicholas
had risen before dawn, eaten a large breakfast, then disappeared to the barn. Liza informed Faith shortly after
Nicholas's departure that the marriage ceremony was
scheduled to take place in Reverend Hicks's parlor at four
o'clock.

Faith glanced at the ticking timepiece, worrying her
lower lip between her front teeth. Already 3:12, and her
bridegroom had not appeared.

Twisting her mother's handkerchief in her lap, Faith
watched the doorway, listening for the sound of Nicholas's footsteps. Was he ever coming?

Her gaze meandered through the Shepherd parlor. The

furnishings were nice, but uncared for. Drab cotton sheets covered most of the upholstery. Everything smelled musty. A rose-colored brocade sofa lined the east wall; two rigid-back chairs in a darker hue sat beside a cold fireplace. The room was devoid of warmth, with nothing to counter the wretched dreariness. Faith wondered what pictures had hung where patched places now spotted the wall. There were no colorful rugs to soften the neglected floor. Heavy drapes blocked a faint breeze that struggled to make itself felt through the open window. Homesickness washed over Faith when she recalled Papa and Mama's cheery home. The Kallahans were as poor as church mice, but their rooms were brightly painted and always smelled of soap and sunshine.

In the brief time she'd been here, one thing was clear: Nicholas and Liza Shepherd were not happy people.

Isolated, nonresponsive to one another, they were so different from the laughing, happy family she'd grown up in. Was Aunt Thalia right when she'd warned her not to pursue this plan? Had she made a mistake by coming here? She glanced at Liza, who hadn't moved in hours. Only the occasional staccato click of knitting needles reminded Faith that she wasn't alone.

Supper last night had been an ordeal. Grace was offered for the food and the hands that prepared it. Then silence settled over the table. Not a word was spoken as they ate a heavy fare of meat, potatoes, gravy, and rich yellow butter spread on biscuits.

Faith winced, still feeling the way the food had lodged in her throat. She'd been exhausted from the long stagecoach ride, barely able to keep her eyes open, but she had made an attempt at polite conversation. Her efforts were rewarded by Liza's reprimanding scowl. Faith had fallen silent, concentrating on the mound of overcooked beef in the center of her plate.

After supper they had retired in silence to the parlor,

where Nicholas conducted the daily devotion from 1 Peter. "Beloved, think it not strange concerning the fiery trial which is to try you, as though some strange thing happened unto you: But rejoice, inasmuch as ye are partakers of Christ's sufferings; that, when his glory shall be revealed, ye may be glad also with exceeding joy." He had looked up, his gaze focusing on her for a moment before turning back to the page.

She'd felt her cheeks burn. Why had he looked up at her? Did he already consider her a "trial" in the short time he'd known her? He hadn't addressed her once since they'd arrived at the Shepherd farmhouse. The rambling two-story house towered between the barn and a few weathered outbuildings. Wealth was certainly not evident in the spartanlike setting with neglected flower beds and the house badly in need of a new coat of paint. There wasn't an ounce of friendliness to welcome visitors. Faith was certain a ranch this size would need hired help, but she'd seen no evidence of a bunkhouse or other lodging.

Nicholas had carried her bags to a small, airless front bedroom, then left without a word. Breakfast this morning had been conducted in the same uncommunicative manner. Fat wedges of ham, eggs swimming in bubbly grease, gravy . . . biscuits washed down with scalding, bitter coffee. Neither Nicholas nor Liza had given any acknowledgment that Faith was at the table. They'd kept their heads bent to their plates, their utensils methodically scraping back and forth across the chipped blue-and-white dishes.

Faith's eyes focused on Liza. The drab calico print she had donned this morning had seen more than its share of washings. How old was she? Sixty? Seventy? Faith wasn't a proper judge of such matters. Once she had guessed Eldora Farthington's age to be fifty, and the poor woman had suffered the vapors. Eldora didn't look thirty-five, as she claimed; still, Papa had instructed Faith to pray for forgiveness for offending Eldora's delicate nature.

Liza couldn't be too old. She seemed to have all her faculties. Faith's eyes skimmed the older woman's hair. Faded blonde braids with streaks of silver were stringently pulled back from her face and secured at the crown with a hairpin. Though the afternoon heat was brutal, she kept a worn black shawl fitted tightly around her shoulders.

Faith sighed. Did she truly intend to see her only son married in that getup?

"Do I have a bird on my head?"

Faith jumped at the sound of Liza's clipped query.

"No, ma'am."

"Then stop staring at me."

Faith blushed, embarrassed she'd been caught gawking.

She pressed her lips tightly together, afraid to speak. Her gaze dropped to her own gown, a pretty white Irish linen Aunt Thalia had paid Rose Nelson, Cold Water's only seamstress, to make. For a surprise, June had saved her egg money and purchased a hat the exact same shade from Edmund Watt's mercantile. She'd presented it to Faith with great flourish, and the three sisters agreed Faith would be the most fashionable bride Deliverance had ever seen.

Faith grinned, thinking about June and the laughter they'd shared so easily. The hat and gown made Faith feel like a princess, but in view of Liza's spartan attire she wondered if she weren't overdressed.

She quickly laid her handwork aside when she heard the back door open. Springing to her feet, she absently smoothed the linen into place, then checked her hair, wondering if Nicholas found her comely. She wasn't, of course. She was rather ordinary, and she couldn't hold a candle to Hope's beauty, but she did her best to keep a tidy appearance.

Nicholas walked to the kitchen counter and deposited

a pail of milk. She heard the metal clang of the handle as he dumped the contents into a large pitcher. The mantel clock struck the half hour. They would have to hurry to be at the Reverend's by four o'clock.

Nicholas glanced toward the parlor, and she smiled.

Dismissing her with a curt nod, he disappeared into the small bedroom just off the kitchen. Of course, he would want to change clothes.

He reappeared moments later, still dressed in the clothing he'd milked in. "I'll hitch the wagon."

Faith nodded, her smile fading as she assessed her bridegroom's attire. Wasn't he going to change into something more suitable for his wedding? The old clothes reeked of barnyard waste.

Liza laid her handwork aside and got up. Pulling the shawl snugly above her shoulders, she sidestepped Faith on her way to the kitchen. "Come along. Nicholas can't dally all day."

Dally! Getting married could hardly be considered dallying! Practically biting her tongue, Faith jerked her white hat into place and trailed Liza through the kitchen and out the back door where Nicholas was bringing the horse and wagon around.

Taking her arm, he helped her aboard. A strong current passed between them, and she whirled, surprised. The strength in his hand was like corded steel. His features softened, and he said, "I could hitch the buggy if you would be more comfortable in it."

"No, the wagon is just fine." Their eyes met. "Thank you." His concern was touching. Perhaps he wasn't as formidable as he seemed, just shy.

Liza settled herself in the middle of the bench, staring straight ahead as Nicholas climbed aboard and set the wagon into motion.

Faith followed the Shepherds' lead and sat quietly beside Liza, her eyes trained on the road.

They'd ridden for over ten minutes when Faith finally squirmed, unable to keep quiet any longer. After all, her wedding day was somewhat of a celebration. "God has provided a beautiful day for our marriage!"

Her cheery observation was met with stony silence.

She studied the scenery, determined to retain a sunny outlook. It wasn't every day that she got married. The Shepherds would warm, eventually.

Overhead a cloudless blue sky provided a lovely canopy. Lush meadow grass waved at her, and bubbling streams glistened in the hot sun. Meadowlarks flitted overhead, and bees drank their fill from the heads of bobbing buttercups. She wondered if she would ever get used to the sight of so many cattle. Nicholas must own every one in the county!

The wagon rolled past field after field of cows that Nicholas called Shorthorns. The animals were strong framed and looked to be of hearty constitutions. They were big cows, with short, sharp horns and a coat of red with white splotches. She stifled a laugh as she watched the playful antics of baby calves leaving their mothers' side to romp through open fields.

As they rounded a bend in the road, Faith heard a loud bellow. The sound was filled with abject misery. Grabbing the side of the buckboard, Faith held on as Nicholas abruptly brought the wagon to a halt in the middle of the road. "There's a cow in trouble."

Faith stood up as he bounded out of the wagon, her attention centered on a cow that was down on its side in the pasture. It was apparent the animal was in labor. Without thinking, Faith hitched up her skirt and climbed down.

Liza slid to the edge of the seat, her face suffused with color. "Young lady! You get back in this wagon! Nicholas will see to the problem!" Liza whipped out her handkerchief, fanning herself, her face glowing beet red.

"Can't! Nicholas needs help!" Faith darted up the embankment and quickly slipped between the wooden fence posts.

The cow, which had been down a minute ago, was now on its feet, pacing in a circle, sniffing the ground. Her tail stood straight out in back of her. Releasing a pitiful bawl, she dropped to her knees and lay down again.

"Tell me what to do." Faith knelt beside Nicholas, her eyes focused on the animal.

"Go back to the buggy. You're disturbing the mother." Nicholas's hands slid along the animal's heaving sides. He frowned. Faith noticed his touch was infinitely gentle.

"I want to help—will she be all right?"

"I don't know; she could be in trouble. The calf is in the birth canal. It'll suffocate if she can't deliver it soon."

Faith remained at Nicholas's side, listening to the mother's rapid breathing. Her sides rapidly rose and fell. Each pitiful bawl brought a gripping pain in Faith's midsection.

Five minutes passed, and Nicholas was getting edgy. "It's not going fast enough." He moved Faith to the front of the cow for safety. "Stay here, and keep out of the way."

Faith obliged, relieved he wasn't going to make her go back to the wagon. She'd witnessed live births before; each one a wondrous new experience.

Ten minutes passed and the cow, though actively straining, was making no progress. Faith continued to edge toward the back for a closer look. Nicholas was pulling on the calf's leg that was farthest back in the cow. The leg would progress a little, and he would switch legs, working slowly, gradually increasing the traction as he pulled with the mother's contractions.

Faith's gaze riveted on his strong arms as, little by little, he advanced the calf out of the canal a little way, then worked on the other leg. Back and forth, back and forth. Nicholas relaxed when the mother relaxed. When the cow quit pushing, it appeared Nicholas was losing ground, but he'd regain it with the next contraction. By now, Faith was on her knees in the dirt beside him, holding the mother's tail out of the way. Occasionally, Nicholas pushed the calf back a little into the mother to correct a position while the mother was resting. Finally, Nicholas got to his feet and motioned for Faith to grasp the calf's left leg. Using both their strengths, they pulled the newborn safely from the birth canal.

Exhausted, Faith dropped to her knees, reeling with exhilaration. Tears ran down her cheeks as she looked at the messy newborn lying on the ground, worn out from its entry into the world. "Praise be to God," she whispered, then waited until the mother prodded the calf to its feet.

Nicholas stepped beside her, and they watched the baby struggle to get to its feet, trying over and over again to gain footing. When it finally did, they clapped, cheering it on.

When the excitement died away, Nicholas checked the mother to be sure she was experiencing a normal birthing process. "She's fine and healthy."

He stepped back, hands on his hips, and surveyed Faith. She could swear she saw a hint of respect lurking in the depths of his blue eyes. "We best get you home. You'll want to clean up."

Faith realized there would be no wedding today. She looked down at her blood-spattered white Irish linen, thinking how appalled Rose Nelson would be if she could see it right now. But dresses were only material, and material didn't matter. With a good scrubbing, she could have the dress presentable in no time. What did matter was that she had felt a bond with Nicholas Shepherd. Albeit a small one, and certainly a precarious one, but they'd managed to make a brief, personal connection. She could hardly ask for anything more this soon. Praise be to God! Nicholas's inclination toward silence had started to worry her.

Chapter Three

THE day she'd most dreaded had arrived.
Lord, I know I should surrender Nicholas gracefully. I just can't.

Liza bent over the stove, suffused with heat. Merciful heavens, the kitchen was a blast furnace this morning! Her back ached, and she felt as if she were coming down with ague. Frustration overwhelmed her. She wasn't supposed to come to the end of her days alone, lonely.

There was no one left to care about her. That was the plain truth. Nicholas respected her, but he didn't need her anymore. He was a grown man, soon to be married.

Married.

The final separation of mother and son.

Oh, Nicholas was an honorable man like his father.

She was his mother; he would dutifully look after her until the end, but marriage would bind him to a wife.

Vigorously stirring the bubbling pot, Liza blinked back scalding tears. Faith thought she was old and cranky. She could see it in her accusing looks. Well, she *was* cranky, and getting worse every day. She didn't like who she'd become, but she couldn't seem to do a thing about it. Her chin rose a notch. Giving up a child fell to all mothers one day. It would fall to young, dewy-eyed Miss Kallahan, too. Was a mother expected to give her son, her life blood, to another woman with a kiss and a smile?

Well, she couldn't. God forgive her, she couldn't.

What did it matter that Nicholas didn't love Faith Kallahan? He would eventually. Siring a child would create an unbreakable bond. And though she knew Nicholas would honor God's teaching to honor his mother, it didn't make her pain any more bearable.

His heart would belong to another woman.

Faith, this stranger—this "mail-order bride"—was about to take the last remaining thing that held any meaning in her life. Without Nicholas, Liza would be completely alone. Abe taken, now Nicholas. The thought rose like bitter gall in her throat.

Pitching the spoon aside, she turned from the stove, stripping off her apron. Why was she feeling so insecure? She had never felt possessive toward Nicholas before. She wanted him to marry and find the happiness she had shared with Abe; it was God's plan. *Forgive me, Father. I don't know what's wrong with me!* Reaching for the small brown vial she kept hidden behind the sugar bowl, she uncapped the bottle and took a sip.

"Desperation, Liza," she muttered. Replacing the cap on the bottle, she held it before her, squinting to read the label: "Lydia E. Pinkham's Vegetable Compound." In smaller letters it read "Restores to vigorous health the lives of those previously sorely distressed." Well, she was "sorely distressed" all right. Oren Stokes had recommended the silly compound, saying it had helped other women to restore vitality. Uncapping the bottle, she took another tiny sip. She didn't need any women's "compound" to see her through her troubles—besides, the tonic only made her feel good temporarily.

Shoving the bottle behind the sugar bowl, she absently checked her hair. Enough of feeling sorry for herself. She had better things to do than sip some useless tonic and blubber all day. Maybe she'd attend the quilting bee. Hadn't been in weeks, and folks were beginning to think she was shutting herself away in the house.

Straightening her dress, she took a deep breath and reached for her bonnet.

"Mama?" Nicholas pushed open the screen door leading to the back porch.

Liza had excused herself during supper and left the table. He was worried about her. This past year she'd gone from being a woman trying to cope with the loss of her husband to being a moody, unhappy shrew. Her moods were getting worse every day, and he didn't know how to help her.

Nothing made her happy. He'd caught her in the kitchen last week crying again. He'd insisted—no, ordered her—to see Doc. So far she had resisted all efforts to get to the bottom of her problem. Was her behavior a sign of a serious illness? Her hand favored her heart a lot lately . . . was that the problem?

One thing he knew for certain: If her strange behavior kept up, he was going to take the matter into his own hands. He was taking Mama to the doctor himself. Maybe then he'd get some peace.

Tonight Liza was sitting on the porch, fanning herself, staring at the moon. Just staring at the moon while Faith

cleared the supper dishes. Letting the screen close behind
him, he joined her. "Mama, are you ill?"

"I'm healthy as a horse. What a thing to ask."

Her tone didn't indicate it. *Mean* as a horse, he'd concede. Lately she snapped at him like a fishwife. At times
he was tempted to snap back, but he held his tongue. For
the sake of peace and quiet, it was better to just let her
have her say and get it out of her system.

Sitting down on the first step, Nicholas glanced toward
the barn. Lantern light spilled from the windows. That
meant a ranch hand was late getting through with his
chores. Mama didn't like the help in the barn after dark.
Once she had been a fearless woman—a wildcat couldn't
intimidate her; lately she was scared of her own shadow.
A year ago she'd insisted the bunkhouse be relocated to
the back of the property in order to keep the help at a
safe distance. The move had been costly and a considerable headache, but he had complied with her wishes in
hopes it would assuage her uneasiness.

It hadn't.

"Glad to see you attended the quilting bee this afternoon."

"Didn't enjoy it."

They sat in silence for a few moments.

"What do you think of Miss Kallahan?" He kept his
tone casual, aware he was wading into quicksand.

"Appears to be a hooligan to me. Wallowing around in
that muck like a man."

Nicholas let the subject drop. Faith had been a help to
him yesterday. Most women would have avoided the
problem. "Nice night."

"It's hotter than a smokehouse." She fanned harder,
wiping drops of perspiration off her forehead.

It wasn't that hot. An earlier shower had blown
through and cooled the air. "Windows are all open.
Should cool down real nice tonight."

Liza dabbed the hanky along her jawbone. "Suppose you'll be inviting Miss Kallahan to services with us in the morning."

"Mama. I am about to marry Miss Kallahan. I can hardly leave her sitting in the front parlor Sunday mornings."

Liza sniffed, reaching for a can of snuff. "Shouldn't have sent for her in the first place. I told you she'd be a peck of trouble—trouble we don't need."

Nicholas eyed the snuff. "I wish you wouldn't do that." His tone was sharper than intended. When Liza had taken up chewing a few months back, he had strongly reprimanded her. Papa would have rolled over in his grave, Nicholas said, but she paid him no mind. Lately, she just seemed bent on being ornery.

Liza shoved the box of snuff aside and promptly burst into tears. Burying her face in her handkerchief, she sobbed, great weeping howls that rendered him defenseless.

Nicholas muttered under his breath. "Mama! Have you seen the doctor about these . . . spells?" He tried to be understanding, but the good Lord knew he was at the end of his rope! He didn't know what to do with her when she got like this!

She looked up from her hanky. "You watch your tongue, young man. You're still not too big for me to take a switch to your behind." Bolting from the chair, she stormed past him, rapping him on the top of his head with her knuckles, then jerked the screen door open and let it slam shut behind her.

Dropping his head back against the post, Nicholas stared at the overhead canopy of stars. Thirty-four years old, and Mama was still thumping him on top of the head. He'd hold his tongue if it killed him—which it likely would if he didn't get to the bottom of her strange moods, and soon.

The sound of rattling dishes drifted from the kitchen and he briefly wondered if Miss Kallahan shared the same disposition for meanness. Was Mama's affliction peculiar to all women? His head pulsed at the thought of two women under one roof—his roof—each afflicted with the same madness.

What did Miss Kallahan think of his letting Mama run roughshod over him? He mentally groaned. Not much, he conceded. But Mama wasn't Mama—hadn't been for a long time now. She was still grieving for Papa, and the Reverend said only time would heal her wounds. Well, almost two years had passed, and she was getting worse.

Quite frankly, it didn't matter what others thought. He had only God and himself to answer to, and he would honor his mother—however weak and indecisive he appeared to Faith Kallahan, or anyone else for that matter.

Sunday morning Faith snuggled deeper beneath the sheet, listening to the sound of rain dripping off the eaves. During the night, thunder and lightning had shaken the old house with the same fury that must have rocked old Noah's ark when the flood came. Toward dawn, heavy downpours had given way to gentle showers. The smell of damp earth drifted through the open window, and she could hear someone moving around downstairs. The fragrant aroma of perking coffee teased her nose.

Stretching, she wiggled her toes, trying to wake up. It was the Lord's Day. It was the first time she would attend services with her new husband. She frowned, remembering the mother cow. Her *soon-to-be* husband, she amended.

Her gaze focused on the white dress hanging on a hook beside the beveled mirror. Ugly blood splotches and grass stain soiled the front of the Irish linen. It would take some time to clean the dress, and even then the gown might be ruined. Sighing, she rolled to her back, grateful Rose Nelson wasn't there to witness the sad sight.

What *would* she wear for her wedding? And when would they attempt to marry again? She owned few garments—a blue-and-white gingham, a paisley green print, a yellow-sprigged cotton, a serviceable dark blue calico, a black wool, two pairs of bib overalls, and a plaid shirt.

She rolled to her side. Maybe the yellow cotton, with a little new lace tacked around the front. . . .

The rooster crowed daylight as she rolled from the bed and descended the stairway for breakfast thirty minutes later. Liza was at the cookstove, turning thick slices of bacon in a cast-iron skillet. She didn't look up when Faith walked into the kitchen.

Summoning her cheeriest tone, Faith said, "Good morning!"

Liza opened the oven door and took out a pan of biscuits. "Make yourself useful. Get the cream and butter from the springhouse."

"Yes, ma'am." Faith glanced out the open back door, smiling when she saw two of the most beautiful horses she'd ever seen standing in the corral. The small dark blotches on a white coat, and striped hooves, took her breath. She knew a ranch this size must have many horses that would be used to pull steel plows, harrows, cultivators, hay rakes and reapers. But the two splendid Appaloosas drinking from the water trough were undoubtedly Nicholas's private stock.

For a moment she forgot all about cream and butter in her desire to take the animals a cube of sugar, touch their cold noses, smell their warm, shiny coats. But one look at Liza's dark countenance made her beat a path hurriedly to the springhouse.

"Shall I tell Nicholas breakfast is ready?" she asked as

she returned, setting the tub of butter and pitcher of cream on the table.

"He doesn't need to be told when it's time to eat."

"Yes, ma'am." Faith dropped into a chair and waited for Nicholas to come in from the barn. Would he let her pet the horses if she slipped out the back and—

She glanced out the window and saw him striding toward the house. She wouldn't be petting any horses this morning.

Breakfast was eaten in silence. Except for an occasional "pass me this" or "pass me that" Nicholas and Liza didn't address each other. Afterward Faith helped Liza wash dishes as Nicholas dressed for church.

Around nine they set off for the church. A gray drizzle peppered the top of the buggy as it rolled into the churchyard. Reverend Hicks, Bible neatly tucked beneath his arm, stood at the door, greeting arrivals.

"Nicholas, Liza, Miss Kallahan." Reverend's pleasant smile lit the dreary morning. "So sorry about the unfortunate turn of events. Is the cow all right?"

"She's in good health," Nicholas said. Liza steered Faith ahead of her as the two men shook hands. Two more wagons rattled into the yard. A crying infant shattered the morning serenity.

"Oh my." Reverend Hicks clucked. "I don't know how Dan Walters does it."

Faith turned to see a stocky, redheaded man climbing out of the wagon, trying to shield a squirmy infant beneath his rain slicker. The man looked harried—and very young; Faith guessed him to be no more than twenty-two. The baby, screaming at the top of its lungs, looked to be only a few months old. A redheaded girl toddler with friendly green eyes was uselessly trying to plug up the noise by wedging a sugar tit between the baby's gums. A dark-haired boy, no more than five, valiantly wrestled to the ground a thick bag crammed with bottles and diapers. It sounded to Faith as if the circus had come to town.

Reverend Hicks cupped his hands to his mouth. "Need any help, Dan?"

Dan glanced up, grinning. One of the baby's shoes was missing. "Thanks, Reverend. I've got it under control!"

Heads turned as the rowdy ensemble entered the church and marched down the aisle, the baby kicking and bucking in protest as Dan settled his noisy brood in the pew.

The Shepherds filed into the church to take their seats as the Reverend closed the double doors. Perched at the pump organ wearing a bright pumpkin-colored dress and hat, Vera awaited the Reverend's signal to begin the services.

Faith leaned closer to Nicholas and whispered, "Who is that young man?"

"Dan Walters and his brood."

She frowned. "Where is Mrs. Walters?"

As the organ music swelled, Nicholas reached for the pew hymnal, whispering, "She died giving birth to the baby."

Faith's eyes returned to the young father who was trying to extricate a strand of hair from the baby's hand. The baby had the head of the poor woman sitting in front of them drawn back like a bow. *Poor man,* she thought.

The opening stanza of "Onward Christian Soldiers" shook the rafters, and the congregation got to their feet. Faith stood beside Nicholas and in a clear, sweet alto sang her Papa's favorite hymn. Closing her eyes, she imagined his booming baritone energetically bolting out verse after verse as if indeed "marching oonn to waaar." She sang with him, matching his tempo, rejoicing in song. When she felt eyes fixed on her, she opened her eyes to see

Nicholas staring at her. She smiled, pointing to the hymnal. "Papa's favorite song."

The singing died away, and the congregation sat down. Reverend Hicks approached the podium, Bible tucked beneath his arm, armed for battle. Baby Walters's muffled frets were the only sound in the room.

Reverend placed the Bible on the podium, then fixed his eyes upon the congregation.

"Brethren, this morning I prayed long and hard about today's message. My first inclination was to bring a message on the joys of giving, and then God reminded me not everyone considers it a joy to give." Relaxing, the Reverend smiled. "Many are unduly upset when the subject of money is broached, but we all know and understand that God doesn't want money; he wants obedience. Better that I preach a message of hope and encouragement to my flock, but the subject of a new steeple weighs heavily upon my mind—"

"Oh, good grief," Faith heard Liza moan under her breath.

"Here now! There'll be no moaning out loud, Liza Shepherd! This is just a friendly discussion before I preach the Word. As unpleasant as the subject is to all of us, we need a new steeple."

"Nothin' wrong with the one we got!" Clarence Watts bellowed. Faith jumped at the outburst. During Papa's services no one ever dreamed of talking back.

A farmer dressed in overalls stood up. "It's gonna fall down round our heads, Clarence, that's what's wrong!"

"It *is* a mite worn," another man conceded before his wife jerked him back to his seat.

"Hush up, Elmer. We cain't afford no new steeple!"

"People." The Reverend attempted to hush the sudden uprising. "The old steeple has served the church well for seventy years, but it's worn out. One good windstorm, and it'll come down, and woe to the unsuspecting soul who is unfortunate enough to be standing beneath it."

He fixed his eyes on Liza.

Faith's eyes pivoted to Liza. If Liza felt the Reverend was speaking directly to her, she showed no sign of backing down.

Whipping out a hanky, she fanned her reddened face as if there weren't a stiff breeze coming through the open windows. She plucked at the top buttons of her blouse, her hand favoring her heart.

Reverend's features softened. "Now I know you don't like to talk about money—none of us do. But there comes a time—"

Liza spoke up. "This is supposed to be sermon time, not business-meeting time, Reverend. If memory serves me, we reserve business matters for Wednesday evenings."

Straightening, the Reverend took a moment to gain his composure. Pursing his lips, he began thoughtfully, "Good people of Deliverance, the Lord has blessed us all in a mighty way. Before I go on with this morning's message, I want you to promise you will go home, get down on your knees, and consult the Lord about his will concerning the new steeple. Perhaps we don't need it— perhaps I'm wrong. But please give it prayerful thought this week. It is my firm conviction that something needs to be done, and done soon."

A young father got up, a severe black suit hanging on his lanky frame. "Times are hard, Reverend. No one is trying to duck responsibility, but I got five kids to feed and clothe. There just ain't anything left over at the end of the month." He sat down, frowning at his wife when she patted his knee in silent support.

"And well I know that, Jim. If the steeple weren't a hazard, I wouldn't be asking that it be replaced. I'm confident we'll all pull together and do what we can."

Faith made herself as small as possible, wondering why

Nicholas didn't speak up. The Shepherds could help with the steeple and never miss it. Instead he sat straight as a statue, eyes fixed on the podium, showing not a sign of emotion other than a muscle working tightly in his left jaw.

"The subject isn't appropriate," Liza declared. "Now if you don't mind, I have a roast in the oven. Kindly get on with the sermon." She crossed her arms, then uncrossed them in search of her fanning hanky.

Vera bounded to her feet, knocking over a sheaf of organ music. Righteous indignation flared beneath her bright orange hat. A young boy darted from his pew to retrieve the fallen sheets. "Liza Shepherd, whatever has gotten into you! Why, Abe would've given the shirt off his back—"

"Sit down, Vera!" Liza's razor-sharp rebuke interrupted Vera. Drawing a deep breath, Liza said more calmly, "Abe is no longer with us. I handle the Shepherd money, and *I* say the steeple needn't concern us. It does not need to be replaced. Repaired, I grant you, but not replaced."

Vera gave a loud hrummph, reached for the sheet music, and sat down.

Defeat settled in the Reverend's eyes as he quietly opened the Bible and instructed in a crisp voice, "This morning's sermon will be taken from Philippians chapter 1, verse 6."

Faith breathed a sigh, relieved the exchange was over. Opening her Bible to Philippians, she read, "Being confident of this very thing, that he which hath begun a good work in you will perform it until the day of Jesus Christ."

Chapter Four

FAITH opened her eyes Monday morning
long before the rooster crowed. Nicholas had spoken with
Reverend Hicks after the service, and Reverend said he
could marry them Monday afternoon at two. Faith could
hardly sleep for excitement. By the end of the day she
would be married!

When finally it was time to get up, she jumped out of
bed and ran to the open window to look out. As far as
the eye could see, it promised to be a perfect day. The
sun was shining, the sky a brilliant blue. Not a cloud in
sight, and a subtle breeze rustled the lace curtains.

The stains on her Irish linen wedding dress were barely
visible this morning. A generous-sized bar of lye soap and
a scrub board had done the trick. She smoothed her dress
and took one last look in the beveled mirror above the

bureau. She'd never thought much about primping, but today was special. She wanted to look especially nice for Nicholas on their wedding day.

Brushing her hair until it shone, she then pulled it to the sides and secured it with pearl combs. It fell to her waist in gentle waves. She considered wearing it in a neat bun. The style would have been more to her liking, and much cooler, but the thought of Mother Shepherd and her taut braids changed her mind.

Pinching one cheek, then the other, she added a touch of color to her face. She'd watched Hope use the trick on many occasions. The feminine ritual had always seemed silly to Faith. Now she knew it was downright ludicrous. It hurt almost as much as the pointy shoes she was wearing. She longed to wear her comfortable brown leather boots that were hidden away at the bottom of her valise.

Turning, she opened the bedroom door. The musty smell from the parlor hung heavy in the air.

Mother Shepherd was sitting in her rocker by the kitchen stove, bent over her sewing. She was wearing a cotton frock just as drab and ordinary as the one she'd chosen for the wedding three days earlier. Once again that awful black shawl rested around her shoulders. No wonder she was so hot all the time.

"Wondered if you were going to sleep all day."

Faith glanced at the clock. It was barely six o'clock. "The wedding isn't until two this afternoon."

"Been changed. Reverend sent word he'd have to do it this morning. Got sick folks to attend this afternoon."

"Sorry," she murmured, resisting the urge to ask why she hadn't been told. Like the Good Book said, "Be slow to anger and sin not." She wanted Nicholas's mother to like her. Their marriage would never be harmonious if his mother disapproved of her. Liza would be her children's grandmother—. She quickly shook the thought aside. First things first. She needed to build a strong foundation with Liza, although it was clear the older woman didn't share the challenge.

"I see you're wearing the white dress." Liza eyed the still visible, but faint, spots. "You think it's appropriate?"

Hold your tongue, Faith. Be kind.

"Are the spots noticeable, Mother Shepherd?"

Liza bit off a piece of thread, switching subjects. "There's ham and biscuits on the stove. Your eggs got cold. I threw them out with the gravy."

So. The first shot sounded.

Faith eyed the cold biscuits. How would Jesus handle this? With kindness and tolerance. Her sister June would seek to win Liza over with a winning smile. Faith's inclination was to sass, which always brought swift restitution from Papa.

"I'm not hungry, thank you." Faith set her jaw. She would just be so nice Liza could do nothing but love her.

"What's wrong with your face?" Liza held the needle up to the light to thread it. "Looks like you've been pinching yourself."

Faith blushed. Drats. Liza wasn't making things easy. OK, tomorrow morning she would come down those stairs looking like death warmed over.

"Oh, for heaven's sake. Whatever you've been up there doing, best get a move on. Nicholas can't surrender another day's work on account of your lollygagging." Liza got up and disappeared into the parlor.

Faith eyed Liza sorely. She bet Liza pinched her cheeks too. She jerked her bodice in place, aware her cheeks no longer needed the additional color.

Faith hurried to keep up with Liza as much as the uncomfortable pointy shoes would permit. She glanced down at the shiny black leather, tightly laced to her ankles. The pointed heel made a woman's life miserable. A body could snap an ankle wearing such things.

Grabbing her white hat, she hurriedly pinned it atop her head as she went out the back door. It didn't matter that it set a tad too far to the left. No one in this house was going to notice.

Pausing on the porch, Faith took a moment to catch her breath. Nicholas emerged from the barn, smiling as he tipped his brown suede Stetson at her. He was wearing work clothes, though this morning they appeared to be clean.

Faith sighed.

No breakfast. Not a single mention of the extra attention she'd given to her appearance. Both Shepherds looked as if they were about to cut hay, not be major participants in a wedding.

She sighed again, then wadded the folds of her dress, expelled another weary breath, and stepped off the porch to join her future family.

Mother Shepherd was already in the buckboard, sitting in the middle of the bench. Faith wondered if she intended to make that her permanent position.

Without a word, Nicholas helped Faith into the wagon and they drove off. Faith thought it would have been nice to ride to the Reverend's house in a real buggy instead of a supply wagon. And she'd have preferred to have a church ceremony, not some indifferent recital in the Reverend's parlor. She studied the bluebonnets growing along the roadside and thought how they'd sure make a pretty bridal bouquet.

She might as well wish for the moon. She wasn't going to have a real buggy, a church service, or a pretty bridal bouquet. This buckboard was as good as it was going to get.

Nicholas suddenly strained forward on the seat, his eyes trained beyond a small rise. In the distance a thick cloud of ominous black smoke boiled upward. Faith saw him stiffen as his eyes scanned the smoke. Even she knew from the direction the wind was blowing, it wouldn't take long for the smallest ember to reach the town settlement.

Snapping the reins, Nicholas urged the team to a full gallop.

Faith gripped the side of the buckboard, holding on to the white hat. The pins flew from her hair, and the dark mass whipped freely in the wind.

"Nicholas—slow down! You're going to kill us!" Liza exclaimed. "What in heaven's name are you—" She fell silent when she spotted the deadly smoke.

Nicholas cracked the reins harder, racing the horses, the buckboard bouncing over potholes and ruts. With each rut, Liza landed hard on the bench, her rigid posture unaffected.

Faith's heart pounded as the wagon sped closer to the flames. Thick smoke teared her eyes now. Each breath produced a sharp stinging in her lungs.

Angry flames lashed upwards, waist high to a grown man. The fire was spreading across the grassland as fast as butter melting on a hot biscuit.

Men from Deliverance were already battling the scorching blaze. In the distance, more could be seen hurrying to join in the fight. Nicholas slowed the horse, tossing the reins to Liza before the wagon came to a complete stop.

Bounding down, he ran to the back of the wagon and took out a handful of empty burlap feed sacks, then raced in the direction of the licking blaze.

"Over there!" Dan Walters shouted, pointing to a waiting buckboard. Two large wooden barrels sat on the wagon, brimming full of water. "Wet your sacks!"

Liza held the team steady, clutching her handkerchief to her nose.

Faith's eyes scanned the unbelievable inferno. Never in her life had she seen anything so powerful. Tossing her hat aside, she jerked the pearl combs free, then wadded her hair into a bun and secured it. Snatching the handkerchief from Liza, she bunched up the layers of her wedding dress and jumped to the ground.

The look on Liza's face would have been comical under other circumstances. Faith refrained from laughing, knowing full well the repercussions of what she was about to do. But she couldn't just sit in some old wagon when a fire like this was going on!

Liza shot to her feet, yelling, "Young lady—you get back in this wagon and stay out of the way!"

Liza's voice was little more than an echo as Faith ran to help battle the blaze. She stopped long enough to scoop up a burlap sack Nicholas had dropped, then raced headlong to the water wagon. The once-clear water was now blackened with soot. Faith dipped the handkerchief into the barrel, quickly tying it across her nose and mouth. Murky water dripped down the front of her white dress, but already the smothering air was easier to breathe. She submerged the burlap sack, hoisting it up soaking wet and dashed to help the men.

Swatting flames with the devil's fury, Faith worked side by side with the men. Cinders and ashes flew. A spark caught the hem of her dress and she quickly doused it, but not before it had burned a good-sized hole. Drats. She glanced down at Mother Shepherd's smoke-blackened handkerchief and frowned. Double drats. For over thirty minutes Faith fought unnoticed alongside Nicholas before her luck ran out. Nicholas was so engrossed in the fire, he hadn't noticed her presence, or most certainly, hadn't expected it.

Passing him on the way to the water barrel, she made the mistake of speaking.

"Terrible fire—wonder how it started?"

He stopped in his tracks, staring at her in total disbelief. "What are you doing out here!"

"Putting out a fire!"

"Get back in the wagon—you're in the way!"

"No, I'm not! Nobody's complained so far!" She doused the sack in the water and brought it up, dripping.

"I'm complaining now!"

"Just a few more sacks." She'd fought the fire for over a half hour. That counted for a respectable amount of experience. Just because he'd just noticed her—well, that didn't mean she hadn't helped.

Nicholas's tanned face blotched with impatience. "Go back to the wagon, Miss Kallahan."

"You need all the hands you can get," Faith argued.

"You're in the way. Get back in the wagon!"

"Let me just take one more sack." She glanced at Mother Shepherd, who was now standing up in the buckboard, watching the exchange. Oh, Papa would blanch at her sass, but Nicholas wasn't being fair!

"Get back in the wagon!"

"The town will be lost!"

"Deliverance was here long before you came! It's up to the men to see that it stays that way!"

Faith stiffened her resolve. He had no right to tell her what she could and could not do! "An extra hand never hurts, Mr. Shepherd."

"A grass fire is no place for a woman!"

"A good wife—"

Nicholas's hand shot to his hip, and Faith wondered if he was going to physically pick her up and haul her back to the wagon. He wouldn't dare. "We are not married yet, Miss Kallahan."

Their eyes locked in a heated duel. "Mr. Shepherd," Faith began. "I am well aware we are not married yet, but when we do say our vows, I refuse to be another Shorthorn that you simply brand and put out to pasture. A wife's place is to be a helpmate to her husband—"

"Get back in the wagon," he ordered.

He hadn't heard a word she'd said! Faith rolled her eyes, more determined than ever to make her point. "Eve was created from Adam's rib. Not from his thick head. Nor from the tip of his boots. From his rib! That's how close I intend to be to my husband, Mr. Shepherd—a part of his rib!"

Nicholas paled, and for a moment she wondered if she'd gone too far. Then her eyes steeled. "You brought me here to be your wife—"

"To be my wife! Not to get underfoot!"

"Nevertheless, I am here. And I intend to stand by your side until death do us part, and that includes fighting this fire with you!"

Nicholas shot her a stern look. She knew what he was thinking. It was going to be a long life.

"Well? What do you say to that, Mr. Shepherd?" Her eyes widened as the muscular Swede rushed her. Squealing, she tried to step aside.

Nicholas lunged, and they tumbled to the ground. Holding onto her, he rolled her on the charred grass.

The jolt knocked the wind out of Faith. She had no idea what possessed him to do such a bizarre thing! She was only trying to make a point! The moment she caught her breath she began kicking and screaming.

Nicholas trapped her in his arms, rolling her on the ground, effortlessly dodging her pointy-toed shoes.

"Mr. Shepherd! You get off of me this instant!"

Liza cupped her hands and shouted from the wagon, "Nicholas Shepherd, you get up from there! The very nerve—my son, wallowing on the ground with a woman—have you lost your mind?"

Nicholas grunted, dodging another kick. "Stop that kicking! I'll personally take those shoes off you!"

They rolled and tumbled through the charred debris as men sidestepped them on the way to the water barrels.

"I'll stop kicking when you get off of me!" Faith tried to squirm from beneath his heavy bulk.

"I'm trying to save your life!"

"Save my life?! You're being stubborn, that's what you're doing!"

Pinning Faith's shoulders to the ground, Nicholas said with a deadly calm, "Your dress is on fire, Miss Kallahan."

Her eyes narrowed. "My dress is what?"

"On fire."

Springing to her feet, she beat the flames out.

Nicholas rolled to his feet, and Faith avoided his eyes.

"The way you came charging at me like an old bull—"

"Get back into the wagon."

She studied the frenzied scene. Men were still fighting the fire, gradually controlling the flames.

Faith glanced down the front of her wedding dress. Even a double dose of Mother Shepherd's lye soap couldn't save it now. The once beautiful garment was now black with soot and scorched beyond repair. She tried to stem the tears but failed.

"Now look what you've done." Nicholas awkwardly brushed cinders from her charred dress.

In his own way, she knew, Nicholas was trying to comfort her. There were just some things a man obviously didn't understand.

"Yes. It's just a dress," she whispered. Her wedding dress. But it didn't look as if she'd ever be getting married anyway.

The fight was gone out of her. Tired and discouraged, she gathered up the scorched hem and walked slowly to the Shepherds' wagon. "You can use my sack if you want," Faith said, refusing to look over her shoulder.

Nicholas dashed off to join the other men.

As she climbed up into the wagon, Liza gave her a

censuring look. Faith knew she'd seen her and Nicholas rolling around on the ground, and the thought left her stricken with shame. She reeked of smoke; she didn't care.

It was late in the evening before the last man dropped to the ground with exhaustion. Faith thanked God the fire hadn't reached Deliverance. Speculation about the cause ran rampant. Old Charlie Snippet, who helped out around the general store, swore it was a lightning storm that did it. Others blamed a couple of gamblers who rode into town early the night before looking for a game. They'd been upset when they found out Deliverance had no saloon. Whatever the cause, Faith was thankful the fire was finally out. She dropped to her knees to thank God for his goodness and mercy.

Worn out, the men headed home. They climbed aboard wagons and saddle horses and scattered in all directions.

On the way home, Nicholas was silent. Faith was too tired and too discouraged to offer conversation. Her wedding had been thwarted twice. She wasn't in the mood to discuss a third attempt.

When the wagon stopped in front of the house, Liza got out and disappeared inside without a word. Nicholas went to the barn to tend chores.

Faith poured a pitcher of water into the wash basin, then discarded the ruined dress and scrubbed herself clean before changing into her nightclothes. Worn out and humiliated, she crawled into bed. The feather mattress felt heavenly against her aching body.

She lay in a lonely bed, in a lonely house, wondering why Mother Shepherd treated her so coldly.

The smell of fried potatoes and bacon drifted to her. She sniffed, her stomach knotting with hunger. She hadn't eaten all day.

When she heard the back door shut, she realized Nicholas had come in from the barn. She heard Mother Shepherd's muffled voice as she shuffled around the kitchen. Faith dreaded the thought of morning dawning, a new day beginning. There was no telling what new disaster awaited.

Oh, Father, grant me more faith, more wisdom, some way to reach Nicholas and his mother. Am I doing something wrong? Am I disappointing you? Is my faith not strong enough? Give me patience to try harder. Reveal your will, dear God. I'll follow as best I can.

Tossing and turning, she finally drifted into a restless sleep.

The sharp rap of knuckles on her bedroom door jolted Faith awake before dawn. It rattled the old rooster off the window ledge, denying him his daybreak caterwauling.

"Breakfast," Mother Shepherd snapped.

At least she was speaking to her. Even if it was in one-syllable barks. It was far more than Faith expected.

Yawning, Faith rolled out of bed. Wearing those torturous pointy shoes another day was out of the question. She buttoned a red-and-black plaid shirt, pulled on denim bib overalls, and put on her old boots. Looking in the mirror, she admitted she wasn't exactly a flattering feminine image. Well, she sighed, looking like a lady hadn't won her any prizes yesterday.

Nicholas was seated at the head of the table when she walked into the kitchen. Liza was taking a pan of biscuits out of the oven. Nicholas briefly nodded to her, smiling. Faith quickly took her seat across from Liza.

Mother Shepherd set the platter of sausage and eggs on the table, her eyes fixed on Faith's attire. "Are we milking this morning?"

Faith ignored the cutting remark. "Sorry I'm so late. I

slept longer than I expected. Is there anything I can do to help?"

Liza unbuttoned her collar and fanned herself. "I can manage my own kitchen, thank you."

Faith pitied Nicholas's predicament. He was a man in the worse possible situation, caught between two warring women, his mother on one side, his intended bride on the other. Liza Shepherd was set in her ways. Faith couldn't imagine her giving an inch, now or ever.

Faith, on the other hand, was young and cheerfully optimistic most times. But she had a fire in her spirit that Papa always said would cause some man a good deal of trouble.

Apparently his prophecy had come true.

"Well, are we going to eat or just stare at our plates all day?" Liza asked. "Nicholas, say grace."

Nicholas complied. "Thank you, Father, for our many blessings and for the food we are about to receive. Amen."

Faith was aware that Nicholas was staring at her over the rim of his cup. She refused to meet his gaze, keeping her eyes trained on her plate. Once or twice she saw him glance at his mother as if she puzzled him. His bitter words still rang sharply in her mind. "Get back in the wagon where you belong!"

Well, she didn't belong in a wagon. She belonged beside him. If that bothered Nicholas, they would have to discuss the situation and find a workable solution. If he wanted a kitchen wife, he'd wasted good money sending for her.

Nicholas pushed his unfinished plate aside and stood up. His gaze focused on Faith. "There will be no wedding today."

Faith nodded, buttering a biscuit. The announcement came as no surprise. She was beginning to think there would never be one.

"Reverend Hicks has been called out of town for the remainder of the week. I've promised the Johnsons I'd help with their barn raising today. Hay needs to be put up while the weather's good, so the wedding will have to wait until a week from Thursday, if you're comfortable with that." For the briefest of moments, Faith thought he looked mildly disappointed.

"Yes, sir," she murmured.

Nicholas pushed his chair against the table. "If you'll excuse me, I'll hitch the wagon." He left the room, and a moment later Faith heard the front door shut behind him.

It was the time of day she'd come to dread. She and Mother Shepherd, alone. Whatever Nicholas's mother said, no matter how mean and petty, Faith vowed to be respectful and patient. Somewhere above, her heavenly Father would be watching.

Liza's mood caught her off guard. As the door closed behind Nicholas, she reached for the coffeepot almost pleasantly. Not a word mentioned about the fire or about Faith's improper behavior. She acted as if Faith were in another room as she quietly began clearing dishes from the table.

Picking up her plate, Faith pushed her chair back from the table. "May I help?"

"No, thank you. I've been clearing tables long before you were born," Liza said. "Besides, you're hardly dressed for women's work."

Faith fought the urge to respond, then tempered her thoughts by reminding herself to respect her elder.

"You're absolutely right, Mother Shepherd. I'll just see if Nicholas needs any help hitching the wagon." A moment later she let herself out the back door, letting Liza wash dishes by herself.

She found Nicholas in the barn, checking the horse's

shoe. When he looked up, Faith smiled, but he went on working.

"You should be in the house getting ready. You'll need to change clothes before we go."

She glanced down at her bib overalls. Perhaps she should; the overalls were a bit wrinkled, but they would get dirty anyway at the barn raising. She couldn't wait to get her hands into that project! Papa had always said she was as good with a hammer and saw as any man he knew. But as silly as it seemed to change clothes, she would meet Nicholas halfway. "I'll change right away." She glanced at the two beautiful horses she'd seen earlier, housed in a stall beside the wagon. "Can I ride one sometime?"

Nicholas glanced up, surprised. "Ride? You're welcome to take the buggy anytime you want."

"No." She moseyed over to pet the horses. Their noses felt wet and moist. "I want to ride one of these fine fellows if you don't mind."

He bent his head, mumbling, "Mama won't approve of it."

"I'll ask her very properly. If she consents, will it be all right with you?"

"If she consents, it will be a miracle," Nicholas grunted, hitching the harness to the wagon.

He might as well know right here and now he's not marrying a parlor lady, she decided. "I've always favored outside work over inside work."

"Yes, I've noticed that."

"And I love animals of all kinds. Don't you?"

"Not real fond of cats." He glanced up, a slow smile spreading across his features. Faith caught her breath, struck by his handsomeness. He winked. "But I guess if you want one, I can learn to live with it underfoot."

Her heart soared. She could finally have that kitten!

"Thank you. That will make me real happy." Giving the horses' rumps a final pat, she moved away from the stall.

A short time later she came out of the house. Liza trailed behind, shaking her head because Faith had donned *clean* overalls.

Nicholas was hitching the wagon.

"Need some help?" Faith called. She trotted out to stand beside him.

"I'm just finishing up here." He scowled at her appearance. He tripped over her feet, trying to get around her.

He might as well know he was marrying a tomboy, too. When she saw his eyes narrow, she said quickly, "I changed my clothes—soiled to clean."

"Don't you own more than one dress?"

"Four or five of them," Faith admitted. "But I can't build a barn in a dress."

He straightened. "You are not going to build a barn."

Well, we'll see about that, Faith thought.

During the ride to the Johnsons' house the silence was so thick it could have been sliced with a knife. The only sound was the rhythmic clop of the horse's pace, passing acre after acre of Shepherd cattle.

Faith's head spun with every turn of the wagon wheels. She could almost read Nicholas's thoughts. Right now he was wondering how he was going to build a barn with her in his way. She didn't care; she was eager to have a hammer in her hand again.

She glanced at Liza. She was probably wondering how she was going to turn a tomboy into a lady. Not very easily. Papa had tried it and failed.

Faith sat up as she spotted a coiled rattler beside the road within striking distance. All Nicholas would need was to lose a good horse. That would surely ruin the whole day. Reaching behind her for the shotgun, she carefully eased it out of the holder. She'd take care of that creature before it did any harm. . . .

Liza turned around. "What on earth—?"

Springing to her feet, Faith blasted both barrels into the coiled reptile. The gun's kick nearly toppled her.

Nicholas jumped as if he'd been shot when the gun exploded.

Liza choked, swallowing the pinch of snuff she'd just stuck in her mouth.

Slapping her hand against her thigh, Faith squealed with delight. "Got it!" The same instant the horse reared. Wide-eyed, Nicholas fought to gain control.

The runaway horse tore off down the road, out of control for over a mile, trailing a cloud of dust the size of a Texas twister behind the buckboard. The old wagon rattled and shook their teeth, threatening to split apart as it careened over potholes and gullies. Liza's hairpins came loose, spinning recklessly in the wind.

Nicholas stood up and sawed back on the reins, using brute strength to bring the horse under control. Gradually the wagon rattled to a jerky halt. The three shaken occupants slowly climbed out.

Liza's braids dangled below her shoulders, her face flushed, looking mad as an old wet hen.

Color rushed to Faith's face. She probably should have warned them before she shot. . . .

Nicholas seemed surprisingly calm. "Is anyone hurt?"

Liza made a strangling sound, and Faith reached over and whacked her on the back. A wad of snuff popped out of her mouth.

"There," Faith soothed. "That feel better?"

Then Nicholas went up like a keg of dynamite. *"What* were you *thinking?"*

Faith stammered, "I-I didn't want the snake to spook the horse, so I—"

"You didn't want the *snake* to spook the horse?" Nicholas said a dirty word. So dirty it brought a blush to Faith's cheeks. He should be ashamed of himself. God would not think highly of that! "You took it upon yourself to fire a shotgun ten inches from my eardrum? Mama, are you all right?"

"WHAT?"

"ARE YOU ALL RIGHT?"

"I CAN'T HEAR A BLASTED THING!"

Well, that did it. She had only tried to help, and they were acting as if she'd committed a crime against the government.

"In the future, kindly refrain from lending your help!" Nicholas tipped his head to the side, trying to clear his ears. "Do you have any idea how idiotic that was?"

"I'm not stupid, Mr. Shepherd." Faith glowered. "I just didn't stop and think."

"In the future—"

"I know! Stop and think!"

Nicholas glowered at her.

"I said I was sorry. What more do you want?"

He pointed to the wagon seat. "I want you to sit on that bench—no thinking, no helping, nothing—until we get to the Johnsons. Do you understand?" His eyes snapped blue fire. Papa had never used that tone of voice with her. "And keep those trigger-happy fingers in your lap where I can see them!"

She nodded.

The three climbed back aboard the wagon, and Nicholas turned the team toward the barn raising.

Faith glanced at Liza. "Mother Shepherd, I'm sorry about your braids."

"WHAT?"

"The bouncing shook them loose." Faith reached over to fix them. "Let me put them back in place—"

"Don't touch me." Liza scooted as far as she could away from Faith.

Faith sighed. Poor Mother Shepherd. Everything Faith did was wrong. At this rate, they were never going to be friends.

Chapter Five

Excitement grew when the Shepherd buggy rolled to a stop at the site of the barn raising. Faith's eyes drank in the sight of buckboards, colorful Jenny Linds and various other conveyances. From the very moment Nicholas had mentioned there was going to be a barn raising, she had looked forward to the social event. She was eager to form new friendships in the community that was to be her new home. She hoped Nicholas would introduce her to women her age.

Young Brice Johnson and his bride, Elga, appeared to greet the new arrivals. The young couple smiled and shook hands, welcoming the Shepherds to their home. Levi Johnson, Brice's father, was the Shepherds' closest neighbor to the south. The two families shared water rights. Faith judged Elga to be two to three years her junior, pretty, with a tousled head of russet hair and sparkling goldish-brown eyes. Elga had been married less than a month, and she still glowed with matrimonial bliss.

Over protests, Brice helped Liza down from the buggy, then took the picnic basket from Faith. His blond, sunny good looks and amicable gray eyes reminded Faith of the air after a summer thunderstorm. Refreshing. If only Nicholas smiled that way once in a while, he'd be every bit as handsome as Brice.

Brice energetically pumped Nicholas's hand. "Glad you could come today. Can always use an extra hand."

The sounds of hammers and saws rang out as Faith trailed Nicholas and Liza through the milling crowd. Nicholas called to several families, who returned the greeting. Faith decided if he wasn't exactly a social butterfly, he was at least a well-respected member of the community.

"Need to talk to you about one of my bulls!" a man in the crowd shouted.

Nicholas waved, promising to get together later as he steered Faith in the direction of the blanket Liza was spreading under a large oak.

"Can't I help?" Faith protested when she realized he intended for her to remain with Liza for the day.

"Women have no place doing men's work," he said.

Her chin tilted with determination. "I've done it before. Once, June and I helped build a whole shed. Mr. Siddons was thankful for our help, said we had the strength of two men, and—"

Nicholas cut her off. "No wife of mine is going to build a barn or a shed. Stay here, and stay out from under foot."

Faith bit her tongue, sorely tempted to remind him she wasn't his wife, but she could see his pride was at stake. He wanted his wife to meet community standards. Well, she resented that he hadn't seemed the least bit upset about their two delayed wedding attempts. When she opened her mouth to argue, he pointed her to the blanket and sat her down.

Handing her a paper fan, he motioned toward the women setting up the food table. "I'm sure Nelly Johnson will welcome some help."

"Woman's work," Faith muttered.

"Nothing wrong with woman's work," Nicholas said. "You can unpack our food basket. It'll keep you out of trouble."

Keep her out of trouble! Jerking her hat in place, she stared at his disappearing back, silently seething. What would it hurt if she handed nails? Or sawed a board to the proper length?

Fanning herself, she looked up to see Liza pulling balls of yarn and crochet hooks out of her sewing bag. Faith saw two hooks, and her heart sank. It was going to be a long day.

"Should I set out our food basket?"

Liza handed her a hook and a ball of thread. "No hurry. Here. Make yourself useful. Idle hands are the devil's playground."

Faith bet the devil himself wouldn't have to sit under a tree and crochet on a pretty day like this. Removing her hat, she set it aside.

Puffy white clouds floated overhead as she made a knot in the yarn and placed it on the hook, listening to the voices of the men, who, on the count of ten, heave-hoed, hoisting the newly framed walls into place. How she envied their camaraderie. *God, I don't question your wisdom, but I sure wish you'd needed more men than women when I was born.* She would have relished the peppery smell of fresh-hewn wood in her hands, adored the feel of a smooth shiny nail.

A faint breeze rustled branches overhead as Faith laid aside her crocheting and sighed. In the distance, a group of children were playing a spirited game of crack-the-whip. Her eyes searched the crowd for Dan Walters and his brood. She finally located the young widower nailing window frames together at a nearby sawhorse. Jeremiah was standing beside him, holding baby Lilly in his arms.

Smiling, Faith waved, and the old hermit tilted Lilly's arm to wave back. Jeremiah's gaze lightly skimmed Liza before returning to the business at hand.

Faith heard Lilly fussing a short while later and quickly laid her handwork aside.

Liza glanced up. "And where do you think you're going?"

"The Walters baby is fussy. I thought I'd see if there's anything I can do to help."

"Dan's capable of taking care of his children."

"Dan's busy right now. I'll only be a minute." Before Liza could stop her, Faith darted off, thankful for the break in the monotony.

She approached Jeremiah and Lilly. "Can I help?"

Jeremiah gratefully handed over the squalling infant. "Thanks." He sniffed the air, wrinkling his nose. "I believe the infant's soiled her didee."

Faith smiled, glancing at Dan. "I'm Nicholas Shepherd's fiancée."

"Yes, ma'am. I saw you in church Sunday morning." Dan's ruddy complexion looked like a boiled lobster from the heat and exertion. "Quite a service."

"Yes—quite."

"There's clean diapers in the wagon. Adam, show Miss Kallahan where they are."

"Faith," Faith corrected, then smiled. "Please call me Faith."

Dan paused, returning her smile. "Thanks. Faith it is."

Adam took Faith's hand and started toward the wagon. With each step, he counted. "One, two, three . . . ."

It was only then Faith realized that little Adam Walters was blind.

Fifteen minutes later the baby was changed and settled on a blanket, quietly nursing a bottle. Jeremiah and Adam had gone off in search of other projects.

Faith sat on the sidelines, shooing flies from the baby as Dan hammered nails into wooden frames. His quick, efficient motions confirmed his carpentry skills, although Faith had heard Nicholas say Dan worked with the blacksmith.

"Have you built many barns?"

"A few." Dan glanced up, using a shirtsleeve to wipe the sweat off his brow. Unlike Nicholas, he seemed happy—almost hungry—for the conversation. "What about you? Ever built anything?"

"A shed once, and I helped my father around the parsonage."

"You're a preacher's kid?"

She nodded. "Papa was the best there is."

They struck up a friendly conversation that lasted until the dinner bell rang. Work ceased as men washed up, then gathered before a long row of tables laden with platters of fried chicken, boiled potatoes, steaming bowls of turnips, ears of corn, green beans, and poke greens. Heaping pans of crispy brown corn bread and bowls of thick, freshly churned butter were started around. Sitting on nearby tables, fat apple pies and rich chocolate fudge cakes awaited.

Levi Johnson gathered the group around. "Father, we thank you for this glorious day and the blessings you have given us. Thank you for friendships, family, and for the bountiful food you've placed before us. Watch over and protect us this day. We ask in Jesus' name, amen."

"Amen!" the crowd responded.

Families and friends broke into small groups to partake of the noon meal. Good-natured laughter filled the air as the hungry workers socialized over talk of weather, grasshoppers, and much needed rain. Faith busied herself helping Dan feed the two smaller children. She filled plates with chicken legs and small helpings of green beans and potatoes, deliberately avoiding Liza's annoyed stare. Nicholas sat beside his mother in silence, the Shepherds keeping a safe distance from the others. Faith knew if she looked their way, she would be obligated to join them, so she purposely looked the other direction.

At one o'clock the bell sounded again. The men groaned, patted full bellies, then pushed to their feet. Minutes later the sounds of hammers and saws once again saturated the air.

The Walters children refused to let Faith go. Adam, who Faith had discovered was born blind, and the three-year-old girl, Sissy, held tightly to her hand as Faith playfully tried to pull free. Laughing, she agreed to stay, then settled them on the blanket and told Bible stories about Jonah and the whale, and David and the giant, Goliath. Clapping their hands, the children stomped around the blanket, mimicking tall giants, until Dan called for them to settle down.

"Has anyone ever read you stories from a make-believe book?" Faith asked as she repacked the picnic basket. She fondly recalled the large, colorful book of fairy tales her mother had read to her when she was about their age.

Adam's sightless eyes lit with expectation. "Papa says we cain't tell no lies."

Faith ruffled his hair. "I'm not talking about lies— make-believe stories. Snow White and Rose Red, Rapunzel, Faithful John?"

Adam and Sissy shook their heads in awe.

"Do you know how to tell make-believe stories?" Adam asked.

Faith nodded, placing his hand on each side of her head so that he could not only hear but also feel her answer. "What am I saying?"

Adam paused, thinking. He broke into a wide grin. "Yes!"

"Yes!" Faith hugged him tight. "That's very good!"

Sissy started prancing again. "I wanta hear stawies!"

As the barn's rafters went up, Faith recited fanciful tales about sisters who loved each other so much they made a vow that what one had she must share with the other; a beautiful girl with magnificent long hair, fine as spun gold; and a servant who strove to be faithful to his king. The children giggled, gleefully pretending to let down their hair for the other to climb down upon.

Sissy's head was nodding by the last story. Faith wiped her hands and face with a cool cloth, then settled her on the blanket beside the sleeping baby.

Disagreement erupted when Adam declared he was too old for a nap. Dan joined the spirited debate, but Adam eventually won out, claiming he couldn't sleep now because Jeremiah had promised to teach him how to spit. Dan looked at Faith, and they both grinned.

"Spitting is an art no boy should be denied," Faith proclaimed.

Dan nodded, playing along. "I think you're right." He pointed the child in the direction of the old hermit.

Hands on hips, Dan paused, studying Faith. "How did you get so good with children?"

Faith shrugged. "Mothering comes natural, I guess."

"Well," Dan said, reaching for the dipper in the pail, dousing his head with water. Sunlight caught the glistening drops cascading off his fiery hair. He wasn't a handsome man, but kindness radiated from every pore. Faith decided kindness was better than handsomeness any day of the week. Kindness and an even temper. "You should have yourself a whole houseful of children," he said.

Faith spotted Nicholas working high above in the rafters, and she wondered if she'd have even one. "Maybe I will, someday."

Dipping back into the water pail, Dan drank his fill. Wiping his mouth with the back of his hand, he gazed at Faith. "Heard you didn't get to say your vows the other day."

"No, one of Nicholas's cows was having trouble birthing. Then there was the fire yesterday."

"That's too bad. Suppose you'll be saying them real soon?"

"Suppose I will." Faith glanced back at Nicholas. "Next Thursday, providing the Lord's willing and the creek don't rise." Or there's another fire or cow in trouble.

Dan grinned. "Nicholas is a lucky man."

She blushed, fairly certain Nicholas didn't think so.

Faith settled on the blanket when Dan went back to work. Her eyes focused on Nicholas, still perched high atop the barn, nailing rafters. Powerful muscles stood out in his arms as he drove nails into two-by-fours. Faith shivered, wondering how gentle those arms would be holding a woman—one he loved and respected. Her gaze meandered through the crowd, and she waved at a few of the church ladies. So far everyone had welcomed her with an amicable smile and an open heart.

"Want to help?"

Dan's offer brought her out of her musings. "Me?"

He stood beside the frame he'd just built, extending a hammer to her. "You said you like to build things."

"I love to build things!" Jumping to her feet, she straightened her overalls. "Are you serious?"

"Serious as buck teeth. Come on. You can help me with the next one."

Faith stepped in closer, helping to hold the board Dan was about to saw.

"Ouch!" She jumped, shoving the piece of wood away as it broke neatly into two pieces. Dan bent down to retrieve the boards, praising her efforts.

"You'll be building a town next."

"I would love it!" She grinned, then picked up a handful of shavings and threw it at him.

Leaning down, he scooped up a handful of sawdust and threw it at her, and a friendly sawdust war erupted. Chips flew, coating hair, faces, and clothes. Faith spit, brushing the swirling fragments out of her eyes as she fended off the attack. She fell to her knees, laughing when a barrage of shavings assailed her.

"Faith Kallahan!"

Faith sprang to her feet, blinking shavings out of her eyes as she glanced up to see Nicholas scowling at her. Staggering to her feet, she blinked again, trying to see through the haze of sawdust. "Yes, sir?"

Hammers fell silent; saws suddenly stilled. The air hummed with tension as workers ceased their efforts. Inquisitive eyes rotated to the direction of the angry voice.

Nicholas, hands on his hips, face as black as a witch's heart, stood in front of her. Liza hovered at his flank, narrow lipped, eyes vibrating with condemnation.

Swallowing, Faith brought her hand up to cover her tripping heart, afraid it was going to thump right out of her chest. Dear goodness. What was she doing? How must a sawdust fight look to Nicholas? She'd forgotten herself and was caught up in harmless frivolity, but how must it look? She hadn't stopped to think about her actions; if she had, she would have realized they were inappropriate. Her eyes locked with Nicholas's and her heart skipped a beat when she realized he was going to make a scene. And by the look on Liza's face, she was about to take a willow switch to her.

She smiled faintly. "Hello, Nicholas. Did you want something?"

Nicholas's eyes turned to blue steel. Faith winced
when she saw a muscle tighten in his jaw.

Stepping forward, he took her by the arm, marching
her through the crowd. Color flooded Faith's face. She
highly resented his barbarian treatment! Who did he
think he was, treating her as if he owned her! She tried
to wrest free of his clasp, but he only tightened his grip.

"Let go—you're hurting me!"

"You are making a mockery of the Shepherd name,"
he said in a tightly controlled voice.

"A mockery? I was only throwing sawdust—"

He hurried her along, refusing to listen.

When they reached the Shepherds' blanket, Liza wasn't
far behind. "Young lady—"

"Mama!" Nicholas took off his hat and pointed it at
her. "I will take care of this."

"But Nicholas, she's—"

"I will handle the matter, Mama. Sit down."

Hurt flashed across Liza's face, but she stepped back.

Nicholas's shirt was soaked with perspiration. Blond
hair lay in damp waves against his forehead. For an instant
Faith was moved by the urge to brush it back. She
warred with conflicting emotions: Concern and compassion fought with the deep temptation to kick him in the
shins. He was a most unpleasant man, determined to take
his resentment out on her!

Then he spoke, and his cold, exacting voice sent any
noble thoughts flying out the window. He was a mean,
boorish brute who delighted in embarrassing her!

"I told you to stay here with Mama and keep out of
the way," he began in a calm, calculated tone.

"Well, you see—Adam and Sissy needed help. I was
only—"

He cut her off. "You were sawing a board!"

"One board!" she defended. "Before that I was helping

with the children. I fed them, diapered the baby, then told Sissy and Adam stories—"

His voice dropped to an ominous timbre. For one brief, elated moment she thought she saw jealousy flare in his eyes. Then it was gone. "You were not brought here to tend Dan Walters's children. And while we're having this talk, I don't want you socializing with Jeremiah."

"But I like Jeremiah!"

"What you like or dislike makes no difference. People will wonder why you are drawn to a drifter, a hermit. The man could be dangerous—he isn't a puppy or a kitten, Miss Kallahan, a stray in need of help. No one knows anything about him, or his past, other than he chooses to be alone."

"But the Lord expects us to be kind to all men."

"You are to keep your distance from Jeremiah. You were brought here to be a Shepherd. A Shepherd does not pick up every stray she runs across."

The air was electrically charged as she turned her back to him. Crossing her arms, she counted to ten. If she were a man . . . how dare he order her around in that tone! Papa had never so much as raised his voice to a woman, and he'd have no patience with a man who did.

Taking a deep breath, she dropped her voice. There was no point in making a spectacle of herself in front of the growing crowd of onlookers. "You don't have to remind me why I'm here."

"Has it ever occurred to you people will talk when they see you cavorting with Dan Walters?"

"Cavorting!" She whirled to face him. "Cavorting?" she repeated. "I was helping Dan—if you recall, I offered to help you, but you told me to sit down and be quiet."

He snorted. "And look where that got me." He glanced at the curious onlookers, then lowered his voice. "Just do as I ask, please."

Liza spoke from the sidelines. "You should be ashamed of yourself, young lady. Have you no regard for Nicholas—"

Nicholas stopped his mother. "I've already spoken to Faith about the situation, Mama. This matter does not concern you."

Turning back to Faith, he repeated quietly but firmly, "You are to sit with Mother the remainder of the afternoon and behave like a lady. Do I make myself clear?"

Her chin lifted. "Do I have to crochet?"

"If that's what it takes for you to conduct yourself in an acceptable manner."

She looked away, crossing her arms again, staring into the distance. "I hate to crochet."

"Look." He lowered his tone. "All I'm asking you to do is act like a lady, and don't embarrass Mama or me. Is that too much to ask?" His dark tone warned her he'd brook no further nonsense. He turned and walked off.

"Apparently so," she murmured.

Nicholas glanced over his shoulder. "What?"

Faith opened her mouth to repeat her declaration, then clamped it shut, words from Ephesians ringing in her ears: *Wives, submit yourselves unto your own husbands, as unto the Lord. For the husband is the head of the wife, even as Christ is the head of the church: and he is savior of the body.*

Nicholas's tone took on a dangerous edge. "Was there something more you needed to say, Miss Kallahan?"

"No, sir." She refused to look at Mother Shepherd.

"You're certain?"

She turned her back to him. "Positive." Her obedience wavered when she added under her breath, "Except that you're not my husband yet."

Liza settled herself on the blanket, then reached for her handwork. "You're asking for trouble."

"Asking?" Faith released a pent-up breath of frustration before picking up her crochet hook. She seared a hole through Nicholas's retreating back. "Seems to me I've already got it."

Chapter Six

FATHER, *I don't mean to be a burden. I'm not proud of my actions of late. It seems no matter how hard I try, I'm short on understanding and long on criticism. Who am I to criticize Liza—or Nicholas, for that matter—when I have so many faults of my own? I truly want to marry Nicholas, and I believe that's your will. Why else would you send me here, among so many strangers? Even as ill tempered and disagreeable as Liza is, I want her to like me. Truthfully, I can be pretty ill tempered and disagreeable myself, and I'm not proud of it. I pray for your forgiveness and the ability to do better. I don't want to disappoint the Shepherds—and I never intentionally do things to upset them. Bless Liza, Lord. Send happiness into her life: She misses her husband so. I seek only to do your will, even if at times I miserably fail. Amen.*

Rising from the side of her bed, Faith quickly dropped

back to her knees. *And, Lord, please tell Papa not to worry. Once Nicholas and I are married, I won't be such a bother. I remain your faithful servant, Faith Marie Kallahan.*

Hay was put up and the wedding scheduled for the third time. Faith followed the Shepherds to the wagon Thursday morning, dressed in a yellow-sprigged cotton with leg-of-mutton sleeves. The gown wasn't as pretty as the white Irish linen, but it was the next best thing she owned. The tatted lace she'd stitched around the collar made it seem like new, although she'd had it for years. The only other hat she had was a thick fur cap with attached earmuffs. Nice for blustery cold winters in Michigan, but useless in sweltering Texas heat.

After the way Nicholas had treated her at the barn raising, Faith wasn't fully able to recapture wedding-day anticipation. Still, she and Nicholas had an understanding, one she intended to honor. Nicholas and she were as different as daylight and dark, but perhaps, in time, there would be more acceptance of each other. The least she hoped for was tolerance.

A smile played at the corners of her mouth, and she felt more optimistic as she remembered the Good Book. If the Lord could heal the sick, raise the dead, and save the most wicked sinner from the fiery pits of hell, he could bless this marriage. All she needed was faith the size of a mustard seed.

Nothing was said on the ride to Reverend's house. Faith watched the countryside roll by, mesmerized by the hum of the wagon wheels. Texas was unbelievably big. Everywhere she looked fertile fields were dotted with cattle, grazing or bunched in herds, seeking the shade of cottonwoods, mesquite, or majestic oaks. She sat up straighter when she spotted one of those strange-looking creatures the elderly gentleman on the stagecoach had called an armadillo. The patterned, plated animal with brown armor on the top and side surfaces of its body darted across the road in front of the wagon.

"Do you see that—that monster?" Faith exclaimed.

"Don't go making a mountain out of a molehill," Liza said. "It's just an armadillo."

"Looks like an armored rat."

In another twenty minutes Faith spotted the church parsonage. She couldn't help comparing it with the Shepherds' dreary dwelling. The quaint white adobe, with porches running the length of the house, radiated warmth and love. Even the stable and chicken coop, with their bright whitewashed boards, captured the Hicks's cheerful spirit.

Though the wagon was still some distance away, she imagined she caught a whiff of the sweetest fragrance. As the rig rolled into the yard she spotted the source. Yellow roses grew in large clusters at the side of the porch. Vera had baskets of lush ferns hanging from every rafter. Lovingly tended flower beds overflowed with bird's-foot violets, buttercups, and spider lilies. Pretty Indian blankets, their russet centers bursting into flared yellow tips, grew generously beneath two huge pecan trees. The heavy branches, like green-leafed umbrellas, provided a shady haven from the blistering sun. Faith longed to someday live in just such a house.

A chestnut mare, lathered and winded from a hard ride, waited by the front porch. A young man in denims and a blue shirt took the steps two at a time and pounded on the door.

"Mornin', Ethan," Nicholas said, helping Faith and Liza from the wagon. Nicholas and Faith started up the steps, Liza close behind.

"Mornin', Nicholas." Ethan paused long enough to acknowledge the ladies' presence. He quickly removed his hat. "Mrs. Shepherd, Miss Kallahan."

Liza nodded. "Something wrong, Ethan?"

"It's Sarah Jane. She's havin' the baby."

Vera came to the door and retreated quickly, then returned carrying a black satchel. Reverend Hicks followed, towering over his wife's short stature. "Hurry along, Ethan. Sounds like your young'un's anxious to make his entrance."

"Yes, ma'am!" Ethan jumped the porch rail and mounted his horse.

Scurrying down the steps to the buggy Reverend Hicks had hitched and waiting, Vera turned to face the wedding party. "I'm afraid Amos will have to conduct the ceremony without me. Sarah Jane's in labor."

"That's quite all right, Vera," Liza acknowledged. "Lord knows there's no stopping a baby when it's his time to come."

Faith turned around to face Liza, surprised at the consideration in her voice. She sounded almost sympathetic. "I didn't know Mrs. Hicks was a doctor."

"She's not. You're in Texas now. Doc's likely to be out on another call, and Vera fills in for him. Many a woman calls Vera before they go for Doc. A mother couldn't be in better hands."

With such praise coming from Mother Shepherd, Faith knew Vera must be miraculous. Since arriving in Deliverance, she couldn't recall Liza saying anything complimentary about anyone.

Reverend helped Vera into the buggy.

"Thank you, dearest."

"You be careful, Mama."

"Can I be of help?" Faith asked. She didn't know much about birthing babies, but she could fetch water and clean linen.

"No, thank you, child." Vera picked up the reins. "Lord knows, I do appreciate the offer. I have everything I'll need in my satchel."

"This is one of those situations where too many cooks can spoil the stew," Liza volunteered.

The observation puzzled Faith. Mrs. Hicks was going to deliver a baby, not fix supper.

Vera and Ethan were about to leave when a frenzied rider, hollering and waving his hat, galloped into view. "It's time! It's time—the baby's a-comin'!"

Faith stepped back to allow the rider plenty of room as he sawed back on the reins, bringing his horse to a stop in a boil of dust. As the grime settled, Albert Finney materialized.

Vera frowned. "Oh dear, Albert. Not Mary Ellen too. Why, she's not due for another week. Albert, are you sure?"

"Yes, ma'am!" Albert grinned. "I'm real sure!"

"Oh, dearie me." Vera bit her lower lip. "I suppose this being your seventh, you would know."

"Yes, ma'am! You gotta hurry, she—"

"See here, Albert! I got here first!" Ethan declared. "My Sarah Jane needs Mrs. Hicks's services—now!"

Albert frowned. "But Mary Ellen's about to pop! The baby's not gonna wait!"

"First come, first served!" Ethan maintained.

"Mrs. Hicks, you know my Mary Ellen," Albert pleaded. "When it's her time, it's her time! Ain't nothin' on God's green earth gonna stop that young'un from comin'! Please! My baby ain't gonna wait!"

"Mine ain't either!"

Faith expected the two men to end up on the ground, going at it.

"Gentlemen, please! You're behaving like children!" Vera interrupted. "I can only be in one place at a time."

"Then let's go!" Albert urged.

Ethan clenched his teeth, "I told you, Albert Finney! I was here first! You're comin' with me, Mrs. Hicks."

"The two of you just calm down a minute," Vera demanded.

Ethan backed off, grumbling, "Guess we could always draw straws."

"Draw straws!" Albert shook his head. "Ethan, we ain't talkin' about who's gonna go first in a horseshoe game! We're talkin' about my baby!"

"No need for straw drawin'." Vera glanced at Liza. "Liza, you're gonna have to help."

"Certainly." Liza sidestepped Faith and hurried back to the buckboard. She motioned for Faith to come along, and Faith blinked, looking to Nicholas.

He nodded. "Go on. Mama needs your help."

Faith wasn't sure what Liza expected of her as she hurriedly climbed aboard the wagon.

Liza picked up the reins, eyeing Faith. "I don't know if you've ever helped birth a baby, but if you're as good at it as you are at pulling calves, you'll do just fine."

Faith's eyes felt as big as silver dollars. "I—I don't know anything about babies—"

Liza snapped the reins, wheeling the wagon around in the direction of the Finney place. "You'll know more by tomorrow." The wagon careened forward. "Albert! Let's get moving!" Liza shouted. "We got ourselves a baby comin'!"

"Yes, ma'am!" Albert grinned, tipping his hat at the ladies as he led the way.

As the dust settled, Nicholas took off his hat, his eyes trained on the fading wagons. Reverend stepped down from the porch, craning his neck for a final look. "Well, we can't have a wedding without a bride."

"Looks that way." Nicholas was beginning to wonder if the wedding would ever take place. Three attempts, and he was still a single man.

Reverend chuckled. "Seems as if you and Miss Kallahan are having a hard time tying the knot."

The thought had occurred to Nicholas.

Reverend laughed, slapping Nicholas good-naturedly on the back. "Sometimes we don't understand why certain things happen. If God made it clear to us, I reckon we'd have no need for faith."

Faith. Nicholas took a deep breath. He prayed God understood Faith Kallahan's ways, because he sure was having a hard time coming to terms with them.

"You eat lunch yet?" the Reverend asked.

"Not yet."

Reverend Hicks opened the front door, motioning for Nicholas to join him. "I don't know about you, but the way I see it, if we can't pray over matrimony, we might as well pray over a good meal."

It was close to midnight before Liza and Faith returned. Light spilled from the kitchen window. Faith could see Nicholas sitting at the table, reading Scripture. When the wagon slowed, he got up to meet them.

"Baby get here all right?" He helped Liza, then Faith down from the buckboard.

"Easiest birthing I've ever tended." Liza yawned. "But I'm tuckered out. See to the buggy, will you, Nicholas?"

Easy? Faith thought, recalling how poor Mary Ellen had labored, it seemed, for hours. Not just for one baby but two. Albert had grinned from ear to ear when she handed him his newborn son. Moments later she handed him another baby—a girl this time. The proud new papa looked as if he might faint. Faith smiled. Twins would be a shock when you had six other mouths to feed.

"Supper's in the oven." Nicholas started for the barn with the horse and wagon. "Reverend Hicks insisted I bring home some of Vera's venison stew and cornbread."

Faith ate two bowls of stew before retiring to her bed-room. Exhausted, she opened the window. The night breeze felt good on her damp forehead. She lifted her hair, allowing the breeze access to her neck.

Stepping out of the yellow wedding dress, she caught her image in the mirror. Three attempts at the altar and still no ring on the third finger of her left hand. It was getting harder and harder to maintain that faith she had boasted to Aunt Thalia about. Then faith had been easy; now it took some doing to believe God had a plan for her and Nicholas Shepherd.

She knelt beside the bed, praying, but tonight for some reason, it felt as if her words went no higher than the ceiling. Papa used to say, "Even though it may feel like God isn't listening, that's when he's working the biggest miracles." She couldn't remember a time when Papa had told her wrong. He'd known the Good Book from cover to cover.

Lying in bed later, Faith's mind refused to shut down. As much as she loved children, what Mary Ellen had gone through tonight made her wonder if she ever wanted babies of her own. Liza had insisted it was an easy birthing, but it had looked difficult to Faith. Liza had taken over in a sure, competent manner during the births while Faith kept the sweat wiped from Mary Ellen's fore-head and tried to keep out of the way. Mary Ellen had squeezed Faith's hand so tightly it still ached.

Just when Faith had felt certain there was no end in sight, cries from the newborns filled the room. In one glorious moment, the anguish was gone from the tired mother's face. All that remained was infinite love glowing in Mary Ellen's eyes as she held her babies for the first time.

Faith remembered something Aunt Thalia once read from the Bible. A Scripture about how the pain of child-birth, which can feel almost like dying, is but a clouded memory after the child is born. She sure hoped that was true in Mary Ellen's case.

She didn't think she'd be likely to ever forget such a thing.

After breakfast on Friday morning, Nicholas went to the woodshed. Faith had her heart set on joining him, but Liza made it clear she had different plans.

"Faith," she called out from the parlor. "I'll be needing your help this morning."

Drats. "Yes, Mother Shepherd," Faith replied, shocked that Liza would admit to needing anyone's help. She glanced up from dusting the parlor to see Liza slip a small brown vial from her apron pocket and take a sip.

Faith flattened her body against the wall. Had she seen what she thought she'd seen? Nicholas's mother chewed *and* imbibed spirits?

Peeking around the corner, she covered a gasp when she saw Liza tipping the bottle back and taking another healthy swig.

She drew back. Oh goodness. Did Nicholas know about this? Should she tell him? Her mind whirled.

Liza came into the parlor and pushed a basket of socks, thread, and a darning needle at her.

"Best get started. We haven't got all day." She frowned. "You do know how to darn?"

"Yes, ma'am," Faith replied, omitting the fact that she detested the chore. As Liza brushed past her, Faith bent close, trying to get a whiff of the liquor.

Liza pulled away, giving her a dour look. "What are you doing?"

"Nothing." Faith grinned.

The weather was beautiful outside. Faith couldn't stand the thought of being cooped up inside. She could hear the sound of the axe biting into the wood. She would much rather chop wood than darn any old day. She'd pricked her finger three times, and it was getting sore. No doubt about it. Darning was more dangerous than wood chopping.

It wouldn't be quite so tiresome if Liza would only talk to her. But the two women sat in the dark room, methodically darning as they listened to the ticking clock.

Faith's eyes roamed the parlor. Every piece of furniture was covered with sheets, even the two straight-backed chairs in which they sat.

The more Faith studied the coverings, the more she wondered why. "Mother Shepherd, why do you keep the furniture covered?"

Liza drew a tolerant breath, concentrating on her stitches. "I'll not have the sunlight fading the furniture. It's wasteful."

"Oh." *As if sunlight could possibly get through those drapes,* Faith thought.

An hour passed without the two women exchanging a word. Faith's toes curled in the pointy shoes she was wearing. She longed for her boots. She should have worn them—and her overalls. At least she would be comfortable.

Her thoughts switched from the furnishings and her foot discomfort to Mother Shepherd, trying to look beyond Liza's coarse exterior. Her eyes were probably once as deep blue as her son's. Faith's heart ached. Did Nicholas have the least suspicion that his mother had taken to strong drink? Perhaps it was only for medicinal purposes. . . . That was possible. There was a woman in Papa's church who contended that a tiny drink every now and then helped her rheumatism. Yes, that was it. Liza was using liquor as a medicinal remedy for whatever plagued her.

Remarkably, Liza's fair skin was barely touched by the Texas sun. Her hair, once blonde but now streaked with silver, could still be attractive if only she would loosen those unbecoming braids.

Faith was amazed to realize that Liza Shepherd wasn't that old—why, she might even be pretty with a little fixing. She stuck her finger and winced.

Drats. She'd rather spit nails than darn socks. Her boredom growing, Faith fidgeted in the chair.

"Must you squirm?"

The woman had barely spoken all this time, and now all she could contribute was, "Must you squirm?"

Faith tried to hide her frustration. "I'm sorry. . . . I need to use the necessary."

She wasn't lying; while she didn't need to go, she needed to *go*. The necessary was the only refuge she'd found to escape monotony.

"Well, don't sit there and squirm. Go do what you have to do."

"Yes, ma'am." Faith laid her basket aside, then stood and stretched like a lazy cat on a hot summer's day.

"And don't take all day. There's plenty of darning left to do."

Faith stepped off the back porch and reached behind the steps for the leather strap she'd been braiding on previous trips. Keeping to the well-worn path, she held the strap hidden in the folds of her dress. Her handiwork wouldn't be appreciated should she encounter Nicholas along the way.

She took refuge in the outhouse, bolted the door, then made herself as comfortable as possible. For over an hour she braided and prayed for patience, more faith, and more guidance. Papa always said, "Don't make a bit of difference where you pray. God hears you no matter where you are."

Well, she sure hoped he was listening now because she was giving him an earful.

I'm running real low on faith, Lord. I don't mean to be

always complaining. I know there's folks a lot worse off than me. Guess I'm just feeling sorry for myself again. My fingers hurt from darning, and I've got a big blister on my little toe from those awful pointy shoes. I know Nicholas isn't as cranky as he seems. I caught him talking real gentle-like to a stray dog the other night. He didn't know I saw him, but he was awfully kind to the lost pet. And one night, he brought a new calf into the house and laid it by the stove. I thought Liza was going to faint. Said she'd just mopped the floor that day! But he didn't budge an inch. Said he wanted to keep a close watch on the heifer in case she got off to a rocky start. Now I ask you, Lord, would a mean man be that considerate? I don't think so. I think he must have other things on his mind, things that don't concern me but that make him the way he is. On the inside, I suspect, he is a kind man. If you'll just provide me sufficient faith to see this thing through, I believe it will all work out. . . . Bless Mary Ellen's new twins. They sure are sweet—

The sudden knock on the outhouse door startled her from her preoccupation.

"Faith?"

She sat up. "Yes, Mr. Shepherd?"

"Mama says you've been in there over an hour. Are you ill?"

"No. I'm fine." Faith felt color heat her cheeks. Of all the humiliating things Mother Shepherd could do! Sending Nicholas to the outhouse to fetch her back to darn those old socks!

An eternity passed.

"Are you coming out?" Nicholas's voice sounded weary.

"Do you need to come in?" Faith asked, wishing he would just go away. Couldn't a woman enjoy a personal moment?

More agonizing silence passed. She knew she'd have to answer him sooner or later.

"Mr. Shepherd? You still there?"

"I'm here."

"Go back to the house and tell Mother Shepherd I'll be there in a moment."

She couldn't come out with him standing there. He'd see the braided strap and be angry. It was one of those "man" things he'd warned her not to do. She exhaled a heavy sigh when she heard the sound of receding footsteps.

Supper that night was fried chicken, milk gravy, string beans, and biscuits and sorghum. Faith cleared the dishes from the table. It was one of the few times Liza consented to let her help in the kitchen. Nicholas excused himself and retired to the side porch. Liza retreated to the parlor to read the Bible.

Faith completed her kitchen chores. Pouring a fresh cup of coffee for Liza and one for herself, she proceeded into the parlor to join her future mother-in-law.

The kerosene lamp burned low. Liza was asleep in her chair, her reading spectacles slipped down the bridge of her nose. The open Bible was still in her lap.

Poor dear, Faith thought. *Drinking and chewing.* How could she help Liza, make her see those were only temporary solutions to whatever was troubling her?

Setting the coffee on a corner table, Faith turned up the lamp for a closer look. Liza's face, peaceful in sleep, looked softer tonight, almost vulnerable. Leaning closer, she sniffed. Not a sign of liquor on her breath. Faith quietly removed Liza's spectacles, placing them and the Bible on the table. Leaning down, she gently kissed the older woman's forehead. *Maybe someday,* Faith thought, *you will grow to like me.*

Gathering the cups, she slipped from the parlor. Out the kitchen window, she saw Nicholas sitting on the porch. No sense in wasting two perfectly good cups of coffee, she reasoned, deciding to join him. She could use some company. There were times when the silence that filled the Shepherd house was unbearable. Tonight was one of those times.

"Mr. Shepherd, I thought you might like some coffee." Faith wasn't sure of the reception she'd receive, but she was willing to risk his rejection.

Nicholas turned to look over his shoulder. She was surprised to see him smile. "Thank you, Miss Kallahan. Coffee would be nice."

Faith handed him the cup. "May I sit for a spell?"

Nicholas made room for her beside him in the swing, glancing toward the parlor window. "Mama asleep?"

"Yes, I just checked on her."

Faith sat down beside him. She knew it wasn't considered proper for them to be together without a chaperone. But Liza was just beyond the window and she felt her presence. By the look on Nicholas's face, he felt it too.

A million twinkling stars filled the sky. Sweet smells and subtle sounds filled Faith's senses; hay cut that morning, crickets, a bullfrog croaking a lonesome love song to his mate. Fireflies flickered in the darkened pasture.

Faith closed her eyes, enjoying the breeze as it gently brushed her hair.

"Miss Kallahan . . ." Nicholas paused. "I'm sorry about the string of unfortunate events. I fear you will think I'm trying to get out of our understanding, but I'm afraid I must once again postpone the wedding."

She sighed, wondering if he indeed regretted sending for her. "Whatever you think best, Mr. Shepherd."

"I have business to oversee. It will be another two to three weeks before we can recite our vows."

Faith kept silent. Three weeks. She wondered if she should offer to return to Michigan and save him the embarrassment of asking her to leave.

"Mr. Shepherd, have you ever been in love?"

Nicholas gazed at the stars, his eyes mirroring distant memories. "Love has passed me by, Miss Kallahan." He glanced at her. "And you?"

"Not really. There were no eligible men in Cold Water, at least none I cared to fall in love with." She thought of Edsel Martin and shuddered.

"Faith—may I call you Faith?"

"Of course . . . Nicholas." She rather liked the feel of his given name on her tongue.

"I know the wedding delays concern you. They concern me, and I fear I have not been fair with you—that at times I've been preoccupied and even short when I should have taken time to explain my concerns." His tone gentled. "This newest delay is because I have cattle to take to market. I'll be leaving for San Antonio first thing on Tuesday and have some business to take care of on Monday before I go. We could marry tomorrow, but I would rather wait until I got back." He smiled. "It hardly seems fitting to get married, then run right off."

"I understand." Faith resolved to be patient. When the time was right, they would marry. Trust, Faith, the good Lord kept seeming to tell her. And she would. "The cattle must come first."

"Well, normally they wouldn't. But this time of year they must."

Faith sat up straighter, encouraging conversation. "Why is that?"

"If I want top dollar, I have to get my herd to market before it's glutted."

"You mean before other ranchers beat you there and demand a higher price?"

He smiled. "Something like that. The more cattle bought, the more prices fall."

Faith could see he enjoyed explaining the procedure to her. She reveled in the secret knowledge that she wasn't nearly as green on such matters as she appeared. She'd always kept up on the stock reports, discussing them with Papa.

Though neither of them had moved an inch, it suddenly seemed they were sitting closer. She could feel the cloth of his trousers brushing her skirt. She wondered if he was aware of it, too.

"So, you'll drive the herd to San Antonio. Can you do that by yourself? You're just one man, and there are so many cattle."

"The ranch hands will help."

"Ranch hands? I've never seen anyone around other than you and Mother Shepherd."

"That's because the bunkhouse is at the far side of the land." He laughed. "Mama wants it that way."

Faith felt fuzzy with warmth. It was the first time she'd heard him laugh, and she loved the sound.

"Why would she insist on such measures?"

His eyes grew distant now. "Mama hasn't been herself lately. I'm worried about her. She has it in her head that our help pose a danger to her. She wants nothing to do with them."

"Are the men dangerous?"

"Most of the men are decent and hardworking. There are always a few who get out of line, but not many because they know they'll be sent packing when they do."

"I imagine it's hard for a man to get out of line in Deliverance. There are no saloons."

Nicholas chuckled, a manly sort of chuckle that made Faith blush. "San Antone has all they need. There have been a couple of times when a cowhand has come back with more cheap whiskey in his belly than pay in his pocket."

Faith wondered if she should mention Liza's brown vial. She decided against it; it would only cause him more worry. "What did Mother Shepherd want you to do about the men?"

"She wanted the bunkhouse moved." He chuckled again.

His mood was infectious. Faith joined in, and they had a good laugh over nothing. Neither meant disrespect toward Liza.

Faith regained her composure. "What happens when you sell the cattle in San Antonio?"

"A broker will arrange for the herd to be driven up the Chisholm Trail. There the cattle will be delivered to the buyer. Usually in Wichita or Abilene."

"I see." Faith paused. "Why don't you just cut out the middleman and drive the herd to the buyer yourself?"

He looked at her a long moment. "Very astute of you, Faith. Because it's a long, hard drive. For years we delivered the herd to the buyer. When my father was alive . . ." Nicholas stared into his empty cup. "Is there any more coffee?"

"Plenty." Faith gathered the cups and disappeared into the house. She glanced into the parlor and heard Liza's soft snores. While the pot was heating, she thought of Nicholas and the way he'd suddenly changed the subject at the mention of his father. Why?

"There's more," Faith offered when she returned and handed Nicholas his cup.

"Thank you."

Sitting down, she gazed at the stars. It was a romantic night. Was he mindful? "Are Texas nights always this pretty?"

Nicholas gazed at the sky. "Seem to be."

"Have you always lived here?"

"I was born here—in this house."

"And your parents, were they born here too?"

Nicholas set the cup aside. "No, they're from Kentucky. Father married Mother when she was sixteen. A year before I was born, they loaded everything they owned into a wagon and headed west. When they reached Texas, they fell in love with the land. Papa staked his claim, then built the herd with hard work and a lot of blood and sweat."

Faith smiled, warmed by the knowledge that he was opening up to her. It filled her heart with joy. She set the swing in gentle motion. "No brothers or sisters?"

"Just me." Nicholas closed his eyes, and she could see him relax. The dim kitchen light shadowed his face, and he looked like a small, tired boy. "The folks wanted more, but no others came along."

"Nicholas?" she asked gently. "How did your father die?"

Nicholas stiffened. A seemingly endless moment passed. Faith wished she hadn't asked. Papa always said she talked too much. She was beginning to think he was right. Some people needed more time to heal than others. At least that's what Aunt Thalia always said.

Exhaling a deep breath, Nicholas said softly, "Papa was shoeing a mule. No one's sure how it happened, but Gus, a ranch hand, was in the barn pitching hay. He said something must have spooked the mule. Said the animal went wild—Papa tried to get out of the way. The mule kicked him in the head. When Gus got to him, Papa was dead."

Faith shut her eyes, in touch with his pain. "I'm so sorry." They sat in silence as the lantern in the kitchen sputtered, then went out.

"Mama took it hard," Nicholas admitted. "She's still taking it bad. That's why I appease her moods."

Faith reached over and laid her hand on top of his. At least he'd noticed them. "I can imagine how hard it must be for her."

"She'd been with him most of her life. Papa used to

laugh and say he'd practically raised her. She hasn't been the same since he died."

Faith looked at the strong, rugged man that sat beside her. Even in the depths of his pain, his concern was for others. Faith was grateful the Lord had allowed her to see a softer side of this man.

Aware that she was still holding his hand, she let go and smoothed her dress. It wasn't proper for a lady to be so forward.

Nicholas stretched, then got to his feet. "It's late— Faith, when I get back from San Antonio, we might saddle those two horses you favor and take a ride. Would you like that?"

Faith thought of those two splendid Appaloosas and beamed. "Very much so."

He offered his hand and helped her up. "Will you be comfortable while I'm gone?"

"I'll be fine. If you don't mind, I'd like to spend time with little Adam Walters." The child had been on her mind since the barn raising. If she could help the sightless boy to experience the world more fully through her eyes, that would make her very happy.

"Dan Walters's boy?"

"Yes—do you mind? I thought with my teaching experience I might be able to help."

"No, I don't mind. The boy's a bright child—just let Mama know what you're doing."

"I will—and Nicholas?" Faith allowed him to open the screen door for her. She gazed into his eyes, picturing their clear blue in the darkness. Her stomach quivered.

"Yes?"

"Thank you for sharing your thoughts with me."

"I was just about to thank you for the same thing." Their eyes met briefly and a silent message passed between them. They could be friends.

As Faith approached the staircase, she turned to Nicholas. "Be careful while you're gone."

"You do the same." He disappeared into his room, softly closing the door behind him.

Chapter Seven

FAITH sat between Nicholas and Liza on the way to the Saturday-night community dance. She'd wished a hundred times she'd been more thoughtful, shown more discretion at the Johnson barn raising, but tonight would be different. She was on new footing with Nicholas after their talk on the porch; she would guard her behavior, although she enjoyed Dan's company and adored his children. When she thought of how excited Adam was when she'd told him stories, she felt she had to share it with someone, so she'd sat up late last night writing long letters to Hope, June, and Aunt Thalia, extolling Dan and his children. God did indeed work in mysterious ways, for if he hadn't sent her to Deliverance, she might never have known the joy of reading to a sightless child. She'd never met anyone who was blind,

93

unless she could count old Mr. Gunnison, who Papa had said could see a little even if he contended he was blind as a bat. Papa said Mr. Gunnison overly enjoyed attention.

As usual, silence prevailed as the wagon bounced along the rutted trail. Faith searched the countryside for signs of trouble, relieved when she saw nothing but a radiant gold-and-blue sunset, though there were clouds looming in the east. The thought of lively music and tasty food quickened her excitement. It had been a long time since she had enjoyed a social evening.

She studied Liza from the corner of her eye, wondering why she'd wanted to come tonight. Faith couldn't imagine her cutting a feisty jig on the dance floor. Yet she appeared to have taken more care than usual with her appearance tonight. Faith bit back a smile, recalling how Jeremiah had started sprucing up lately. He'd looked right dapper at the Johnsons'. Clean shaven, smelling of soap and water instead of donkey. And he was wearing new clothes. Was it possible Jeremiah was smitten with Liza?

A laugh bubbled in Faith's throat when she thought of the unlikely pair: dour-faced Liza and good-hearted Jeremiah. She laughed out loud, remembering how she'd complimented Jeremiah on his new haircut. He blushed, dismissing the compliment as if it embarrassed him. Had Jeremiah ever been married? Did he have children of his own?

Faith glanced at Liza. Had she ever once laughed or had fun? What had Abe Shepherd been like? Debonair? Jovial? Rowdy and fun loving? Cranky, like Liza? The picture sitting on the parlor table portrayed Nicholas's father as a handsome man with a handlebar mustache and a brisk twinkle in his eye.

She laughed out loud again and jumped when Nicholas elbowed her and gave her a stern look.

"Sorry," she muttered, straightening the skirt of her

dress. But the thought of Jeremiah and Liza together was funny.

The air was close, with an occasional flash of light in the east. Faith loved a good thunderstorm with jagged lightning and gusty wind. As a child she used to stand in the rain, arms outstretched, experiencing God's awesome power.

Jeremiah stepped off the porch when the Shepherd buggy rolled to a stop in front of the community hall. If Faith was surprised by his improved appearance at the Johnsons', she was thrilled with his appearance tonight. He was clean shaven and wore a sedate lightweight brown suit and white shirt. He looked different, distinguished, not at all like the shaggy recluse who had given her a ride into town on his mule.

Jeremiah reached for the horse's bridle, smiling. "Looks like we're in for a good soaking."

"We can always use rain." Nicholas set the brake, then wrapped the reins around it. "Surprised to see you in town tonight, Jeremiah."

Jeremiah smiled, his eyes openly admiring Liza Shepherd. "I never miss the opportunity to be with a pretty lady." He lifted a hand to help Liza down. When her foot touched the ground, she broke the contact, primly adjusting her dress into place, refusing to meet Jeremiah's eyes. "May I say you look fetching tonight, Mrs. Shepherd?"

Liza's eyes narrowed. "Don't you have anything better to do with your time than annoy folks, Mr. . . ." She paused, her face going temporarily blank.

"Montgomery." Jeremiah supplied. "Jeremiah Wilson Montgomery. And I have a variety of interesting ways to spend my time, but I would rather make the effort talking to you."

Adjusting her shawl, Liza sidestepped him and disappeared into the brightly lit community hall, where the sounds of fiddles and guitars filled the air.

Faith stepped from the wagon, wondering why Liza was so bent on acting ugly. Jeremiah was only trying to be sociable, and Liza did look . . . well, nice tonight . . . softer, less daunting. The particular shade of green she was wearing complimented her . . . made her hazel eyes look more . . . human-like.

Faith softened as Nicholas took her arm and they climbed the wooden steps. The polite contact sent her heart racing. At times he acted as though he didn't like her, much less want to marry her. At others he seemed polite, almost gentle. His moods were a puzzlement.

The brightly lit hall was crowded. Faith spotted the town's eligible women quickly. They surged toward Nicholas, smiling and gesturing. A young, very pretty, brown-haired woman waved to him from across the room.

Nicholas smiled at her, acknowledging her greeting. Faith was startled when she felt a twinge of jealousy.

A group of ranchers who were gathered around the punch bowl called to Nicholas, motioning for him to join them.

Settling Faith on a bench, he said quietly, "Please try to remember your place."

Faith's eyes focused on the colorfully dressed dancers whirling around the floor. Her foot automatically tapped to the beat of the lively music. "My place is to sit here on this hard bench all evening?"

"That isn't amusing, Miss Kallahan."

"Neither is being the dance wallflower, Mr. Shepherd."

"We're here for you to become better acquainted with our neighbors, not necessarily to dance." Nicholas straightened. "I'll be nearby if you need me."

Faith didn't doubt that. Between him and Mother Shepherd, she would be watched like a hawk.

Nicholas wandered off as Faith settled her skirts, prepared to endure a long evening. A quick search of the dance floor confirmed her suspicions: There were few men her age in attendance. A lanky youth with a rash of angry-looking pimples looked her way, but she quickly averted his gaze. Tonight she was intent on behaving properly. She would not give Nicholas or Liza one morsel to fault her. She located Liza conversing with Vera Hicks and two other ladies gathered around the refreshment table. Jeremiah was standing to the side, talking to the Reverend. Faith giggled, wondering if Liza was aware she had an admirer . . . no, she wouldn't be. Having an admirer would border on frivolity, and no one could accuse Liza Shepherd of having a frivolous bone in her body. Actually she was downright rude to Jeremiah, and Faith wondered why. Jeremiah was the epitome of politeness. Until recently he could have taken more care with his appearance, but Faith had been taught to look deeper than the outside. She knew Liza would be horrified to know how intently Jeremiah's intelligent eyes followed her around the room.

A small group of men and women stood at the back of the hall, discussing the needed new church steeple. Their remarks caught Faith's attention. She strained to hear their conversation.

"One good wind and it's gonna come down," a stout-looking man proclaimed.

"We're still hundreds of dollars short from being able to replace the steeple," his wife said. "Everybody's given all they can." Eyes swiveled to Liza, who was ladling herself a cup of punch.

"Looks to me like someone ought to just open up their moth-eaten pocketbook and donate a new steeple." The woman's voice dropped to a whisper. "The Shepherds have all the money they'll ever need. Why Nicholas doesn't put his foot down with Liza puzzles me. If Abe were alive, it'd be a different story, I'm here to tell you."

"Now, Geraldine," her husband patted his wife's arm. "If it weren't for Nicholas, the Brunson family wouldn't have a roof over their heads. Wasn't he the one who paid to have their house built back after the fire? As I recall, Liza didn't like it, but Nicholas did it anyway."

"Yes, and remember Liza paid for Whit Lawson's little girl's leg braces. Poor little mite would have been a cripple if Liza hadn't stepped in," a silver-haired woman added.

"Liza was a different woman then. Abe was alive."

"If the Shepherds are so blamed charitable, why don't they offer to replace the steeple?"

"Well, we all know Liza's a good woman and serves the Lord. Seems a new steeple isn't high on her list of priorities these days."

The women looked at each other and tittered. "Doesn't seem like anything's high on her priorities these days," one observed.

The woman's statement was met by a round of good-natured laughter, and Faith wanted to go to them and tell them to stop whispering about Liza! Faith couldn't imagine why Liza didn't want to help with the steeple, but maybe she had her reasons.

Why *didn't* Liza buy that steeple? Seemed to Faith the Lord had poured out a blessing on the Shepherd family the likes of which most common folks had never seen. Papa would say, "The more God blesses a body, the more responsibility that person has to use his gifts wisely."

A disturbance drew Faith's attention to the doorway, where Dan was just coming in. Baby Lilly was screaming at the top of her lungs. Adam trailed behind Sissy, dragging a lumpy bag, which Faith assumed contained diapers and bottles.

Faith started to get up and help the new arrivals but quickly sank back down to the bench, remembering Nicholas's warning to keep her place. If she disobeyed, he would be angry.

Dan weaved toward her, holding Adam's hand and maneuvering Lilly on his right hip. The crowd moved back, allowing the noisy family plenty of leeway, a few shaking their heads in sympathy. Sissy spotted Faith and started running, dragging Adam along with her. The sightless boy tripped over his feet, and the bag spilled to the floor. Faith caught her breath as she heard the sound of breaking glass.

Before she thought, she was up, running to help the child. Milk bubbled out of the sack and pooled in a widening puddle on the floor.

Dan stooped down to pick up the broken bottle amid baby Lilly's deafening cries. "Stay back, Sissy! You'll cut yourself!"

Faith searched the room for Nicholas, relieved to see he'd barely looked up at the commotion. Taking a deep breath, she reached for the baby. As long as she didn't have fun, he'd have no reason to be upset with her. If ever a man needed help, it was Dan Walters.

Jiggling the baby up and down, Faith tried to calm her as Dan accepted a towel and mopped up the spilled milk. Adam and Sissy darted into the crowd, ducking between unsuspecting legs and creating general havoc.

Faith's heart went out to Dan as he sank down on the bench, trying to catch his breath. His discouraged thoughts were reflected in his eyes: The Walters family had been at the dance for less than five minutes, and the room already looked as if a cyclone had hit it.

Faith sat down beside him, lifting Lilly to her shoulder.

The baby's cries dwindled to soft mews, and she began to suck her fist.

"Maybe she's hungry." Faith glanced at Dan. "Do you have a bottle?"

"Not anymore. They were all in the sack."

"Well, I'm sure we can come up with something." She smiled. "Raising children isn't easy."

Sighing, Dan leaned back, bracing his head against the wall. He closed his eyes, and Faith knew he was relishing a rare quiet moment. "I do the best I can, but they need a ma."

Mary Ellen handed Faith a fresh bottle and smiled. "I always pack a spare, just for Lilly."

"Thank you, Mary Ellen. I don't know what I'd do without you." Dan grinned sheepishly.

Faith gently cradled Lilly's soft mound of carrot-colored hair as she fed her. The infant smelled of soured milk. Faith wished she could give her a good bath and sprinkle cornstarch on the heat rash dotting the baby's face. "You must miss your wife very much."

Dan laughed softly. "I miss her so much at times that I don't think I can stand it."

"You had a good marriage?" The question was intensely personal, and Faith hoped he wouldn't think her brash. They barely knew one another, certainly not well enough to confide their personal lives, yet in an odd way, she felt as if Dan were the only person in Deliverance she could talk to. The town women were polite, but they kept their distance. Nicholas ignored her, and Liza spoke only to criticize or reprimand.

"The best," Dan conceded. "Carolyn was real young when we got married . . . barely fifteen. We ran off. . . . Her pa had a fit . . . threatened to turn a double-gauge shotgun on me, but Carolyn stood between us and vowed he'd have to shoot her first." Faith pretended not to notice the moisture that suddenly filled his eyes. "I surely did love that woman." He glanced up. "I may be out of place askin', but what's a pretty lady like you doing marrying a Shepherd?"

"A Shepherd?" Faith frowned. He made it sound worse than a medieval curse.

"Oh, Nicholas is a good catch, I suppose . . . but he's older than you—"

"Not much. He's thirty-four."

"Thirty-four?" Dan shook his head. "I thought he was older."

"No," Faith conceded. "He just acts that way." Recognizing her disloyalty, she blushed. "I'm sorry. Sometimes I speak before I think. Nicholas is just very serious minded and worried about his mother. He feels a responsibility to Liza."

Dan snorted. "Surprised Liza is gonna let him get married. She's kept him on a choke chain since Abe died."

Faith's eyes were drawn back to Nicholas, who was standing at the punch bowl. The pretty brown-haired lady he'd smiled at earlier had him cornered. Nicholas's laughter floated to her.

Sitting up straighter, she watched the exchange, amazed by the difference a smile brought to his face. He lit with animation as he talked, eyes sparkling. The transformation was startling.

"Dan, who's Nicholas talking to?"

Dan's eyes traced her gaze. "That's Rachel. . . ."

"Who's Rachel?"

"Rachel . . . the woman Nicholas almost married. Hear tell, folks around here thought they'd tie the knot when they were younger, but she ended up marrying Joe Lanner." Dan lowered his voice. "Lanner drinks, and he gets real mean when he's under the influence. . . . She ought to leave him, but she won't."

About that time Nicholas threw his head back and laughed uproariously at something Rachel said.

Faith stiffened. "Is he still in love with her?" She had a sinking feeling he was—he'd never laughed at her remarks that way. A man didn't look at a woman the way Nicholas was looking at Rachel if he didn't feel something.

"You'd have to ask him. Story goes Rachel got tired of waiting for Nicholas to propose, so she up and married Lanner."

The woman, married or not, was standing rather close to Nicholas. Where was that Shepherd sense of propriety?

"You didn't answer my question." Dan's voice broke into her thoughts.

"I'm sorry. . . . What was the question?" Baby Lilly had settled down and was now dozing on her shoulder.

Dan was about to repeat the question but winced instead at the sound of chairs overturning. "Sissy!" he roared, coming to his feet. "Come here!"

The frisky three-year-old darted out the front door and made a beeline for the street. Annabelle Grayson latched on to the girl's shirttail to thwart the escape.

"I'm doing my best, but I guess I'm not hard enough on them," Dan confessed, sitting down. "Well, what about my question?"

She knew the one he meant. The whole town was buzzing about her situation. "It isn't that I wanted to be a mail-order bride, but my sisters and I didn't have a choice." She briefly explained the circumstances that had brought her to Deliverance. "Aunt Thalia can't afford to feed three more mouths forever, and the meager funds I made teaching school wouldn't support my sisters and me. So we answered an ad, and very shortly all three of us had offers of marriage."

"You answered an ad?"

She nodded. "It seemed the only sensible solution."

"I can't picture Nicholas running an ad. . . . What's the name of the journal?"

Faith told him, wondering at his sudden interest. "Would you like the address? I'm sure I have it somewhere. . . ."

Dan shrugged. "I've never heard of running an ad for a wife. . . . Cold Water has no eligible men?"

Faith thought about Edsel Martin and shivered. "Not really."

Dan shook his head in sympathy. "Real shame. A nice lady like you deserves the love of a good man."

Faith smoothed the baby's hair, silently agreeing. Just then Nicholas laughed again, and she bristled. Nicholas Shepherd was seeming less and less the likely candidate.

"Well, you're lucky to have part of Carolyn still with you. Lilly's a beautiful child."

"Yes, ma'am, she is. Looks exactly like her ma."

Lifting Lilly to her shoulder, Faith gently patted her back. "You've got your hands full. How do you handle three children and work every day?"

"Old Man Dickson's real understanding. He lets me bring the young'uns to work with me on the days I can't find anyone to look after them. The town ladies have been real good. Many a night I've come home to find supper waitin' on the table and the wash ironed and folded."

Adam darted toward the food table, tripping over Eldorene Hardy's foot. Eldorene's punch went airborne, landing in Lawrence Hardy's lap. Lawrence sprang up wide-eyed, muttering under his breath as he gingerly fanned the wet front of his britches.

Sissy raced to the punch bowl and grabbed the ladle, wielding it recklessly. Sticky red punch showered the occupants standing close by.

Faith could see the pride fairly oozing out of Dan as he watched the chaos. "Them kids are sure independent, got to hand it to 'em. Being blind don't stop Adam from doin' anything he sets his mind to."

"Yes," Faith agreed faintly. "He's spunky." The community hall was a shambles, chairs overturned, punch staining the once pristine white tablecloth, cookies ground underfoot, but Adam was independent, all right.

Dan shoved slowly to his feet. "Well, guess I better corral the young'uns. Can I get you a cup of punch?"

"No, thank you. I'll just sit here with the baby." Faith doubted there was a drop left in the bowl anyway.

"Well, much obliged." Dan wandered off in the direction of the sound of more shattering glass.

As Dan left, Jeremiah excused himself from Reverend Hicks and walked in Faith's direction. She smiled as he approached.

"What's a pretty little thing like you doing sitting on the sidelines?"

Patting the bench beside her, she motioned for him to join her. "I am behaving myself," she announced. "What's a handsome gentleman like you doing all alone? I should think the eligible women would be fawning over you."

Jeremiah chuckled, his eyes traveling to Liza. "Do you think a certain beautiful lady would box my jaw if I asked her to dance?"

Liza? Beautiful? Faith strained for a closer look at the dour-faced woman chatting with a group of women. Well, maybe she had been, once. Or maybe Jeremiah just needed spectacles.

Jeremiah's focus centered on the baby. "Heard her crying a minute ago. . . . Seemed a mite out of sorts."

"She's hungry, and her bottles are broken. Mary Ellen brought a spare, but Lilly drank it all."

Shaking his head, Jeremiah watched Dan trying to break up a food fight between Sissy and Adam. "Spirited children."

Faith nodded. "Real spirited."

Jeremiah settled down on the bench. "Well, at least

Dan's determined to keep them with him. He'll have to learn discipline, but he's not much more than a boy himself."

Faith nodded. "It's a shame Adam's energy can't be channeled. He's a bright boy."

"Exceptionally bright." Jeremiah reached in his pocket and took out a pipe. "Do you mind?"

Faith shook her head. "Papa always said it was the devil's habit, but I always kind of liked the smell of tobacco smoke."

Jeremiah opened a pouch and tapped tobacco into the bowl. "Bad habit, all right. Tell me about yourself, Miss Kallahan. You appear to be a highly intelligent young woman. Have you a formal education?"

She nodded. "Papa saw that his children were educated. My sisters and I were lucky. My mother graduated from one of the first women's colleges."

Jeremiah drew on his pipe. "I understand you've taught school?"

"Only for a couple of years; then Papa died. But I loved it, loved the children and seeing them learn."

Jeremiah puffed, sending billowing smoke spiraling toward the ceiling. The smell of tobacco floated pleasantly in the air.

"It's a real shame there's no one here in Deliverance who can teach Adam Braille."

"Braille?" Faith brightened. "Are you referring to the Frenchman Louis Braille . . . the man who invented the Braille system?"

"The same." Lighting a match, Jeremiah touched it to the tobacco, drawing deeply, whorls of white smoke mushrooming over his head. "Have you heard of him?"

"Heard of him! He was a dear friend of my grandpapa—Grandpapa Troy." She remembered how Grandpapa had said Louis had been blinded at the age of three in an accident. While studying in Paris at the National

Institute for Blind Youth, he'd witnessed an army officer demonstrate a military code for night communications. Grandpapa told how the code used dots and dashes but was too complex and inconvenient for the blind to use. The Institute's founder had developed cumbersome texts with large raised writing, but that, too, proved too complicated. When Louis was only fifteen years old, he improved the dot system, teaching it throughout his life.

"You don't say." Jeremiah drew on the pipe thoughtfully. "Then I'm sure you recognize the potential a child like Adam has."

"Yes, but I'm afraid I don't know anyone who teaches Braille." Louis Braille first published his dot system in 1829, but few, if any, in the rural communities taught it.

"Yes, yes," Jeremiah concurred, "Louis Braille's techniques are different . . . but I would imagine an illustrious person like yourself could pick them up easily enough."

Faith glanced over, and suspicion nagged her. From the moment she'd met Jeremiah, she thought there was more to the man than what appeared. Talking with him now, she detected a vein of intelligence and knowledge far superior to that of most men she knew. Did Jeremiah have a secret past? A past he kept well hidden beneath a scruffy exterior?

"Yes, I suppose one could learn Braille. . . . Have you personal knowledge of Braille's teaching?"

"Me? Oh, no. I've only read about his work."

"Really?" Faith eyed him suspiciously. "Do you have access to magazines and journals concerning the subject?" She couldn't imagine that he would, but his eyes belied his protestation.

"Oh . . . suppose I might be able to come up with something. . . . Why do you ask?"

Faith winced at the sound of silverware clattering to the floor. "What you say is true. Adam is exceptionally smart, and he was very responsive when I told him stories. A whole new world would open for him if he were able to read for himself. If you could provide material on the subject, perhaps I could teach Adam Braille. I would be happy to donate my time."

"That would be most gracious of you, Miss Kallahan."

"I would enjoy the challenge. Will you help?" Was that a mischievous twinkle in Jeremiah's eye?

"I'll certainly do whatever I can, but I can't promise I'll come up with anything. . . ."

Faith was elated at the thought of applying her teaching skills. She'd have to discuss the plan with Nicholas and Liza, of course, but surely they couldn't object to such a noble gesture. Her spirits sang. The outings would relieve her from household chores, and she'd do almost anything to get out of darning.

"Please see what you can find out, Jeremiah, and let me know."

"I'll do whatever I can, but right now I think you have bigger problems." Faith saw what he meant. Old Man Zimmer was threading his way across the room, his faded blue eyes zeroing in on her.

Rollie Zimmer was deaf as a board and missing every tooth in his head. He stopped in front of her, holding an earpiece to his right ear. "WANNA DANCE?"

Faith glanced at Jeremiah.

"COME ON, GIRLIE! LET'S YOU AND ME CUT A JIG!" He handed Jeremiah the horn, then grabbed Faith's hand and jerked her to her feet. Faith shot Jeremiah a frantic look as he reached for the baby. Shaking his head, he motioned for her to dance.

When they reached the dance floor, Rollie jumped straight up in the air and clicked his heels. He landed flat on his feet, his weathered face splitting into an impish grin. "HOWDY!"

"Howdy," Faith murmured, aware that every eye in

the room was on them. She located Nicholas and smiled lamely. He wouldn't care if she danced with Methuselah.

The music started, and Rollie whirled her around, then caught her in a breathless dip. Inspired, Faith tried to follow his lively steps. He jigged and jagged across the floor, pulling her along with him. She felt pins fly out of her hair when he suddenly paused and spun her around in the middle of the floor like a toy top. The room tilted, she staggered, flailing the air as she tried to regain her balance.

"YOU'RE A GOOD DANCER, HONEY PIE!" The old man energetically gave her another spin.

Faith blushed, wishing the dance floor would open up and swallow her. By now the other dancers had cleared a path, laughing at the funny spectacle. She, with her hair loosely flying, trying to match the spry old man's steps. She flew past Liza and witnessed her mortification at the unseemly exhibition.

Suddenly a large arm firmly encircled Faith's waist, halting the fiasco. She looked up to meet familiar cool blue eyes.

"May I cut in, Rollie?"

"EH?"

"Cut in—dance with my fiancée!"

"EH? DIDN'T SAY NOTHIN'! I'M DANCIN'!"

Nicholas leaned closer and shouted in Zimmer's good ear. "I WANT TO DANCE WITH MY FIANCÉE."

"WELL, WHY DIDN'T YOU SAY SO?" Rollie relinquished his hold on Faith, his ferretlike eyes spotting Widow Cumming sitting on the sidelines. When she saw his intentions, she bolted from the bench and headed for the front door. Rollie followed, hot on her heels.

The music slowed to a calming waltz. Nicholas lightly held Faith in his arms at a proper distance. She was surprised to find he danced flawlessly, gliding her effortlessly around the crowded floor. She wondered who had taught him the art. Beautiful Rachel, perhaps?

"Thank you," she murmured, remembering her manners.

He gazed down on her, amusement creasing the corners of his eyes. "For what?"

"For coming to my rescue. I . . ." He smiled, distracting her. Her stomach did somersaults. Why didn't he do that more often?

"I must say, you and Rollie made a pathetic sight."

She bit back a grin. She liked him immensely when he wasn't so serious. "I don't suppose we'd win any contests."

He drew her closer, renouncing propriety. "I can't imagine anyone letting you enter one."

Faith felt strangely right in his arms. She could smell the tangy scent of soap, the sun-dried scent of his shirt. She quickly located Liza and grinned when she saw that Jeremiah had her cornered.

Resting her head on Nicholas's broad shoulder, Faith sighed. Perhaps the evening wouldn't be so boring after all.

Thank you, Lord. Faith. That's what I've needed, to hang on in faith. I'm believing that you're going to keep helping Nicholas to come around.

Chapter Eight

LIZA placed a steaming bowl of gravy on the table, then took her seat. Nicholas said a prayer, and the day's routine began.

With Rachel's image still vivid in Faith's mind, she had dressed in the blue gingham this morning. She might as well have worn a burlap sack for all of Nicholas's interest.

The memory of Rachel's beauty haunted Faith. Rachel was so pretty, and Nicholas had once been in love with her. Was he still?

Well, one thing Faith was grateful for—if Nicholas didn't acknowledge her appearance this morning, he certainly wasn't going to notice the brown boots hidden beneath the hem. She couldn't wear those pointy shoes one more day.

Faith took a bite of biscuit, reviewing her talk with

Jeremiah the night before. Teaching Adam to read excited her. She had always eagerly embraced a challenge—especially when nothing but good could come of it. In this particular situation her direction wasn't quite clear, but her mind was made up. If Jeremiah could provide a channel by which she could purchase the Braille teaching material, she would teach Adam to read.

She had a small nest egg from her teaching funds. Aunt Thalia had insisted she keep the money she earned, so she'd set aside as much as she could spare from her daily expenses. She could think of no worthier cause for the money. She'd spent the better part of the night praying and asking God's guidance. Knowing she'd have the Shepherds to deal with, Faith had searched her mind for all possible arguments. She took comfort in knowing that, regardless of the outcome, her priorities were in proper order.

Last night Jeremiah had planted some powerful images in her mind. Little Adam, unknowingly, strengthened those thoughts. The idea of teaching Dan's son to read Braille quickly escalated. One little boy . . . then maybe another child, and then another. How many blind people lived in the area? Perhaps adults would come; perhaps she could start a school. . . . She pondered the creation of an institution that would serve hundreds of others.

She had been tempted to share her enthusiasm with Nicholas and Liza during the ride home last night. But Liza had seemed on edge. She sat in her usual place between them, fanning and grumbling about how close the air was. Faith wasn't sure if Liza's annoyance was due to Jeremiah's obvious attraction to her, or to Rollie Zimmer's spectacle on the dance floor. Whatever the reason, Faith hadn't mentioned her talk with Jeremiah.

She must wait for the proper time to discuss her idea of teaching the blind. . . . Studying Liza's and Nicholas's stoic faces, she feared there might never be a proper time. Her excitement couldn't be contained another moment. She had to tell someone before she burst!

Lifting her napkin, she blotted her mouth with the stiff muslin. "Nicholas, I've been thinking. . . ."

Nicholas and Liza lifted their heads in unison.

Faith's courage momentarily flagged, then revitalized. "Is this an appropriate time?"

Liza frowned. "We don't discuss trivialities during mealtime."

"My thoughts aren't trivial, Mother Shepherd." Faith tempered her inclination to scream.

Nicholas calmly poured cream into his coffee. "Mama, let her speak."

"Nicholas, we—"

"Let her speak, Mama." Nicholas nodded to Faith. "What is it, Faith?"

Faith hoped her gratitude showed in her eyes. "Thank you. Jeremiah and I had a talk last night. If it's all right with you and Mother Shepherd, I would like to teach Adam Walters to read." When objection flared in Liza's eyes, Faith hurried on. "Of course, I'll have to speak to Dan, but I'm hoping that if I'm successful in obtaining his permission, then I might teach other blind in the area to read."

"Hogwash and dishwater."

Nicholas pushed the cream pitcher aside. "You surely have a way with words, Mama."

"Don't use that tone with me, Nicholas Shepherd! You'll be taking your breakfast outside to eat with the dogs!"

"We don't have dogs."

"Well, let me tell you—if we did, you'd be eating with them. I'll not tolerate disrespect!"

The conversation was disintegrating. Faith didn't intend to be dissuaded from her purpose. Her mouth opened, intent on saying something she'd no doubt regret. But

Aunt Thalia's calming words of biblical wisdom reverberated softly in her spirit. *Be slow to anger, and sin not. . . .*

Biting her bottom lip, Faith moderated her tone, "My
family always shared conversation at the dinner table—"

"Well, this isn't dinner," Liza said.

"I'm *going* to teach Adam to *read.*" There. She'd said
it. Faith waited for the explosion.

To her relief, none was forthcoming. Liza's mouth
dropped open; Nicholas simply eyed her with curiosity.

She could see they both clearly thought she had lost
her mind.

"In all my born days—are you addled? Dan's boy is
blind." Liza shook her head. "How do you propose to
teach a blind child to read?"

Faith blushed. "I'm going to learn Braille and then—"

"Braille? Those dot things?" Liza shook her head
again. "Doesn't make a bit of difference what you learn,
you can't open that boy's eyes."

"By using Braille, Mother Shepherd, Adam can learn
to read. And not just Dan's son, others can too."

"What others? I don't know any others."

"Maybe not in Deliverance. But there are undoubtedly
many in Texas, and once the blind school—"

Nicholas interrupted. "Are you saying a blind child can
be taught to read?"

"Yes," Faith said proudly. "And taught many other
things. Learning to read is only the beginning."

Liza looked faint, sitting back in her chair to fan herself.

"You call this method Braille?" Nicholas asked.

"Yes, Braille."

"And how is it you seem to know—"

It was all the encouragement Faith needed. Sliding to
the edge of her chair, she explained. "Grandpapa was
born in Coupvray, near Paris. As children, he and Louis

Braille played together in the village. When Mr. Braille was very small, he was blinded in an accident."

She was pleased to see that Nicholas was listening closely. She relayed the story of Louis and how he had developed the Braille system.

"Grandpapa took great pleasure in telling of his boyhood friendship with Louis. As the years passed, they didn't spend as much time together, but they continued to correspond with each other. They did so until Mr. Braille died in '52."

"If this Mr. Braille was blind, how was he able to teach others like him?"

"Blind leading the blind," Liza muttered.

"Mother." Nicholas sent her a censuring look.

"No—she's right, Nicholas. In a sense, that's exactly what happened."

"How did Louis Braille teach blind children to make sense of a bunch of dots on a piece of cardboard?" Liza exclaimed.

Faith was more than happy to tell her. "It only took Louis five years to develop the system. From what I've read in journals, Mr. Braille created his dot system using six dots. From sixty-three possible arrangements of the dots, he devised an entire alphabet, punctuation marks, numerals, and later even a means for writing music!"

Faith knew Liza would never admit to it, but even her curiosity was obviously kindled. "From a bunch of dots?"

"Not just dots. Each letter, numeral, or punctuation mark is indicated by the number and arrangement of one to six dots in a cell, or letter space, two dots wide and three dots high."

Liza's skepticism returned. "Dots, spots, or knots! The blind can't see to read them."

"That's true. But Braille books are pressed from metal plates. The sightless read Braille by feel—running their fingers over the dots."

"I think you were out in the sun too long yesterday." Liza reached for a second biscuit. "And just how far will running fingers over a bunch of dots help that poor Walters boy?"

"Plenty," Faith defended herself. "Louis Braille was an outstanding student, excelling in science and music. In fact, he became famous in Paris as an organist and as a violoncellist. Not to mention a *church* organist."

Liza's eyes softened with respect. "He learned to play organ in the church?"

Faith nodded. "Yes, and other blind children can be taught to do the same, and more."

Nicholas studied her. "But you said you'd need to learn this Braille?"

"My, yes. Coupvray was long before my time. When Mother was a baby, her parents immigrated to this country. I was born in Michigan. Grandpapa used to tell us stories about Louis Braille. I was always fascinated by Grandpapa's good friend and paid attention to every detail. But I've never had access to a Braille book. I intend to exhaust every opportunity to find one. With Jeremiah's help, I know I can learn."

"Jeremiah! What could that old coot know about Braille?" Liza snapped.

"I don't know—but I have a feeling he knows more than he's saying. He's promised to do all he can to help me."

Liza cleaned her plate and pushed back from the table. "Helping little Adam Walters is one thing, but a blind school—that's a horse of a different color."

"Blind children should have the same advantages as sighted children."

"An entire school for one blind child? That's nonsense."

"The school wouldn't be just for Adam. We could invite others."

Nicholas laid his fork aside. "You know, Mama, there are some other blind people I know about. What about Gregory Hillman, and that Bittle girl? Are you thinking you'd teach children and adults, Faith?"

"Yes, children and adults!"

"Nonsense! A school costs money, money the town doesn't have. Nicholas, talk some sense into her."

After a moment's thought, Nicholas said, "A blind school makes more sense than a steeple. You would need a building—I suppose we could look into the Smith place."

Faith could barely contain her excitement. "The Smith place?"

"It's been abandoned for years and getting to be an eyesore. It could serve as a school," Nicholas conceded. "The old schoolhouse has plenty of room. Until the blind school has enough pupils to keep you busy, perhaps the school can be used not only for the children but, if you're willing, also for teaching adults who don't know how to read. Lord knows, there's enough men and women around here who can't read a thing." He smiled. "I think your idea is sound, Faith."

Liza was predictably quick to spoil the mood. "And who's going to pay for cleaning up that eyesore, not to mention acquiring the property?"

Faith glanced to Nicholas for support. "Wouldn't the town help—?"

Liza cut in. "Help, help, help. That's all I ever hear. Why is it when people holler help, what they really mean is money! Why don't they just come right out and say what they mean? Money. You know why. Because a fool and his money are soon parted."

Faith was sorely tempted to stand up and fight for her cause, but she declined. Papa said you shouldn't kill a fly on a friend's head using a hatchet, and though Liza wasn't exactly a friend, she did control the Shepherd purse strings.

Faith allowed the subject to drop. But she wasn't about to forget it. If she could teach Adam and others like him to read, that's what she was going to do. The Lord had laid the mission on her heart, and she gladly accepted it.

When breakfast was over, Nicholas excused himself and left the house. Faith knew he was getting ready for the upcoming cattle drive. For the first time she resented Liza for having such a hold on her son, and Nicholas more, for allowing it. She'd had Nicholas on her side until Liza threw on the wet blanket.

"The morning's near spent," Liza said, clearing the table. "We have chores."

Faith reached for an apron. "I'll feed the chickens."

"Don't stay out there all day."

"No, ma'am. I won't."

Faith barely finished sprinkling feed in the chicken coop when Liza rounded the corner. Her unexpected visit startled Faith. The hens set to cackling and flapping their wings. Faith snickered, thinking how Liza could intimidate even the least of God's creatures.

"It's butchering time. There's pig's feet waiting to be put up," Liza informed her. "I need your help in the kitchen."

Pig's feet. Faith's heart sank. That would take all day. She hated pig's feet. The mere sight of those boney-looking hoofy paws made her sick.

"Yes, ma'am." She set aside the feed bag, latched the weathered gate, and followed Liza into the house.

As she entered the kitchen, she tried not to look at the huge pan of feet. Jars lined the counter. Did Liza intend to feed an army? She would be stuck in this kitchen forever.

Liza sat down across from Faith at the table, and the two women set to work.

Faith stuffed pig's feet into jars until her fingers ached. Still, her pan was half full. Liza finished her share with remarkable speed.

She eyed Faith's pan, sighing with impatience. "I'll wash more jars. You fetch more water."

Faith drew two buckets of water from the open well and hurried back inside. Though her heart wasn't in it, she knew the harder she worked, the quicker she could escape the kitchen and those hateful feet.

Liza washed and dried the remaining canning jars. Stuffing the last foot into a jar around noon, Faith drew a sigh of relief. Her fingers ached, not to mention her sore back.

It took both women to carry the cumbersome load to the stove.

As the water started to boil, Liza picked up a basket of dirty laundry. "I'll be doing wash. Don't let the pan boil dry."

"Yes, ma'am."

Faith was amazed how quickly her enthusiasm rekindled about the school for the blind. She would just explode if she didn't tell someone.

Hope and June. They were happily married now, without all the problems she faced; still, they would understand her excitement about the school.

Her sisters would be delighted to hear of her grand adventure. Faith glanced at the pot of boiling pig's feet. Liza's "don't let the pan boil dry" sounded in her mind. The pan looked just fine, she determined, before going to her room for the stationery Aunt Thalia had given her.

Sitting back down at the kitchen table, she wrote Hope first.

My dearest Hope,
It is with great sadness that I write, for I sorely miss you. You are always in my thoughts and my prayers. Have you

any word from June or Aunt Thalia? I pray for a letter. I suppose it takes a good many days for such correspondence to reach Texas. This land is so big; most of the time I feel as though I've gone to another country.

There are so many times my heart aches for the three of us to be together again, with Aunt Thalia, in Cold Water. I often wonder if Deliverance will ever be my home . . . a home like the three of us shared, with laughter and happy times. There is very little laughter and virtually no happy times here.

I have no intention of doubting the good Lord's ability to know what is best for me, but I admit that at times my faith falters. I wonder if I have made a mistake in understanding his direction. Deliverance seems to be anything but a place where I belong.

Dreary is a word that describes my present situation. Now that I think about it, the calamity started mere miles before I arrived. The stagecoach broke down just outside of Deliverance. A kind man named Jeremiah was generous enough to bring me into town on the back of a donkey. . . .

I am yet to be a bride, though several attempts have been undertaken. You will not believe the obstacles; still, I will share them with you. Perhaps in doing so, we may have ourselves a hearty laugh or two. It's far more uplifting than crying, which I'm often tempted to do.

Faith then wrote all about the wedding delays, her spoiled dress, and Mary Ellen's birthing twins. As she wrote, she sometimes wiped away a tear, and sometimes giggled.

Now Nicholas informs me the wedding must be postponed yet another two weeks. He is leaving soon to drive cattle to San Antonio, where they will be sold and herded up the Chisholm Trail to somewhere in Abilene or Wichita. Nicholas is a puzzling man, but one I think I could grow to love.

At times he seems tied to his mother's apron strings, but I think he only appeases her because he's worried about her. If I didn't believe that, if I didn't believe there was still hope for us, I would be on my way back to Michigan this very moment.

I know this letter must leave you disheartened. But blessings do abound. There is a very nice young widower, Dan Walters. His struggles are many. But he's taken time to be very kind to me and is a perfect gentleman in the truest respect. His wife died giving birth to his daughter. The baby's a darling nine-month-old named Lilly. Dan says she is the image of her mother. Dan also has two other children. Sissy, who's three years old and full of vinegar, and Adam, as rambunctious as any five-year-old, except that he is blind. He has been since birth.

But don't be sad, my precious Hope. This is where the good news starts. I have the utmost intentions of learning Braille, and as quickly as possible. Jeremiah, the hermit I told you about, is trying to help me get some Braille books. I want—I have a burning need—to teach Adam to read. Perhaps that is my calling, the true reason God has brought me to Deliverance. After all, the way things are going, it's beginning to look like a wedding isn't the purpose for my journey. Ha. Yes, you may laugh. But not hysterically.

Hope, whatever the Lord has me do, I willingly rejoice in his labor. When I think of Adam and all of the possibilities, my heart sings. I think of the Scripture "and a child shall lead them." Perhaps, though Adam's eyes are now darkened, he will yet be able to shed light, giving hope and a measure of deliverance to others with the same affliction. You can see how desperate I am to be even the smallest part of that miracle. And not just for Adam, though I love him dearly. There are many who live in darkness, longing for a brighter way. I have this dream of starting a school to help all the blind who will come learn how to read.

My dear sister, I ask that you unite with me in prayer

concerning this matter. I know that you will, and God's will shall be done.

I truly wish that Nicholas would stand up to his mother more. He has the patience of Job with that woman. Although I pray every night for God to give me more patience, I still find it very hard to still my fiery tongue.

Faith penned a similar letter to June. Writing to her sisters eased the homesickness she'd been battling for days. She addressed and sealed each envelope with care. It felt so good to share her feelings with someone who would understand.

She suddenly sat up straighter, catching a whiff of a foul odor.

The pan! Faith sprang from her chair and dashed to the stove. The pan was bone-dry. Jars exploded, sending a plume of steam and pig's feet spiraling toward the ceiling. Feet belched from the pan like hot ash.

Throwing her arms over her head, Faith ducked as thousands of boney particles rained down on her. When the explosion died off, the room turned deadly silent.

Horrified, she viewed the carnage. Shattered glass from broken jars littered counters and floors. Pieces of pig's feet hung from the ceiling. Nothing could be salvaged. Not even the pan.

Smoke stung Faith's eyes; the odor was sickening.

Fanning with a dish towel, she glanced outside and groaned when she saw Liza coming toward the house, empty laundry basket tucked beneath her arm.

Sinking into a chair at the kitchen table, Faith braced herself for the approaching storm.

It was likely to be a dandy.

Chapter Nine

DUSTING the oak sideboard, Liza's hands suddenly stilled. Picking up a small picture frame, she smiled. "Good morning, Abe. I miss you, darling." Her fingertips lovingly traced the features of her beloved's face smiling back at her. Abe. Husband, lover, best friend. When would the awful pain ease? Friends said, "Time, Liza. Time will heal your loss." But time had failed to change anything. Would she ever go to bed at night without automatically reaching for the comfort of Abe's arms? He had been her protector, her mentor, the reason she got up every morning. And he was gone.

Evenings she used to look up from her handwork and see him sitting beside her, reading a journal, spectacles riding on the bridge of his nose. Tonight when she looks up, she will see his empty chair.

She kept the furniture covered now, unable to cope with memories. Abe had made every single piece; worked for years to build whatever she wanted. She couldn't bear to look at the furnishings now; it just inflicted fresh wounds.

She had prayed—oh how she had prayed—that when it was time, God would take Abe and her together in order to spare the other agony. It was a selfish wish; she knew that. God had called Abe first. Now only she remained to look after their son.

Nicholas was a dutiful boy, but a son couldn't take his father's place. Not in matters of the heart.

Alarmed, Liza's hand came to her throat as the familiar thump vibrated in her chest. She needed to see Doc about her worsening condition, yet she was frightened, afraid Doc would tell her there was something horribly wrong: She was going to die.

At times she felt she'd welcome death. Since Abe had died, Liza thought of the grave more as a friend than an enemy. Dying didn't concern her, for she knew in whom she believed. Her concern lay with Nicholas. If she were gone, who would see to his needs? Who would love him, care for him? She'd prayed daily for the Lord to send a good woman into Nicholas's life—a woman, not a scatterbrained child from Michigan! Her heart skipped erratically. *Oh, Abe, I'm in desperate need of assurance that our child will have someone to rely on when I'm gone—and God has sent a twit.*

Liza wanted a home for Nicholas, a wife, children. She wanted to die with the certainty that he was happy, surrounded by those he loved. But Nicholas no longer believed in love. She saw the way he looked at Rachel, as though still convinced that she was the one woman who would have made him happy. Liza didn't for a minute agree with him. Rachel's passive nature would never mix with Nicholas's proud spirit Actually, Faith was more suited to Nicholas's nature. . . .

Odd how that just came to her. Of course, those pig's feet. . . . A grin hovered at the corners of her mouth. Land sakes . . . all those pieces of feet clinging to the ceiling. Her smile died.

Liza knew her "condition" made her impossible to live with lately, but she still had a clear mind—most of the time. More often than not, her conversations with her son ended in arguments. Lately, Nicholas had been predisposed to silence; she supposed it was an effort to keep the peace.

Her fingers tenderly retraced the photograph of her smiling husband, arm in arm with his son in the field. The photograph was old and tattered, like her heart. Abe was very handsome. . . . Nicholas looked so much like his father. She bit back tears, aching to hear her husband's voice, the sound of his silly laugh. . . .

Tears rolled down her cheeks, and her heart thumped. Emptiness settled in the pit of her stomach as she blindly set the picture down and dusted around it. All the tears in the world wouldn't bring Abe back. He was gone. When was she ever going to face it?

She missed Nicholas. Faith was startled by the admission, but it was true. She missed Nicholas. This strange man she'd agreed to take as a husband had been gone for over a week, and the days were endless without him.

Though Nicholas had barely acknowledged her presence, when he was around, the house seemed warmer, more bearable.

On the rare occasions when she experienced his smile or enjoyed his laugh, she was filled with the outrageous need for him to like her. She enjoyed seeing him read his Bible at night by the fire, looking so strong and confident. And she was sure his submissive way toward Liza was out of kindness, not weakness. Given the slightest encouragement, she might easily fall in love with this tall, somber man.

Nicholas practiced his faith more quietly than most men, yet it ran true and strong in his veins. True, there were times it seemed mother and son were set upon by the devil himself, determined to suck every shred of Christian joy out of their lives.

And yet . . . he could be kind. She smiled when she recalled how Nicholas had pulled her aside just before leaving. Concern colored his eyes, and he'd instructed her in a strong, confident voice, "You take care of yourself— don't be delivering any calves or shooting any snakes while I'm gone. Be in before dark, and if Mama gets on your nerves, go visit Mary Ellen. You hear?"

She'd nodded, feeling all warm inside. It had sounded almost as if he cared—honestly cared—about her welfare. He was such a puzzlement: stern one minute, irresistible the next.

Faith had known other Christians like the Shepherds. Papa had called them suffering Christians. Those who accepted Christ but took no joy in living. All was law, and Christianity a sentence to be practiced conscientiously until God called them home. Faith felt that Christians should be the happiest folks around. What loss God must feel when his children failed to live a rich, full life.

Rinsing a skillet, Faith laid it aside. Perhaps Nicholas liked her more than she thought. There'd been times lately when he had acted like a smitten suitor. When other men had shown her attention—particularly Dan— Nicholas's mouth tightened, and he made her stop whatever she was doing and join him. The corners of her mouth turned up. She shouldn't take delight in his insecurity, and she certainly didn't encourage it; but she had to admit she rather enjoyed Nicholas's attention.

Dan was always grateful for her help. Considering the failed wedding attempts, Faith wondered if God had maybe sent her to Dan . . . to be a mother to his children rather than an unappreciated guest in the Shepherd house.

Folding the dishcloth, she draped it over a drying rack, then bent to pick up a stray piece of pig's feet she'd missed the day before. She never would have dreamed the chaos those exploding jars of pig's feet could cause. She'd thought Liza would faint when she saw the kitchen. But after her first bewildered stare, she had begun to grin, then chuckle, and before they knew it, the two women were laughing until the tears trickled down their cheeks. Faith shook her head. There was no figuring that woman out. After their laughter died down, Liza had said, "Of course, you'll have to clean it all up. Nicholas will be disappointed; he loves pig's feet." A grin hovered around the corners of her mouth. "To tell the truth, I've always detested them. But the neighbors know how much Nicholas likes them, and they supply him with all he can eat." Then, before Faith could say a word, she had turned around and left the kitchen.

Straightening, Faith focused on the small tin of snuff sitting on the counter. Such a tasteless habit. Why did Liza insist on chewing? Reaching for the tin, she quickly disposed of it. Perhaps Liza would rid herself of the habit if temptation weren't so readily at hand. If Faith could find that brown vial Liza kept in her apron pocket, she'd throw that away too!

She called to Mother Shepherd in the parlor. "Would it be all right if I took the buggy into town this morning?" Closing her eyes, she held her breath, waiting for the answer. It would be her first outing alone since she'd arrived in Deliverance, but if she didn't escape Liza's critical eye for a few hours, she was going to scream. She would hitch the buggy and go into town. She needed a few personal items from the mercantile, and while she was at it, she wanted to visit the land office to inquire about the Smith house. Nicholas and Liza hadn't approved her starting the school for the blind, but they hadn't forbidden her to start one either.

Liza poked her head around the kitchen doorway. "Why do you want to go into town?"

"Well . . ." Faith worried her teeth against her lower lip. She could fib. She could pretend she desperately needed something personal from the mercantile, and Liza wouldn't know the difference unless she went out of her way to check with Oren Stokes.

Papa's voice echoing Leviticus rang in her mind: "Ye shall not steal, neither deal falsely, neither lie one to another."

Drats. "Well . . . I thought it might be neighborly to stop by Mary Ellen's and see if she needed help with the new babies."

Not exactly her intended purpose for going into town, but neither was it an outright lie. She could easily stop by the Finney place.

Liza took a hanky from her bodice and fanned herself. "Nonsense. Mary Ellen can see after her own children. Have you seen my box of snuff?"

"No, ma'am." Faith's cheeks burned with the falsehood. *Forgive me, Lord; it's for her own good.* She stepped aside as Liza entered the kitchen, the older woman's eyes searching for the familiar tin.

Faith clasped her hands behind her back and trailed behind her. "I was thinking that Mary Ellen and her family might enjoy a fresh-baked cherry pie."

Liza's muffled voice floated down to her as she rummaged through a drawer. "Flour and sugar don't grow on trees, Miss Kallahan."

"But cherries do, Mother Shepherd." Liza had seen

enough canned cherries in the pantry to feed a horse. "May I go?"

"Oh, very well." Liza closed the drawer. "You may take the buggy, but don't be wearing out your welcome, you hear?"

"Yes, ma'am. Thank you! I won't be long!"

Faith ran to change into a dress with Liza's strident voice close on her heels. "Can't imagine what happened to my snuff lately. I've bought three cans this week!"

It was past noon by the time Faith hitched up the buggy, then tucked the fresh-baked pie into a secure corner. The crusty brown pastry was still hot to the touch. Climbing aboard, she picked up the reins, aware that Liza was standing in the doorway, watching her departure.

"You be back here before dark!"

"Yes, ma'am."

Snapping the reins, Faith set the horse into motion. The animal trotted briskly out of the barnyard as Liza stepped out on the porch, cupping her hands to her mouth. "And don't be running the wheels off that buggy!"

"Yes, ma'am! No, ma'am." Faith leaned out the side and waved. "I won't!"

Glorious sunshine beat down on the top of the buggy. Faith drew a deep breath, inhaling the sweet scent of honeysuckle growing wild along the roadside. Free at last! The horse stepped high as if he, too, welcomed the unexpected freedom.

The buggy rolled by fertile pastures and running creeks. Faith waved at a farmer in a nearby field, busy putting up hay. The tangy scent tickled her nose and made her sneeze. The farmer rested on his scythe, tipping his hat to her as the buggy raced by.

Mary Ellen was hanging wash when the Shepherd buggy rolled to a stop in front of the small dwelling. Chickens milled around the front stoop. Two coonhounds lay beneath the porch, cooling their bellies against the packed dirt.

Leaving her basket of wash, Mary Ellen ran to greet her. Children streamed out of the house, and the dogs set up a loud ruckus.

"Glad you stopped by!" Mary Ellen brushed a piece of hair out of her eyes. "It gets real lonely with no one but the kids to talk to."

Faith handed her the cherry pie, then patted a youngster on the head. "I can't stay long, but I'll be glad to do anything I can to give you a rest."

Time flew as the women chatted and folded diapers. Faith hadn't wanted to put the babies down, but she knew if she was to complete her mission in town and be home by dark, she couldn't linger. It was close to two when Faith climbed back into the buggy.

As she entered the land office, a cheerful-looking lady glanced up from behind a battered wooden desk. The gold nameplate read "Evelyn Williams." Evelyn's friendly blue eyes immediately put Faith at ease. "You're Nicholas's new bride."

"Not yet, but I'm trying." Faith grinned.

The matronly woman chuckled, shoving her considerable bulk to her feet. "Heard you two are having a hard time tying the knot."

"I never realized getting married could be so hard." Faith briefly explained the three delays and how Nicholas had now taken his cattle to market.

"Well," the woman said with a wink, "Nicholas is a man well worth waiting for. Why, half the women in Deliverance have been waitin' on him."

Faith frowned. "For what?"

"For him to make up his mind who he's gonna marry!" Twinkling eyes scanned Faith, and Evelyn's smile widened. "Looks like he's picked a real beauty."

Faith blushed, clearing her throat. No one had ever

accused her of being a beauty. Hope was the only Kallahan who could claim that distinction. "I've come to inquire about the Smith house."

"Bert and Betty's place?"

"Yes, ma'am . . . I was wondering what the state planned to do with the homestead."

Evelyn grimaced. "Land sakes, don't rightly know. Are the Shepherds interested in buying it?"

"No," Faith said. "And I'd appreciate it if you wouldn't mention my interest just yet." No use stirring up a hornet's nest with Liza if she didn't have to. "I've been thinking about starting a school, and the house looks ideal for what I have in mind."

Evelyn frowned. "Town's got a school."

"Not this kind of school. I want to start a school for the blind."

"A school for the blind?" Evelyn's brows bunched tighter. "A school for the blind. Well, guess there's a few in the area who'd benefit by a school for the blind."

"There might be lots."

"Yes . . . there's Dan Walters's boy. Land sakes, that boy's got ants in his britches! He'd not sit still long enough to learn anything!"

"Adam's exceptionally bright, Mrs. Williams. He just needs his energy channeled. I want to teach Adam, and others like him, to read and write and cipher as good or better than children with sight." Faith could feel her excitement rising every time she thought about it. To be able to make a difference enthralled her. "And if at first there aren't enough blind students, then I can teach adults in the community to read and write."

"Yes, guess you could. There are a few around here who'd like to learn to read. The Bittle girl's blind, you know—old enough to go to school now—and Gregory— he'd like going to school. Sixteen years old now, hard to believe."

Evelyn stepped to the file drawer and rifled through a stack of folders. Moments later she extracted a file, her eyes scanning the contents. She glanced up, smiling. "Looks to me like Bert's place can be bought for back taxes."

Faith's smile faded. Back taxes. Her heart sank. She had her teaching money, but that probably wouldn't be enough. Nicholas and Liza hadn't said she couldn't start the school, but she knew without asking that Liza would never back the project. She swallowed. "How much?"

Evelyn shook her head, still perusing the sheet of paper. "Doesn't say . . . but I'll find out." Slipping the file back into the cabinet, she shut the drawer. "Come back Saturday, and I'll have the information for you."

Faith smiled. "Thank you . . . and Mrs. Williams?"

"Call me Evelyn, dear."

Faith nodded. "Don't forget what I said about not mentioning my visit to anyone."

Evelyn brushed her concern aside. "I'll not say a word, but you'll have a difficult time keeping something like this from Liza very long."

Faith was in a good mood when she left the land office. In a few days she'd know for certain whether the Smith house could be purchased. She had no idea where she'd get the money, but she planned to pray long and hard about it. If the school was meant to be, God would provide the means. Faith brightened when she spotted Jeremiah unloading a wagon in front of the mercantile.

Waving, she ran to meet him as the hermit heaved a large crate off the wagon. For a man his age, he still had remarkable agility.

He smiled as she approached. "You look pretty as a rose in January. What's put the bloom in your face this fine day?"

Faith could barely contain her enthusiasm. "I was just talking to Mrs. Williams at the land office. She says the

Smith place might be bought for as little as back taxes! Isn't that wonderful! I can start my school for the blind there."

Setting the crate on the steps, Jeremiah pulled a handkerchief out of his pocket and mopped his forehead. The late afternoon sun bore down on the town. "Sounds reasonable enough—if a body had the money for the back taxes."

Faith sat down on the lower step of the porch to visit. "It might not be so much. Mrs. Williams will know the exact amount in a few days."

Jeremiah removed his hat, wiping the brim with a kerchief. "It's a worthy goal you're attempting, but a mighty big undertaking you've set upon, young lady. Have you talked to Dan about your idea? Might be he won't allow Adam to attend your school."

"What father wouldn't want to see his child educated and offered a better life?"

Reaching the back of the wagon, Jeremiah lifted another crate onto the sidewalk.

"Don't suppose you've mentioned your plans to Nicholas or Liza."

"I mentioned it," she admitted.

"And?"

"No use getting them all upset until I see if the Smith place is affordable." She sat up straighter. "Have you been able to locate Braille teaching material?"

Jeremiah glanced away. "I wired a friend . . . he might be of help, when everything else is in place."

"Well." Faith sat back. "If all goes well, I plan to start teaching Adam by fall. And I'm going to send out letters to the other people Nicholas told me about, inviting them, too. I can teach folks to read while the blind school is getting started." As she spoke, she realized she'd just decided. There was no use delaying the project.

"Fall, huh? That's pretty optimistic thinking, young lady. Aren't you forgetting something?"

Faith looked up.

"What if Nicholas doesn't want his wife running a school for the blind? What if he forbids you to open the doors?"

Faith hadn't considered the possibility. Nicholas was a God-fearing man, and God-fearing men were committed to do all within their power to help others. . . . Besides, Nicholas had encouraged her. But Liza hadn't. What if Liza forbade her to teach? Would Nicholas stand by her if Liza opposed her?

"Guess I'll cross that bridge when I come to it," Faith admitted. She fervently hoped she wouldn't have to cross it at all.

Jeremiah paused, resting on the side of the wagon. "Lot of work to be done before a school can materialize. You'll need three paying students just to open the doors."

Faith stared off into the distance. Dan was preparing to shoe a horse in front of the livery. The rhythmic clang of his hammer against the anvil filled the air. "And it'll take a lot of hands to repair, paint, and fix up that old house."

Jeremiah nodded. "We're not just talking about donated time. You'll need food, cots, blankets, supplies. Then there are Braille books, wood for heating and cooking, kerosene for the lanterns. . . ."

Faith listened as the list went on and on. Everything Jeremiah said was true, but she held fast to the belief that God had sent her to Deliverance for a purpose, and that purpose was looking less and less like she was intended to be a helpmate to Nicholas.

Sighing, she got to her feet. "There's still a lot of work to be done, but my mind is set, Jeremiah. When Nicholas gets back, I'll ask his help."

"That should be interesting." Jeremiah turned to load another crate.

Faith brushed dirt off the back of her dress. "I have to be going. I promised Liza I'd be home before dark." She brightened. "Would you like to eat dinner with us?"

When Jeremiah met her suggestion with a wry look and a quick shake of his head, she giggled, thinking of Liza's reaction should he accept such an invitation.

"Well, perhaps another time."

Jeremiah nodded. "Perhaps . . . if hell ever freezes over."

A week later, Liza made her purchases at the feed store and started home. She felt faint from the heat. Mopping her forehead, she wondered what was wrong with her lately. The sudden waves of heat ignited her body, as if she'd been soaked in kerosene and had a lit match thrown on her. She was jolted awake in the middle of the night, drenched in sweat, her heart pounding. Was her heart giving out? Yes, that was it. The Lord had heard her prayers. Once Nicholas married, God planned to call her home.

She looked in the opposite direction as the wagon rolled past Doc's office. She couldn't tell a man her problems. He'd laugh and tell her to go home and rest. Rest. She hand-fanned her face as another hot spell assaulted her. She'd like to see him rest with the fires of Hades licking at his britches. She could consult Vera, but Vera would tell Molly, and Molly would tell Etta, and the whole town would know her problems by morning.

The wagon passed the mercantile, and she quickly averted her head. Jeremiah. That old fool. Why had he started coming around? For years he had avoided people, but lately he was everywhere she looked. He dressed decently these days; his hair was cut to a respectable length. Her lips thinned. He must have his eye on Widow Blackburn. The old fool.

The wagon rolled past the land office, and wheeled out of town. Liza's heart hammered against her ribs. She felt as if an invisible hand had hold of her throat. She had to get home to be by herself!

Whipping the horse, she pushed the animal on. The wagon flew around the bend in the road, and the Smith house came into view. Faith's buggy was parked at the front stoop!

Sawing back on the reins, Liza slowed the horse. What would Faith be doing here? She was supposed to be helping Mary Ellen churn this morning.

Clicking her tongue, she turned the horse up the rutted lane.

Faith was down on her knees, humming as she scrubbed the worn floor. Plans for the school were moving much faster than she had expected. Evelyn had given her permission to clean the old house this morning. Even if the house never became a school for the blind, Evelyn agreed the town eyesore needed a good cleaning. Faith was thrilled. It was a monumental task, but once the town saw how the blind school was beginning to take shape, Faith hoped more people would get excited about it.

She was badly in need of able-bodied men to repair the outside, and Evelyn promised if the men came, the women would soon follow. She could use all the help she could get. Right after she helped Mary Ellen churn butter, she had left and gone directly to the land office, thinking Evelyn would have the information on the taxes. Instead, Evelyn had handed her a key and told her she was free to start cleaning whenever she wanted, predicting the money and help would come in.

Faith suddenly froze at the sound of Liza's strident voice.

"What is the meaning of this?"

Scrambling to her feet, Faith brushed damp hair back from her forehead. "Mother Shepherd! What are you doing here?"

Liza's eyes coldly assessed the bucket of suds.

Faith swallowed and hurried on. "I—I thought the place needed cleaning."

"You thought an empty homestead needed cleaning?"

"I . . ." Faith knew that sounded ridiculous. "Evelyn gave me permission."

"Why would Evelyn give you permission to trespass on the Smiths' property?"

"I'm not trespassing."

Liza's eyes narrowed. "Does this have something to do with your insane idea to open a blind school?"

Faith sighed. "Mother Shepherd, it's not an insane idea. Jeremiah's promised to help, and I—"

Liza cut her off sharply. "Get into the buggy."

"Mother Shepherd—"

"Into the buggy, young woman! You are making a laughingstock of the Shepherds! I won't have it!"

Faith had never once shown disrespect to an elder. Papa would've taken a switch to any one of his daughters who dared to talk back to a senior, but she didn't think he'd object to her standing up for herself.

"No."

Liza's brows shot up. "What did you say?"

"I said no . . . ma'am." Faith met her glacial stare. "I don't mean any disrespect, and it troubles me to disobey you, Mother Shepherd, but I've been given permission to start work on the school, and I intend to see it through."

"Have you lost your mind? Just where do you think you're going to get the money to start this school?"

"Well, I've been praying. . . ."

"The Lord isn't a fool, young lady. He doesn't answer every whim a headstrong young woman throws at him— and if you've got it in your mind the money's coming from Nicholas, you can just get it right out again! People around here think we're made of money! All this talk about new steeples and blind schools—it's enough to make a body want to scream. Now pick up that bucket and get in the buggy. I'll hear no more talk of this school for the blind. Do you understand me?"

"Yes, ma'am." Faith didn't move.

"Well? Pick up that bucket!"

"No, ma'am, because I'd just have to set it down again." Faith felt faint. She'd never stood her ground in such a bold manner, but the school was important—so important she was willing to fight for it.

Liza's face suffused with color. "Do I have to take a switch to you?"

Faith blushed. "No, ma'am. If you would only listen to reason—"

"Very well." Liza pinned her with a final look. "You will either pick up that bucket and come with me, or you needn't come home at all."

The threat hung between them.

"I can't do that," Faith said softly.

"You will do it, or you will be sent packing, young lady. You are not Nicholas's wife yet. This . . . this blind school is a matter that will require considerable thought—you can't just come in here and turn our lives upside down."

"I'm not starting the school today, Mother Shepherd. I'm only cleaning—"

"Don't sass me. Either get up and come with me now, or don't bother coming back to the house."

Faith mulled the ultimatum over in her mind. Where would she go? She couldn't go back to Aunt Thalia's. Aunt Thalia would turn her over her knee for certain when she learned Faith had deliberately disobeyed an elder, but she couldn't stay and live in a household where she wasn't wanted, either.

Liza tapped her foot. "Have you forgotten your purpose, Miss Kallahan? You were bought—purchased, by my son. Have you forgotten that?"

Faith recoiled from the spiteful words. *Purchased?* The hateful word was hostile, repugnant. God had sent her to Deliverance; Nicholas had sent for her, and Liza had no right to ask her to leave. When Faith married Nicholas, she had every intention of being an obedient wife. To Nicholas, not Liza. Was that what was bothering Liza? Was the school for the blind the real issue, or was it the knowledge that her son would soon belong to another woman that incited her?

"Are you going to answer me?"

Faith dropped to her knees and started scrubbing, closing her eyes against the sound of Liza's audible gasp. She had no idea where she would go, but she wasn't going back to that cold tomb the Shepherds called home.

"Very well. Your belongings will be on the front porch when you decide to pick them up. You had best find another place to stay, Miss Kallahan. You are no longer welcome in my house."

"What about Nicholas?" Faith murmured, afraid to look up.

"My son will do as I say." Liza turned to walk off, then turned to give Faith a cold stare. "I'll expect the buggy to be returned immediately."

Biting back tears, Faith scrubbed harder. The floor was old and chipped, but with work it would come clean. She looked up only when she heard Liza's buckboard rattle out of the yard.

Dear Lord. What would she do now? She had just been thrown out of the Shepherd house. She had failed God; she had failed Nicholas.

Burying her face in her hands, she sobbed.

Chapter Ten

I'M already missing home, Rusty."

As foreign as homesickness was to Nicholas, the realization was clear: He wasn't looking forward to the long trip. He was going to miss Faith. The thought was even more sobering when he conceded he barely knew the woman. Yet he was going to miss her. Her infectious zest for life, her spontaneous nature, her radiant smile had brought sunshine into the Shepherd household, something sadly missing for longer than he cared to remember.

"Well, it won't be long before the cattle are ready, Boss." Rusty whistled, steering a stray heifer back into the herd.

For six weeks the men had worked hard before Nicholas joined them, searing hot branding irons into the cattle's sides, marking them Shepherd beef. Sunup to sundown, the men worked, readying the cows for the cattle drive.

Nicholas smiled, missing his comfortable bed and hot meals already. The roundup was taking longer than Nicholas liked. For the past few days he'd worked the back range and shared a cabin with Rusty Treson, the trail boss. This morning the two men rode to the main bunkhouse. The men were up and saddling their horses, loading their Winchesters and securing bedrolls. Cook, Gabby Masters, was busy stocking the chuck wagon with beans, flour, cornmeal, coffee, lard, salt pork, bacon, and beef jerky. The drive was finally under way.

Thirteen days later Nicholas took off his Stetson, wiping sweat from his forehead as he eyed the hardy group. He studied the men, proud of his help. The men knew their jobs and always gave him a full day's work. There were a couple of tenderfeet in the crowd this year, but by the end of the drive, they'd be seasoned drovers. One cattle drive, even a short one, could determine a man's calling in life.

Nicholas's features sobered as he faced the cowboys. "You each know how much I appreciate the job you're doing. You've put in long hours and had little rest. But we still have our work cut out for us. Tonight's activities are bound to cause problems, but you men need a break from the tedious work. Have a good time, but remember, you're paid to work, not to play."

Nicholas knew that a few hours of relaxation would see them back, rested and brimming with enthusiasm. "Bear in mind the rules. No one comes back drunk, and everyone is to be in his bedroll by ten o'clock."

A good-natured groan went up.

"Ten o'clock," Nicholas reiterated. "There'll be a brief prayer service at sunup."

"How about extendin' the time to ten-thirty, Boss?"
Gabby Masters grinned. A gold tooth glistened in the
predawn light.

Nicholas gave the weathered old cook a good-natured
frown. Nicholas couldn't recall Gabby ever leaving camp.
"You know what's expected of you, Gabby. Just keep the
biscuits and gravy coming."

Rusty spoke up. "We'll be on our best behavior, Mr.
Shepherd. I guarantee it. Ain't that right, boys?"

A few nodded; some mumbled as they adjusted their
spurs, tightened their chaps, and mounted their horses.

"Let's head 'em out!" Nicholas ordered, his high-
spirited Appaloosa stirring up a trail of dust as he led the
way.

This year's herd was larger than usual. The cattle plod-
ded along with riders ahead, behind, and on both sides.
Gabby, eating a lot of dust, followed behind the herd
with the chuck wagon. At the end of the day, there
wasn't a man in the pack who wasn't ready to climb out
of his saddle and chow down. Gabby set up camp at the
edge of a small, clear stream. By the time the men had
washed up, supper was waiting.

The hungry drovers lined up at the chuck wagon.

"I've eaten more dust today than a cyclone," one of
the men joked.

"A meal, fifteen minutes of shut-eye, then I'm headin'
into town!" another declared.

Cook piled tin plates with salt pork, steaming beans,
and biscuits. Gabby's generous helpings were guaranteed
to stick to a man's ribs.

Nicholas poured scalding hot coffee into a tin cup,
then leaned against a rock. He hoped the drive would
end in San Antonio in a few days, maybe less. Faith filled
his thoughts. Were she and Mama getting along? He
grinned, taking a sip of the biting coffee. He sure hoped
so.

The women reminded him of two ornery bulldogs staking out their territory. It had been slow coming, but now that he wasn't around, maybe they'd get along better. Mama needed to accept Faith; after he and Faith were married, she would be a comfort to Mama. He pictured them sitting in the parlor, stitching handwork as they talked about whatever women talked about. Later Mama would fix that tea she favored—maybe put a few of those lemon cookies on a fragile plate, and the two women would warm to each other.

He felt a twinge of guilt, realizing he hadn't been fair to Faith. He should have taken time to court her, let her get to know him. But with Mama acting so strange, hay to be put up, and the cattle drive, he'd neglected his intended bride. He planned to change that when he got home.

Pitching the remainder of his coffee into the fire, he decided to join the men in town.

As the cowboys crawled into their bedrolls later, they fell asleep listening to the night watch sing to the herd. A few weary snickers sounded from nearby bedrolls. Even Nicholas had to smile. No matter how off-key a cowboy sang, his voice had a soothing effect on the herd.

Camp had been asleep not more than an hour when the wind suddenly rose. In an instant, bolts of lightning lit up the churning sky. Thunder reverberated through the ground, and rain fell in blinding sheets.

"Watch the herd!" Nicholas shouted, and the men ran for their horses.

Cattle moved about restlessly. *Father, don't let the herd spook,* Nicholas prayed as he rode the perimeter of the camp. The storm passed, and the weary men spent the remainder of the night rounding up stray steers. The electrical storm would throw them yet another day behind schedule.

The men, worn out from lack of sleep, broke camp before dawn.

"Just look at all that mud." Rusty took off his gloves, eyeing the swollen river. "Think we should try and cross it?"

"We're not camping here another three days. Better warn the men." Nicholas took off his hat, studying the churning rapids. They'd crossed worse, but he didn't like to test the animals.

The chuck wagon mired down twice in midstream. Cowboys tied ropes from their saddle horns to the rig, using the horses' weight as leverage. Cooking utensils banged and rattled as the wagon rocked back and forth but refused to budge.

Gabby shook his fist, hollering, "Don't you cockleburs bust up my pots and pans! I'll have your skins in a skillet!"

The men kept at it until the wagon broke free from the mire and surged onto the bank. Gabby inspected every last pot and pan before saying with a grin, "Thank ya, boys. Right nice of ya."

"Never rile the cook!" one of the tenderfeet observed dryly.

"Pretty smart feller, for a knucklehead." Gabby ignored the men's good-natured ribbing as they tipped their Stetsons and galloped off.

Toward dusk a lone rider rode up. "Got a man down!"

"What's wrong?" Nicholas turned his horse, trying to hear the drover.

"One of the tenderfeet broke his leg!"

Spurring his horse, Nicholas rode ahead. Dismounting before the horse came to a halt, he ran to a young man lying on the ground, writhing in pain. The boy's leg was shattered, the bone poking through the skin.

Nicholas shook his head. "It's going to have to be set."

The boy cried out in pain.

"Gabby, Rusty and I will hold him down. You pour some whiskey on that wound. We don't want it getting infected." Nicholas scouted the area until he found a two-inch stick. Wedging it between the boy's teeth, he apologized. "Sorry to have to do this, son. It's going to hurt."

Gabby made a splint and then poured a shot of rotgut down the screaming youth's throat.

"As bad as it is," Nicholas muttered, "it could be worse. God was looking after you. You could have lost your leg. Rusty, have someone take him back to camp."

"Sure thing, Boss."

Nicholas hated to lose the cowhand. Shorthanded or not, the help's welfare came first. That was Abe Shepherd's cardinal rule and one Nicholas was glad to follow. Whether they realized it or not, many of the men were like sons to him. He would never sacrifice their safety for his own financial gain.

A few miles farther up the trail, Nicholas spotted one of his men on a ridge a couple of hills away, signaling with his Stetson.

Rusty rode up beside him. "Trouble?"

"Riders, eyeing the herd from a distance."

Signaling back, Rusty let the cowboy know they'd gotten the message.

That evening they made camp beneath a scattering of mesquite trees a few miles south of San Antonio. A full moon hung overhead like a huge lantern. Millions of stars twinkled in the darkness as the tired drovers fell into their bedrolls, dropping off to sleep to the sound of lowing cattle.

At dawn Nicholas and the trail boss rode into town to meet the buyers. Nicholas groaned when he learned the cattle buyers from Abilene were delayed.

"That could take another week!"

"Can't be helped," the man told him. "Been delayed by rain and swollen streams."

Nicholas had no choice but to stay until they arrived.

Three days passed. When the buyers finally arrived in San Antonio, they sent a rider to camp. Nicholas and the men drove the cattle into the stockyards and finalized the purchase. The cattle brought a high return, and though Nicholas was pleased, his thoughts were not on profit. They centered on home.

That night he spread his bedroll on the ground. Though Nicholas was tired, sleep would not come. Instead, his mind was on his approaching wedding. Now that the cattle were sold, he could take care of personal matters.

Rolling to his side, he stared at the stars. Faith was a Christian woman, strong in her faith.

Under Mama's influence, she would be domesticated. Her fiery spirit tested his patience, but he wouldn't want her any different. She was well mannered, and though he hadn't thought so at first, he realized now that she was pretty, real pretty, with a cloud of dark hair and those striking violet-colored eyes.

Desire stirred, a feeling he didn't often acknowledge.

Yawning, he closed his eyes in weariness. Home. He was going home. It was comforting to think Mama and Faith would hit it off while he was gone. Why, he could almost smell the biscuits baking in the oven. . . .

"She's *what!*"

Nicholas took off his hat and hooked it over the peg beside the door. Liza kept her back to him, beating flames from a pan of biscuits she'd just taken out of the oven. The stench of burnt bread hung heavy in the air.

His gaze roamed the empty kitchen. "Faith's gone?"

Liza bounced a burned biscuit off the stove. "I sent her packing."

"You *what?*"

"Are you deaf? Since when did I have to start repeating myself? You were born with two good ears—use them." Liza slammed the pan of biscuits on the table. "I told you, I sent her packing. Believe me, that isn't the half of it. She's moved in with Mary Ellen."

Nicholas's face fell. What nonsense was Mama babbling this time?

"Don't stand there like some love-struck pup! Sit down. Supper's ready."

Nicholas sat down, trying to assess the situation. Mama was mad; Faith was gone. What had happened? "What do you mean, you 'sent her packing'?" He couldn't imagine Mama acting so unchristian. Had she taken permanent leave of her senses?

Liza scraped blackened crust from her biscuit and added butter. The butter wadded into a gooey ball. She pitched it aside. "I've made a mess. Hand me a dish towel."

Nicholas handed Liza the towel. She took a long time wiping butter from her fingers. He waited.

"What happened? Where's Faith?"

Dissolving into tears, Liza buried her face in the dishcloth. "She was awful to me, Nicholas. I had no choice but to do what I did. She took it upon herself to clean the Smith house—after all we said about not wanting to get involved with her foolish talk of a blind school. Does she think we're made of money? I begged her to wait and talk it over with you, but she refused. She's gone—moved in with Albert and Mary Ellen Finney."

"Finneys?" Nicholas glanced around the room, bewildered. "Why would she do that?"

Liza worried the end of the dishcloth, shrugging.

"Mama. Why would Faith move in with Albert and Mary Ellen?"

"Well, she just left—taken a shine to those twins. That's all she wants to do—look after those babies."

Nicholas didn't believe that for one minute. Faith was definitely a Good Samaritan, but to leave his house to help with babies?

"Are you sure about that, Mama?"

Liza took a deep breath, dabbing the dishcloth at the corners of her eyes. Her face was mottled from crying. "I think I would know. You don't see her, do you?"

Nicholas fixed his gaze on his mother's face.

Liza averted her eyes and wiped the table around her plate. "I tried to stop her, Nicholas—she—she just won't listen to me!"

Nicholas frowned. Faith and Mama didn't get along, but Faith had never disobeyed Liza, not in his presence.

"Used my sugar, my flour, and my cherries, the week before. Said she was taking a pie to Mary Ellen."

"So?"

Liza folded and refolded the damp material. "So, what?"

"Did she take a pie to Mary Ellen?"

"I doubt it. She's wily, I tell you. Plain wily."

Frustrated, Nicholas ran a hand through his hair. Faith didn't have a wily bone in her. How could the situation have gotten so out of hand? "Mama, what do you think she did with the pie—how could you let this happen? Have you prayed about this?"

"Of course I've prayed about it. Faith lied. Said she was going over to help Mary Ellen with the babies, and she knew all along what she was going to do. Nicholas, I told her to leave and not to come back. I should have known better than to let her go that day. . . ." She suddenly softened. "You're right; it was my fault. I'm sorry I didn't watch her more closely."

Nicholas stiffened. "What is going on here! You told her to leave?"

"I did—it was a horrible thing to do, but when I found her cleaning that old house, intent on that blind school, I just exploded. Told her to leave, she wasn't welcome here any longer." Burying her face in her hands, she wept. "Lying, sneaking around behind my back—I'll not have it, Nicholas."

Nicholas's insides churned. "Exactly what did you say to her, Mama?"

Tears rolled unchecked down Liza's cheeks, and it was obvious she was starting to get worked up again. "I told her she wasn't welcome here any longer."

Nicholas's heart sank. For a brief moment he felt his loyalty shift to Faith. Why would Mama do such a thing? She had no right!

"Over there cleaning that house like a woman possessed. Oh, you'll hear it all from the town gossips. Molly and Etta will tell the whole town! Then come Sunday morning they'll sit like saints in the amen corner, shouting hallelujah at the top of their lungs."

Nicholas stared at Liza in disbelief. "Mama, stop it— Molly and Etta are your friends."

Liza's eyes darkened. "I don't have friends, Nicholas! Can't you see that? Haven't since Abe died—not one friend has stuck by me. When Abe was alive, we had more couple friends than we could shake a stick at, but now . . . now, I have nobody." She flung her hands to the ceiling. "They've all drifted away—every last one of them." Spent, she buried her face in the dishcloth and sobbed.

"I'm sorry, Mama, that you feel you don't have friends. I happen to think you do; you just haven't cultivated them lately, but I fail to see what this has to do with Faith."

"She lied to me, Nicholas!" Liza shouted, pounding a fist on the table.

Nicholas stared at her. Her face was flushed a bright

red. Tiny beads of sweat trickled from her forehead, and she looked as if she were going to burst. He'd only seen her this angry on rare occasions. Her distress went deeper than Faith.

"Mama." His tone tempered. "Have you done as I asked and seen Doc?"

Liza exploded and evaded the question, "What's Doc got to do with anything? There's nothing wrong with me! Faith Kallahan is the problem here. Not me!"

"I'm trying my best to understand the situation," Nicholas snapped. "Did Faith tell you she wasn't going to the Smith's house?"

"Of course not!"

"Well, then, she didn't lie."

"Oh, for heaven's sake! It's blazing hot in here." Liza sprang from the chair and jerked the window open wider. "Hot as Hades in this kitchen."

"Faith didn't lie," Nicholas repeated.

"Maybe it wasn't an out-and-out lie." Liza hesitated, holding her handkerchief to her throat. "But she deliberately led me to believe she was going to help Mary Ellen. She didn't say a word about going to the Smith house—she knew I would forbid it!"

"So, she did go to Mary Ellen's, and then she went to clean an empty old house that's been nothing but a community eyesore for years." Nicholas's patience was wearing thin.

"She defied me. I refuse to be treated with such disrespect—How can you defend her, Nicholas? A stranger? I'm your mother!"

"And from what you say, Faith was only scrubbing a dirty floor—hardly grounds for a firing squad."

Liza reached over and thumped him soundly. "Are you sassing me?"

He winced and silently asked God to give him patience. "No, Mama, I'm trying to make sense of what you've done. I'm not defending Faith; I just find it hard to believe she would disobey you without a reason."

"Well, she did. She wouldn't budge an inch from that bucket—even after I threatened to take a switch to her."

"A switch? You threatened to take a switch to her? At her age?"

"Yes, a switch! If she's bent on sass, then she needs a good switching."

Like the occasional thump on the head Liza found necessary to inflict on his noggin!

Liza folded the dishcloth and laid it aside. "I gave her a choice: Come home and forget all about the blind school, or stay and finish that floor. If she chose the floor, then I told her not to bother to come home at all. She scrubbed that old floor as if she hadn't heard a word I said. Even after I reminded her she'd been purchased to—"

"Purchased!" Nicholas roared. He sank down in a nearby chair. "You told her she'd been *purchased?*"

"Well? Wasn't she? Have you forgotten who paid for her ticket out here?"

Nicholas got up to look out the window. *Purchased.* How must that make Faith feel? Purchased, like beef on the hoof. He had been disrespectful to Faith; Mama even more so.

Liza rearranged the sugar bowl. "Nicholas, have you seen my snuff? I can't find it."

"Good."

"Nicholas!"

Nicholas held his tongue. He was too angry to talk sense. Mama was out of hand. He was personally taking her to see Doc first thing in the morning. Meanwhile, he needed time to think this mess through.

Liza was muttering under her breath now, fanning. "Came straight home, packed Miss Kallahan's belongings, and set them on the front porch, I did. It was after dark when Albert came for her things. Told me not to worry about her; she'd be all right with them. I just bet she will. She'll be going full steam ahead with those blind-school plans."

Liza wiped her forehead. "At least Albert was thoughtful enough to return the horse and buggy. Miss Kallahan would not likely have thought about it."

Nicholas turned from the window, trying to temper his rage. "I can't believe you've done this."

"I haven't done anything. It was Faith Kallahan's doings, not mine. I've done nothing that any good mother wouldn't do." Liza pushed back from the table and got up. "Most likely she's over there cookin' supper for the Walters family. You've seen the way Dan looks at her."

The declaration was like ice water in Nicholas's face.

Liza sniffed. "Supper's getting cold. Sit down. You're worn out from the long trip."

Nicholas was more heartsick than tired. "I've lost my appetite." He snagged his hat from the peg and went out the back door, slamming it behind him. The lace curtain gyrated wildly.

He entered the barn and quickly climbed the ladder to the loft. Exhausted, he lay back on a bale of hay, allowing familiar sounds and smells to calm him. How had his life gotten so complicated?

The thought of Faith in another family's house stung. The thought of her with Dan hurt even more. He had seen the way Dan looked at her, relied on her. Was Nicholas falling in love with her? No. Would he ever be able to love again? Did he know Faith well enough to love her? He'd loved only one woman, Rachel. But he'd had to let that sentiment die once she was married. Now he felt sorry for her, and guilty that she was married to a man who treated her badly. He was sorry she didn't have the life she deserved.

His thoughts returned to Faith. Why wasn't he happy

to have her out from under his feet? Nicholas started a slow burn. *I paid for her ticket out here; she's promised to me.* The angry thought jarred his senses. He was no better than Mama, using hateful thoughts to justify his short-comings. *Father, forgive me. My thoughts are so muddled on this situation.*

Why should he let Mama send Faith away? Why didn't he march into that kitchen right now and tell Mama that since she was the one who'd told Faith to go, she had to be the one to bring her back?

Faith was told to leave; how could she just waltz back into his house?

She should never have left; she should have stood her ground until he got back and could straighten this thing out.

Had she been looking for a reason to leave? Was that reason Dan Walters? Mama's words rang in his head: *over there cooking the Walters's supper.*

Well, he'd see about that! He'd saddle his horse and bring Faith back to the Shepherd ranch where she be-longed. Then he'd deal with Mama's absurd accusations and get to the bottom of all this nonsense.

Climbing out of the loft, he saddled the Appaloosa, his thoughts on his mission. His hands suddenly paused.

Regardless of Mama's interference, Faith had chosen to move in with Mary Ellen. What if she had been looking for a reason to leave? Liza's rash demand and Faith's deci-sion, no matter how warranted, made him feel like a downright fool now that she'd left him.

Jerking the saddle off the horse's back, he sat down, torn. What would make him look the bigger fool in the town's eyes? Faith's remaining with the Finneys, or his going after her?

Dropping to his knees, he prayed. *Father, give me guid-ance. Forgive my pride; give me the strength to do what's right.*

Getting to his feet, he swung the saddle back on the

horse and mounted, then slid back down and jerked it off again.

The answer was obvious. He wouldn't go after her even though he wanted to. And, God help him, he did want to. If she had a shred of decency, she would come home, try to straighten this out—at least consult him about it! If she didn't . . . well, it would just prove that she didn't want to stay with him after all. Mama had no right to humiliate Faith, but Faith had no right to humiliate him. A man had his pride.

Exhausted, he curled up on a bale of hay, shivering in the night air. It wasn't the most comfortable place to sleep, but he had his pride. Let Mama wonder where he'd spent the night. She should never have sent Faith away.

So much for his mail-order bride. He rolled into a tighter knot, prepared to endure a miserable night.

Liza paced the kitchen floor, occasionally parting the curtains to look out. Where was Nicholas? He'd been gone for hours, and there wasn't a sign of light in the barn.

Dropping the curtain back into place, she resumed pacing. She'd gone too far. Her acid tongue had betrayed her one too many times. Nicholas had never spoken to her in such a shameful way. The sound of the slamming door echoed in her mind. She glanced around the empty kitchen, feeling the full brunt of her loneliness.

Bursting into hot tears, she wondered how Nicholas— her own flesh and blood—could treat her so badly. What evil possessed him to side with Faith Kallahan? He barely knew the woman. How dare he choose an ungrateful mail-order bride over his own mother?

He had deserted her. She had lost him. Just like she'd lost Abe. Only her son's abandonment hurt more; he had a choice. He'd angrily slammed out, leaving her to wonder if he'd ever come back. Abe was never coming back; she understood that, but Nicholas—he couldn't leave her. She would have nothing, nothing to live for.

Liza sobbed, certain she was losing her mind. Had Abe lived, would he have left her too—in the most wretched time of her life? She couldn't think straight anymore. It was as if the world had gone crazy.

The way she'd been acting, she wouldn't blame Nicholas if he left and never came back.

Kneeling, she prayed for forgiveness. *Help me, Father, help me.*

She rocked back on her heels, burying her face in her hands. *Oh, Abe, what should I do?* If only Abe were here to protect her, comfort her, hold her close. Where could she go for refuge? Bitterness rose in her throat. *Why, God, why did you take Abe and leave me? Worthless me, who can do nothing but cry and sweat and hate the world!*

Where had her little boy gone? Where was the laughing child she'd once cradled in her arms, sprinkling butterfly kisses on his tiny forehead as she gently rocked him to sleep? Her little boy was gone, and oh, how she missed the sound of tiny feet scurrying through the house.

Wiping her tears, she got up and looked out the window. She missed the boy, but she was proud of the man he'd become. Nicholas was so like Abe . . . so like her Abe.

Everyone was gone now. Abe was dead. Nicholas had walked out. And Faith . . . she'd shoved her away, too . . . and Nicholas would never forgive her. The image of Faith sitting in the middle of the Smith floor, trying to restore the dirty wood to decency, tore at her conscience. What harm could scrubbing an old floor cause? She had been irrational, cranky, and unreasonable. What had she been thinking?

"Oh, Lord," Liza cried out to the empty kitchen. "What's happening to me? What have I done?"

She felt insufferable heat rising in her chest, a hellish fire that ignited her. For a moment she thought she might not catch her breath. As quickly as the fire imprisoned her, it released her, leaving her exhausted and drenched in perspiration.

Taking a deep breath, she dried her eyes, then lifted her head with dignity. She would not give in to this strange malady, or the others inflicted upon her.

She would not.

Chapter Eleven

MISS Kallahan? Will you read to me?"
Faith let the front curtain drop into place. Adam had caught her looking again. She'd been hoping—no, praying—Nicholas would come. But she'd looked down that road until she couldn't look anymore. He wasn't coming; she must accept this cruel twist of fate. Could this be God's will? Why was she brought out here—to be rejected by the family who'd asked her to come? Was there some other purpose for her being in Deliverance, or should she return to Cold Water? She sighed. Would she ever understand God's will? Accept it she could, but understand?

When she'd discovered that Dan was having trouble finding someone to care for the children while he worked, she talked to Mary Ellen about the situation.

Mary Ellen said Dan needed Faith's help more than she did, and to go on over. It was a way to feel useful, so she'd gladly offered Dan her help.

She enjoyed spending her days taking care of Dan's children, but it was becoming increasingly difficult to keep her thoughts away from Nicholas. How could she miss the Shepherd home so? It had never really been her home—though it was the only home she'd known in Deliverance. Then there was Liza. She had always been so difficult. And Nicholas.

Was she at fault in some way? Had she not tried hard enough to win Nicholas's love? Should she have tried harder with Liza? *Father, forgive me if I have not followed you closely enough, paid enough attention to what you wanted me to do. I just don't know what to do now. I wait on you. Please give me patience, and help me to know what you want me to do.*

Did Nicholas think about her? Not that he should be concerned about her welfare. She had disobeyed Liza, and for that she was sorry. In retrospect the school for the blind was a worthy cause, but her stance may have been too rash. It looked like that stance would cost her her marriage to Nicholas. The thought saddened her. In the short time they'd had together she had come to respect him—at times even like him. Most assuredly she'd looked forward to their occasional talks.

Now she was faced with a dreadful decision. If Nicholas didn't come after her—and she felt certain he wouldn't—she would be forced to return to Cold Water. Perhaps she would even have to marry Edsel Martin. She shuddered. Daniel was asked to face mere lions; would the Lord ask her to face Edsel?

"Miss Kallahan, would you read to me?" Adam repeated patiently. His sightless eyes stared expectantly back at her, and she was reminded that her situation was not without blessings. And, she had made a choice. She could have gone home when Liza demanded it. Now she had to live with her choice.

Faith didn't know what was going to happen, or when, but for as long as she remained in Deliverance, she intended to make herself as useful as possible. She would help Mary Ellen with her children, and Dan with his. Oddly enough, word was spreading about the school for the blind. Many were offering to help; even some donations were dropped off at the Finneys'. Where was her faith, the faith she'd promised God to uphold?

Her thoughts returned to the child by her side. "Of course, Adam. What would you like to hear?"

"That story about that boy that killed that big old giant with one tiny stone."

"Go get the Bible. I believe I left it on the stand next to your bed."

Adam knew his way around the house with amazing accuracy. Within a few moments he returned, carrying the book. Lifting him onto her lap, Faith gently placed his fingertips on the pages, urging him to familiarize himself with the paper's texture. "Feel how smooth and worn it is?"

Adam nodded, running his fingers over the pages. "It feels like mommy's dress."

"I'd never thought of it that way, but yes, the soft parchment feels like fine silk or soft cotton." Faith rewarded him with a hug. God had given him much to overcome in his five short years. Inability to see and the loss of his mother. On the other hand, Dan was more than a father to his children, he was a friend. Faith saw how hard he worked to try to hold the family together.

Papa would have liked this righteous man Dan Walters. He would have said Dan was the salt of the earth.

"The pages are worn because your papa reads the Bible every day."

Adam nodded. "Uh-huh. And he tries to live by it, but he says sometimes it's powerful hard."

Powerful hard, Faith thought, recalling Liza. Sometimes nearly impossible.

Sissy and Lilly napped on the nearby couch as Faith retold the story of David and Goliath, Philistines, swords, five smooth stones, and a sling. When she finished, Adam turned to her, cupping her face in his small hands.

"Are you pretty?"

"Some say my eyes are an unusual shade, but no, I wouldn't say I'm pretty." She laughed. "Maybe passable, on a good day." Papa said eyes revealed a person's soul. If Adam could see her eyes, would he see a woman who longed for a child just like him? "Adam, do you understand color?"

Adam shook his head. "Papa's tried to 'splain them to me, but he's not very good at it."

"Would you like for me to try?"

"Would you?"

"Of course. Let's see—where should I start?"

Adam quickly decided. " 'Splain me the color of *your* eyes."

Faith smiled. "Better yet, why don't I let you *see* the color of my eyes."

Adam cocked his head. "I *can't* see!"

"Maybe not with your eyes, but you can see with your hands."

The expression on the child's face clearly said she must be teasing.

Taking his right hand, she placed it on her left cheek. "Tell me what you see, Adam."

Adam carefully ran his fingertips over her cheekbones, frowning. "I see . . . lumps." He grinned.

"Now my eyes."

His fingertips lightly traced her eyelids, the tips of his fingers exploring her lashes, the shape of her nose.

"My eyes are violet," she said.

"Violet?"

"Violet is a cool color, like the lilacs blooming next to the porch step."

"*Those* smelly things?"

"Those *lovely* smelling things." He was so like a man. "Do you know the feel of cool, Adam?"

Adam shook his head.

Lifting him off her lap, she took his hand, and they walked outside and down the path to the icehouse. A draft of cool air washed over her as they entered the building.

Holding tightly to her hand, Adam edged closer. "I know where we are!"

"Yes, we're in the icehouse." She led him to a block of ice, then carefully took his hand and ran it across the cold, moist surface. "This is how cool feels."

Adam broke into a wide grin as he ran first one hand, then the other, over the icy surface. "Cool," he murmured. "Cold!"

"Very cold!" Faith laughed. "Now, let's feel warm."

"Like the stove? Papa said the stove's *hot!*"

"And Papa's right!"

Returning to the kitchen, she guided him to the cookstove. As trusting as a puppy, he allowed her to hold his hand above the burners. Heat radiated from the cast iron. "This is hot."

"Hot." He nodded. "Once I burned myself on hot, real bad."

"That can happen. Hot is best left alone." She opened the warming oven and took out a biscuit. Placing the bread in the child's hand, she said softly, "This is warm. Yellow is a warm color. Butter is yellow; sunshine is yellow."

They both turned as the back door opened and Dan walked into the kitchen.

"Papa!"

Grinning, Dan ruffled his son's hair as he made a bee-line for the washbowl. "What are you two up to this fine day?"

"Faith's teaching me how to see colors!"

"She is!" Dan glanced at Faith appreciatively. "I've tried to explain colors to him, but I guess I don't do a very good job."

Faith dished up his dinner as he toweled dry.

"Where are the other young'uns?"

"Sissy and Lilly went down for naps earlier."

"I got tied up at the livery. Thought I wasn't going to get a dinner break at all."

Faith set a plate of chicken and dumplings in front of him, watching him eye the fat dumplings swimming in rich gravy with an appreciative sigh. "That sure looks good. Haven't eaten this good since Carolyn was alive."

They bowed their heads, and Dan said grace. Picking up his fork, he dug in. "Have you eaten?"

Faith nodded and poured coffee into a thick mug. "The children and I ate earlier."

Dan's eyes met hers across the table. "Much obliged. It's real nice to have a woman in the kitchen again." He took a bite of dumplings, then observed, "You know, I promised Carolyn I wouldn't pine away—I'd remarry someday, give the children a mama."

"I shouldn't think Deliverance has a shortage of women who'd be proud to look after them." Faith glanced away, careful not to acknowledge the tender look in his eyes. He was a good man, and he needed a wife more than any man she knew. Why hadn't God chosen her to be that wife? There could never be anything but friendship between them. If Nicholas didn't want her, she would return to Michigan. She would not shame Nicholas by marrying another man here in Deliverance.

The past week had opened her eyes regarding marriage. Vows could be bought and paid for like a sack of grain, but she discovered that she needed—wanted—more. She wanted to be in love with the man she married. If she were to explore a relationship with Dan, love would come. He was far too good a man not to love. As she'd cared for them these past days, his children had started to feel like hers. And Dan, well, he would make some lucky lady a wonderful husband. But she couldn't stay.

She and Dan had talked about their individual situations. He understood her insecurities, her doubts, her fears that Liza would never allow Nicholas to marry her, her dread of Edsel Martin. The wistfulness in Dan's tone when they talked about marriage had wrenched her heart. More than once he'd asked for the address of the journal in which Faith had placed her ad. She always steered the conversation to safer ground, fearing it was his subtle way of conveying that he, also, was in the market for a wife. Perhaps—perhaps if it weren't for shaming Nicholas. . . .

"There are a few women around, but none that I'd marry," Dan continued, buttering a piece of bread. "Jenny Petersen's looking to get hitched, but Jenny's got a temper like a chafed bull." He took a bite of chicken. " 'Course, there's always Maggie Lewis, but Maggie's like her ma; she clings to a man like a summer cold. And not real trustworthy, either. I couldn't count on Maggie to get the kids in out of the rain." Dan bit into the bread. "Nicholas stopped by the livery this morning."

He'd changed the subject so quickly that Faith wondered if he'd read her earlier thoughts. She calmly took a couple of cookies from the jar and put them on a plate. "Oh?"

"Asked how you were doing."

She worked to keep her tone impartial. "I trust he's fine and his cattle drive was successful?"

"Fit as a fiddle, and richer." Dan reached for the sugar bowl. "Asked about you—did I say that?"

"Yes, it's always nice to hear you're being thought about." Nicholas might *ask* about her, but he'd certainly shown no interest otherwise. She set the plate of cookies in front of Dan. "What brought Nicholas to the livery today?"

"Said his horse was limping, but I couldn't find a problem." Dan looked up, grinning. "I think he's snooping."

"Snooping?" Faith scoffed at the unlikely assumption. The last thing Nicholas Shepherd would do was *snoop* on her. "Dan, I need to ask you something."

"Sure." He motioned with his fork for her to sit down.

Taking a seat opposite him, she folded her hands, studying them thoughtfully. "What does . . . well, this is a rather difficult question." Papa had done his best, but there were a few things he'd neglected to explain—like, what a man wanted in a woman, what he expected. Obviously, she didn't possess a single thing that attracted Nicholas.

Dan appeared curious. "What's the question?"

"Men. What do they want in a woman?" She bit her lower lip when she saw a red blush creep up the back of his neck. Was she being frightfully forward?

She didn't mean *what* did they want; she was old enough to know all about the birds and the bees, and she'd seen enough tomfoolery with friends to know that you didn't give a man everything he *wanted,* at least not without the sanctity of marriage. What she meant was: What did a man look for in a woman? Beauty? Loyalty? A hard worker? She shook her head, answering her own question. Nicholas certainly wasn't looking for a hard worker to make him happy. He had a bunkhouse full of men who were paid for that service.

Stirring cream into his coffee, Dan studied the question. "You mean, what makes a man fall in love with a woman?"

"I suppose that's what I mean."

"We're back to talking about Nicholas, aren't we?"

"Yes," she admitted, then released her breath in a disgusted whoosh. "I might as well be as freckled as a turkey egg the way Nicholas fails to notice me."

"A turkey egg?" Dan shook his head, sobering. "I don't think any man would think of you as a turkey egg. I've caught Nicholas looking at you a few times out of the corner of his eye."

"But his other eye was on Rachel."

"Rachel?" He frowned. "She's married to Joe Lanner, although I don't know of a person who'd fault her if she decided to leave him."

"I overheard someone in the mercantile say Joe mistreats her. Is that true?"

Dan nodded, taking a bite of dumplings. "She refuses to admit it, but she shows up every week with a new bruise or broken bone. Says she falls, but no one believes her. Joe Lanner should be taken out and hung from the highest limb. A man's got no right to treat a woman that way."

"Well?"

He glanced up.

"You haven't answered my question."

Pushing back from the table, Dan took a deep breath, loosening his belt. He'd eaten as if it were his last meal, but Faith was proud he enjoyed her cooking. "Let's see. What does a man want in a woman? That was the question."

"Yes, except for the obvious."

"Except for the obvious—well, I guess he enjoys a pretty face—but if she were as ugly as sin, guess that wouldn't matter as long as she had a kind heart and a humble spirit.

"A fine figure helps, but she could be fat as a hog, and if her man loves her, it wouldn't make an ounce of difference. There'd just be more to love—but you've got no problem there. You're a handsome woman, slim as a reed.

"I guess when it comes right down to it, a man wants someone who'll share his life, be his best friend, bear his children; and it wouldn't hurt none if she could make dumplings as good as his mama." He winked. "And you got *no* problem at all in that area."

She waited for him to go on, fascinated. When he didn't, she frowned. "That's all?"

His sincere chestnut brown eyes met hers. "What I'm sayin' is, Nicholas would be a fool to let you go, so stop your frettin'. Nicholas is a lot of things, but he's not stupid. He knows he's got a rose; it'll just take a while for his pride to allow him to admit it."

Faith fiddled with the end of the tablecloth. "Maybe Liza won't let him admit it."

"Nicholas is his own man. He's been real good to Liza since his papa died, indulged her more than he should, but that doesn't mean she runs him. It may look that way; but I've known him all my life, and he doesn't do anything he doesn't want to do."

Faith wasn't as sure about Nicholas's independence. From all appearances, Liza ruled the Shepherd roost.

Tuesday morning Faith was down on her hands and knees polishing the banister at the Smith house when she looked up to find Nicholas standing in the doorway. Her heart shot to her throat. He looked so handsome standing there, tanned, wearing a blue shirt that matched his eyes, his tall frame filling the opening.

Dropping her gaze, she went on polishing. "Is there

something I can do for you?" It was the first time she'd seen him since he'd gotten back from the cattle drive, and the moment was awkward.

A muscle worked tightly in his jaw as his eyes fixed on her. "One of Dan's bulls is out."

No pleasant "How are you?" or "I'm sorry you and Mother disagreed." Not even an "I think we should pray about this." Just "Dan's bull's out."

She kept her eyes trained on the banister. "Did you tell Dan?"

"I'm not going into town. You tell him this afternoon, when he gets home." She winced at his apparent willingness to be on with his business.

Deliberately keeping her voice pleasant, even though she wanted to bite his head off for caring so little about her, she said nicely, "I'm not going to be seeing Dan today; I'm going back to the Finneys'. Can't you put it up for him?"

"It's not my bull."

"It's not mine, either." *Nor my stubborn pride,* she reasoned. Pride goeth before a fall, the Good Book says. Papa would take a switch to her for her impertinence, but Nicholas's outward calm infuriated her! Wasn't he going to ask why she'd left? Didn't he even *want* to hear her side of the story?

The air was electrically charged with raw, masculine power. Faith kept her head bent, carefully working the rag along the railing, thanking the good Lord that Nicholas was a Christian man, able to keep his anger in check.

Pride might prevent him from saying he was disappointed and angry with her, but she could see it in his stance—stiff, unyielding. And in the stubborn set of his jaw. Why didn't he just put the bull back himself? Why bother her at all? He certainly hadn't troubled himself to come around all week. Why now?

"Tell *Dan* his bull will be in the north pasture."

"Thank you. I will tell *Dan* his bull is safe the moment I see him, which may not be until tomorrow," she returned in a voice as stiff as a bullwhip. When she glanced up, he was gone.

Dropping the rag, she sat back on her heels, fighting tears. She would not cry! She wouldn't. Nicholas Shepherd was a stubborn man who would go to his grave lonely and alone!

She reminded herself of that when she bumped into the arrogant rancher a few days later. She'd used the last of the cleaning supplies and several of the church ladies had promised to help with the cleaning Saturday morning.

Nicholas was rounding the corner of the livery when Faith collided head-on with him. Packages flew in all directions as she dropped to her hands and knees, her head spinning. She sat for a moment, trying to orient herself. Color flooded her face when she realized the noisy collision had drawn a crowd.

Strong hands latched on to her waist and effortlessly lifted her up, allowing her feet to dangle in midair. For a moment she stared into amused cobalt blue eyes.

"Shopping again, Miss Kallahan?"

Aware of the chuckles around her, she gritted her teeth and ordered, "Put me down."

"Why, of course, Miss Kallahan." He stood her back on her feet, none too gently, then knelt to pick up the scattered packages. Stacking parcels like cordwood in her arms, he stepped back, removed his hat, and affected a mock bow. Faith felt like a ninny. Every time he saw her lately she was either on her hands and knees or in the process of getting there.

"Might I be of further assistance?" he inquired.

Hugging the packages to her chest, she hurried off, sourly eyeing him over her shoulder. "May I be of further assistance, Miss Kallahan," she mimicked. Oh, she'd tell him *exactly* how he could be of further service if she weren't afraid of the Lord's wrath. The—the arrogant buffoon!

Saturday night, Community Hall was unusually crowded. Faith arrived late with the Finneys.

She caught herself searching the crowd for Nicholas. Liza was standing on the sidelines, vigorously fanning herself as she visited with friends. Faith's gaze traveled the room, stopping when she found her point of interest. He was standing in a group of both men and women. Rachel was standing beside him, smiling as she listened with rapt attention to what he was saying.

Envy sliced through Faith's stomach, and she prayed for understanding. Nicholas was free to talk to whomever he wanted, but Rachel wasn't. She was a married woman, yet she'd heard Liza mention that Joe refused to attend socials.

Seeing the Walterses arrive, Faith hurried over to help out. Taking Adam's and Sissy's hands, she ushered them to the bench lining the wall and seated them.

"My belwee hurts," Sissy complained.

Adam instinctively turned his head in the direction of the refreshment table. "May I have some punch?"

"I'll bring you a cup," Faith promised, recalling the chaos he could incite when left to his own devices.

When the children were settled with cups of punch and a cookie in each hand, Dan pulled Faith toward the dance floor with a teasing light in his eye. When she protested, Vera Hicks offered to hold Lilly, promising she'd keep an eye on the two older children.

Faith realized it would only cause a scene if she refused Dan this dance, but she didn't feel right about it. The whole room would be watching, including Nicholas and Liza, and the last thing she wanted to do was cause the

Shepherds further humiliation. Thanks to Molly and Etta, the town was already buzzing with the news that she had moved off the Shepherd ranch.

She could hear the murmurs and speculations now. "Does Faith Kallahan intend to throw Nicholas Shepherd over for Dan Walters?" "Didn't Nicholas bring Faith to Deliverance to be his bride?" "Is her insistence on opening the blind school causing the problem?"

Before Faith could make a polite refusal, the band struck up a lively reel, and Dan swung her onto the dance floor.

"Really, Dan, I'm a little tired tonight!" she called out as the fiddlers instituted a lively rendition of "Turkey in the Straw."

"You'll get your second wind soon!"

Faith whirled, then began the allemande left, threading her way through the dancers. When her hand came in contact with a solid steel grip, her heart tripped like a drum, but she kept her head low, trying to keep her composure.

"I trust you're enjoying yourself, Miss Kallahan?" Nicholas inquired as they passed.

"Exquisitely so, Mr. Shepherd. And you?" She smiled, determined to be pleasant if it killed her.

"Couldn't be better. Thank you for asking." They continued to allemande, completing a full circle.

A moment later they passed again. Faith bit her lip; she would not fire a return volley. He was only trying to antagonize her, and she wasn't about to fall for it.

"Mrs. Lanner looks lovely tonight, don't you agree?" She bit her tongue hard. Drats and double drats! Did she have to say that?

As they rounded a corner and were forced to join hands to dance through a tunnel of widespread arms, Nicholas returned quietly, "Funny, I was just about to comment on Dan's appearance tonight. He looks mighty dapper."

They reached the end of the archway where he gracefully twirled her, then caught her to him. She landed against the solid wall of his chest. Their eyes met, and for a moment she couldn't catch her breath.

His eyes made his point. "At least Rachel is obedient to her husband."

"As I will be," she volleyed, aware the conversation had just taken a personal turn, "but surely you've forgotten." She leaned closer and whispered, "I'm not married yet."

He whirled her a second time, and she moved on. Seconds later she was back.

"Perhaps if you weren't so stubborn, you would be," he observed nicely.

"Perhaps if *you* weren't so *thickheaded,* you would have asked to hear my side of the story." She smiled prettily, locking hands with him as they joined other dancers to form a bridge.

The caller shouted for the dancers to change partners. Faith whirled with first one man, then another, until the caller reversed the instructions and she returned to Nicholas's waiting arms.

"You, Miss Kallahan, have gone back on your word."

"And you, Mr. Shepherd, are allowing your mother to control your life."

"Nonsense."

"Truth." If only he'd come after her, she would have apologized from the bottom of her heart! She wouldn't promise to give up on the school for the blind, but she would listen to his concerns and address them.

They whirled, then whirled back to face each other.

"Don't deny it. You have your cap set for Dan—have had since the day you got here," he accused.

"I do not!" She stopped, tripping a row of dancers

close on their heels. Men reached out to steady women who staggered clumsily to regain their balance. How dare he accuse *her* of disloyalty! Dan was a good friend, and she didn't like Nicholas talking bad about him. Had Nicholas asked, she would gladly have explained her relationship with Dan, but now, *now* wild horses couldn't drag it out of her. "Sorry, Papa," she muttered, "but you've never dealt with a man like Nicholas!"

Nicholas drew her closer, his eyes riveted with hers. "May I remind you *I* brought you here to marry me, not Dan Walters?"

"It's the money, isn't it?" She sighed. She had never seen two stingier people in all her born days, these Shepherds. "Well, I'll pay you back."

He scoffed. "Where would you get that kind of money?"

"I'll use my nest egg!" she shouted.

He blanched, and she realized she'd struck a nerve.

Lowering her voice, she apologized. "I'm sorry . . . it's just that I feel I owe you an explanation—" She wavered as Nicholas took her arm and ushered her off the dance floor. Dancers looked momentarily confused, but quickly confiscated a couple standing on the sidelines to replace the void.

Bursting outdoors, Nicholas marched Faith to a corner of the porch where a lantern burned low.

"Let me go!"

"You are, undoubtedly, the most stubborn woman I've ever had the misfortune to meet!"

"And you are the most stubborn man." She tried to rub feeling back into her wrist.

Nicholas started to pace. "Is this any way for a grown man and woman to act?"

"You started it."

Her anger gradually dissipated as Papa's voice singed

her conscience. "Faith Marie! That temper's going to earn you a good switchin'!"

"Sorry, Papa," she muttered. *Forgive me, Lord.* "But he just makes me so mad."

Nicholas turned. "What?"

Faith jerked the bodice of her dress into place. "I was talking to *Papa.*"

Running a hand through his hair, Nicholas paced the length of the porch. Faith supposed he was sorting through his thoughts. She turned to face the road, crossing her arms. Well, he had a powerful lot of sorting to do. Did he intend to marry her or not? Was he going to stand up and tell Liza that he meant no disrespect but he was the man of the house, that he'd brought Faith here to marry her, and he darn well was going to live up to his end of the bargain? Or was he not?

"Faith. Are you interested in Dan?" Nicholas asked the question so softly, reluctantly, Faith wasn't sure she'd heard it correctly.

"Am I interested in Dan?"

He looked up, and their eyes met in the moonlight. A soft breeze tossed his hair, making him look boyish. Her anger melted.

"No," she whispered, then wiped a strand of blowing hair out of her eyes. Clearing her throat, she repeated more firmly, "No. I like Dan, and I love his children, but there's nothing romantic between Dan and me."

Relief flooded Nicholas's features but vanished so quickly she wasn't sure it had ever been there. "Are you certain?"

She looked down at her hands, at the empty space, third finger, left hand. "I'm certain. I came here to marry you. If that can't be, then I want to go home, back to Michigan." She closed her eyes, waiting, praying he would say there was no need for that. That he didn't want her to go.

But he didn't.

The silence stretched. Overhead a hoot owl called to its mate. The moon slid behind a cloud, shadowing the honeysuckle-scented porch. It seemed like an eternity before he finally spoke.

"They'll be wondering what's keeping us."

Nodding, she whispered, "Well, we can't have that, can we."

She turned to leave and suddenly felt his hand on her arm. Turning her gently to face him, he gazed at her for a very long time. "I'm sorry if I've been anything other than a gentleman."

Her voice caught as she took a deep breath, reminding herself that love and respect must be earned, and she didn't warrant either from this man. Papa would have been deeply ashamed of her behavior, and in the stillness of the soft summer night, she regretted her outburst on the dance floor. The Lord would be even more disappointed with her. How could Nicholas love a woman who embarrassed him? "You haven't . . . been so bad."

Cupping her face between his large hands, he gazed at her, then kissed her lightly. The kiss was simple, reserved, mysterious, but so utterly galvanizing that it struck a cord deep inside Faith. Why did happiness flood her very being with the touch of his lips? Could she possibly be falling in love with this man? She knew God's plan for her life was perfect, without flaw, but, oh, how her faith needed reassurance.

How was she to take that kiss? she wondered, as Nicholas took her arm and ushered her inside. Was it his way of saying good-bye?

Chapter Twelve

No one can leave Deliverance until after the Founder's Day celebration."

Faith glanced up from packing to see Mary Ellen standing in the doorway. Her friend's unexpected appearance startled her. "Good morning. I thought you were in the kitchen."

"I was, but I knew I had to talk you out of leaving today. It's Founder's Day." Mary Ellen stepped into the small cubicle and slid her hand across the dark blue calico folded in Faith's valise. "Carl Lewis's sister is here from San Antonio, Oren's brother's visitin' from Dallas—no one would miss the celebration."

"But, Mary Ellen," Faith protested.

"Don't do this, Faith. Don't leave in haste. Wait a few more days, and see what Nicholas does."

Faith shook her head. "I've taken advantage of your hospitality for over a month. It's time for me to go home."

"You've been a godsend." Mary Ellen's sober look vanished and her sunny smile returned. "Stay, if only for the day. I'm not even sure if the stage operates on holidays."

Faith felt stricken. It had taken days to convince herself that the time had finally come to leave. She'd seen Nicholas twice since the community dance—once at the mercantile, and last Thursday afternoon when she was crossing the street to attend Bible study. On both occasions they'd nodded politely and gone about their business. Sundays, Nicholas and Liza attended church services but left immediately after the sermon. Nicholas gave no indication of the slightest interest in her.

"Powder your nose; then help me get the food ready. Then we have to get the children into clean clothes." Mary Ellen gave Faith's shoulder a pat and ran to the bedroom door. "Albert, get the buckboard ready. We're going to a celebration!"

For weeks everyone in town had taken part in planning the anticipated event, scheduled to take place today. Faith knew Nicholas and Liza would be there, and Rachel as well. She just couldn't bear to run into those people again. She had to leave now. She'd wrestled with the issue, and it wasn't clear what God would have her to do. She just couldn't face a public situation where she would see Nicholas and Liza.

Then again, she really hadn't gotten the go-ahead from God to leave. . . . Oh, it seemed that every way she turned she faced insurmountable problems! Yet in her spirit, through all the chaos, she felt as if God was telling her to wait . . . to hold on.

"Mary Ellen, if I do go to the celebration today . . ."

"No 'if'—you're going."

"OK, I'm going. But I must go by and help Dan get the children ready. I told him I would help before I caught the stage."

"Yes, I know you promised to help him. We'll drop you at his house on our way."

The two women busied themselves gathering the food for the day's picnic. Faith was caught up in the excitement of the hectic household. She refused to worry about Nicholas and his relationship with her today.

She arrived at Dan's shortly before noon. For weeks now Sissy and Adam had talked about the Founder's Day festivities. Adam's voice filled with excitement as he chattered about the annual fireworks display. As she watched the excitement that radiated from a child who would never experience the spectacular display of brilliant colors and splendid designs exploding in midair, Faith realized how many blessings she took for granted.

Adam and Sissy burst through the doorway, clamoring for the washbowl.

"Papa said we're going to a sellobration!" Sissy shrieked.

"We're going, we're going, we're *going!*" Adam chanted. "Faith, will you help me see the fireworks colors?"

"You bet I will, Buster!" Faith paused long enough to embrace the little boy.

"Hey, my name's not Buster!" Adam grinned. "But you can call me anything you want—long as you promise to come with us!"

"I wouldn't miss it for the world!" Faith realized that was true, and she silently promised herself that tonight, somehow, someway, she would make Adam *see* the fireworks. She'd find a way to describe every detail, every magnificent, glorious, colorful burst. Though young Adam had been to previous Founder's Day displays, tonight she'd make certain he experienced the performance through her eyes.

The Walterses' buckboard rolled into town around twelve-thirty as the stage was just departing the depot. Faith's mouth dropped open, and she looked at Dan.

"Mary Ellen said she didn't think the stage ran today."

He shrugged, grinning. "We all wanted you to stay."

As the wagon drew closer to the church, Faith caught sight of the much discussed steeple. Liza still wasn't going to give money to replace it. But as she looked more carefully, she thought that with a little paint and some nails it would last for another few years. An idea hit her. She liked the townsfolk; most had made her feel wanted and welcomed. If she couldn't bring a school for the blind to Deliverance, she could leave a small legacy behind when she left.

She would fix the steeple. She and Dan. She was sure Dan wouldn't mind. Between them, they could have that old bell tower looking like new. It would mean she would have to stay in town a few more days, but what would that hurt? After all, she'd promised to head the steeple committee in exchange for the women's help cleaning the Smith house. Dreams for the school for the blind were gone, but she could still fulfill her duty. Once the steeple was repaired, she would be free to purchase her stage ticket. It would take every cent of her nest egg, but it was worth it.

The quaint Church of Deliverance was nestled in a shady grove of pecan trees. It was one of those rare summer Saturdays when the weather was comfortable. Reverend Hicks stood at the front door, shaking hands as his flock packed into the small church.

Faith noticed Joe and Rachel Lanner's pew was empty today. Nicholas and Liza were already stationed in their usual front seats.

Faith followed Dan and the children into their pew and sat down.

Liza briefly turned to look over her shoulder as the Walters entered the room. For a split second, she met Faith's gaze. Faith's heart turned over. Liza looked very old and tired this morning, her eyes sad. Could it be, Faith wondered, that Liza regretted her reckless conduct? Bowing her head, Faith asked the Lord for forgiveness for both her and Liza. Neither had been acting as God wanted. If Liza would show one ounce of encouragement, Faith would gladly set their differences aside. Faith still believed God had sent her to Deliverance for a purpose. *I will never fail you. I will never forsake you.* Lifting her eyes ever so slightly, Faith offered Liza a tentative smile.

Liza nodded toward her, then turned in her seat as the service began.

Children squirmed throughout Reverend Hicks's oratory about how Deliverance had been founded by a small band of Ute Indians. The tribe had fallen ill from a strange malady, and J. W. Delivers had fed and cared for the ailing tribe. All died except the chief. In gratitude for Delivers's kindness, the chief had proclaimed that the land belonged to Delivers. The town sprang up some twenty-five years later.

Even baby Lilly got restless during the long talk, squirming on Dan's lap. He bounced her up and down on one knee, trying unsuccessfully to quiet her. Faith finally reached over and took the fussy infant. Lilly immediately stuck her fingers in her mouth and surrendered to a peaceful sleep.

Faith looked up to see Nicholas watching the exchange with eyes as cold as granite.

After the service, the congregation gathered for the long-awaited celebration. With all the colorful blankets spread on the ground, the churchyard resembled a giant, multicolored quilt.

Activity was everywhere. Hardworking farmers and ranchers who seldom saw each other gathered to discuss crops and herds. Others tossed horseshoes or swapped tales so windy that the Reverend jokingly said next year they'd follow Founder's Day with a Liars Festival.

Children, like miniature whirlwinds, ran in every direction. Little boys in their best knickers and white shirts played snap-the-whip or engaged in marbles, using shiny agates and cat's eyes. Little girls in their frilliest dresses, with matching pinafores and bonnets, skipped rope or played ring-around-the-rosy. Their hearty laughter filled the air.

Women chased rowdy toddlers while others preferred to sit in the shade, issuing idle threats. Single girls discreetly scouted for potential suitors, smiling and charming their way through the groups of young men whose ears flamed a bright red under all the attention. Women, young and old, traded recipes and gave advice on gardening, canning, and dressmaking. Conversations grew more animated as several women huddled to share the latest bit of gossip.

Adam was full of the need to help. Faith steadied his hands as he poured lemonade into glasses. When each glass was filled, he was thrilled with his accomplishment. A huge grin wreathed his face.

Dan gathered his brood and said grace, then Faith filled plates with fried chicken, baked beans, corn on the cob, and sourdough bread. Lilly got a bottle. A fine-looking chocolate cake and browned apple dumplings awaited them for dessert. During the past month, as Faith helped cook for Dan and for Mary Ellen, she was delighted to learn that although she still didn't like cooking, she was pretty good at it.

"Thank you for helping me, Adam." Faith smiled at the child as they cleaned up.

"Ahhhh, weren't nothin' to it." He grinned broadly.

"And what, young man, did you do to help Faith that was so special?" Dan asked, playfully ruffling the boy's carrot top.

"You want to tell him, Adam? Or should I?" Faith asked.

"You tell him." Adam's freckled face blushed a russet red.

"Your handsome son filled every last one of our glasses with lemonade!" Faith said. "And without dribbling a single drop!"

Dan patted Adam's shoulder. "Is that right?"

"Yes, sir." Adam beamed. "But Faith helped me."

"All I did was guide your hand, just a little. You did the rest. Pouring was the hardest and most important part."

Dan winked his appreciation at her. Father's pride glowed in his eyes at his son's latest success. Faith knew exactly how he felt. She was feeling a bit of pride herself.

"I suppose we should show this young man our appreciation," Dan said. "Don't know about the rest of you, but as for me, there's nothing quite as satisfying on a hot day as a cool glass of lemonade."

"I absolutely agree," Faith replied. "I suggest we make young Adam king for the day and seal his new title with a round of applause." They fashioned a crown of twigs and placed it on his head.

Faith, Dan, and Sissy clapped so loud and long that they drew attention from the crowd. Even Lilly made a couple of decent swats with her chubby little hands, squealing loudly. Faith could see by the sparkle in Adam's sightless eyes that he truly felt like a king. The young boy reveled in even the slightest accomplishment. An ache gripped Faith's heart when she thought about the school for the blind that would never be. Adam was so bright, so starved for knowledge. Little Adam Walters would someday make his mark in this life, she'd wager on that— and Papa never let her wager. Ever.

Midafternoon, musicians gathered to provide lively tunes and soul-wrenching gospel. Albert Finney played harmonica; Sarah Jane's husband picked banjo. Another man fired up a toe-tapping fiddle. Beside him, a young boy played spoons.

The foursome regaled the crowd with "My Old Kentucky Home," "Tenting on the Old Camp Ground," and "Oh! Susanna."

Faith's favorite was "Amazing Grace." No matter how often she heard the song, it was so beautiful, so heart-rending, that it brought tears to her eyes. June had sung "Amazing Grace" a cappella as they lowered Papa into his grave.

Late in the afternoon Sissy played with a ball that had seen better days, its torn leather having been stitched for the last possible time.

Lilly demanded all of her father's attention. The baby was determined to inch her way off the blanket. Just as Dan blocked her path or took hold of her diaper to slow her down, she turned and crawled in the other direction. The rambunctious baby kept Faith and Dan busy.

Nicholas, Liza, Vera, and Reverend Hicks sat on a blanket nearby, watching the display of family unity. Faith was uncomfortable with their close perusal, but she vowed not to let it spoil her day.

"Afternoon, good people." Jeremiah wandered by and paused to tickle Lilly under her chin.

"Hello, Jeremiah," Faith replied. "Would you like to join us?"

"You're more than welcome, Jeremiah. We've got more food than we could eat in a week," Dan invited. "I do believe you'll find Faith's cookin' to be the best around."

Jeremiah nodded, smiling. "I'm most certain it is, and I do thank you for the tempting invitation. But I was just about to pay my respects to Liza."

Dan winced. "Good luck."

Faith glanced over to see that Liza was now sitting alone. Reverend Hicks and Nicholas were setting up a table in the brush arbor. Vera hauled out watermelons.

"Thank you, my good man. I'm sure I'll be needing all the help I can get." Jeremiah smiled and continued toward the Shepherd blanket.

"Poor Jeremiah." Faith sighed, her gaze following him as he approached Liza, sitting under a tree. "If he isn't careful, Liza will serve him up for lunch."

"I have a feeling Jeremiah can hold his own with Liza." Dan leaned over and snagged Sissy by the hem of her dress. "Who wants to play ball with me?"

"I do!" Sissy screamed.

"Me too!" Adam shouted.

Dan tossed the ball to Adam. He threw it wildly to Sissy, who scurried to catch it.

Faith lay down on the blanket, cradling her head on folded arms, watching Jeremiah. She'd been taught not to eavesdrop, but the temptation was just too great.

Jeremiah removed his hat. "Afternoon, Liza."

Liza lifted her arm, shielding her eyes against the glare. Her eyes skimmed Jeremiah, and she grumbled, "What's so good about it?"

"Why, everything!"

"Too hot," Liza snapped. "What do you want?"

"Nothing more than the pleasure of your company."

Faith strained to hear the conversation. The idea of Jeremiah trying to win favor with Liza—she didn't know whether to laugh or cry.

"May I sit with you a spell?"

Liza brushed an imaginary fly away from a plate of chicken. "You most certainly cannot."

Jeremiah smiled, rubbing his chin. "I'd be no bother."

The poor man. He obviously didn't know Liza the way Faith did. Jeremiah would have better luck trying to lasso the moon than winning Liza Shepherd's favor.

"Well, then, would you do me the honor of sharing a cool glass of lemonade?" Jeremiah motioned toward his blanket spread generously with food, a pitcher of fresh lemonade, and a single yellow rose in a crystal vase.

"Are you out of your mind?" Liza busied herself with her handwork. "Go away—people are staring—go away, you old goat!"

Jeremiah politely bowed. "As you wish, madam. Please accept my apologies. My intentions are most honorable. You see, I thought I was inviting a lady to share an idle moment with me, but sadly I was mistaken. I didn't realize I was extending an invitation to an *old crab!*"

Liza's jaw dropped as Jeremiah turned and walked off.

Biting her lip, Faith lowered her head, her body shaking with mirth. *Old crab.* Jeremiah had called Liza an old crab!

Adam shouted for Faith to join them in the ball game. Collecting herself, she sprang to her feet, catching the ball Dan tossed to her. She threw it to Sissy, who missed. Sissy chased the ball and threw it back to Faith. Running backward, Faith stretched as tall as she could but missed the reckless throw. She heard a dull thwack and whirled to see Nicholas rubbing the back of his head. For a moment her steps faltered, and she wasn't sure what to do.

Nicholas calmly bent down and picked up the ball. Faith backed up as he walked toward her, cupping the ball in the palm of his hand.

"Does this belong to you?"

Faith nodded, for once speechless. Nicholas handed her the ball. Their hands brushed during the brief exchange, and Faith felt a current. For a moment she was certain Nicholas felt it too.

"Try to keep it in your court."

"I'll do that."

Oooohhhhhh, he was so *infuriating,* she thought as he walked away—so downright smug!

Faith's temper gave way and she reared back, hurled the ball, and hit him squarely in the back of the head, hard. Nicholas spun around and shot her a look of disbelief.

"Faith, I wouldn't do that," Dan cautioned. "Nicholas will only put up with so much."

Faith met Nicholas's stern look with one of her own. "I could have knocked him cold if I'd tried."

Dan looked mildly amused, then cleared his throat. "Get the ball, Sissy!"

"Anyone care for watermelon?" Reverend Hicks shouted.

Picnickers made a beeline to the brush arbor. Amos and Vera were busy slicing watermelon, serving adults first, then children. Sissy and Adam were anxious to get their piece of the juicy pink melon. Dan took them by the hand and asked Faith, "Want me to bring yours?"

"No, thanks." She brushed grass from the back of her dress, glancing at Liza still sitting alone on her blanket. On closer look, Faith saw the woman was crying. Liza, crying? She looked again, just to make sure. Liza was silently sobbing into her handkerchief.

Regardless of their differences, Liza's tears softened Faith's heart. God would not want her to ignore another's pain. She had no idea how her presence would be received, but she couldn't just stand here without offering help. If Liza sent her away, so be it. It certainly wouldn't be the first time she had been rebuffed by Nicholas's mother. It surely might be the last.

Edging toward the Shepherd blanket, Faith proceeded

with caution until she was able to kneel beside the older woman. Liza quickly dried her eyes.

"Liza, may I get you a slice of watermelon?" Faith asked softly.

Liza refused to look at her. "I'm surprised you'd offer."

Faith sighed, gently touching her shoulder. "Well, I care about you, Liza. I wish we could be friends."

Liza's gruff demeanor evaporated, and vulnerability took its place. Tears spilled down her cheeks. "Oh, Faith, how *could* you care about me? After the way I've treated you—the way I've treated everyone. I'm so ashamed . . . so ashamed."

Papa always said Faith was blessed with a forgiving spirit. She knew she wasn't, but in this instance she found it easy to forgive. She knew Christians weren't perfect, just forgiven.

"Liza, I know I'm impetuous at times, and I'm not the easiest person to get along with. I have a stubborn streak a mile long," Faith admitted. "But I've never meant you or Nicholas any harm."

Liza reached out for Faith's hand, and held it. She trembled like a small child. "You've done nothing wrong. You stood up for something you believed in. I've been so impossible, so vile to you. And I'm sorry I came between you and Nicholas." She broke off, sobbing into her handkerchief. "It's just that I don't know what's wrong with me. I don't mean to be hurtful."

Faith put her arms around the broken woman and held her tightly. "Sometimes we just need a good long cry," she comforted. "Cry, Liza. I'll hold you."

And cry she did, until Faith felt there were no more tears left to fall. Liza must have had them stored for a powerfully long time.

When the storm passed, Liza sat up, wiping her swollen lids. "I'm sorry. I haven't always been like this." She drew a deep, shuddering breath, then gave a faint laugh. "Always a little headstrong, but never this mass of weeping emotions. The death of a loved one is devastating. I miss Abe so much! Sometimes the pain just takes my breath away."

Nodding, Faith tenderly brushed a lock of hair stuck to Liza's damp cheek. "It must be difficult to accept." Nicholas was a dutiful son, that Faith knew only too well; but Liza needed another woman, a daughter, to comfort her when she hurt, to understand the depth of her pain, to hold her hand during uncertain times.

Liza brought her hand to her mouth, whispering, "I know God is to be the center of our lives, but oh, how I long for my husband. When Abe died, a part of me died with him—my best part. Sometimes I feel so empty that I rail against God, wishing he had taken me, not Abe."

"I know it's not quite the same, but I felt empty and lost when Papa died."

Liza blew her nose, and her gaze centered on Jeremiah. "What must he think of me? I've treated him so badly."

Faith smiled, thinking how strange life was. Never in a million years would she have thought she'd be having this conversation. Not with Liza. Especially not with Liza. "Well, I can't speak for Jeremiah, but I suspect he doesn't think badly of you."

"The whole town thinks badly of me. They can't understand that it isn't the money. . . ." Liza paused, drained of emotion. "I can't recall when I wasn't on the front pew come Sunday mornings. I've been there for revivals, christenings, baptisms, never failed to give the Lord his 10 percent and thank him for his bountiful blessings. I've tried to raise Nicholas in a Christian home, but oh, I've fallen short so many times. I'll be the first to admit to that. For so long now, I've been in this awful deep valley. I'm not sure why, or how, to find the strength to climb out."

"Papa said sometimes God takes us through the darkest times because he's preparing us for a higher mountaintop." Faith reached for Liza's hand, squeezing it. "Something in my spirit tells me you're not in a hopeless valley; you're just getting ready to climb a new mountain."

"How can you say that, child?" Liza questioned softly. "My husband is gone. I've lost my youth; my body betrays me. Nicholas will be married—another woman will take my place in his life. I have nothing. I have no one."

"Yes, Abe is dead. But you'll always have his memories; nothing can take those away from you. And you know he's with the Lord now. Why, he's probably smiling down on you right now, saying, 'Hold on, Liza; we'll be together again soon.' And, Liza, you'll never lose Nicholas. You have raised him well. He's a good and godly man who will always honor his mother. And his family will be your family."

Faith drew the woman back to her breast and gave her a good hug, something she'd obviously not had in a long time. "As for youth, don't cry over lost youth, but glory in the knowledge that each year that passes brings you one step closer to going home to be with our heavenly Father, home to be with Abe."

Liza's shoulders heaved as tears fell anew. "Right now I just feel very old, old and tired, unloved, and horribly forgetful. I misplace everything, and I'd forget my name if I didn't write it down."

Liza's admission brought Faith a pang of guilt. "I'm afraid I have a confession to make. . . ."

Liza looked up. "A confession?"

"You're not as forgetful as you think. I've been hiding your snuff—not out of spite. I hid it because I thought if it wasn't there to tempt you, you might decide to give up the habit." Faith wrinkled her nose. "I hid it behind the mantel clock."

Liza patted Faith's hand. "I know, dear. I found it each

time I rewound the clock. You're lucky, young lady, I didn't take a switch to you." Liza shyly grinned through a veil of tears. Faith was stunned to see she wasn't old at all. Quite pretty, actually.

"I hope you aren't upset with me."

"Quite the contrary. I haven't touched snuff for weeks now. And I have you to thank for making me think about what a bad habit I had developed."

Should she mention the brown vial? No, they were making progress on their friendship. She didn't want to spoil the effort by introducing more problems.

The women shared a good laugh. Then Faith grew serious. "See, you're not as forgetful as you think. And you're not old, either. You're still beautiful and—" she raised her eyebrows—"there's a certain gentleman who would very much like to know you better."

Liza blushed, her gaze fixed on Jeremiah sitting across the yard. "Well, I doubt that he likes me any longer. I've managed to run *him* off, too."

"Oh, I have a feeling he won't be gone long. Jeremiah knows a good thing when he sees it. I doubt he'd let you slip away without a good fight."

Liza blushed. "Faith, I—I don't know how to thank you. I realize now that I haven't turned my problem over to God, haven't let him heal my pain. I know better; I read God's Word every day. It's odd how easy it is to forget his promises in the midst of one's pain."

"God loves you, Liza, and he's waiting to give you peace." *My yoke is easy, and my burden is light,* Faith remembered. She hugged Liza again briefly. Her sister, Hope, always said she hugged the life out of people, but she didn't care. She never got enough hugging herself. "If you're feeling better, I had better be getting back. The children will be looking for me."

"Run along . . . and thank you for listening to an old woman's problems."

Faith pointed a stern finger at her. "You're *not* old."

Faith was about to walk away when Liza latched onto the hem of her skirt. "All the apologies in the world aren't going to correct what I've done. Nicholas is stubborn, so like his father. It seems you've wounded his pride by turning to Dan—although I accept full responsibility. I'm so sorry, Faith. As much as I would like, I doubt that I can undo the wrong I've done. Pride destroys all it touches."

Faith nodded. "I know. It doesn't matter anymore. I've decided to return to Cold Water. Perhaps when this is over, Nicholas will find a woman here in Deliverance to marry." She thought of Rachel, taking no joy in the thought. "A grandchild is just what you need to take away your loneliness."

Faith said good-bye and rejoined Dan and the children. Now she knew the reasons Liza had erected so many barriers—to protect herself from further loss. The woman she thought she could never like, now appeared to be someone she could truly love.

But it was too late. Too late for Liza, and too late for Nicholas and her.

Toward sunset, Nicholas wandered down to the pond. Faith and the children were sitting on the bank, fishing; Dan and the baby were napping at the church ground.

Watching Faith bait her hook, Nicholas felt a tightening in his throat. With stark clarity he realized God had not sent Faith to him; he'd sent her to Dan Walters. Dan's children loved her—Dan was in love with her himself; it didn't take a wise man to see that. And Faith was falling in love with him. Nicholas saw the blush in her cheeks, heard her bubbly laughter. What a blind fool he'd been. He'd sweated blood over their situation, wondered, prayed if he should ask her to come back. Ironically, today he realized the state of their relationship was no longer in his hands. Faith belonged to Dan.

"Looks like Adam and Sissy could use some help baiting those hooks."

Faith looked up, surprise crossing her sun-kissed features when she saw him. Like Lilly, he thought, Faith refused to wear her bonnet. "Oh, we'll manage." She jerked, missed a catch, and brought her line back in.

The moment felt awkward and strained. Where was her earlier laughter; the laughter she shared so easily with Dan?

"Tried your luck lately?" she asked.

It wasn't exactly an invitation, but Nicholas took it as one. Walking to the edge of the water, he stood for a moment, watching water skimmers on long, comical legs skitter across the pond. He'd never noticed how nice Faith looked in a dress. The blue-and-white gingham brought out the violet in her eyes. Had she worn the dress before?

Adam jerked, and his line snarled around a nearby stump. He pulled back, popping the hook. It shot by Sissy's ear like a bullet. She screamed and dropped her pole on the ground.

The boy whipped the rod in the opposite direction and caught the brim of Sissy's hat, yanking it into the water. Bending over, Sissy picked up a rock and hurled it at him.

Nicholas moved in. "Hold on now—no rock throwing." As he walked past Faith, he leaned down, his breath warm against her ear. "I'd like to call a truce."

Faith looked up. "A truce?"

"If you're agreeable."

He could see she must surely be tempted to remind him of the past month, a month when he had managed to torment, tease *and* ignore her; but she didn't. Would she be willing to call an end to their childishness? *Blessed are the peacemakers.*

"If that's what you want."

"I'd like that very much." He missed her, more than he thought he'd miss any woman. The thought left him unsettled. "Shake on it?" Nicholas extended his hand.

They shook, sharing forgiving smiles.

"Sorry I was so short with you."

"Sorry I've been such a twit."

Sissy and Adam reminded Nicholas that he needed to bait their hooks. Nicholas reluctantly released Faith's hand. "I'm sorry our arrangement hasn't worked out."

"So am I."

Why hadn't they tried harder to make it work? Why hadn't *he* tried harder? Pride? Was pride blinding him the way it so often had Papa?

"No hard feelings?"

Faith deserved a husband closer to her age. As much as Nicholas hated to admit it, Dan would be good for her. Nicholas was older, more set in his ways. He couldn't imagine playing ball with young children, frolicking around the churchyard like frisky colts, running hand in hand with Faith through fields of bluebonnets. But for one irrational moment he wanted to. A thought hit him like a thunderbolt. What would their children have looked like—blond and fair like he was, or dark and ol-ive-skinned like Faith? He had never pictured himself as a father, but he realized either would suit him just fine.

"No hard feelings," she granted.

"Mr. Shewperd, are yew gonna put this woorm on my hook or not?" Nicholas was jolted from his thoughts to find Sissy, cane pole in one hand, an ugly-looking night crawler dangling in the other.

He frowned. "Are you sure you want that hearty fella on your line?"

Sissy solemnly nodded.

Nicholas looked at Faith and wrinkled his nose. "That's what I was afraid of."

Time passed too quickly. Before Nicholas knew it, the sun had set in a purple-streaked sky.

"Faith, it's almost time for the fireworks!" Adam breathlessly announced after his fourth journey to the churchyard.

"Adam, you come on now," Dan yelled, holding Lilly in his arms and standing on a small rise at the back of the churchyard.

"Be there in a moment, Adam," Faith promised. The little boy allowed his sister to take his hand and lead him up the steep embankment.

Nicholas helped Faith gather poles and other tackle. "Kids love those fireworks."

"Adam's been looking forward to them all day."

As they started up the incline, Faith suddenly stopped, whirled, and reached up to give him a little peck on the cheek. Then she simply gazed at him. "I'm sorry, but I can't leave without doing that."

Surprised, Nicholas didn't know what to say. "I'm glad you didn't . . . leave," he clarified. "Without doing that."

She released a breath of what sounded like relief. "I hoped you'd see it that way." Playfully rubbing the goose-egg-sized knot on the back of his head, she confessed, "I need to say I'm sorry about hitting you with that ball. That was most impolite of me."

"If that's what it takes to get a kiss from you, you have my permission to fell me with a ball bat."

He heard her say softly, "Well, actually, my kiss was about more, but that's neither here nor there."

He frowned.

She stopped his next question by resting a fingertip on his lips. "The fireworks will be starting. I promised I'd watch them with Adam. I don't want to disappoint him."

As they started up the steep incline, Nicholas reached for her hand. Hand in hand, they climbed the hill. When they reached the top, he reluctantly released her hand and headed back to his mother.

Nicholas had thought that once he apologized to Faith and settled their dispute, he'd feel better.

Oddly enough, he felt worse.

Before the fireworks started, Faith shredded paper and bunched it into a loose ball. She told Adam to hold out his hand.

"Why?" Adam questioned.

"It's a firework," Faith answered. "Not a real one, but a pretend one. I want you to *see* what one looks like."

"Really?"

"Really. Are you ready to use your imagination?"

"Yes, ma'am!"

"OK, here we go." Faith stood over Adam. "Feel all the little bits of paper, rolled into a ball?"

Adam carefully examined the paper ball with his fingers. "Yes."

"Well, that's a firework before it's lit. But when its fuse is lit, the firework shoots far up in the sky, exploding into a hundred million brilliant colors and shapes as it falls back to earth."

"What are the colors?" Adam asked excitedly.

"Blue—"

"Cool," Adam squealed. "Like the ice!"

"Red—"

"Hot!"

"Like the stove," Faith said. "Now close your eyes, and we're going to shoot off our pretend firework. You'll feel the little pieces of paper when they fall on your face. Imagine the real ones falling from the sky, only they're hot and burn themselves out before they reach the ground."

"That's a good thing, huh, Faith?" Adam turned sober.

"A very good thing. If they didn't, we'd all have little blisters. . . ."

" 'Cause they're red-hot!"

Faith laughed. "Are you ready? The fireworks are about to begin!"

"Yes!"

"Are you using your imagination?"

"A whole bunch!"

Faith made a sizzling, sputtering sound like a rocket about to take off. Loosening the paper ball, she clasped his hand to hers. They tossed the tiny pieces in the air, letting them burst free and cascade down on Adam's face as the first rocket went up. The crowd ooohhed and ahhhed as the missile soared into the heavens, exploded, then rained down in a myriad of spectacular colors.

"Fireworks! Red, blue—hot and cold—I can see them, Faith! I can see them in my 'magination!"

Tears sprang to Faith's eyes. Adam didn't need eyes to see the beauty. God had given him a lively imagination, one where virtually nothing was out of his reach. "Aren't they beautiful!"

"They're *beautiful*," Adam repeated, jumping up and down. "So *beautiful!*"

Dan looked at Faith, his eyes filled with gratitude. "You're amazing."

Faith shook her head. "No. Your son is the amazing one. And I like to think that somewhere your wife, Carolyn, is looking down, so very proud of him right now."

Just then the sky lit up with another explosion. Faith sat beside Adam as the rockets burst in midair, their dazzling colors a stark contrast to the nighttime sky. Sissy squealed with delight, hopping on one foot, then the other. Lilly bawled, wanting her bottle. Hand in hand,

Adam and Faith watched with a new appreciation for Deliverance's Founder's Day fireworks display.

The celebration came to an end. Weary mothers and fathers loaded sleepy children into wagons. While Dan packed the buckboard, Faith stepped over to talk to Jeremiah.

"Jeremiah, may I have a word with you?" she asked, not exactly sure how to broach the subject of his relationship with Liza.

"You most certainly may." Jeremiah smiled. "How can I help a pretty little thing like you?"

"I couldn't help overhearing you and Liza earlier today. . . ."

"Water under the bridge, I assure you."

"Jeremiah, maybe it isn't." Faith searched for the right words. She didn't want to make the situation worse. "I think perhaps Liza realizes she was a little . . . shall we say, brusque with you today?"

"Oh, I believe she made herself quite clear." He laughed, but his eyes exposed deep hurt.

"I don't think she meant to be so harsh. In fact, I think you should give Liza another chance."

Jeremiah eyed Faith. "Another chance to insult me and turn me down?"

"No. I have a feeling you'll be getting a different response from now on."

"And what makes you so sure?"

Faith had no intention of betraying Liza's confidence. But she believed that once Liza surrendered her hurt to God, he would be swift to lighten her burden. She winked at Jeremiah. "Just trust me on this one. Please?"

Jeremiah hesitated, absently stroking his beard. "Well . . . I'll take the matter under consideration."

"Thanks, Jeremiah." Faith stood on tiptoes and kissed him on the cheek.

"My," Jeremiah said. "What's brought this on?"

"Nothing." Although Faith wanted to tell him she was leaving, she feared she would get emotional. She gulped. Better to warn him now than to betray his friendship. "I must leave, and you must keep my secret."

He frowned.

"Nicholas has left me no other choice."

"Child, with time—"

"Please, as my friend, allow me this."

He nodded.

When they arrived back at the Walters home, Mary Ellen and Albert waited as Faith helped Dan get the children into the house.

Less than an hour later, exhausted but happy, the two women sat at the Finneys' kitchen table, each thinking about the strange day.

Faith had fallen in love with Nicholas Shepherd.

She had realized it this afternoon at the pond. Nicholas had tried to smooth things over, but it just made her want more of him. Somehow he had seemed more relaxed, at peace, and he was wonderful with the children. Her heart ached. She supposed worse things could happen than falling in love under these circumstances. But the thought somehow failed to cheer her.

Chapter Thirteen

Liza?" Doc got up from his desk and motioned Liza into his office.

"Hi, Doc. I took a chance you weren't busy."

"Never too busy for you." Doc pulled up a chair and invited her to sit down. Perching on the edge of the desk, the portly, silver-haired gentleman smiled. "How's Nicholas?"

"Fine, just fine."

"Heard that he and Miss Kallahan are having quite a time gettin' the knot tied."

Liza didn't care to discuss Nicholas's personal problems. Molly Anderson and Etta Larkin were doing a fine job of that. "Seems that way."

Doc's features sobered. "Something I can do for you, Liza?"

It was the moment she'd dreaded, yet now she fully welcomed it. It was the first step to relinquishing all her hurts and disappointments to God. The thought no longer frightened her; she felt a peace for the first time since Abe's death. But she had to know how much time she had left. There were matters to be set in order.

"I . . . haven't been feeling myself lately."

"Oh?" Doc frowned. "How long?"

She shrugged. "A couple of years . . . since Abe . . . since Abe left. At first I thought it was grief. Now I know it's much more than that."

Doc's mouth fell. "Liza!"

"You know I don't hold with doctors," she snapped.

Getting to his feet, Doc eyed her sternly. "Tell me what you've observed about your health. Think this through. I need to know everything that has been going on with you and when each symptom began." He picked up his pencil and paper and settled in a chair close to her.

Liza burst into tears, ailments pouring out of her like lava: night sweats, hot flashes, loss of memory, bouts of depression, paranoia. When the flood subsided, she dried her eyes and braced herself for the worst. "I know I don't have long, but I need to know how long, so I can make plans."

Doc nodded, listened to her heart, looked down her throat, peered into her ears, thumped here and there as she talked.

"Hummmm."

When the examination was over, she gazed up at him. "How long, Doc?"

Doc shook his head and moved to the medicine cabinet. "Hard to say, but listening to your heart, I'd guess no more than thirty, forty years."

Liza nodded. Thirty to forty years. That's what she'd thought. . . . She sat up straighter. "What?"

"How old are you now, Liza? Fifty? Fifty-one?"

"Fifty-two in November."

"Monthlies ceased?"

She blushed, then nodded.

"Cross as a settin' hen?"

She nodded, miserably wringing her hands. She hated to think how regularly she'd pinned Nicholas's ears back.

Doc took a bottle off the shelf, then closed the cabinet door. "You're going through the change of life, Liza. Nothing to be worried about. It falls to every woman. The symptoms are uncomfortable and annoying, but it won't kill you."

He put the bottle in her hand, squeezing her fingers shut. "Pinkham's Tonic. A lot of physicians think it's hogwash, but I don't. I have women who swear by it. Take a couple of teaspoons three times a day, and you'll be your old self in no time at all."

"Change of life? That's what *Grandma* went through."

Doc nodded. "And her mother, and her mother, and her mother. I suppose even old Eve gave Adam a fair run for his money when she hit the right age."

Liza stared at the brown vial of *Lydia E. Pinkham's Vegetable Compound.* "I'm not going to die?"

He chuckled. "Not any time soon—now, of course, you understand, I don't make those kinds of decisions. I leave that up to the Lord."

Liza rolled the bottle of medicine in her hands and took a deep breath. "I . . . I've been using . . ." She couldn't look Doc in the eyes.

"You've been using Pinkham's Tonic?"

"I had heard, uh, had heard it might help."

"What dosage did you use, Liza?" the doctor asked gently.

"I only took a swallow when I really needed it." She straightened, and her chin shot skyward. "I knew I could handle whatever trials the Lord sent to me. Until Abe . . . until Abe left . . . died." There, she'd finally ad-

mitted it. Abe was gone, residing now with his heavenly
Father. "I thought perhaps it was grief that made me feel
so awful."

"Liza, trust me. Take the medicine and follow my instructions. You'll be over this before long." He squeezed
her shoulder. "Nature makes these changes in your body,
and once you understand what is happening, it's much
easier to accept. Now, I want to hear from you soon
about how you're feeling."

Leaving the office a few minutes later, Liza closed the
door and sagged against it. She wasn't going to die.

Clutching the full bottle of tonic to her chest, she
lifted her face to the afternoon sun, letting the glorious
assurance wash over her.

She *wasn't* going to die.

"Mama!" Nicholas burst through the back door and
slammed it shut. The cat, sunning on the windowsill,
jumped as if shot. "The chickens are in the garden
again!"

Liza glanced up from the stove. "Well, put them back
in the pen."

"*You* put them back in the pen." He threw his hat on
the kitchen table, rattling a cup and saucer. "It's your job
to keep them out of the garden."

Slicing a beef roast, Liza calmly motioned him toward
the washstand. "Wash up. Dinner's almost ready."

Nicholas reached the washbowl in two angry strides.
When Papa was alive, if a chicken went near the garden,
it would have been swimming in a pot of dumplings that
night!

Reaching for the bar of soap, he lathered his hands and
elbows. The image of Faith swam before his eyes. Muttering under his breath, he forced her image aside. The
woman was on his mind day and night. What was hap-

pening to him? It was almost as if she'd cast a spell over him, a spell he was powerless to escape.

She was a curse—had been from the moment she rode into town on the back of Jeremiah's mule. Stirring up the town with talk of a school for the blind, spending time with Dan Walters—she, and she alone, was responsible for all these hushed whispers and sympathetic stares coming his way.

How soon was Miss Kallahan going to make it worse?

Nicholas wondered how soon she was going to marry Dan and make Nicholas look like an even bigger fool. Paying her way here, putting her up all those weeks—he should never have gone on that cattle drive. That's when the problem had started. If he'd stayed home, he and Faith would be married.

He scrubbed harder. He'd bet Walters took his meals at his own table with Faith at noontime. His stomach spasmed with the thought as he scoured his arms so hard they hurt. The woman just plain made him mad. He couldn't eat, couldn't sleep. Toweling off, he stalked to the table.

Setting a bowl of greens on the table, Liza eyed him. "My, aren't we in a temper."

"Chickens don't belong in the garden." Nicholas reached for an ear of corn and slapped butter on it.

Taking her seat at the opposite end of the table, Liza bowed her head and quietly blessed the food.

"Seems to me," she continued as she shook out her napkin, "you've had a burr under your saddle lately."

"I don't know what you're talking about."

"I'm talking about Faith."

Nicholas froze at the sound of her name. The mention of Faith Kallahan had been banned in this house. Why Mama chose to bring it up now escaped him. "Well," Nicholas said as he reached for the platter of roast, "I'm *not* talking about her, Mama. So let's eat in peace."

Liza took a bite of meat with her eyes still fixed on her son. "Saw Faith today while I was in town."

Was she going to wear out that name right here at the dinner table? Nicholas grumbled, "What took you to town on a weekday morning?"

"A little this, a little that." Liza thought about the new brown bottle of Pinkham's Tonic hidden at the bottom of her bureau drawer and smiled. Picking up the bowl of greens, she spooned a helping onto her plate. "Faith's fixing the town steeple."

"She's what?"

"Fixing the town steeple. There she and Dan were, on the church rooftop, big as you please, Faith dressed in overalls and men's boots, hammering and painting to beat the band. I must say, the old steeple's going to look a sight better."

"Fixing steeples, sawing wood, delivering cows—what next?" Nicholas shoved a bite of meat into his mouth.

Liza casually speared a slice of tomato. "Seems she and Dan were meant for each other. They have the same interests; Faith takes to those kids like a moth to a flame—wouldn't surprise me if Dan didn't snap her right up."

"I thought he already had."

"Nicholas . . ."

"Mama, I'm trying to eat."

"I was wrong about Faith, Nicholas." Liza's humble admission rattled him. She had been *wrong?* Well, now was a fine time to admit it.

"No, you weren't wrong, Mama. Your instincts about Faith were right. I'm just glad I found out she was fickle before I married her."

"This whole misunderstanding between you and Faith is my fault. I'm sorry I was so unreasonable and that I didn't try to befriend her—perhaps if you were to start over—"

"Don't be foolish. You were right about the steeple, and I'm right about Faith. No caring woman would have left the moment my back was turned."

"I could be right about the steeple, but not about Faith. And she didn't just up and leave. If you blame anyone, blame me. My irrational ultimatum left Faith little choice but to seek refuge at the Finneys'. I treated her unfairly, Nicholas—and I indicated she was feeling something for Dan that I don't think she's really feeling. I deliberately planted that seed in your head, and I was wrong, so wrong. I'm sorry . . . if I had it to do over—"

Nicholas cut her off. "What's done is done." He was tired of talking about Faith Kallahan. Six days out of seven they ate their meals in silence. Why, of all days, did Mama have to pick this particular meal to philosophize? He bit into an ear of corn and wiped juice off his chin.

Liza took a bite of roast, her eyes fixed on him. What was she looking at? Couldn't a man eat his dinner in peace?

"You feeling all right lately, Nicholas?"

"Fine."

She reached for a biscuit, breaking it open. "Good dose of Epsom salts now and then never hurt a body."

He lifted his head and eyed her sourly.

They lapsed into silence, their focus on their plates.

"Reverend Hicks stopped by earlier."

"What did he want?"

"Money for the holiday baskets. He's starting the drive early this year."

Nicholas forked a bite of greens into his mouth. "Give it to him. Make a generous donation this year. We've got more money than we can ever spend." Lord knew they'd been miserly enough the past couple of years.

Liza reached for her fan as color saturated her face.

Nicholas watched the familiar red flush creeping up her neck.

"Are you hot again?"

"It's a little warm in here." She sheepishly avoided his stare. "Don't you think?"

Nicholas shook his head. "Feels comfortable to me."

The flush receded, and she snapped the fan shut. "Eat your dinner before it gets cold."

Late that afternoon Nicholas was loading an order of feed at the mercantile. Oren Stokes and Jeremiah were discussing the weather. Hot, could use a good rain, the two men decided.

Jeremiah was another person on Nicholas's short list. If he hadn't encouraged Faith, she wouldn't have gone off half-cocked to open a school for the blind. Jeremiah knew Nicholas hadn't endorsed the idea, yet he had continued to encourage Faith.

Nicholas had been at the store last week when two large crates arrived from Boston. Jeremiah had hurriedly loaded the bins onto a cart, and hauled them off. Nicholas suspected the boxes had something to do with the proposed school, but Jeremiah refused to say.

Just then Jeremiah came out of the store and down the steps. He smiled at Nicholas, nodding pleasantly.

Heaving another sack aboard the wagon, Nicholas grunted what passed for a civil greeting. He didn't feel very "civil" at the moment.

Jeremiah paused on the lower step to light his pipe. Giving a hearty puff, he gazed up at the flawless blue sky. "Hot, isn't it?"

Nicholas swung another sack onto the wagon, hoping Jeremiah wasn't going to start in on the weather again. How much more could be said about a hot June day? Oren had pretty much exhausted the subject.

"Yes, sir." Jeremiah patted his vest, drawing on the pipe. White smoke swirled above his head. "Fine time for traveling—though it could get a mite dusty."

Hefting the last grain sack onto the wagon, Nicholas took off his hat and wiped the sweat off his forehead. "Suppose it could—if anyone was going anywhere."

Jeremiah cocked a brow. "You haven't heard?"

"Heard what?" Nicholas reached for the dipper in the water barrel.

"Why, Miss Kallahan is leaving us soon."

The statement hit Nicholas like a cannonball. His hand paused, the dipper suspended in midair. His eyes darkened to a troubled hue. "You must be mistaken. She doesn't intend to leave; she intends to marry Dan."

Drawing on the stem of the pipe, Jeremiah shook his head. "No, don't believe she does. She's leaving on the stage in the morning. Saw her purchase the ticket myself, couldn't have been more than thirty minutes ago."

Nicholas tried to find his voice. Faith leaving? Lifting the dipper to his mouth, he took a long, thirsty drink. If Jeremiah expected a reaction, he wasn't going to get one. This whole mail-order bride mess left a bad taste in Nicholas's mouth. She had told him at the dance that she didn't intend to marry Dan Walters but to return to Michigan. But when he'd seen her at the Founder's Day celebration, with Dan and his children, he'd been sure that she was in love with Dan and had changed her mind. Apparently she had decided to keep her word to him.

The thought should have left him with a measure of satisfaction; instead, he felt empty, as if he'd lost something rare and irreplaceable because of pride and stupidity.

Jerking the brim of his hat low, he said quietly, "That's too bad. I'm surprised Dan would allow her to go."

Jeremiah struck a match and frowned at his cold pipe.

"I'm sure if Dan had any say in the matter, he would insist that she stay." He touched the match to the rim, puffing, "Unfortunately, he doesn't. Faith came here to marry you. Since that no longer seems likely, she's decided to return to her aunt in Michigan."

Nicholas removed his gloves, stalling for time. "What about the school for the blind?"

"Pity," Jeremiah said. "Faith's a fine figure of a woman—smart, too. The town would have benefited greatly had she been allowed to open the school."

Nicholas slapped the gloves against his thighs, his features taut with frustration. "No one's running her out of town. She can stay if she wants."

"Oh, I think she'd find that entirely too awkward." The pipe flared to life again. "True, Dan would marry her in a heartbeat, but she doesn't love Dan." He fanned the match out, smiling. "Love's a strange thing; never know where it's going to pop up, or with whom."

Jeremiah's tone implied she was in love with him, Nicholas. Nicholas inwardly ridiculed the idea. It was not only wrong, it was laughable. How could Faith love him? He'd given her every reason to feel the opposite.

Swinging aboard the wagon, Nicholas released the brake. "Tell her I wish her the best."

"Why don't you tell her?"

He couldn't. He didn't wish her to leave at all.

Nicholas rolled to his back and hurled a boot at the open window. Blasted crickets! They'd kept him awake half the night.

Settling back on the pillow, he closed his eyes, only to see Faith's face for the hundredth time. Why should he care if she left tomorrow . . . yet he did. How could he ever make up for all that had happened between them— and all that hadn't happened?

Shifting to his side, he wadded his pillow under his head, soundly thumping it. He heard the clock strike two; then, what seemed like hours later, it struck three, and he sighed.

Twisting to his back, he stared at the ceiling. He'd done the work of ten men today trying to put Faith and her fickle nature out of his mind. He should be sleeping like the dead, but instead he was staring at the ceiling, wondering what he'd done wrong.

He had been polite, respectful, careful to make Faith comfortable during the time she was under his roof. Their brief talks on the porch at night had made him think they were warming to each other. Their wedding was delayed twice—no, three times—well actually four, but she'd seemed to understand why. A man wasn't expected to lose a good herd of stock for a ten-minute wedding ceremony, was he? Faith hadn't expected him to let the town burn to the ground, had she? Babies had a way of coming at the most inconvenient time—he'd heard that himself. Miss Kallahan couldn't pin that one on him. And the herd, well, that was pure common sense in the cattle business.

He switched back to his side. It was Dan Walters's fault. From the moment she'd arrived, Dan had his eye on her, and Carolyn barely cold in her grave. He listened to the pesky cricket near the windowsill.

Walters needed help. Three small kids under the age of five—one blind. He guessed he'd be looking for help too if he were in Dan's shoes.

He rolled onto his back and frowned in the darkness. Faith certainly hadn't lost any time making herself useful to Dan. Naturally he'd take to her—no, he was being unfair. Dan didn't just *need* Faith; he was attracted to her. That was the hardest to admit, and it stuck in his throat. He'd seen the admiration in Dan's eyes, the expectant way he looked at Faith, the way the two of them shared a confidential smile when the children did something cute.

Why hadn't Faith looked at him that way? Or had she, and he'd been so busy trying to solve Mama's problems that he failed to notice? Questions nagged him. He thought he'd gotten Faith out of his system, but she was back, haunting his thoughts, making him feel as though *he* were at fault, not her. He professed to be a Christian, but where was his faith now? What had become of his initial trust—the belief that God had sent Faith for him, not for Dan?

Faith had brought sunshine back into his life. She brought laughter into the house. After Papa's death the house had become a tomb. Mama went about her work, he went about his, and two years passed by. One day he woke up and realized he was thirty-four years old. Thirty-four. Before long, life would pass him by.

If he'd had any idea that posting that blasted ad would bring this kind of grief, he would have cut the journal in a hundred pieces and fed it to the hogs. What had he been thinking? Just because he was thirty-four and single, did that give him license to order a bride? Send off for a wife like he would send for a new plow? Well, it hadn't worked. He'd only served to make a fool of himself.

If he had it to do over, he'd try harder with Faith. He would marry her before the problems ever got out of hand. Pride, ugly pride, had kept him from going to her. When was he going to turn that pride over to God?

It wasn't easy to welcome a stranger into his home, and it took time to build a union between a man and a woman; but they had struck a bargain. He'd given his promise; she'd given hers. If he'd married her the moment she got off Jeremiah's mule, he wouldn't be going through this! He punched his pillow. Pride be hanged. He should have seen this thing through. It wasn't the worst idea he'd ever had. The worst was when he'd decided not to go after her the moment he returned from San Antonio.

Sitting up in bed, he realized his mistake. He was obligated to keep his promise. The town would see his rationale and not hold it against him. He'd sent for Faith to be his bride, and a man wasn't much of a man who refused to honor a commitment.

Tossing the sheet aside, he got out of bed and reached for his trousers.

Faith lifted her head off the pillow, roused from a deep sleep. The sound of Nicholas's raised voice behind the closed bedroom door startled her.

"I want to talk to Faith!"

Albert's hushed voice tried to quiet him. "She's asleep, Nicholas, has been for hours—"

Faith cringed at the note of authority in Nicholas's voice. "*Now,* Albert."

Climbing out of bed, Faith dressed quickly, then twisted her braid on top her head. Pinching color into her cheeks, she slipped out the door.

"Nicholas?"

Nicholas's eyes burned with intensity. "I want to talk to you."

Faith glanced questioningly at Albert. "Certainly—Albert, would you mind—"

"Not here," Nicholas said. "Horses are waiting outside."

"Nicholas, that's highly improper," Albert reminded him. "Faith is without a chaperone—"

"Faith and I are both adults. I can assure you I have no intention of dishonoring Miss Kallahan."

"It's all right, Albert." She reached for a light shawl. "I'll only be gone a short while."

"Do you want me to come with you?"

"No, you stay with Mary Ellen and the children. I'll be fine, really." She brushed coolly past Nicholas on her way out of the door.

Her mind whirled. Where was he taking her? Was it wise for her to entrust her well-being to this man? A new, hopeful thought dawned on her. Had he discovered she was leaving and come to stop her? No, the only ones who knew she was leaving were Dan and Jeremiah. Dan had promised to keep quiet until she was safely gone, and Nicholas would never have talked to Jeremiah.

She paused when she saw the two Appaloosas standing by the rail. For a moment she wanted to cry. *Now* he was taking her for that promised ride.

"Pick the one you want. I promised you a ride when I got back."

Faith nuzzled a warm, black nose. "Do you keep promises, Nicholas?"

"I try, Faith. I try very hard."

Biting her lip, Faith picked the animal on the left. They were both magnificent creatures. But she didn't want a horse. She wanted Nicholas.

Nicholas lifted her onto the saddle, and their hands brushed. She felt a thrill of anticipation and quickly smothered it. Tucking her dress between her knees, she flicked the reins. The horses galloped out of the yard and into the lane. A full moon hung overhead. Nicholas rode beside her, his jaw set in determination. Whatever had prompted this nocturnal visit, she guessed she'd soon know.

An hour, then two, the horses traveled back roads and forded dry creek beds. Faith shivered, hunched beneath her thin shawl. How dare he burst into the Finneys' house and demand to see her at this time of night? He had no right—no right at all to act as if he owned her!

The animals climbed steep inclines and picked their way through valleys dotted with Shepherd cattle.

The moon sank lower and lower in the western sky as the horses clopped along dirt roads. The silence was altered only by the changing cadence of hooves, fast, then slower. And still, Nicholas didn't speak. For what reason had he come calling for her tonight? His stern features seemed at war with himself. Did he want to say something? Tell her something? Confess something?

Darkness gradually gave way to dawn. The sky lightened, spreading tendrils of pastel pinks and golds across the distant horizon. Faith dozed, her head bobbing with the horse's easy gait.

The animals came to a stop, and Faith sat up, trying to orient herself. They were back in the Finneys' yard. She looked at Nicholas's tired features and knew that indeed a war raged within him, but he seemed determined not to permit her to know his enemy.

"Nicholas," she said softly, wanting to erase the pain she saw in his eyes. "What is it?"

Shaking his head, he refused to answer. She'd known all along he wasn't a man who easily expressed his feelings. But she was powerless to help until he exposed the demons that drove him.

Getting off the horse, he came to stand beside her mount. She waited, holding her breath.

"I'd like to kiss you," he stated quietly.

"All right," she agreed in a hushed whisper.

Lifting her off the saddle into his arms, he kissed her, his kiss even more bewildering than his actions. Tentative, yet possessive. Needy, yet reserved. What was going through his mind?

When their lips parted, he said softly, "Good night, Faith."

"Good night, Nicholas."

The rooster crowed the beginning of a new day as she let herself in the back door, still wondering what he'd wanted.

The sun was coming up as Nicholas closed the door to his bedroom. Sitting on the edge of the bed, he thought about the past few hours and realized that Faith must think him loco. No matter how hard he'd tried, words had failed him. How could he tell her what was in his heart? How could he explain blind pride and what it does to a man when he fails to turn it over to God? What kind of man takes a woman on a long ride in the middle of the night and doesn't say a word? Papa would have carried on a conversation, wooed the woman he loved . . . but he wasn't Papa. Had he caught the same strange affliction that plagued Liza? He wasn't good at expressing himself—with Faith, he was completely inadequate.

He sat staring at the floor. He hadn't treated Faith respectfully. He had been too proud, too quick to judge. Papa would never have treated Mama like he'd treated Faith. He'd acted like a blind fool, let envy, jealousy, and pride rule him. He should go to her, get down on his knees, and confess his love, and ask her and God to forgive him for the way he'd acted.

His mind churned. Why? Why couldn't he do that? *Please, Father, take away this horrible pride. Don't let me lose Faith.*

He'd fallen in love with Faith. And he prayed to God that she loved him back. That's what he'd wanted to tell her tonight. For the first time in his adult life, he was in love.

Heaving a deep sigh, he ran his hands through his hair and accepted the truth. He was deeply in love with Faith, and he prayed that God would allow him to correct his mistakes, that it wasn't too late to win her love, to give her the honor and respect she so justly deserved.

Springing off the bed, he threw open the door and

yelled. "Mama! Get up! I'm going to ask Faith Kallahan to marry me!"

Slamming the door shut, he sat back down on the bed, drawing a shaky breath.

After a while, a smile started at the corners of his mouth and quickly spread to an ear-to-ear grin.

He amended his declaration silently. He was going to *get down on his knees* and ask Faith Kallahan to marry him.

Chapter Fourteen

WHAT had Nicholas tried to tell her? What words did he find so impossible to say?

Faith packed her bags dispiritedly. The Irish linen was the last item folded and tucked away in her satchel. The dress was ruined, and the thought of Aunt Thalia seeing what had happened to the once beautiful garment broke her heart. Tears misted her eyes. She wished she had listened to wise-and-wonderful Aunt Thalia. Perhaps she would have been spared the agony of the past two months.

Faith changed into the green paisley print and laced up the pointy shoes. Studying her image in the mirror, she shook her head. She would help at Dan's one last morning before Jeremiah took her to catch the stage.

But could she face Dan looking this way? Her face was

blotched and swollen from crying and lack of sleep. Dipping a washcloth in the basin, she pressed the moist cloth against her eyes. By the time she had hugged all the Finneys and said her long good-bye to Mary Ellen, and Albert had delivered her to Dan's house, the red was almost gone.

Faith sat at Dan's kitchen table, fortifying herself with strong coffee.

One by one the children entered the kitchen. First Adam, who begged her to stay in Deliverance. It was difficult to explain the delicate situation to a boy so young and innocent of the world's heartaches.

Then Sissy climbed onto her lap, eyes filled with tears, and pleaded with her not to go. Faith tried to comfort the children, but it was impossible when her own heart cried out to stay. Lilly made her presence known from her crib. Faith went to get her, sitting back down at the kitchen table to cradle the infant to her breast. She looked at Adam and Sissy. "I'll write often. I promise."

"But I can't read," Adam said, shuffling his feet against the oak floor.

"Me can't wead needer," Sissy sobbed.

"Well, your papa can read." Faith struggled to keep a brave front. "He'll read my letters to you."

"It won't be the same as you being here," Adam said.

"No, not the same, but we can make a game of it. I'll write each letter like a story."

"Don't want no story. Can't play no games with yew. Yew be in Wishigan." Sissy sobbed harder.

Faith gathered the child in her arms. "Sissy, Michigan isn't so far away, not when you're right here in my heart. Each of you will always be in my thoughts and in my prayers."

"No, me *won't!*" Sissy wiped her nose on the sleeve of her gown. "Papa says me can't go out of the yarrd."

Faith laughed. "And you must always listen to your papa, young lady. He wants to keep you safe."

Adam's lower lip trembled as he fought back tears. "I love you, Faith."

"Me loves you too!" Sissy cried.

"And I love both of you, so very, very much. More than you could ever know," Faith whispered. Baby Lilly made cooing sounds as Faith held the infant close to her heart.

She was going to desperately miss Dan and the children. She prayed someday, somehow, Adam would have an opportunity to attend a school for the blind. Adam was capable of so much. She wished she could have opened the world to his eyes.

Around noon Jeremiah arrived in a buckboard. Dan and she agreed there would be no good-byes at the depot. No sense in making it any harder than it already was. But Dan seemed at ease about the arrangements.

She sat solemnly next to Jeremiah as he drove the wagon into town. Faith bit her lower lip, resigned that marriage to Nicholas Shepherd, and the school for the blind, were not God's will after all. She'd prayed until her lips were blue, knelt until her knees felt callused, and the answer was either no, not now, or wait. She wasn't sure which, but she felt certain it wasn't the "wait." Once she returned to Michigan, she would never be back to Deliverance.

The vast countryside blurred as tears gathered in her eyes. Everywhere she looked, there was something to remind her of Nicholas. She passed the field where they'd helped the mother cow birth her calf; charred grass, reminders of the fire; Reverend and Mrs. Hicks's house. She thought of the cattle drive; four failed attempts at marriage. She saw the pond embankment behind the church where she'd kissed Nicholas during the Founder's Day celebration. Each crossroads reminded her of the previous night's strange ride. She wasn't sure which of the many forks they had taken, but she felt certain they'd encountered every last one of them.

The stagecoach was just pulling into town when Jeremiah and Faith arrived. Already there was a good number of people gathered at the station.

Faith still harbored the tiniest shred of hope that Nicholas would be there, like a knight in shining armor, ready to profess his unrequited love at the last possible moment. Her eyes scanned the crowd, and her heart sank when she saw his wasn't among the familiar faces.

"Faith, I wish you would give this more time," Jeremiah said. "Are you sure you won't change your mind?"

"Oh, Jeremiah. We both know there's nothing in Deliverance for me. I've prayed about the situation, and it's clear to me that if Nicholas doesn't want me, I need to go home. Other than Dan and the children, there's no purpose for me here." When Jeremiah opened his mouth to respond, she stopped him with a quiet reminder: "I know Dan would marry me today, but I don't love Dan."

"You didn't love Nicholas, but you came all the way here to marry him," Jeremiah gently rebuked.

"But I love him now," she whispered. "That's the difference." Fresh tears swam to her eyes.

Jeremiah handed her a handkerchief. "Now, now. God has a way of working things out in spite of his children's hindrance."

Faith nodded, wiping her eyes. But she didn't think he was going to work this one out to her satisfaction.

"Are you going to be all right?"

"Yes. Thank you. You've done so much for me. I'm sorry about the school for the blind."

"Well, you tried, child." Jeremiah patted her hand.

Tears rolled in rivulets down her cheeks.

"Good land," he said as he tried to stem the flood

with the hanky. "Are we going to have to build an ark? If you love the man that much, why don't you tell him?"

"Why don't you . . ." she hiccuped, "tell Liza you love her?"

Jeremiah paled. "I value my life."

"See." Faith took the handkerchief and cleared her eyes. "I can't tell Nicholas I love him. He has to tell me."

"Is this a new rule I'm not aware of? The man must tell the woman?"

Faith nodded.

"Huh." Jeremiah scratched his head. "I'd like to know who makes these rules."

Jeremiah handed her bag to the stagecoach driver, then came back to the buckboard for Faith.

"Are you sure?" His gentle eyes pleaded for her to stay.

Faith knew he hoped she would have a last-minute change of heart. She wished she could. But if she stayed, knowing the way she felt about Nicholas and the way he didn't feel about her, she would only be hurting herself.

Helping her from the buckboard, Jeremiah walked her to the stage. She smiled at the gathered townsfolk: Vera, Lahoma, Oren Stokes, Molly, Etta, Reverend Hicks, Rollie Zimmer. She frowned. What was Rollie doing here?

Rollie gave her a toothless grin, waving at her.

Faith waved back, then awaited her turn to board as passengers started to descend from the stagecoach.

A heavyset mother rocked the stage as she stepped down with two rowdy children, calling out to her husband. Obediently a tiny, thin man scurried through the crowd to take her bags.

The second traveler to get out was a flamboyant-looking man with shifty dark eyes and a long, black handlebar mustache. For a long time he stood by the stagecoach door, scanning the crowd. He wouldn't be staying in Deliverance long, Faith predicted. Even to her naive eyes, *carpetbagger* was written all over him.

She looked closer when the last passenger departed. A petite young woman stepped gracefully out the door, her tiny foot daintily pausing on the step. Faith contrasted this comely vision with her own unorthodox descent upon Deliverance. She had been hot, disheveled, and riding with Jeremiah on the back of his mule.

The young woman wasn't the least bit in disarray, although she must have been traveling for days. Her bustled emerald dress made a striking contrast against her long, copper-colored hair and almond-shaped eyes. Jade, Faith noted. Her eyes were the color of jade. The latest Paris hat fashion shaded her delicate complexion from the harsh Texas sun. Even the bonnet feathers were dyed to match her gown, as were her suede shoes, pointed, Faith noticed. She seemed to have no problem walking in them.

The beautiful stranger had "city girl" written all over her. What did she expect to find in Deliverance? Jeremiah helped Faith into the stagecoach and closed the door. "I'm not very good at good-byes," he told her through the open window.

"Neither am I." Faith's eyes welled. "Thank you for everything."

Jeremiah nodded. "You write when you can."

"I promise."

"I need to move the buckboard. There's getting to be a crowd." Jeremiah reached out and lightly brushed a knuckle over her cheek. "Nicholas doesn't know what he's losing." He nodded. "You take care of yourself."

Faith sniffled. "You too."

Jeremiah turned and walked away but not before Faith caught a glimpse of the moisture suddenly misting the old man's eyes.

She waited for the driver to climb aboard his seat. As

she waited, she stared out the window. The fashionable young woman was anxiously searching the crowd, apparently looking for someone.

Faith sat up straighter when she heard a ruckus break out in the crowd. Peering to the far left, she saw Dan hurriedly threading his way through the onlookers, his gaze anxiously searching the area. Was he looking for her? They had already said their good-byes. . . .

Dan stepped into the clearing and even from her vantage point, Faith saw his eyes lock on the beauty. The woman broke into a radiant smile, and she ran to meet him.

As the implication of Dan's appearance hit Faith, her hand came to her mouth. Heavenly days! Dan had ordered a mail-order bride!

His inquiries had been so subtle, so minute, that she never once suspected what he'd had in mind. But there was no mistaking the look on the young couple's faces as they met for the first time. In a moment the children were climbing all over the woman. She didn't seem to mind, patiently smiling at them and Dan.

Dan Walters looked like a besotted suitor.

Scooting back in the seat, Faith fumed. *Liza's happy. Nicholas is relieved to see me go. Dan replaced me before I'd even left town.* If she thought her heart was broken before, she felt as if it might explode now.

As the driver and guard climbed atop the stagecoach, Faith blinked back tears.

An old woman entered the coach and took the seat opposite Faith. "There, there, dear. Don't cry," she comforted, bending forward to pat Faith's hand. "Why, you'll be back before you know it!"

Faith burst into tears.

"Oh, gracious me." The white-haired woman looked startled. "I hope I haven't said anything to upset you."

Shaking her head, Faith sobbed uncontrollably. "It's just—that—I'll *never* be coming back."

"Dear child, one mustn't ever say never." She smiled angelically, a sparkle in her warm brown eyes. "We never know what the Lord has in store for us. Why, our next miracle could be waiting just around the bend. Yes, just around the bend."

"The only thing waiting around the bend for me is Michigan," Faith sniffled. "And Edsellllll Martinnnnnnn!" She leaned over, sobbing harder as the stage lurched and wheels started to roll.

Suddenly a buckboard wheeled wildly down the road. A familiar voice shouted, "Stop that stage!" Faith jerked upright in her seat. What was that?

Jeremiah looked up, then whirled and shouted. "Driver! Hold that stage!"

The driver tightened back on the reins, bringing the four-horse team to a halt. "Somebody better have a mighty good reason! We got a schedule to keep!"

Jeremiah grinned, looking in Faith's direction. She could barely hear his words. "Well, thank you, Lord. I was beginning to wonder if you were listening."

Nicholas sprang from the buckboard, followed by Liza. Running toward the stage, his legs covered the ground with long, powerful strides.

The stagecoach jerked forward as the horses threatened to bolt. "Driver, wait!" Nicholas shouted.

"I ain't goin' nowhere. You're spookin' the team!"

Bounding aboard the stage, Nicholas jerked open the door. Faith was face-to-face with him. For a moment nobody spoke.

"Faith, you can't leave."

"Why not?" she sniffled.

"Because . . . I'm in love with you. I . . . I want us to start over."

She opened her mouth to speak, but he laid his hand

across her mouth. "I'm a thickheaded, opinionated man. Sometimes I say too much; other times I don't say enough, and rarely do I get out what I actually mean. My pride has cost me something very rare and precious. I surrendered that pride to God this morning, Faith, asking him to free me of that burden. I love you, Faith. I thought I could marry you and Mama would have someone to keep her company, but instead I fell in love with you. I hope—no, I have prayed, all night, that you will someday feel the same about me."

Their eyes met and held for what seemed like an eternity.

"I take heart that you're leaving town," he admitted.

"Pardon me?"

"You're leaving town; that means you really can't be in love with Dan."

"No . . . I don't love Dan," she conceded, glancing at the Walters family happily gathered around the stylish young woman. "I've told you that before, Nicholas. Dan is not the issue."

"Then could you ever love *me?*" Nicholas inquired softly.

Pride, the same that had affected Nicholas, made her want to say no, but her eyes—and her heart—gave her away. Lowering her eyes, she whispered, "Yes, I just don't like you very much sometimes."

Nicholas's features turned as solemn as a hanging judge's. "I can safely promise that I will spend the rest of my life working on that."

The old woman leaned forward and whispered under her breath, "See, dear? Always a miracle waitin' just around the bend."

Faith's eyes steeled as she recalled the torturous weeks Nicholas had put her through. "How do I know you're not doing this out of obligation?" Nicholas was foremost an honorable man.

"You don't. You just have to trust me on this one." He looked so needy, so repentant. How could she do anything but trust him?

"Will you marry me?"

She nodded. "Yes."

"Right now?"

"Now?"

"The sooner the better! I love you! And I've already checked. Reverend Hicks is in town today, and he is standing by for a wedding tomorrow." He threw his head back and laughed. His mood was infectious. Faith found herself laughing with him. In the years to come, she planned to make him laugh more often. A lot more often.

His laughter gradually receded, and he reached for her hand. Love shown brightly in his eyes. "Tomorrow, we will be married, regardless of birthing cows, raging fires, needy mothers, cattle drives—this time in a church ceremony, dressed in our finest, with the whole town looking on."

Faith's eyes glowed with wonder. *Ceremony.* Now that was so much nicer than "recital of vows."

She rested her fingers lightly against his cheek and silently thanked the Lord for this hour. Her faith had seen her through. She had prayed for faith that she and Nicholas would be married, and sure enough, God was listening. It finally made sense now why she'd always felt that God meant her to marry Nicholas. She'd prayed for the faith to believe that, but as circumstances had changed, she'd lost that faith and had begun to believe she had been mistaken all along. But now, at the last hour, God was giving her her heart's desire after all.

"Yes, my darling. . . . Tomorrow I will marry you." It wouldn't be in her finest, and they'd have a lot of inviting to do if the whole town was to be there—but, yes! she most certainly would marry him.

"All in God's plan," the old woman sitting across from her observed.

Faith took a closer look at the old woman. Her silvery white hair framed her angelic face like a halo. Faith remembered passages from the Bible about how the Lord sometimes sends special messengers.

Faith asked softly, "Are you an angel?"

"An angel? Me? Mercy no, child. I sell eggs. I have a chicken ranch just outside San Antonio." She leaned forward, a merry twinkle in her eye. "I'm Bessie Lewis, Carl Lewis's sister. Been visiting my brother, and we sure have been praying hard for you young people." She winked. "Where one or more are gathered to pray?"

"Oh, thank you—but please, you *can't* leave now."

"She's right. You have a wedding to attend," Nicholas said.

The old woman beamed. "Why, I reckon I can stay around a spell longer. It would do my heart proud to see you young'uns finally tie the knot."

Nicholas helped Bessie out of the coach. Carl Lewis and his wife were there with welcoming smiles. They expressed brief congratulations, then escorted Bessie back to their wagon.

Nicholas gently lifted Faith from the stage, momentarily holding her in midair as he kissed her.

"Why, Mr. Shepherd!" Faith accused breathlessly as their lips parted.

"Nick, to you, Miss Kallahan." He kissed her again.

"Oh, yes—Nick," she murmured against his mouth. "That sounds so much better." Faith's senses were reeling. So this was what love felt like. *Thank you, wonderful, merciful God!*

The roar of applause from the crowd quickly brought her back to earth. Her face flushed bright red. She'd been so in love with Nicholas, so swept away, knowing he loved her right back, that she'd forgotten they were standing in the middle of town. And kissing, of all things.

Nicholas turned to the waiting crowd. "My friends! I'm getting married! And you're all invited!"

"It's about time!" Dan shouted, hand in hand with his mail-order bride.

Dan's pleasant features sobered as he pulled Faith aside. For a long moment he just looked at her. "Nicholas has held your heart from the beginning. I knew that—everyone can see it." His unspoken words were clear to Faith. "I needed to move on, to find a woman I could love— one who could love me back."

Faith smiled. "I understand, Dan. I hope you will be wonderfully happy!" She hugged him tightly. Then she turned back to Nicholas and hooked her arm in his.

Everyone, young and old, shouted in ear-piercing unison, *"It's about time!"*

Faith gazed up at Nicholas. "Did you hear that, Mr. Shepherd?"

"I heard." His eyes openly adored her. "But they're mistaken."

"Mistaken?" She frowned.

"It's *past* time." He kissed her again, long and hard. It really mattered not that she would be married in her second-best dress.

The embrace ended, and Faith slipped her arm through his. She felt as if she were walking on clouds as they strolled to the buckboard. So love must be the secret to walking in pointy shoes, she mused, realizing her feet didn't hurt at all.

Liza sat in the wagon, smiling. As Nicholas helped Faith aboard, Liza quickly scooted to one end of the bench. She had been strangely quiet during all the activity, but Faith realized the sparkle in her eyes looked downright cagey.

Liza patted the bench beside her. "Hello, dear. I believe your place is here, beside Nicholas."

Faith smiled, waiting for the other shoe to drop. "Thank you, Liza."

"No." Liza's features softened. "Thank you, Faith. You've made my son very happy."

Everything was happening so quickly that Faith wasn't sure if she was dreaming. But if by chance she was, she hoped she'd never wake up.

"And, Nicholas, I want to thank you for bringing Faith into the Shepherd family. You've made me very happy. Your father would have been proud of your choice of a bride."

"Thank you, Mama. For the first time in years, I agree with you." Nicholas glanced at Liza, smiling. "And whatever's in that brown bottle you've been sipping out of, I think it's helping." He clicked to the horse, and it trotted off.

Faith gasped. "You knew all along about her drinking?" she tried to whisper to Nicholas.

A hearty laugh from Liza caused another gasp. Was the woman mad?

"Oh, my dear, dear girl. That was medicine in the bottle. Doc told me it would help my . . . my—" she turned bright red, then took a deep breath—"Doc explained that my actions were not only a result of my grief when I became a widow. My age had a lot to do with my emotions. It really is part of God's plan."

"But why did you hide it?"

"That was before I saw Doc. I wasn't taking enough of Pinkham's Tonic to help me . . . and I didn't believe medicine would help. I know now I was foolish. And I caused a great deal of grief by being so bullheaded. The Lord and I have had a good long talk, and I've turned all my hurts, all my sorrows over to him. Should have done that all along."

Faith's arms tightened through Nicholas's as the wagon rolled along. He refused to let her go now that they had found each other.

Liza reached over and patted Faith's hand. "I know I've said it before, but it bears repeating. From the moment you arrived in Deliverance, I have made life difficult for you. I've whined, complained, and been a downright—"

"Mama!" Nicholas cautioned.

"Pain," she finished. "I didn't consciously set out to be so difficult, and I'm not sure I've fully explained why I've acted this way. We'll save that for tea and cookies. I only know I'm sorry for all I've put you through. I pray you can find it in your heart to forgive me."

Liza's words touched Faith's heart even more deeply than those spoken in confidence at the Founder's Day picnic. Her heart swelled with love. She knew that from this day forward they would share a solid relationship, based on respect. After all, they loved the same man.

Who said mother and daughter-in-law couldn't be friends?

"Mother Shepherd, you are forgiven, and all is forgotten." Faith gently squeezed Liza's hand. "As long as you remember your place." She flashed an impish grin. "And that's right here, beside Nicholas and me."

Liza shook her head with wonderment. "Thank you, Faith. I'll try to be a good mother-in-law. When my grandbabies come along—"

Nicholas glanced over. "Whoa! Is there a conspiracy going on I should know about? Did you say grandbabies?"

Liza's eyes lit up. Faith could see that Mother Shepherd liked the thought of grandchildren as opposed to grandchild. "Yes. Grandchildren!"

Faith chimed in. "At least one boy and one girl. Or maybe two of each. And kittens, lots and lots of kittens!"

They all laughed. This time as Faith rattled on about cats and babies she could tell the Shepherds loved the sound of the warmth and laughter. Faith's eyes fell on a familiar wagon ahead.

Jeremiah, who was watching from his buckboard, waved as the Shepherds' wagon approached. His gaze focused on Liza, and Faith could have sworn she saw Mother Shepherd blush.

Liza quickly averted her head and pinched both of her cheeks, hard. "Ouch." She muttered under her breath, "Now I remember why I stopped doing that."

Faith grinned. "Mother Shepherd!"

Liza winked. "At my age, a woman needs all the help she can get."

Faith noticed that the usually taut braids strapped tightly across Liza's head were now styled into a loose French braid. A few wisps of hair softly framed her face.

"Mother Shepherd, you look absolutely—stunning!"

A natural blush colored Liza's face. "Thank you, dear. A certain wise young woman once told me, 'You're only as old as you feel!' " Liza grinned. "And right now, I feel about as young as a body can—for my age."

She turned and waved at Jeremiah as the wagon flew past.

His hand shot up, returning the greeting.

Faith suddenly stood up in the wagon floor, shouting over her shoulder. "Hey, Jeremiah! I'm not leaving after all! Sorry to have troubled you! *I'm getting married!*" She made pointy jabs with the tip of her finger at Nicholas. "To Mr. Shepherd!" she silently mouthed, almost losing her footing as the buckboard whipped around a sharp bend in the road.

Chapter Fifteen

A SPLENDID sunrise ushered in Faith Kallahan's wedding day. The air smelled sweetly fragrant from rain that had fallen intermittently during the night.

Early morning sunlight filtered through the open window, spreading rays of warmth across the quilt Faith snuggled beneath. She lazily stirred, thinking how symbolic the rising sun was to her heart. Warm and wonderful. Not a single doubt to be found. She had never thought Nicholas Shepherd could produce such a fuzzy feeling inside her, but he did—oh, how he did! Smiling, she stretched, wiggling her toes. *Father, your goodness takes my breath away!*

To know Nicholas loved her in return made her heady with delight. Liza, willing and eager to accept her as her daughter—it was more happiness than one woman could expect in a lifetime.

Faith took ample time to count her blessings and the way God had intervened at the last possible moment. She was reminded that often that was his way. She smiled, knowing his way was divine and perfect. "Just around the bend," Bessie Lewis had predicted.

A gentle knock at the door broke into her musings. "Faith?"

Nicholas. She'd warned him the night before that the groom was not to see the bride on their wedding day until she walked down the aisle. That tradition was strictly adhered to on Papa's Irish side of the family. As for her French heritage, those customs had never been explained to her.

"Are you awake?" Nicholas called.

Clutching the quilt to her neck she called back, "Yes, Nicholas. I'm awake. Is something wrong?" She would *not* permit anything to interfere with the day's festivities, no matter how dour. By nightfall she was going to be Mrs. Nicholas Shepherd.

"No, I just wanted you to know I'm leaving now."

Faith bolted upright in bed. "Leaving?"

"I'm going to the church."

She glanced at the sunrise. It couldn't be much past six. "Isn't it a little early? The wedding isn't until two o'clock."

"Are you getting cold feet?"

Tension drained, and she grinned sheepishly. "No, Mr. Shepherd, *I* don't have cold feet."

"Neither do I." His voice dropped to a low timbre. "Make sure you're there on time. I'd hate to put on my Sunday best to be jilted at the altar," he teased.

Her breath caught and shivers raced down her arms. "I promise you won't be jilted. Why are you leaving so early?"

"There are a few things that need my attention. And you're the one who insisted I am forbidden to lay eyes on you until the ceremony."

"You can't." She grinned. "And don't you be forgetting it."

His tone sobered. "I love you—be at the church on time."

"I love you, too." Faith toyed with a strand of her long dark hair. "But it's going to cost you."

"Cost me? I've already spent a fortune on this wedding!"

Faith playfully tossed a pointy shoe at the door, hitting the target with a dull thud. "That was merely a down payment."

"Name your price, darling." His voice was soft and sincere. "Whatever the price, I'll pay."

"The rest of your life," she murmured. "For richer, for poorer. In sickness, in health. Until—"

"Death do us part."

"That long and more," she returned softly. "I'll meet you at the church, Nick." Her eyes welled as she slid back on the pillow, listening to the sounds of his footsteps receding down the hallway.

Throwing the covers back, she jumped out of bed, eager for the day to begin. No more talk of recitals of vows and parlor weddings. On this very day, Nicholas Shepherd and Faith Kallahan would be joined together in the sight of God. As she pulled her bag from beneath the bed, she heard the sound of Nicholas's horse leave the yard. For a fleeting moment she was tempted to rush to the window to sneak a last peek at this wonderful, handsome man who would soon be her husband. How she wished Hope and June and Aunt Thalia could be here to share her happiness, to meet Nicholas and Liza.

Faith hefted the satchel onto the bed and opened it.

Reality hit hard when she unwrapped the soiled Irish linen.

She forced a smile. As painful as the loss of that gown was, she wasn't about to let anything spoil the joy of this blessed day. Besides, it wasn't the dress that formed a happy union. God bound the soul.

Sorting through her limited wardrobe, she selected the blue-and-white gingham. She'd worn it the day she'd kissed Nicholas at the pond. Spreading the dress on the bed, she smiled, thinking, "married in blue you'll always be true." And that's exactly how she felt. She would always be true to Nicholas, in every way.

A second knock sounded at the door. "Faith, may I come in?"

"Of course, Mother Shepherd."

Liza entered the room and joined Faith at the bedside. "I always thought you looked so pretty in that dress, dear."

Faith was surprised by her candor. Liza'd never commented on Faith's appearance other than to scowl when she wore overalls.

"I should have told you before." Liza lightly traced a hand over the pretty material. "But as nice as you look in this one, you were stunning in the white linen. Did your aunt make it for you?"

"No, she had it specially made by a seamstress in Cold Water, Rose Nelson."

"Such a waste. . . . I wish there were some way of repairing the damage, but I'm afraid it's impossible." Liza picked up the dress, studying it. "I imagine you had your heart set on wearing it on your wedding day."

Faith sighed. "Rose worked very hard to finish it before I left."

"I can see she did. Rose is an excellent seamstress."

A companionable silence filled the room.

Finally Liza spoke. "Faith, my dear. You will be a most beautiful bride no matter what you wear."

Faith smiled. "Thank you, Mother Shepherd."

"Even should you decide to wear those disgraceful overalls!" Liza's eyes twinkled playfully.

Faith joined in the good-natured teasing. "I don't think Nicholas would be too happy about me showing up at the church wearing overalls."

"Nicholas would be proud to marry you, regardless."

"Well, I'll play it safe and go with the gingham," Faith promised. "I'd hate to be left standing at the altar!"

As their merriment faded, Faith looked at Liza. She hated to ask, but she had to know. "Mother Shepherd, do you think Rachel will be there?"

Liza looked puzzled. "At your wedding?"

Faith nodded, her face flaming.

"Oh, no dear." Liza took Faith's hand. "Haven't you heard?"

She shook her head. "Heard what?"

"Yesterday, after we left, Rachel boarded the stage."

"Why?" Faith was confused. "Has she gone to visit kin?"

"Oh, Faith. There's no easy way to say this. Rachel's husband was killed in a bar fight in San Antonio. Rachel has gone to bury Joe. Afterward she plans to return to the East to live with friends."

"I'm sorry . . . I didn't know." Faith felt very sad for Rachel. How tragic her marriage had been.

"I'm sorry no one told you. In all the confusion . . ."

Faith suddenly felt sick to her stomach. "What about Nicholas?"

Liza busied herself straightening the bed. "What about Nicholas?"

"Well, Joe being dead does change things."

Frowning, Liza plumped a pillow. "I can't see how."

"Joe is dead. Rachel is no longer married."

Faith waited for Liza to make the connection.

"Oh . . . oh, my goodness, Faith. Nicholas was over Rachel years ago." Liza took her by the shoulders and gently shook her. "Look at the poor man; he's a besotted fool! I heard him singing this morning as he shaved. *Singing,* Faith. He hasn't sung since Abe died. He's in love with you, darling. He doesn't know other women exist."

Faith hugged her. "Thank you."

Liza's features sobered. "Faith, I came to see you for a reason. I'm not sure how to approach the subject, but I know I've beaten around the bush long enough."

Faith studied her, but there wasn't a clue in the woman's eyes as to what she was thinking. "Have I done something—"

"Heavens, no!" Liza patted her hand. "It's just that I . . . Well, I can show you much better than I can tell you. If you will come with me?"

"Of course. Just give me a minute to change."

"Oh, you needn't bother. We'll only be a minute."

"But, I'm still in my nightclothes, and someone—"

Liza smiled. "It's just us girls. And besides, you might want to change again." Taking Faith's hand, she pulled her toward the door.

"Shouldn't I at least put on shoes?"

"I don't think so, dear. You might be wanting—oh, never mind. You'll see. Besides, you look like a child on Christmas morning in your nightgown, barefoot and sleepy eyed." Her eyes softened. "Just like the daughter I always longed for."

Faith trailed Liza as she led her to the end of the hallway. Removing a brass key from her apron, she slipped it into the lock and jiggled the door open. Streaks of sunlight lit the narrow staircase.

"Don't fall," Liza cautioned as they climbed the creaking steps to the attic.

Ornate sunburst windows were cut into each gabled

end of the house, bathing the rustic room with more light than Faith had ever seen in the Shepherd house. She thought it odd that such beauty was hidden away in a dusty attic. It was even stranger that she'd never noticed the lovely windows from outside.

Faith's eyes roved the huge attic. She glimpsed their reflections in an intricately carved cheval mirror abandoned in an alcove. The room was filled with crates, portraits, and discarded-but-beautiful pieces of furniture. Treasures tucked away for no telling how long.

Liza located a large steamer trunk and turned, motioning for Faith to join her.

"Now, before you say yes or no, just let me say, the choice is entirely yours. But, my dear, you would honor me greatly if you would accept my gift."

Liza opened the trunk, removing an exquisite ivory satin wedding gown, lavishly trimmed in the finest Belgian lace. As she held the dress for Faith to see, her eyes grew misted, and her voice fell to a whisper. "This is the gown I married Abe in."

"Oh, Mother Shepherd!" Faith cried, "I've never seen anything so beautiful!"

"Yes, it's quite lovely." Liza sighed, a faraway look in her eyes. Faith sensed Liza's thoughts were drifting back to her own wedding day.

"This is the gift?"

Liza nodded, handing the gown to Faith.

"May I wear it today?" Faith couldn't contain the excitement in her voice.

Liza's eyes lit with expectation. "You would do this?"

"Oh, it would be my honor!"

"Wonderful!" Liza clasped her hands together, then she reached back into the trunk.

Faith held the gown up to her and looked in the mirror. It was breathtaking.

"Faith," Liza called, carefully removing items and setting them aside. "Come see if you like this."

Faith hurried to see what other treasures Liza had pulled from the steamer trunk. Gently placing the gown on a rocking chair, she knelt beside Mother Shepherd.

"This is my veil," Liza said, unfolding the many yards of lacy material. "It's made from the same Belgian lace as the gown."

"Oh my!" Faith sighed.

"Let's see how it looks." Liza secured the lacy veil on Faith's head with two combs decorated by tiny gold leaves and pearls.

"My goodness!" Faith smiled beneath the floor-length veil. "I feel like a princess!"

"And you're every bit as beautiful as one," Liza said.

Faith gathered the folds of her nightgown and waltzed before the mirror. The sight of the bride-to-be, dancing barefoot in a dusty attic, hours away from her wedding, stirred laughter from both women.

"Do you like these?" Liza asked, holding up ivory-colored pointy shoes that laced up the side, with mother-of-pearl buttons on the front.

"Do I like them!" Faith exclaimed. "Those have got to be the most beautiful pointy shoes I've seen in my life! And you know how I feel about pointy shoes."

Liza laughed. "Yes, I've noticed! But they don't hurt half as much—"

"When you're in love!" Faith smiled.

"I remember well." Liza agreed. "There's also a pair of white silk stockings in here somewhere. Do you see them, dear? I wrapped them in paper. I know they're here. . . . Ah, here they are."

Faith hugged Liza close. "Liza, I don't know how to thank you for everything you've—"

"Child, you are marrying my son." Liza dabbed at Faith's tears. "And you are soon to be my daughter. I'm

the thankful one. I only want to see Nicholas happy.
Now, we best get busy!" Liza smiled. "We don't want to
be late for the church!"

Faith, bathed and dressed in her new wedding attire,
stood in her bedroom before the mirror, unable to believe the radiant image reflected back at her. Liza's gown
was truly the most beautiful creation she'd ever seen.

"May I come in?" Liza asked, tapping at the door.

"Yes."

"Oh, my dear!" Liza said breathlessly. "You're every
bit as beautiful as I knew you would be!"

"Thank you, Mother Shepherd!" Faith whirled. "And
thank you, again, for the wedding dress. I can't believe
I'm wearing something so elegant."

"It fits as if it were made for you!" Liza's eyes glowed
with excitement. "Now, let me help you with the veil."

"Oh, I almost forgot!"

"It's those wedding-day jitters! They'll sneak up on
you every time." Liza laughed, slipping the combs into
Faith's long, dark hair. "There. What do you think?"

Faith looked in the mirror, tracing a nervous hand
down the length of the lace sleeve, scalloped at the wrist.
Suddenly she turned to Liza. "I think you look beautiful,
Mother Shepherd."

And she did, dressed in a fashionable powder blue
dress, accentuated with a blue-and-white cameo pin. Her
hair was loosely secured with matching combs.

Liza blushed. "Oh, as good as an old woman can
look."

"Liza, have you been pinching your cheeks?" Faith
teased.

"No, but I suppose we should."

Liza and Faith turned to face the mirror in unison and
gave themselves a quick pinch.

"Ouch!" They laughed simultaneously.

The sound of a wagon pulling to a stop outside Faith's window broke the moment.

"There's yet another surprise awaiting you!" Liza took Faith by the hand.

Faith followed Mother Shepherd to the front porch. The driver stepped down from the buggy, tipping his Stetson at the ladies.

"Oh, my goodness!" Faith cried.

"Do you like it?"

"Like it?" She stammered like a schoolgirl, looking at the elegant buggy with its fixed roof and curtains. "I love it!"

"I thought you might, so I had Nicholas send for Rusty to fetch it from the barn. It's been stored there since Abe—"

"Liza, it's lovely. But are you sure? We could always take the buckboard."

"No buckboard for my daughter-in-law!" Liza's eyes glowed. "It's too special a day not to bring out the Jenny Lind. Abe wouldn't have it any other way. And neither would I."

Hand in hand the women walked to their waiting buggy. Rusty opened the door. Liza introduced Faith to Rusty as he helped them onto the fine leather-upholstered seats.

Drawing back the curtains, Liza leaned her head out the window. "Thank you, Rusty."

"My pleasure, ma'am."

"Are the rest of the boys coming?"

"Wouldn't miss it for the world!"

As the buggy pulled up in front of the church, Liza reached for Faith's hand and held it tightly. "I know how fond you are of Jeremiah. I've taken the liberty of asking him to walk you down the aisle today."

Faith had been silently wishing her father were here to give her away. Mother Shepherd's last gift was truly the nicest of all.

Tears glistened as she tried to speak.

Liza nodded knowingly. "The next time we meet, we will officially be family. But in my heart, we already are."

Moments later Jeremiah came for Faith. His kindly face glowed with pride. "Hello, my dearest. Are you ready?"

"Oh yes, Jeremiah."

Jeremiah helped Faith from the buggy. Sissy was standing beside him with a basketful of yellow rose petals.

"Hi, Faith! We're gettin' marrwid!"

"Yeah," Adam said. "And I get to *see* you get married!"

Faith hugged the two children. She looked over to see Dan and his mail-order bride smiling. Forming an O with thumb and forefinger, Dan winked.

Vera, Molly, and Etta were waiting for Faith on the church steps.

"You look beautiful, dear." Vera beamed.

"Yes, you do," Etta added, handing Faith a flowing bouquet of yellow roses and ivy. "These are from my garden, for you."

Faith was speechless at the generosity.

"Thank you," she murmured, overcome with emotion. God had truly given her a new home.

The church doors swung open, and heavenly music poured from the foyer. Sissy walked ahead of Faith, sprinkling rose petals. Jeremiah placed Faith's arm through his, and they started down the aisle. The church was packed. Some folks had to stand. But the only thing Faith saw was her handsome groom, waiting for her at the altar.

Twenty minutes later Mr. and Mrs. Nicholas Shepherd sealed their union with a kiss, lingering perhaps just a little too long as guests began to giggle. The next thing

Faith knew, they were headed out the door, rice being thrown from every direction.

Rusty had the Jenny Lind waiting. The bride and groom were escorted to their reception in grand style as children ran alongside the buggy.

Nicholas had made the arrangements for their reception to be held on the church grounds. The brush arbor was elegantly decorated; every kind of food imaginable filled the long tables, in addition to a four-tiered wedding cake and bowls of bright red sparkling punch.

"How did you do all this so quickly?" Faith exclaimed.

Nicholas winked. "You'd be surprised what money can buy."

As the townsfolk and Shepherd hired hands gathered around the reception table, Nicholas turned to thank them for coming.

When the crowd quieted, he spoke. "I want to thank each of you for coming to help me share the happiest day of my life." He gazed at Faith, and she blushed.

The guests applauded the newlyweds.

"Faith and I thank God for his presence in our lives and for the miracle of bringing us together." Grinning, he handed Faith a gaily wrapped box.

"For me?" she asked.

"For you. Open it."

Faith glowed as she slipped the ribbon off the package and opened the deep blue velvet box to find a key.

"Oh, by the way," Nicholas handed her an important-looking piece of paper. "This goes with it."

She looked up. "I don't understand. . . ."

"Read the piece of paper; it will explain."

Faith unfolded the document. It was a deed, and as she quickly scanned the legal writings, she realized it was to the Smith place. She squealed with joy, hugging her husband around the neck. "Does this mean what I think it means?"

Nicholas held her tightly. "If you're talking about a school for the blind, it does."

Faith was speechless for a moment. "Oh, Nick."

"But," Jeremiah stepped forward. "What good is a blind school without Braille slates?"

"Oh, yes." Faith's face fell.

"But then, I just happen to have a few crates on hand."

"Jeremiah! However on earth did you get Braille slates?"

"Young lady, I used to be a schoolteacher at an exclusive boarding school for boys. But I got real tired of seeing parents dump their kids off and go on to pursue their own pleasures. It hurt to see bright young boys neglected while their parents stockpiled earthly treasures and neglected their most important treasure—their children. I tried to make a difference, but nothing I did seemed to do any good. So I came here, asking for nothing more than to be left alone.

"You, however, have helped restore my faith in humanity. I think you'll do real well with Adam Walters, and with others God will bring your way.

"Now, about those Braille slates. . . . I suppose I could donate them if a certain woman in the crowd would agree to let me court her."

Liza's head shot up.

Jeremiah grinned, stepping over to take Liza's hand. "How about it, young lady? Want to squire around with me?"

A smile spread over Nicholas's face. "Professor Montgomery is a good catch, Mother. The two of you could spend the rest of your lives helping Faith teach the blind to read at the Faith Shepherd School for the Blind."

"Oh, Jeremiah." Liza blushed, squeezing his hand. "You old . . . sweet-talker, you."

Nicholas leaned over and stole another kiss from Faith.

Jeremiah frowned at Liza. "I take that as a yes?"

"It's an 'I'll give it some thought.' "

"Well, don't hem and haw too long. At our age—"

"At our age, Jeremiah, you're only as old as you feel!" Liza winked at her new daughter-in-law.

"I think 'The Liza Shepherd School for the Blind' sounds better." Faith smiled at Nicholas.

"No, Faith." Liza said. "The school should bear your name. After all, you are the one who envisioned it—"

"I insist, Mother Shepherd. It's my gift to you."

"I don't know what to say."

"That's a first." Jeremiah playfully yanked a lock of her hair.

"Say yes!" Little Adam shouted from the crowd.

Liza turned to look at the precocious boy. "Yes!"

"Does that go for my proposal, too?" Jeremiah teased.

"I'd be right proud to 'squire around' with you, Jeremiah Montgomery," Liza said.

Nicholas cleared his throat. "I think Mother has something she wants to say."

"Oh, yes. I almost forgot." Liza faced the guests. "With this day being such a joyous occasion, and one with many gifts, I feel the Lord should share in our offerings. I would like to announce that the Shepherds will pay the full amount to have a new steeple erected."

For a moment, a stunned hush fell over the crowd.

"Faith and Dan repaired the steeple," someone in the crowd reminded.

"Repaired, yes, but the steeple's not good enough for Deliverance." She looked at Reverend Hicks. "It's going to fall on somebody's head one of these days. A new steeple, the finest money can buy, will be in place for Thanksgiving services." Liza glanced at Faith. "If there's one thing I've learned, money can't buy happiness."

Suddenly everyone was cheering and applauding.

Cake was cut and punch served. Children played on the church grounds, and laughter filled the air.

It was late afternoon when the guests began departing. Night would be upon them soon. It was a long drive home for most, and many of the guests still had chores to do.

Best wishes and hugs were exchanged. Faith and Nicholas met Dan's mail-order bride. Her name was Ruth. Faith decided they were meant for each other. When she saw the way Dan looked at Ruth, she was reminded of one of Papa's favorite sayings: "If you want to make God laugh, tell him *your* plans."

Most important, Dan's children adored Ruth as much as she did them. Faith had a very good feeling about Dan and Ruth. And Liza and Jeremiah as well.

But most especially about Nicholas and Faith.

The moon was rising as the newlyweds were driven home. Soon a full "Shepherd's Moon" hung suspended in the sky. Faith glanced out the carriage window.

"Look at that moon. It has to be the brightest moon I've ever seen."

Nicholas's head touched hers as he bent to look out. "It's a beauty."

"Yes, tonight it seems extra special. The way it lights up the road reminds me of the light that the school for the blind will bring to so many children."

Drawing her back in his arms, Nicholas said softly, "God has brought us together to be more than just man and wife. This light you talk about, it's as though God has turned a light on in all of us, especially me. I thought I was walking close with the Lord, but I realize now that my light was dim until you came along." Nicholas gently kissed her.

Snuggling closer, she sighed. "Do they really call it Shepherd's Moon?"

"Most do," Nicholas said. "But I plan to change that."

"Why is that?"

"Well, before, I guess I never quite understood the full meaning behind it."

"You mean being known as the richest man around?"

"Exactly."

Faith remained silent.

"I think I would like to be known for something more important than money."

Faith grinned, wiggling closer to her husband. "And how would you most like to be remembered, my darling?"

Nicholas answered softly and without a moment's hesitation. "For a Shepherd's faith."

A Note from the Author

Dear Reader,
What a joy it is to see my first Inspirational book in print! It certainly isn't my first book. God has so richly blessed me over the years; I've published more than fifty novels, both historical and contemporary, in the general market. But in many ways, *Faith* is my proudest achievement—if you will, my personal best for my Savior. In the story of Faith and Nicholas, I have drawn from the humor God has given me, my conviction of his unfailing love, and my own sometimes-shaky, sometimes-steady faith walk. I hope you have enjoyed this lighthearted novel and will look forward to *June* and *Hope,* the other Kallahan sisters' stories in my Brides of the West series.

Zephaniah 3:17 says that God "will rejoice over you with great gladness," that "he will exult over you by singing a happy song." God rejoices over us, and he says that his joy is our strength (Nehemiah 8:10). God rejoices in our laughter. In a troubled world, what better way to celebrate his love?

Lori Copeland

LORI
COPELAND

Brides of the West 1872

HEART
QUEST™

Romance fiction from
Tyndale House Publishers, Inc.
WHEATON, ILLINOIS

Visit Tyndale's exciting Web site at www.tyndale.com

Copyright © 1999 by Lori Copeland. All rights reserved.

Cover illustration copyright © 1998 by Michael Dudash. All rights reserved.

Author photo taken by Sothern Studio © 1998. All rights reserved.

Scripture quotations are taken from the *Holy Bible,* King James Version.

HeartQuest is a trademark of Tyndale House Publishers, Inc.

Edited by Diane Eble

Designed by Melinda Schumacher

3 in 1 ISBN: 0-7394-0809-7

Printed in the United States of America

A Note from the Author

Dear Reader,

Thank you for the overwhelming response to book 1 in my Brides of the West series, *Faith*. I hope you will enjoy June Kallahan's story as she travels all the way to Seattle to marry her husband-to-be—whoever that turns out to be! Life can sometimes be unpredictable, but by keeping our eyes on Jesus Christ our Savior, we can rest in the assurance that he works all things together for our good and his glory.

Lori Copeland

Prologue

Cold Water, Michigan, late 1800s

Billows of white smoke rolled from the train's stack as a shrill whistle announced its imminent arrival. Turning to give Aunt Thalia a final hug, June Kallahan blinked back tears.

"I'll write you the moment I get settled, Aunt Thalia."

The old woman's arms tightened around June's neck, holding on longer than necessary. "I'm going to miss you, child."

"Don't worry about me," June said softly. "It's you I worry about."

"I'll be going to a better place someday very soon. No need for anyone to worry about me. But *of course* I'll worry about you. My age ought to afford me *some* rights. And I'll worry about your sisters. Faith gone off to Texas, Hope to Kentucky." Thalia Grayson shook her head. "Sakes alive. You've all taken leave of your senses."

June lovingly patted her old aunt's back. "God will take care of us, Auntie."

The engine came to a halt amid a *whoosh* of steam and squealing brakes. Passengers got off while others hurried to board. The stopover in Cold Water was brief. Smiling, June blew Aunt Thalia a final kiss as she reached for her bag. "Don't worry! I'll be fine!"

Running toward the coach, June determined to keep up her brave facade. Auntie would worry enough without sending her off in a flurry of tears. The conductor caught her hand and lifted her aboard as the train slowly pulled out of the station. Standing on the car's platform, June smiled and waved until Aunt Thalia's stooped frame faded into the distance.

Fighting her tears, June made her way into the coach, wondering if Faith and Hope had felt the same insecurities when they left, two weeks earlier.

A gentleman got up and offered his seat. Murmuring her thanks, June sat down, then buried her face in her handkerchief and bawled. Was she doing the right thing? Should she stay and take care of Auntie—let Faith and Hope be the mail-order brides? Aunt Thalia was old. Who would look after her?

The gentleman leaned forward. "Are you all right, miss?"

June wiped her tears, sitting up straighter. "Yes, thank you. I'm fine."

The enormity of what she was about to do overwhelmed her. She was off to Seattle—hundreds and hundreds of miles from Cold Water, about to marry a man she knew only by the few letters they'd exchanged.

She was about to marry Eli Messenger, and she didn't even know him.

The idea had made so much sense a few weeks ago. With their father, Thomas Kallahan, dead and Aunt Thalia unable to bear the financial responsibility of three additional mouths to feed, she and her sisters knew they must be keepers of their own fates. The decision to become mail-order brides had not been made easily, nor without a great deal of prayer.

June stared out the window, listening to the wheels clacking against the metal rails, wheels carrying her away from Cold Water to a brand-new life. She thought about her soon-to-be husband, Eli Messenger, and the unfamiliar world that awaited her in Seattle. Eli was a man of God, associate pastor to the famed Isaac Inman, of the Isaac Inman Evangelistic Crusade. Everyone had heard of

Isaac Inman—of his unflagging dedication to God, his charismatic personality, how he led hundreds of thousands of lost souls to find salvation. Goose bumps rose on her arms when she thought about meeting the world-renowned minister in person. Not only would she meet Isaac Inman, but she would work beside him! Papa would be so proud of her, were he still alive.

Removing Eli's letter from her purse, she scanned the last paragraph.

> *Together, we will work for God's kingdom. Our life will be good, June. I know you must experience moments of doubts about your venture, but I believe God has destined us to be together, to work together for his glory. I eagerly anticipate your arrival and the beginning of what surely promises to be our wonderful life together.*

She refolded the letter and tucked it safely back in her purse. Resting her head on the back of the seat, she willed herself to relax. Everything was as it should be.

Clickety-clack, clickety-clack.

Every turn of the wheel carried her farther and farther away from the only life she had ever known.

Biting down hard on her lower lip, she prayed that Eli Messenger was right and that God did, indeed, intend them for each other.

Otherwise, she was heading straight for the pits of—

She caught her wayward thoughts. She would surely, at best, be heading straight for trouble.

Chapter One

RAINING again?" June Kallahan stood on tiptoe to look out the ship porthole. "Doesn't it ever let up?"

Samantha Harris pressed closer, elbowing a larger peephole in the dirty pane. "Can't allow a bit o' rain to spoil your day, lovey. Do you see your intended?"

June anxiously searched the landing area. Eli had said to look for a man, five foot ten, fair skinned, with sandy brown hair and hazel eyes. As she scanned the milling crowd, her heartbeat quickened. Where could he be?

"Do you think he'll like me, Sam?"

"Oh, 'ow could 'e *not* like you?" Sam gave June's arm a jaunty squeeze. "You bein' so comely and all."

"Comely?" June laughed. She'd struck up an instant friendship with this charming English waif the moment they boarded ship in San Francisco. Sam was en route to Seattle to assist her ailing aunt, who ran a small orphanage. Sam's accent was pure delight—a touch of cockney and Irish brogue amid the English, with Sam's own particular manners of speech thrown in for color.

"Goodness, Sam. There isn't a comely thing about me. My nose is too long, my eyes are too close-set, and this hair! Just look at it, Sam! It's a bundle of frizz."

"Shame on ya! It's beautiful! So dark and curly. Truly, lovey, it is. And those big brown eyes o' yours are sure to melt his heart."

June gave a quick shake of her head. "The only comely daughter my papa sired was my sister Hope, although Faith had her share of gentleman admirers." June patted her hair. "I'd give my Aunt Thalia's prize setting hen for a hot bath and clean clothes before I meet Eli."

Sam jumped up and down. "Is that him?"

Flattening her nose against the pane, June squinted. "I don't think so—" Disappointment flooded her. The short, portly man standing at the railing looked nothing like Eli's description. Did Eli neglect to mention his true age? His letters said that he was twenty-three, but the man standing at the side of the railing, his gaze eagerly skimming debarking passengers, looked older than her papa had been.

Sam pressed closer. "Oh dear. He's a bit older than I 'spected."

"Yes . . . he is—a bit." A good twenty years older, but it wasn't the age that mattered so much. What mattered was the trickery. She didn't approve of trickery— not in any form. Eli was an old man!

She clamped her eyes shut, then quickly reopened them. The man on the dock was still there. Closing her eyes again, she silently prayed. *Please, please, please don't let that be Eli.*

Again opening her eyes, she sighed. Well, perhaps Eli

thought himself young. What did Aunt Thalia say? Age was a state of mind; if you didn't mind, it didn't matter. But then, Aunt Thalia wasn't marrying Eli!

"You say he's an assistant pastor?"

"Yes, to Isaac Inman, the evangelist."

Mustering a stiff upper lip, she gathered her belongings and prepared to meet Eli Messenger.

Sam trailed behind as June descended the gangplank. June dreaded parting company with the young cockney girl. Sam had been a comfort during the seven-day voyage, and June had grown very fond of her. She hoped they would see each other from time to time.

"I'll miss our teatime talks," Sam confided as she hurried to keep up.

"As will I." June smiled. "Once you're settled, perhaps you can attend services one evening. You can go with Eli and me. You'll be our guest."

"Oh, I'd not be knowing lots about godly men. Met more of the other kind, I have. But Auntie's written of Mr. Inman's Evangelistic Crusade and the wonderful work he's doin'."

June was awash with pride. "Eli is proud to be working with Reverend Inman. He raves about the man's dedication."

"Well, I'll not be in church often. Me mum says me old auntie is a good woman but a very sick one. I suspect I'll have me work cut out, taking care of orphaned tykes. There'll be no time for churchin'."

"There's always time for churching, Sam."

June returned Eli's smile as she stepped off the gangplank. He had kind eyes—dare she hope he had a youngish heart, too? The man extended his hand with a warm smile. "June Kallahan?"

Nodding, June switched her valise to the opposite hand and accepted his outstretched hand. "Eli Messenger?"

The man appeared momentarily abashed before breaking into hearty laughter. "Oh, my, no! I'm Isaac—Isaac Inman, Eli's employer. But thank you, young lady! You've certainly brightened my day!" He pumped her hand vigorously.

Relief flooded June. "You're not Eli! That's wonderful!" She was instantly ashamed. Her cheeks burned, but Reverend Inman just laughed harder.

"Oh—no, I didn't mean 'wonderful you weren't Eli'; I only meant—" Realizing she didn't know *what* she meant, much less what she was saying, she simply returned his smile. "How nice to meet you, Reverend Inman. Eli speaks highly of you in his letters." Drawing Sam to her side, June introduced her. "Reverend Inman, I'd like for you to meet Sam—Samantha Harris."

Reverend Inman grasped Sam's hand in a friendly grip. "I didn't expect to find two lovely creatures coming off that boat."

"Sam and I met on the voyage." June anxiously searched the crowd. "Where is Eli?"

Reverend Inman's features sobered. "Eli has taken ill. He's asked that I escort you to your quarters."

June frowned. "Ill?"

Taking her arm, Reverend Inman turned her toward a long row of waiting carriages. Departing passengers milled about, carrying heavy baggage. "Nothing serious," he assured her. "He's been afield most of the week, and the weather's taken a nasty turn. Seems he's caught a bit of a chill. He thought it best that I come to meet you." Reverend Inman reached for the women's valises. "May I take you somewhere, Miss Harris?"

Sam searched the rows of waiting wagons. "Thank you ever so much, but me auntie said she'd send a driver. . . ." She broke into a grin. "Ow, there 'e is now!" A weathered buckboard with *Angeline's Orphanage* spelled out in large, colorful letters was parked at the back of the row. A white-haired Indian man stood beside the wagon, waiting.

"Are you Angeline's niece?" Reverend Inman asked, surprised.

Sam brightened. "You know me old auntie?"

"Know of her," Reverend Inman said. "Fine woman doing a good job with the children. I understand she's not feeling well."

"No, sir, that's why I'm here. Goin' to 'elp her, I am."

Giving June a hug, Sam reached for her battered valise, her youthful face radiant with excitement. "Promise you'll come see me? And soon!"

Hugging back, June promised. "The orphanage is located where?"

"On the outskirts of town—not far from the crusade grounds. Me auntie says every man, woman, and child in Seattle 'as heard of Angeline's Orphanage."

The two women shared a final brief, warm embrace.

"I'll be keepin' you in me prayers, June Kallahan," Sam whispered.

"As I'll keep you in mine," June promised.

Sam walked to the waiting wagon, and Reverend Inman helped June into the carriage, then took his place behind the reins. As the buggy pulled away, June glanced over her shoulder for a final glimpse of Sam. The elderly driver was loading her valise into the buckboard. Scared and filled with apprehension, she turned back to face the road. Homesickness nearly felled her.

Look on the bright side, June! Soon she would be married, taking care of her new husband.

Tomorrow she wouldn't miss her sisters so much.

Tomorrow she wouldn't listen so intently for the sound of Sam's lyrical cockney accent.

Tomorrow God would remove all her fears.

The pungent air reeked of the vast forests of Douglas

firs and red cedars. The smell of wet vegetation stung her
nose. The rain had slowed to a light drizzle.

"Oh, my! Just look at those mountains! Aren't they
spectacular!" She'd seen pictures of mountains but had
never hoped to actually see one.

Reverend Inman clucked, urging the horse through a
muddy pothole. "To the east we have the Cascades. To
the west, the Olympics. They are quite magnificent, some
of God's finest work."

From the moment June had accepted Eli's proposal, she
read every book she could get her hands on concerning
Seattle. She learned the town was located on a hilly isth-
mus on Puget Sound. Seattle served primarily as a lumber
town and was noted for its abundant natural resources of
water, timber, and fish.

"Have you been here long?"

"Seattle is my home. I left for a while, but when my
wife passed on, I returned." His eyes grew distant. "The
area is fertile for harvest."

The clouds lowered, and a cold wind blew off the
inlets as the buggy traveled deeper inland. June burrowed
into her cloak, wishing she'd worn something heavier.
The worsening weather made it impossible to talk. Instead she watched the road, praying God would safely
deliver them from the inclement weather.

It was some time before Reverend Inman finally drew
the horse to a halt. June's breath caught at the sight below. A tent, the size of which June had never before
witnessed, spread out like a vast city before them. Men,
dressed in yellow oilcloth slickers, wrestled with heavy
ropes and cables. The heavens suddenly opened, and the
drizzle turned into a deluge. Lightning forked, and the
mountains reverberated with the mighty sound of thunder.

June gripped the side of the wagon as Reverend Inman
urged the team down the slippery incline. Aunt Thalia's

warning rang in her ears. *You're making a mistake, young lady!*

The wagon finally rolled to a stop in front of an unusual-looking octagon-shaped dwelling. June stared at the odd-shaped cinder-block building, thinking it looked very out of place among the ocean of canvas. Sitting low to the ground, the earth-tone complex zigzagged in varying directions, covering at least a half acre of ground. The land surrounding the house unit was barren, with not one blade of grass. In the summer, colorful marigolds and asters might relieve the naked landscape, but today the rain only made it look more bleak.

"We're here," Reverend Inman announced. "Home— for now."

June looked about, fighting another wave of homesickness. The immense revival tent flapped like a giant, awkward bird, two hundred yards to the right of the complex. Home. The connotation sounded peculiar to her, almost frightening.

Climbing out of the buckboard, Reverend Inman extended his hand. "Hurry now, let's get you inside, where it's dry!"

June gathered her damp skirt and stepped down. Thankful to be on solid ground again, she hurried behind Reverend Inman into the shelter of her strange-looking new home. Shivering, she trailed the minister through the corridor and emerged in a brightly lit parlor where a coal stove burned in the middle of the octagon-shaped room.

Reverend Inman shrugged out of his wet coat, then reached for a small bell and rang it. "I'll have Ettie bring tea."

Momentarily a tiny woman appeared, wearing a flannel nightgown and wrapper. Salt-and-pepper strands peeked from beneath the nightcap framing her weathered face and friendly blue eyes. As Papa would say, she couldn't weigh eighty pounds soaking wet. "You rang, Reverend?"

Reverend Inman smiled with weary gratitude. "I know it's late, but Miss Kallahan and I could use a cup of tea, Ettie. Do you mind?"

"Mind? Of course I don't mind, Reverend. I've been worried about you." She tsked. "Not a fit night for man or beast." She crossed the room, snagging a crocheted throw from a wing chair beside the fire. "You must be Eli's intended."

June nodded, trying to still her chattering teeth. "Yes, ma'am."

"Ettie keeps my house and cooks my meals," Reverend Inman explained. He viewed the wiry woman with open affection. "But, of course, she's much more than a housekeeper. I couldn't manage without her."

"And I couldn't do without you, Reverend. Here now, we need to get you out of those wet clothes. Rain, rain, and more rain," Ettie clucked. "My old bones can't take much more." Pointing to a door on the right, she ordered June, "Go on, now. I'll bring your things in to you. When you've changed, I'll have tea waiting. Reverend, take off those wet shoes." Scurrying purposefully across the floor, she bent down and stoked the fire. Sparks flew up the stovepipe as the embers caught and the flames grew.

June did as she was told, returning a short time later dressed in a dry pewter-colored wool. The smell of fresh-baked bread drew her to the small table Ettie had set. A heaping plate of scones, blackberry jelly, and a bowl of rich yellow butter surrounded a colorful clay pot of steeping tea. June realized she hadn't eaten since breakfast—a meager fare of tea with toast and butter.

"Come. Sit," Ettie ordered.

Reverend Inman appeared through a second doorway. June wondered how many rooms the quaint-looking building had. "Ahh, Ettie, my dear. Hot scones on a rainy night. How did you know that's exactly what I prayed for on the way home?"

Ettie winked at June. "You've prayed the same prayer for the thirty years I've known you, Reverend. By now, the Lord knows it by heart."

Reverend Inman chuckled, holding his hands to the crackling stove.

Ettie poured cups of steaming tea, adding a generous dollop of cream to the reverend's cup. June listened to the affectionate banter between Ettie and the reverend, deciding she was going to like the friendly housekeeper and the gentle evangelist.

Heavy rain pelted the windowpanes as they drank tea and buttered the hot scones. The room was cozy, with an overstuffed sofa, wing chairs, and wool rugs on the pine floors. Reverend Inman's private quarters, June surmised. A long row of bookshelves on the east wall contained books concerning the ministries of Dwight L. Moody and other prominent evangelists of the time. June thought of how eager Papa would have been to read works about these great men. He'd spoken often of Moody and chorister Ira Sankey. The two men traveled the country, preaching to huge crowds and converting thousands to Christianity.

Ettie fussed around the warm room, setting damp shoes on the brick hearth and draping wet coats over a line strung behind the stove. The room smelled of baked bread and steamed wool.

"Will you be needing anything else, Reverend?"

"No, thank you, Ettie. Is Eli awake?"

"Yes, sir. Parker is with him."

"Parker?" The reverend lifted his cup thoughtfully. "Terrible night for visiting."

"Yes, sir. Terrible. But you know how Parker feels about Eli. He refuses to leave his side."

"Yes, yes. He and Eli are good friends."

"That they are, close as bark on a tree. I'll be taking them both tea and scones now."

"You do that, Ettie. Tell Eli we'll be in to say good night shortly."

Ettie left through yet another doorway, which June assumed led to the kitchen. Swallowing the last bite of scone and jelly, she stood up, anxious to meet her intended husband. The trip had been long, and her curiosity was blooming. Who was this man she was about to marry? Was he as kind and gentle as Reverend Inman? Was there anything she could do to hasten his recovery?

Wiping his mouth on a white napkin, Reverend Inman smiled. "I see you're anxious to meet your fiancé."

June smoothed the folds of her skirt, hoping her excitement didn't show. "Yes, sir, I am most anxious to meet Eli."

"Then we must delay no longer." Pushing back from the table, the reverend got slowly to his feet. "Follow me."

June accompanied him through a fourth doorway leading down a long, winding hallway. They passed many closed doors before finally stopping. Rapping softly, the reverend called, "Eli? Do you feel up to visitors?"

Momentarily the door opened, and June shrank back when a man so tall, with shoulders so broad she suddenly felt breathless, blocked their way.

His eyes—incredibly blue eyes—looked past her and fixed on the reverend. He nodded. "Isaac."

Reverend Inman met the man's steady gaze. "I know it's late, but Eli's bride has arrived. Does he feel up to a brief visit?"

The man turned and spoke quietly. June couldn't make out his words. In the background, a weak male voice answered.

Stepping aside, the man ushered them into the room.

June walked past him, aware of the faint smell of soap and water. The red-and-black flannel shirt and dark trousers he wore were neatly pressed.

Moving to the bedside, Reverend Inman adjusted the wick on the lamp higher. Shadows danced off the walls as rain pelted the windowpane.

A figure on the bed stirred. "Is that you, Reverend?"

"I've collected your bride safely, Eli."

"Thank you, Brother Isaac. Bring her closer to the light," Eli murmured.

June was troubled by the tremor in his voice. He sounded so very weak. What had the reverend said? Eli had taken ill suddenly? He had caught a chill—well, a chill could take the starch right out of a body. If Eli would permit her, first thing tomorrow morning she would concoct Aunt Thalia's poultice, made from garlic, honey, and herbs. Very unpleasant to smell but guaranteed to cure whatever ailed a person.

Reverend Inman reached for June's hand and drew her closer to the light. Smiling, she focused on the man who was soon to be her husband. Illness shadowed his lean face. Hazel eyes—much too bright—searched the shadows for her. His boyish features were flushed red, and an inadequate reddish growth that passed for a beard covered his youthful chin. A line of angry sores dotted his bottom lip from the high fever.

Groping for her hand, he said softly, "Hello, June."

June squeezed his fingers, hot to the touch. "Hello, Eli. I'm sorry to hear you're sick. Is there anything I can do to make you more comfortable?"

He shook his head, closing his eyes. "No . . . no, they're taking very good care of me. I'm sorry I wasn't able to meet you. I trust the voyage from San Francisco was uneventful?"

"Yes, quite uneventful—with the exception that I met—" June stepped back as Eli dissolved in a fit of coughing. The attack was so violent, so all-consuming, that she immediately grew concerned. Reaching for the pitcher on the bedside table, she steadied her hand and poured a glass of water. "Perhaps some water . . ."

The man with the broad shoulders suddenly blocked her efforts. She glanced up to meet his stern look. "Water only makes it worse."

She immediately set the glass down. "I'm sorry."

"This is my friend Parker. Parker Sentell," Eli whispered. "Parker, my intended bride, June Kallahan. She's come all the way from Michigan—" Another round of coughing interrupted the introductions.

June lifted her eyes to meet Parker Sentell's. For a moment their gaze held. Shivers raced down June's spine, and she suddenly felt chilled. He was scrutinizing her—looking her over closely, and she detected resentment in his stormy blue eyes. An awkward moment passed before he briefly inclined his head, silently acknowledging the introduction. A man of few words, June decided. Instinct told her that Parker Sentell was trouble.

She wondered how two complete opposites could form such a close friendship, yet Eli had written that the bond between Parker and himself was as strong as that of brothers.

Parker stationed himself at the doorway, crossing his arms over his massive chest. The width of his biceps was as impressive as the breadth of his shoulders.

He fixed his cool eyes on her.

When the coughing refused to abate, Reverend Inman gently eased June toward the doorway. "We'll return in the morning when you're feeling stronger."

"Thank you . . . Reverend." Eli feebly lifted an imploring hand to June. "I'm sorry. . . . Perhaps tomorrow . . ."

"Of course. Tomorrow. I'll come and sit with you—all day if you'd like."

Nodding, Eli doubled up in another coughing spasm.

As June slipped past Parker Sentell, their eyes met again. She resisted the urge to assure him that nothing would change for him once she and Eli married. She would have many friends, as Eli would. Parker needn't feel threatened by her presence.

But he did. She could see it in the cool depth of his eyes.

Accusation? Animosity? She wasn't sure what was mirrored in his eyes. Nor was she sure why, but the implication was clear: She was an intruder.

Brushing past him, she made a mental note to ask Reverend Inman why this man, this powerful-looking man who was Eli's best friend, was so hostile.

She glanced over her shoulder and shivered at the sight of his intimidating stature. Then again, maybe she didn't want to know.

The reverend retraced their steps through the corridor, and he showed her to her room. The cubicle was adequate but sparse. Octagon-shaped, the small space held a single bed, a washstand, a simple clothespress, and a stove. Wind whistled around the cracks in the walls.

She shivered, spying her valise sitting on the bed.

"Breakfast is at seven."

"Thank you, Reverend." Saying good night, she closed the door and leaned against it as the long day closed in on her. Rain battered the windowpane with unrelenting velocity. What a week this had been. The long trip from Cold Water, Eli's unexpected illness. She sank to the side of the bed, trying to organize her thoughts. Tomorrow she would sit with Eli, and they could talk. They would tell one another all about themselves, and she would get to know her soon-to-be husband. The same intuition that told her Parker Sentell was trouble also told her she was going to like Eli Messenger. He seemed a gentle soul, and he had been most polite, even as bad as he felt.

Yawning, she slipped off the bed and rummaged through her valise for pen, ink, and writing paper. She wanted to share this first exciting day in Seattle with Aunt Thalia.

Dear Auntie,

I am so weary I can hardly keep my eyes open, but I wanted to inform you I have arrived in Seattle without incident. The Lord protected my way, and I made a new friend, Samantha Harris. Sam is here in Seattle to assist her ailing aunt, who runs a small orphanage not far from the crusade grounds. I hope to visit there one day soon.

A few minutes ago Isaac Inman, of the Isaac Inman Evangelistic Crusade, introduced me to my husband-to-be, Eli Messenger. Eli is presently under the weather, but Reverend Inman assures me he will be fit again very soon. Eli's friend, Parker Sentell, was visiting Eli tonight. I understand the two men are good friends. Although I like Eli very much, I personally didn't take to Mr. Sentell. He's certainly one giant of a man, tall, powerfully built, with arms so large they resemble small hams, and eyes . . . eyes, Auntie, so blue they remind me of that robin egg I found one day when I was six. Remember? I brought it to your house for safe-keeping.

I sense Mr. Sentell resents my presence here, though why I can't imagine. I will pray that he will be of comfort to Eli during his illness and that in time he will consider me a friend. That said, Auntie, I will say an extraspecial thank-you to the Lord that he has sent me to be a helpmate to Eli and not to a man like Mr. Sentell.

I hope this letter finds you well and happy in the Lord. I miss you, and I hope I can send money for your passage to Seattle very soon. We will have a long visit and rejoice in my new life.

Your loving niece,
June Kallahan

Blotting the letter, she folded it, then laid it aside. Stretching out on the bed, she listened to the rain pelting the window, wishing she were home in Cold Water, in her warm bed in Aunt Thalia's normal-shaped attic.

Chapter Two

Tʜᴇ rain refused to let up. It came in heavy sheets, nearly blinding June as she picked her way along the thin board sidewalk. She was chilled to the bone, and it was getting dark. Gripping the lantern tightly in one hand, she bunched her skirt in the other and cautiously made her way to the complex. The ground was a quagmire.

Sighing, she paused to get her footing, her attention diverted to the activity taking place around her. Mules, the biggest she'd ever seen, pulled wagons heavy-laden with tents, poles, pews, and equipment necessary to operate the massive church crusade. Once-lush, green Seattle countryside was mired in thick ruts. Someone had laid boards end to end for a makeshift walkway. Unfortunately, the raw-pine planks didn't always meet in the center. Twice, June snagged the hem of her dress and almost plunged headfirst into the dank mire.

The gloomy weather only added to her growing melancholy. She'd been in Seattle two days, and Eli was still ill—so ill they had yet to have their promised talk.

Each day she made the trek down the hallway to his room, but each day Parker Sentell turned her away, saying, "Eli isn't up to visitors today. You'll have to come back tomorrow." He was polite, but June had the feeling he didn't like her.

Well, who did this Parker Sentell think he was? He protected Eli as if he needed protection from her—*her, his wife-to-be.* She'd spoken to Reverend Inman about the matter, but he only shook his head and suggested she pray that Eli would soon enjoy robust health again. As Eli's intended wife, she had a right to help. She had always been good at nursing people back to health. Parker had no right to exclude her from Eli's illness.

June took her eyes from the board for an instant, and her foot slipped. Hopping around on one foot and waving both arms, she did a desperate dance in an attempt to steady herself and keep from sitting down in the muck. She managed not to fall down. But one foot landed on the board; the other sank up to her ankle in gray slime. Muttering under her breath, she jerked free, but her boot remained buried.

Heaving a huge sigh, she glanced around to see who, if anyone, had witnessed the spectacle. Men whistled and called to their mule teams, but most seemed unaware of her predicament.

With a great sucking sound, she broke the mud's hold and pulled her boot free. She was drenched, chilled to the bone, and feeling more than a little foolish. It would take an hour to scrape the mud off that boot.

She continued down the walk in an uneven gait, wearing one boot and holding the other in the hand that held the lantern. The saturated planks were icy beneath her stockinged foot.

As she approached her quarters, lightning split the sky. A clap of thunder jarred the ground, and the clouds opened up and poured. She quickly ducked inside the complex, wondering if coming to Washington had been the right thing to do. She thought of Aunt Thalia's parlor in Cold Water. The old house was drafty but always comfortable. It was nothing like the strange-looking complex that was supposed to be her new home.

Scraping mud off her boot, she swallowed against the thick lump forming in her throat. She thought of her sisters; Faith was in Texas, Hope in Kentucky. They might as well have been at the ends of the earth. How long would it be before the sisters were reunited? She didn't want to think of how long. Right now, it felt like an eternity.

Lord, forgive me for fretting over material things like warm parlors and happy talks with my sisters when you've given me a new start.

Taking a deep breath, she brightened. She might be barely seventeen, but she was about to marry a preacher—or almost a preacher. Eli was only an assistant pastor, but he would be a preacher someday. And as a minister's wife, certain things would be expected of her.

She vowed to relinquish her selfish thoughts and endure whatever it took to be a loving wife and devoted helpmate to Eli. A supportive wife, wholeheartedly involved in his ministry. Shivers ran up her back just thinking about it. She, June Kallahan, a preacher's wife. And one day, the mother of Preacher Eli's children. Growing up as a preacher's kid, she had dreamt of marrying a wonderful man like Papa. Now here she was, a mail-order bride to a preacher. God had provided her with her dream.

Dropping the lantern on the tabletop, she shrugged out

of the raincoat and hung it up to dry. The long braid she'd so carefully plaited earlier was now plastered to her back. Releasing the buttons on her wet dress, she stepped out of it and draped the wet garment across the back of the chair. She suddenly recalled the letter Parker Sentell had thrust through the partially opened door, stating that it had arrived that morning from Eli's mother. "Read it somewhere dry," he'd said. As if she would sit down in the middle of a downpour and read mail!

June admitted that her thoughts about Parker Sentell weren't exactly charitable, and she had to bite her tongue to remain civil whenever she saw him. If Eli considered Parker a friend, she would like to share that friendship too. But it didn't look as if it would be easy.

Rummaging through her satchel, she located her flannel gown and robe and quickly changed into the warmth of the dry nightclothes. Wrapping her wet hair in a towel, she stifled a sneeze, praying she wasn't coming down with a cold.

She removed the envelope from her dress pocket and sat down on the side of the bed.

Eli filled her thoughts, and she wondered if he thought often of her. What was his impression of her? She considered herself somewhat of a plain soul even if Sam didn't. Even more so, when compared to her sisters, Faith and Hope. She often wondered why Papa hadn't just named her Jane. Plain Jane. But instead he named her June. June, though a pretty month, seemed rather uninspired for a name. Charity—now that would have been more appropriate. Faith, Hope, and Charity. But Mama had died giving birth to her, and Papa, in blind grief, hadn't felt very charitable toward his new infant daughter. June, he declared. Her name would be June. So June it was, but charity was close to June's heart. Helping others gave her a peace she couldn't explain. It was an intricate part of her, a part she needed to fulfill in order to feel whole.

Deep down, it didn't matter that she was rather ordinary looking and without any remarkable strengths. The heavenly Father may not have seen fit to make her as independent as Faith or as beautiful as Hope, but he had blessed her with a singing voice. More than one kind soul had remarked that she had a voice superior to most, young or old. She didn't think so, but she hoped the good Lord saw fit to let her use her talent—however small—in Eli's ministry.

Slipping her fingertips along the envelope seal, she carefully opened the letter. Eli's mother had sent the letter all the way from Ohio for her son's new bride. But there was more than just a letter enclosed. Inside the pages was a neatly folded handkerchief. June admired the pale blue fine linen, crisply starched and trimmed with delicate white lace. For a moment she held the gift close to her heart, inhaling its subtle lavender fragrance.

As nice as the present was, she couldn't wait to read Mrs. Messenger's words. She quickly unfolded the pages.

Dearest June,

I hope you won't mind my taking the liberty of addressing you by your first name. When Eli wrote, telling us of his plans to marry, his father and I were elated. We wish you and our son great happiness. Perhaps when you're settled, we can come and visit you.

When Eli wrote last year, informing us of the accident, we were gravely concerned. Eli explained how a tree had fallen on him and crushed his leg. Parker Sentell, Eli's boss and very good friend, took Eli under his care and secured for him the services of the finest surgeon to be found in Seattle. After the operation and much time spent recuperating, Eli says his limp is only slightly noticeable.

We were very grateful to the Lord and Parker Sentell. And, of course, to Reverend Inman. I'm certain you can imagine our joy when Eli wrote that he had accepted the

Lord's call to preach the gospel. It was the answer to our prayers. To have a son in the ministry! And now, to know he has chosen a wife who shares his love for the Lord. Well, it doesn't get any better! Except, of course, when the grandchildren start to arrive.

I hope you like the enclosed wedding gift. It was Eli's paternal great-grandmother's, and was given to me on my wedding day. I want you to have it.

I pray many happy and prosperous years embrace your marriage. We are anxiously waiting to hear from you.

Love,

Ruth and Paul Messenger

June sat for a moment, holding the letter. Ruth Messenger's thoughtfulness already made her feel a welcomed part of the family.

Folding the letter back into the envelope, June placed the handkerchief inside her satchel with the rest of her wedding attire. She would carry it on top of her Bible as soon as Eli was well enough for the ceremony.

Kneeling beside the small cot, she prayed for Eli's health to be restored, for his family, and for their forthcoming marriage.

Slipping beneath the cool sheets, she fell asleep to the sound of rain hammering the roof, content in the belief that morning would bring Eli's first real signs of recovery.

Early the next morning she stepped out of the house, pausing to lift her face to the sun. Sunshine streamed down, and the rays felt gloriously warm! Not only had the rain ceased, but the sky was a brilliant blue—so blue, she thought of Parker Sentell's eyes and frowned.

Deep green forests, towering Douglas firs, Sitka spruce, and western redwoods soared into the heavens.

Drawing a cleansing breath, she spun around and

around, lifting her arms in praise. *Thank you, heavenly Father! A day this beautiful can be nothing but special!*

Hurrying back inside, she quickly covered the distance to Eli's room, thinking she would mention Aunt Thalia's poultice if he weren't greatly improved this morning.

Pausing before his door, she rapped twice, hoping Mr. Sentell had decided to go to work today. He must work—a man with arms the size of fence posts didn't just sit all day.

"Come in."

June couldn't believe her luck when she recognized Eli's voice. She opened the door a crack and peeked in. Eli was propped up in the bed, looking very pale but improved from the first time she saw him. His voice was weak, yet the illness had done nothing to erase the friendly smile now hovering on his full mouth.

"You are looking much better today," June assured him with a warm smile.

"I'm feeling much better," Eli said. "I'm feeling almost human this morning."

His color reminded June of a time Faith was gravely ill with the fever. They'd almost lost her. Brushing the disturbing thought aside, she reminded herself to be thankful Eli had a little color now. June closed the door, then approached the bed to fluff his pillows. "Have you eaten?"

"Ettie brought a tray in earlier. I managed to eat some hot cereal."

"That's a start!" She poured a glass of fresh water and handed him the cup.

He looked up gratefully, his hand trembling as he drank. "Thank you. I'm trying to force myself to eat—I need the strength."

June waited until he drank a few swallows before she leaned over to steady his hand.

"Thank you."

23

She smiled.

"Did Isaac meet the ship on time?"

"Yes, he was waiting when it docked. Thank you for sending him. It was very thoughtful of you."

Eli dismissed her gratitude. "I'm sorry I couldn't be there to meet you myself."

"I understood. I wish you could have met Sam."

"Sam?"

"Yes, she's here to help her aunt, who runs the orphanage not far from here."

"Oh . . . yes, I've seen the place. Angeline's, isn't it?"

"Yes, Angeline is Sam's aunt."

He took a last sip, then set the cup aside. "I was afraid you were ready to run back to Michigan when you got your first look at me the other night."

"No, not at all! Why would you think that?"

He chuckled softly. "I fear I must make a pitiful sight."

"Don't be silly." Her cheeks grew warm. "You're very handsome. I'm not at all disappointed." She straightened the mussed blankets, then sat down in the straight-back chair next to the bed. He obviously was going to need nursing; maybe he would allow her to help. Crossing her hands in her lap, she studied the pattern on the rug on the floor.

The silence stretched. Her mind raced with a million thoughts. Now that he was feeling better and able to get a clear look at her, was *he* having second notions? Had he expected someone prettier? Thinner? More outgoing?

No, she reasoned away the insecure thought. She'd been completely honest with Eli Messenger when she responded to his ad. She had enclosed a small tintype of herself, so unless he were blind—which she could clearly see he wasn't—he would have known she was no raving beauty. She glanced up to find Eli studying her.

He gave a wan smile. "Penny for your thoughts."

June blushed. "You wouldn't be getting your money's worth."

"Oh, I don't know about that. You look very serious."

If he only knew her wayward thoughts, she'd die of embarrassment. Thank goodness Eli was an assistant preacher and not a mind reader.

"Would you like for me to read to you?" she asked.

"Not now. I'd like to just talk."

"Of course." She shifted in the chair, crossing and then recrossing her hands.

"You met Parker, didn't you?"

She frowned. "Yes."

With an attempt at another smile, Eli lay back against the pillow. "Is that a frown I see?"

"I'm sorry. It is. Parker doesn't seem to like me."

Eli closed his eyes. "You and Parker aren't getting along?"

"Oh . . . it isn't that." She could hardly tell him that she didn't like his friend. She barely knew Mr. Sentell. She would allow she might be misjudging him. "If you like him, that's all that matters."

Eli lay for a moment, gathering the strength to speak. "When I'm stronger, we'll talk about Parker and what an exceptional friend he has been to me. No man could have any better. Parker's accustomed to working with loggers—I'm afraid he overlooks etiquette when he's around a woman. Too, Parker and the reverend don't see eye to eye on Isaac's tabernacle. When Isaac's around, Parker tends to be difficult to get along with."

Once again silence lapsed between them.

"Well, I don't want to overly tire you. I'll be going along—unless, of course, there's anything you need." June stood up, ready to leave.

Eli opened his eyes. "Resting is the one thing I'm getting very tired of doing."

"I know it must be difficult to be confined to a sick-bed. It won't be long before you're up and around again."

"Yes . . . I'll certainly welcome that. But don't go—I want you to stay."

June started to protest, but the sincerity in his hazel eyes touched her.

"We've barely begun to talk. I'll rest for a moment; then we can visit. Please . . . stay."

Moving the chair closer, she sat down again. "Of course, I'll be happy to stay."

She returned his attempted good-natured smile. Was he courting her? She wasn't sure because no one had ever courted her before. But she supposed he could be. After all, they were about to be married. It would be proper enough. She smiled. "Your mother sent me your great-grandmother's lovely handkerchief for the wedding. It was so thoughtful of her."

"That's Mama. . . . Always eager to do something nice for someone." He appeared to doze for a moment.

If she had harbored any lingering doubts about coming west, these past few moments with Eli erased them. It was surely God's plan for her life—a life devoted to Eli Messenger.

"Do you think you could eat again? I could have Ettie fix something light."

Eli shook his head. "No, she'll be bringing lunch soon. Fusses over me like an old mother hen." He lay still for a moment, and June could see his strength fade. "Has Isaac shown you around?"

"No, he's been very busy. It seems he works day and night."

"Yes, he does. He cares so much for his people."

"My, the crusade tent—it's the biggest tent I've ever seen. Why, it's even bigger than the one I saw when Aunt Thalia took us to a circus in Lansing one year."

Eli smiled, and June realized she was babbling. She must go now and let him rest. He obviously wasn't out of the woods. "Not that I'm comparing the revival tent to a circus—but then, you're tired. I really must go," she said, rising.

"No, please . . . I want to talk."

June liked his gentle ways and the way he made her feel at ease. It was going to be a very good marriage.

Against her better judgment, she took her seat a third time. "Just a little longer."

Eli opened his eyes, and they'd taken on a sudden shine. "I want to tell you about Isaac. He's been preaching over thirty years, traveled the revival circuit, been practically everywhere." He stopped for a moment, then began again. "He was with Jeremiah Lanphier at one time. You've heard of Lanphier? Jeremiah started weekly noon prayer meetings in New York City. Within months there were over six thousand people participating in daily prayer services."

June listened to the warmth in Eli's voice. He loved Reverend Inman deeply. "I don't think I've ever seen that many people in my whole life."

Eli smiled. "In May of that same year, fifty thousand people were converted."

"Praise God."

"The next year, Isaac traveled with a crusade to England."

"My . . . all the way across the ocean?" June couldn't imagine that, yet Sam had heard of Reverend Inman's ministry.

"All that way. Tragically, his wife of forty years passed away on the voyage back. Katherine had a powerful dream, one she and Isaac shared. A vision, actually."

"A vision?"

"The tabernacle. When Katherine was in New York, she saw the cathedrals of Saint Patrick and Saint John the

27

Divine. Both she and Isaac were deeply moved, but it wasn't until they traveled to England and saw the Lincoln and other cathedrals that Isaac was truly inspired."

"Inspired to do what?"

"To build his own church. But not just a church. A tabernacle, a magnificent place to worship and glorify God," Eli said, with great pride reflected in his voice. "Katherine shared that dream. Her dying words were, 'Build our cathedral, Isaac. Build it for the glory of God.' " Eli's eyes closed momentarily, then opened.

"A cathedral? Here? In the middle of the woods?"

June's question seemed to renew his strength. "Here— on the land Isaac and Katherine purchased a few years back. Seattle is growing, June. The growth is precisely what's needed to accommodate the large congregation Isaac is acquiring."

"The only kind of church I've ever attended was one room—"

"Visualize it, June! See it—dream about it. Isaac, like King David in the Old Testament, desires to build a splendid tabernacle to the Lord, using only the best be-cause the Lord deserves the best. Isaac and Katherine wanted to build something that would attest to the great-ness of God."

"Yes, I *can* see it," she murmured.

"Every detail. An elegant handcrafted altar, made from the finest mahogany. Scarlet fabric cushioning the multi-tude of pews. A choir stall. Brass pillars. Stained-glass windows, each telling in mosaic beauty the story of Christianity. Magnificent materials and detailed work-manship, right down to candlesticks made of pure gold. Nothing but the best for the Lord."

June was spellbound. She'd never heard of such gran-deur, let alone seen anything as splendid as the church Eli described. It was a wonderful dream—a glorious tribute to God's presence. "When does Reverend Inman plan to build this church?"

"Tabernacle. And we'll build it as soon as there are sufficient funds. If God continues to bless as he has, it will be within the year."

"You must be very excited to be a part of the dream," June said.

"Yes . . . yes. I want to give God my best. Once the people see the magnificent building, it is our belief that they will experience God's grace as well."

Eli was clearly exhausted. Rising from her chair, June straightened his pillows. "I've worn you out. Thank you for sharing your dream." When he voiced a weak protest, she said softly, "I'll come back first thing in the morning."

"I'll look forward to it." Eli grasped her hand warmly. "Thank you for spending this time with me. It's been one of the nicest mornings of my life."

"Thank you, Eli. Sleep well. I'll visit again tomorrow." She touched her fingers to her lips, then lay them across his forehead. It felt hot to her touch. "Sweet dreams."

Chapter Three

ELI was recovering, and they could be married soon. June wanted to get on with the Lord's work with Eli at her side. After their talk yesterday she, too, could visualize the tabernacle. What a tribute to God's glory! She wanted to be part of building the monument, part of the dream. In a small way she would be building a tribute to Papa for all the years he'd spent preaching the gospel. Papa's name wouldn't be on the tabernacle, but in her heart she would know that the monument represented a part of him.

It would take a good while for Eli to regain his strength, even longer to collect sufficient funds to build the tabernacle. He had seemed so much weaker after their talk than when she entered his room. She would keep her visit brief today.

She brushed her hair until it crackled, then tied it back with a pink ribbon. Papa would have been proud to have Eli for a son-in-law. Sitting for a moment, she stared at her mirrored reflection. Eli Messenger was everything Ruth had written about her son, and more.

June's plainness had no effect on him.

Her heart swelled when she realized that Eli was one of a rare breed of men who looked beyond the exterior and sought a person's inner beauty. "Thank you, God, for giving me such a perceptive husband. And a handsome one, too. You're far too good to me."

She pinched her cheeks for a little color. She must write both sisters immediately after her visit with Eli this morning. If Eli felt up to it, they could both write. Faith and Hope would be happy to hear from their new brother-in-law.

Moments later she walked down the corridor carrying a basket of oranges. Ettie had purchased the fruit the day before, saying they were Eli's favorite. Humming under her breath, she smiled when she saw Reverend Inman walking toward her. It was his custom to visit Eli early before he started the busy day.

"Good morning, Reverend—"

Isaac took her by the arm and turned her around, urging her back down the corridor. Puzzled, she followed, wondering why he was acting so strangely.

Steering her back into her room, he closed the door.

"Reverend Inman—?"

Drawing a deep breath, he ran his hands over his ashen features. June's heart tripped as she sank to the side of the bed. The reverend looked as if he'd just seen a ghost! Something must have happened with the crusade.

Edging forward, her eyes anxiously searched his. "What's wrong, Reverend?"

"It's—" his voice cracked, then steadied—"It's . . . Eli."

"Eli?" She felt the blood drain from her face. "Has he had a setback? He seemed to be feeling much better when I left yesterday—"

Shaking his head, the reverend took her hand. Tears filled his eyes, and he said softly, "There's no easy way to tell you, June. Eli is gone."

"Gone?" June's mind whirled. "Gone where?" Her heart sank. Oh, dear Lord. Gone. Eli had started thinking about the marriage and her plainness and decided to go back to Ohio—

"But he was so weak—he wasn't able to travel—"

Reverend Inman bowed his head, his voice barely a whisper. "Gone." The silence was unbearable. A million images raced through June's mind. Eli gone? Even if he were feeling better, where could he have gone in the middle of the night?

"When . . . when did he leave?" June struggled to maintain her composure. The news was devastating. How could she have been so taken with Eli—felt so good about him and the marriage—and been so wrong?

"A few moments ago," the reverend said softly. "I'm sorry. . . . It was so unexpected. . . . There was no time. . . ."

June's anger swelled as the implication of Eli's actions hit her. "You don't need to apologize for Eli. If he didn't have the decency to say good-bye—"

"June." The solemnity in the reverend's voice stopped her. "My dear—" he bent forward, squeezing her hand gently—"I'm so sorry—you misunderstand. Eli's gone home . . . to be with the Lord."

For a moment June couldn't comprehend the enormity of what he was saying.

"I am so very, very sorry." The reverend's face crumpled, and he began to weep. "Eli was like a son to me."

Sliding off the bed, June held him as his sobs filled the

room. She had never witnessed such pain. The exhibition tore at her heart.

"We don't understand God's ways," Reverend Inman said brokenly, "but we have to believe there's a reason for everything that happens." His features constricted. "God forgive me, I can't imagine what it would be . . . taking Eli when. . . ." Words failed him.

"Eli . . . gone," June whispered as the realization sank in. Eli was dead. "But why? Why?" she cried. "Yesterday he was feeling . . . I prayed . . . prayed so hard for him."

Reverend Inman fumbled in his pocket for his handkerchief. "I have no explanation. . . . He seemed to be improving. Toward dawn his fever came up again, and he was having trouble catching his breath. He rang for Ettie. She came for me, and . . . an hour later he slipped away."

June bit her lip, shaking her head. Tears welled to her eyes. Eli gone? Why did God bring her to this faraway place to marry such a wonderful man, only to call him home before their life together ever started? June experienced something foreign to her. Doubt. Why would God do something so unfair to Eli? His life had barely begun. . . . There was so much he wanted to do to help build the reverend's tabernacle.

"Oh, Reverend Inman." She held the older man as he broke down again. What a grievous loss this kind man must feel. She barely knew Eli, and she was overcome by news of his death. What must the reverend be feeling?

When the wave of sorrow receded, he got unsteadily to his feet. Blowing his nose, he shook his head, trying to regain his composure. "His family must be told."

June thought of Ruth Messenger's glowing letter, Eli's great-grandmother's lovely handkerchief—the family would be heartbroken.

She patted Reverend Inman's shoulder, fortifying herself for the terrible task that lay ahead. "I will tell Eli's parents of his death and make arrangements for his burial."

"I can't allow you to do that, June. You've only just arrived."

"Please, Reverend Inman. I need to do this. I know Eli and I weren't married, but in a way I feel as if we were. Let me do this, for both you and Eli."

"Parker—"

She swallowed, steeling herself for the most onerous task of all. "I will inform Parker." It wouldn't be the easiest thing she'd ever done, but then, it wouldn't be the hardest.

Coming to grips with the knowledge that she was a widow before she was ever a bride was the hardest thing.

My dear Mr. and Mrs. Messenger:

It is with the deepest regret that I write this letter. Your beloved son, Eli, passed away early this morning. He had been ill for nearly a week but expected to fully recover. We tended him and prayed for his healing; still, God saw best to call him home.

Eli was everything you said and more. And though we had yet to marry, I shall forever feel the loss of this wonderful man I was given the pleasure of knowing for even a brief time. I pray God will give you and your family abundant comfort in your time of need.

You will remain in my thoughts and prayers, as Eli will always hold a special place in my heart.

Yours in Christian love,

June Kallahan

Before sealing the envelope, June gently tucked the handkerchief inside.

Her bravado slipped, and she really wept for the first time, still unable to believe that Eli was dead.

Later that morning June sat on a horse, looking down on Pine Ridge Logging Camp. This was Parker Sentell's world. Teams of oxen were skidding logs from the cutting area to the landing. June could hear the sound of axes biting into trees and the occasional shout of "Timber!" in the distance.

Parker's camp appeared to be hacked out of the dense woods, and one of the bigger, better managed outfits. Beyond the string of bunkhouses and the cookshack/dining room were the office/living quarters for the bosses and a large barn containing oxen and what looked to be a milk cow. June spotted the river. Logs were stacked high on miles of rollways along the banks, where they awaited the spring log drive to the mills.

Reverend Inman had told her that Parker ran Pine Ridge and oversaw four smaller camps. Men respected him, if not for his size and position, then because they knew they were dependent upon him for work. Loggers came and went. If a man didn't work for Sentell now, he eventually could.

June couldn't imagine women in camp. Not many would subject families to such primitive living conditions.

Nudging the horse's flanks, she rode down the small incline into camp and stopped in front of the office.

"A little far from home, aren't you, Miss Kallahan?"

Her horse shied at the sound of Parker's voice as he reached out and grasped hold of the bridle. She was met with distant blue eyes.

Her arrival attracted a small crowd. Shantyboys stopped what they were doing to stare at the newcomer. June didn't want to break the news of Eli's death to Parker in front of others. Eli's sudden passing would be hard enough for Parker to accept. "May I speak to you in private, Mr. Sentell?"

His eyes narrowed with impatience. "Concerning what?"

"In private, please." She started to dismount, surprised when she felt his hands lifting her slight weight off the saddle.

"What's this about? Is Eli worse?" Concern tinged his voice.

She glanced around, spotting the cookshack. "Can we talk in private there?"

He directed her toward a long, low building with smoke curling from the chimney. It was warm inside, and in spite of the spartan interior, the pleasant aroma of coffee mingled with fried potatoes, sowbelly, flapjacks, and molasses syrup.

"Coffee?"

"No, thank you."

Long tables flanked by plain benches stretched the length of the room. At one end a thin man with a knitted cap stood in front of the big iron cooking range and stirred a huge pot.

Motioning for her to take a seat at the far end of a bench, Parker took the seat opposite her.

"What's this all about?"

June folded her hands, then took a deep breath. "It's Eli."

"What's wrong? He was better yesterday."

"I know. . . . I'm sorry, Parker." There was no easy way to tell him. She was feeling what Reverend Inman must have felt when he broke the news to her. That seemed like days ago. Better to get it out, then try to offer him comfort and prayer. "Eli passed away early this morning."

Color drained from his face, and compassion flooded her. He and Eli had been close, yet, because he was a man, he couldn't cry; he would be expected to buck up.

"We'd hoped . . ."

Parker's fist slammed against the table, and he got up.

June patiently waited for the initial storm to pass. Papa's emotions had flared easily, but he got over it just as quickly.

"No," Parker said tightly. He strode to the window, rubbing his clean-shaven chin. Gripping the top of the window frame, he stared at the activity going on outside.

June wished she had the proper words of condolence. Eli's death was so sudden, so unexpected, that she could barely grasp it herself. "I'm sorry. I know you had a great deal of respect for Eli—"

Parker turned. "Why?"

"Why?"

"Why did God take him?"

June sighed. She had expected sadness, yes, even disbelief, but not anger. She could never understand why the bereaved were often so quick to blame God for what appeared to be senseless tragedy. "Parker, are you a Christian?"

His shoulders filled the breadth of the small window. For a long time he didn't answer. Finally he said in a low voice, "I accept Jesus as my Savior, if that's what you're asking."

"Then how can you blame him for Eli's death?"

A muscle in his jaw firmed. "Eli's death doesn't make any sense. I get mad, Miss Kallahan, when a man is taken in his prime for no reason at all."

"Eli's passing doesn't make sense to us, but it does to God. He always knows—has always known—what is right, what is best."

His expression closed. "There's no purpose for Eli's death. It shouldn't have happened."

She chose not to get into a discussion of whether God knew what he was doing. There was no point in such a discussion. God was always right. Parker must know that. Grief was speaking.

"We may not always agree with God, but he doesn't make mistakes."

Parker turned from the window. "Isaac is responsible for this."

"Isaac? Reverend Inman?" What could he possibly have to do with Eli's death?

"The 'dream,' the tabernacle!" Parker snapped. "Eli was consumed with the thought—spoke of nothing else but his dream of building Isaac's tabernacle, some great shrine to draw people." Bitterness tinged his voice. "Perhaps, as I've argued all along, it wasn't *God's* plan but Isaac's."

"Of course you're at liberty to believe whatever you like."

Parker paced back and forth, his hands gripped at his sides. He talked more to himself than to her. "God's not interested in buildings or any of the other trappings that people say they need to glorify him. This is for Isaac's glory."

How could this man call himself Eli's friend and have such thoughts? It was for God's glory, not Reverend Inman's, that Eli dreamed of the tabernacle.

"I understand you're overwrought, Mr. Sentell." June stood up so she didn't have to look up quite so far to talk to him. "I understand your grief and share it—"

"How can you share my grief? You barely knew Eli."

That was true. But she'd known him long enough to know he would be appalled at his friend's reaction. "I knew him long enough to know that I could have loved him deeply." For Eli's sake she couldn't let the issue of the tabernacle go unchallenged. "Reverend Inman's dream is to provide a place of worship, a place like no other. Eli shared that dream, worked hard to fulfill it. God deserves our finest."

"Don't give me that. God doesn't require monuments."

"Of course, that's true—"

"People around here aren't used to grand buildings, Miss Kallahan. Life is hard. I don't know about Cold Water, Michigan, but life in Seattle, Washington, is hard. Most of the community works in one of the logging camps. And life in a logging camp is hard. It's all a man can do to hold it together. They work six days a week and don't see wives and families until spring breakup or the end of the log drives."

He gestured toward the door. "Most come from distant parts and have few contacts with the fairer sex because of the isolation. That can make a man testy, Miss Kallahan. Real testy. The men earn between twenty-five and thirty dollars a month, plus board. They live in drafty cabins built from lumber they cut themselves. We're common folk, Miss Kallahan. We believe in God, and we can worship him in a tar-paper shack if necessary. I never doubted Eli's sincerity, but we don't need a tabernacle to make us feel better about ourselves."

June could hardly disagree. She believed in all the things he'd listed, but there was nothing wrong with building a monument to God. Reverend Inman was a man pure of heart. His tabernacle would be a glory to God, not a hindrance to his Word.

"The tabernacle will be a place set apart, a place where people from far and wide will come to worship."

"A place Isaac builds in his wife's memory—worse yet, as a tribute to himself."

"The building is a tribute to God," she retorted, irritated that he would have such thoughts. He simply didn't understand what Reverend Inman was trying to do. "It's saying we love God enough to build a special place in which to worship him."

"The Bible says we're to worship God in spirit and in truth. Nothing is said about a fine building being a requirement."

"I cannot believe you are saying this—wasn't Eli your friend?"

Parker leaned toward her, spearing her with a sharpened gaze. "Eli's gone. The matter no longer concerns you. You're entitled to your opinion, but you're not entitled to mine. Go home, Miss Kallahan. There's nothing here for you any longer."

Until this very moment she hadn't considered what she would do, but now the answer was abundantly clear. "I plan to stay on and continue Eli's work with Reverend Inman."

Bracing his broad hands on the tabletop, he leaned in closer, his voice low. "Go home."

"I'm staying on." June raised her chin a notch and met his fixed gaze. "I'm going to help the reverend raise the funds to build the tabernacle."

Parker looked at her for a long moment, then turned on his heel and strode out of the building, anger clear in the set of his shoulders. The door slammed behind him, rattling dishes.

Sinking to the bench, June released the pent-up breath she hadn't realized she'd been holding. No one needed to tell her the battle lines were drawn. She would rather have Parker Sentell as a friend than a foe, but even his boorish and decidedly rude manner wouldn't stop her.

God had a purpose for her in Seattle. She'd thought it was to marry Eli and help in his ministry. With Eli gone, she must wait and pray for God to reveal his will. Meanwhile, she would assist Reverend Inman. . . .

Her eyes followed Parker Sentell's angry gait, watching him march toward his office.

. . . And avoid Parker Sentell whenever possible.

Eli was dead. Parker's hands shook as he jerked the knot on his tie free and started again.

In a few hours he would bury his best friend. Grief washed over him, so forceful he nearly dropped to his knees. *Why, God?* his soul cried. *Why Eli?* Parker bit back bitter tears. *Why would you take Eli when he worked so diligently for your kingdom?* Parker might not have approved of Eli's goals, but he loved Eli like a brother.

Taking a deep breath, he forced his thoughts to Eli's bride. June Kallahan. What should he do with her? She wasn't his responsibility, yet Eli would expect him to look after her welfare. He swallowed around the tight lump crowding his throat. Blast Eli for being so idealistic! What man assumed he could just send for a bride and eternal bliss would reign? Didn't he know that wasn't the way love worked? A man and a woman needed feelings— strong feelings you couldn't buy as a result of an ad in a journal. What was Eli thinking? He jerked the tie and started over.

His angry thoughts tumbled over each other. *Working himself to death to serve Isaac Inman—going from dawn to dusk in an effort to build that temple that was Isaac's obsession, not necessarily God's will.*

Parker had never approved of the tabernacle, and he never would. And he didn't approve of Isaac Inman. Some said he was wrong about Isaac, that the evangelist was a true man of God. But Parker saw little indication of that. He saw a man consumed by his own wants. As far as he was concerned, Isaac should have stuck to his traveling crusade and should not be trying to force his dreams of grandeur off on Seattle. Folks here didn't need his kind. He'd made that clear to Eli, but Eli never argued. He just smiled that good-natured smile and asked Parker to pray about it. Parker had given up trying to talk sense into him. Eli's mind was bent on helping build that temple, and nothing Parker said changed it.

Well, where is endless bliss now, Eli? And what do you expect me to do with the woman you ordered?

The harsh thought faded as the crushing loss closed around him. What would he do without Eli's friendship to brighten the long days? How he would miss his friend's smile and his sense of goodness. The times they'd spent in prayer and fellowship. He blinked, clearing the moisture now clouding his view.

What would God have him to do about Miss Kallahan? She looked as delicate as an orchid, a citified woman, all sweet and helpless.

He frowned at his reflection in the mirror. She wouldn't have lasted more than six months in these wilds—a year at best. And he'd bet she would be gone before the first shovelful of dirt hit Eli's casket.

Somehow the thought made him feel better.

Yes, June Kallahan would return to Michigan or Minnesota or whatever "M" state she was from, and he wouldn't have to worry about her. Out of every tragedy emerges a purpose—isn't that what his mother contended? Who knows? Maybe Eli's death would even cause Isaac to reappraise his objective, and Parker would be rid of two nuisances—June Kallahan and Isaac Inman.

Closing his eyes, he said softly, "The marriage might have worked, Eli, but your new bride seemed a little bossy to me."

The morning of Eli's funeral dawned cool, the sun hidden behind clouds just as death hid Eli's light from the world. How appropriate, June thought, considering the sadness of those who knew and loved the young, aspiring pastor. Everyone June met said how they'd cherished his warmth, his genuine concern, his love of God. Many said that with his passing it was as if a part of them had been taken with him.

For herself, she was determined to dwell on the knowledge that Eli was today with God. His pain was gone, his hope in eternal life realized. She smiled to herself, thinking of the day she would see Eli again and walk with him in that perfect place made for all who belong to God. Keeping her thoughts centered made the day ahead bearable.

She busied herself with preparations for the ceremony. Today, more than ever, she thought about those she loved. Aunt Thalia kept coming to mind, and Papa. What would Papa think of this misadventure? Would he think the building of a tabernacle a worthy cause? She wasn't sure he would. Papa had the soul of a humble man, and any sort of venture that might be deemed "glorious," as Reverend Inman was wont to describe his vision of the tabernacle, would immediately be suspect as a prideful idea. But Papa would look at the motivation behind the desire for the tabernacle. Was it truly for God's glory? Then, likely, Papa would approve. Certainly Eli's motives had been pure.

Today, more than she usually allowed herself, she missed Faith and Hope. Beautiful Hope, in Kentucky; tomboy Faith, in Texas. How were each of her sisters faring? It would take so long for letters to reach her.

Sometimes she worried about whether her sisters were safe and happy, but then, the Kallahan girls had always relied on God to take care of them. She had no less faith that he would continue to do so.

Quick on the heels of that thought came the wish that she herself would one day find the man God intended for her. She was awash with sadness when she thought of Eli, lying so still and pale in a simple pine box in the large crusade tent. All day long, friends and mourners filed past, laying floral tributes and simple tokens of love at the base of the casket.

Eli no longer occupied his earthly body; she knew that. Eli sat at the feet of God, and she was heartened in the knowledge. As the time for the funeral approached, the tent began to fill. Eyes reddened, heads bowed, and voices turned to reverent whispers.

June sat on the front pew beside Reverend Inman and Parker Sentell. When she glanced at Parker, she saw his jaw working with emotion, but his eyes remained dry. She smothered the urge to lean closer and comfort him.

Every seat in the tent was filled by the time Reverend Inman rose to address the mourners. As his gaze moved across the gathering, he conveyed a private message of comfort to each one. Without looking at the Bible, he began speaking.

"We are gathered today to pay tribute to a dear friend. Eli was not just a good friend, a beloved husband-to-be, a community spiritual leader, a brother in Christ. Eli was so much more." The reverend's eyes softened. "To me, he was the son I never had. To his intended bride, he was the hope of a shining future. To others, he was a confidant, a safe harbor from life's storms. We will miss him deeply.

"Some will ask, why? Why would a man so young, living his life so purposefully, be called home when his work had barely begun? We do not know why. God's timetable is not our timetable. Shall we wring our hands and weep for understanding, or will we join hands and rejoice in the knowledge that Eli's work here on earth has been fulfilled?"

As Reverend Inman went on to relay touching stories of Eli's ministry, June was painfully aware of Parker's grief. He remained dry eyed, but she knew it was an act of will. People had told her Parker had never supported Eli's work. He came on Sunday to hear him preach on occasion. No doubt to Parker, Eli was a loyal friend who had been plucked from Parker's life too soon, and he saw no purpose or meaning in such a loss.

June's thoughts returned to Reverend Inman's compelling voice.

"Together we will carry on Eli's dream, the dream he so fervently shared with me. We will build the tabernacle. With God's help, we will erect this monument." Isaac wiped his eyes, then continued. "Shall we worry how we'll carry on? No, Eli would say no. Far more important, God says no. 'Thou wilt keep him in perfect peace, whose mind is stayed on thee: because he trusteth in thee,' it says in Isaiah 26:3. Jesus admonishes us not to let our hearts be troubled or afraid. That implies we have a choice in the matter. 'These things I have spoken unto you, that in me ye might have peace. In the world ye shall have tribulation: but be of good cheer; I have overcome the world,' John 16:33.

"Eli Messenger was a gifted man, a man who asked for little here on earth, but a man who is rich beyond measure in the treasure he has laid up for himself in heaven. He was a man who asked little *for* himself, but asked much *of* himself. He offered cool water to the thirsty, comfort to the sorrowing, hope to the hopeless. Friends, 'let not your hearts be troubled,' " Reverend Inman repeated softly. "Together we toil on. Together we will plant seeds and reap the harvest. 'I can do all things through Christ which strengtheneth me,' Philippians 4:13.''

Tears rolled down his cheeks now. "Brother Eli sits at the feet of God today. He is feasting at the table of the Lord. And he is hearing God say, 'Well done, good and faithful servant.' "

Bowing his head, he prayed. "Father, let our tears be of joy rather than of frustration. Let us move on, glorifying your name, building your kingdom. For the days allotted us here upon earth are precious and few."

Lifting his hand, he intoned, "Now, may the peace of

God which passeth all understanding keep our hearts and minds through Jesus Christ. Amen, and amen."

June lowered her eyes as mourners rose and began to file silently past Eli's casket. Reverend Inman had requested that Eli be buried in a peaceful valley on the grounds where the tabernacle would be erected. In his words, "Eli will still be a part of the dream."

Later, June stood with the other mourners as the pine box was slowly lowered into a gaping hole in the muddy ground. When she saw tears unabashedly rolling down Parker's cheeks, she leaned closer, pressing a clean handkerchief into his right hand. He took it, refusing to meet her eyes. Her heart ached for his pain.

"Dust to dust," Reverend Inman intoned softly. "We are all but dust. Brother Eli, you will be sorely missed, but by your devotion you have given us a measure to live up to; by your faith you have given us a light, and by your faithfulness you have given us courage and a greater conviction toward the work we have yet to accomplish."

June wept openly, feeling more than ever that she was called to be a part of something miraculous. Something destined to be a lasting tribute to God, to Eli and Reverend Inman, and, yes, even to Papa, for generations to come.

At the moment, she asked for no more.

Chapter Four

Iт was settled. June would stay on in Seattle and help raise funds for the tabernacle.

As she dressed the following morning, June thought about the conversation she'd had with Reverend Inman over supper the night before.

"I want to stay on and work to see Eli's dream realized."

Reverend Inman had laid his napkin aside, obviously surprised by her decision. "I thought you would want to return to Michigan."

"No. No," she repeated more softly. "I thought God brought me here to Seattle to marry a wonderful man. Now that Eli's gone, I feel God has a more defined purpose. You know my papa was a pastor."

Reverend Inman nodded. "So Eli said."

"Well, Papa never so much as thought about building anything so grand as a tabernacle, but I believe he would approve of your and Eli's dream. When Eli told me about the dream you and he shared, something moved in my heart, Reverend Inman. Something so deep and so profound that I believe God wants me to stay here, to do all I can to help carry on Eli's work."

Leaning back in his chair, Reverend Inman appeared to weigh her suggestion. "You're most welcome to stay if you feel this is where God is leading you. The ministry can use all the hands we can get."

June could see he was touched that she had caught Eli's vision. "I've prayed about it, and I believe this is what I am to do. In a small way I'll be doing it for Papa, too. I think he would be proud of my being part of such a grand endeavor."

"Then, of course, you must stay. Might I hope you will remain here at the complex?"

June nodded. "If that would be all right with you."

"I would have it no other way." He patted her hand. "Oh, my dear, you are indeed a godsend. Eli would be overjoyed to know that you're carrying on in his footsteps."

June sighed, pushing her half-empty plate aside. "Do you think Eli knows, Reverend Inman?"

Reverend Inman smiled. "I think Eli's joy knows no bounds, my dear. Could we ask for anything more?"

"No, nothing more," she agreed. "I thought I would begin tomorrow morning. I have an idea for raising funds I would like to talk over, if I may."

"Certainly." Reverend Inman reached for his coffee. "What's this idea you have?"

His eyes widened as she chatted on. He stirred four teaspoons of sugar into his coffee instead of his usual two, his jaw slackening on occasion. When she was finished, he took a fortifying sip of coffee and leaned back in his chair.

"Well." He cleared his throat. "It is a most uncommon approach, but I can think of nothing scripturally wrong with it—provided you in no way imply the men should give out of guilt."

"Oh, no! I would never imply that. Giving should be from the heart—a freewill offering. It's just, that's where so many men go—and I think they'll be happy to donate to the tabernacle if given an opportunity."

"Well, they could attend services nightly," Reverend Inman pointed out.

"Yes, but they don't, Reverend. So I'll go to them."

The following afternoon June stood in front of the saloon, gazing up at the large, crudely constructed sign nailed to a weathered-looking shack.

The Gilded Hen looked downright sinful.

She shook her head, wondering if Eli would have approved of her scheme. More important, would God object? Reverend Inman had said he could think of no scriptural reason not to. . . .

Piano music spilled through the double swinging doors as she balanced on tiptoes to peek in. Scruffy men sat around tables playing cards while others stood at the bar and flirted with scantily dressed women with flaming rouged cheeks. Oh, the shame of it all. What would Aunt Thalia say about such goings-on?

When June first thought about a plan to raise funds for the tabernacle, the saloon had immediately come to mind. She and Reverend Inman had driven past the establishment the day he met her ship. Stationed beside the door of The Gilded Hen, she could sing and ring a bell. When the men started home after a long night of drinking and . . . well, whatever a man did in an establishment like The Gilded Hen, she could offer them an opportunity to contribute to a worthwhile community project. If they didn't want to give, they didn't have to. Nothing ventured, nothing gained, Aunt Thalia would say.

Positioning herself to the left of the wood porch, June hummed a few practice notes, then began to sing "Amazing Grace" in a strong, clear alto. The tones were as sweet and pure as the message. Ringing the tiny silver bell, she flashed passersby her sweetest smile. "Donations for the Isaac Inman Crusade! Would you care to give?"

A passing matron responded immediately. "The Isaac Inman Crusade thanks you, and God thanks you," June said as the woman dropped a coin into the cup and walked on.

"Thank you, sir. God bless you."

"Thank you."

"Your kindness is deeply appreciated."

By the end of the first hour she'd emptied the cup once and sung "Amazing Grace" fourteen times. Her mouth was as dry as the floor of a chicken coop, but she'd collected five dollars and twenty-two cents for the Inman Crusade.

Darkness closed around her, and the wind picked up. Huddling deeper into her wool cloak, she rang the bell, keeping an eye on the saloon doorway. The door swung open, and a group of men emerged, holding on to each other for support.

Straightening, she sang louder, "that saaaaaved a wretch like meeeeee. I once was lost . . ."

The men stumbled down the steps, barely sparing her a glance.

She watched them walk on down the street, then eyed the half-empty cup. Drats. The door opened again, and two large men—loggers, she assumed by the impressive width of their shoulders—teetered out.

Lifting the bell, she rang it harder, extending the tin cup. "Can you spare a coin for the Isaac Inman Crusade, sir?"

"For what?" One man stopped to focus on her.

"For the Isaac Inman Crusade. Reverend Inman intends to build a tabernacle right here in Seattle—the likes of which you've never seen." She smiled, holding the cup a little closer. "Can you spare a coin?"

The man leaned unsteadily against the saloon wall, squinting at her.

"The Isaac Inman Crusade," June repeated. "Donations are gratefully appreciated."

He finally focused. "What's yer name, girlie?"

"June, sir."

The two men obediently fished in their pockets and came up with a few coins. Dropping them into the cup, they draped their arms around each other's shoulders and teetered on. She could hear their deep voices singing in disjointed harmony:

"Oh, in 1869 in the merry month of June,
I landed in a vanzousi one sultry afternoon,
Up stepped a walking skeleton with his long and lantern
*   jaw. . . ."*

"God bless you, sirs!" June called.

"Well, well. Now, what's your name?" a man sporting the remains of his supper in his unkempt white beard asked a while later.

"God's emissary!" June replied, holding out the cup.

The man gave generously, but his unwarranted winks and ribald remarks brought a blush to June's cheeks. Blowing on her icy fingertips, she thought about calling it a day. Donations had been good, and evening services would be starting soon. Reverend Inman would be delighted when she dropped the day's contributions into the offering plate. The men, for the most part, had given from the heart, pausing occasionally to ask her to remember them in her prayers.

She turned to look over her shoulder when she heard hoofbeats approaching. A huge man rode up and swung out of the saddle, tossing the reins around the hitching post. June frowned when she recognized Parker Sentell.

A shiver raced up her spine. What was he doing at The Gilded Hen?

She had no explanation for what happened next. It was if an invisible force gave her a shove from behind. As the big logger stepped onto the saloon porch, she blocked his path. Her gaze collided with his silver belt buckle, then lifted to follow the long, long row of buttons on his shirt. The man was as tall as a mountain! Lifting the bell, she rang it. "Care to spare a coin, sir?"

Taken off guard, Parker stepped back. June grinned as recognition, then disbelief, dawned in his eyes. She lowered the cup. "Good evening, Mr. Sentell."

Parker eyed her sternly. "What are you doing in a place like this?"

"Collecting donations." She shook the cup, and the coins jangled. "They've been quite good. Care to make a contribution?"

His scowl reminded her of her childhood and Aunt Thalia's disapproving looks. He stepped around her, and she resumed her position by the steps. She didn't care if she annoyed him. Now maybe he would realize she was serious about her intentions to carry out Eli's work. Jingling the tin cup, she called, "Donations for the Isaac Inman Crusade!"

A logger dropped a coin into the cup and walked on. "God bless you!"

Giving her a look of pained tolerance, Parker pushed through the doorway and disappeared into the saloon.

Anxious to see what he was doing, she scrambled to

the swinging doors and peeked inside. Parker stood at a table of young men playing cards. They looked to be very young—no more than early teens. Towering over the boys, the logger issued a few curt words. Chairs overturned as the boys darted toward the door.

June jumped back to avoid being trampled as the four burst out and struck off down the middle of the street in a dead run.

Wow! What had Parker said? Whatever it was, she was glad it hadn't been directed at her.

Her curiosity got the better of her, and she stepped back to the doorway. The sound of heavy boots hitting hardwood floor met her ears as Parker forcefully strode out, almost bowling her over. Stumbling, she reached out to grasp the railing.

Giving her a hard look, he walked down the steps, reached for the reins, got on his horse, and rode off.

Leaning against the rail, she took a deep breath, sourly eyeing his disappearing horse. He was such an unpleasant man.

Thirty-five dollars and sixty-two cents for the tabernacle. June lay back on her bed and stared at the ceiling, exhausted. She'd been in Seattle a little over two weeks, and already she was well on the way to helping Reverend Inman and Eli achieve their goal. Her heart sang with accomplishment. The only damper on her enthusiasm was Parker Sentell. What would it take to make him warm up to her? His continuing aloofness was like ice water on her joy.

Until she came to Seattle, June had never been more than fifty miles in any direction outside of Cold Water.

Now she was hundreds of miles from home, separated from family, close friends, and the only life she'd ever known. Everything that once felt safe and familiar suddenly seemed to have existed eons ago.

Even with her efforts to raise funds, she found it difficult to fill the hours in the day. She spent late afternoons and early evenings in front of The Gilded Hen, but days like these, when the skies poured down heavy rains, prevented her from going at all.

She clung to the belief that God had sent her to help with Reverend Inman's ministry. With Eli gone, God surely must mean for her to carry out the important work Eli had started.

One minute she was certain, or at least practically certain, that she was destined to remain in Washington.

The next minute she definitely knew, or at least was pretty sure, that she should return to Michigan.

Maybe if she talked to Reverend Inman about her jumbled feelings, he could help with the many questions that burdened her heart.

Above all, she desperately wanted to do the right thing. If only the Lord would speak to her spirit and grant her guidance and wisdom, she would gladly follow wherever he led.

Full of determination to do better, she headed for Reverend Inman's room late Monday morning. When she arrived, however, he was gone.

"If you're lookin' for the reverend, he's . . . he's not here," a childish voice informed her.

Startled, June looked around to see who was speaking.

Ben Wilson, a crusade usher, was sweeping the hallway with a large broom. Ben, a thin, big-boned man, towered over the heads of other men who worked with the crusade.

Fellow workers good-naturedly teased Ben that he was as slow as molasses. Rudy Silas, Ben's best friend, quickly spoke up and said that whatever Ben lacked upstairs he made up for with his unshakable willingness to do God's work.

June had silently agreed, wishing that she'd had the courage to speak in Ben's defense. Ben was a little odd at times, but he was a kind man. She recognized his total devotion to the Lord and felt a kindred spirit with Ben Wilson from the moment she met him.

"Hello, Ben." June smiled and smoothed her dark blue wool skirt in place.

"Hey, Miss June." Ben shuffled his big boots against the floor.

"Do you know where I might find Reverend Inman?"

"Yes."

A moment of silence passed without Ben's saying.

"Can you tell me?" June prompted.

"Yes," Ben said, raking a calloused hand through his thick gray hair.

"Where, then, is Reverend Inman?"

"The reverend went to Sea—Sea—Sea—" Ben's face throbbed a bright red as he struggled to pronounce the words.

"Seattle?"

"Yes, Miss June. That's where he went." Ben grinned, revealing a missing front tooth.

"Did he say how long he'd be gone?"

"Yes."

"How long will he be gone, Ben?" June asked patiently.

"Said he'd be gone 'til dark." Ben's eyes glowed with pride. Sometimes Ben forgot things. June could see his self-esteem elevate, if only briefly, from having remembered the reverend's promise.

"Hey, Ben!" A man stuck his head around the corridor doorway. "Buddy, we need your help outside."

"I'm their buddy," Ben said. His smile widened. "They need me."

"Thank you for your help, Ben." June smiled as Ben put on his hat.

"You're welcome, Miss June." The big man headed toward the door, reminding himself with pride, "They need you. You have to go, Ben. They need you."

June watched out the window as Ben pitched in to help erect a large pole. He was eager to work, doing anything, from the dirtiest, heaviest tasks to running the simplest errands. All anyone had to do was tell Ben where he was needed.

Sighing, she focused on the large crusade tent. What should she do with all her time? The crusade had all the services it needed. People came from far and wide to hear Reverend Inman preach.

June admired the landscape lining the crusade ground. Trees, tall and majestic. As far as the eye could see, trees.

Trees . . .

Lumber . . .

Lumber camps . . .

Lumberjacks . . .

Families of lumberjacks . . .

Parker said men had to wait until spring breakup to see their families, but surely there were a few women and children privileged to live with their men.

Services.

"That's it!" June shouted. She quickly glanced over her shoulder to see if anyone had heard her. Ettie was nowhere to be seen. The building was deserted this morning.

Her direction was now clear to her. How could she have missed the obvious? Gathering the folds of her wool skirt, she hurried toward the area where Ben was working. She knew exactly what she wanted to do. Big, rowdy lumberjacks rarely came to the crusade meetings. Some promised to attend services, telling her they would do so for "God's little emissary." Five actually came one night, but she was still waiting for the others.

The way she figured it, their wives and children would enjoy informal services if the services were brought to them.

Her hope spiraled downward.

The plan would obligate her to deal with Parker Sentell. He ran the largest camp around and oversaw four others. She wouldn't be able to go into those camps without his knowledge. She sat for a moment and thought about the problem. Resolve stiffened her shoulders. God's work was more important than her rocky relationship with Parker Sentell.

Enthused by her plan, she hurried to find Ben. He was busy helping a fellow worker pick up leaflets in the crusade tent. She drew him aside so they could speak privately.

"I need your help."

Ben's face lit from ear to ear. "Miss June needs my help?"

In no time at all, the man with the intelligence of a ten-year-old had the buggy hitched and waiting. He carefully helped June climb aboard the driver's seat.

"Thank you, Ben." June reached for his hand and squeezed it. "You're a true gentleman."

"Miss June is welcome." Ben grinned, his eyes brightening. "I am a gentle man."

"That you are." June picked up the reins. "Ben, please tell Reverend Inman I'll be back before dark."

He nodded and returned to his earlier task. June heard him reciting, "Back before dark. Back before dark."

She drove directly to Pine Ridge. She wasn't sure how to approach Parker about holding services in the camp, but with a hefty measure of the Lord's help, she would think of something.

She'd never seen such spectacular beauty. The deepest

green pines, the bluest sky, the most vivid browns dotted the meadows. As she traveled deeper into the piney forest, she noticed the path narrowed to bumpy ruts. The route must be one of many logging roads cut through the heart of the woods. The ground beneath the towering trees was blanketed with a cushion of ferns. She smiled, recalling the briars she had endured as a child, racing through Cold Water's brambly groves.

A bend appeared in the road, and June spotted the sign proclaiming Pine Ridge Logging Camp. Reining the horse to a stop, she sat for a moment, collecting her thoughts. God as yet hadn't given her the insight about how to approach Parker. Well, maybe at this point she wasn't supposed to know. Perhaps this was a time when the Lord wanted her to travel by faith, not by her instincts, which more often than not proved to be troublesome.

If only she had started off on better footing with the obstinate logger, she wouldn't be facing this uphill battle. There must be something good about the man; she just had to find it.

Five minutes later June stopped the buggy in front of a small log building. *Pine Ridge Company Store,* she read.

The sound of razor-sharp axes biting into wood echoed through camp. The rhythmical grind of crosscut saws, or, as Papa had called them, misery whips, filled the air. In the distance a logging road ran parallel to the forest. Teams of mules labored to drag heavy loads of logs chained to a skid. Somewhere deep within the woods, a man shouted a warning. The next thing June knew, the ground beneath her shook from the weight of a felled tree. The jolt spooked the horse.

Holding tightly to the reins, she struggled to control the animal, yet it was obvious that it was only a matter of time before the frightened horse overcame her weakening grip. Her arms burned as she wrestled with the reins.

In the midst of the frenzy, she glimpsed Parker darting from the camp office. His long legs effortlessly covered the ground as he raced toward the swaying buggy. The horse whinnied and reared on its hind legs, threatening to overturn the small conveyance.

Parker's hand snaked out and grasped the bridle, putting him dangerously close to the animal's powerful hooves. Gripping the leather, he calmed the wild beast.

"Whoa, girl. Easy, there."

The animal pranced wide eyed and gradually responded to his soothing tone.

June was shaking. Meeting Parker's stern gaze, she smiled weakly.

"Are you OK?" Parker walked around the horse, giving the animal a gentle pat. It took a moment for June to compose herself.

"Yes . . . thank you—I didn't realize the horse would spook so easily." She touched her hand to her hair. Well, she'd certainly made a fool of herself! "I don't like to think what might have happened if you hadn't come to my rescue."

Parker crossed his arms and stared at her. "That's what I'm here for."

She was relieved that he seemed to be in a better mood than at their previous meeting. She tried to move, but couldn't. "I think I'm paralyzed."

Before she realized it, he had lifted her down from the buggy. The strength in his arms amazed her.

Their gaze touched briefly, and he set her gently on her feet. She quickly looked away. "Your camp . . . it's very nice. I forgot to mention that on my last visit."

Parker studied the long, neat row of bunkhouses as if seeing them for the first time. "The men work long hours; they deserve a decent place to live."

"You should be congratulated." Other logging camps she'd seen in the area weren't as nice. Most looked as if

they'd been thrown together with spit and baling wire.
Parker took her arm and steered her toward the office. "I
don't suppose you came all the way out here to comment
on the condition of my camp."

Color flooded June's face. "No, I didn't."

"Then to what exactly do I owe the pleasure of this
visit?"

"Well, first of all, I'd like for us to be friends." There.
She'd said it. Bold as brass. He could either recognize her
attempt to reconcile their differences, or they could continue at sword's point. She'd much prefer the former. "I
think we've gotten off to a bad start, and I want to apologize if it's my fault."

He simply stared at her, weighing the offer. After a
moment he said, "All right. Apology accepted. I guess I
owe you one too." He extended his hand, his smile almost pleasant. "I have nothing against you, Miss Kallahan.
I don't approve of the tabernacle or your part in it. But,
I'm willing to let bygones be bygones."

She smiled, tremendously relieved. They shook on it.
His grip was firm and confident.

"Now, Miss Kallahan. What's on your mind this afternoon?"

Drawing a deep breath, she said quietly, "I have a
proposition for you."

His eyes narrowed. "A what?"

"A proposition. Interested in hearing it?"

"Should I be?"

"Yes. I think so." He smiled, and she suddenly felt
flushed. The sun was warmer than expected. She needed
to remove her cloak.

"Why am I almost certain I *don't* want to hear this
proposition?"

"You may not, but I'm going to present it anyway."

Recrossing his arms, his guarded blue eyes studied her.
"I'm listening."

June quickly tried to choose the best approach to argue her request. She needed to be tactful. She didn't want to scare him off her idea. "I understand you oversee many of the logging camps in the area?"

He conceded with a nod. "A few."

"The work must be very arduous."

"Most work is."

"Long days—the men are worn by the end of the week—much too weary to travel much farther than the bunkhouse."

"You looking for work?"

He wasn't making her job any easier, but she didn't discourage easily. "No, but I've noticed that not many loggers attend revival services."

He shook his head, shifting his stance. "Not many."

"Well—I've been thinking that perhaps the men's wives and children would like services—maybe even some of the men would, if services were brought to them."

He stared down at her with his arms folded across his chest in a fighter's stance. "That's what you think."

Taking a deep breath, she continued, "That's what I think—and I'm also thinking there's no reason they should be deprived of services when I am quite willing to provide them."

It seemed to take a moment for her implication to sink in. When it did, his eyes narrowed. "Are you asking to set up a tent revival here? In camp?"

"Oh, no," June assured him. "Nothing like that. Just an informal Sunday service—"

"No."

Her jaw dropped. "But you haven't heard—"

"I've heard all I need to hear." He shifted positions, and June could see a stubborn set forming along his jawline. "We've gotten along fine without outside services; there's no reason to start one now."

"Mr. Sentell—"

"I didn't say we don't have services; I said we don't have *outside* services."

She eyed him skeptically. "You have services?"

"Hoss Barlow reads a couple of Scriptures before breakfast Sunday mornings."

"A couple of Scriptures? You call that services?"

"The amount of Scripture isn't a problem with God; why should it be a problem for you?"

June's confidence was shaken, but not her spirit. "Every man, woman, and child should keep the Sabbath holy. The men, especially, need to hear more than 'a couple of Scriptures.' I'm sure—"

"You haven't been here long enough to be sure of anything." He straightened, his arms dropping back to his sides. "But I have, and I want no part of Isaac Inman's Evangelistic Crusades *or* his tabernacle. I thought I made that clear."

June opened her mouth to argue, but he stopped her.

"What Isaac does on crusade ground is his business. Pine Ridge is my business. We don't need you coming in here, stirring up trouble under the guise of Sunday services."

"Mr. Sentell!"

He lifted an imperious brow, his eyes issuing her a challenge. "I'll tell you the same thing I told Eli. There are far greater needs, Miss Kallahan. Open your eyes and look around you. Now, if you'll excuse me, I don't believe we have anything more to discuss. I have work to do—unless, of course, you can't find your way back to Inman's camp, in which case I'll have one of my men drive you."

Why—the man had more gall than starched long johns! June straightened, refusing to let him shake her. "I am perfectly capable of driving myself back, thank you."

"I'm sure you are." Parker turned and walked off.

Seething, she watched him disappear into the office and shut the door.

So that was it. He was mad at Reverend Inman. Eli had said as much, but if Parker thought for one moment his mean spirit would deter her work for the tabernacle, he had another think coming. His obstinacy only made her that much more determined to succeed. She *would* start Sunday services for women and children—if not at Pine Ridge, then at some other camp—with or without his approval.

Logging camps were all alike. The needs were the same, and she felt now, more than ever, that leading a morning worship service was something she needed to do. The Lord said to pick up the cross and follow him. He didn't say it would always be easy to carry or that she wouldn't meet any Parker Sentells along the way.

Climbing back into the buggy, she spotted a lumberjack leaving Parker's office. Springing to her feet, she called out, "Sir? Excuse me. Can you help me?"

The man glanced up, smiling. June shivered. All the men in this camp were giants. This one was even taller than Parker Sentell, if that was possible.

As the logger approached, she encountered a pair of earnest brown eyes. When he spoke, the manly rumble made her think of rich, warm honey. "Yes, ma'am?"

"Where's the next nearest logging camp?"

He paused, glancing toward the west. "Tin Cup, about a mile up the road."

Smiling, she turned the buggy. "Thank you!"

"Ma'am," he called, "you don't want to go there! It's no place for a lady—"

"Thank you," she called gaily. "But it's exactly where this lady wants to go!"

Chapter Five

THE buggy rattled along the rutted road, jarring June's skull. Surely the kind lumberjack had pointed her in the wrong direction. *Might as well turn back. But . . . perhaps it's just around the next bend. . . .*

As she debated with herself, she finally spotted an obscured, weathered sign reading "Tin Cup."

Breathing a sigh of relief, June trotted the horse through the crudely built log arch.

The difference between Pine Ridge and Tin Cup was shocking. A foul odor met her nose and stung her eyes. As the buggy rolled farther into camp, she was sickened by the deplorable living conditions.

Moldering garbage dumps fouled the air with a rotting stench. Trash littered the ground—slivers of broken bottles, discarded tins, and pieces of broken furniture. Pigs and dogs ran loose. Chickens roosted on housetops.

Houses consisted of ragged tents and unkempt shacks. The area reminded June of the aftermath of a bad storm that had once torn through Cold Water.

The buggy rolled deeper into camp. June saw a small, barefoot boy dart out, shouting at the top of his lungs, "Stranger's a-comin'!" The child quickly ducked back into one of the shacks, where a woman peered curiously from behind tattered curtains. When June looked her way, she quickly allowed the material to drop back into place.

The camp was eerily quiet for a Monday. No piercing saws or rattling chains, or logs rolling toward the river. June glanced over her shoulder as the sound of men's laughter, tongues thick with drink, floated from a nearby tent.

She swallowed. What *was* this place?

Whirling to look behind her, June considered turning the buggy in search of a more civilized camp.

A man's head suddenly appeared in the opening of the tent flap. His frowning glance swept the camp, coming to a halt on June and the buggy. His eyes narrowed.

June's heart pounded. Gripping the reins, she ran her tongue over her dry lips. She had made a huge mistake. She should have listened to the logger who had warned her not to come. She jumped at a surly voice.

"You want somethin'?"

The tall, skinny man, his beard thick with tobacco spittle, studied her. Her heart hammered against her ribs. Where had he come from?

He stepped closer. "I'd be more than happy to accommodate."

A second logger approached; he was almost as big around as he was tall. Five or six huge, dirty men drifted out of the tent. Their eyes greedily assessed her.

Please, God, June prayed silently. *Make my words bold.*

"Well, sir, I'm . . . I'm here for a purpose." She cleared her throat, trying to think of it. "I've come to bring you good news!"

Please, God, let them consider Sunday services good news!

"What good news?" The skinny man eyed her up and down, then bent at the waist to hawk up a wad of tobacco.

"Very good news." She tried to smile confidently. "Wonderful news."

A man pushed his way to the front of the crowd. He was so slovenly that the smell of him reached the buggy before he did. "What do you want, woman? Spit it out."

June turned away from the stench and silently implored God to give her strength. "I've come to offer you services—Sunday services—for you and your families—"

The men's laughter overpowered her faint voice. She glanced from man to man. Scraggly beards, dirty hands with nails bitten and broken to the quick, clothes that reeked of unwashed bodies. Should she turn around and leave?

She summoned the courage to continue. Her voice rose. "I want to come to your camp on Sunday mornings and share with you and your families preaching, prayer, Bible study, singing—"

The rounded man approached the buggy, fingering the hem of her blue wool skirt. He leered at her. "What is it you're offering to share, little lady?"

The men broke into laughter, elbowing each other.

June reached out and firmly removed the man's fingers, determined to keep her head. She had done a foolish thing. She couldn't afford another mistake. Staring straight ahead, she reiterated her intent. "I am with the Isaac Inman Crusade. I'm here this morning to see if your camp is in need of Sunday services—"

"You're one of those preacher women? One of those crusaders?"

The men roared. "That's a good one!" someone called.

"She's here to see if we need any churchin'! What say, men?" A man held out his suspenders, winking. "Do we need any churchin'?"

Leaning back in his chair, Parker stared out the office window. For some reason he couldn't shake the thought of the morning's visitor.

He was surprised at how quickly June had given up. He didn't know her well, but he did know she was pushy and somewhat naive. He'd gotten the feeling that she wasn't easily swayed from a purpose. So why hadn't she tried harder to persuade him to hold services at the camp? His gut feeling told him that deep within June Kallahan there burned a fire that would not easily be extinguished.

"Parker, I need your signature on these documents. There's a shipment of new saws due out of Seattle first thing tomorrow morning." Simon Hendricks handed his boss a stack of papers.

Drawn from his thoughts, Parker looked up. "What?" he asked absently.

Parker's clerk rattled the sheaf of papers. "Your signature? On these?"

"The new saws?"

"The new saws. Where's your mind today?"

Parker leaned across the desk and took the papers. His mind was on June Kallahan, Eli's mail-order bride. With Eli gone, she should go back to Michigan. His jaw tensed when he thought about her declaration that she wanted to see Eli's dream realized. He mentally snorted. Eli's dream—building that tabernacle was Isaac's dream, a dream to glorify Isaac's work. If Inman wanted a cause to promote, he need look no further than the poverty in the area. Families going hungry, the orphanage where children were going without proper food and clothing. That old woman, Angeline, who was trying to raise a houseful of kids with no help except that old Indian. Inman's "tabernacle" wasn't going to put food in folks' bellies, or shoes on those orphans' feet.

"Is something wrong, boss?" Simon eyed him with a concerned frown.

Parker leaned back, stretching. "Nothing's wrong. Just a little tired, I guess." But something was wrong. Something nagged at him.

Simon's hand was on the doorknob when Parker stopped him. Something told him not to ask, that he didn't really want to know. Common sense dictated he'd better.

"Did I see you talking to the Kallahan girl earlier?"

"The woman in the buggy?" Simon nodded his head warily.

Parker's heart sank. Simon had a heart of gold. If *he* was worried, Parker's instincts were on target.

"She wanted to know where the nearest camp was. I told her she didn't want to go there, but—"

Parker slammed his fist on the desk and got up. "Blast that woman!"

"Trouble, boss?"

"Saddle the horses, Simon."

"Right away." Simon hurried out the door, pulling on his coat.

Parker took a deep breath. June was naive, but was she crazy? Riding into Tin Cup, spouting the gospel? They'd have her for supper. For a moment he considered letting her learn the hard way. Going off, half cocked, to a camp known for its . . .

Reaching for his coat, he shrugged into the fleece lining. Regardless of his aggravation, he couldn't allow anything to happen to her. Loyalty to Eli, as well as his own judgment, forbade it.

⌒

"Gonna preach to us, girlie?"

Trying desperately to hide her fear, June swallowed hard. Intent on drowning out the suggestive words of the vulgar men, she turned Papa's words over in her mind. *The Lord will take what the enemy has intended for harm and turn it to good.*

"Well, now, yo're a purty li'l thing, ain't ya!" A burly man grinned up at her, showing rotting teeth. "All dressed up and smellin' so fine!"

Fear is not of God. Fear is not of God, June told herself. Springing to her feet, June pointed a commanding finger at the man as he closed in. "You stop right there!"

"Fiery, too!"

In her mind Papa's voice, clear as a bell, shouted, *Sing, June! Sing!*

June opened her mouth and belted out one of the songs she'd sung in front of the saloon yesterday.

> *"We give Thee but thine own,*
> *Whate'er the gift may be:*
> *All that we have is Thine alone,*
> *A trust, O Lord, from Thee."*

The words tumbled out crisp and clear. From the corner of her eye she saw the men were listening.

> *"May we Thy bounties thus*
> *As stewards true receive,*
> *And gladly, as Thou blessest us,*
> *To Thee our first fruits give."*

Two men slowly removed their hats and laid them over their hearts.

> *"O hearts are bruised and dead,*
> *And homes are bare and cold,*
> *And lambs for whom the Shepherd bled*
> *Are straying from the fold."*

June's knees were knocking so hard that she thought the men would surely hear it. She silently thanked God for the power of song and her singing voice. Without this talent, she would surely be thrown over one of these bullies' shoulders and hauled off to who knew where. She shuddered, and sang louder.

> *"To comfort and to bless,*
> *To find a balm for woe,*
> *To tend the lone and fatherless,*
> *Is angels' work below.*

> *"The captive to relieve,*
> *To God the lost to bring,*
> *To teach the way of life and peace—*
> *It is a Christlike thing.*

> *"And we believe Thy word,*
> *Though dim our faith may be:*
> *Whate'er for Thine we do, O Lord—"*

She glanced at the men and finished with a rush.

> *"We do it unto Thee."*

She was running out of verses! Now what should she do?

"I have found a friend in Jesus, He's everything to me,
He's the fairest of ten thousand to my soul;
The 'Lily of the Valley,' in Him alone I see,
All I need to cleanse and make me fully whole.
In sorrow He's my comfort, in trouble He's my stay,
He tells me every care on Him to roll;
He's the 'Lily of the Valley, the Bright and Morning Star,'
He's the fairest of ten thousand to my soul—"

She wavered at the sound of approaching hoofbeats, going limp with relief when she saw Parker Sentell gallop into camp, along with the giant she'd asked directions from earlier.

Parker shot her a look that told her he was angry with her, but even with his caustic glance, June was relieved to see him.

The men cleared a wide path for the big Pine Ridge foreman. June dropped weakly to the buggy seat. Her knees were so watery that she hoped he wouldn't ask her to get out of the buggy.

The man who had grabbed her hem grinned. "Howdy, Mr. Sentell."

Parker nodded to the camp foreman. "Herschal." His eyes scanned the group of rough men. "What's going on here?"

"Just singin', Mr. Sentell."

Parker gave him a dubious look. "Singing?"

Herschal hung his head. "Aw, me and the boys was jest havin' fun with the little lady. Don't mean no harm."

Parker glanced at June, then back to Herschal. "Then I suggest you apologize to the lady."

Herschal whipped off his hat, nervously twisting the dingy brim in his fingertips. "Sorry, missy."

"The lady's name is Miss Kallahan."

Herschal shot Parker a pained look, then tried again. "Sorry, Miss Kallahan. Didn't mean no harm."

Parker dismissed Herschal with a cold look and turned to June. She swallowed, feeling like a disobedient child caught in the act and about to be punished.

His eyes pinned her. "Shouldn't you be getting back?"

Afraid to further aggravate him, June nodded. Giving Herschal a withering glance, she turned the buggy and followed Parker and Simon out.

When they reached the arch, Parker motioned for her to follow him back to Pine Ridge. She caught her lower lip between her teeth and bit down, wondering about the wisdom of obeying. She would probably be well advised to keep going, but she couldn't. After all, he had rescued her from a frightening encounter.

During the brief ride back to Pine Ridge, she counted her blessings and thanked God for his protection—even if it *had* come in the form of Parker Sentell.

When Parker swung off the black stallion, he handed the reins to a shantyboy. Then he turned to his assistant. "Simon, please stay with our 'guest' until I can figure out what to do."

Simon nodded. "Yes, sir."

Parker stalked into his office and went to his desk. Blast that Miss Kallahan! She was a burr in his side. Stubborn as all get-out. He had been right—she didn't give up easily.

He sighed. It wasn't that he really minded if she brought the loggers services—Lord knew, it might do the men good. He just couldn't stand the thought of connecting his men in any way with Isaac Inman's crusade. Now, if she would take a collection for the orphans, that would be a different story. But she was so set on carrying on Eli's dream, he was sure she would be just as blind to other needs as Isaac was.

He looked out the window at her. She sat quietly in

the buggy, waiting for his decision. Why didn't she go back to Michigan, where she belonged? In spite of himself, he felt a sense of responsibility for her while she remained in Seattle. Out of loyalty to Eli, he couldn't let anything happen to her. And he had to admit that Eli probably would have been proud of her for what she wanted to do.

Expelling a heavy breath, he shoved his chair back from the desk and bellowed out the door. "Simon!"

"Yes, boss?"

"Get in here!"

"Yes, sir!" Simon left his post beside the buggy and strode to the office.

Parker stood at his desk. "What do you think of this cockamamy idea of hers?"

"You want my honest opinion?"

"I don't expect you to humor me."

"I think you're wrong . . . about this Sunday service thing."

Parker nodded. "Go on."

"I think women and children, and some of the men as well, would appreciate a Sunday service. I know I would."

"Are you willing to accompany her to every service and see that she doesn't get into trouble?"

"Yes, sir, I'd be willing to do that."

Parker rubbed his chin, staring in June's direction. "I'd just as soon ship her home as deal with her."

"Yes, sir, but you can't."

Getting up from the desk, Parker moved to the window and stared out. Much as he hated to do it, he knew what he had to do. Finally he turned around to Simon. "Ask Miss Kallahan to step in here."

Simon appeared in the doorway, meeting June's apprehensive gaze. He grinned. "Boss wants to see you."

Gathering her skirts, she climbed down from the wagon, wondering if Parker intended to make a scene before he gave his permission to hold services. She hoped not. One embarrassment a day was quite enough.

Entering his office, she glanced around at the furnishings. Two battered desks, a stove with a large pipe extending through the ceiling, three wooden chairs, and a battered file cabinet. A big window faced east. "Sit down, Miss Kallahan."

She sank down in one of the wooden chairs, her legs still wobbly from the earlier experience.

As Parker paced the wood floor, hands behind his back, his features remained stoic. She remembered his smile earlier in the day and wished he'd engage in the act a little more often. It softened the tight lines around his mouth.

He paused, facing her. "You are sorely trying my patience."

She slid to the edge of the chair. "I don't mean to. For the life of me, I don't know why I anger you. I'm only trying to help."

"Help?" He snorted. "You're determined to hold these services on Sunday?"

There was no need to bear false witness. His friendship with Eli gave him the right to know her intentions. "Yes, sir, I truly am."

She saw there was disapproval on the tip of his tongue. He seemed to war with frustration, then continued pacing.

"You're a stubborn woman, Miss Kallahan."

She didn't know what to say about that. She *was* stubborn. Especially when she was forced to defend a cause she strongly believed in, and she believed strongly in Sunday services for camp women and children, whether he did or not.

"Yes, sir. I've been told that before."

He paced to the window, where he stood staring out, hands still behind his back. He was silent for so long that she was certain he'd forgotten her.

Finally he said in a carefully modulated voice, "If you're so all-fired set on doing this, I won't stop you. A man should be allowed to worship on Sunday. But . . ."

His "but" resonated through the room.

"Only if Simon accompanies you to the services."

"Every one of them?"

"Every one in surrounding camps."

Her pulse leaped. The punishment could be worse. From what she'd seen of Simon, the gentle giant would be more than adequate protection and a delight to be around. After today's experience, it was easy to accept Parker's pronouncement.

"Logging camps are no place for single women." Parker turned from the window, meeting her gaze. "Men tend to forget they're in a lady's presence. I warn you, I can't be responsible for the men's language."

"Perhaps after a few services, they'll be more conscious of their shortcomings."

His face remained stony. "I assure you they won't. The first sign of trouble will be the last of your services." His gaze nailed hers. "Do I make myself clear?"

"Quite clear," she conceded. "I won't be any trouble—I hope to be an inspiration."

He laughed as if she'd said something funny.

She laughed back. She'd show him she could be an inspiration if she wanted.

They stared at each other for an uncomfortably long time until June gave in first. Heaving a defeated sigh, she broke eye contact. "Now that we have that out of our systems, I need to thank you."

"For what?"

"For coming to my rescue earlier. I realize I acted foolishly, and I won't be doing that again. And thank you for allowing me to hold services. I thank you, and others will thank you once the services commence."

"I'm not interested in thank-yous, Miss Kallahan. I'm only interested in keeping the peace. I don't have time to be rescuing you from any more situations like we just walked out of."

"I understand, and I promise that you don't have to worry about me. I'll not go anywhere without Simon."

She leaned forward to hear his mumbled words but could only catch the clipped phrases: "flighty women" and "Simon having to spend his Sundays looking after her" and "what was Eli thinking?" Well, anyway, she was happy he was going to cooperate.

"I promise you won't regret it."

He started out of the office, then turned back to face her. Bracing his large hand on the doorframe, he dropped his bombshell. "By the way, while you're in camp, you are not—and I repeat, *not*—to take up a donation for the Inman Crusade. Not one cent, Miss Kallahan."

She opened her mouth to protest, and his censuring look stopped her.

"Not one cent, Miss Kallahan. Do I make myself clear? Nothing for the tabernacle."

Nothing? How could he be so cold? He was within his rights to forbid her to solicit money, but the tabernacle was for the Lord. Couldn't he see that?

Resigned, she nodded. It was his camp, and after all, money wasn't the issue. The issue was bringing the gospel to others, and he was allowing that. She wouldn't ask for more. Like Aunt Thalia said: "Never look a gift horse in the mouth."

"All right. No offering. You have my word."

Nodding, he walked out, leaving her to savor her small-but-nonetheless-sweet victory.

She had a hunch that wouldn't happen often with Parker Sentell.

Chapter Six

THE crusade tent was filled to capacity. Benches strained beneath the weight of the faithful who returned night after night. June waited for Reverend Inman to mount the platform and take his seat on the right before she slipped onto one end of a wooden bench toward the back.

Someone toward the front stood up and began the first verse of "Praise Him! Praise Him!" in a clear baritone, which was soon joined by the congregation. The richness of the worshipers' efforts more than made up for the scarcity of musical talent.

By the end of the first chorus, most of the people were on their feet, lifting their voices toward heaven.

"Praise Him! Praise Him! Jesus, our blessed Redeemer!
For our sins He suffered, and bled and died.

He our Rock, our hope of eternal salvation,
Hail Him! Hail Him! Jesus the Crucified."

Mixed emotions flooded June. Even though she had never attended a meeting with Eli, she felt his presence strongly. She missed him, though she'd known him so briefly. She couldn't help feeling that the work would suffer.

"Love unbounded, wonderful, deep and strong."

Eli had loved his work, and she'd caught a glimpse of how much he seemed to have loved people. She hoped to fill an infinitesimal part of the gap left by his untimely passing.

She opened her eyes as the voices blended sweetly into "I Must Tell Jesus," a hymn that spoke directly to the heart.

"I must tell Jesus all of my trials
I cannot bear these burdens alone."

Creases etched in careworn faces lifted toward heaven as each, in his or her own way, told Jesus a particular trial or burden. What a blessing it was to come together and know that no concern was ever too small for Jesus to care about. June found herself questioning why a godly man like Eli was allowed to die—She caught herself. Surely Eli would not want her to question. God was in control.

She drew a resigned breath and slowly released it. It would dishonor Eli if she, even for a moment, doubted that his life, as well as his death, could, and would, be used by God for the good he intended.

She joined with the chorus, "I must tell Jesus! I must tell Jesus!"

As the words faded, the crowd fell silent. When the last rustle, the last foot scrape, had settled, only then did

Reverend Inman approach the front of the narrow stage.
June thought he looked tired tonight, drawn, as if the
weight of the world rested on his shoulders.

His eyes scanned the crowd. Then he spoke. "I quote
from Hosea 8:7. 'For they have sown the wind, and they
shall reap the whirlwind: it hath no stalk: the bud shall
yield no meal: if so be it yield, the strangers shall swallow
it up.' "

Rubbing his hand across his face, he continued softly,
"It is we, the believers, the ones chosen by God to do his
work, who must work for his kingdom. We must build
the vessel in which to rescue those who are lost in sin."

June listened to the message, fully understanding why
Eli had nearly idolized this dynamic man of God. His
words, his reflections, his crisp, clear commands gleaned
from the Word brought goose bumps to her arms. He
brought heaven down to earth during the ensuing hour
and a half.

"And I say unto you: The Lord's work will be done! Will
you be there?" Reverend Inman's voice rose to a fever
pitch. "Will you be the one to build the vessel? Will you be
there to throw out the lifeline?" The crowd swelled to their
feet, their voices lifted in praise.

"Throw out the lifeline!
Throw out the lifeline!
Someone is drifting away."

"Will you close your eyes against the light? Will you
harden your heart against the work? Or will you help
build the tabernacle?" Reverend Inman's voice swept the
crowd, bringing men and women to their feet. They
continued singing in unison while making their way to
the altar. Collection baskets were passed around. People
dug deep, tossing coins, some dollars, into the baskets.

The Spirit of the Lord was moving, and his people responded with open hearts.

June recalled Eli's glowing praise of Reverend Inman, how he was a visionary, able to see and do great things. He propelled God's people to action. Workers extolled his goodness, his purity of heart. He was a man devoted to God, a man who worked unceasingly to bring hope to the lost and weary.

June dropped a coin into the passing basket, wishing she could contribute a king's ransom. She'd heard of people who accused Christians of placing too much emphasis on money. Papa once explained that giving was necessary to a Christian's spiritual wellness. God did not need a person's money, but giving for the kingdom was a way his child could become more Christlike and less self-centered. Papa contended that a person's attitude toward giving reflected where his or her heart truly was.

Friday dawned cool and overcast. Pewter gray edged the horizon and promised more rain. As the day wore on, the gray deepened. During the afternoon, June prepared for her visit to the logging camps on the coming Sunday. Filled with the prospect of bringing the gospel to those who were hungry to hear it, she selected Scriptures and fashioned colorful paper chains with Bible verses written on them.

As time for the evening services drew near, the wind picked up. Fingers of lightning embroidered rolling clouds. By five o'clock the lamps were lit in order for people to find their way into the tent.

Hanging lamps oscillated crazily on wooden pegs as the wind battered the tent. Sides and top flapped like a great, angry canvas bird. June pulled her shawl closer as she threaded her way through the milling crowd.

"Good evening, Miss June." Ben doffed his hat when he spotted her, bowing from the waist.

"Good evening, Ben. Looks like we're in for a storm." Ben's childlike features folded. "Ben don't like storms."

June reached to grasp his hand. His skin was cold and rough from hard work. "Are you frightened?"

Lifting his head, he smiled. "Ben's not afraid. God loves Ben. Ben loves God. My Father tells Ben not to be afraid."

Squeezing his hand, June wondered at his perfect innocence. "With God on our side, who can be against us?"

Ben nodded with childlike zeal. "No one against us when God is for us."

He wandered around, checking each lantern to make certain it was secure in the rising wind. June busied herself with the offering baskets, placing them beneath the correct pews, out of the way but easy to locate by those taking the nightly contribution.

Half an hour before services, there wasn't a seat left. June thought the threatening weather might keep some worshipers away, especially the older citizens and those with younger children, but the faithful didn't let a little rain stop them.

The rumble of thunder accompanied voices lifted in song as Reverend Inman took his seat on the platform. Bright lightning flashes illuminated the tent, and the wind continued to rise, snapping canvas in time with the beat of the song. Ben and other workers prowled the outer aisles, keeping a close eye on the lanterns and the elongated canvas.

With impeccable timing, Reverend Inman stood up, and June felt the crowd's energy surge. Resolute voices became even more forceful with musical praise.

How did Reverend Inman accomplish such a miraculous transformation? Eli and Papa were mighty workers for the Lord. But Reverend Inman . . . Reverend Inman hummed with charisma—literally compelling the worshiper to follow God, to respond.

Tonight the offering baskets were passed again and again. June spotted Parker sitting toward the back. He was accompanied tonight by Simon and two other loggers. The big loggers filled the wooden bench. Parker looked over to catch June's eyes as the basket passed in front of him. She smiled, but his mouth tightened and accusation colored his features.

Disappointment swept over her. Parker had a powerful influence over his men. If he weren't so stubborn, so *thickheaded,* he would support, not hinder, her work— Eli's work—and more importantly, God's work. Bitterness over Eli's death still twisted Parker's opinion of Reverend Inman. She had to concede that perhaps Reverend Inman was caught up in his dream—at times to the point of obsession—but it was still a worthy dream.

Jesus, she breathed, closing her eyes, *touch Parker's heart. Soften it toward your work. Allow him to see that Reverend Inman is only doing your will; his dream is to provide a place that will demonstrate the glorious splendor of God, a place like no other where people can worship God. Open Parker's eyes so that Reverend Inman's dream can be realized. Let him be a help instead of a hindrance.*

"Well, well, God's little emissary! You're gettin' to be a pest." Anthony Riggings dropped a coin in June's tin cup, and the teasing light left his eyes. "Wish it could be more, girlie."

"God will stretch it, Anthony. Remember the two fish and five loaves of bread?"

"Thought it was two loaves of bread and five fish."

"Nope," she teased. "Two mackerel and five loaves of cracked wheat." She grinned good-naturedly at the burly, redheaded logger. "Haven't seen you in services all week!"

Anthony faked a bad cough. "Been laid up, I have."

"You'll be back soon?"

He coughed again, more convincingly this time. "Shore plan to try."

June grinned, shaking her head as he wove down the street. She guessed she couldn't expect money *and* a miracle.

Dumping the coins into a bag, she buttoned her cloak and hurried to the waiting buggy. She'd promised to go to the tabernacle site with Reverend Inman this afternoon.

Visiting the site had turned into a daily ritual for him. Reverend Inman seemed to draw sustenance from the rite, as if seeing the land it would occupy, visualizing the tabernacle again and again, kept the vision alive in his mind.

"I can see it," Reverend Inman said, sweeping his hand parallel with the horizon as they stood at the site. "The auditorium will be there—so the morning sun will stream through the windows."

June knew the planned structure by heart. Reverend Inman would go on and on about building plans. Wooden stakes surrounded the construction area. Reverend Inman had staked the site with such joy, such adoration, it was exhilarating to watch.

"Come spring, ground will be broken," he promised. "We will build the tabernacle from lumber taken from these very woods so the people will feel a part of it all." His eyes burned with fevered conviction. "I've patterned the tabernacle after a cathedral Katherine and I once saw in England—have I mentioned that? People will come by land and by sea to witness this glorious spectacle." Arms spread wide, he obviously envisioned the wondrous sight.

"Across the front will be three sweeping gables: one over the double front door and one over each portal.

"Over the front door I see a rose-colored window, a circle, representing eternity. Flanking the window, two multifoil windows over double lancet windows. Stained glass, yes, beautiful stained glass. When the sun streams through the colored panes, the interior will be bathed in heaven's light.

"Here—above the stained glass, I'll build a cross erected between two towers." He clasped a balled fist to his mouth, choked with emotion. "I wish—how I wish the towers could be marble, but the money—always the money."

Turning, his eyes reviewed the uneven ground. "I'll place the altar here, seats for the clergy and choir in the chancel. The pulpit here." His gaze centered on the area where the front wall would stand.

"When the doors are thrown open, the altar will be in full view, the choir loft behind. Behind the choir I picture a pristine white wall with a wooden cross. The grain of the wood will imitate bloodstains."

June was momentarily disconcerted, frightened almost, by the reverend's intensity. His eyes burned with fanatical zeal. Reverend Inman's words became Eli's, or was it the other way around? Eli had used the same grand description when he visualized the shrine. She thought it was his dream too, but was it possible Reverend Inman had imagined the tabernacle aloud so many times that the words had become ingrained in Eli's mind?

When June left a short while later, she felt a sense of unease. Something troubled her. Something that remained, nagged, hung on the rest of the day.

After services that evening, June collected the baskets and took them into a small alcove behind the stage.

Reverend Inman swept into the small space as she finished, his features animated tonight.

"God moved among his people tonight!"

"Yes," June murmured absently, stacking coins into one-dollar piles.

Reverend Inman peered over her shoulder. "The offering doesn't look as generous as previous nights."

"It's most generous," she assured him.

He frowned as his eye skimmed the piles of coins. "No, no, I'm sure it isn't. Were all the baskets passed? If the offerings fall off, the tabernacle will suffer. We can't allow that to happen. God's people must be involved." He started to pace the cramped space, speaking to no one in particular. "It's imperative—the people must be a part of this great venture."

He paused, pinching his lower lip between his thumb and forefinger. "I must enhance the commitment. I must be more adamant about the tabernacle's significance."

June glanced up. There was something about his demeanor. Gone was the charismatic, commanding figure who had spoken so eloquently from the pulpit earlier, a man who knelt and prayed with the sick and the hurting. A man who, with tears streaming down his cheeks, prayed with the sinner for redemption. Now he spoke as if the tabernacle were all consuming, as if nothing else mattered.

Reverend Inman ceased pacing. "Tomorrow night I will preach on the man who built bigger barns." Digging his pocket watch out of his vest, he snapped it open and noted the time. "It's late. Will you be all right here alone?"

"Of course—"

"When you're finished, you will put the offering into the safe and lock it. Do you understand?"

"I understand." She followed the same ritual every night. "Ben always helps me."

"Good. Ben's a good man. I'll go over the ledgers in the morning."

When Reverend Inman left, June sat for a moment, staring at the piles of coins covering the scarred wooden table. So much money—staggering amounts—and yet Reverend Inman was distraught with the shortfall. For the life of her, she couldn't understand why. Was Reverend Inman beginning to lose perspective? She'd heard Papa talk about good men who lost sight of their intent and became caught up in their eagerness to achieve. She shook the troubling thought aside. She'd been in a strange mood all day. Why should she question Reverend Inman's motives? She had been so sure God had sought Reverend Inman out to build the tabernacle. Eli had been sure.

Funds must be raised to further God's kingdom, and that was her purpose now. She'd never heard Reverend Inman purposely ply guilt in order to spur healthier offerings.

She finished counting the money, entered the final tally into the ledger, and put it and the money into the safe. She turned the lock.

She jumped when Ben unexpectedly poked his head through the tent opening. "Do you need Ben, Miss June?"

Hand over her heart, June met his expectant gaze. "No, I've taken care of the money, Ben. You can go home."

Ben grinned. "Thank you." His childlike eyes scanned her dress. "You look so pretty tonight. I like blue."

Her cheeks grew hot at the compliment. "Thank you, Ben."

"Mr. Parker was here tonight?"

"Yes, he was here." She recalled the way Parker's eyes had turned on her in silent accusation during the offering. Did he attend services to be her accuser, or did he attend in order to worship his heavenly Father?

Reverend Inman's earlier mood clouded her mind as

she slipped into her cloak. Parker clearly wanted no part of the tabernacle, yet he attended Reverend Inman's services. Did he honestly feel the tabernacle was an obsession for Reverend Inman—that Reverend Inman, without knowing it, was consumed with the project?

Had he seen in Reverend Inman something she had barely glimpsed tonight?

She blew out the lamp and let herself out. Waving good night to Ben, she walked toward the complex.

Parker must be wrong about Reverend Inman. The reverend was a man of God. His people adored him, and he loved them back. He would never compromise God's work to gratify his own desires.

Given enough time, she would prove Parker wrong—make him see that Reverend Inman's dream was God's plan.

Chapter Seven

JUNE was dressing Saturday morning when a knock sounded at her door. She hurriedly fastened the last hook on her black wool dress. Who could be calling so early?

"Hey in there! Open up! You got yourself a visitor!"

"Sam!" June squealed with delight, nearly tipping over the vanity as she rushed to open the door.

"And who else could it be with a voice like this?" Samantha Harris challenged.

Flinging open the door, June threw herself into Sam's arms and hugged her. The two girls giggled and danced a half circle, holding each other. June finally stood back for a good look at her dear friend. "If you aren't a sight for sore eyes!"

Sam grinned, her big hazel eyes rich with mischief. "Look like somethin' the cats dragged in, ay?"

Laughing, June pulled her into the room and closed the door. "What do you think of the complex?"

"Interesting, lovey—a bit confusin' to live in, is it not?"

Squeezing Sam's hand affectionately, June drank in the sight of her. She hadn't realized until this moment how very much she missed her. "It's so good to see you."

"It's good to see you too, lovey! Sorry it took so long." Her freckled features sobered. "I've been wantin' to come see you, desperately so, I 'ave. But me Aunt Angie . . . well, she's been quite ill these days, taken to her bed, she 'as."

June wanted to console her. "I'm so sorry. Is there anything I can do?"

"No . . . not much anyone can do," Sam admitted.

June drew her back into her arms for another close embrace. "Oh, Sam! God can! Tonight I'll request special prayer for her at services."

Sam brightened. "Would you, lovey? I'd be most appreciative!"

"I'd pray regardless, but don't you worry. God can have your aunt feeling better in no time." Draping her arm around Sam's boyish shoulders, June steered her to the only chair in the room.

Sam glanced around the small quarters, grinning. "Got yourself a quaint little place here."

Regardless of the size of her new home, June was grateful for the shelter it provided. The complex was old and drafty, and Ettie was forever saying Reverend Inman desperately needed to build a new one—but, of course, that would take money, money the ministry didn't have. "I'm comfortable here, truly I am. And everyone is so good to me."

Sam elbowed her with a knowing wink. "Suppose that

includes 'ubby! I'll wager all of London 'e's not complainin'. Considers it to be quite the cozy place for 'im-
self and 'is smashing new bride."

June's face fell. In all the excitement she'd forgotten
about Eli. "No . . . Eli isn't complaining. Didn't you
get my message?"

"Message?" Sam tilted her head, a sly grin on her face.
"Are you pullin' me leg? I didn't get any message." Her
features suddenly sobered. "Is somethin' amiss?"

"Sam . . . my husband-to-be—Eli Messenger—passed
away before we could be married."

For a moment the words didn't appear to have registered. Then Sam's hand shot to her heart, and the color
drained from under her freckles. "Passed away? As in
. . . died?"

June sank to the side of the bed. Poor Sam, the news
must have come as a shock. She'd paid a messenger one
nickel to go to the orphanage and inform Sam about Eli's
death, but apparently the scallywag had fled with the
money. It was still difficult for her to think about Eli's
untimely death, much less talk about it. She reached for a
hankie on the nightstand.

Sam knelt by the bedside to console her. "Come on,
now. 'e isn't really dead, a young man like 'im. You can
be honest with me, lovey."

June shook her head. "He's gone, Sam."

"Well, 'ow dare 'e!" Sam stood up, ready to fight. Her
eyes scanned the tiny quarters. "Now where did the
rogue run off to? Never you worry, lovey, 'e'll not get
away with breakin' your 'eart. We'll hunt 'im down like a
dog, we will, and when we find the scoundrel we'll—"

June took a deep breath and interrupted her tirade.
"Eli is dead, Sam. When I arrived, Eli was very sick.
Remember? Reverend Inman met us at the dock? Every-
one thought Eli was getting better. We barely had time to

95

introduce ourselves before . . . well, before the Lord called him home."

Sam whistled under her breath. "Oh, dear. Then 'e is . . ."

June nodded. "Dead."

"Oh my . . . how awful. So sorry, lovey. What a bloomin' rotten turn of luck."

"I'm trying not to question what's happened. God called Eli home. I don't understand why, but I know there must be a reason."

Nodding, Sam blew her nose, which was suddenly red with emotion. "Aye, me auntie says there's just some things we aren't supposed to question." She was silent for a long moment. "Still, it's a bloomin' shame. Just a bloomin' shame."

June nodded. "A bloomin' shame." Once the tabernacle was built, she would feel obligated to return to Cold Water.

Sam sat down at the table, toying with June's hairbrush. "So, what will you do now?"

"I'm going to stay on and finish the work Eli started."

Sam looked up expectantly. "And what work is that, lovey?"

June explained the tabernacle and how Eli and Reverend Inman shared the same dream. There was so much she wanted to tell Sam, so many hopes, so many fears. "I've collected over two hundred dollars in the short time I've been here."

"Ow, now that's lovely. It's like me mum says. There's nothin' a woman can't do if she sets 'er mind to it."

June dried her tears, hope overtaking her pessimism. If God had a purpose for her, he would sustain her. Leaning across the table, she clasped Sam's freckled hand. "We have so much to talk about. Can you stay the afternoon?"

"Yes, today is one of Auntie's better days. I needn't be back till time for evenin' chores."

"Wonderful! Are you hungry? Would you like to go for a walk? I'll ask Ettie to bring—"

"Whoa, whoa! I'm not 'ungry." She patted her flat stomach. "Gettin' fat as a hog, I am. All those beans and potatoes. A nice, brisk walk would do me heart good!"

Elated to be reunited, June happily agreed. A day with her best friend was exactly what she needed.

On the way out, the women stopped by the kitchen and pilfered two large buttermilk biscuits, generously spread with Ettie's blackberry jam. In between sticky bites, they giggled and caught up on the news.

"Has your Aunt Angie been sick long?"

"Aye, but she's worsened over the month. Some days are better than others. To look at 'er you'd think there was nothing amiss." Sam licked blackberry jam from between her fingers. "Doc says it's 'er 'eart. Plumb worn to a nubbin, it is. I'm not surprised. She's given a 'unk of it to everyone who's ever needed it. And she is gettin' on in years, you know."

"How old is she?"

"She says seventy-three, but I think it's more like eighty." She took a bite of biscuit, chewing thoughtfully. "Me mum says it's only a matter of time. Can't bear the thought of losing me auntie, but it's the children's plight that pains me more."

"The orphans?"

"Aye, the poor wee tykes. Don't know what will happen to them when Auntie passes on. She takes in stray kiddies like some folks take in abandoned kitties."

June was afraid she knew the answer. Cold Water had a small orphanage. It was run down and needy, managed by an elderly couple who loved children. When Edward Rugby died and then a year later his wife, Millie, passed away, the poor babies were left with no one to look after them. If Aunt Angeline died, her orphans would undoubtedly be fated to be uprooted again. "What will happen to the children?"

Sam's face firmed. "They'll stay together, if I have me say about it."

"You? Sam, you can't possibly take on such a responsibility by yourself. How old are you?"

"Seventeen, come next winter."

Barely sixteen, and this girl with a heart of gold was willing to give her life in service to the orphanage. Sam stiffened with pride. "I can do it, I can! Sick as Auntie's been, she barely pulls 'er share of the load now. Taught me a thing or two, she has. Besides, I got Ol' Joe." She grinned. "And even though Joe might be pushing eighty, he ain't goin' nowhere. Leastways, not anytime soon. He's fit as a fiddle and strong as an ox."

"Ol' Joe who?"

"Ol' Joe—the Indian man. You remember—he came to fetch me the day we got here."

June did recall an elderly white-haired gentleman standing beside a wagon with *Angeline's Orphanage* painted on the sides.

"Sam—is he dangerous?"

"Dangerous?" Sam had a good laugh. "Ol' Joe? 'e's about the nicest Yakima you'd ever want to meet."

June paled. "What's a Yakima?"

Sam laughed all the harder. "You're a bloomin' innocent! Yakima is a native tribe that live in these parts."

"Where did Aunt Angie get Ol' Joe?"

"Where did she get him? Ain't like she fetched 'im from the mercantile along with the rest of the supplies."

June felt incredibly foolish. "Of course not. I just meant—"

"Ow, I know what you meant, lovey. No matter. Ol' Joe just showed up on Auntie's doorstep one day, cold, hungry, nowhere left to go after the war."

"War?"

"The war—you know, the nasty dispute the settlers had with the Yakima a long time ago."

June was impressed with Sam's knowledge of the area's heritage. She didn't know a thing about any war.

"Joe was much younger then. 'Course Aunt Angie was too. 'e needed work, and Aunt Angie sure needed 'elp, so she took 'im in and 'e's lived there ever since. Been a real godsend, 'e 'as."

"If an Indian ever showed up on my doorstep, I would be scared to death," June confessed. "Here's one of my favorite places." She stopped at the edge of a small pond.

Sam rolled her eyes. "Ya big scaredy. It was a bit spooky at first. Neither Auntie nor Joe could speak each other's language. And their customs were so different from each other's. They must have made quite a sight."

June smiled, picturing the colorful aunt and the Yakima. "But it all worked out?"

"This is a beautiful place, June." Sam leaned over and picked up a rock to skip across the pond. The water shimmered like glass in the bright sunshine. "Worked out quite well, actually. First they taught each other their native language, which, according to Auntie, was no easy task. But I suppose the most difficult part was adapting to each other's customs. Auntie Angie reads the Bible every night. As soon as Ol' Joe could understand the words, 'e couldn't get enough. 'e used to be called by his Yakima name. Auntie thought it proper he be given a Christian name. She settled on Job. Joe liked that, liked it real well. But it didn't take long to see it wasn't fittin'.

"Joe didn't have a whole lot of patience; still doesn't. So, on one of 'is particularly testy days, Auntie jerked the Job off, and she's called 'im Joe ever since."

June laughed, recalling how Aunt Thalia lacked patience too. "Did Joe make her smoke a peace pipe?"

"Ol' Joe? He'd been choked if 'e'd dared to try, but Auntie did make 'im do the dishes. Took 'im forever to get the knack of it. 'ates it, 'e does. Been tryin' to get out of it ever since!"

June sighed. "I don't know, Sam. It all sounds so scary to me."

Sam paused to look at her. "Joe doin' the dishes?" She giggled. "Nothin' scary 'bout it, lovey. Joe teases that 'e's the only Yakima in these parts with dishpan hands!"

"No, no, Ol' Joe doesn't sound scary; it's scary that your aunt is ill and the children will have no one if something should happen to her."

"Aye, that part is scary, it is. They'll have Joe and me, but we won't be able to do much to 'old it together. Auntie's barely able to keep food on the table and shoes on the kiddies' feet."

"You're sure Ol' Joe is harmless?" June kidded.

Sam solemnly crossed her heart. "Honest Injun!"

Both burst into laughter. June was relieved to lighten the mood.

"Seriously," Sam said with great certainty, "Joe's real good about helping. Chauffeurs Auntie and the children anywhere they need to go. Tends the garden, chops wood, hauls water. Whatever needs doin', he's right there. I don't even think of him as an Indian, a Brit, or a Yank, for that matter. He's just a decent man."

June agreed. Yakima, white, or any color of the rainbow, he was one of God's children. He need be nothing more, and certainly he was nothing less. She stood. "Come on. I have something I want you to see."

The two young women walked across the meadow and turned to climb a small rise.

"Where are we goin'?" Sam bent over and rubbed the backs of her legs. "Me dogs are killin' me."

"Your dogs?" June glanced behind her. She hadn't seen any dogs.

Sam lifted a heavy boot and pointed. "Dogs."

"Oh, your feet!" June laughed. "Well, let's shed these boots."

Sam didn't need a second invitation. She dropped to the ground and stripped off the heavy leather boots. Her feet were generously sprinkled with the same russet freckles as her face.

June quickly joined her, and soon they were both barefoot, wiggling their toes with newfound freedom. Tying their boot strings together, they slung the shoes across their shoulders and started up the grassy embankment. It was far too cold to be going barefoot; the abrasive blades of grass were like icy needles beneath their toes.

"Isn't this the grandest thing!" Sam wiggled her freckled toes in ankle-tall weeds.

"It's marvelous!" June felt lighthearted and carefree for the first time in weeks. Aunt Thalia would have apoplexy if she knew June was going barefoot this soon.

"You never did say where we are 'eading."

"You'll see." June wanted to surprise her. "I'm taking you to a special place that will suck the breath right out of you. A sight unlike any you've ever seen!"

Sam eyed her curiously. "I'm not terribly sure I want to 'ave the breath sucked out of me."

June laughed. It was wonderful to feel young again! "Look, Sam! Another pond. This one has cattails!"

"Cat's what?"

"Cattails—come on. Let's pick some!"

"Have you lost your bloomin' mind! What would we do with a bouquet of animal tails!" Sam protested as June pulled her toward the water's edge.

"You'll see!"

The girls busied themselves picking cattails, arranging them in a huge brown bouquet.

Sam waded out of the water and handed hers to June. "Here, lovey. I think you've lost your bloomin' mind."

Smiling, June took her hand, and the two girls raced

back to the rise. When they reached the top, they paused to catch their breath. June pointed below. A single white cross stood alone in the peaceful meadow.

"They're for Eli. I try to bring fresh ones whenever I can."

"Oh, lovey—" Sam took her hand—"I'm sorry."

"You needn't be." June smiled. "Eli's in a far better place. I bring the cattails to remind passersby what a wonderful person he was."

Sam frowned. "Shouldn't you be bringing flowers?"

June gave her a pained look. "Sam, where would I find flowers this time of year in Seattle?"

"I say, I quite forgot for a moment where we were. Cattails are just fine."

The two women placed the bouquet on the mound of fresh dirt beneath the white cross. For a moment they stood in silence, paying their respects to Eli Messenger, a young man buried beneath a simple cross with a crudely engraved marker that read, "Asleep in Jesus."

June's hand crept into Sam's. "He would have been a very good husband."

"Aye, that 'e would, lovey. The best."

Halfway across the meadow, the ground sloped to a tranquil valley. The view was mesmerizing. Tall pines stretched into the flawless blue sky. The spicy scent of pine perfumed the air.

"Wow!" Sam murmured. "Do you suppose heaven must look a bit like this?"

June glowed. "Do you like it?"

Sam's eyes welled with appreciation. "Like it? It's so lovely it makes me puddle."

"Not a prettier place this side of heaven."

"I bloomin' well reckon not!" Sam sniffed, wiping her eyes with the sleeves of her dress.

"This is where Reverend Inman plans to build the tabernacle."

"Clean down there!" Sam exclaimed. "He must be off his nut! How will he ever—?"

June laughed. "Not down there. Up here. Right here—on the very spot where we're standing."

"I'm not one to know much about such matters," Sam admitted. Her freckles stood out in the harsh, cold light. She glanced around uneasily. "Should we be standing on such sacred ground?"

Nodding, June took a deep breath of the sweet air. "We're God's children. We can stand on any ground we want, 'cause we're heirs to the kingdom!" she proclaimed proudly.

"That's so beautiful, it makes me want to pray," Sam said solemnly. "And that's something I don't do a whole lot of."

"Shame on you, Sam Harris." June took her hand and pulled her to her knees. "We'll pray together, right here, right now."

Sam groaned as her knees met the grassy knoll. June looked over at her solemnly. "Do you want to start?"

Sam shook her head.

"Then I will. Bow your head."

"Me toes are cold," Sam murmured. "Bloomin' well should have stayed 'ome today."

"Father, we bow before you, thanking you for this marvelous day, for shared friendship, for unspeakable beauty. We thank you for Eli Messenger's life, and for his death, for we know you can work both for your glory. Bless Reverend Inman; grant him wisdom and strength to bring hope to the hundreds of lost and lonely who gather every night to hear your Word.

"Forgive us our sins, and protect us from harm. Bless Aunt Angie, and allow her to remain with us a while longer, Lord. She's needed so very much. Bless the children, Lord. Keep them safe and happy and protected.

Bless Ol' Joe, and keep him healthy so he can serve the children.

"Most of all, we praise you for your love, for sending your only Son to die on the cross so that we may have eternal life. Forgive our sins, and help us to do better. We ask in Jesus' name. Amen."

Pulling Sam to her feet, June smiled. "Now, that wasn't so hard, was it?"

Sam rubbed her aching knees. "Not as long as you do the talkin'. Do you come here every day?"

"Every day. Come, let me show you the tabernacle."

"Show me? It ain't been built yet, 'as it?"

"No, but I can make you see it."

Sam listened intently as June described the temple, its beauty and opulence, how Reverend Inman planned to pattern it after a great European cathedral, with the three magnificent arches, the stately portals, the beautiful stained-glass windows.

"It will surely cost a bloomin' fortune to build something like that!" Sam said.

"I suppose it will, but Reverend Inman says the Lord deserves the best."

"That's exactly what 'e'll be getting when this tabernacle is finished." Sam looked off in the distance, trouble coloring her features.

"Is something wrong?" June asked. She had detected a tone of sadness in Sam's voice.

"No, not really." Sam sat down, wiggling her toes. "It's bloomin' cold, it is."

"Want to put your boots on?"

"Not yet."

"Then what's wrong? Does something about the tabernacle bother you?"

"No—it's just all that money. When I think about what that amount of money, or just a smidgen of it, could do for the orphanage. . . . It could buy new shoes, schoolbooks, a woodstove for the upstairs. We 'ave a small one downstairs, but it can't begin to heat the entire house. And clothes. Nice warm coats and mittens. Clothes at the orphanage 'ave been 'anded down from one to the other so often that they're threadbare and hardly serviceable. Doesn't take long to go through clothes with all those kids—and more comin' every day. They come in all shapes and sizes, you know. From the oldest, twelve, right down to the toddler, who turned two last week."

June knew it must be difficult to feed and clothe so many children. "Others help, don't they? Donate money and food?"

Sam shook her head. "Aye, you'd think they would, and Auntie says they used to 'elp a sight more than they do now. The loggers are kind to the little ones, but nobody gives as much as they used to." She tsked. "There are so many in the community who could help. . . . Such a bloomin' shame."

"I know it must be difficult." Raising money for the tabernacle was hard enough. "Is there anything I can do to help?"

"Oh, lovey! Do you mean it? We can always use help!" Sam exclaimed.

"Then consider me an extra pair of hands. I have lots of free time, and I'd be more than glad to help. I haven't any money to offer, but I have a heart full of love, and Aunt Thalia says I can take a stove apart and black it as good as anybody. I can mop floors and hang wash. Not to be prideful, but you should taste my elderberry jelly. Papa said there was none better!"

"God bless you, June Kallahan! Not only can we use your help, but it will allow you and me to spend more time together. You'll love Auntie and the kids."

"I'd love to help, but I'll need to consult Reverend Inman. Then I'll need to rearrange my schedule—perhaps

I can spend mornings at the orphanage, afternoons in front of The Gilded Hen, and evenings at tent services counting the nightly offering. I have to keep my previous commitments, but I think I should be able to help you out too."

Excitement welled in June. She would love the children. And it wouldn't interfere with her work for Reverend Inman or the tabernacle. She'd make sure of it. *Glory be! Praise God and alleluia!*

"I can't wait to get started!"

"When can you start?"

"Soon, Sam. I can't say exactly when—but soon."

Sam's face fell. "Ow. I was rather gettin' me 'opes up you could start tomorrow."

June shook her head. "Tomorrow is Sunday, Sam."

"Ow, yes—I suppose you'll be wanting to attend services."

"Not attend, teach."

Sam frowned. "Aye, now you be pullin' me leg."

"Sam, I would never pull your leg. I'm serious." June explained her plan to hold Sunday services at nearby logging camps, starting with Pine Ridge, Parker Sentell's camp.

"Well, that does sound admirable." Sam thought for a moment. "Who's Parker Sentell?"

Taking her arm, June turned her around, and they started back. A cold wind had sprung up, and clouds were rolling in. "Now that's a story that will take more than an afternoon to tell."

"Ow." Sam winked. "A right 'andsome one, ay?"

"Most handsome," June conceded. "And incredibly stubborn!"

"How on earth did you get those loggers to agree to church services? 'ear tell, they're real rascals."

The observation reminded June of the day she had disregarded Parker's warning and gone into the rival camp alone. She shuddered. The men were rascals all right. Depraved ones. She didn't know what would have happened if Parker hadn't rescued her. June suddenly stopped, bringing her hands to her hips as she fixed Sam with a stern look. "Would you like to attend Sunday's service?"

"Ow, no, lovey. . . ." Sam looked doubtful.

"Wonderful!" June slipped her arm back through Sam's. "And someday very soon, you can take me to meet Aunt Angie and the children. Meanwhile, you can start coming to services. It will do you good."

"Ow dear, I've fell in it now, 'aven't I? Well . . . OK, I'll come to your services when I can—because you're such a good friend." Her eyes swept the darkening sky. "And if we've got a pound of smarts between us, I say we be 'eadin' back. From the looks of those clouds movin' in, we're apt to get caught in the middle of a gully washer."

June studied the bank of dark rain clouds. "I think you're right. And I think we'd best be putting our boots back on—in case we have to make a run for it."

"Or a swim for it," Sam groused.

The two women sat down on the grass and laced up their boots. When the last knot was tied, Sam sprang to her feet. "Race ya!"

In no time at all, Sam was little more than a speck in the distance. June was just getting to her feet.

When June reached the revival tent, a rested-looking Sam was perched jauntily on a bench, eating an apple. "Where you been, slowpoke?"

Trying to catch her breath, June leaned forward, panting. "Are you part rabbit?"

"Lynx," Sam conceded.

Exhausted, June dropped to the bench and tried to catch her breath. "I'm so glad you're here, Sam."

"Me too, lovey. Me too." Sam lifted her eyes to the

threatening weather. "But I best be going. It's about to open up and pour any minute."

"I'll ask Ben to drive you home in the buggy."

"Nah, I got Sissy." Sam pitched the apple core away, then brushed dust from her skirt.

"Sissy?"

"Me mule." Pulling June to her feet, she propelled her to the side of the tent, where she'd tied the animal earlier. "Meet Sissy, one fine mule."

"But you'll get soaked!" June protested as she felt the first sprinkling of raindrops hit her cheek.

"Not me." Sam bunched up her skirt and slid bareback onto the mule.

"You will unless you've got feathers like a duck!"

"Got me something even better." Sam reached across Sissy's bridle and prominently displayed her treasure. "I got me a bumbershoot."

Sissy turned her head, staring at June with big brown eyes that would melt a stone.

With a flick of her wrist, Sam proudly snapped the faded red umbrella open.

The sudden noise made June jump. She doubted anything so tattered would protect Sam from a sprinkle, let alone a downpour. The umbrella was so small, it scarcely covered Sam's head.

"Are you sure you don't want Ben to drive you? It'd be no trouble."

Sam gently nudged Sissy's flanks. "See you tomorrow then . . . at services. Pine Ridge, you say?"

"Nine o'clock."

"Nine o'clock."

"Sharp."

"Sharp."

The big gray mule obediently trotted off. "See you tomorrow!" Sam waved with her left hand, holding the reins and umbrella in her right, bouncing high on Sissy's back.

An hour after revival services, people still milled around the tent. The altar call had lasted unusually long; fifty or more had come to profess their faith. June had a difficult time keeping her mind on business. Hard as she tried, she kept seeing Sam on the back of that old mule, waving that silly "bumbershoot." She prayed that her friend had made it safely back to the orphanage and that Aunt Angie wasn't any worse. . . . If anything happened to Aunt Angie, the orphans would have to find new homes. . . . They had worn-out shoes—improper heating. They needed so much.

When the tent eventually cleared, June disappeared into the small room behind the pulpit to count money. Ben and several other ushers piled the overflowing collection baskets on the large wooden table. Tonight's service was large and required that even more baskets be passed. The offerings seemed endless.

Counting the donations, June's mind returned to the orphans. Sam's words about the needs at the orphanage turned over in her mind. Shoes, clothes, food.

June shook the troubling thoughts aside. The tabernacle was important too. The orphanage served the needs of a pitiful few. The tabernacle would serve thousands.

The kerosene lamp burned low when she finally finished. She penciled the amount in the ledger, tucking it and the money inside the safe.

Pulling on her cloak, she thought of the orphans again. New shoes, warm clothes, adequate food, a stove for upstairs. Hardly selfish needs—important ones, that desperately needed to be addressed.

Her gaze focused on the safe. The outpouring of love had been so large tonight. Perhaps if she were to bring the children's needs to Reverend Inman's attention, he would help. Just a portion—perhaps twenty dollars? The amount would purchase staples for the orphanage for a month, if nothing else.

As she was about to snuff out the lamp and go in search of the reverend, he suddenly pulled back the curtain and entered the room.

"Reverend."

"Hello, my dear. Wonderful service tonight—so many responses. The angels surely are rejoicing."

Reverend Inman removed his wire-rimmed glasses and polished them with his handkerchief. June noticed that his worn overcoat had seen better days.

"Reverend, you should buy yourself a new coat. The one you're wearing isn't adequate protection against the cold wind."

"Nonsense. It's fine—any spare coin I have goes toward the tabernacle." He rubbed his hands together to warm them. "Did you see the crowd tonight? Did you see how they came to hear God's Word, to receive his blessings? Praise God!"

"Oh, yes, Reverend Inman, I saw." June's eyes focused on the safe. So many needs. Warm clothes, adequate food, a stove for the upstairs.

"God's been good to his people."

"Very good."

The reverend hooked his glasses over his ears, then looked around. "You're awfully quiet tonight. Have a big day?"

"Yes. . . . Reverend, I'd like to speak to you about a personal matter."

His eyes softened with concern. "Of course—please, say whatever's in your heart."

"You know the small orphanage on the outskirts of Seattle?"

"Oh, yes. Angeline's. Wonderful woman doing an admirable job with those children."

JUNE

"My friend Sam—Samantha Harris—you remember Sam? She was with me the day you met me at the dock."

"Yes, I remember Sam. A bright child, freckle faced and precocious."

June grinned. "That's Sam."

"What about her? Does she need special prayer?"

"That would be nice, Reverend, but Sam's not the problem; it's her Aunt Angeline. She cares for the orphans, and she's very ill."

"Yes, you requested prayer for Angeline this evening. I'm sure the Lord will hear her needs."

"Yes, I believe he will." June paused. "But the orphanage has dire needs right now, needs that have to be addressed."

"Did you pray for those needs to be met?"

June glanced at the safe. "I prayed, Reverend, and I'm hoping we can do more than pray. I thought perhaps the ministry might be willing to give the orphanage a small donation. The children need shoes and warm clothing. There's only one stove in the drafty house, and they desperately need a second stove for the upstairs bedrooms. If the crusade could share even a small portion of tonight's offering for the children—not a lot, maybe twenty dollars. Just enough to help—"

She faltered when Reverend Inman shook his head sadly.

"I'm afraid that would be out of the question. The crusade money is for the tabernacle."

"Yes, I know. But twenty dollars—the money would hardly be missed."

Reverend Inman shook his head again. "My heart goes out to the children, and I deeply wish the ministry could be of assistance, but there are so many needs, and so few funds to meet them. No, we cannot use tabernacle funds for other purposes."

June's spirit sagged.

The reverend's features gentled. "I understand your concern, June dear, but we must keep our focus on the tabernacle. God's work must be our first priority. The tabernacle will portray his glory to all who see it. Glory be to God."

June wanted to help the orphans as well as see the tabernacle built. Both were worthy causes.

"But twenty dollars, Reverend. The people give so generously—all they can spare."

Patting her shoulder, the reverend busied himself reading the night's tally. Obviously he considered the matter closed.

June sighed. She'd lost this battle. She was a mere lamb, and Reverend Inman was the shepherd. He was wiser than she, and he knew the most urgent need. He would never lead his followers astray. . . .

Her heart was heavy as she let herself out of the tent a few minutes later and closed the flap behind her. Reverend Inman had promised to extinguish the lamp.

The children needed warm clothes, shoes, proper food. The concern refused to leave her.

Twenty dollars was a lot—but so little to ask for the orphans' sake.

Perhaps if she mentioned the orphans' needs to Parker tomorrow, he would allow her to. . . .

No, he'd forbidden her to take up an offering. She could hold services, but she wasn't allowed to accept donations.

When she blew out the light and climbed into bed a short while later, her mind was still on the orphans. Clothes. Nourishing food. A second stove to warm a cold bedroom floor.

Rolling onto her back, she stared at the ceiling.

Souls saved. God's Word proclaimed to thousands. The tabernacle.

Which was the more worthy need?

Chapter Eight

PIGS! June had never seen so many pigs! White pigs, black pigs, big pigs, little pigs, white sows with their litters beside them, all rooting beneath the pines for acorns.

June shook her head at the comical sight. Pine Ridge Logging Camp was alive with pigs!

"Did ya ever see so many 'ogs in your life?" Sam sat up straighter, straining to get a better look. "Does Mr. Sentell raise 'ogs or cut timber?"

June frowned. "Apparently a little of both."

Sam tucked a lock of windblown hair beneath her bonnet as June drove the buckboard through an open gate. "There won't be none of that carryin' on and prayin' out loud, will there now, lovey?"

June swerved the buggy to avoid a boar sprawled sideways in the middle of the road. "Some—but I won't call on you to pray aloud."

"Right ducky of you," Sam grumbled. "Don't know 'ow I let meself get talked into this."

June made a face at her. "Samantha Harris, the Lord loves you despite your heathenish attitude." Sam needed a little spiritual tune-up, and June happily accepted the challenge.

The wind was nippy this morning in spite of a dazzling blue sky overhead. June welcomed the change to dry weather. Above, geese flew in a pretty, symmetrical formation. June concentrated on the message she wanted to bring to the women.

"I'll be speaking on faithfulness this morning."

Sam's mouth dropped open. "Be steppin' on a few toes, I'll wager."

"I'll do my best to avoid yours." June patted Sam's head and laughed.

The logging camp was active for Sunday morning. June frowned when she recalled that Parker hadn't attended a single crusade service this week. Where had he been? Eli had said Parker wasn't married, but she wondered if perhaps a woman occupied his thoughts. The idea intrigued her. That might explain his odd conduct, his lack of patience, his downright boorish behavior at times. Of course at other times, he could be very nice.

She was surprised when her thoughts took off in a new direction. Exactly what sort of woman would interest the gruff, opinionated logger—perhaps one of the scantily dressed women employed at The Gilded Hen? The notion left her feeling unsettled, though she couldn't imagine why.

Simon met the wagon as it rolled to a stop in front of the camp office. A shy grin spread across the giant's rugged features as he extended a hand to help June down.

"Good morning, Miss Kallahan. I've been expecting you."

"Good morning, Simon." June gave him a warm smile as she removed her gloves. It was interesting how Simon's gaze fixed solidly on Sam.

June glanced at Sam. It was clear to see she had no objections to the intense perusal.

"Simon, this is my friend, Samantha Harris. Sam is helping with services this morning."

Smiling, Simon effortlessly lifted Sam out of the buggy and set her lightly on her feet. The two continued to stare at each other as if this were their first encounter with the opposite sex.

Clearing her throat, June brought the moment back to the business at hand. "Simon, there's a box of study material in the bed of the wagon. If you would be so kind as to carry it in for me?"

"Yes, ma'am." Simon's eyes remained riveted on Sam's.

"Simon?"

He glanced up. "Yes, ma'am?"

"Please, don't call me ma'am." That made her sound like an old woman. "June will be fine."

"Yes, ma'am—June." Simon reached for the box of study material and hefted it onto his wide shoulder. A sea of ridged muscles played in his forearms. June hid a smile when Sam gaped at the display of brawny masculinity.

June fell in step with Simon, aware of the curious eyes now focused in their direction.

Men paused in front of sudsy washtubs, watching the entourage as they moved through camp. Others were playing cards on a nearby porch. Two men in barber chairs lay back in the warm sunshine and enjoyed a shave.

"Don't mind all the gawking," Simon called over his shoulder. "We don't get many women up this way."

"But you have some?" June questioned. Otherwise, her purpose to hold camp services would be useless. Surely

Parker would have said if there were no women in camp! Her footsteps momentarily slowed. She started to fume. She wouldn't put it past him to let her come all the way up here for nothing.

"Well?" she prodded.

"Oh, there are a few," Simon conceded. "Eddy Crager's wife, Mary. She's a cook. Loren Jacobs's and Jim Bushy's families live up here, though Ellen Bushy doesn't like it. Come spring, she'll be leaving. Can't take the isolation anymore."

Sam turned to peer over her shoulder at the activity. "Why are the men washing their clothes on Sunday?"

Simon flashed her a friendly grin. "Sunday's boil-up day—the day the men delouse their blankets and clothing."

"Sunday's the Lord's day." June wrinkled her nose at the peculiar tang that saturated the air. "What's that smell?"

"Laundry soap, scalding water, and Peerless tobacco. It's the only thing we've found to kill lice."

June shuddered. "Lice."

"Yes, ma'am." His features sobered. "We try real hard to get rid of them." Simon headed for the cookshack. "Parker said for you to hold services in here. We eat dinner at eleven on Sundays. You'll need to be through by then."

They entered the cookshack, and June deeply inhaled the pleasant aroma of fresh-baked cinnamon rolls.

Setting the box on the table, Simon looked at Sam. "I have a few things left to attend to. I'll be back for the services."

Sam flushed a pretty red.

The door closed behind him, and June laughed. "I think he likes you."

"Ow, what a crock of rubbish. The bloke barely knows me."

"Still—" June stripped off her bonnet—"by the gleam in his eyes, I think he'd like to know you better."

A few minutes before nine, Mary Crager removed her apron, hooked it over the back of a chair, and took her seat at the long table. June welcomed her with a friendly smile.

"Mary?"

The woman nodded. She was painfully thin, with shoulder-length brown hair that could stand a good washing. June recognized shyness in her doleful nut brown eyes. Her hands were rough and reddened from hard work and scalding dishwater. In her right one, she clutched a small, worn Bible.

"I'm glad you could come," June said, and meant it. She hadn't known how many to expect in the first service. One was a promising start.

Sam fished in the box and handed Mary a colorful chain of Bible verses. "Here, lovey. June made 'em herself, she did."

Mary's smile was saintly as she modestly accepted the gift. "Thank you. . . . I've . . . looked forward to you coming all week."

"God bless you," June said softly.

The door opened, and two women entered. Ellen Bushy and Amy Jacobs walked to the table and sat down at the end of the bench, their eyes darting around the room. They clearly were uncomfortable with the situation.

Sam forced a paper chain on them, though they protested, each trying to give Sam a coin in return.

"It's free, lovey. June made 'em."

The women perused the paper chains, exchanging dubious looks.

"It's all right," June explained. "They're Bible verses. You can refer to them during the coming week."

The women slowly nodded as if that was acceptable.

By ten minutes after nine, Simon and two men who introduced themselves as Pete Ridges and Arnold Atkinson joined the service. June stood up, her gaze encompassing her small flock, and her heart swelled with joy. She expected the services to be small; size didn't matter. Where two or more gathered in his name, God promised to be there also.

She glanced up expectantly as the door opened again, hoping Parker had decided to attend. Instead she saw a burly logger carrying a fifty-pound sack of potatoes on his shoulder. He walked past the bench and strode back to the kitchen.

Opening her Bible, June sighed, ignoring a prick of disappointment. She glanced up when the door opened again, and this time her hopes were realized. Her heart thumped when she saw Parker standing at the back of the room, arms crossed, waiting for services to begin. For the life of her, she didn't know why his approval should matter to her. But oddly enough, it did.

Releasing a pent-up breath she hadn't realized she was holding, she reminded herself that at least he was here. That was more than she'd expected.

Smiling, she welcomed the small group. All in all, the services were off to a promising start.

A month later Parker stood at his office window, arms akimbo, watching Simon load a box into June's buggy after the morning worship service. Services were going better than he had expected, but he still thought he was going to live to regret allowing her into camp. If he got wind she was attempting to raise funds for Inman, she would be gone before she could say, "God bless you."

Guilt nagged at him for not participating in the services. He attended because Sunday was the Lord's Day and up until now worship opportunities had been pretty slim. But wild horses couldn't make him tell her he actually approved of her interference. From the time he'd been knee-high to a grasshopper, he'd attended church services. Uncle Walt had insisted on it; Aunt Lacey upheld the edict with a stiff hickory switch. Stubbornness was the only thing keeping him from actually taking part in Miss-High-and-Mighty Kallahan's service.

The memory of Uncle Walt sobered him. Where had Walt gone wrong?

June must think I'm a cold, cantankerous man, Parker mused. She couldn't be more wrong. . . . Not that it bothered him a bit what her opinion of him was. He was a thinking man. And he happened to *think* Isaac Inman, just like Uncle Walt, had let his desire to serve the Lord get out of hand.

Building that fancy tabernacle, using money to construct an extravagant exhibition that would bring thousands of strangers streaming into the area to view the spectacle! Thousands of people would be crowding the streets, overflowing the hotels, making a nuisance of themselves. The church itself would be miles from the logging camps, but it would still interfere with everything.

He rubbed the back of his neck. Why would he care what June Kallahan or anybody else thought of him?

He glanced out the window again. Why was he so restless today? His eyes focused on the gentle sway of June's skirt as she climbed into the wagon, chatting with Simon and Sam. Deep down he knew why. He wasn't able to get those orphans out of his mind.

The community did little anymore to help their plight; and for the past year, he and his men hadn't been able to keep up with the necessities. A few baskets of groceries here and there, a few monetary donations. It wasn't enough. The children's needs were not even close to being met.

"Mr. Sentell."

Parker looked up to see one of his men standing in the doorway. "Hello, Chester. What can I do for you?"

Chester King was a tall, lanky man. He was one of Parker's oldest employees, as well as one of his most trusted.

Chester paused in the doorway, red faced. "I hate to ask, Mr. Sentell. But I was wonderin' if I might be able to get a draw on my pay. Just a small one. I wouldn't ask, but the wife's mother came down sick, and my Betta needs to go to Portland to look after her. I know payday's still a ways away—"

Parker opened the desk drawer and took out the cash box. "How much do you need, Chester?"

"Just enough for a stage ticket. I figure payday will roll around before Betta's ma gets better. I can send her money for the stage back."

"That won't be necessary." Parker counted a generous stack of bills onto the table. "Your wife will be needing a round-trip ticket and money for expenses while she's gone?"

"Yes, sir. . . . Mr. Sentell, I—"

Parker handed him the money. "Don't argue with the boss. You're one of my best workers, and if you have a need, I want to know about it."

Chester accepted the money with a humble, "Thank you, sir. You be sure and hold it out of my next pay."

Parker closed the desk drawer. "That's not necessary. We'll settle up when things are back to normal for you."

"I really appreciate it, Mr. Sentell." Chester reached to shake his hand. "Can I put my X on a paper for you?"

"No, you take care of your family's needs."

"Much obliged." Chester put his frayed hat back on and turned to leave.

"Chester." Parker stopped him. "There is one thing you can do for me."

"Yes, sir?"

"See if you can find Simon. Tell him I need to speak to him."

"I shore will, Mr. Sentell." Chester left, closing the door behind him.

Parker turned back to the window. He wished mere money could ease the orphans' problems as easily as it had Chester's.

Six weeks. June had been in Seattle six weeks, and Sunday camp services were growing. She felt a tingle of anticipation as she unloaded the picnic hamper and located a nice big tree near the riverbank. Twenty had attended the service this morning, and next week there promised to be even more.

Bright sunshine streamed through bare branches of the old oak. Overhead a red-tailed hawk soared to catch the light breeze.

June unpacked the wicker picnic hamper, keeping an eye on Simon and Sam. The besotted couple strolled the banks of the running stream, hand in hand.

Setting a loaf of bread on the blanket, June wondered how love happened so quickly. Sam had known Simon such a short time, but already the two were inseparable.

According to Sam, Simon could quite probably be the man she wanted to spend the rest of her life with, although June didn't see how anyone could arrive at such a significant decision in so brief a time. She smiled, remembering Eli. Of course, she had come hundreds of miles to marry a man she'd never met.

Unscrewing the lid from a jar from Ettie's pantry, she extracted a pickle, then leaned back, biting into its sweetness. Juice squirted and ran down her chin. She lapped it off with her tongue, wondering if she'd ever find love as easily as Sam had.

Simon's eyes had lit up like Christmas candles when Sam invited him to share their lunch after today's services. He readily agreed, and from that moment on, June ceased to exist in the couple's eyes. She was now reduced to watching the picnic basket.

She took another bite of her pickle, sitting up straighter when she saw Parker covering the distance on horseback.

Now there was a man not easily swayed by love. She blushed when she recalled how effortlessly he'd refused Sam's invitation to join them today. Apparently business held a higher priority than his stomach.

Swinging off the stallion, he nodded toward her.

Hoisting the glass pint jar, she smiled. "Pickle?"

To her surprise, he took one and bit it in two. "Good. You make them?"

"No, Ettie did." She was tempted to add that hers were just as good, but she didn't. That would be bragging.

Parker finished the pickle, his eyes focused on Simon, who was skipping stones across the water. "Do those two know it's lunchtime?"

June laughed. "Food is the last thing on their mind."

"Simon not thinking about his next meal? It must be love."

Fishing in the basket, June took out a plate of thickly sliced ham. She set out potato salad, pickled beets, deviled eggs, and a bowl of beans and bacon swimming in blackstrap molasses.

"Change your mind about joining us?" June asked lightly. She didn't want to make much over the fact he'd decided to come, for somewhere deep within her, she relished the unexpected treat. When Parker tried, which admittedly wasn't that often, he could be quite pleasant.

"Not exactly. Business brings me out this way, but there's no reason I can't stay and eat."

June handed him a filled plate. He studied the mound of ham and potato salad, frowning. "You could spoil a man, Miss Kallahan."

She smiled, thinking if that's all it took, he would be an easy man to spoil. She filled a plate for herself as Parker sat down. They bowed their heads, and he said grace.

Unfolding his napkin, Parker said, "Shouldn't the lovebirds be warned we're starting without them?"

June took a bite of ham, chewing thoughtfully. "Do you think they care?"

He chuckled. "Not really."

They managed to carry on a pleasant conversation about the weather and topics that required little thought for the remainder of the meal. Polishing off the last of his potato salad, Parker lifted the lid on the wicker basket and looked inside. "You don't happen to have a chocolate cake in here, do you?"

"No, apple pie." Though Sam had wanted to fix lunch, the orphanage couldn't spare the food. So Ettie had allowed June to commandeer the kitchen this morning. The pie was baked and cooling by the time the sun came up.

Two sizable slices later, Parker lay back against the tree trunk and closed his eyes. June was happy to see he'd loosened his belt a couple of notches. "That, Miss Kallahan, was one fine meal."

"Thank you, Mr. Sentell, but I happen to know Mary is an excellent cook. I ate one of her cinnamon rolls before services this morning, and I've tasted none better."

"Yes," he murmured drowsily. "Mary's a good cook, but I can't remember when I've eaten a better apple pie. Reminds me of my mother's cooking."

She couldn't think of any higher praise. "Cinnamon."

He cracked one eye open to look at her.

"I use extra cinnamon—and chunks of fresh-churned butter."

"Well, keep it up." His eyes drifted closed again.

"Does your mother live around here?"

"No. She's been dead for many years."

June settled back, listening to the birds chirping overhead. "This is my favorite time of year. What about you?"

"It's all right." He appeared to doze, but she knew he wasn't sleeping. She studied the large hands folded contentedly over his broad chest. He always looked clean and freshly shaven. She wondered how he did that. Did someone do his laundry for him? If so, who?

"Mary," he said.

"Huh? . . . What did you say?"

"Mary does my shirts. I pay her to clean once a month and do my laundry."

She blushed. Now *how* did he know what she was thinking?

"You have an expressive face," he answered, tiny lines appearing at his eyes. If she didn't know better, she'd swear he was about to laugh.

Straightening, she covered the bowl of potato salad. In the future she would have to guard her thoughts more carefully.

Silence closed around them. Birds fluttered in and out of tree branches. Sam and Simon had wandered farther down the creek, but they were still in sight.

Shaping her hands into a pillow, June rested her head on the blanket. Here she was, in the company of a very handsome man, and she had put him to sleep.

Full of potato salad, she, too, started to succumb to drowsiness.

"You're doing a good job."

Starting, she lifted her head. Bright sunshine blinded her. "Did you say something?"

"I said, you're doing a good job. The women—and men, too—appreciate Sunday services. I was wrong."

She sat up, basking in his compliment. "Well, thank you. I enjoy leading the services. I haven't started services in other camps yet—but I will." She glanced over and saw his eyes were still closed. "I'm sorry we disagreed about it."

"Don't be sorry. I like a woman who knows her mind and isn't afraid to speak it."

It was just too much. Both compliments *and* praise from Parker Sentell?

"Is that ham I smell?"

June looked up to see Simon and Sam approaching, contented smiles on their faces.

"Parker?" Simon grinned. "Thought you were working."

Without opening his eyes, Parker grunted. "All work and no play makes a man—"

"Dull," Sam finished. She winked at June. "Ain't that right, lovey?"

"You don't have to see me home."

Simon ignored Sam's protests as he hitched the buggy. "It'll be raining soon. I'll see that Sissy is brought back to the orphanage." He winked at Parker. "Parker and I have nothing better to do than see you ladies home."

June glanced at Parker, who was tying the mares to the back of the wagon. "Are you sure?" What about that business he'd mentioned?

Straightening, Parker came around the buggy. "Rain's coming up. Don't want you to get wet." He helped her aboard, then took the seat beside her. She felt very small and very important sitting beside him—almost as if they were courting. The thought made her laugh out loud.

Parker turned to look at her. "Care to share what's funny?"

She shook her head. No, she did not care to share that. Not with him.

The orphanage came into view half an hour later.

"Oh, Sam!" June exclaimed. "I'll finally get to meet your aunt."

When the buggy rolled to a stop in front of the towering old house, children poured out the door. June caught herself before she jumped to the ground to run to them. The children ranged from early teens to a blond-haired, blue-eyed toddler.

A frail woman with a mass of snow white hair appeared in the doorway, holding on to the doorframe. She squinted. "Is that you, Sam?"

" 'Tis me, Auntie." Sam waited until Simon lifted her down. "Come meet me dear ol' auntie and the children." She extended a hand to June.

An elderly man carrying an ax came around the corner.

"Hi, Joe—just me, and me friends. Come meet them!"

The old man approached, his faded eyes taking in the newcomers.

"Chopping wood again?" Sam asked.

Joe nodded. "Running low."

June took in the squalor, appalled. The roof was patched in so many places it looked warped. Random placement of large sheets of tin were held down by rocks, adding to the dilapidated appearance.

A young boy edged out to meet them. His solemn brown eyes stared up at June. He was painfully thin, and barefoot.

"Hello." She smiled. "What's your name?"

"Peter."

"Peter. That's a wonderful name."

"It's from the Bible."

June nodded. "I recognized that. Peter, one of Jesus' disciples."

Some of the smaller children held back. They cowered behind Angeline, peeking around her skirt.

Sam urged her friends closer to the house. "Aunt Angeline, I want you to meet June, my friend, and Simon"—Sam's face flamed—"the man I've been telling you about." She blushed, her freckles standing out like measles.

Simon shook hands with Angeline. "Good to see you again, Angeline."

Angeline smiled at the big lumberjack. "Where you been keepin' yourself lately? Haven't seen you around."

Sam's eyes widened. "Do you know me old auntie?"

Simon nodded. "We've met."

June stepped forward to shake the old woman's hand. "Sam's told me so much about you. It's nice to finally meet you."

The old woman's tired eyes looked the young people over. "Good to see you, Parker. Can't thank you enough for all those supplies you been dropping by. Couldn't make it without them."

Parker nodded. "The men want to do more, Angeline."

June turned to look at him. "You know Sam's aunt too?"

He smiled at Angeline. "I manage to get out here every now and then."

June glanced at him accusingly.

"Good of you to bring my niece home, Parker. Won't you come in and sit a spell?"

Simon gave Sam a warm smile. "I'd like that, but it looks as if a storm's about to break. We best be going along."

While Simon and Sam took a private moment to say good-bye, Parker took June's arm and led her back to the buggy. June smiled over her shoulder at the orphans. She'd never seen a more pitiful lot.

"The children break my heart," she whispered. "Sam said the orphans' situation was deplorable, but I've never seen children living in such poor surroundings."

"The community does all it can, under the circumstances." June was glad that he didn't directly accuse Reverend Inman of taking food out of the children's mouths, although the implication was thinly veiled. "Someone needs to step in, close the orphanage down, and find the kids foster homes."

When they drove away a few minutes later, June was still looking over her shoulder, appalled by the sight. One thing was certain—she would be keeping her promise to help Sam all she could. And she would be starting first thing tomorrow morning.

Chapter Nine

SIMON'S massive frame darkened the office doorway Monday morning. "You wanted to see me, boss?"

Parker motioned for his clerk to sit down.

The chair squeaked under Simon's considerable bulk. "Got a problem?"

A problem? Yes, there was a problem. His name was Isaac Inman. "Something's been bothering me."

Simon's brows knotted with concern. "You comin' down with something?"

Parker shook his head. "I wish the solution were that simple."

Simon leaned back, scissoring his arms behind his head. "You're thinking about those kids, aren't you?"

Parker turned to the window to look out. Simon could

read him like an open book. "What are we going to do about that situation?"

"I don't know. I've been praying about it for some time now. It's a pitiful situation out there."

"It's despicable the way the kids are forced to do without basic necessities. Things we take for granted—food, shelter, clothing—warm clothing that hasn't been worn threadbare by others first. A decent-fitting pair of shoes—shoes that don't rub their feet raw by the end of the day."

"They deserve better," Simon agreed. "They need proper schooling, a chance to learn to read, write, and do arithmetic. Maybe study history."

A muscle tightened in Parker's jaw. "Children need a penny's worth of candy every once in a while. Jawbreakers, licorice whips, jelly beans, or peppermint sticks. I've watched the orphans at the mercantile. They stand back, pretending not to care, when you know they do."

Simon shook his head. "There sure should be something we can do. The men are concerned about the situation, but Inman's got them all fired up about building that tabernacle. Then June caught their eye. They're partial to 'God's little emissary.' Their spare coins go to her."

Parker stared out the window, wracking his brain. The loggers were a generous lot, but Simon was right. Their minds were on the tabernacle.

"I know Angeline would appreciate any help she could get." Simon paused for a long moment. "I noticed a lot of things yesterday that needed fixing, but when it comes down to it, money is what they need most."

"Yes, money would solve a lot of problems."

Simon absently scanned a work order. "Those children haven't had the proper food for years."

Dropping into his chair, Parker propped his boots on the desk. "Or anything else they need."

"True. Well, I'm willing to pitch in a month's pay. If we explain the kids' needs to the men, they'll chip in all they can."

"I have a better idea."

Simon met Parker's steady gaze. "What's that?"

"Inman could help out here."

"Reverend Inman?" Simon frowned. "You can't be serious."

Parker felt his blood pressure rise. "Yes, I'm serious. Why not? He needs to think of the community's needs first, for a change."

"There you go again, boss—you're bullheaded, you know that? You judge every evangelist by your Uncle Walt's shortcomings. You know the reverend feels he's been called by God to build that tabernacle. That doesn't make him crooked."

"We're not talking about my Uncle Walt," Parker snapped. "We're talking about the orphanage. Isaac should see the need without having to point it out to him. After all, it's his community."

"And we're all God's children." Simon shook his head. "Isaac's a good man, whether you want to believe it or not. I've talked to his people. They say he's the salt of the earth, will do anything in his power to serve the Lord. But he's fixed on erecting that tabernacle in his wife's memory. No doubt he sees the orphanage's need, undoubtedly sympathizes with them, but he won't stand for a penny of the contributions to go toward the orphanage—you know that."

"And that's Christianity?"

"Well, Christianity walks a fine line. In one man's mind, what Isaac's doing is the height of servitude; in another's, it's heresy. Men like Isaac confront needs every day—dire, unimaginable needs. Inman's not a miracle worker, Parker; he's one man, a man with a mission—a worthy mission, whether you like it or not. The taberna-

131

cle will serve thousands, the orphanage only a handful of children."

"Only a handful of children." Parker found that a bit ironic. "Wonder if that's how God sees it—only a handful of his children?"

Simon got up to pour a cup of coffee. "We could argue all day about what's needed where, and the most, and never come up with a solution. It's up to you and me to find a way to help these particular children." He warmed Parker's cup, then set the pot back on the stove.

Parker sat for a long moment without speaking. The church served the community. The community's future lay with its children. Isaac was obsessed with building the tabernacle, blinded by intent. Couldn't anyone else see that?

"I'm going to have a talk with Isaac."

"You? Talk to Isaac? That would be a first. Thought you didn't approve of him or the tabernacle."

"I don't, but he serves the community's spiritual needs, and the orphans are part of the community. For too long he's turned his back on them. Someone needs to point that out to him."

Simon stirred sugar into his coffee. "The tabernacle's blinded Isaac to a lot of needs."

Parker pushed away from the desk, stretching. "I'll talk to him. If he doesn't like it, that's his problem. Meantime, we're going to have to do more. Have the men take up an offering and send it over to the orphanage— or have Miss Kallahan deliver it."

Simon grinned, and Parker gave him a sour look. "Something funny?"

"Yeah, you and Miss Kallahan. You cross swords more than Sioux warriors. What's wrong with you? She's a pretty woman—available now that Eli's gone. You're single. Why do you want to argue with her?"

"Let's just say I don't like pushy women."

Simon grinned, then quickly recovered when Parker shot him a dark look. He watched his boss drain his cup and set it on the desk, then shrug into his coat.

"Think I'll have that talk with Isaac while it's on my mind. Can you take care of things here while I'm gone?"

"I'll give it a try. If you see Sam, tell her I said hello."

Parker paused at the door. "Seems to me you're getting mighty interested in Sam Harris all of a sudden."

Simon took a sip of coffee, grinning. "Seems that way to me, too."

"Sam's worried about your shyness—thinks the cat gets your tongue."

Simon scowled. "Who told you that?"

"I overheard June and Mary discussing it the other day."

"Women!" Simon shuffled the work orders. "You know talking to women don't come easy for me—except talking to Sam. I feel comfortable around her, even if I don't talk her leg off."

Parker frowned. "If it's talking you're worried about, you should have Miss Kallahan help you with that. She talks enough for two people."

"Isaac, I want to talk to you."

Isaac glanced up, and upon seeing Parker standing in the doorway, returned to the papers he was reading. "That's surprising, since you haven't been so inclined now for several years."

Parker ignored the rebuke. He wasn't here for scones and a tea party. "I want to discuss the orphanage."

Isaac frowned. "The orphanage. Is that all that's on people's minds these days? The orphanage has been here for years. Why all the sudden concern? The children are healthy, aren't they? They have a roof over their head, and food on the table."

"Healthy, maybe; food, occasionally. The roof's a laugh. Something has to be done about their situation."

"I have no argument with that, but you must realize there are so many—"

Parker's deadly tone stopped him. "Cut it out, Isaac. It's me—Parker. Remember? Of course there are many needs, but the orphans are *our* particular problem. I want your ministry to help them."

Removing his glasses, Isaac polished them, refusing to look up. "How can I help?"

"Give the orphans at least one Sunday-night offering a month. That's an insignificant amount compared to the overall picture. The kids will have proper food and clothing, and the community can rest in the knowledge they are taking care of their own."

Isaac stuffed the handkerchief in his pocket, his features tight. "I'll have the elders prepare more food baskets and deliver them—"

"The children need more than food baskets. They need a steady income. The old woman is sick. She isn't able to drum up donations like she used to. Provide those kids funding, Isaac. If the tabernacle is God's plan, he will see it built."

Isaac's eyes centered on the window, where outside a gray drizzle fell. "My heart goes out to those children— to needy children throughout the world. If I could, I would see to it that not one single child would go to bed hungry tonight. But it isn't within my power. I'm only one man, Parker. You must know a minister's task is overwhelming. As much as I want to help, I cannot take money from the crusade and give it for another cause, no matter how worthy that cause might be. Donations received from this ministry must go to build the tabernacle."

A suffocating tightness squeezed Parker's chest. *Remem-*

ber, you're here for the orphans, not to chastise Isaac, he reminded himself.

"You're wrong, Isaac. You know that. My men do all they can, but they're following you, and forgetting their responsibilities toward those less fortunate."

Parker saw the way the loggers gave outside the saloon, but all collected funds were channeled toward the tabernacle. The orphans were getting trampled in the shuffle.

Isaac stared straight ahead, refusing to meet Parker's eyes. "I wish I could help, but I stand firm in my conviction—my knowledge of what I have been called to do."

They were getting nowhere. "Those children need your help. Read your Bible."

"I am aware of their needs, and I read my Bible daily, thank you. I am concerned about the orphans, but God has called me for a different purpose. God has called me to build a tabernacle. I will abide in his Word and see my mission accomplished. I must keep my eyes focused on the tabernacle. A place of worship that will feed the spiritual needs of thousands, not just the everyday needs of a few."

"OK." Parker realized he couldn't argue with a fence post. Isaac's mind was made up. If the children were to eat properly, he'd have to find another avenue. "I hope *you* can sleep warm tonight, Isaac, and aren't kept awake by the knowledge there are babies down the road who can't."

Isaac never raised his eyes. Parker walked out.

Chapter Ten

MARY, what a pretty necklace!" June admired the chain of colorful glass beads before handing it to Sam. "Did you make this?"

Mary blushed. "Oh, it's nothing, really."

"Ow, lovey, it's smashin', it is! I didn't know you did such handiwork!"

Color deepened in Mary's cheeks. "Oh, go on—it's only cheap baubles woven onto golden thread. My grandmother taught me how to do it."

Sam closely examined the trinket, her eyes bright with admiration. "Where do you get such lovely beads?"

"Oh, my Eddie buys them when he goes to visit his mother in Spokane. I'll make you one, if you like."

"I'd love it!" Sam grabbed the skinny cook around the neck and hugged her. "It would be ever so nice o' you."

137

Mary glanced at June. "I'll make you one too. I'll have them both finished by next Sunday."

The women admired the necklace as the cookshack filled with morning worshipers. Twenty-eight, in all, sat around the long table. June mentally calculated the multicolored paper chains left in her box, glad she'd brought extra.

After services, June and Sam repacked the box, and Simon carried it back to the wagon. June looked the other way when Sam leaned over and whispered something in Simon's ear. The gentle giant turned beet red and nodded.

"What did you say to him?" June whispered under her breath as they walked off.

"I told 'im 'e looked right smashing today, 'e did, and told 'im 'e looked good enough to kiss."

"Oh, Sam." June punched her in the side. "Stop—you'll embarrass the poor man."

"Too late." Sam's features turned solemn. "Already did." The women burst into laughter, June's fading when she spotted Parker through the office window. He was leaning back, boots on the desk, engrossed in a handful of papers.

"Ow, look, lovey." Sam punched her. "There's your sweetie."

Sweetie, June scoffed, ignoring Sam's mischievous grin. Parker wasn't her sweetie—though the thought wasn't that unappealing.

"Oh, Sam, I wish he would just once look at me the way Simon looks at you."

"Maybe 'e would, if you'd be a bit more friendly."

"I try to be friendly, Sam. He just plain doesn't like me. Since I'm working with the crusade, he equates me with Reverend Inman. It's so unfair. Parker acts as if Reverend Inman doesn't care about anything but the tabernacle, but it's not true. Reverend Inman mentioned the orphanage twice this week, and just yesterday he sent Ben over with two bushels of apples and three hams."

Sam tsked. "Such a pity. Hardheaded as a rock."

"Those two remind me of hardheaded Christians who—" June's footsteps slowed, and she turned to face Sam. "Why, that's exactly what they remind me of. I hadn't realized it until this very moment, but Reverend Inman and Parker have forgotten what Christians are supposed to do when one or the other is overcome by sin. They are to gently and humbly help that person back onto the right path. Reverend Inman and Parker are trampling each other in their efforts to prove the other wrong!"

"Don't know what you can do 'bout it. Until they both realize what they're doing, their warrin' won't cease."

June gathered her skirt and climbed into the wagon. "That may be, but perhaps it's my duty to remind them." Sam took her place on the board seat beside her. June continued, "It was nice of Mary to offer to make us a necklace. They are lovely."

"Breathtakin', to be sure," Sam agreed. "I wouldn't have thought poor little Mary was so talented, 'er being so mousey and all. Why, what woman wouldn't love to own such a pretty? I've seen nothing in the mercantile like it."

June squealed, hauling back on the reins. Sam grasped June's arm and held on for dear life. "What's wrong? More pigs?"

"No, you! Do you know what you just said?"

Sam frowned. "More pigs?"

"No, before that!"

Sam concentrated, her face a mask of confusion.

June prompted her. "You were talking about Mary's necklace."

"What about it? I said it was pretty—"

"And other women would like it too. You said there's nothing like it in the mercantile!"

Sam released June's arm. "June Kallahan, 'ave you lost your bloomin' mind? What does Mary's necklace 'ave to do with anythin'?"

"Don't you see? I've been wracking my brain for days for a way to raise money for the orphanage other than using crusade funds. We can sell necklaces! Mary said the beads were inexpensive. I have a small nest egg, not much, but if the beads are inexpensive and the necklaces simple to make, perhaps Mary will teach us how."

June sat back, plotting her strategy. "I'll use my savings to buy the beads and thread, and we can sell the necklaces to the loggers. Most all have wives and girlfriends waiting at home. I'll bet the men would love the chance to give their sweethearts a present to make up for their absence. And for those who don't have sweethearts, they surely have mothers! Just think, Sam! If business is good, we can buy that stove for the upstairs bedroom in no time at all!"

"But using your life savin's, lovey—are you sure you want to do that?"

"I'm positive! It's not much, but it will multiply three-fold if the men like the necklaces."

"Mary might not be anxious to share 'er secret."

"Oh, but she will, once we explain what we're doing. Come on, Sam! It's a brilliant idea. We'll take the necklace money and use it for the orphans' needs. I won't be taking money from the crusade, so Reverend Inman can't object, and I won't be angering Parker, because I'm not soliciting donations for Reverend Inman." June flung her arms around Sam and hugged her right there in the middle of the road. "It's perfect!"

"Ow, I don't know, lovey." Sam pried June's arms loose, choking.

"We'll talk to Mary." June reached for the reins and wheeled the buggy around in the middle of the road.

"Now? But I'm hungry!" The clattering wagon drowned out Sam's protests.

June gripped the reins and planted her feet. This was too important to wait. Much too important!

Within a month, necklace sales had exceeded June's wildest expectations. Mary had opened her heart and her cookshack to assemble the colorful trinkets, and the men opened their wallets and splurged on the jewelry. Luther Medsker even bought one for his mother-in-law.

Lying back on her bed, June thought of all the exhausting work she, Sam, and Mary had put into the entrepreneurial venture. But it was paying off! In just the past three days they had collected over thirty dollars. This morning June was taking the oldest children to the mercantile to be fitted for new shoes. And not one cent had come out of the tabernacle fund.

Glory be to God! June hugged her pillow, elated with the progress. In no time at all, the children would have the new stove *and* winter coats.

The mercantile was empty when June led three children in later that morning. Peter shot straight to the shoe rack and began inspecting the merchandise, his eyes wide with wonder. Allowing the others equal time to browse, June purchased peppermint sticks for the smaller children.

"I threw in a couple of extra sticks," the clerk confessed with a conspirator's wink.

"Thank you." June smiled. "You can't possibly know how much your kindness will be appreciated."

Picking up a bolt of red hair ribbon, she laid it on the counter. The girls would have a squealing fit when she tied the ribbon in their hair tonight.

Stepping to the Home Fire stove displayed on a

wooden platform, she admired it. It was a fine stove—the finest she'd ever seen. Running her hands over the shiny cast iron, she mentally calculated how many necklaces she would have to sell in order to purchase it. A lot, she decided, after numerous attempts to cipher the amount.

The front door opened, and June glanced up to see Reverend Inman coming in. The reverend took off his hat, his eyes casting about the room. When he spotted June, he broke into a smile. "June!"

"Good morning, Reverend," June called.

Reverend Inman hurried over to her, mopping his brow. "It's too soon to be this warm." His eyes brightened when he saw the orphans. "My, my. Who have we here?"

The children gathered around the minister, the youngest hanging on to his leg.

"What brings you children out on such a warm day?"

"We're gettin' new shoes!" they chorused.

"New shoes!" Reverend Inman looked surprised. He addressed the storekeeper. "I think we should have three of those nice, plump candy balls to go with those new shoes, don't you, children?"

The children nodded their unanimous, enthusiastic endorsement.

Reverend Inman dug in his pocket and laid a coin on the counter. "Let the children select the color they want."

The clerk nodded. "Come along, children. Who wants a red one?"

"Me, me," they clamored. Footsteps echoed across the wood floor as they made a beeline for the candy jar.

June turned back to face Reverend Inman. "That's generous of you, Reverend. The children rarely get such a treat."

Reverend Inman's eyes followed the children and softened with compassion. "Poor tykes. I wish I could do more."

June selected a tin of sugar and laid it on the counter. "What brings you to town so early?"

"Ettie's running low on coffee. I promised to bring some home before dinnertime." Reverend Inman glanced at the bolt of red ribbon and the peppermint sticks lying on the counter. "Looks like you're doing quite a lot of shopping today." He turned to look at the children, who were busy now trying on the new purchases. "Did the orphanage come into a windfall?"

"Oh, no," June said. She paused, biting her lower lip. She'd supposed he'd already heard about the necklaces she had been selling. But perhaps he was so preoccupied with crusade business that he hadn't heard. "No windfall."

His features sobered. "You're not using tabernacle funds, are you? I thought we'd discussed this and agreed where our priorities lie."

"We did—and I'm not using ministry funds without your knowledge. I wouldn't do that."

Reverend Inman's eyes swept the room, the children, the peppermint sticks, and the red ribbons. "Then where is all this money coming from?" June was troubled to hear a note of urgency in his voice.

"Sam, Mary, and I have been selling necklaces."

Reverend Inman's brow lifted. "Selling necklaces?"

"Just frivolous trinkets. The men buy them for their sweethearts. The money from the necklaces goes toward the orphanage."

She wanted to make it abundantly clear that the orphanage proceeds had absolutely nothing to do with tabernacle funds.

A shadow crossed Reverend Inman's face. "No wonder I don't see you around very often. You must keep very busy, collecting funds for both the orphanage and the tabernacle. That's quite an undertaking for one person."

June couldn't miss the new coolness in his voice. "Not really—I have plenty of time for both."

He gazed down his nose at her, his features stern. "Perhaps, but I wouldn't think you could do proper service to two causes. Do you?"

"Yes, sir, I think I can. I work as hard for one as I do for the other." Opening the string on her purse, she rummaged around and came up with a handful of coins. "I collected this in front of The Gilded Hen yesterday. You can see the men's dedication to the building fund hasn't changed."

Reverend Inman lowered his voice. His features took a somber look. "June, it isn't the money. It's your loyalty I seek. You are being torn between two needs—both great, both important. While I applaud your generosity, I wonder about your motives. Giving has dropped off lately. This concerns me greatly. What would Eli think of you funneling money away from the crusade?"

June dropped her eyes submissively. "I would never do that."

"This must stop. Immediately."

The force of his words stunned her. He couldn't mean that he believed she would take from the tabernacle funds. "Are you asking me to choose between the orphans and the ministry?"

Please, God, don't let him be asking that. The choice would be impossible. Both were just causes. Why couldn't Reverend Inman—or Parker, for that matter— see that?

The front door opened, and as if the devil had summoned help to further her dilemma, Parker and two other men walked in. When Parker spotted her and the reverend, he stalked to the back of the store.

"I'd best be getting that coffee to Ettie." Reverend Inman selected a tin and set it on the counter.

"I'm sorry, Reverend."

Reverend Inman turned away, directing his attention to the clerk.

Edging to the back of the store, June sought out Parker. As gruff as he could be, she needed his insight. She needed to know why he was so against Reverend Inman. Did he see something that she was blind to?

Parker was squatting on his haunches, sorting through a pile of hand implements, when June came up to him.

"Miss Kallahan."

"I didn't expect to see you here this morning."

He glanced up. "That makes two of us." He returned to the job at hand.

"Can I ask you something?"

"Since when do you need permission to ask me anything?"

Casting a glance toward the front of the store, she lowered her voice. "It's about Reverend Inman."

Parker didn't look up. "What about him?"

Kneeling beside him, she dropped her voice to a whisper. "I'm puzzled. I know you don't approve of Reverend Inman or the tabernacle. You don't attend services as often as you should. On top of that, Eli was your best friend, and Eli shared Reverend Inman's dream—to the extent that he worked through all sorts of weather, acquiring donations to build the temple—literally giving his *life* in order to achieve the dream. How can you explain all this?"

Parker sorted through the hand tools. "Why do I have to explain it?"

"Well, because. I think you and I are at odds over something, but I'm not sure what. Don't you think it would profit both of us if *I* knew what we were arguing about?"

Shoving a hammer aside, Parker looked at her. Anger darkened his eyes, and she wondered if she was wise to confront him—yet she had to know. Why was he so dead set against Reverend Inman's efforts?

"Men like Isaac burn me."

She stared back at him. "Burn you? What do you mean?"

"I had an uncle like Isaac. Man of the pulpit, smooth talker, fleecing the flock for money to be used for *his* glory."

June's heart sank. Nobody wanted to confront the issue of an evangelist who'd lost his way. It happened, but no Christian was proud of it. Bad things happened.

"And you think that's what Reverend Inman's doing?"

His gaze met hers stoically. "What do *you* think? God doesn't require that great monuments be built in his name."

"No, that's true. But is it wrong for Christians to honor their Lord by erecting churches befitting his name?"

Parker shook his head. "I'm not going to argue religion, Miss Kallahan. I read my Bible. I know what's commanded of us."

"So, you're saying that as Christians, we should interpret God's Word only as he reveals it to us."

"That's what I'm saying."

"Good, because this is a good place to remind you to read Galatians 6. Then come back, and we'll discuss this rationally. Did you feel this way about Eli's involvement with the tabernacle?"

"Eli knew how I felt about the tabernacle."

"You talked about it?"

"Many times, but I knew Eli's heart was in the right

place. Eli let Isaac influence him. Isaac let his wife, Katherine, influence him. It was a bad mix."

"Have you spoken to Reverend Inman about your feelings?"

He gave her a sour look.

"You haven't, have you?"

"I haven't spoken to Isaac about anything other than the orphans. I must say, Miss Kallahan, his true spirit was evident."

June ignored his sarcasm. "Well, shame on both of you. You're Christian men acting like children. You should be working just as hard to build the tabernacle and support the orphanage as I am."

Impatience flared in his eyes. "I wouldn't collect a penny for Isaac."

"Ah—then you're judging."

"No, I'm not judging. That's my opinion."

"And your opinion is, all evangelists—Reverend Inman included—are dishonest."

"I didn't say that."

"But you did. You said your uncle was confused, lost his way; therefore, all evangelists are bad."

Parker stood up. "I *didn't* say that!" A logger examining a flannel shirt turned to stare at them.

June rose to face Parker. "You did too!" She controlled the impulse to raise her voice. She could see she was severely testing his control. Good. She wanted him to stop and think about his prejudices and put a face on them.

"I am saying, Miss Kallahan, that I think there are far more pressing needs in this world than erecting an expensive monument meant to glorify Isaac Inman's name."

"And that's the only reason you forbid me to take up a collection in your camp on Sunday?"

He crossed his arms. "That's precisely why."

147

"But you agree there are other needs, more worthy needs even in your eyes, when a collection is acceptable."

"Of course. I know it takes money to carry on God's work."

"Then you wouldn't care if I took up a collection for—say—the orphans, on Sunday mornings."

"Why would I object to that?"

"I don't know. Would you?"

"No."

"Then I can?"

His eyes narrowed with suspicion. "Why do I have the impression I've just been had?"

She grinned. "A tiny collection—to go toward the orphans' needs alone." She couldn't sell necklaces anymore, not without risking Reverend Inman's disapproval. She had to regain those funds some way.

She thought she detected a tolerant smile twitching at the corners of Parker's mouth. But she couldn't be sure. It would be so unlike him to smile.

"All right. You can take a collection for the orphans on Sunday mornings, but don't think for one minute you've talked me into anything. I was just getting ready to suggest the idea myself."

She presented her most somber face. "No, I would never think that."

Nodding, he picked up a shovel and walked to the counter. Reverend Inman and Parker eyed each other disagreeably.

"Good morning, Sentell."

"Morning, Reverend."

Reverend Inman paid for his purchase, tipped his hat to Parker, and left the store. The door closed behind Parker a moment later.

Those two need to talk, June decided, unwrapping a peppermint stick and taking a lick. They were both wrong.

Chapter Eleven

I'M worried, June," Sam said as she and June prepared food in the orphanage's kitchen. "I feel like we're running out of space here. You know the wee tykes need not only space but clothes, toys, shoes, books, food. ' Come winter, they'll need warm coats and mufflers. Where's it all to come from?"

June sighed. "I know. I'm worried too. The extra clothing I collected helped some, but it's not enough. People don't seem to have much left over to give."

"You two worry too much."

Sam and June jumped in surprise. They hadn't heard Simon approach.

"Just feeling a bit sorry for meself, love." Sam stood on tiptoe to accept his kiss. "What brings you out this way today?"

"You." Simon smoothed her creased brow with his forefinger. "I thought we might eat our dinner together."

She grinned, stealing another quick kiss. "Can't think of anything I'd like better."

Simon unknotted the corners of a cloth bag and took out two thick ham sandwiches and laid them on the table. June busied herself making a pot of fresh coffee.

"How're things going?" Simon asked.

"Not so good. The wee ones need so much. The camp offering Parker allows June to take helps, but it's not nearly enough. The roof needs fixing, the baby needs special medicine. . . . The list is endless."

"If Isaac would share a few of his offerings, it would make things easier," Simon grumbled.

June looked at him. So Parker wasn't the only one who felt this way. She herself had begun to feel confused. Hadn't God sent her to Eli, and then to carry on his work? Yet as she saw the needs of the orphans, she felt more and more pulled toward helping them. What was her call? She'd thought she knew, but when Reverend Inman asked her to choose, she began to question everything.

"June's done her best to talk to 'im; Parker's done his best to talk to 'im. But Reverend Inman can't see his responsibility 'ere."

"Then he's blind."

Sam shrugged. " 'e is, in some ways. Can't see beyond 'is wife's dream."

Simon turned to June. "What do you think?"

"I'm not sure," she admitted. "Perhaps the tabernacle Katherine envisioned has become his obsession."

"It's not right. . . . Don't know what the orphans will do when you're forced to shut this place down."

Shut down? Would it come to that? Much as June hated to face it, that did seem the likely scenario—if something more couldn't be done. "There should be a

way to support both the orphanage and the tabernacle,"
she said. "Why does everyone think that's so impossible?"

"Well, it seems like it should be possible, but those
kids still need a decent roof over their heads and a stove
to warm the upstairs. I know you've been working real
hard, Miss June, but still the needs are too great."

Sam turned to Simon, her eyes ablaze. "Well, June's
'elping me not to lose faith in the power of God. Reverend Inman may come through yet."

"I wouldn't hold my breath."

Sam grinned. "That's not sayin' we might not all 'ave
to give God a wee bit of 'elp."

Simon lifted his cup, and June filled it with hot coffee.
Cocking an ear, Simon listened. "What's all that pounding?"

"Ow, that. Joe's putting a new floor on the back
porch. Harold Stinson donated lumber from the old cabin
'e tore down last week."

Sam lifted the curtain window to look out. The children were playing in the yard with the few wooden toys
Simon and Joe had made for them. She let the curtain
fall back into place. When a knock sounded at the back
door, Sam sprang up to answer it.

"Parker! I didn't expect you this morning."

"I hear Joe's working on the porch—" Parker looked
over her shoulder. "Simon?"

Simon waved from his place at the table. "Guess you're
here to help build the porch too?"

Parker nodded. "Thought Pine Ridge could do without me for a day."

Sam noticed the twinkle in his eyes. "Have you
brought someone with you?"

"Oh, there are a couple of wagons outside. They just
happen to be full of shingles that my men cut—"

"Shingles!" Sam flung her arms around his neck and
held on. "The roof! You're goin' to patch the roof." Sam

couldn't imagine not having to sidestep pots in the middle of the floor.

She stepped back, aware Parker was straining to see around her.

June lowered her eyes, blushing at Parker's gaze. "Hello, June."

My, it was awfully warm in here all of a sudden! "Parker," she said. "How good of you to come and help with the roof."

He smiled at her. Never taking his gaze from her, he said to Sam, "Think I can tear Joe away from the porch long enough to help unload those shingles?"

Sam fairly danced out the back door. "Joe! Come quick! Parker just brought shingles!" She raced back to the table and flung her arms around Simon's neck. "Glory be! You hear that, love? Shingles!"

Looking at Parker, June said, "You have no idea what this means. I wish I could think of some way to thank you."

"The smiles on your faces are thanks enough." Parker glanced at the fresh pot of coffee. "And maybe a cup of whatever that is that smells so good."

Simon finished off his sandwich and stood up. "Guess those shingles won't unload themselves."

Parker settled his hat back on his head. "Guess not."

"And I'll pray that God will hold back the rain until you're finished," June promised.

Before sunup the following morning, Parker and Simon returned with four other loggers in tow. While Angeline rested in her attic room, the men began tearing off the old roof.

Warning the children to stay out of the way, Sam and June planned to cook all morning in preparation for the noon meal. Parker had delivered two boxes of groceries the day before.

"When I unloaded the boxes, guess what I found," Sam asked June.

June couldn't guess.

"Ten whole dollars in the bottom of the basket!" Sam slid four loaves of white bread dough into the oven to bake.

"Who do you think put it there?"

"I 'spect it be Parker—or me Simon. When I asked Simon 'bout it, he just shrugged and said the tooth fairy most likely did it."

"Did you know today is Parker's birthday?" June asked as she wiped a bowl and set it back on the shelf.

"Is it, now?" Sam dumped pea pods into a bucket. "Then we have to do something special for him." She handed one of the orphans, Mary Ann, the bucket. "Empty it outdoors, lovey."

"Well, I know Parker favors chocolate cake."

"Chocolate cake, eh? I'll need to check the pantry, but I think we have the proper ingredients for a chocolate cake."

"I'll make it," Mary Jane volunteered, "if you'll show me how."

"I'll be glad to." June grinned. "I'll tell you what to do, and you do it. It'll be a great surprise for Parker."

June had decided the older girls needed tutoring in the basics of cooking and sewing. Together they'd repaired sheets, learned to darn socks, and were now starting to knit sweaters for the younger children's Christmas presents. June knew it would take all summer to finish the items since most of the girls were under the age of twelve.

Aunt Angeline, though failing, often came downstairs to sit with them, providing a critical eye, advice, or direction on a proper stitch. June enjoyed Angeline's pres-

ence. It reminded her of the hours she'd spent under
Aunt Thalia's watchful supervision.

With June standing by, Mary Jane sifted flour, cocoa,
baking soda, baking powder, and salt into a large bowl.

Cracking three eggs into the dry ingredients, the child
added sugar, vanilla, and thick buttermilk.

In no time at all, a heavenly aroma rose from the oven.
Mary Jane skipped off to tell the other orphans about the
special treat she'd helped make for Mr. Sentell.

June poured two cups of coffee and took a seat across
the table from Sam.

"You're so good at this, lovey. I don't know 'ow you
cope so well."

"I love children—I hope to have a whole houseful
someday."

"Ever give any thought to who the proud papa will
be?"

"If I did, I wouldn't tell you," June teased.

Sam brushed a handful of unruly red locks back from
her face. "I wish I had your confidence. Seems I'm having more than me share of doubts of late."

"Simon?" June guessed.

"No, not me Simon. 'e's the salt of the earth, 'e is.
No, I'm thinkin' if anything happens to Auntie, I'll have
to go back to England."

"And you don't want to?"

"Ow, it's not that I don't love me country; it's just
I've grown to love the children. Feel like me own, they
do. Would break me 'eart if they had to go to foster
homes."

"Yes, I can see that."

"June, when we first came here, we believed God
wanted us here. But when we first came, we thought
we'd be doing somethin' entirely different than what
we're doin' now. Does that mean God was wrong?"

June's eyes softened. "I've wondered the same thing

myself, at times. But I do believe that God is never wrong, Sam. He doesn't make mistakes."

Sam took a sip of coffee. "If that be true, then you think he'll make all this trouble and woe work for his glory?"

"I have to believe that. And if Reverend Inman has temporarily lost his way, God will make him aware of it. In his own time."

"I certainly hope so, lovey—I certainly hope so."

Thirty minutes later June stepped out the back door and into a hubbub. The children danced around in the yard, playing spirited games. Men crawled over the orphanage like bees on a honeycomb. It wasn't quite noon yet, and they'd already torn off half the old roof.

"Dinner's ready," June called.

"Good thing," Parker yelled back.

She shaded her eyes against the sun, looking up to where he stood on the tallest roof peak.

His silhouette was clear against the sky, and June's heart skipped a beat. He was incredibly big and strong. They might not see eye to eye on Reverend Inman or the tabernacle, but there was a lot of good in Parker. As hard as he tried to hide it, it was there. It would be so very easy to fall in love with this man—She caught her errant thoughts as Aunt Angeline appeared and slowly made her way to a chair sitting beneath a tree in the backyard, where she could oversee the younger children.

"Are you all right, Auntie?" June called.

The old woman waved, covering her lap with a light blanket.

"She's so frail," Sam fretted as June returned to the kitchen. "But she wants to 'elp."

"I worry about her."

"You shouldn't, love. She's 'ad a good life, and she's lookin' forward to meetin' the Lord. I try to make 'er rest—lately she's been more willing. I think she's just plain wearin' out."

The men washed up and took their places at the large table set up in the backyard. They dug in, filling their plates with roast beef, chicken swimming in rich broth with dumplings, peas, corn, turnips, mashed potatoes, and loaves of fresh-baked bread.

"You're going to make us all fat," Parker teased, shoving back from his plate a while later. June smiled, pleased that he'd eaten four servings of everything.

The men visited for a while to let their food digest. Parker finally stretched, then said, "I guess the work won't get done with us sitting here."

June sprang up. "Don't go yet!" She gave Mary Jane the prearranged signal. Shortly before, three of the older girls had disappeared to the kitchen to slice wedges of chocolate cake with thick fudge icing.

They now carried trays of dessert out to the makeshift tables in the yard.

"What's this?" Simon exclaimed.

"Happy birthday, Parker!" Sam shouted.

Parker looked genuinely stunned and a little embarrassed. His eyes fastened on June. "How did you know?"

"Simon looked it up in the camp records." She blushed. "I hope you don't mind. I always like to know a person's birthday."

He took in the cake and the festive icing as if he still couldn't believe it. "I haven't had a birthday cake since, well, I don't remember when." He dipped a large spoon into the icing and closed his eyes to savor the taste. "This is good." He opened his eyes, grinning. "Really good."

After dessert the men settled on the porch to rest before climbing back onto the roof. The weather was mild, and some shed their shirts. Some of the boys joined them, and June was appalled when a spitting match began.

Although she didn't want to encourage their antics, she couldn't help but see how the little ones gravitated to the men. After a while the older boys took out the pocket-knives they had received as Christmas gifts and attempted to carve toys for the younger children. Parker and Simon knelt on the ground, showing them how to carve whistles.

Before long the air resonated with the shrill sounds.

"I hope this doesn't get to be a habit," Sam complained, wincing as another screech split the air.

June laughed. "Isn't it wonderful to see the children having such a good time?"

Soon the sounds of hammers filled the air. The men nailed new shingles on the half of the roof they'd exposed that morning. June helped Sam settle the younger children for naps, though she seriously doubted that sleep was possible with all the racket.

Angeline, though, seemed to have no problem sleeping through the noise.

It was late afternoon when the men came off the roof and settled in the grass to eat sandwiches made from roast beef and bread left over from lunch.

"It's been a good day of work," one of the loggers commented, looking up at the new shingles.

"It's been a very good day of work," Sam agreed. "I wish I could think of some way to thank you for all you've done."

Parker was sitting on the grass, a sandwich in one hand, a glass of cold well water in the other. Sweat ran in rivulets down his face, and he wiped it away with his forearm. June watched, thinking he'd never looked more handsome. He finished the food, stretched, and pushed himself up. He said a few words to the men, smiled June's way, and started toward the front yard.

Groaning, Simon and the other men got to their feet

and headed toward the wagons. Sam ran to catch up with Simon.

June quickly ducked into the house, exiting the front door as Parker rounded the corner.

"Parker?"

When he turned, the setting sun washed his face in golden color, defining his rugged features. June inhaled sharply. How handsome he was! "Happy birthday."

"Thank you for the cake," he said. "I don't know when . . ." He paused. "Well, my birthdays come and go with no fuss. In fact, I'd forgotten the date myself."

"How old are you?" she teased. The records said he was twenty-nine.

"Too old for birthday cake," he said dryly.

"Nobody's ever too old for birthday cake." June wished the butterflies fluttering in her stomach would set-tle down. "I made something for you."

"More surprises?"

She handed him the package and waited while he opened it. He held the quilted squares up to the light, examining them. Her heart sank. Why didn't he say something? Didn't he know what they were? Or did he know and just not like the idea of her giving him a gift?

"They're . . . hand warmers." She stepped closer, aware of his masculine scent, all warm and musky. "See? There's a round stone for each finger. You warm the stones on the rail around the stove, then when you go outside, you slip them inside your gloves. Or when you come inside, you hold the stones for a few minutes to warm your hands—"

He looked up, and she could swear there was a strange mist in his eyes. "I—no one has ever made me a gift."

June smiled. "No one? Ever?"

"No one. Ever. I've been on my own since I was fourteen, June. And even when Ma and Pa were alive . . . well, there were a lot of kids at home." He looked at the hand warmers. "This is . . . the warmers will come in handy come fall and winter. Thank you."

"Happy birthday."

He hesitated, and for a moment she thought he would kiss her. She realized she'd like that, very much. But then he turned on his heel and strode quickly toward the wagon.

Think of me, Parker, every time you see those hand warmers, every time you hold them.

She returned to the house to finish cleaning up the kitchen, wondering what kind of childhood Parker had endured. If he'd never been given a gift, if birthday surprises were foreign to him, no wonder he was so touched by the orphans' plight.

No wonder he found a tabernacle a poor substitute for caring for God's children.

"Parker Sentell, if you belonged to me, you'd have gifts every day of the week," she whispered as she poured boiling water into the sudsy dishpan. "And I'd bake chocolate cakes and apple pies until they were coming out your ears. We'd worship in an open field every Sunday morning, if that suited you."

She washed a cup and set it aside to drain dry. "God loves you; Eli loved you, Parker Sentell. And I could love you too, if you'd let me."

Chapter Twelve

No matter how bad things are, they can always get worse.

Until yesterday June hadn't thought much about Aunt Thalia's old adage, but today it was back to haunt her.

Standing beneath an umbrella, she listened to Reverend Inman recite Psalm 23 to the small group of assembled mourners. Overnight, things had gotten worse. Much worse.

"The Lord is my shepherd; I shall not want. He maketh me to lie down in green pastures: he leadeth me beside the still waters. He restoreth my soul. . . . ."

The fiery man of God's Word seemed uncharacteristically subdued this morning as Reverend Inman finalized Angeline's simple graveside service with a heartfelt whispered "Amen and amen."

June drew Sam into the comfort of her arms while the young girl sobbed quietly into a frayed hankie. Rain clouds hovered overhead, and the mourners sank deeper into the lining of their coats. A cold rain began to fall.

June focused on the mourners gathered to eulogize Angeline Ferriman, the woman known to many as "that poor soul responsible for all those children."

In life Angeline hadn't cultivated many close friendships; in death, neighbors and community members gathered to pay homage to the slightly eccentric woman who had run the local orphanage. Heads bowed, dressed in Sunday best and spit-shined shoes, they stood before the simple casket and prayed.

Where had they been when Aunt Angie was alive and in desperate need of their help? June wondered.

"Judge not, that ye be not judged." Jesus' words shamed her thoughts, and she banished them, wondering instead how Sam would keep the children together now that Angeline was gone.

Ol' Joe stood next to June, dressed in a thin coat that afforded little protection from the chilly wind. The children huddled in a group on his right side, bracing themselves against the driving rain.

It seemed to June the person who'd known Aunt Angie the least was taking her passing the hardest. Tears rolled down Ben Wilson's face as he stared at the casket.

Death had come swiftly for Angeline. Though everyone suspected she had been failing for some time, her passing came as a shock. Perhaps it always does, June thought.

Angeline had asked to be buried at the edge of her property, beneath a large Douglas fir she'd planted herself, forty-two springs ago.

Pallbearers, some who had been with Reverend Inman's crusade in the earlier days when he traveled, others from Pine Ridge Logging Camp, gently lowered the plain pine coffin into the muddy ground.

June was painfully aware of the children's tear-streaked faces. Though Aunt Angeline had taught them about the Good Book, the joys of Christianity, death, and heaven, most were too young to comprehend.

The older ones understood enough to know that Aunt Angie was never coming back. June wondered about the anguish, the multitude of questions and fears that must be playing through their minds.

When the last prayer was issued, Simon stepped forward and led a weeping Sam from the gravesite.

June was surprised and grateful when Parker took her arm, and they fell into step behind the young couple.

"Terrible day for a funeral," he observed quietly.

"Sam's taking her aunt's death awfully hard."

"Well, she's here in a strange community, her family overseas. I imagine she's scared."

"She'd grown very close to Angeline."

"There must be something more I can do to help," Parker said.

June paused, turning to look at him. He constantly surprised her with his compassion. "If you truly mean that, I'm sure there is."

"You need only to let me know what's needed." He reached for her hand, and his eyes softened as he clasped it tightly in his. "I'll do what's possible to keep the children together. Simon and I have already discussed it."

June's stomach felt all knotted and strange, a feeling she often had in Parker's presence these days.

She squeezed his hand, thankful for his comforting presence.

The townspeople provided food for the bereaved. The orphanage's huge oak table held more food than the children had ever seen at one time, yet the children didn't seem eager to eat. They sat or stood staring, seemingly unaware it was dinnertime.

Reaching for an apron, June tied it around her waist and approached Mary. "What can I do to help?"

Mary paused, then resumed cutting squares of piping hot corn bread. Brushing a lock of hair off her forehead, she pointed the tip of the knife at a pile of plates. "You can get the children started."

"That sounds like a job I can handle."

June turned to see Parker filling the doorway, looking very big, and very out of place in a kitchen. She smiled. "You want to start with the smallest ones first?"

Parker picked up a plate, studying the heaping bowls of mashed potatoes, green beans, turnips, carrots, fried apples, sweet potatoes, and a myriad of other dishes lining the table.

"Fill their plates as you would your own." June handed him a heaping platter of golden brown fried chicken. "But remember, they don't eat as much as you."

Parker grinned. "Nobody eats as much as I do."

When the plates were ready, June and Parker corralled the children to a corner table. The kids began to eat, methodically swallowing as if they barely tasted the food. June noticed the younger ones' eyes occasionally searching the room. How they would miss Angeline.

Simon insisted on feeding the youngest child, who was delighted to have the honor of sitting on the big logger's lap.

Once the children were settled, June drew Sam aside. It might be too soon to discuss the matter, but it weighed on her mind. Steering her friend into the kitchen, June threaded Sam to the far end of the pantry, where they could talk in private. "Sam, is Joe going to stay on and help with the children?"

Freckles stood out on Sam's pale features. Her eyes were red from weeping. "I'm not sure, lovey; I haven't been about askin' 'im, yet." She walked to the small window and stared out. A heart-wrenching sadness filled her voice. "I suppose he will. . . . I just assume he'll be stayin'. Ain't like he's got a bloomin' lot of places to be goin' . . . if you know what I mean."

June nodded. The orphanage was the only home Joe had known for many years. He was an old man now; starting over would be difficult.

"If he's not set on stayin' . . . suppose I could send for me mum. . . . But she's up in years herself. As white headed as the snow on them mountains. Done raised her family, she has. And a second one as well, what with me bein' born so late in life. Don't think she has the energy to take on all these kiddies." Sam wiped her hands on her faded apron. "No . . . wouldn't be right to ask me mum to do such a thing. Would be the death of her, I'm thinkin'."

June chose her words carefully. Papa had always said, "Say what you mean, and mean what you say, lest you live to regret it." That's how she tried to live her life: meaning what she said. "Well, regardless of whether Joe does or doesn't stay, you're going to need help."

"Ow, that be the gospel for sure. No blasphemy intended." Sam's words faded to a whisper. "But I'll tell you this, June Kallahan: I'll be doin' it meself if necessary."

"Sam, that's a frightening responsibility for one person to assume."

The familiar spit-and-vinegar spirit Sam ordinarily possessed suddenly bloomed with a vengeance. "I'll not be shippin' them poor kiddies off in a million different directions! They may not be me blood kin, but they're family. *We're* family. And we'll stay a family no matter what."

June grinned. That's what she wanted to hear! The old

Sam was back. "And I'll be right beside you," she declared.

Sam blew her nose. "You're a good woman, June Kallahan." Her thin shoulders trembled beneath her thin dress. "Sorry I'm so blessed testy. I should've known you had somethin' up your sleeve. But, me dear, dear friend, you've already given so much of your free time helpin' out 'round here. Not to mention time making those pretty necklaces so the kiddies can have shoes and peppermint sticks. You got your responsibilities with the crusade, and Sunday services at the loggin' camps. I don't see how you can manage to spare another hour."

"Don't worry about me. I can fit in a lot more when it comes to the Lord's work." June met Sam's teary gaze. "I've been thinking. I want to help more around the orphanage—and I could, if I spent less time traveling back and forth."

Sam wiped at her eyes. "I expect that's true."

June gently squeezed Sam's hand. "The complex is old and drafty. So is the orphanage, for that matter, so I wouldn't be any better off there than here. I want to stay here awhile—if you'll have me."

"Have you?" Sam started laughing and crying at the same time. "I'd be plumb off me bean to refuse the offer! Oh, June. The kids love you so. And you're the best friend I've ever had. A sister to me, you are. A real sister. Of course I'll have you!"

"Then it's settled. I'll move in first thing tomorrow morning."

"Me prayers have surely been answered!"

"What prayers?" June teased. "I thought you didn't like all that praying."

"Out loud, lovey. When I be by meself, me and the Lord have jolly good talks."

June was proud of the progress Sam was making. It was

the Lord's doing, but she liked to think she had a small hand in it.

"Sam, I know sometimes it doesn't always feel like it, nor do circumstances always go according to what we want, but God answers prayers. In his own time and in his own way—sometimes he says yes; sometimes he says no; sometimes he says wait. But always, always, Sam, he answers us."

"I know he surely does, lovey." Sam playfully pulled June's nose. "Lord knows he's makin' me see that more and more lately."

June spotted Joe standing outside the kitchen doorway. "Do you think Joe would mind helping me fetch my things from the complex?"

"I'm sure he wouldn't." Sam frowned. "But what about Reverend Inman? What's he gonna think about all this movin' about?"

June toyed with a loose strand of hair, avoiding Sam's anxious look. What *would* Reverend Inman think about her moving into the orphanage? She didn't want to hurt his feelings, and she would work just as hard or even harder for the crusade. Sam desperately needed her help, and other than counting money and collecting donations, she wasn't really needed at the complex. She could be at nightly services; her job with the ministry would be unaffected. How could Reverend Inman object to her helping a friend in need?

Sam's hazel eyes widened with disbelief. "You mean you haven't talked with him about movin' in with a bunch of bloomin' ragamuffins?"

"You're not ragamuffins!" June chided. "Besides, it isn't like I've deliberately kept anything from him. I really haven't had a chance to talk to him. He isn't a monster, Sam. He'll recognize the need and insist that I help out."

"He'll throw a tizzy fit, he will." Sam shook her head. "He might be a godly man, but he's a stubborn one, wearing horse blinders when it comes to that tabernacle. He'll be hurt, he will."

A rush of pity washed over June. Her decision to move into the orphanage probably *would* hurt Reverend Inman's feelings. After all, he'd been gracious enough to take her in after Eli's death. But surely he would understand her motives, especially now that Aunt Angeline was gone.

"Reverend Inman will understand. He will consider the circumstances and agree that it's the only Christian thing to do."

Sam eyed her skeptically. It was easy to see she didn't agree with June's logic.

"Oh, stop worrying. If my decision bothers him—well, I'll just have to cross that bridge when I get to it."

"You best be mindin' your crossin' and don't go fallin' off that bridge," Sam cautioned.

"And what's that supposed to mean?"

"The reverend has a way—how do you Yanks say?—a way of wantin' his own way. Just like a man, eh, lovey?"

"Reverend Inman would never try to talk me out of doing charitable work," June defended.

"Maybe. Maybe not. But if it comes down to you not bein' as involved with the crusade—"

"It won't. My work with the crusade won't be affected. I'll make very sure of that."

Sam's silence was more eloquent than any words.

June's impatience surfaced. "Everyone seems to think the tabernacle is all Reverend Inman is concerned about. It isn't. He cares about his flock—about his people." June was suddenly trembling, and she didn't know why. Parker, and now Sam, had implied that Reverend Inman was blinded by greed.

Sam patted her hand. "Maybe I'm bein' a tad hasty. Who am I to judge the reverend? You know him better than anyone, what with the time you spend with him."

"I do, and I've seen how he works from daylight to dusk, down on his knees day after day, praying for guidance. Everyone connected with Reverend Inman wants to see the tabernacle raised. But that doesn't mean we aren't allowed to carry on God's work in other ways."

"You don't need to convince me," Sam assured her with a warm smile. "I may not know Reverend Isaac Inman, but I know *you* like the back of me hand. You wouldn't defend anyone not worth defendin'."

"Thank you, Sam." June got so heated when she talked about the tabernacle. She was tired of defending it and Reverend Inman.

"I knew the very day we met on the steamer that our friendship was a keeper."

June laughed softly. "Kindred spirits, that's what we are. Everything happens for a reason, Sam. Nothing happens by chance. The Lord brought our paths together for a specific purpose."

Sam added with a serious note, "You've certainly been a godsend to me and the children."

It was nearing dark when the last wagon rolled out of the orphanage yard. June stayed to clean up while Sam put the children to bed. Parker was one of the last to leave, offering June a ride back to the complex. She thanked him but declined his offer. His day had started before sunup. By the time he waited around for her to finish, took her to the complex, then rode back to camp, it would nearly be time for his new day to start.

Reverend Inman stopped by the kitchen to offer his assistance. June expressed her gratitude but insisted he go ahead, explaining that she wanted to keep Sam company for a while.

Part of her reason was that she wasn't ready to discuss her plans with Reverend Inman yet. She needed time to digest her decision, think it through, prepare a valid argument.

When she defended Reverend Inman, she meant what she said. He was caring, and giving, and concerned about others. But some of what Sam contended was true as well. Reverend Inman could be very persuasive when he wanted. It wasn't that she was afraid he'd talk her out of moving to the orphanage; she had her mind made up about that. She just didn't want a confrontation, especially after the emotionally draining day.

The rain had stopped, and a cold moon hung low in the sky when Ol' Joe stopped the wagon in front of the complex. The Indian waited until she was safely inside, then waved and drove away into the night.

Stretching out across the bed, June closed her eyes, her head swimming. The day had been long and difficult.

Eventually she rose, changed into her flannel gown, then said her prayers. *Lord, help the children. . . .* She fell asleep before she could complete her train of thought.

The sun was peeking over the horizon when she awoke, feeling as tired as when she'd gone to bed. Quickly she washed and dressed, then set about packing her few belongings.

She spread the worn patchwork quilt on the single bed and fluffed the pillow, stood back, and then rearranged them, realizing she was procrastinating.

You're being silly. Reverend Inman will be awake now. Go to him, tell him your plans, share breakfast with him, then ask him to come with you to the orphanage—possibly spend the day with the children. Ol' Joe will be coming soon. She had no reason to feel such dread. What she was doing was right. The children needed her. And it wasn't as though she would be neglecting her other responsibilities.

She'd delayed the inevitable as long as she could. Even at this early hour she knew exactly where to find Reverend Inman. He would be in the revival tent, absorbed in his morning devotions. Leaving the complex, she hurried to the tent.

Reverend Inman was kneeling at the altar in prayer. He started each new day in the same manner before preparing the subject of his nightly message. June slipped into the front pew to wait.

When Reverend Inman finished and stood up, he looked around, and a quick smile crossed his face. "June. I didn't expect to see you up and about so early. You must have stayed at the orphanage quite late. I listened for your return, but I was overcome by exhaustion."

"It was late when Ol' Joe brought me home."

Tight lines around Reverend Inman's eyes made him look older this morning. June worried that he wasn't getting enough rest.

He nodded. "I'm told we can expect another large crowd tonight."

"Praise God."

"Yes, indeed. Praise his name. Seems there's a new logging camp not far from the grounds. As unusual as it is, most of the men have brought their families with them. The foreman rode out just yesterday, and we had a pleasant visit. Said he'd heard about our revival all the way to Portland. He's excited about joining us in worship and promised that others from the camp would be accompanying him."

"That's wonderful, Reverend."

"Yes, it's exciting to know God's work is being recognized throughout this great land."

"Reverend Inman." June cleared her throat. She needed to get this over with. "I have something I need to tell you."

His smiled faded, and he suddenly looked very old. Shoulders slumped, he sank to the bench. "I suspected as much. You're leaving me, aren't you?"

"No, no, Reverend, I'm not leaving you."

"No, I know you are. I've been expecting this."

June knelt beside the pew, wanting to ease the terrible pain creasing his face. "Reverend Inman, now that Sam's aunt is gone, she can't care for all those children by herself. Even if Ol' Joe stays on, the responsibility is too much for her." She paused, and the silence was deafening. "I'm moving to the orphanage."

Sadness played across his face. It seemed an eternity before he spoke. "You want to live at the orphanage?"

"Yes. Sam desperately needs my help. Ol' Joe is old and not able to keep up with the younger children."

"But you're needed here. You give the orphanage hours of service each week." Reverend Inman ran his fingers through a rim of silvery gray hair. "I don't understand. Why would you want to abandon Eli's work? Have you forgotten your calling? Have I been unkind—insensitive?"

"No, you've been wonderful, but I am called to do the work of the Lord—"

"Yes!" His voice lost its timidity and swelled with conviction. "And the Lord's work is here! Have you forgotten the tabernacle?"

No, she hadn't forgotten the tabernacle, but at times she wished she could. For just one sane moment, she wished she could forget the madness, the sense of urgency that consumed them all. "I'll contribute no less time—"

"Oh, child! You can't *contribute;* you must *commit*— completely and wholeheartedly commit—to this endeavor. Your every effort *must* revolve around its completion!"

"Reverend Inman, building the tabernacle is my vision as well as yours, and it was Eli's. But I feel the Lord has also called me to help care for those children. They have no one but Sam."

Reverend Inman buried his face in his hands. His

shoulders shook with emotion. "I cannot believe I'm hearing this. Has Parker influenced your decision? He doesn't approve of the tabernacle—is this your reason for leaving?"

"No, Reverend. Parker doesn't know about my moving. I only made the decision late yesterday afternoon."

Shaking his head, Reverend Inman stared at the altar. "I can't begin to tell you how disappointed I am."

"But you needn't be." June wanted desperately for him to understand. "I'll spend just as much time with the crusade. Moving to the orphanage won't alter my dedication. I'll still collect donations at The Gilded Hen, and I'll stay late after the services—"

"No," Reverend Inman murmured. "No. It won't be the same. Eli had complete dedication to the project. You—you will be pulled in a different direction."

"I don't mean to hurt you," June said, feeling sick to her stomach. She didn't want it to end this way.

"No." Reverend Inman straightened. "I'm sure you don't. Go, go to your orphanage. Eli's dream will live on, with or without your commitment."

"Please, Reverend. I promised to help Sam only until other arrangements can be made. In the meantime, my work with the crusade will continue. I promise you, I'll be just as dependable as ever. My enthusiasm won't wane. Nor will the vision of the tabernacle diminish in my heart."

Reverend Inman released a weary breath. "I can't hold you here. You must do what you feel best."

June stood up, her legs trembling beneath her. She'd expected his disappointment; she had not expected his condemnation. Why must he and Parker see only black and white?

Hanging her head, she said softly, "I'll be moving my things this morning."

The reverend appeared to succumb. He sat quietly, looking at nothing. "I'll have Ben hitch the wagon."

"Thank you, it won't be necessary."

Reverend Inman looked up, as if to confirm her insanity.

"Ol' Joe's coming back for me."

Reverend Inman nodded. "Ol' Joe." Hurt rang hollow in his voice. Guilt gnawed at June. She was torn between loyalty to Reverend Inman and devotion to Sam. If Reverend Inman only understood that she wasn't choosing, that she truly could do both well. "I think I hear Ol' Joe's wagon now. I'm sorry if I hurt you. I never meant to."

Reverend Inman turned away. "You mustn't keep Joe waiting."

June edged toward the doorway, torn between going and staying. "I'll be at services tonight. Just like every night before and every night to come. You'll see. Nothing will change. I promise you."

Chapter Thirteen

SUNDAY night services were continuing to draw large crowds. Twenty minutes before the sermon that night, latecomers had to search for an empty seat. Loggers from Tin Cup, Pine Ridge, and Cutter's Pass filled the back pews. June's work in front of The Gilded Hen had finally borne fruit. Familiar faces were popping up.

No matter how many times the congregation heard Reverend Inman preach, each service hummed with anticipation. Whether he condemned sin, warned of the consequences of straying from God, or admonished the worshipers to seek God's guidance in every decision, people were ready to listen, to examine their heart for shortcomings.

Tonight Reverend Inman's message was on the Christian walk: What did God expect of his children? June listened attentively, wondering if Reverend Inman ever listened to his own message. If so, how could he fail to see the catastrophic need less than two miles from his own back door?

After services June counted the offering and entered the total in the ledger. Moments later she let herself out of the tent, closing the flap behind her.

Someone stepped from the shadows, and her heart flew to her throat.

"Don't be frightened. It's Parker. I didn't mean to scare you."

"Parker!" She drew a steady breath, trying to get her bearings. "What are you doing here this late?"

"Waiting for you."

He stood in the half shadows. Pale moonlight bathed his face, throwing his strong features into relief. His coat was open, revealing a blue chambray shirt open at the neck. Her pulse tripped erratically. She self-consciously smoothed her skirt. "Is something wrong?"

"No—I just wanted to see you."

Her heartbeat quickened. "You did?"

He smiled, stepping into the light. "If you have no objections."

"No—no objections." She couldn't think of a single one, even if she tried.

"I heard you'd moved into the orphanage. I thought I might give you a ride home. And, what with all the commotion of moving, I wasn't sure you had eaten a proper supper. So I packed us a picnic."

She frowned. "A picnic?" Was he serious? A picnic? At ten o'clock at night? In a million years she'd never have thought of him asking her to go on a moonlit picnic!

"Yeah—I hear you can work up a powerful appetite chasing little tykes around."

She bit back a grin. This was an impetuous side of

Parker. He was full of surprises. "Well, they sure can wear a body out."

"Then let's let you relax some."

Parker drew her in front of him, his hand warm in the middle of her back as he guided her toward a waiting buggy. Lifting her into the carriage, he stepped in behind her as she settled her skirts.

"Comfortable?"

"Very—thank you."

"Are you warm? Nights can still be pretty chilly."

"I'm fine." She leaned close, her face only inches from his now, playfully whispering, "Now, will you stop fussing over me, and let's see what you've got in that picnic basket."

He quirked a brow. "Getting pretty sassy, aren't you?"

She grinned. "Sassy and stubborn. That's me!"

Flipping the reins, Parker set the buggy in motion. She longed to ask what had brought about his sudden good humor, but she didn't want to break the spell. Whatever it was, it was fine with her.

Moonlight washed the landscape, the pines casting gentle shadows across the road as the horse trotted by the river. It was a perfect summer night. Stars overhead, a cool breeze. "It's beautiful," June said softly.

"Yes, it is."

"Have you lived in Seattle all your life?"

"Not yet," he confided with a wink. "But I was born not far away."

She shivered against the cool breeze, and he leaned closer, drawing her into the warmth of his arm. She looked up at him, surprised, afraid to move for fear he would abandon the idea.

"Is this better?"

She smiled, snuggling closer. "Much better."

"I could drive you straight home to the orphanage, but I was thinking that perhaps you might want to see a spot that Eli and I often enjoyed. It's here by the river. If you're not too tired."

She didn't feel the least bit tired. "The river?"

"Yes, Eli and I used to go fishing here." A mischievous gleam showed in his eyes. "How would you like to try your hand at fishing?"

"Fishing?" The man was still full of surprises!

"Yeah—I hear they're biting."

"Nothing I like better than fresh panfish."

"Then let's go catch some."

Twenty minutes later Parker stopped the carriage beneath a bare oak and lifted June out of the buggy. Taking a feed bag from beneath the seat, he slipped it over the horse's head.

June wandered down a small incline, following the sound of running water. Moonlight played on the gurgling stream, making pretty diamond-shaped patterns on the water.

"I brought something to sit on," Parker said when he joined her. He spread a heavy blanket on the ground and set a basket at one corner.

"What's in the basket?"

"Supper." He grinned. "In case you're a bad fisherman."

She suddenly felt flirtatious, lighthearted. "Is that a challenge?"

"Didn't your papa warn you not to wager?"

She laughed. "Yes, I do believe he mentioned that one or a hundred times."

Parker handed her a baited fishing pole. "I can even be persuaded to bait this for you."

"Such a gentleman," she teased, but thankful for the offer. The thought of threading a hook through a worm's entrails didn't excite her.

Sitting down on the blanket, she watched the cork on her fishing line bob in the water. Fishing had never interested her. Long hours spent waiting for a poor fish to bite seemed a waste of precious time. She would rather talk—have Parker tell her about himself.

They sat side by side, sharing a quiet camaraderie. For the first time in a long while she felt at peace.

This new side of Parker was nearly as disconcerting as it was pleasant. In her wildest fantasies she would never have imagined this man capable of planning a lovely late-night picnic by the river.

They'd argued about Reverend Inman's plans, disagreed over his motivation, mourned Eli's passing. She had alternately been angry with him—accused him of having a blind spot when it came to Reverend Inman—and had been drawn to his strength, to his dedication to Eli, to his ability to keep a hundred or more lumberjacks in line with a mere evenly modulated command.

One side of Parker she hadn't experienced was fishing with him. And now, here she was, pole in hand, wondering what she was doing here.

"Hungry?"

She hadn't thought so, but, yes, she was hungry. "Yes. What did you bring that's good to eat?"

Parker opened the hamper and set out a tin of soda crackers, a wedge of cheese, and a plate of what looked to be oatmeal cookies. Very dry oatmeal cookies.

"I packed it myself."

Somehow she managed to seem properly impressed. "It looks very—dry."

He produced a pottery carafe. "Fresh water," he said. And a second—"Coffee, in case you get cold."

Handing her a wedge of cheese, he bit into a cracker. "Go ahead—taste it."

She took an experimental bite and was surprised to find the cheese exceptionally good. "Very tasty."

He cut off another slice and handed it to her. She

179

smiled, shifting it to the other hand. A two-fisted eater. That was sure to make an impression on him.

They ate in silence, sitting opposite one another on the blanket. This was such a different Parker, a side she found extremely attractive.

A side she could learn to love.

Love. A small word that held such enormous implications.

"This is very nice," she commented, reaching for a cookie. She bit into it, watching her cork bob up and down on the rippling water.

"This was Eli's favorite fishing hole."

She took another bite of cookie, looking at him from the corner of her eye. He was lost in memory, thinking back to a simpler time. Lying back on the blanket, she gazed at the sky. It was such a lovely night—millions of stars overhead. Warm enough, despite the brisk breeze. Was Eli watching? *Hello, Eli. You were right. Your friend is nice—very nice.*

"How did you meet Eli?"

Parker laughed, a masculine rumble coming from deep inside his chest, and she thought how comfortable she was with the sound.

"I nearly ran him down."

"You what?"

"I was driving a wagon back into town. Eli was walking along the road, head down, deep in thought. As the wagon approached him from behind, he stepped out as if he were going to cross the road. I thought there was no way I could keep from running him down."

"Did you?"

"No—he stepped back in time. We laughed about it later, but it could have been serious. Dead serious."

June smiled. "God at work again."

"That's what Eli said, and I couldn't argue it. He came to work for me a few days later."

"So how did you two become such good friends?" she asked.

"Eli had a bad accident—nearly severed a limb. But again, God led us to a doctor who was developing new methods in that field of medicine. I visited him often in the long weeks during his recuperation, and we became close friends. During his recovery, Eli began attending Isaac's meetings and caught his vision. Since he could no longer work in the logging camp, he felt called to join Isaac's staff.

"He told me about his work with Isaac, what he wanted to accomplish. I didn't agree, but we agreed to disagree. We spent our spare time together, talked hours about God, about God's work, about faith. I found Eli to be a man of great faith, and I wanted to have his sense of assurance, his absolute belief that God was at work in his life and in the lives of others. Even mine."

"You doubted that?"

"Sometimes," he admitted. He gazed at the gurgling stream. "Often. I suppose you don't?"

"Oh, yes, I do. Not my faith, but whether I'm follow-ing God's direction and not my own."

"And you worry about that?"

"Sometimes. I think sometimes I'm not doubting God but myself, my ability to discern his direction."

"I think we all worry about that." He drew his line in and rebaited his hook. "I miss Eli."

"So do I." She sat up, resting her chin on her drawn knees. "Sometimes I want so badly to talk to him again, ask him why things happen the way they do. I know it's silly, but I talk aloud—just as if he were here. I knew him so briefly, yet when he died, I felt as if I had lost my husband."

"Yeah—I find myself talking to him every now and then, too. Isaac's name usually comes up."

"Parker." She frowned. "You really are wrong about

Reverend Inman. He's dedicated but . . . granted, maybe to the wrong thing."

He made a disagreeable grumbling sound in his throat, and she changed the subject. "Let's talk about Sam. I wish I could be as certain about what I'm doing as Sam is. As soon as she learned of the need at the orphanage, she knew immediately that was where she belonged."

"You aren't sure what you're doing is right?"

"I know it's right, that I'm filling an important need. I just wonder if that's why I was brought here. Eli is dead, so God must intend me for another purpose."

"Well, maybe the orphanage is it."

"Maybe—but still, it seems like there's more."

He grinned. "I don't see you being unsure about anything. Seems to me you know your mind real well."

She made a playful face at him. "Don't tell anyone, but most of the time I haven't a clue what I'm doing. I just go by that small, still voice that says, 'Do something, June, until you can figure out what you're doing.' But Sam needs help, and I'm it for right now."

June lifted her pole to check if a clever fish had stolen her bait. "I don't like it when I'm uncertain. My papa was a preacher. A good one. A pulpit-pounding, hellfire-and-damnation preacher who never wavered. He made me believe that once your course is set you never stray from it. I set my course for Eli, then his dream . . . and now it seems like maybe I should stray from that. I'm not sure how it all fits together—Eli, the tabernacle, and the orphanage."

"How did you meet Sam?"

"On the ship. We were excited to discover we were both coming to Seattle." She set her pole aside. "Strange, isn't it, that both of us were drawn here by outside forces? Her aunt, and Eli. Now they're both gone." She sighed. "But Sam has Simon now."

"Simon's in love. He's a man of few words, but he's

off the deep end with Sam. I wouldn't be surprised if he leaves me and goes to work at the orphanage."

June sighed, rather liking the thought that love changed lives. "Wouldn't that be nice?"

"For Sam maybe—not for me. Simon's my right hand, but if he wants more time at the orphanage, I can arrange it."

June debated whether to ask her next question. But since they were being so candid . . . "Do you suppose this was God's plan all along? Bringing Sam here so she could meet Simon?"

"Do you think your coming here was his plan?"

She glanced away. "What do you think?"

"I think that remains to be seen." He playfully wedged a cracker into her mouth.

Biting into the crisp texture, she mused, "I truly do worry about the orphans' welfare. Sam can't keep them forever."

If Sam had her way, she'd keep them together, but if she and Simon decided to marry, the care and custody of all those children would be too much for a young married couple. She couldn't stay on at the orphanage—the couple would need their privacy. And Simon would have to keep working, to provide food for his family. In spite of what Sam might say, or even Simon, they couldn't be expected to assume such responsibility for the orphanage.

If she could, June would open a new orphanage and work even harder to convince Reverend Inman and others in the community to support her work.

She longed to talk to Faith about the matter. She smiled when she thought about her sister. She'd just received a letter from Faith, who had not failed to mention the number of eligible young men in the community— men of faith, upstanding men, with solid jobs in stores and banks or who owned their own businesses. Gentlemen. Potential husbands, June read between the lines.

The idea of visiting Faith tempted her. Sometimes she thought she should go—pour out her problems and have a good cry. But then she'd look at Parker, and Sam and the orphans, and she wasn't so ready to go.

"This is very nice. I'm glad you thought of it."

"It's been a long time since I enjoyed a pretty woman's company." He turned to look at her. Moonlight softened his features. "Thank you for remembering my birthday."

She reached over and laid her hand over his. "You don't have to thank me. No—actually, you should be grateful," she amended. "The hand warmers could have been a necklace." She grinned.

Sobering, she gazed at him, refusing to look away. Leaning closer, he kissed her lightly, and it seemed as natural as rain.

"Thank you for the picnic," she murmured.

"Thank you for the hand warmers." He kissed her again softly, on the nose, then on her forehead. "Can I tell you something?"

"Anything."

"You're a lousy fisherman."

She swatted him on the shoulder. "I know. Why do you think I avoid it like the plague?"

How could it be that just a short time ago she had thought this wonderful, perceptive man was such an oaf?

Sam had left a light burning in the front window of the orphanage. When the buggy rolled to a stop, it was very late.

"Thank you for sharing your supper with me."

When Parker didn't immediately respond, June reached over, turning his face to meet hers. He looked at her, and she had the feeling that he was trying to decide what to think about her. But apparently he couldn't decide.

Brushing the backs of his fingers against her cheek, he

smiled. "You may not fish worth a hoot, but you're good company." His gaze softened. "Thank you for having supper with me."

Looking into his eyes, June felt a sense of rightness—that Parker was her destiny, even if he didn't know it yet.

Chapter Fourteen

Isaac Inman was tired. Services were still hours away, yet there were Scriptures to review, final preparations for tonight's sermon. He was usually cognizant of the familiar hustle that preceded other services, but tonight . . . tonight he was just too soul weary to notice.

Settling himself at the table, he waved aside Ettie's offer of tea and scones. "I'm not hungry . . . but thank you, Ettie. You're a good woman."

"You work too hard, Brother Isaac." Ettie brought his slippers and adjusted the damper on the stove.

"I'm fine, Ettie. I'd like to be alone."

"Of course, Reverend."

The door closed, and Isaac bowed his head, praying for

187

God's guidance for the evening sermon. When he finished, he opened the Bible to Psalm 32:8.

A familiar peace settled over him as he entered into God's Word. "I will instruct thee and teach thee in the way which thou shalt go: I will guide thee with mine eye."

"Oh, Lord," Isaac whispered. "This is all I ask of thee. Show me, Father. Show me what you would have me do."

The passage so moved him that he slipped to his knees in prayer, giving thanks and praising God's holy name. Rising again, he sat back down.

Every bone in his body cried out for rest. Removing his wire-framed spectacles and faded black jacket, he rubbed his eyes. Was there time for a short nap before services? Perhaps. The mantle clock sounded five soft, melodic chimes as he crawled into his bed and pulled the soft down coverlet to his chin.

His body surrendered easily to sleep, and yet he tossed and turned, thrashing about on the cot.

When he woke, he sat up with a start. Looking around the small room, he felt confused.

Rolling off the bed, he hurried down the corridor, around the corner, and returned to his desk. Turning to Matthew 5:1–16, he read the Scriptures aloud, savoring the words as if he'd only just heard them.

"And seeing the multitudes, he went up into a mountain: and when he was set . . . "

It was a full thirty minutes later when he prayed for guidance and finished the Scripture.

"Neither do men light a candle, and put it under a bushel, but on a candlestick: and it giveth light unto all that are in the house. Let your light so shine before men, that they may see your good works, and glorify your Father which is in heaven."

When he was finished reading, he closed the book. He

sat for a long while, staring into the fire's slow-burning embers.

Finally he reached for a silver bell and rang it.

Ettie appeared momentarily.

"Yes, Reverend?"

"I'll have that tea now, Ettie."

"Yes, Reverend . . . will you be wanting your supper too?"

"No. Just tea. Thank you, Ettie."

June arrived at the tent a little before six. She'd driven the orphanage wagon. Sam and Joe thought it best to keep the children home tonight. One of the younger ones was running a fever.

She tied the horse to the hitching post, where Ben Wilson was waiting to escort her into the crusade.

"Evenin', Miss June." Ben smiled.

"Hello, Ben." June gave him a quick hug. "It's good to see you again. I've missed you."

"Yes, you missed me!" Ben giggled.

"I haven't seen you at the orphanage for a few days."

Ben hung his head. "Ben misses you." He perked up again just as readily. "The people here, they need me!" He thrust his chest out proudly as they entered the tent.

June was relieved to see that the service was going to be packed again. Every pew was filled to capacity. Men and women were milling around outside the tent in a standing-room-only crowd.

By six-thirty, songs of praise filled the air. Young and old alike clapped in rhythm to the powerful message found in the music.

Gazing out on the audience, Reverend Inman lifted his arms, commanding silence.

The noise subsided, and every head bowed.

The silence stretched. Finally, in a compelling voice, Isaac said, "Father, we gather tonight to praise you!"

At first, Reverend Inman seemed in command, but as the service wore on, June noticed a change. He seemed preoccupied, searching passages from the Bible as if he were speaking more to himself than to the congregation. Even his demeanor was different. His intense blue eyes skimmed the worshipers, yet he seemed to be oblivious to them.

Gone was Reverend Inman's familiar fiery message. No raised shouts, no prowling the altar, no raising his arms toward the heavens as he preached.

June became concerned. Was he ill? His features were pale, and he looked tired—incredibly tired. Guilt assaulted her. Was she responsible for his fatigue? In the weeks she'd been gone, she'd worked as hard as ever for the ministry. Only yesterday three loggers had donated an entire month's salary toward the tabernacle.

Reverend Inman's voice drew her back.

"If the congregation will turn with me in their Bibles to Matthew, chapter 25, verses 29 through 46."

The rustling of turning parchment filled the huge tent.

Standing behind the pulpit, Isaac put his spectacles on. "Earlier I prepared a sermon . . . but God has led me to deliver a different message."

Silence prevailed. Every eye steadied on the reverend.

Reverend Inman cleared his throat and began with an uncharacteristic softness. "For unto every one that hath shall be given, and he shall have abundance: but from him that hath not shall be taken away even that which he hath."

He paused, and June saw tears well in his eyes.

"For I was an hungred, and ye gave me meat," he read softly. "I was thirsty, and ye gave me drink: I was a stranger, and ye took me in."

There was a faraway look in his eyes, and Isaac ignored the tears that streamed down his cheeks.

"Naked, and ye clothed me: I was sick, and ye visited me: I was in prison, and ye came unto me."

Still not referring to the Bible open before him, he continued.

"Then shall the righteous answer him, saying, Lord, when saw we thee an hungred, and fed thee? or thirsty, and gave thee drink? When saw we thee a stranger, and took thee in? or naked, and clothed thee? Or when saw we thee sick, or in prison, and came unto thee?"

Isaac looked up, openly weeping now.

"Verily I say unto you, Inasmuch as ye have done it unto one of the least of these my brethren, ye have done it unto me."

Reverend Inman closed his Bible.

Not a sound was heard throughout the tent.

The ushers exchanged questioning looks. Ben got up and hurried to distribute the offering baskets.

"If the ushers would please return to their seats," Isaac commanded softly.

The activity ceased. The men sat down. Ben looked confused but obediently returned to his bench.

Isaac focused on the congregation, tears rolling down his cheeks. "Tonight it would give me great pleasure if we would stand as a congregation and give thanks for the countless blessings already given in the Lord's precious name."

A man got to his feet, then a woman, then two men. One by one, from all over the tent, the worshipers stood in prayerful gratitude.

What is troubling Reverend Inman? June wondered as she rose from her seat. The service had taken on a surreal atmosphere.

She gradually became aware of sounds outside the tent, and she strained to hear. Was it thunder that shook the earth beneath her? One by one people in the congregation heard the commotion and lifted their heads to listen.

It was the sound of rapidly approaching horses. The hoofbeats were muffled at first; then they shattered the stillness, followed by men's raised voices.

"Fire!"

"The orphanage is burning!"

"Help! Come quickly—there'll be nothing left to save!"

June raced from the tent, threading her way through the crushing crowd. Outside she could smell the deadly smoke.

"Ben!" she shouted.

"Miss June!" Ben was suddenly at her side, eyes wide with fear. "Please don't go. You'll be hurt!"

June raced breathlessly toward the wagon with Ben trailing a few feet behind. "Unhitch the wagon. I can get there faster on horseback. Ben, quickly! Please!"

Ben passed her and quickly unhitched the quarter horse. He picked June up and swung her lithely onto the animal. It was the first time June had ever ridden bareback, but there wasn't time for a saddle.

"Ben—Ben," Ben struggled to get the words out. "Me—me—me come, too! I—I—I can help! You need me!"

June glanced at the orange glow along the horizon, then back at Ben's earnest gray eyes. The orphanage needed all the help it could get.

June steadied the prancing horse. "Ben, I do need you. Ride to the orphanage, and help carry water."

"Yes, Miss June! Ben carry water!" Ben ran for a horse, reciting under his breath, "Carry water, lots of water. Hot. Fire!"

"Ben!" June shouted above the roar of panic. "Don't go into the house! You carry buckets of water, OK? Just buckets of water!"

Ben nodded, reciting as he climbed aboard the horse. "Just buck—buck—buckets of water!"

Parker and Simon had to be told. The stretch of rutted road leading to Pine Ridge was dark and frightening. Bending close to the horse's neck, June gave the animal his head.

Galloping into the sleeping camp, she rode to the bunkhouse, shouting, "Parker! Simon! Help!"

A breathless moment passed, and she shouted again, "Parker!"

A lantern flickered to life. June watched the bunkhouse door until she saw Parker stagger out. Roused from a deep sleep, he hitched his suspenders over his shoulder.

"June?" He struggled to focus on her. "What are you doing out here at this time of—?"

"Come quickly," June pleaded. "The orphanage is on fire!"

Parker blindly reached for the big brass bell hanging from the bunkhouse rafters.

Within moments lights flickered in darkened windows, doors burst open, and loggers poured out into the cold night.

Pine Ridge was all but deserted, save for women and children, when June led a large contingency to the fire.

Horses galloped through the night, hooves pounding.

Simon rode up beside June. "Where's Sam?"

"At the orphanage! She stayed home with the children tonight!"

Skirting her horse, Simon rode ahead.

When the riders arrived at the orphanage, Sam and the children huddled beneath blankets on the road, tearfully watching the old two-story house go up in flames. Though neighbors, along with Joe, Ben, Isaac, and the men from the congregation, had tried to contain the fire, they were powerless against the flames. All anyone could do was watch helplessly as the fire raged, flames angrily eating up the weathered lumber.

June bit back tears of anger. What would the children do now? Hadn't they been through enough? Was there no end to their misfortune?

"Ow, June," Sam blubbered. "Me old auntie's gone, the orphanage is gone—where is this merciful God that's always so good to everyone—where is he, June?" She pounded June's chest, her voice a raised wail.

"Come on now," Simon said, gently prying her away. "This isn't June's fault, Sam. You know that."

Sam dissolved against him in tears and allowed Simon to lead her away.

Reverend Inman was making his way through the chaotic scene, trying to still the younger children's cries. In the midst of the disaster someone remembered to thank God that their lives had been spared.

"Oh, Parker," June whispered as he appeared at her side. He was covered in soot, his clothes singed from going too near the flames. "What's going to happen to those children?"

Drawing her into his arms, he held her close. The front of his shirt dampened with her tears.

With the fire clearly out of control, Reverend Inman took hold of the situation. He dispersed men to gather up frightened children and load them into waiting wagons.

"There's nothing more we can do," he said. "I'll take them to the complex for the night. Tomorrow we'll make proper arrangements."

June couldn't find her voice. What proper arrangements? The only home they knew had burned. Aunt Angeline was dead. No one wanted the orphans on their hands.

Holding June close, Parker questioned Reverend Inman. "Is there room enough at the complex?"

"Ettie will make room."

"We can take a few back to camp with us."

Reverend Inman looked to June for permission.

"No, they should be together—especially tonight."

"They'll be taken to the complex. Workers are waiting to see to their needs. You and Sam must come too."

June wiped her eyes. The matter was no longer in her control. It never had been. "I'll get Sam."

The men were downcast as they walked away from the charred remains. Ben helped load children into the wagons and cover them with blankets.

As the pitiful caravan rumbled off into the night, whimpers were heard from frightened children as big, gruff loggers held them tightly in their arms and tried to comfort them.

Papa's words thundered in June's head.

There's a reason and due season.

Sometimes he comes through on the brink of the midnight hour.

Nothing is left to chance.

He knows our needs before we ask.

Though he sometimes makes us wait, it's all part of his plan.

Remember, June, as big as our dreams are, they can't compare to what he has in store for us. We can't out-dream him, any more than we can out-give him. He'll always give us his best. He's never late, Daughter. No matter the hour, he's always right on time.

Kicking a smoldering piece of wood out of the way, June was assaulted by doubt. Where was God tonight? Why had he heaped even more trouble on poor, defenseless children? The strange sense of faltering belief left a bitter taste in her mouth.

"What are you thinking?" Parker asked, drawing her aside.

"That I don't know about God, Parker. All my life I've trusted, believed that, no matter what, he was there to look after us. Why would God let something this unspeakable happen? Haven't Sam and I fought hard enough just to keep shoes on the kids' feet and a roof over their heads? Why did God have to go and burn down the orphanage?"

"You know, June," Parker said, hesitating only slightly, "I can understand how you feel. When God took Eli, it didn't make any sense to me. But we may not always understand God's way. We have to trust that he sees the big picture, and then say, 'In his own way, God knows what's best for all his children.' "

"Right now I'm finding that very hard to do."

Parker avoided her eyes and went on. "The situation here at the orphanage was impossible. Sam has tried to make a rundown house a home for—how many children? She couldn't run this place alone. She's lost Angeline, and Joe's old. The fight to build that blasted tabernacle and keep the orphans clothed and fed is draining the whole community. With the orphanage gone, the settlement will have no choice. They will have to do something with the children."

June felt her hackles rise. "Why don't you just come out and say what you mean, Parker, instead of reciting all these nice platitudes?"

Parker sobered. "I've said what I mean. You're not thinking straight. You can't run an orphanage on a hope and a prayer, June."

"Well, I can, Parker. And I'll fight with every last breath in me to see that those children are not packed up and carted off like some abandoned livestock. They aren't pieces of property! They are God's children."

A muscle tightened in Parker's jaw. "What God?"

She kicked at another ember. "You know I didn't mean what I said a minute ago. I'm just mad at God right now—it doesn't mean I believe for one moment that he isn't here, watching this whole fiasco."

June's emotions were running the full gamut. She was tired, frustrated, heartbroken. When the full meaning of Parker's earlier statement hit her, she seethed.

There was no mistaking his underlying meaning. He wasn't just glad to be free of the orphanage, he was glad to be getting rid of *her*. He knew that the only thing keeping her here was the orphanage. He was feeling pure-and-simple—relief!

He cocked a brow and looked at her. "What?"

June Kallahan, the mail-order bride from Cold Water, Michigan, no longer had a reason to stay in Seattle. In Parker Sentell's hair.

Well, Eli Messenger might be dead. The orphanage might be smoldering ashes. Her part in Reverend Inman's dream might be over, but she still had her pride. She backed away. Anger left her speechless. She would not let Parker see her cry; she would not! She had foolishly fallen in love with him, and now look what happened.

In love.

The thought hit her harder than Parker's betrayal.

She was in love with Parker; she had been for weeks. Why hadn't she realized it? For some time now, she'd known he wasn't like any other man she'd ever met. He didn't have Eli's sensitivity or easy kindness, but she loved him all the same.

Parker shifted stances, his anger evident now. "Where are you going? Just once I'd like to have a conversation with you that didn't end in a disagreement—June—"

She hadn't realized how slippery the ground beneath her was. Papa's stern, "Pride goeth before a fall," flashed through her mind as she felt her feet fly from under her.

Parker reached out to break her fall, but it was too late. The next thing June knew, she was lying facedown in the mud.

She groaned, clamping her eyes shut in humiliation. Why must she always behave like a bumbling fool in front of him? She rolled to her back to see Parker standing over her, grinning.

"What's so funny?"

"You are." He took her by the arm and set her on her feet. Using his handkerchief, he wiped mud out of her nose. "You're a pretty sight."

June jerked her arm free. "You've made your feelings perfectly clear, Mr. Sentell—stop wiping my nose!" She yanked the handkerchief out of his hand and threw it on the ground. "I don't need your help!"

"You need somebody's help." Parker crossed his arms over his chest and stared at her. "What's wrong with you? Surely you don't blame God *and* me for starting the fire."

Her tears got the best of her. How could he be so nice one minute and so—so blasted infuriating the next? "I don't blame you for anything," she cried. Tears started down her cheeks.

"June—" His stance softened. "What's wrong, sweetheart? Look, I'm sorry about the fire—I'd have done anything to prevent it, but it's over. The orphanage is gone, but the children are alive and well. You should be thanking God instead of accusing him of being in cahoots with me."

June swung around, searching for her horse. Where could he be? Someone had taken him, or the animal had tired of waiting and headed back to camp on its own. Whatever the reason, it was just more bad luck, the same bad luck that had plagued her from the moment she stepped off the steamer in Seattle three months earlier.

There was only one thing to do. Walk. And she certainly wasn't looking forward to that. It was pitch dark, she had no lantern, and the crusade camp was a long, long way from the orphanage.

Gathering her muddy skirt, she struck out.

"Hey!" Parker fell into step with her. "Where do you think you're going?"

"Back to the complex."

"I don't think so—not by yourself, you're not."

"Ahh, ahh, ahh! Watch it! You sound concerned, and we both know that's not possible. I can take care of myself just fine, thank you."

June kept walking without a single look in his direction.

"Is that right?"

"That's right."

"Those are mighty brave words for a woman who can't even find her horse."

"I know exactly where my horse is." June kept walking although at the moment she couldn't see her hand in front of her face and she *didn't* know where that silly horse had gone.

She was suddenly walking alone, and she felt a shiver of anticipation. Well, fine. She'd known he was a cad from the beginning.

In the distance, she heard approaching hoofbeats.

"Give me your hand," Parker said dryly from atop his perch on the stallion.

"No."

"Give me your hand, June. Don't make me get off this horse and put you on this animal."

"Parker Sentell, don't you dare threaten me!"

His snort made it clear he was put out with her behavior. "I'm not going to leave you out here in the middle of nowhere. And I am not riding this horse behind you as you walk!"

June's footsteps slowed. It *was* awfully dark out here. Something hooted in the distance. And she glimpsed something with big yellow eyes. . . .

She could accept his ride, she reasoned. But she didn't have to talk to him.

"Are you going to get on this horse?"

Glaring up at him, she reached for a hand up. When he hoisted her up behind him, she teetered on the saddle.

"I don't bite," he said dryly.

Catching him around the waist, she latched on. "Well, I do."

He laughed, and touched his heels to the horse's flanks.

She needed time to think and sort her emotions. She must leave Seattle! She must go to be with people who loved her. Family that she didn't have to second-guess all the time. It was time to visit Faith. A weight lifted from her chest. Yes, she would go to Deliverance, Texas, to see her sister and meet her new brother-in-law. She had to get away.

She had had all she wanted of Seattle, and of Parker Sentell.

Chapter Fifteen

JUNE stared at her reflection in the vanity mirror. How had her life gotten so complicated? What seemed like a lifetime ago, she'd sat with her sisters in Aunt Thalia's parlor and felt proud of herself. Proud that she would no longer be a burden to her aunt, proud to be going west to marry an upstanding man who shared her faith. Now here she was, back in her old room in Reverend Inman's complex. Sam was in another area. Townsfolk had agreed to help with the children until arrangements for them could be made.

Throughout the night June had prayed and sought God's counsel. Her mind had exhausted every conceivable option. As darkness turned to dawn, still no word came from the Lord.

By nature she wasn't impatient, nor was she prone to

acts of extreme stubbornness. She thought of herself as submissive, forgiving, charitable when needed. She'd carefully considered her next step, and she was left with no other choice. Eli was dead, she had failed Reverend Inman, and Parker gave no indication that he wanted her to stay.

Parker. How she wished God had sent her to Parker— illogical as that seemed. She felt a closeness to him, an attraction she was powerless to understand. Yes, even a deep love.

She must leave Seattle now, before she made an even bigger fool of herself. Parker was a man content to live life alone—he never once indicated she had a permanent place in his life.

Oh, he had been affectionate toward her at times— even, perhaps, teetering on the edge of being loving. But never, not even once, did he suggest she become a part of his life. Except for the moonlight picnic, he had never initiated an encounter with her.

She still had a small portion of her savings left. She would purchase ship passage to San Francisco. From San Francisco, she would board the stagecoach that would take her to Deliverance. She'd be done with the whole unpleasant situation before week's end.

Sam would be disappointed, but she would understand. Now that the orphanage was gone, it was only a matter of days before the children were placed in foster homes.

Reaching for her hairbrush, she drew it through her tangled locks. She was comforted at the prospect of seeing Faith again. They would laugh and talk and try to figure out why June's plans had never materialized. Faith's steadfast belief was exactly what she needed.

She slipped out before anyone was awake and rode to Seattle to purchase her ticket. There was so much commotion at the complex, no one seemed to notice her absence. When she returned, she packed her meager belongings, then took a moment to sit and compose herself, staring at the ticket. The ship sailed at five o'clock that afternoon. There was still time to say good-bye to Sam. Then she could put the past behind her.

Setting her bag by the door, she stepped outside the complex. Joe and Ben were playing with the children, kicking a ball around the empty crusade grounds.

Ettie was trying to keep up with the toddler, who seemed to always be a step or two ahead of her.

Surrounded by baskets of overflowing laundry, Sam was up to her elbows in sudsy water this morning. Three wooden tubs encircled her, and she rubbed the children's smoke-stained clothes up and down on the large scrub board.

"Aye, lovey!" Sam sighed when she spotted June. "What are you 'bout so early this mornin'?"

June forced a smile. She dreaded telling Sam she was leaving. No one else knew—she wanted it that way, hoping to discourage attempts to talk her into staying.

Sam dried her hands and walked to meet her. "Ow— are you angry with me for spoutin' off last night? I didn't mean it, lovey—"

"No, Sam. That isn't it."

Sam eyed June curiously. "So, are you gonna tell me what's bitin' your back, or do I 'ave to drag it out of you?"

"Oh, Sam . . . since when did you become so perceptive?" Tears welled in June's eyes, and she tried to avoid Sam's concerned look.

"Ain't smarts, lovey." Sam patted June's hand. "Just know a saggin' soul when I see one. You tell Sammie what's troublin' you, other than the fire. That's troubling us all."

June glanced at the children, swallowing around the thick lump suddenly crowding her throat. "Coming to Seattle was about the dumbest thing I've ever done!"

"Hey, now! Don't you be talkin' like that! I know things didn't exactly turn out the way you'd hoped. But if you hadn't come, we'd never got thick as thieves!"

"You remind me of Papa, only he used to say 'tight as ticks.'" June dabbed at the corners of her eyes with her handkerchief.

"Ah, thieves, ticks . . . makes no never mind. Thick is thick and tight is tight. We'll always be close—"

"Sam, I'm leaving."

"What?"

"Leaving. I'm going to Texas to stay with my sister Faith for a while—at least until I can determine what God would have me do. There's really nothing left in Seattle for me anymore."

"Oh, June. Me dear, dear friend!" Sam wrapped her arms around June's neck and held on tight. "There's plenty for you to do 'ere. We'll find another house for the kiddies—"

June shook her head. "No, Sam. I thought Seattle was my calling. But look at all the terrible things that have happened since I arrived. Eli's death, the orphanage burning. I no longer feel a part of Reverend Inman's crusade, and he thinks I've lost faith in the tabernacle. I haven't; I still believe, but I also believe in other needs as well."

Sam was silent for a long moment; then she spoke. "Much of what you're sayin' is true. I'll not be denyin' that. But you're makin' it sound like every bad thing that's happened 'as been your fault."

June bit her lower lip, wiping at tears that refused to stop. "Sometimes I suppose I do feel responsible."

Sam flared. "Well, if that's not 'bout the most ridiculous thing I ever 'eard! I suppose the next thing you'll be believin' is you're responsible for 'angin' the moon and the stars as well! I got a bit of news for you, missy. Good or bad, you didn't 'ave a bloomin' thing to do with any of it. Not everything is of *your* doin'."

June was stunned. Sam had never talked so harshly before. Her words chafed.

"Eli Messenger, God rest his soul, would 'ave died whether you were 'ere or in Cold Water. It was 'is time to go. As for the tabernacle, you know Reverend Inman will see it through, with or without you—or anyone else for that matter. The orphanage was failin' long afore you got 'ere and long afore the fire brought it down. But because of Reverend Inman's generosity, the kids is eatin' better and sleepin' warmer than they ever were before."

"Yes . . . I told you Reverend Inman is a good man—"

"That he be. But we can't keep our needs dependent upon the crusade's charity." Sam's lips parted with a sly grin.

June eyed her suspiciously. Sam was hiding something, and June had a feeling it was something good. "Are you going to tell me what's behind that mischievous look of yours?"

"Well, I wish you'd come bearin' better news. But still, I'll share me lot with you."

"I could use a bit of good news."

"It's me and Simon," Sam exclaimed, love flooding her words. "The bloke's done asked me to be 'is bride, 'e 'as."

"Sam, how wonderful! Did you accept his proposal?"

"Of course! Told 'im the sooner, the better."

June hugged her and they did a jaunty dance around the washtubs. "Congratulations! I'm so happy for you and Simon."

"Thank ye kindly. Simon is a good soul, and me 'eart is filled with much love for the man. We want desperately to take care of the children. As soon as new quarters can be arranged, we'll work 'ard to give the children a real home. Joe's agreed to stay on. And even sweet Ben has offered to 'elp, 'e 'as."

"That's marvelous, Sam."

Sam's smile died, and her features sobered. "Be more of a hoot if you'd be stayin' on."

"I wish I could, but it's time for me to go." June squeezed her hand. "Truly it is."

"Can't stay even long enough for the weddin'?" Sam chided. "Fine friend you are."

"I would like nothing better, but it would only make my leaving more difficult. I'm leaving today, Sam. This afternoon."

"This very afternoon?" Sam's eyes widened. "You surely can't be meanin' *this* afternoon!"

"It's for the best. But we'll keep in touch. I promise."

"You bet we will. I'll see to that." Sam's voice grew stern. "And what about you and Parker?"

June hesitated, then said quietly. "What about me and Parker?"

"Have you told 'im you're leavin'—this very afternoon?"

"No, why should I?"

Sam shook her head in disbelief. " 'Cause you're crazy in love with 'im, and you know it!"

June blushed. "And what makes you think that?"

"It's not what I think. It's what everyone, includin' you, already knows."

"Don't be ridiculous."

"Ridiculous? Me? Aye, lovey, you're the one who needs a good dose of reality." Sam's lips thinned. "You've got to tell 'im; got to swallow your pride and tell Parker Sentell how much you love 'im!"

June felt as though the breath had been sucked out of her. "I could never tell Parker that!"

"Sure you could. If you'd pack that pride as quickly as you did your valise."

"But you don't understand—"

" 'Course I do. There's a fire 'twixt the two of you, burns bright as a torch, it does, every time you get near one another."

"That's not a fire; it's a facade!" June defended. "It's the only way we can be around each other without arguing."

Sam shook her head. "Nah, it's a fire all right. I know smoke when I smell it."

"Sam, you're not old enough to recognize—"

"Aye, that's where you're wrong," Sam warned. "I know all about love, no matter my age."

Sighing, June conceded, "Maybe in the past, but this time you're wrong."

"And what would it 'urt if I am? Which I'm not," Sam added. "Just tell the bloke you love 'im. Your heart will never be truly at rest, 'til you do. I know 'e feels the same. And if 'e doesn't, what 'ave you lost? At least you'll know for certain."

"You don't understand, Sam. Last night when the orphanage burned, Parker came right out . . ." For a moment, she couldn't speak.

"Yes?"

"Well, Parker came right out and said the orphanage burning was probably for the best. He kept talking about how the responsibilities were draining everyone and now something would have to be done. If he meant that, then he meant he thought it was time for me to go home."

"Ow, I'm sure 'e didn't mean it that way. You're just borrowin' trouble."

"Well, I was there, and I know what he said. And there's no mistaking what he meant. It was as if he couldn't wait to finally be rid of me."

Sam shook her head. "I think you misunderstood. From what you've told me, it doesn't sound anything at all like the mountain you're makin' it out to be."

207

"I thought you'd be on my side, Sam!" June burst into fresh tears. "Don't you realize how humiliating it is for me to even tell you about—?"

"Ow, now!" Sam stepped closer to comfort her. The smell of lye soap and wash water swept over June. "I'm always on your side. But I'll always be tellin' you the truth the way I see it. And this time I think you're wrong about Parker and 'is intentions. For the sake of love, I'm beggin' you to go see 'im. Ask 'im straight-out to make 'is feelin's known."

"Sam, I can't do that." She just couldn't. That would just confirm that she was an utter fool. "I understood his remarks all too well. He will be relieved to see me go."

Sam sighed. "Well, I guess there's no convincin' you."

"No, Sam." June wiped her eyes and put the handkerchief back in her pocket. "I know when I'm beat. I want to leave with some measure of my pride intact."

"Would you like for Simon to drive you to the dock?"

"Thanks, but that isn't necessary. Ol' Joe will. I'm sure he won't mind." June paused. "Besides, if Simon took me, Parker would know. And I'd just as soon be gone when that happens."

Tears glistened in Sam's eyes. "I'll miss you."

"I'll miss you, too."

"We'll stay in touch?" Sam's voice cracked.

"Always."

The women hugged, and June left in search of Reverend Inman, but she couldn't find him anywhere.

Joe was next. He was shocked when she told him she was leaving, but he said he would be glad to be of service and drive her to the dock. Ben openly cried when he heard the news. With her ride secured, June returned to her room, where she paced the floor and counted the hours until time to leave.

Each tick of the clock was louder than the one before. As hard as she tried to rid her thoughts of Parker, his image filled her mind. Sam's words haunted her. What if Sam was right? What if Parker cared that she left? What if he actually cared about her? The thought brought both hope and despair.

In a moment of weakness, June grabbed her cloak. She glanced at the clock. A little over two hours remained before the ship departed. She hurried out the door before she had a chance to change her mind. She found Ben playing with the children.

"Ben!" June shouted as she quickened her steps.

Ben waved. "Hey, Miss June! You come to play with us?"

June frowned. "No, Ben. I need a favor of you."

Ben turned to the children. "Miss June needs me. I'll be right back."

"Ben, could you hitch the buggy for me?"

"No trouble for Ben." He smiled, then sobered. "I will miss you."

"I'll miss you, too." She hugged him, teary eyed.

His sunny disposition returned. "OK!"

Ben quickly hitched the buggy and helped June climb aboard.

"Thank you, Ben."

"Miss June welcome. Ben go play with his friends."

June headed the buggy toward Pine Ridge at a fast clip. Her stomach felt as knotted as a sailor's rope, and her mind raced with every conceivable reaction Parker Sentell might have to news of her leaving. She alternately quaked and prayed as she whipped the horse to run faster.

The buggy bounced along the rutted road, and she reminded herself she was only going to tell Parker goodbye. It wasn't as though she'd had a change of heart. She *would* be on that ship when it sailed at five.

Parker was just leaving the office when June pulled the horse to a stop. He waved and walked in her direction.

She waved back, her heart heavy with the knowledge that this was the last time she'd ever see him. Blast that Parker Sentell anyway. Why did he have to be so good looking? So tall, and so sweet when he wanted to be, so ornery when he didn't.

Why hadn't he fallen in love with her as she'd fallen hopelessly in love with him?

Parker reached the buggy, smiling. "Hello. I was just on my way to check on you and the children. Is everyone all right?"

"Yes—no one seems worse for the wear," she admitted.

"Good."

He smiled, and she faltered. Last night he'd called her sweetheart. The term was apparently meaningless to him, but she had rather enjoyed it and wished he'd said more. A woman, any woman, would be likely to take a remark like that to heart. How could he call her sweetheart in one breath and in the next, wish her gone?

Their moment of truth had come. She prayed that when she explained why she was here, Parker would admit his love and forbid her to go—but she thought that terribly unlikely.

"I . . . I'm leaving." June avoided his eyes, afraid she might see relief written there. Her heart couldn't accept such open rejection.

Parker's smile faded. "Leaving?"

"This afternoon," June said softly. "I'm leaving Washington, and even though you and I never really saw eye to eye on much, Sam thought you should know." She took a deep breath, refusing to meet his eyes. "Sam also thought I shouldn't leave without saying good-bye." She watched the muscle in his jaw tense.

"Sam thought that."

"Yes, Sam . . . and, I guess, I did too."

He took her chin and made her look at him now. "This is kind of sudden, isn't it?"

"No, I've given the matter sufficient thought. The time has come—"

"What do you mean 'the time has come'? And how much thought could you have given it? The orphanage only burned last night."

"There's no longer a reason for me to stay on. With Eli gone, the orphanage gone—"

She flinched as his eyes darkened, and his voice lowered. "Did you ever consider there might be other reasons for you to stay?" Each word was an accusation.

"If you're referring to Reverend Inman's crusade, I'm not needed there any longer either. I still believe in Eli and Reverend Inman's dream for the tabernacle, but deep in my heart I know the Lord will bring that vision to pass without my help."

Parker studied her, his eyes reflecting none of what he was feeling. How could he just stand there and say nothing? She longed to cry out, beg him not to let her go.

The silence was unbearable, his face unreadable.

"Where are you going?"

"To Texas, to be with my sister."

"And you hope to find what there?"

"Peace—a sense of purpose. I've had neither in a long time."

He looked away, as if to sort his thoughts. She bit her lip. Blast that Sam! This was a foolish idea at best. She should have just left and let him find out later that she was gone.

"Well, I need to be on my way." June smoothed her skirt and renewed her grip on the reins. "I—" She blinked back tears. "Good-bye, Parker."

Parker's mouth tensed when he turned back to face her. "You're sure this is what you want?"

June fought back scalding tears. "Truthfully? I'm not certain of anything anymore."

The moment stretched. Would he let her go so easily? If he did, then he surely didn't return her love.

Finally he took a step back. "I wish you Godspeed."

June's lip quivered ever so slightly. "Thank you. And I pray the same for you."

The buggy started to roll, and Parker reached out to grasp the bridle, stopping the horse. June's heart pounded like a tribal war drum. Every nerved tensed. He didn't want her to go! He needed her in his life as much as she needed him in hers!

"Before you go I have something I need to give you."

Her enthusiasm waned. Of course. Probably her box of Sunday service supplies.

"Wait here. I'll only be a minute." Parker turned and strode through the open office doorway. He was back in a moment. "I want you to have this. I've been meaning to give it to you for a long time now."

June accepted the small burlap sack, having no idea what it contained. "Thank you."

"Go ahead, open it. There's a story behind it. I know your ship is leaving soon, so I'll keep it as simple as possible."

June opened the sack and dumped a single sizable gold nugget into the palm of her hand. "Oh, Parker. I can't accept this. It's far too expensive—"

"It's fool's gold."

June shot him a look of disdain. Was he now implying she was a fool? He certainly had his nerve.

"Well, if it's fool's gold, perhaps you should keep it for yourself." She handed it back.

Taking her hand, he folded it gently around the glistening nugget. His blue eyes confronted hers evenly. "You don't understand. When Eli and I first met, we had big dreams of striking it rich. We went panning for gold

every opportunity we got. Tales of other dusters hitting
the mother lode abounded. Finally one day, when we
were just about ready to call it quits, Eli panned this
beautiful nugget. We hurried into town to stake our
claim and weigh the nugget we were certain was worth a
king's ransom."

June smiled despite her best efforts to keep a solemn
face. It was so obvious Parker had loved Eli like a
brother.

"When they appraised our good fortune, we quickly
found out it was nothing more than fool's gold."

"I'm sorry. . . . You must have been terribly disappointed."

"Yes and no. Seems we were the only panners in these
parts to hit fool's gold. But Eli was quick to assess the
situation. Said that material riches didn't matter, that only
love endured."

"Eli was a wise man."

"Yes, he was." Parker's voice dropped. "He and I kept
this nugget as a reminder. Now that he's gone, I want
you to have it."

"Oh . . . no, I couldn't—"

Parker squeezed her hand shut around the nugget.
"Take it, and think about its meaning."

"I have to be going." June still prayed for his last-
minute confession—anything that would encourage her to
stay.

Parker let go of the bridle and stepped back. "Have a
safe trip."

"I'll try." June snapped the reins, and the horse trotted
on. Hot tears rolled down her cheeks. *Thank you, Lord, for
helping me contain them as long as I did.*

Chapter Sixteen

As a cool gray dawn streaked the eastern horizon, Isaac retreated to the solitude of the mountains, something he often did when he was in earnest search of God's answers.

He found a special place of quiet seclusion where he could be alone with the Lord, seeking communion and counsel for his divine purpose in life.

It was late evening when Isaac returned, his heart burdened with unanswered questions.

Ben came running to tell him the sorrowful news. June Kallahan was gone. Hours ago Ol' Joe drove her to the docks in the orphanage wagon.

"Did she say why she was leaving, Ben?" Isaac asked.

Ben thought long and hard, his face a tight mask as he

tried to remember Miss June's exact words. "To visit her faith."

June had gone to visit her sister. "Thank you, Ben."

"Will Miss June come back, Reverend?"

"What did she tell you, Ben?"

Ben's eyes were confused. He nodded his head. "She will come back. Ben knows she will."

"Pray that she does, Ben."

It was past midnight before Isaac finally crawled between sun-dried sheets. As tired as he was, sleep was slow to come. He tossed and turned, throwing covers aside. Toward dawn he was awakened from a fitful slumber.

Climbing out of bed, he reached for his spectacles and hooked them over his ears. Moving to the window, he looked out, trying to see what had awakened him. Dawn was just breaking over the deserted crusade ground. Nothing was stirring but Ben's old coon dog just coming in from a night of prowling.

His faint reflection gazed back at him from the windowpane, and again he examined his heart. All he'd ever wanted was to glorify God, to give God his best without question or doubt. Had he lost sight of God's will for his life, his ministry? Had the vision of the great tabernacle somehow gone from a powerful edifice for the Lord's work to a personal obsession?

Was he building the tabernacle as a monument for God or for the wife he'd adored for forty years?

Isaac stirred, confused for a moment. Something had brushed his heart. Something light, something intangible, something so sweet and so pure he could have no doubt about its source.

God had just made his presence known.

Tears rolled from the corners of his eyes, and he knew. Knew with crystal clarity that his intentions were pure but somehow he had been obsessed with the tabernacle.

He had misinterpreted God's instruction.

The sermon he'd begun the night the orphanage burned resonated in his mind. That message, more than any other message he usually preached, held the answer.

"For I was an hungred, and ye gave me meat: I was thirsty, and ye gave me drink: I was a stranger, and ye took me in: naked, and ye clothed me. . . ."

The faces of children appeared before him. Thin faces. Unsmiling faces. The beseeching eyes of orphans asking for no more than the necessities of life.

As the Scriptures and images flooded his mind, he dropped to his knees. *Father in heaven, how could I have been so blind?* His heart was overcome by the shame of it.

He remained in prayer until a knock sounded. He got slowly to his feet and shuffled to answer the door. A grim-faced Parker awaited him.

"We need to talk."

Nodding, Isaac gestured him inside and complied in a soft voice. "Yes. It's time."

The long passage to San Francisco seemed endless. June spent hour after hour prowling the decks, wondering if she was being too hasty. Should she have stayed longer, given Parker more time to sort through his feelings? He obviously cared for her in his own way. But did he care enough? Now she would never know that answer.

Each time she felt she was making progress at putting the past behind her, everywhere she turned she saw young lovers holding hands, openly displaying their affection. Strolling the deck in the romantic moonlight, they whispered words of love.

On this voyage there was no Sam to give her a warm smile and a comforting hug. No Sam to share cookies and tea. No Sam, period. Sam was with Simon, and June was happy about that. Though it had been only a few days since they said good-bye, she already missed her friend terribly.

Ensconced in her misery, June sought refuge in her small cabin, hoping that behind closed doors she could somehow come to terms with her loss and her questions. But she sat on the small bunk, tears rolling down her cheeks, grieving for Sam, for Reverend Inman, for the children, and for Parker, the man she had loved and lost.

When Ol' Joe drove her to the dock, she had prayed Parker would ride up at the last minute with a shout, proclaiming his deep and everlasting love. Plead for her hand in marriage.

But he didn't.

Ol' Joe saw her safely on board, and she'd felt that surely, this being the last minute . . .

Still Parker had failed to appear. As the steamer made its way through Puget Sound, Ol' Joe was the only one standing on the dock, waving back at her perch on the high deck.

She wiped her eyes. She would miss Sam, Simon, Reverend Inman, the children, Joe, and Ben. And . . . Parker. Especially Parker.

Something Joe said to her as they'd arrived at the harbor haunted her. He didn't have a lot to say, but he had repeated the phrase *by and by* several times.

What did he mean by that? *By and by. By and by.* The phrase rolled over in her mind. When curiosity had overcome her, she'd asked him the meaning of his strange chant. She would never forget the wise look in the old man's eyes as he turned to face her and simply repeated, "By and by."

Joe was a man of few words. Anyone who knew him agreed. Yet June felt an odd stirring in her spirit by the simplicity of his response. Something told her it meant more.

She searched her heart during the days of passage,

looking for a single explanation for why God had sent
her to Seattle in the first place.

Eli's death.

The senseless fire.

The incomplete tabernacle.

Parker Sentell.

Answers refused to come.

When the ship docked in San Francisco, June traded
modest comfort for a cramped stagecoach, continuing her
journey to Deliverance.

Squeezed between a portly, balding man and a pencil-
thin young woman wearing a large hat fashioned from a
dozen bright peacock plumes, she stared morosely ahead
of her. The conveyance occasionally hit a particularly
deep rut, violently rocking the coach. The woman's ridiculous hat fell sideways across her face, and June found
herself repeatedly blowing a feather away from her nose.

A new morning found her sitting next to the window.
Texas was as different from Washington as night from day.
She supposed it was pretty, in its own right. The cows
were interesting, with those horns that looked like racks
strapped across their heads.

Day after day she watched unfamiliar landscape roll
past. One afternoon, she suddenly sat straight up, staring
at what looked to be a huge rat in armor scurrying across
the road. The animal had to be the ugliest thing she'd
ever seen!

Sitting back, she wondered if the odd creature was
dangerous. She made a mental note to ask Faith.

Although the coach was crowded, no one seemed to
care for conversation. That suited her just fine. There
wasn't much she wanted to talk about anyway.

The stage stopped at every pothole in the road—weigh
stations, the driver called them. Passengers got off, and
new ones boarded. At night June slept in a small,

crowded room with others and got up before dawn to start out again.

The long trip passed slowly. June felt as if she'd eaten at least a crockful of dust since the onset of the journey. Just when the cramped conditions became intolerable, the stage finally rolled into Deliverance, Texas.

June scanned the crowd. Her heart soared when she spotted her sister standing between a tall, handsome man and a kind-looking older woman. Faith stood on her toes, wildly waving. She was the best sight June had seen in a long time.

"June!" Faith shouted above the confusion, threading her way to the coach.

When the stage door opened, June climbed out and flew into Faith's arms. A lifetime passed before they found the strength to let go.

"Oh, June!" Faith cried. "You look wonderful!"

June blushed. She looked like the wrath of God, having traveled for days in a bowl of dust.

"Mother Shepherd!" Faith motioned for the older woman. "Come meet my sister June."

June extended her hand, but the kind woman with graying hair was quick to embrace her with a warm hug. "It's so nice to finally meet you, June. Faith has told us so much about you."

"Thank you," June replied, looking at Faith. She wasn't sure what she should call the woman who was her sister's mother-in-law.

Liza Shepherd smiled. "You may call me Mother Shepherd if it suits you."

"I would like that, Mother Shepherd."

Faith latched onto the arm of a tall, handsome man who was standing beside her. "June, this is Nicholas."

June shook her brother-in-law's hand.

"Oh, give him a kiss," Faith ordered. "You're going to love him every bit as much as I do."

Nicholas Shepherd's face turned a crimson red.

June settled for a polite handshake. The kissing would have to come later—much later. "I'm delighted to meet you, Nicholas."

"My pleasure." Nicholas shook her hand, and she noticed his grip was firm and confident, like Parker's. "I'll collect your bag while you ladies catch up on your gossip."

The carriage ride to Faith's home was luxurious compared to the stage. The stylish coach rolled along the verdant countryside with hardly a bump. June listened attentively as Faith pointed out the endless acres and hundreds of cattle that comprised the Shepherds' ranch.

Nicholas halted the buggy in front of a towering two-story house. Various porches held dozens of ferns swaying from the rafters. Colorful flowers bordered the stone walkway. Everything about the Shepherd house reflected love.

Nicholas helped the ladies from the buggy, then reached for June's valise.

"Are you hungry?" Faith asked.

June's stomach knotted as she remembered all that dust. "Not really."

"Well, you will be when you taste my pot roast," Mother Shepherd promised.

"Mother Shepherd, I'll show June to her room; then I'll be down to help you," Faith said.

"Not tonight, dear." Liza smiled. "Tonight you'll spend time with your sister. It's been a long time since the two of you had a moment together. I'll not have you wasting precious time with biscuit dough up to your elbows."

"Are you sure?" Faith asked, excitement dancing in her eyes.

"Absolutely!" Liza headed for the porch. "You young people enjoy yourselves. I'll let you know when supper's ready. Keep an eye out for Jeremiah. He'll be eating with us tonight!''

June glanced at Faith. "Jeremiah?"

"Mother Shepherd's beau."

Nicholas pointed the horse toward the barn, taking a moment to steal a kiss from his wife. Faith grinned and kissed him back.

Turning, she reached for June's bag, and the two women disappeared into the house. "You can't believe how different Mother Shepherd is now compared to how she acted when I first arrived in Deliverance. She's a completely different woman."

"Looks like you and Nicholas have definitely warmed to each other. You two act like newlyweds," June teased, recalling Faith's own earlier trials and tribulations. If only June's had worked out so happily.

"We are newlyweds! And I've never been happier. I've had to teach Nicholas a thing or two though. A month ago he would have died from embarrassment if we kissed in front of his mother. What a difference even a little time makes."

"And love."

"Yes." Faith beamed. "Most definitely love."

"Oh, Faith . . . I am so happy for you." If only June had found the same love in Seattle, with Parker . . .

"Your room is down the hall from ours," Faith explained as she pointed toward a huge oak door. "If you need anything, just call."

June's bedroom was exquisite. The walls were painted a pale yellow. The warm afternoon sun set the room aglow.

"It's a wonderful room, Faith," June said. She was determined to hold back her tears. "I'll be most comfortable here."

Faith gave her a quick hug. "I had Nicholas paint it your favorite color."

"Thank you." June turned in her sister's arms. "Oh, Faith, it's so good to be with you. I've made such a mess of things!"

Faith gently led her to the bed and sat her down on the yellow patchwork quilt. "Oh my. Don't cry. It can't be that bad. Believe me. You should have seen the mess of things I made when I first tried to fit in here."

June wiped at her tears, recalling the letters Faith had written her in the beginning, expressing her doubts.

"Yes, but look how well everything has turned out for you. You have a loving husband, a wonderful mother-in-law, and a beautiful home."

"I thank God every day. But it wasn't always this way, and it almost didn't happen at all," Faith confided. "Your time will come. I promise. No matter how hopeless things look, when you least expect it, God will deliver a blessing even greater than you can imagine."

June sniffled. "I know you're right. But sometimes the waiting, the not knowing—it's so hard."

"Ah, but those are the times God is teaching us patience and encouraging us to grow in our Christian walk. Without trials we would still be babies, crawling around in the dirt, instead of adults, standing tall and proud."

"It's so good to have a sister like you to hold on to until then," June confessed.

Faith handed her a dry hankie. "Now, tell me everything! I want to know about Parker, and Reverend Inman, the tabernacle, Ben, and Simon, and Sam, and the orphanage. Everything!"

June smiled through her tears. "Are you sure you want to hear everything? It's pretty discouraging."

"Everything."

June told Faith everything she could think of. All the disappointments she'd encountered from the day she stepped off the ship in Seattle poured out. She dwelled longest on Parker Sentell.

Her words were forced at times, bitter at others, but June knew the love and warmth reflected in her heart must show in her eyes each time she spoke his name. Parker.

"I don't understand, Faith." June sniffed. "Why would God send me all the way to Washington and then allow all those horrible things to happen?"

Faith held her close. "You know, it sounds to me as though this Parker Sentell may have been an integral part of God's plan for you."

June was shocked. "Don't be ridiculous! God isn't cruel."

"I don't think I'm being ridiculous. Just look at you. You're an emotional wreck. You're in love with this man, deeply in love with him."

"Well, Parker isn't in love with me. He's in Washington, and I'm here in Texas, a world away."

"For right now. But Texas isn't the end of the earth. You must bide your time, wait for the by and by."

There was that phrase again. The same phrase Joe had used when he saw her off at the dock.

By and by.

First Joe. Now Faith.

Was God speaking to her through them? And if so, what did he mean?

June had promised to stay no longer than a month, but the Shepherds made her feel such a comfortable part of the family, it would be easy to wear out her welcome.

Mother Shepherd treated her as well as a mother would. And Nicholas was the brother she never had. June and Faith grew closer than ever, if that was possible. On Mondays June accompanied Faith to the school where Faith taught three blind students. June fell in love with Adam, the youngest. They became the best of friends.

The weeks passed, and June realized her month was coming to an end. She would have to book passage back to Cold Water and Aunt Thalia.

She was down on her knees, weeding the vegetable garden one afternoon when Nicholas returned from Deliverance with a letter postmarked to her. He handed her the envelope, his face solemn.

"I believe it's from your reverend friend."

Nicholas left her alone to read the missive. Several moments passed before June found the courage to open it. Finally tearing into the envelope, she scanned the message.

My dearest June:

I pray this letter finds you healthy and happy in your new surroundings. I deeply regret we didn't have the opportunity to say good-bye. Perhaps it was not in his plans for us to part. Perhaps his will is that our paths will cross again someday. I would like nothing more. You are truly a woman after God's own heart.

The Lord used your charitable spirit to teach me many important lessons. For this I am grateful, not only to the Father, but to you as well, for your faithfulness in his following.

It shames me to admit though, that as good as my intentions were, somehow I had lost sight of God's will as opposed to my own. All I've ever wanted was to glorify God, to give him my best without question or doubt. But I fear I lost sight of God's will for my life, his ministry. The vision of the great tabernacle somehow went from a powerful edifice for the Lord's work to a personal obsession.

I have prayed for his forgiveness, and Parker and I have made a reasonable peace.

Consequently I've been led to revise the plans for the tabernacle. I will build a more modest church. One with large quarters in the back for a new orphanage. I united Sam and Simon in holy matrimony, and they have agreed to stay and help care for the children. Through their unselfish efforts, and with the help of the lumber camps and the crusade, the children will stay together.

I know the orphanage held a special place in your heart. I could not allow another day to go by without sending you the good news and asking you to return to friends who love you. You have a place in our community, an important place. As well as in this foolish old man's heart.

For being such a young Christian, you certainly taught this old preacher a valued lesson. My heart will always hold you in great fondness.

By and by, all good things come to those who wait patiently upon the Lord. May his tender mercies and great blessings be upon your life always.

In Christian love,
Reverend Isaac Inman

June's eyes filled with tears of happiness. She should never second-guess God. All things work for his glory. Her heart rejoiced in Reverend Inman's good news. She smiled, refolding the letter with a sense of peace.

She *knew* Reverend Inman was a godly man, and now others knew.

There would now be a home for the children, a house of worship that would serve the spiritual needs of many . . . the immediate needs of a few. The Lord had certainly blessed the work of Isaac Inman's hands.

Did Parker know——? She quickly shook the thought aside. Of course he did! She didn't want to even think of Parker.

Kneeling, she jerked a weed from the garden, unaware she spoke out loud. "And this, Mr. Sentell, is for kissing me in the moonlight and calling me sweetheart!"

Yank!

"And this, Mr. Sentell, is for being more handsome than any man has a right to be!"

Yank!

"And this, Mr. Sentell—"

"Ouch."

June froze at the sound of the masculine voice. Not just any man's voice. She would know this voice anywhere.

Wiping a stray lock of hair out of her eyes, she let her gaze slowly travel the length of a long, long trouser leg, looking up, up . . . up to see Parker towering above her. Her heart sank when she realized he'd witnessed every spiteful yank.

Squatting beside her, he met her astounded gaze. Without breaking eye contact, he yanked a weed and tossed it aside. It landed in the pile with the others. "And that, Mr. Sentell, is for letting the only woman you ever loved walk out of your life without attempting to stop her." He stared deeply into her eyes.

June's breath caught as the meaning of his words sank in.

"Oh . . . Parker," she whispered, feeling so ashamed of herself. She had been such a fool. Pride. Foolish pride could be such a hurtful thing. His presence here—he was in love with her, too. She should have recognized that all along.

"Can you ever forgive me for being so—?"

"Wonderful," June finished. She sighed, laying her head against his broad chest. Her answer had come. She was home now. "Of course. If you can forgive me."

"I love you, June. I should never have let you go that day." His hold tightened. "I won't let you go again," he whispered, stroking her unencumbered hair.

"Oh, Parker! I never wanted to go. I was praying you would stop me—I only left because I was prideful and stubborn and I really thought that's what you wanted."

"What I wanted was to take you in my arms, carry you to Isaac, and make you my wife."

"But you never said—"

He gently touched her mouth with his forefinger. "I've been a fool, and it's almost cost me something very important in my life."

Setting her gently back from him, he gazed into her eyes. "June Kallahan, may I kiss you?"

"I do believe I'd die if you didn't."

Pulling her gently to her feet, he kissed her. The kiss was long and sweet and devoid of reserve. He towered over her, but it didn't interfere with his ability to hold her tightly in his big, powerful arms.

When the embrace ended, he dropped to one knee. "Will you marry me? Come back to Seattle with me— share a life with me?"

"Oh, Parker! So many questions!"

Parker cocked a brow, waiting.

"Yes, yes, and yes!"

"I'm the luckiest man in the world."

"Yes, you are." June grabbed his hand, relieved to have that settled. "Come with me. You have to meet my sister Faith and her wonderful family."

"I've already had the pleasure. How do you think I knew you were out here yanking my head off?"

June looked past Parker to the front porch. Faith, Nicholas, and Mother Shepherd watched the two of them with smiles of approval.

Parker sobered. "Isaac told me he'd written you about the orphanage. I know how much the children mean to you."

"Parker—about you and Reverend Inman—"

"Isaac and I have settled our dispute. We've prayed together, and we realize our mistakes. I was judging Isaac by my Uncle Walt. I've asked Isaac to forgive me. We're working together to build the new church."

"I'm so glad."

"Once we're back in Seattle, I think Simon and Sam

might welcome our help . . . that is, until our own babies come along."

"Our own babies?"

"You do want babies?"

June stared up into the eyes of the man God had so richly designed for her. Only for her.

"By and by," she replied, finally knowing exactly what God had been trying to tell her.

LORI
COPELAND

Brides of the West 1872

HEART
QUEST™

Romance fiction from
Tyndale House Publishers, Inc.
WHEATON, ILLINOIS

Visit Tyndale's exciting Web site at www.tyndale.com

Check out the latest about HeartQuest Books at www.heartquest-romances.com

Copyright © 1999 by Lori Copeland. All rights reserved.

Cover illustration copyright © 1998 by Michael Dudash. All rights reserved.

Author photo taken by Sothern Studio © 1998. All rights reserved.

HeartQuest is a trademark of Tyndale House Publishers, Inc.

Edited by Diane Eble

Designed by Melinda Schumacher

Scripture quotations are taken from the *Holy Bible,* King James Version.

3 in 1 ISBN: 0-7394-0809-7

Printed in the United States of America

To my family,
the source of
my greatest earthly joy.
I love you all so very much.

Preface

This book is a work of fiction. Thomas White Ferry (1827–1896) of Grand Haven, Michigan, had a long career in politics. He was a member of the Michigan House of Representatives from 1851 to 1852; a member of the Michigan Senate, 31st District, from 1857 to 1858; a U.S. representative from Michigan's 4th District from 1865 to 1871; and a U.S. senator from Michigan from 1871 to 1883, when this story takes place. I'm not sure the senator had a daughter; she's as fictional as Big Joe Davidson.

Prologue

December 1871

"You're a Christian, Dan."

At the odd remark, Dan Sullivan looked up. Franklin knew Dan had accepted the Lord several years ago. It had taken a lot of hard knocks to get to that point, but now his convictions were strong.

Franklin chuckled. "You're going to need the patience of Job for what I'm about to ask you to do." The general reared back in his chair, his scruffy boots propped on the scarred desk. The smell of reams of periodicals wedged in the floor-to-ceiling bookshelves permeated the room. The office was cramped and perfectly reflected Franklin Talsman. The old gentleman absently drummed his stubby fingers on the belly of one who'd partaken of too many of his wife's biscuits.

Dan studied the man who'd been more like a father to him than a commanding officer. There wasn't much Frank could ask that Dan wouldn't try to oblige. One more job wasn't going to hurt. God had been good, kept him alive all these years. One last favor for the general wasn't out of place.

"I'm not sure I like the sound of that. What do you need, General?"

"Oh . . ." Franklin pretended sudden interest in his ink blotter as he fidgeted with the inkwell. Dan frowned. Then again, maybe he shouldn't be so quick to offer his services.

"Just a small job—shouldn't take more than a week or

two at the most." Franklin kept his eyes on the blotter. "Maybe three."

Two or three weeks. Not much of a delay for an old friend. Still leaves plenty of time to buy that farm, get a small crop into the ground before summer hit.

Leaning back in his chair, Dan recalled the time he first met the general. Had it been fifteen years ago? Frank had waded into a rowdy New Orleans street brawl to save his neck. Dan would never forget the favor.

He'd been a headstrong, cocky nineteen-year-old spoiling for a fight and never had trouble finding one. He was lucky that the general liked that in a man. He took Dan under his wing, drew him into the military, and became both friend and mentor. By the end of Dan's military stint, Franklin bragged openly that Dan Sullivan had matured into one of the army's most prized possessions.

Three years ago Franklin had formed a small but elite group of men for high-risk jobs like the recent rash of government payroll robberies. Dan was part of that unit—at least until he retired at the end of the month.

"Interested?"

"As long as it's no more than two to three weeks."

No one was more surprised than Dan when he recently came to the realization that he wanted out of the service. Two years ago, he'd have laughed at the idea. But he was thirty-four now, long overdue for roots—somewhere to call home. Last month he'd informed Franklin he was leaving. He planned to go back to Virginia, buy a piece of land he'd had his eye on, and start a new life. Both parents were dead, and his one sister lived in England. All of a sudden he needed something other than a cold bedroll and a lonely campfire.

Franklin pushed away from his desk and stood up. "It's the Davidson gang. They're on the move again. They've robbed three government payrolls in the past six weeks. You've got to find these men and stop this piracy."

Dan frowned. "The Davidson gang? Aren't they—"

"Nuts?" Franklin shoved a sheaf of papers aside. "Nuttier than Grandma Elliot's fruitcakes. But they're smart enough to rid the government of a good deal of money lately."

Getting out of his chair, Dan moved to the window. Outside, twilight settled over the barren ground. In another few months, Washington, D.C., would come to life. Ugly patches of snow would give way to tender blades of new green grass. Crocuses and lilies would push their heads through rich, black soil. Tulips and daffodils would bloom along the walks and roadways.

"You know, Dan, Meredith and I have been hoping you'd reconsider your resignation. Why not take a few months off—take a well-deserved break, then come back." The old man chuckled. "After the assignment, of course. The army needs men like you."

Dan watched the streetlights wink on in the gathering dusk. Carriages rolled by outside the window, men going home to families. Six years ago he'd stood at this window and watched the Union army parading up Pennsylvania Avenue in a final Grand Review. That same month, April 1865, he'd watched the funeral cortege of his beloved president, Abraham Lincoln, led by a detachment of black troops, move slowly up the avenue to the muffled beat of drums and the tolling of church bells. Dan had stood in the East Room of the White House earlier that day and said good-bye to his old friend. Mary had pressed a large white linen handkerchief with A. Lincoln stitched in red into his hand as he'd offered his condolences. Most of his life had been here in Washington. It wasn't going to be easy to leave, to start over. "Thanks, Frank, but it's time to go. Move on with my life."

The older man moved beside Dan. "Next thing I know, you'll be getting married."

Dan didn't have to look up to know humor danced in

his friend's eyes. Married? For the past fifteen years there hadn't been time for a wife. There was no time for a personal life at all. Besides, he'd been in love once. The brief episode had ended in dissatisfaction and heartache. He wasn't interested in marriage; he planned to live the remainder of his life in peaceful solitude.

"Right now I'm more concerned about buying a few head of good beef cattle." Dan sank back into the hard wooden chair in front of Frank's desk. "Exactly what is it you want me to do, Frank?"

Franklin sat down again, shuffling more papers and handing them to Dan. "Wouldn't be our kind of thing except that military payrolls are involved. Seven total, to be exact."

Dan frowned. "Seven?"

"Seems this gang of three scruffy ne'er-do-wells has been able to intercept seven payroll shipments—three in the past six weeks. Witnesses say the gang is a bunch of inept fools—don't seem to know what they're doing— but that could be a cover." He pushed a sheet of paper across the desk. "We've tentatively identified them. One is Big Joe Davidson. Spent some time in Leavenworth for armed robbery. A bank. Tall, strong as an ox, got one eye that wanders. Isn't known to be real bright, but that could be a cover, too. The second is Boris Batson—don't know much about this one, just that he's ridden with the gang two years.

"The third one is called Frog. He sustained a bad throat injury in a fight several years ago. Ruined his voice." Frank leaned back in his chair. "He's been in prison once that we know of. Apparently he doesn't talk much. At least hasn't during a holdup, and from what we've heard, never spoke while he served his time."

Dan studied the wanted posters. The three faces that stared back at him didn't appear to be overly bright.

"I want you to hook up with them. Gain their confidence, find out where they're getting their information. We'll put the word out on you." Frank grinned. "In fact, you'll be one dangerous character. Name's Grunt Lawson, and you're lightning fast with a gun, even faster with women, and mean as a woodpile rattler. We hope the Davidson gang gets wind of you, so that when you meet up, they'll be begging you to join them."

"You think someone on the inside is feeding this gang information about the payroll shipments?"

"That's what we think. Only two or three people know when those shipments go out and how much. So far, the gang has hit the three largest ones. Someone has to be filtering information. Your job is to find out who and make the arrest."

It was a standard request. Dan had followed the procedure more than a dozen times over the years. But he was tired. Tired of being someone else, tired of cozying up to outlaws, then moving in for the arrest. Tired of living a lie. He tossed the flyer back on the table. "Where's the next shipment?"

"Kentucky."

"When do I leave?"

"First light. You accepting the job?"

Dan pushed out of the chair and stood up. "For you, yes. But it's my last one, Frank."

Frank's smile widened as he rounded the desk to walk Dan to the door. "Your orders will be ready in the morning. Be careful, Son. This gang may be stupid, but they're also dangerous. I'd hate to lose you over something foolish."

"I'm always careful, Frank. You know that."

The general clapped him on the back affectionately. "Gonna miss you, boy. Sure you won't reconsider and stay on? I can arrange for a desk job if that's what you want."

"No, thanks. I'm going to simplify my life."

"Simplify your life, huh?" Franklin grinned.

Dan didn't know what the general found so amusing. One last job, and Dan Sullivan's life was going to be dull as dishwater.

"I'm tired of moving around, Frank. From now on, I'm going to live a quiet, uncomplicated life, alone—with a few head of cattle on my own piece of land with nobody telling me where to go or what to do."

Franklin's grin widened.

Dan eyed him sourly. "What's so funny?"

"You."

"Me?"

"Got your life all planned out, do you?"

"Sure. Why not?" Dan prided himself on control. Control of his life and his actions. God took care of the big picture; he took care of the details. "What's so odd about that?"

Franklin shrugged. "My mother, God rest her soul, had a saying: 'Want to hear God laugh? Tell him what you got planned for your life.'" He winked. "You take care of yourself, Son. It's going to be real interesting to see if God agrees with you."

Chapter One

HOPE Kallahan pressed a plain cotton handkerchief to her upper lip and shifted wearily on the hard wooden seat, bracing herself against the wall of the coach.

Her bones ached.

She'd have given all she owned for a pillow to cushion her backside. Never had she sat for so long on such a hard wooden bench, not even in church. The pews in Papa's house of worship were softer than this device of torture.

"Are you feeling poorly, Miss Della?"

The young woman sitting opposite Hope peered anxiously into the sickly face of her elderly companion.

"I'll be fine, dear. Just having some mild discomfort.

Don't worry your pretty head, Miss Anne. I'll be just fine."

Della DeMarco, the young woman's escort, fanned her flushed face. The poor woman had taken ill the moment she boarded the coach, but she insisted on continuing the journey. Her charge, Miss Anne Ferry, daughter of Thomas White Ferry, U.S. senator from Michigan, was traveling to Louisville to visit friends.

Pressing back against the seat, Hope counted the tall trees lining the road. Miles of countryside rolled by, bringing her closer and closer to her new home.

And a new husband. To think that a man like John Jacobs wanted her as a mail-order bride—well, it was answered prayer. After Papa died, Hope and her sisters, Faith and June, were in desperate straits. They knew Aunt Thalia couldn't afford to feed another mouth, much less three. With no resources of their own, the girls felt they had no other choice but to find suitable mates. And since Cold Water had no likely prospects, they were forced to look elsewhere.

Faith had moved to Texas to marry Nicholas Shepherd, a fine upstanding rancher; June would soon travel to Seattle to marry Eli Messenger, an understudy to the powerful evangelist, Isaac Inman of the Isaac Inman Crusade.

Of course it was too soon for Hope to have heard from either Faith or June, but she hoped to very soon. She was anxious to see how each sister fared with her new husband.

Ordinarily, Hope would be frightened by such a long and perilous journey undertaken without the security of her sisters' companionship, but she was resigned in the knowledge that she was doing the right thing. She simply had to trust that God had ordained this marriage. Soon she would marry John, and they would live happily ever after.

Would she be a good wife, one John would be proud

to claim? Papa had spoiled her shamelessly, but she was perfectly capable of being a dutiful wife. She reached up to pat her ebony hair into place.

If matrimony wasn't too demanding—and Medford had a decent hairdresser.

Anne Ferry edged forward in her seat. Large brown eyes saved the petite blonde from being plain. "I just don't know what to do. Miss Della shouldn't be traveling, but she insists."

"Well—she's the best judge of that," Hope murmured, but she uttered a silent prayer for the woman's impediment anyway. Papa always said that folks sometimes weren't the best judges of their own resources, meaning that they depended upon themselves far too much and not enough on the Lord.

Papa. She sighed, still feeling his loss. So much had changed since his death. One moment he had been preaching a fiery lesson, and the next, he was lying cold and unresponsive in the pulpit. Now she was leaving everything and everyone she knew to marry a man she didn't know.

She closed her eyes, her forced enthusiasm waning. From now on her life would be just plain dull. She'd be a tired old married woman with three or four young ones hanging on her skirts. She sighed.

She knew little about this man she was about to marry. They'd become briefly acquainted through letters exchanged over a few short weeks. John's picture depicted a rather plain face, dark hair neatly trimmed and parted on one side, a handlebar mustache. She'd never cared for mustaches, but then perhaps she'd learn to like one. John looked a bit uncomfortable in the photo, as if his collar were too tight or his britches too snug in the get-a-long.

Sitting up, Hope opened her compact and peered at her image in the mirror. Everyone said she was beautiful, but Papa said that was the Lord's doing, not hers. She studied her violet-colored eyes and dark hair gleaming like black coal in the sunlight. Indeed, she had been given high cheekbones and a rosy, full mouth. Lots of people were pretty . . . but maybe she was extraordinarily blessed. . . . She snapped the compact closed. Papa had warned her about being vain.

"Ohhhh, who would have ever thought this would happen?" Anne glanced at her chaperone. "Miss Della was in blooming health when we left."

"One can't always anticipate these things." Hope was more concerned about the slightly green tinge that had come on Anne's companion than about her persistent cough. The old woman was dozing, her head bouncing against the rolled upholstery.

"Have I told you that I'm visiting old friends from the Ladies' Seminary?" Anne asked. "We share such wonderful times together in Bible study and discussion." She leaned closer. "There are very few, you know, who can discuss the Scriptures intelligently. Most are inclined to frivolous things, parties and such. Even Father. Why, there's this one man on our staff who is positively decadent. He dresses well, but his hair is much too long and he has this, well, this 'look' to him." She shivered. "He's taken a shine to me, but I fear he hasn't much interest in Scripture." She glanced at Miss Della, whose dry snores resonated off the coach walls.

"I've wanted to visit friends for some time now, and now Miss Della has taken ill." She fanned her face with a small fan she kept in the turquoise bag in her lap. She glanced back, her pretty blonde curls bobbing with each jolt. "But it's been a joy to travel with you. I do hope that your Mr. Jacobs isn't too far from Louisville, so that we might see each other often while I'm in Kentucky. I want you to meet all my acquaintances, perhaps even join our Bible studies."

"That would be nice, but Mr. Jacobs said Medford is

some fifty miles from Louisville." Hope shifted, trying to get more comfortable. The miles seemed endless now. She'd been traveling for over a week, and she was anxious now to reach her destination.

Though she had little in common with Anne, she had been excited to have someone her age on the long journey. Papa had been a preacher, and she'd heard whole chapters of Scripture every day of her life, but she wasn't as dedicated to Bible study as Anne.

And her memory was just awful. She couldn't remember a thing she read.

June was more to Papa's liking when it came to spiritual matters—and Faith, too. They recalled every single thing they read. It seemed a natural thing for her sisters to accurately quote Scripture, but though she tried, she got hopelessly confused.

Blessed are the peacemakers for they shall . . . they shall . . . find peace? No, they would be called something, but she wasn't sure what.

She studied serious young Anne Ferry. She bet Anne would know—she'd quoted the Bible since boarding the stage, and it all sounded perfectly flawless to Hope.

The coach slowed noticeably, and Hope straightened to look out the window.

"We're coming to a way station."

"Thank goodness," Anne breathed. "I am so weary of all this lurching—and the dust. Perhaps a stop will make Miss Della feel better."

Hope doubted it, but then, as bad as Miss Della was looking, most anything was likely to help. She automatically braced herself as the stage drew to a swaying halt. Miss Della jarred awake, looking around dazedly. Her small round face was flushed with heat. Hope feared she was feverish.

The driver's face appeared briefly in the coach window

before he swung open the door. "We'll be stopping to change teams and eat a bite, ladies."

Hope settled her hat more firmly on her head. "Thank you, Mr. Barnes." She clambered out of the coach, then turned to assist Anne with Miss Della.

"Oh, my," Miss Della whispered, her considerable bulk sagging against the two young women. "I don't feel well at all."

Hope gently steadied her. "Perhaps you can lie down until we're ready to leave."

"Thank you—yes, that would be nice. Oh, my. My head is reeling!"

With Anne on one side and Hope on the other, they supported the elderly woman's bulk inside the way station. The log building had a low ceiling and only one window. The interior was dim and unappealing, but the tempting aroma of stew and corn bread caught Hope's attention. Breakfast had been some time ago.

Anne waited with Miss Della while Hope asked the stationmaster if there was a place for the woman to rest. The tall, thin man pointed to a narrow cot that didn't appear to be all that clean. But beggars couldn't be choosers.

When Della was gently settled on the small bed, Anne and Hope sat down at a long wooden table. A haggard-looking woman wearing a dirty apron set bowls of steaming hot stew and squares of corn bread before them.

Hope cast glances at the cot, concerned for Della's comfort. "She seems very ill."

"Yes—if only she could see a physician. . . . Sir!" Anne called.

The stationmaster paused in the middle of refilling the drivers' coffee cups.

"Is it possible that a physician might look after my chaperone? I fear she's running a fever."

"Sorry, lady. Ain't no doctor around here."

"How far is the nearest one?"

"Twenty miles—maybe more."

Anne met Hope's eyes anxiously. Picking up her spoon, Hope began to eat.

It seemed like only moments had passed when the two drivers pushed back from the table and announced they would be leaving shortly.

Della thrashed about on the cot, moaning.

"She isn't able to go on," Anne said. "We'll have to return home."

"Might be for the best," one of the drivers observed. "I got to stay on schedule."

"Don't worry about me," Hope said quietly. "You just see to Miss Della. I suggest that you send for a doctor immediately."

Anne looked uncertain about her new role—that of caregiver rather than receiver. "Yes—I'll have to forego my trip—but there will be others. I would never forgive myself if anything happened to Della. The moment she's able, we'll return home and have our family doctor assume her care."

"Got to get back on the road." Mr. Barnes picked up his hat and left.

"I'm coming." Hope rose and embraced Anne, then touched Miss Della's unresponsive hand. With a final glance over her shoulder, she returned to the stage.

Dear Lord, please restore Miss Della to health. And please watch over Anne and keep her from harm.

The coach lurched forward, and Hope's gaze fell on Anne's turquoise bag lying on the seat. Picking it up, she moved to call out the window for Mr. Barnes to stop the stage but then realized that she could arrange for the purse to be returned. The driver had made it clear that he intended to stay on time. Hope opened the turquoise tote. Inside were a few of Anne's calling cards, some spare hairpins, a gold locket engraved with Anne's initials, and a small mirror, also engraved. Valuable treasures, but nothing Anne couldn't do without for a few weeks.

The day seemed endless without the senator's daughter's conversation to break the monotony. Hope's clothing was covered in dust, and she'd have given nearly everything she owned to be able to take her hair down and brush it out. A headache pounded between her eyes.

In spite of the discomfort, she finally dozed, dreaming of Kentucky, a hot bath, and a bed that didn't rock.

Dan Sullivan wearily urged his horse down the steep incline. Up ahead, the Davidson gang wound their way through the narrow pass. Four months. He never planned on this assignment taking four long months. Was Franklin nuts, sending him on this wild-goose chase? The Davidson gang was a threat, all right—to anyone who came near them. How they'd managed to lift twenty thousand dollars in army payroll he'd never know. They moved at a whim, choosing a target by chance, never with apparent forethought. Yet their luck was uncanny. Or else someone was feeding them information. But if this was the case, Dan had been unable to identify the source.

Joining up with the gang had been easy. Frank had done an admirable job spreading the word about the legendary Grunt Lawson. Grunt was accepted into the gang and given the job as lookout.

But Dan was tired.

Tired of cold food and sleeping on hard ground. Tired of washing in cold streams and tired of watching his back.

Weary of living with imbeciles.

This case had no apparent end in sight. The gang had hit several payrolls, but Dan considered it blind luck. If something didn't happen soon, he was going back to Washington and tell Frank he was through. Spring was here, and he didn't have a potato in the ground. The thought irked him. His plans were made, and he didn't like interruptions.

Big Joe drew his bay to a halt at a wide place in the trail. "This is it."

Boris and Frog reined up short. Boris's mare jolted the rump of Big Joe's stallion. Big Joe turned to give the outlaw a dirty look.

Boris blankly returned the look. "This is what?"

"This is where the stage'll be comin' through. We wait here until we see the dust on that second rise over there. Back yore horse up, Boris! Yore crowdin' me."

Boris grudgingly complied.

Dan studied the road below. It was the third stage the gang had attempted to rob in as many weeks. Somehow, their luck had soured lately. Yesterday Boris broke a stirrup. He rode it to the ground, and the stage flew past before he got the horse stopped and his foot untangled.

The week before, Frog had burst out of the bushes and had ridden straight into the oncoming coach. He was thrown fifty feet into the air and was lucky he hadn't broken his neck. His horse ran off, and they still hadn't found her. Frog had to steal a horse to replace the missing one; he also nursed some pretty ugly bruises for days, vowing that from now on Boris was leading the charges. A heated disagreement erupted, with a lot of name-calling Dan didn't appreciate.

"I'll wait here." Reining up, Dan settled back into his saddle to wait. With any luck, they'd botch this one, too.

"Nah, you ride with us. Don't need no lookout for this one. Ain't nobody around these parts for miles." Big Joe's left eye wandered wildly. "The drivers usually whip up the horses when they come through this pass, so be ready."

Dan shifted in his saddle. "What if the stage isn't carrying a strongbox?"

"Don't matter. This one's carryin' somethin' better."

Boris leaned over and spat. A grasshopper leapt clear of the sudden onslaught.

Better? That was a strange statement. What did this stage carry that the men wanted more than army payroll?

The four men waited in silence. A dry wind whipped their hats, and the horses grew restless.

Dan shifted again. "Maybe it's not coming."

"It'll come," Big Joe said. "Somethin' must be keeping it."

"Yeah, somethin's keeping it," Boris echoed.

"Shut up, Boris."

"Can talk if I want to."

"Shut up."

"Can't make me."

Dan shifted again. "Both of you dry up."

Frog hunched over his saddle horn, staring at the horizon. Dan decided Frog didn't speak much because it wasted too much effort. Frog was lazy. Lazy, and he smelled like a skunk. The only time Dan had seen him take a bath was when his horse fell in a river and Frog was sucked under. Dan had begun to pray for river crossings.

He studied the motley group. Big Joe was questionably the brain of the outfit. Joe had difficulty deciding which side of his bedroll to put next to the ground. Frog was like his namesake, easily distracted, his attention hopping from one thing to another so quickly that it was impossible to follow his reasoning—if he had any. If this was the dangerous gang that was so adept at robbing the army-payroll coaches, their success had to be more fluke than finesse. These three had a hard time planning breakfast.

Big Joe suddenly sat up straighter. "There she comes!"

The others snapped to attention. Boris craned his neck, trying to get a better look.

"Where?"

"There."

"Where?"

"There!"

"Wh—" Boris winced as Big Joe whacked him across the back with his hat. Dust flew.

"Oh yeah. I see it."

Flanking the stallion, Joe started down the narrow trail. The others followed, Dan bringing up the rear. This had better be resolved soon.

Dan had had just about enough of this job.

Hope was dozing, her body automatically swaying with the motion of the coach. The sound of pounding hooves pulled her into wakefulness. One driver shouted and the reins slapped as the team whipped the coach down the road.

Scooting to the window, she peered out, wide-eyed.

A sharp crack rent the air. Clamping her eyes tightly shut, she swallowed the terror rising in the back of her throat. The crack sounded again and again. Gunshots! Someone was firing at the coach!

Horses pounded alongside the window. Hope's fingers dug into the crimson upholstery, gripping the fabric. She craned, unable to see who was chasing the stage. Then four men rode alongside the coach, hats pulled low. Her heart hammered against her ribs. Robbery. The stage was being robbed!

"Stop the coach!"

The harsh yell was accompanied by another gunshot. Hope's lips moved in silent prayer. *Don't let this be a holdup. Let me get to Medford safely. Protect the drivers. Oh dear—if only I could accurately remember the Lord's Prayer . . . the part about walking the fields of death . . . .*

The coach came to a shuddering halt, dust fogging the open windows. Hope sat still as a church mouse, terrified to move. She heard the sound of someone cocking a

11

rifle, and her heart threatened to stop beating. Dear Lord, what if she were killed before she reached John Jacobs? Would anyone find her? Faith? June? Aunt Thalia?

Our Father, who art in heaven, how now be thy name. Thy kingdom come, thy . . . thy . . . something or other be something or other . . .

"Stay where you are!" a hoarse voice called out.

"You ain't gettin' the box!" Mr. Barnes yelled.

Another harsh laugh. "You totin' cash money? Throw it down!"

"Stay back, Joe! Yore horse is gonna—"

A gun exploded and a horse whinnied. Hope carefully edged back to the window. One of the bandits was now lying spread-eagle on the ground, rubbing his noggin.

"Git back!" the grating voice yelled to the drivers who'd gone for their guns.

The drivers stepped back, still shielding the strongbox.

The second rider eyed the outlaw sprawled on the ground. "Git up, Joe. This ain't no time to be foolin' around."

The man sat up, nursing his head between his knees. "Fool horse. Pert near knocked the thunder outta me."

A third man rode in, his gun leveled on the drivers. His voice was steady, unyielding. "Throw down the box, and no one gets hurt."

Hope shivered at the sound of the strong, confident tone. It was nothing like the others. She timidly poked her head out the window, her heart skipping erratically. The outlaw with the calm voice wore a mask across his face, but the disguise couldn't hide his dark good looks.

The heavy metal box bit into the dirt beside the coach.

"Whooeee! Look at that!" The big man on the ground shook his head to clear it, then got to his feet. "We got us another U.S. Army money box!"

The second outlaw climbed off his horse and approached the cache. "Yes sirreeee. That's sure nuff what

it is, all right—got us another army payroll! Money and
the woman too! This must be our day!"

"Lemma have it."

"No way. Frog's gonna carry it. You cain't even stay
on yore horse."

Frog urged his animal forward, and the outlaw slid the
cash box across his lap.

"Now, let's see what we got inside here." The big
man, undaunted by humiliation, walked over to the coach
and yanked the door open. Hope stared into the face of
one of the strangest-looking men she'd ever seen. Thick
body, bowed legs, square face. It appeared as if someone
had fashioned a seven-foot man, then pushed him down
into a six-foot-three body with a wandering eye.

"Well, howdee do! Here's what we're lookin' for!" Big
Joe's mouth split into a tobacco-stained grin. "It's
Thomas Ferry's daughter! And ain't she pretty."

Dan's eyes switched to the frightened girl. "Senator
Thomas Ferry's daughter?" He urged his horse closer to
the coach. "What are you doing?"

Joe looked back at him. "This here is the daughter of
the big politician from Michigan. Read in th' paper that
she was on her way to visit friends in Louisville—"

"You cain't read!" Boris accused.

"Oh, all right! I had someone read it to me! What's
the difference?" Joe's good eye rested on the prize. "Bet
her daddy will pay a fine ransom to get his little girl
back. A fine ransom."

The young woman drew back, slapping the outlaw's
hand when he reached for her.

"Now don't be spunky, little gal. Come on out here
and let us have a look-see at what's gonna make us rich."

Boris grinned. "Yeah, rich—even if we cain't spend
any of the money."

"Not yet, we cain't. But in a few months, when we

got all we want, we'll lie back and let the stink die down; then we'll hightail it to Mexico and live like kings."

Big Joe reached inside the coach, but the woman scooted to the far end of the bench. "Why, Boris, she don't want to come out," Big Joe complained. He grinned. "Guess I'll jest hafta go in and git her."

One boot was on the metal step when the occupant apparently decided it would be better to exit the stage herself than have him inside with her.

"I'm coming out!"

"She's coming out," Joe repeated loudly.

"Could be she don't want anywhere near you!" Boris laughed.

Dan backed his horse away from the coach as a bronze-booted foot searched for the stage step.

Dressed in a brown traveling dress with a straw hat perched atop her ebony hair, the young woman slowly exited the stage. For a moment, Dan couldn't take his eyes off her. He'd seen his share of good-looking women in his day, but this one was a rare jewel. Safe on the ground, she brushed at her skirt, glancing from one gang member to another, her gaze finally fastening on him.

Dan drew a resigned breath, looking away.

There was only one problem: This woman wasn't Anne Ferry.

Chapter Two

THE dark-haired beauty struggled against the burly outlaw who had slung her over his shoulder like a sack of feed. Dan watched the exchange, helpless to intervene. If he tipped his hand, he and the girl would both be shot.

"Stop fighting me, girlie!" Big Joe dragged Hope toward his waiting horse. "Frog, tie up that driver and guard!"

"Hold it a minute." Joe whirled at the sound of Grunt's voice. Dan met his eyes with a grave warning.

"How do we know she's Thomas Ferry's daughter?"

Dan had met Anne Ferry at a social event at the senator's mansion in Lansing a couple of years back. While Anne was an attractive young woman, she couldn't hold a candle to this dark-haired beauty pummeling Joe's back.

15

Slim and fine boned, she was a striking enchantress. A cloud of black hair framed her pretty heart-shaped face. Eyes—an unusual shade of violet—were wide beneath her flowered straw hat, but not with fear. Stubbornness. Dan could spot obstinacy a mile off. This woman was going to fight Joe Davidson every step of the way.

"It is Miss Ferry—paper said so," declared Joe.

Dan met the girl's headstrong gaze as Big Joe let her down off his shoulder. "Are you Anne Ferry?"

"Certainly not!"

"She is too!"

Dan shot Boris a short glance. "She says she isn't."

"Well, she's lyin' through her teeth. Look here." Boris picked up the turquoise purse lying in the coach seat and rummaged through its contents. Holding up a gold locket, he asked smugly, "What's this say?"

Dan frowned when he read the initials: *A. F.* How did this young woman come to be in possession of Anne Ferry's personal effects?

Hope watched the spectacle, tapping her foot. "Anne was on the stage, but she had to leave when her chaperone fell ill and—"

"She's lyin'!"

"I am not!"

"Are too! You'd say anythin' to save yore hide!"

Dan's sharp command broke up the spirited debate. "We can't just take a woman hostage without knowing her identity." That's all Dan needed—a woman thrown into this insane mission to up the ante.

The girl wasn't Anne Ferry, but he had little choice but to play along and stay close enough to keep her from harm. Thomas Ferry wasn't going to pay money for a daughter who wasn't missing.

"Well, well." Big Joe rubbed his beefy hands together, studying his prize. "Yore a purty little dish. Papa's gonna pay a handsome sum to get you back."

Crossing her arms, Hope glared at him. "I can't imagine why. I'm not Anne Ferry. My name is Hope Kallahan."

Big Joe snickered. "Is not."

"Is too."

"Is not!"

"I am not Thomas Ferry's daughter!" Hope stamped her foot.

" 'Course you'd say that!"

Dan shook his head, turning his horse. Now he had four of them on his hands.

"Frog! Get Miss Ferry's valise," Big Joe ordered. "She'll need duds."

The silent outlaw climbed atop the stage and started rifling through the baggage. Grinning in triumph, Frog lifted up a green carpetbag a moment later.

Joe nodded. "Says *A. F.* That's hers all right."

Dan watched the exchange. Where was Anne Ferry, and why was her bag still on the stage? Was foul play involved? He studied the young woman, who was engaged in another heated dispute with Joe. Exactly what was going on here?

Frog pitched the valise to the ground, then climbed down. A moment later the gang mounted, and Boris and Frog fired their guns in the air. The sudden explosion spooked Big Joe's horse, and it reared, spilling Joe and the woman to the ground. In a flurry of screeches and petticoats, Hope landed hard on top of the outlaw. The breath whooshed out of him. He lay for a moment, staring blankly up at the sky.

Bounding to her feet, Hope kicked dust at the outlaw. "How dare you!"

Joe's face flamed, and he rolled awkwardly to his feet. "Doggone it."

Brushing dust off the back of her dress, Hope glared at him. "Can't you ride a horse?"

17

He swore and glared at her. "The fool thing spooked."

Boris eyed the stage drivers warily. "Quit messin' around, Joe. We gotta get outta here."

Joe climbed back on the horse, swung Hope up behind him, and the gang rode off in a boil of dust.

Hope's heart hammered as the horses galloped down the narrow road. Fear crowded her throat, but she refused to give in to its paralyzing effects. She was scared—more frightened than she'd ever been in her life. Were they going to kill her? How soon before someone found her bones that the buzzards had picked clean and shipped them back to Aunt Thalia? *Pray, Hope. Pray!* But her thoughts were frozen.

She quickly weighed her options. She couldn't convince these men that she wasn't Anne Ferry. Perhaps that was good. When they discovered that she *was* Hope Kallahan and not the senator's daughter, they'd have no further use for her. But she could identify them. They would be forced to do away with her in order to save their rotten hides.

She had to pretend to be Anne until she could escape. That's what she had to do. Pretend to be Thomas Ferry's daughter until she could get away from these horrible men.

The men pushed the horses hard, up ravines and through narrow passes. Hope lost track of time. She concentrated on staying astride the animal though her limbs were numb. They rode at a feverish pace, but the one called Grunt controlled his horse effortlessly. He was different from the others. His body was hard and lean. His shirt and denims—even his bedroll looked clean and well kept.

Hope found herself hypnotized by the horse's rhythm beneath her. Surrendering to exhaustion, she lay her head against Big Joe's back and closed her eyes. Her mind refused to rest. She wasn't Anne Ferry. What would happen to her when these men discovered their mistake?

Toward dark, she became aware that the riders were slowing. She sat up straighter, trying to focus.

The sun was sinking behind a row of tall pine trees as they rode into a small clearing. A shallow stream gurgled nearby. Hope peered around the outlaw's shoulder and saw a ramshackle cabin set in the middle of the meadow, the front door sagging half off its hinges. Her pulse quickened, and her arms tightened around her captor's waist.

"Home sweet home, girlie." Big Joe swung out of the saddle, pitching the reins to Boris. The desperado stalked toward the cabin, leaving Hope to dismount for herself.

As she attempted to climb down, a pair of strong arms grasped her around the waist. Grunt lifted her out of the saddle and onto the ground. His touch was surprisingly gentle.

Yanking free of his grasp, she marched toward the rickety shelter.

"Whooooeeee. Got us a fireball!" Joe stood on the front porch, mock fright on his face. "Hurry along, darlin'. You got to write a note to yore daddy."

"I don't know how to write," Hope said, trying to meet his one-eyed gaze. One eye kept going south.

He managed to focus. "Stubborn, ain't ya?"

"Your effort to extort money from Mr. Ferry is useless."

Big Joe bent forward, and Hope fought the urge to run. His good eye pinned her. "We know who you are, so jest stop sayin' that unlessin you want to get me riled. Your luggage says you are, your purty gold engraved locket says so too. Yore her, lady."

Hope stiffened. "Maybe."

The bowlegged outlaw spit over the porch railing. She saw Grunt back away from the conversation, watching the exchange from beneath the lowered brim of his black felt hat.

"Git on in there." Big Joe grabbed Hope's arm and tried to shove her ahead of him. He kicked the front door open and stepped inside. Frog followed him, carrying Hope's suitcase.

When Hope saw the room's condition, she caught her breath. Stopping dead in her tracks in the doorway, she wrinkled her nose. She'd never seen anything so filthy. Broken furniture, dishes with remnants of dried food still on them. Something furry skittered out of a bowl and raced down the table leg. She shuddered. Surely they didn't expect her to stay here!

"This is unacceptable!"

Cobwebs dangled from the ceiling. The only window was obscured by dirt. The woodstove, used for both cooking and heating she assumed, had rusted from neglect. Trash littered the corners, and the rodents had brought nuts in from the outdoors. Her gaze traveled to the only bed in the room, a single cot with a dirty quilt wadded up on the bare ticking. Her eyes switched to the ceiling, where holes large enough for a good-sized animal to slide through were apparent.

She whirled at the sudden movement in a corner and cringed. The room was infested with rodents and who knew what else? Fear constricted her throat.

Big Joe came back to physically try and pull her into the room. "Come on, git in here, girlie."

Hope planted her feet and refused to move. "Never."

Big Joe peered at her menacingly. "What'd you mean, never? You gotta come in. I say so."

She shook her head, refusing to budge. "I'm not going in there—not until someone removes those—those things."

Frog and Boris exchanged quizzical looks. Boris scratched his head. "What things?"

Joe tried to yank her into the room, but she dug her heels in.

"Now yore rilin' me, girlie!"

Crossing her arms, Hope planted herself in the doorway. If Big Joe wanted to shoot her he could. She wasn't going into that pigsty. They would either clean it up, or she would stand here all night.

Big Joe, hands on his hips, big stomach hanging over his belt, glared at her. "You get yoreself in here, Missy. Right now!"

Hope shook her head. She was scared—she didn't know if Joe would shoot her on the spot, but she wasn't going in that room. "I will not subject myself to that . . ." *They think you're the senator's daughter,* an inner voice reminded her. "My daddy wouldn' 'low it."

That wasn't a lie. Papa wouldn't have allowed her to breathe air in that room, let alone stay in it.

Big Joe grabbed her arm. "You'll do as I say—"

"No," Hope screeched, stomping his foot.

Grabbing his toe, Big Joe did a painful jig.

The two struggled, Hope's boot connecting with the outlaw's shins. He whooped, dancing in circles now.

Grunt calmly stepped in to break up the fray. Grasping Joe's arm, he moved him to safety. "If she wants to stay out here and let the coyotes get her, that's her choice."

Hope shot him a sour look. He didn't scare her. He might act nicer than the others, but he wasn't.

Well, she could stand anything. Besides, they wouldn't want a coyote near the cabin. Their hides would be in danger, too.

Grunt brushed past her. "Leave her alone. She'll come in soon enough."

Ha. They didn't know Hope Kallahan. Papa said she had a one-track mind. No one could make her do anything she didn't want to do. And right now, she didn't want to go into that dirty room. Crossing her arms, she rooted herself in the doorway.

Boris tried to close the door, but Hope braced her weight and refused to budge.

"Git outta the way so I can shut the door. It's gonna git cold in here tonight."

"No."

Boris took a step back, hunched his shoulder, and burst toward the door, his face filled with determination.

Hope calmly stepped aside.

The outlaw shot through the opening and barreled headlong across the porch, slamming into the porch railing. The impact threw him into the air, and he landed flat on his back. Groaning, he rolled to his side and lay there.

Joe and Frog stood on tiptoe, gaping at the standoff.

Hope resumed her position. Recrossing her arms, she stared at them. They just didn't know Hope Kallahan.

Finally Big Joe gave in. "Hang it all! If she don't want to come in, she don't want to come in!"

Frog tossed her suitcase on the cot. A cloud of dust rose and fogged the air.

"What else could we expect from Ferry's daughter? Livin' in that big house with all kinds of servants," Big Joe grumbled. "Have folks waitin' on her, hand and foot. Spoiled rotten, that's what she is."

Hope shot him an impatient glare.

"Spoiled rotten," Boris groused, rolling to his feet. He stretched, and bones popped.

The men dismissed her, going about their business.

Frog walked to the stove and lit it. He cut carrots and potatoes. Before long, he stirred them into a bubbling pot. Hope's stomach knotted with hunger. It seemed like days since she'd eaten at the way station.

Grunt removed his gun belt and hung it over a hook. Her eyes followed him as he moved about the room.

There was something different about him. He seemed more in control, less volatile. Miles smarter. Why would he choose to ride with these miscreants?

The men ate—a thin watery stew with crusted slices of buttered bread. The smell of coffee made Hope faint. The men's spoons mesmerized her. She could almost taste the potatoes, carrots. . . .

"Hungry?" Boris asked without looking up.

"No." She looked away.

"Hummm, mighty tasty vittles, Frog." Joe dipped up a large spoonful of stew and held it out in front of him. Steam rose off the food, the heavenly smell wafting across the room. Hope swallowed and looked at the ceiling.

Minutes ticked slowly by. The wind picked up, blowing a gale through the open doorway. Her thin cloak fluttered. Goose bumps welled on her arms.

The men gulped down their food, shooting resentful glances at her and huddling deeper into their jackets as the wind whistled around their ears. Their breath formed frosty vapors in the air.

An hour passed, then two. Hope couldn't feel her legs now. The men were getting ready to bed down for the night, their teeth chattering as they rummaged for blankets.

"Cold enough to hang meat in here," Boris grumbled.

"Leave her alone. She cain't stand there all night." Big Joe jerked a rug off the floor and wrapped it around his shoulders.

Hope's chin rose a notch. She could stand here forever or until she froze stiff. Whichever came first.

"We take shifts watching her." Big Joe unrolled his bedding. "Grunt, you and Frog take first shift. Me and Boris'll take second. I want her watched ever' minute until we get that ransom."

"She'll have to have privacy, Joe." Grunt pitched the remains of his coffee into the fire.

"We'll string a blanket—she'll hafta make do. This ain't no fancy hotel."

Grunt stared into the fire. "No one touches her. Is that understood?"

When Big Joe opened his mouth, Grunt reiterated the order. "No one touches her. She's to be treated like a lady at all times. We don't want Ferry accusing us of hurting his little girl."

Boris bent down, trying to coax more heat from the old stove. "Maybe we ought not to ask so much for her. She's mean—real mean. Her daddy might not want her back."

Big Joe grunted. "He'll want her—he has to want her. She's his daughter."

Hope choked back an angry response. If they thought the ransom wouldn't be met, they might easily abandon her here alone, without food or water. She'd die in this filthy hole. She swallowed her complaints.

"Cat got your tongue, Miss Ferry?" Boris grinned, rolling deeper into his blanket.

Hope refused to look at him.

Getting up from his chair, Joe stretched, then scratched in places a gentleman didn't scratch in front of a lady. Stretching out on the cot, he lifted his head off the dirty ticking and grinned at Hope. "Yore welcome to the best bed in the house, Miss Snooty Ferry, if yore a mind to sleep tonight."

Eyes of violet steel chilled him. "I'd sooner eat dirt."

"That can be arranged, too." Joe yawned, then sank back on the pillow. "Nighty, night."

Grunt took up watch beside the fire, huddling deeper into his coat. "Leave her alone, Joe."

Arms akimbo, Hope stood in the doorway.

Soon the only sounds were the groan of the cooling stove and Big Joe's snores.

Grunt sat beside the fire, his dark eyes trained on

Hope. Frog kept watch from the table, blowing to warm his stiff fingers.

Lord, Hope prayed, closing her eyes against the sight of four strangers sprawled about the filthy room. *This isn't my fault; I only wanted to get to Medford to meet my future husband. I don't know why you've involved me in this horrible mistake, but please help me.* She opened her eyes, then shut them again. *It isn't fair, Lord. I've done nothing to deserve this. Where are you?* Her feet ached, and she was so hungry she could eat dirt. What would Faith and June do? They'd pray, just like Papa; they'd pray and trust the Lord to deliver them.

Did she really believe there was a kind, benevolent heavenly Father living in a place with streets of gold, forgiving people of their sins, rescuing them from evil men who kidnapped people?

Did she really, truly believe that?

There'd never been a time when she wasn't aware there was a Lord, a higher being. Papa had made sure of that. But honestly, she'd never thought much about her beliefs. Papa believed—it only stood to reason she did, too. She believed in her own way . . . but belief like Papa had? Tears stung her eyes. She was cold and hungry and alone and scared.

If you're there, show yourself, Lord. Papa was a righteous man. He did enough praying for both of us—have you forgotten? Deliver me from this . . . this travesty.

She reached out to grip the edge of the door frame to steady herself. Grunt and Frog had their eyes closed now. Boris and Big Joe were snoring loud enough to wake the dead. A chair was just three feet from her.

Three short feet away.

The more she looked at it, the more she longed to sit down.

She shifted from one foot to the other. Better. Now if she could just reach that chair without making a noise.

She edged one foot forward, then the other, holding her breath. She was nearly there. Carefully, slowly, she lifted the chair, then turned and silently crept back to the door.

Sinking down, she gratefully leaned her head back, closing her eyes. Glorious. And she hadn't compromised her position one iota. She wasn't exactly "inside" the cabin. She was still at the door.

Blinking hard, she fought to stay awake. She'd be on her feet when the men awoke in the morning. Hummpt. Grunt and Frog were disgraceful guards. They were dozing—sleeping on the job. They'd never know she sat for just a moment . . .

Her eyes flew open. Why, she could stay awake for days if necessary. Everyone knew she was a fighter. She'd stay awake until she escaped these horrible men. Tipping her chair back, she closed her eyes. Ahh. It felt so good. Just for a moment. . . .

Her eyes flew open again, and she frantically flapped her arms as the chair upended and hit the floor with a thunderous crash.

All four men sprang to their feet. Hair standing on end, they stared at her, glassy-eyed.

Swallowing, she stared down the barrel of Big Joe's pistol.

Oops. Now they'd know she'd sat down.

Picking herself up off the floor, she righted the chair and set it back into place. Stepping back to the doorway, she recrossed her arms, blinking back tears.

Are you there, Lord?

Chapter Three

SOMEWHERE toward dawn Hope heard a rooster crow. Fingers of orange and gold unfolded, then gradually spread a hand the width of the eastern skyline. One by one, the outlaws began to stir. Big Joe sat up on the cot, scratching his head. His mat of tousled hair stood on end.

Hope, arms crossed, swayed with exhaustion. She'd stood for eight hours. Her legs felt like two wooden posts. It had been the longest night of her life. Focusing on her captors, she wondered what would happen next. Would they stick a gun to her head and make her come inside? Physically drag her into the cabin?

Her eyes locked with Grunt's as he stood at the stove pouring coffee. She wasn't stepping a foot into that room unless they cleaned it; they, on the other hand, didn't seem threatened by her stubbornness. That was as plain as the nose on her face. How long could she stand here? Her puffy feet told her not much longer. She'd have to eat—and use the necessary. She hadn't used the necessary in hours.

Her gaze switched to Big Joe, sitting on the side of his cot in a dazed stupor. He seemed to be the leader. Boris and Frog followed orders. Grunt—she wasn't sure what Grunt did.

He robbed stages and abducted an innocent young woman, that's what he did.

The men began moving about. Frog reached for the water bucket and pushed past Hope on his way to the creek. She'd been captive for over fifteen hours, and this man hadn't spoken a word. Could he talk? Did he have a tongue?

Big Joe gave a whining yawn and scratched his belly. He eyed Hope's stance sourly. "You this stubborn all th' time?"

She nodded. More, if the truth were known. One time she'd sat up two nights straight to prove to June that she could do it. She'd wanted to make it three, but Papa had cut a hickory switch and told her he'd use it if she didn't get herself to bed.

Frog returned with the water, his heavy boots tracking mud to the stove. Picking up the poker, he stoked the fire, threw in some kindling, and slammed the lid back in place. She watched as he lay thick slices of bacon in the skillet, wondering how long it had been since he'd washed his hands. If ever. Within minutes, the meat began to sizzle, filling the room with a delicious aroma.

Her stomach ached with hunger. She glanced at Grunt, her eyes sending him a silent plea. *Don't let that bacon burn.*

Grunt finished pulling on his boots and stood up. "Frog, watch that bacon."

Hope closed her eyes. *Thank you, Father.*

The outlaw took a tin cup off a hook beneath the shelf and poured coffee. Hope watched as Grunt approached. He extended the steaming cup to her.

"Drink it."

She might be stubborn enough to stand in the doorway forever, but she had sense enough to know that she had to eat. She was already faint from lack of nourishment. She took the cup, refusing to meet his gaze.

"That'a girl. We can't have our ticket to prosperity gettin' sick on us." Big Joe reached for the coffeepot, his eye shooting west. "We want our little Annie healthy as a horse when her pappy pays us all that money."

"I'm—"

Grunt's eyes sent her a silent warning, and her mouth clamped shut.

I'm not Anne Ferry.

She peered into the cup. The tin cup was burning her fingers. Desperation made her drink the potent black brew. The bitter liquid was scalding and strong enough to walk, but it felt heavenly to her parched throat. Shivering, she took another long drink. Maybe she was being foolish by refusing to eat. A piece of bacon—two pieces. She would eat two pieces of that heavenly smelling bacon and drink one cup of this horrible coffee. She'd need her strength to escape. She sipped and thought.

Anne was a Bible scholar. Would the outlaws know that? Anne had talked of memorizing whole chapters of Scripture. Hope knew Scripture, but she certainly hadn't memorized much. So if the subject came up and she was going to pretend to be Anne, she would have to be careful not to trip herself up. Faith and June knew the whole first chapter of Revelation by heart—she'd heard them recite it once when they were trying to outdo one another. Now that was something—one whole chapter. If anyone asked her to recite verse one by memory, she'd be in trouble. Right now, she was none too proud of that. She sincerely wished she'd been a more dutiful student.

"You gonna just stand there like a mule?" Big Joe asked.

Hope tried to look brave, but her thumping heart told her she had the courage of jelly. Still, she could see her obstinacy was having an effect on the outlaws—it made them uncomfortable.

Boris slammed his fork on the table and got up. Eyes narrowed, teeth clenched, he confronted her. She pressed tighter against the door frame.

"You think yore better than us just because yore papa's in politics and you have all them fancy clothes. But you won't be so uppity if—"

Hope lifted her chin. "You are being most rude."

She wasn't afraid of him—she was terrified, but she couldn't show it. These men understood force. She had to make them see things her way. "I'm not budging until this room is set to order."

"You—" Boris's big hand circled Hope's neck.

Hope dropped her coffee, and the cup rattled across the floor, the hot liquid splashing on the outlaw's trouser leg.

"Leave her alone," Grunt warned from the corner where he sat drinking his coffee.

"She's too persnickety." His fingers sliding off her throat, Boris mocked, "The room's not clean enough, the food's not good enough."

Grunt looked away. "She's got a point."

"You complainin'? Then you do the cookin' and cleanin'," Frog bellowed.

The three men's heads snapped to look at Frog.

Frog's face flamed. "Can talk when I want—just don't want that often."

Grunt got up to refill his cup. "It wouldn't hurt to clean this place up some."

"What? You some girly-girl, want your linens washed?" Boris chided.

"No, but she's going to make herself sick standing in that doorway. So we clean up the room? She comes inside, we shut the door and get warm for the first time in sixteen hours, and she writes the note to her papa. Seems like a fair enough exchange."

Big Joe turned sullen. "I ain't doin' no cleanin'. That's woman's work."

Grunt shrugged. "I don't see any women here, except her. It doesn't seem smart to have her down scrubbing floors, does it?" He stood up, stretching. Hope's eyes involuntarily followed the play of his muscles beneath his heavy shirt. "If you want her papa to pay that ransom, you'd better make sure his little girl's alive and well."

Hope mentally added, *Amen.* Grunt was smarter than the other three put together. She was going to hold out until the cows came home. Grunt could see that.

Boris studied the disheveled room. "Can't say a good cleanin' would hurt."

Big Joe's eye wandered the room. "Nah, guess it wouldn't kill us to clean it up some—knock out a few cobwebs. Ain't like we got anything else to do 'cept wait to collect from Ferry."

The four men looked at each other.

Finally Frog nodded. Then Boris and Big Joe.

Heaving his bulk out of the chair, Big Joe reached for a stack of dirty plates. "Suppose she'll want us to heat water—do this thing up right."

Grunt took a piece of fried bread from the skillet, broke it, and stuck two strips of bacon between the pieces. "Might as well."

He carried a plate to Hope. "You win," he said, extending the peace offering.

She eyed the saucer. It appeared cleaner than the others. At this point it didn't matter. She'd eat anything that didn't eat her first.

The men sat down and began to wolf down their food. Hope dropped into a nearby chair. For a moment she just stared into space. One problem down—a multitude to go. Bringing the bread and bacon to her mouth, she bit into it, sighing with pleasure. *Thank you, Lord, for sustenance. And forgive me for thinking my troubles are greater than your power.*

Big Joe glanced up from his plate. "Once you eat, girlie, you're gonna write that ransom note."

Boris and Frog grunted their agreement around mouthfuls of bacon.

Closing her eyes, Hope took another bite. She'd write the silly ransom note as soon as they cleaned this cabin.

And not one minute sooner.

Dust smoked the air as Frog wielded a broom. Big Joe took a bucket of hot water, dumped in half a bar of soap, and proceeded to scrub the window. At the sink, Boris and Grunt had their hands in suds up to their elbows.

Hope sat at the table, holding the pencil stub to her mouth pensively, her brow furrowed in thought. What did one say when trying to extract ransom money from a senator for a daughter who wasn't missing? Her thoughts turned to Della, and she wondered if the kindly old chaperone was feeling better. By now, Anne was back home and Della would have proper care. When this ransom note reached Thomas Ferry, his daughter would be safely back in her own room in Lansing.

A bowl slipped out of Boris's soapy fingers, and he let out a string of vehement curses. She flushed at the foul language. Why, Papa would say Boris needed his tongue cut out and fed to the hogs for such blasphemous talk.

Grunt shot Boris a warning look. "There's a lady present."

Boris swore again, dumping more suds into the pan. Bubbles rose up, threatening to overflow the sink. "Don't like doin' woman's work."

Laying the pencil aside, Hope cleared her throat. "I have to use the necessary."

The four men stopped what they were doing and stared at her.

She smiled faintly. "The . . . necessary. Please."

Big Joe flushed a bright red. "Grunt, you take her."

Grunt quietly set his dustpan aside and reached for his rifle.

"While you're out there, see if you can scare up somethin' to eat," Boris grumbled. "I'm tired of stew."

Getting up from the table, Hope preceded Grunt out the door.

"And don't be gone all day!" Big Joe kicked the door shut with his boot. A second later, Hope saw him back at the window, scrubbing the pane.

The morning air was brisk as Grunt hurried her across the clearing toward a row of heavy thickets. She shivered, drawing her cloak tighter around her. Dark clouds skittered overhead, and the wind was picking up again.

Grunt stopped at the first thicket. "This is good enough."

She hurried toward the hedge, turning when the tone of his voice stopped her. There was no humor evident now. His eyes pinned her to the spot. "You understand the situation, don't you? If you attempt an escape, you're a long way from anywhere. It's dangerous—suicidal even—for a young woman to travel these parts alone." His dark eyes refused to release hers. "Do you understand what I'm saying? Now is not the time to show your independence, Miss . . . Ferry."

"I understand you," Hope muttered. She didn't appre-

ciate the sermon. Given a chance, she'd be gone in a
second and worry about the consequences later.

As if he read her thoughts, he said quietly, "Don't be
foolish. You won't make it alone."

"I'm here to use the necessary. Do you mind?"

Nodding, he tugged the brim of his hat. "I'll wait
down by the creek. You might want to wash when you're
finished."

She might at that. If she looked half as bad as she felt,
it must be scary. Pushing her hair out of her eyes, she
straightened regally. "If you'd be so kind as to allow me
privacy?"

His eyes sent her a final warning before he pushed his
way through a hedge, the sound of his movement evident
long after his broad shoulders had disappeared from sight.
Releasing a pent-up breath, Hope disappeared behind the
bushes.

When she returned, she followed the path to the creek.
She found Grunt squatting beside the stream, deep in
thought.

"Are you going to hunt before we go back?"

He rose slowly, his eyes assessing her. Apart from the
others, he looked like an ordinary man. One Hope might
even like, under different circumstances. Might like a
whole lot.

"You can't be tired of stew."

"No, but Boris said—"

"You don't want to go back yet."

She didn't want to go back ever. "It is nicer out here."
She could breathe again.

"All right. We'll stay for a while." Picking up his rifle,
he started off. She fell into step, threading her way
through the heavy briars. Anything was better than
spending time in that cabin.

She couldn't detect a path, but he seemed to know
where he was going. After a few minutes, he paused,

gesturing for her to keep her distance. He disappeared into the thicket ahead, and it got very quiet. If he was moving, he was doing it silently.

Suddenly it occurred to Hope that he might leave her out here. He wasn't like the others—what if he had tired of the game and decided to move on? What if he knew—actually knew that she wasn't Anne Ferry and there would never be any ransom money? She'd be hopelessly lost in this thicket, probably be eaten by wild animals. . . .

Her eyes anxiously scanned the area.

Grunt was nowhere in sight. Her heart pounded in her chest. She should run, as fast and hard as she could. She wouldn't be missed for a while. Blood pumped feverishly through her veins.

She jumped as a rifle went off, then again. Gunshots. Grunt had shot something. She closed her eyes, thankful it wasn't her.

A few minutes later she heard something moving back through the brush. Grunt appeared in the clearing, holding two fat squirrels in one hand.

"Dinner."

Feeling faint, she smiled lamely at him. "More stew?"

"Fried, with gravy—if we can find a cow."

She followed him back to the creek and sat on a flat stone while he skinned and cleaned the squirrels. His hands were large and capable, manly hands, tanned dark from the sun.

Hope picked burrs off her skirt, tossing them into the creek. A thin watery sun slid from behind a dark cloud. The air was damp, like it could rain any moment. "You're not like them."

"Um."

"They're not nice men."

"I'm not either."

She studied him, trying to decide what made him different. "You bathe regularly, and your speech is more educated. Did you attend school?"

"Did you?"

"Don't change the subject." If she were Anne Ferry, of course, she would be well schooled. He knew that. It was as if he was testing her—weighing her answers. Well, she was smarter than that. He wasn't going to trip her up.

"Why do you ride with them?"

Tossing a skin aside, he spared her a brief, impersonal glance. "Do you always talk so much?"

Leaning back, she closed her eyes, listening to the early spring morning—the gurgling creek, birds chirping in a nearby tree. Everything seemed so normal, and yet her life was in an upheaval. She was here, with this puzzling man, and almost enjoying it. She should be frightened half out of her mind, but she wasn't. The Lord gave her peace. "You're doing it again."

"Doing what?"

"Changing the subject."

"Um-hum."

Straightening the hem of her dress, she sighed. For some unfathomable reason, she felt she could be honest with him. If she were mistaken, her fate lay in his hands. "I'm not Thomas Ferry's daughter."

He didn't respond, just went on cutting skin away from the carcass.

"So there won't be any money coming, even if I do write that silly note. Mr. Ferry will read it and think a simpleton wrote it. Anne Ferry is probably home this minute, safe in her own bed."

He rinsed the knife in the water, his eyes meeting hers now. "If I were you, I'd keep that bit of information under my hat."

Her eyes narrowed with suspicion. Who was he? He

wasn't a part of those other men; he was too perceptive. Too . . . real.

"The others will find out soon enough."

He tossed the entrails into the stream and rinsed his hands. "The longer they think you're Anne Ferry, the better off you are. Remember that."

"Then you're not—"

His look silenced her. "In any position to help you," he finished her sentence. "Take my advice. Go along with the circumstances for now. Don't cause any trouble."

"I don't understand. Whoever you are, I want you to help me—"

"I can't help you." He stood up, holding the two skinned squirrels. His dark eyes skimmed her coolly. "Write the note and wait to see what happens."

"It's the money, isn't it? That's why you're with them. You want that money as much as they do, but you won't get it. I'm not Anne Ferry."

A mask shuttered his features. "Just do as I say if you want to get out of this alive."

She got up, smoothing the back of her skirt. "What's the profit if a man has the whole world but loses his soul?"

He frowned. "What?"

"The Bible." She repeated the misquoted verse.

"Is that supposed to mean something?"

"It's Scripture. Mark 8 something."

He looked none too happy, and she knew why. The mention of Scripture induced feelings of guilt, as well it should for a man in his profession.

" 'What's the profit if a man has the whole world but loses his soul'? That's found in Mark?"

She nodded gravely. "My papa was a preacher."

His eyes narrowed. "Mine is the Lord, and I imagine he'd prefer you get the Scriptures right."

She crossed her arms. "God isn't mocked. What a man sows, he'll get back," she retorted, hoping that was correct.

If a man sows he'll get it back—no, if a sow throws—no, no, there was nothing in the verse about a pig.

Disbelief filled his face. It irritated Hope that he—of all people—challenged her.

" 'A fool despises instruction!' " Dear me! Had she misquoted that? Oh, she hoped not—besides, how would he know? Indignant, she paced back and forth.

"I don't understand any of this. I was on my way to Medford, minding my own business. You . . . and those terrible men . . . stopped the stage, dragged me off—"

A clap of thunder shook the ground. Hope glanced up as the first raindrop hit her cheek. "Great. Rain."

"At least you got that right."

Hope planted her fists on her hips. "I don't know who you are or what you plan to do with the money you hope to steal, but I do know that a fool despises instruction—"

"Misquoting again, Miss Ferry."

"My papa—," she began, then gasped as the heavens opened up and poured.

Grunt grabbed her by the arm, and they started running for shelter. He steered her toward a rise with a long outcropping of rock. The ground beneath was dry.

"We'll hole up here until it slacks off." He settled Hope into the cramped space, then crawled in beside her. For a moment she couldn't breathe. She'd rarely been so close to a man—a man this . . . masculine, with such overpowering presence. He was all muscle and brawny strength.

Scooting toward the back, she tucked the hem of her dress around her ankles. Grunt took off his hat and shoved his fingers through his dark hair. The two sat, staring at the falling rain. The minutes ticked by. The space shrank, becoming incredibly small and personal. Her arm brushed the fabric of his shirt, their bodies only inches apart in the tiny space.

She focused on his clean profile. His jaw was firm, not soft and flabby like the others; his nose straight, his mouth well defined. And he had the most incredible dark brown eyes that looked right through her. A sigh escaped her.

He looked over. "Did you say something?"

"No." Such a waste of manhood. He might have made some lucky woman a wonderful husband, been a doting father. Had he implied his "father" was the Lord, or had she imagined it? No self-respecting man would tolerate the likes of Big Joe, Boris, and Frog.

Aunt Thalia's voice echoed in her mind: *Let those without sin hurl the first rock.* She could hear the admonition clearly. Aunt Thalia was a saint; Hope wasn't.

"I'm not without sin, Aunt Thalia, but unlike some people, I don't steal money and terrorize innocent people," she muttered.

Grunt turned to look over his shoulder. "I know you said something that time."

Hope realized she'd spoken her thoughts out loud. Her face flamed. "I was talking to myself, if you don't mind."

The rain came down in blowing sheets. They pressed back into the shelter and huddled as lightning split the sky and the ground rumbled beneath them. *Dear Lord, why must I be a prisoner of a man I find so appealing? Why couldn't Grunt look and act despicable, like Big Joe?*

It might take weeks—months—for the men to recognize their mistake. The ransom note would have to be delivered. Thomas Ferry would know that someone was playing a cruel trick and strike a match to the absurd request. Then the outlaws would have to wait more weeks before they were sure their demands weren't going to be met. She couldn't survive months here in that one-room cabin! Even if she could keep the men fooled into thinking she was Anne Ferry, when they received no response to the ransom note they'd investigate and discover she wasn't Ferry's daughter. Then what? Fear constricted her throat as another clap of thunder rocked the ground.

Grunt shifted. Was her presence unnerving to him? She hoped so—she sincerely hoped so. It would serve him right.

Settling himself in a dry spot, he tipped his hat over his face and appeared to sleep. Hope's eyes gauged the distance between her and where he rested. It was now or never. Grunt's warning rang in her ears. *It would be suicide for a woman alone in these parts.* But it would be suicidal of her to remain in his custody.

It was pouring rain—she could hide in the bushes, make her way back to civilization under the guise of darkness. It wasn't the smartest plan, but then she'd never been in this situation before. Desperate times called for desperate measures.

Was that Scripture?

No, Uncle Frank used to say that to Aunt Thalia.

Springing from beneath the rock outcropping, Hope ran. As fast and as hard as she could run. Faster than she'd ever run in her life. Her breath came in gasps as she leaped puddles and dodged prickly bushes. Disoriented, she beat her way through thick underbrush. Rain sluiced down, blinding her. She could hear Grunt shouting at her.

"Come back here, you little fool!"

She ran on, praying that the thunder would cover the noise of her flight. Turning to look back, she plowed headlong into a tree. The impact threw her into a bush, and she lay on her back, stunned.

"Anne! Don't be foolish—you can't make it alone!"

Rolling to her side, she doubled up, holding her breath. Grunt's voice boomed above the downpour.

"Miss Ferry! Anne!"

Squeezing her eyes shut, she prayed. *Don't let him find me; please, please, don't let him find me.*

"You can't get away—don't try it!" His voice sounded nearer at times, then farther away.

"I can, if I escape you," she whispered.

The minutes crept by. Her legs began to ache, but she couldn't move. Any sound, even in the pouring rain, would alert him. She was chilled to the bone now. How long before he would give up and return to the cabin for help? By then, she would be so far down the road they'd never find her.

She lay for hours, listening for footfalls, terrified to move. Toward evening, the rain slowed to a cold drizzle. Teeth chattering, she listened to small animals moving around foraging for food. A raccoon crept close, and she shooed it away with her hand. Two more appeared, their beady eyes wide with curiosity.

Her voice was barely a whisper. "Hungry, fellows?" She didn't blame them. The thought of bacon and bread and rich, black coffee haunted her.

She scavenged beneath the bush and came up with a handful of acorns, then gently pitched them several feet away. The coons darted off, investigating.

She hadn't heard Grunt calling her name for some time. She'd made it. *Thank you, God, thank you, God, thank you, God—*

She yelped when she suddenly felt herself yanked to her feet and a large, warm hand clamped over her mouth.

"You are sorely testing my patience," a rough voice rasped in her ear.

Her heart was thumping a mile a minute as he whirled her around and steadied her on her feet, none too gently. She blinked, weak with relief when she saw it was Grunt, not Big Joe, Boris, or Frog. His face was a storm cloud. "Don't you have a lick of sense?"

41

She tried to break his hurtful hold. "Let me go! You're not like the others. You're intelligent; you have a quality the others don't have—" She wrenched free. "Don't do this!"

"If I let you go, you'll be dead by morning." He took her by the shoulders and gently shook her. To her surprise, she saw concern in his eyes. "Why did you disobey me?"

"Please—"

"No."

She clamped her teeth together. She was wrong about him. He was just as mean and ornery and bullheaded as Big Joe, Frog, and Boris put together. Her heart sank. She was doomed. She had failed at her escape, and they would watch her closer than ever now.

"Come on. You're going to catch your death out here." Keeping her firmly in check, he turned her in the direction of the cabin. Stopping at the shelter, he picked up his rifle and the squirrels, then continued forcing her ahead of him.

Despair enveloped her. She was going to die here in these awful woods. No one would know where she was or what had happened to her. If Grunt didn't strangle her, the others would.

"Please let me go," she chattered between breaths.

"You're staying with me." He latched onto her ear and marched her toward the cabin.

"Ouch . . . you're hurting me!"

"Just walk, Miss Ferry."

She was sopping wet, and her teeth were knocking together so hard she couldn't argue. It seemed like hours later when he finally shoved her inside the cabin. "Ouch, ouch, ouch!" Wrestling out of Grunt's grip, she stood in the middle of the floor, thick mud caked on her thin shoes, the hem of her dress dripping a stream.

Big Joe sprang up from the table, overturning a chair. His features were tight. "Where have you been!"

Lifting her chin, she crossed her arms.

She stumbled when Grunt pushed her closer to the fire. "Had a bear tracking us. Fired off a couple of rounds, but he dogged us most of the day. Had to hole up until we could shake him."

Hope gravitated toward the fire, seeking its warmth. His excuse barely registered with her. She needed blankets, hot coffee.

"A bear?" Boris sat up from his bedroll. "Did you git 'im?"

Grunt motioned toward Hope. "She needs dry clothes and something to eat. Now."

Boris grumbled but rolled to his feet and stoked the fire. Big Joe opened the suitcase and pushed it across the floor to her. She fished around for a clean dress and underclothing.

The men busied themselves with the squirrels. Grunt rigged a rope and draped a blanket over it, then heated water on the stove. Stepping behind the makeshift curtain, Hope removed her wet clothing, shaking so hard her hands refused to cooperate.

"Wrap a blanket around yourself." She froze when she heard Grunt's deep baritone on the other side of the blanket.

"What?"

"Wrap a blanket around yourself. I have a hot bath drawn."

Hope closed her eyes, so grateful she wanted to cry. Hot water. She picked up a second blanket and secured it tightly around her. A wooden tub slid behind the curtain.

She heard the front door close as the men stepped outside to allow her privacy. Climbing into the water, she sank down, allowing the steaming vapors to envelop her.

Her body cried out with relief and she sighed, sliding deeper into the comforting warmth.

It occurred to her that Grunt had been out in the cold rain all day searching for her. He must be every bit as chilled as she was.

Soon heavenly smells filled the cabin. Rain pattered on the windowpane as Hope brushed her hair dry before the fire. Grunt was cutting up the squirrels and dipping them in flour. The meat sizzled when he laid the pieces in a skillet of hot grease. Boris mixed cornmeal and water— bannock, she heard him say—cakes of Indian meal fried in lard.

She listened as the men talked among themselves. Big Joe questioned Grunt about the bear. She thought she detected a hint of skepticism in his voice, but Grunt was adept at holding to the story. He was protecting her, but why?

As the mouthwatering smells permeated the room, Hope grew a little light-headed. She was so tired and so very hungry. And so grateful to Grunt for rescuing her. She might well have perished out there alone.

She stood up and walked to the table.

Grunt glanced up, continuing to dish up plates of hot food. The cabin looked spotless. The curtains had been washed, the floors scrubbed. "Sit down, Miss Ferry. Supper's ready."

Big Joe, Boris, and Frog scraped their chairs to the table and lit into the fried squirrel and johnnycakes like a pack of wild animals. Stunned, Hope watched them strip meat off the bones with their teeth, wipe their mouths on their sleeves, and belch between bites.

She had yet to pick up her fork.

When they noticed that she was staring, Big Joe glanced up, utensil paused in midair. "What?"

Her eyes silently condemned their atrocious table manners.

Boris lowered the squirrel leg he was gnawing on. "What's wrong now, Miss Snootypants?"

"Must you eat like mules?"

"Hum?" Frog asked, his mouth full.

"Your manners—they're disgraceful."

The men exchanged quizzical glances. "What's she yakkin' about now?" Boris complained, a piece of meat falling from his mouth as he talked.

"Somethin' 'bout manners. Cain't please her."

Picking up her fork, Hope looked at each of them. "It seems to me you would be interested in improving yourselves."

They gawked at her, mouths slack. Grunt moved to the stove and poured a cup of coffee.

Hope took a small bite of her meat. "Chew with your mouth closed, and if you take small bites you'll enjoy the food more. Besides, swallowing it all in one gob will give you indigestion."

Big Joe frowned. "Indi-what?"

"A sour stomach," Grunt said, sitting down at the table. Boris swore under his breath.

"And please watch your language." Hope picked up the plate of johnnycakes. "It isn't necessary to curse in order to properly express yourself." She selected two nice brown cakes and arranged them neatly on her plate. "Papa says only a fool opens his mouth and proves it."

Forks and knifes clanked as the men returned to their meals. Hope quietly laid her fork aside and folded her hands next to her plate. A minute later, Big Joe glanced up, frowning when he saw her staring. His bushy brows lifted.

"Grace," she said.

"Who?"

"Grace. We haven't said grace."

Boris let out a blue curse, and Big Joe kicked him under the table, hard. Boris pinned Big Joe with a sour look; then, fork standing at sentinel, he bowed his head.

Hope began, "Oh, Lord, we are so grateful for the food you've provided, though we are so unworthy."

Frog snickered.

Hope's voice rose an octave. "We know your mercy is endless, Father, and I ask that that unbiased mercy be extended to these poor heathen souls—Big Joe, Boris, and Frog—" she glanced up to meet Grunt's eyes and hurriedly added—"and Grunt, who knows no better. Amen."

Opening her right eye, Hope studied Big Joe, who seemed to be trying to decide if he'd just been insulted.

Raising his coffee, Grunt quietly ended the prayer. "Amen."

When the meal was over, Big Joe pushed back from the table and walked over to his saddlebags. Hope felt as if she'd eaten with a pack of buzzards. All except Grunt. His table manners were flawless. Joe lumbered back to the table, looming above Hope with pencil and paper in hand as she savored the last bite of meat, allowing the tasty morsel to slide down her throat.

"Now write that note, girlie. We've waited long enough. We want five thousand dollars from Ferry by the fifth of next month."

"Fifth of next month! That's only two weeks away!" Hope protested. She set her fork on the table. "There isn't time—"

"Write the note."

Hope glanced at Grunt expectantly. He shrugged, draining the last of his coffee. "Write the note, Miss Ferry."

Well. He was no help. Did she dare to hope that was compassion she had seen in his traitorous eyes? Of course not. He wanted money, just like the others. What she saw was desire—the urge to be rid of her, no matter who she was.

Grasping the piece of paper, she smoothed it against the table. She held her hand up for the pencil.

Big Joe slapped one into her open palm.

Venturing a last withering glance at Grunt, she prayed that he'd intervene, stop this nonsense. He didn't. Instead, he got up for more coffee.

Sighing, she positioned the pencil. *God forgive me, but I fear even your power isn't enough right now.*

Biting her lower lip, she wrote: "Dear Daddy . . ."

Chapter Four

SENATOR, sir, your morning mail."

The butler set the silver tray on the corner of the desk. Thomas Ferry reached for his coffee cup, eyes glued to the newspaper article he was reading. A moment later he laid his paper aside and glanced at the three letters on the tray.

"An unusually small offering this morning."

"Yes, sir. Would there be anything else, sir?"

"No, thank you. Send Miss Finch in, will you?"

Thomas was a creature of habit. Rising early, he bathed, shaved, ate breakfast, and then finished reading the morning news in his office over a third cup of coffee. While reading the morning mail, he dictated responses as necessary, thus saving his secretary and himself valuable time.

Mardell Finch kept her employer on time. She was respected throughout the Ferry camp as efficient, loyal, and hardworking. A spinster of some forty-plus years, she was dedicated not only to Thomas but also to the office itself. Miss Finch was no slacker.

As Miss Finch entered the study, notebook in hand, Thomas opened the first letter. After ten minutes of dictation, he reached for the second envelope. Examining the missive, he frowned.

"Crude paper, but the writing is quite delicate. Hmmm, no return address."

He slit open the envelope and removed the creased paper.

Then he blinked.

"Great day in the morning! Listen to this, Mardell: 'Some very dangerous men are holding me captive. They demand a ransom of five thousand dollars, payable in paper money within ten days once you receive this note. The money should be placed in plain wrapping and addressed to Joe Smith in care of Louisville, Kentucky, Post Office. When the money has been received, I will be released unharmed. At that time I will travel back to you. Love, Anne.' "

Thomas glanced at Miss Finch. "What do you make of that?"

"It must be a joke," Miss Finch responded.

"Bernard!"

The double study doors opened immediately. "You called, sir?"

"Go upstairs and make sure Anne is in her room."

The elderly white-haired gentleman frowned. "In her room, sir? The doctor left not fifteen minutes ago—I'm quite sure she's still abed with the sniffles."

"Check on her anyway, Bernard. I want to be certain of my daughter's whereabouts."

"Yes, sir." The door closed. Bernard's footsteps could be heard receding down the hall.

Thomas drummed his fingers on the desk, checking his watch fob every few minutes. Snapping the face closed, he got up to pace.

Miss Finch shut her notebook, primly crossing her hands in her lap. "I'm sure it's just someone's idea of a cruel joke, Mr. Ferry."

Footsteps once again sounded outside the door, and Bernard reappeared. "Miss Anne is resting comfortably, sir. She took some tea and toast a short while ago and said to tell you she plans to nap the morning away."

Thomas Ferry's face sagged with relief. "Thank God." He tossed the note into the wastepaper basket. "That will be all, Bernard. Now—" he turned back to address Miss Finch—"where were we?"

Hope pointed to a corner. "You missed a cobweb."

Boris picked up the broom, his beady eyes trying to pinpoint the offender. He swung the broom in the general direction of her finger. "Satisfied?"

She shrugged, smothering a cough. These pesky sniffles were getting worse. And her throat was scratchy this morning. It was this infernal drafty cabin. She'd be deathly ill if she didn't get warm soon. Her feet were like two blocks of ice. "It's still there."

"I can't git this stupid broom into corners," Boris groused.

"You can if you gently push, instead of jam," Hope explained for the third time that morning.

Boris rammed the head of the broom in the cracks, trying to dig the dirt out. "What do you think this is, some ladies seminary or somethin'?"

"No. I think this is a miserable excuse for a living establishment!" Hope snapped, then immediately repented. If the Lord could love Boris, surely she could put up with him awhile longer. "Though it is a great deal better than it was."

Which wasn't saying much.

One month. Had it been only a month since this unending nightmare had begun? It seemed like years. The men had kept their distance well enough. Grunt had seen to that, but she wanted out. She tried hard to keep up her spirits. Papa would say that everything that happened to a person was meant for a reason—though she couldn't imagine what good would come of her mistaken abduction.

Grunt continued to puzzle her with his soft-spoken commands and almost protective attitude toward her. Was he only looking after his interest? It was increasingly hard to maintain the belief that he was a ruthless outlaw when at times he seemed the exact opposite. Just last night he'd made sure she had the biggest piece of venison. That was nice—even if she did hate venison.

"Well, this ain't no boardinghouse, and I'm tired of washin' dishes, and I ain't sweepin' no more floors. And if I have to take another bath in that creek, I'm gonna prune up permanent-like."

Hope looked up as Grunt came in the front door. His dark eyes took in the confrontation. "If you're tired of keeping house, Boris, why don't you take these rabbits and dress them for supper?"

"Fine. Anything to get away from Miss Bossy." Boris grabbed the rabbits and stomped out the door.

Big Joe sat up on the cot, scratching his belly. "What'd you find out in Louisville?"

"Nothing at the post office." Grunt moved to the sink to wash up.

Big Joe frowned. "Nothin'." His eyes pivoted to Hope. "It's takin' too long—don't yore daddy care what happens to you?"

Her daddy had indeed cared for her. Unfortunately, Thomas Ferry didn't.

"Perhaps the ransom's been lost. That happens to mail, you know. Maybe—"

"Maybe you should just keep quiet."

"Well, maybe you shouldn't ask so many questions and make me have to talk."

"Well, maybe I like to ask questions!"

"Well, maybe I don't want to answer them."

"Maybe both of you should find something more productive to do with your time," Grunt snapped.

Hope rinsed the dress she was washing, then squeezed the water out. She flicked a few drops at Frog. He stiffened, shooting her a lethal look. Stepping around him, she announced, "I'm going to hang my wash."

"Good," Joe mumbled and dropped his head back to the pillow. "With any luck you'll hang yoreself."

Or you, Hope thought. He was just sore. She'd made him wash his filthy shirt yesterday, and Joe didn't take kindly to soap and water. He'd griped for hours afterward, complaining that he smelled like a girl. She relented and rewarded him by washing dishes last night.

As she hung the dress on the line, she heard the men talking among themselves.

"Boris, maybe you ought to ride back to Louisville and git a paper—see if there's anything in there about Ferry's daughter being held for ransom."

"Why me? Grunt was jest there."

" 'Cause Grunt didn't git no paper. Cain't you take orders no more?"

"What makes you think there'd be anything in the Louisville paper?" Grunt's voice drifted through the open doorway.

"News that the senator's daughter's been kidnapped will be in every paper!"

"Maybe Ferry's kept the news quiet."

"No way! He'll have every Tom, Dick, and Harry in the county lookin' for her."

After all the arguing, Boris was elected to ride back to Louisville the following morning. They waited for him to return with news of Ferry's distress.

On the third morning, Hope awoke with a splitting headache, a hammer pounding between her temples. She emerged from behind the blanket that afforded her privacy. She was aware of Grunt's eyes on her as he put sausage in the skillet to fry. Concern tinged his features. "Are you ill, Miss Ferry?"

"I have a small headache." Hope sat down at the table, feeling a little light-headed. The scratchy irritation had turned into a ferocious sore throat, and she felt hot all over. She got up to put plates on the table.

Big Joe and Frog were stirring by then, grumbling about all the racket. Five adults in one cramped room wasn't the most pleasant way to spend a life. They were getting on each other's nerves.

By the time breakfast was over, Hope was feeling decidedly worse.

Aware that Grunt was still watching her, she got up from the table, leaving her plate of food virtually untouched. She couldn't let them know she was ill. She had her bluff in on Big Joe, and she intended to keep it that way.

"I'll wash the dishes," she volunteered, forcing herself to sound perkier than she felt.

"Sit down," Grunt ordered.

"I want to wash—"

The outlaw sat her down in a chair, then touched his large hand to her forehead. "She's got a fever."

Big Joe turned from the mantel. "Sick? She's sick!"

"I'm not sick. . . . I'm only feeling slightly unpleasant." Sick as a dog, actually, but she couldn't, just couldn't, give in to whatever had her feeling so bad.

54

They turned as the door opened and Boris stomped in. Giving Hope a dark glance, he strode into the room, shrugging out of his coat.

Big Joe frowned. "Well?"

"She ain't Ferry's daughter!" he declared hotly, throwing his hat onto the table. Hope shrank back as he glared at her.

"What?" Big Joe's head snapped up. "What d'you mean, 'She ain't Ferry's daughter'?"

"She ain't his daughter!" Boris repeated.

"Who told you that?"

"This." Boris tossed a copy of the *Louisville Courier-Journal* onto the table.

Big Joe glanced at the paper, then colored a bright crimson. "You know I ain't got no learnin'. What's it say?"

Grunt picked up the paper, his eyes scanning the headlines. He read, "Distinguished Kentuckian Honored by Michigan Senator.

"William Campbell Preston Breckinridge, distinguished Kentucky lawyer, editor, soldier, was a special guest in the home of Michigan's Senator Thomas White Ferry. Mr. Breckinridge was the honored guest at the annual Spring Ball held last week, where he was accompanied by Miss Anne Ferry, the senator's daughter—"

The outlaws turned to look at her.

Hope slid out of the chair in a dead faint.

Angry voices tried to penetrate her thick fog. Hope struggled to consciousness, wondering what those awful men were squabbling about this time. She felt as hot as a firecracker, and her head threatened to split in half. If only the voices would go away. They were angry, full of rage.

"No arguin'. We gotta get rid of her!" Boris declared.

"Who is she?" Frog asked. "If she ain't Anne Ferry, who in the blue blazes have we had to cotton to for the past month?"

"She must be that Hope . . . what'd she say her name was?"

"Who cares who she is?" Big Joe said. "Boris is right. We gotta git rid of her."

Grunt? Where was Grunt? Did he want to get rid of her, too? Hope coughed, a racking hack that brought all conversation to a halt.

"She's gettin' sicker. Maybe we won't hafta do away with her. Maybe she'll just croak on her own."

"She's too mean to croak on her own." Big Joe's voice filtered through the deep fog.

"What's wrong with her?" Frog asked.

"How should I know?" Big Joe shot back. "I ain't no lady's maid."

Cool fingers touched her forehead. Her eyes refused to open, but she sensed it was Grunt. The touch was infinitely gentle.

"Her fever's rising. We've got to get it down."

She heard Boris back away. "She got somethin' I'm likely to catch? I git the ague real easy—"

"Shut up, Boris."

Hope whimpered when she felt a cold cloth pressed to her forehead.

"She's caught cold. Frog, get some more blankets."

Hope moaned. She didn't want those dirty old blankets on her. They weren't fit for an animal, let alone a lady. She pushed at the gentle hands that now securely held her captive.

"Don't waste time with blankets. Put her outside and let's be done with it. She'll be dead by mornin'."

"Boris is right," Frog said. "Put her outside and lock the door. Good riddance."

"No one come near her," Grunt warned. "We're not going to let her die."

"She ain't Ferry's daughter, what do you care?"

Grunt's voice firmed. "No one lays a hand on her." She heard him do something. Cracking an eye open, Hope saw Grunt reach for his gun belt and strap it on.

With a sour look Big Joe returned to the fire.

"I still say we get rid of her," Boris growled. "She ain't no use to us! Jest a millstone around our necks."

The outlaws' voices faded as Hope slipped back into unconsciousness.

She was running now from something dark and sinister. Glancing back over her shoulder, she stumbled over rough ground, trying to make out the shadowy form that was chasing her. She opened her mouth to scream, but no sound came out. Just incredible heat, a furnace filling her whole body. She didn't know where she was; everything was so black and closing in. Hot. She was so hot! Water. She needed water . . . cool water. The murkiness drew her deeper, covering her mouth. She was choking, clawing at this thing. . . .

Suddenly her fear was reality. The darkness was real, and there was something hard and persistent across her mouth. She clawed at the thing, trying to rip it away. She heard a grunt as she was tossed over a man's shoulder like a sack of flour. Awake now and terrified, she kicked and lashed out, trying to free herself. The darkness she'd desperately tried to escape was real, and someone was carrying her off into the night. Hope's worst fears were coming true. The outlaws were going kill her.

Bile rose to the back of her throat, and she struggled with all her might. The man was large and strong, his shoulder pressing into her middle. She was going to die, and no one would know. Murdered somewhere in the

Kentucky wilderness. Was she still in Kentucky? She couldn't be sure . . . she didn't even know! Mr. Jacobs would think she had abandoned him, changed her mind about marriage. Her sisters wouldn't know what had happened to her. Aunt Thalia would take to her bed when she learned that Hope had disappeared and never been heard from again.

This isn't fair; it isn't fair, Lord! I never asked for anything more than a husband so I wouldn't be a burden to Aunt Thalia. And now she was going to die at the hands of ruthless outlaws, and not even her family would know what had happened to her. *Why, God, why did you let this happen to me? God isn't there. He truly isn't there!*

Her captor laid her across a saddle, then climbed on the horse behind her. The moonless night was so black it was impossible to identify her abductor. Was it Frog? No, Frog smelled like rotting garbage.

She was chilling now, her teeth chattering in the night air. It felt like there was an anchor sitting on her chest. The man kicked the horse into a gallop, and then they were riding headlong down a long lane. She drifted in and out of consciousness, aware only of the jarring motion. Whoever he was, he was taking her deeper into the wilderness. Boris? Big Joe? A shudder escaped her, and she felt the man's hand on her back, soothing her. Not, not Boris. He was never gentle. Her fear began to ease. Grunt. Why was Grunt taking her away?

It seemed hours before the horse slowed. Hope mumbled incoherently as she was lifted off the saddle and gently eased onto a pallet.

"Cold," she murmured. "Please, I'm so cold. . . ."

The sweet scent of rain teased the air. Then it was raining hard . . . rain falling in blinding sheets.

A blanket settled around her, then another. She groaned and sought its warmth.

"Thank you . . . thank you . . ."

Throughout the long night, Hope was aware of kind hands alternately holding her head and forcing her to swallow something warm and salty, and bathing her face and neck with cool water.

She was only vaguely aware when a new day dawned. Outside, the storm raged. Hope drifted in and out of consciousness, her fever soaring. Tender hands ministered to her needs, hands that she occasionally associated with Grunt. But he'd wanted to harm her, not help her. . . . She didn't understand.

On the third morning Hope slowly opened her eyes. She lay for a moment, trying to orient herself. She was in some sort of shelter . . . a cave? Was it a cave? She heard the fire pop, and she turned to see her captor's eyes fixed on her. She groaned, bringing her hand to her fevered forehead. "Grunt?" she murmured.

Dan closed his eyes. "I thought you were . . ."

She struggled to sit up. "Where am I? . . . Where are the others?"

He was by her side, pressing her back to the pallet. "Lie still. You've been sick."

"Where—where are we?" She ran her tongue over her dry lips, surprised they were cracked and swollen. "I'm so thirsty."

"Drink this."

Tilting her head, he held a cup of water to her mouth. She drank deeply.

"So good," she whispered, then lay weakly back on the pallet. Her eyes scanned the dim interior. "Where are we?"

"I'm not sure—somewhere near the Kentucky line."

A frown creased her brow. "It was you . . . you were the one—" She coughed, pain distorting her features. "You took me away during the night."

"I felt it necessary to remove you from the situation."

"Yes . . . I remember now. Boris found out I'm not Thomas Ferry's daughter."

"Yes."

"So you . . . kidnapped me again?"

"I moved you to safety."

"But why?" Nothing made sense to her. Grunt was one of the outlaws. Why was he being so kind to her?

Settling her head in the crook of his arm, he said quietly, "Listen to me, Hope." He took a cool cloth and bathed her forehead. "I'm not a part of Joe's gang."

She stared at him blankly for a moment. "I didn't think so—you're different."

"I work for the government."

"But why—"

"I'm on assignment. I've been riding with Joe, Frog, and Boris, trying to learn how they've successfully captured a number of army payrolls."

"Joe and Frog? Those imbeciles have actually done something right?"

"It's hard to believe, but yes. Actually, they've stolen a good deal of money."

"With your help," she reminded him. He'd been there the day they took her off the stage and stole the strongbox.

"Not really. I just don't do anything to stop them. My job is to find out who's filtering information to them on the payroll shipments."

She struggled to sit up. The fever must be making her delirious. "I don't believe you." But oh, how she wanted to believe him. Though he'd spoken sharply to her at times, she'd sensed it was for her welfare. She tried to focus on him, but his large form was wavy, fading in and out. "You're not an outlaw?"

He shook his head. He looked very tired, she realized. A dark beard coated his handsome face, making him seem more dangerously appealing. "I don't expect you to take my word for it, but I'm not."

No, he wasn't, she realized with a start. She'd known that in her heart from the moment they met. He wasn't like the others.

"I'm not an outlaw. A rebel at times, but not on the wrong side of the law." He smiled, and Hope was reminded how sorely tempted she was to like him.

Closing her eyes, she thanked God for placing her in Grunt's hands. "I'm glad. I knew you were different."

A smile touched his eyes. "How could you tell? I've treated you badly. I hope you understand—"

"It's all right," she whispered. "You were trying to protect me."

"Speaking of which—exactly whom am I protecting?"

"My name is Hope Kallahan. I was traveling to Medford to meet my husband-to-be, John Jacobs, when the stage was attacked. Mr. Jacobs and I are to be married soon."

"You're promised to this man?"

Was there disappointment in his voice? Her heart soared, then plunged. Or did she only want to hear it? Nodding, she motioned toward the cup. He brought the water back to her lips, and she drank thirstily. She pushed the tin aside and met his gaze. "What do we do now?"

"We wait here until you're stronger, then we'll move out under cover of darkness."

"And then?"

"Then I'll escort you to your fiancé in Medford, and I'll return to Washington. My cover is blown; there's nothing more I can do here. Until you're better, I'll sleep just outside the doorway. You'll be safe, for now."

"I can't ask you to bother with me." He'd protected her these past weeks, kept her from certain harm. She couldn't impose on his generosity any longer. "I've inconvenienced you quite enough. If you'll be so kind as to see me to the next town, I'll catch a stage."

"No. No stage."

"Why not?"

"Because it isn't safe. Big Joe is still in the area. He'll be bent on taking you hostage again."

"But why? I'm worth nothing to him. I'm not Anne Ferry; they'll get no ransom for me."

"You're still of great benefit to these men, Hope. Trust me."

She pulled the blanket tighter around her. At the moment she had no choice but to trust him with her very life. "They'll be after you too," she murmured sleepily, feeling her strength drain. "And they'll be angry that you took me away from them—furious, should they learn that you're working for the government."

He shrugged. "Their anger doesn't concern me as much as getting you safely to Medford. As far as I can tell, Medford's still a good fifty miles away. A lot can happen in fifty miles."

Hope closed her eyes; fatigue was beginning to overtake her. Her mind refused to absorb what he was saying. An incredible peace came over her. Grunt was here, offering to help her. Could she trust him? Was he actually a government official, or was this just another cruel hoax? She sighed. Whether she believed him or not made little difference. God had seen fit to place her earthly life in this man's hands. They were both in danger from Big Joe, Frog, and Boris. If only she could believe that God would deliver her . . .

The absurd situation suddenly struck her funny, and she burst into laughter.

Grunt glanced at her, frowning. "I'm glad to see that you still have your sense of humor—but what's funny about our situation?"

"You don't know?"

"No, I'm afraid I don't."

"I've spent a month in your company, my life is in your hands at the moment, and I don't know your name."

"It's Grunt."

Her merriment increased, causing her to break into another fit of coughing. Dan gently lifted her to a sitting position.

When the spasm subsided, she lay weakly back against his chest. "I'm reasonably sure your name isn't Grunt. I doubt any mother would do that to her poor, helpless newborn."

"No?" He grinned. "You don't like the name Grunt?"

She shook her head. "It's truly inappropriate."

He carefully settled her back on the pallet, and she sighed. His blanket smelled of wood smoke and lye soap. "My name is Dan Sullivan."

"Dan." She closed her eyes, testing the feel of his name on her tongue. "Daniel?"

"Daniel."

It was a good, strong biblical name. And they'd surely both been in the lions' den.

"How did you know I wasn't Anne Ferry?"

He reached for a stick of wood and laid it on the fire. "I met Anne Ferry at a Christmas soirée a few years back. Thomas Ferry is a personal friend of my commander." He moved back to the pallet and knelt beside her, gently smoothing hair back from her face with the cloth. "I knew the moment I saw you that you weren't Thomas's daughter. You're prettier than Anne."

Prettier than Anne. She felt a pang of envy for Anne, who had probably danced with this handsome man, been held in his arms. She wanted to hold his words close to her heart, but she was so weary she couldn't think at all. She couldn't imagine why Dan Sullivan's flattery meant so much to her. She was betrothed to John Jacobs, and Mr. Jacobs must be worried sick about her whereabouts.

Dan's voice was solemn now. "Hope, what were you doing with Anne's bags and her personal effects?"

When she heard uneasiness in his voice, she smiled. "Anne and her companion, Della DeMarco, had been traveling with me earlier. Miss DeMarco took ill, and Anne returned home in order for Miss Della to have the proper care. They left so suddenly that Anne forgot to get her things."

Hope smiled when she heard him exhale with relief. A moment later, she drifted off, his words tucked neatly inside her heart: *You're prettier than Anne.*

She awoke later, aware that she was alone now. Dan? Had he left? *Please, Dan . . . no . . . stay with me.* If he left her, there would be nothing she could do. She had no idea where she was nor one single way to care for herself. He'd surely take the horse.

She lay in the light of the flickering fire, waiting, listening, and praying that he wouldn't abandon her. He was, after all, a government agent . . . now she was part of that job.

Hot tears slipped from the corners of her eyes and rolled down her cheeks. Her thoughts—about God, about Dan Sullivan—were confused and jumbled. *Lord, please help me trust you like Papa did. Help me to believe—*

A sound caught her attention, and she opened her eyes. For one brief, elated moment, she saw Dan standing at the cave's entrance with two fat rabbits in his hand.

"You're back."

"Sorry it took so long. Game's scarce."

"It's OK." Giving him a smile, she closed her eyes again. Dan hadn't left her. Perhaps God was still watching out for her after all.

"Dan?"

"Yes, Hope?" His voice seemed to come from a long way off.

"Do you honestly think I'm prettier than Anne?"

The soft, masculine chuckle made her blush. "Well, Miss Kallahan, if I were to say who's the prettiest . . ."

She drifted off without ever hearing him finish the sentence.

Chapter Five

JOHN Jacobs teetered on a wooden ladder propped against the wall case of the Jacobs Mercantile, straining to reach the top shelves with the feather duster. No one could ever say they'd purchased a single item from Jacobs Mercantile that was the least bit neglected.

No sir. When one bought from Jacobs, one got quality product, down to the last needle and spool of thread. He paused on his perch to glance around the store, mentally cataloging each aisle of merchandise. Fresh goods and perishables were toward the front where people could see for themselves that Jacobs had nothing but the freshest. Of course, part of his strategy was moving the stock around a bit each day, but that never detracted from quality.

Canned goods were centered on the right; material,

spools of thread, cards of ribbons and the finest laces neatly piled on tables—center aisle. Ready-made dresses to the left. Hand tools, men's pants and shirts were at the back, near the stove where men were prone to gather while their wives shopped.

Stepping off the ladder, John nodded absently to himself. Yes, he ran a tight ship. He was proud of his accomplishments, and rightfully so. It was a solid start for his soon-to-be family. The family he hoped to build with Hope Kallahan.

Hope. How often he thought about his mail-order bride. Concerns whether she'd like him or could ever care deeply for him were never far from his mind. Betrothal to a man she'd never seen, had only seen a poor likeness of, must be a matter of discomfiture. Nevertheless—and the fact was of no small satisfaction to him— she had answered his ad.

The ad.

Wonder filled him anew. Placing that want ad in the Heart-and-Hand column of the *Kentucky Monthly*—then having that journal miraculously make its way to Michigan and into Miss Kallahan's possession. . . . He drew a deep, shuddering breath. Well, it was just a miracle, that's what it was. Just one more of God's abundant blessings, and there had been many of those in John Jacobs's life.

The moment he'd placed the ad, he'd been assailed with doubt. What madness had driven him to do so? He was reasonably happy with his life, though admittedly lonely since Mother had passed on two years ago. But life had settled into a comfortable routine. He went to work each morning. Then at night, with his trusty hound, Oliver, he climbed the stairway to his apartment above the store.

He'd told no one about the ad. In fact, he'd been so abashed about having put his private life in the public eye that he'd tried to forget about his impetuosity. But then Hope's letter arrived.

John shook his head in wonder. He'd been so taken aback by the letter, by the delicate spidery script on the envelope, that he'd waited a whole day and a half to open it. Hope had introduced herself, telling him about her Aunt Thalia and about her sisters embarking upon their own mail-order-bride adventures. John had felt encouraged. It took him another two days to compose a letter in return. With mail service between Michigan and Kentucky so slow, it took forever, or so it seemed, to receive her reply to his letter.

If Hope were nearly as beautiful as the picture that had accompanied her third letter, then he was the most fortunate man on earth! That is, unless she took one look at him and got back on the stage.

The picture he'd sent to her had been a poor image, but he wasn't a handsome man. He was a loyal man, moral, read the Good Book and did his best to live by it. But by no stretch of the imagination was he a handsome swain.

Oh, he knew full well the gamble he was taking, hoping that a woman of Miss Kallahan's exceptional beauty would agree to travel all the way to Medford to form a union with him, John Jacobs.

John stepped to the front window of the store, trying to see the town as Hope might perceive it. Medford had fared well during the war, with minimal damage from marauders. Like most towns of its size, Medford had a main street with two crossroads. The Basin River ran the length of the community. During heavy rains, it overflowed its banks and caused more than its share of headaches for the townspeople. Most, if not all, of the shop owners in town lived above their businesses. A spattering of town residents, generally the elderly or widowed, resided in small two- or three-room dwellings interspersed between storefronts. The larger portion of the population lived on the outskirts and ventured into town once a month for supplies.

Would Hope find Medford too . . . dull? too confining? There wasn't much here. Besides the Mercantile there were Pierson's Hotel, Hattie's Millinery and Sewing, Porter's Feed and Grain, Grant's Smithy, the livery where he boarded his own team and buggy, the church, and, of course, the school. Townsfolk took great pride that the school went to the eighth grade.

It was a simple, unassuming, friendly town. He was a simple, unassuming, friendly man. Would Hope find it in her heart to make her home here with him? *Father, I pray you will send a woman whom I can make happy, for indeed I will do my best to be a good husband.*

With both hope and trepidation, John stored the duster under the counter, then bent to retrieve a new roll of wrapping paper from the bottom shelf. About to heave it onto the countertop, he spied Veda Fletcher crossing the street, scurrying toward the Mercantile. Tucked beneath her arm was a familiar package. Even from this distance, he knew it was a towel-wrapped, glass casserole dish. He'd seen that particular sight many times.

"Oh, no," he muttered, quickly ducking down behind the counter. He dropped to his knees, lifting his head for an occasional peek over the countertop. Veda was still on target, her plump, rouged cheeks puffing with exertion.

The spunky, rotund widow had lost her husband some years back, and she now spent most of her time officiating as town matchmaker. Veda was just one of a whole list of town "mothers" who tried to initiate a match between John and their daughters or, in Veda's case, her spinster niece.

Attending town social functions had become more of a burden than a joy, what with mothers plying him with food while parading eligible daughters in front of him like prize mares. Why, at the church picnic, he'd ended up with no less than nine pieces of dried-apple pie after Mrs. Baker discovered it was his favorite. He'd taken to eluding any community gathering whenever he could to avoid being up all night, gulping down soda water for indigestion.

For the past couple of years, Veda had been fixated on John carrying on a long-distance courtship with that niece of hers. Fortunately, Ginger lived in San Antonio. Unfortunately, Veda lived at the edge of town.

Being a social swan herself, Veda made her way to the store at least twice a week, each time managing to drag Ginger's name into the conversation. John had explained no less than a hundred times in the last few weeks that he was betrothed, but Veda didn't listen.

It was his fervent prayer that with Hope due to arrive any moment, the campaign—no, outright war—waged by the mothers of Medford to get him married off could end. True, Hope was a month overdue, but surely she was en route. He clung to the hope much like a drowning victim clings to driftwood.

Attempting to avoid another "visit" with Veda, John crept on his hands and knees toward the front door, pushing a sleeping Oliver out of the way. He didn't want to hurt the woman's feelings, but he just couldn't face her again. Not today.

Just as John peeked from his hiding place, Veda put on the brakes and stopped to peer in the window of Hattie's shop. Seizing his chance, he bounded to his feet and slipped the lock on the front door, then hurriedly crept back behind the counter.

Shortly, he heard the doorknob turn and the door rattle. A moment later someone pecked on the front window. John wished she'd just go away. But not Veda. She knocked, rapped, and jiggled the knob loudly. John peeked around the edge of the counter, only to glimpse her cupping her hands on the glass to peer inside, her parcel tucked securely beneath her elbow.

John held his breath. *Go away, Veda.*

"John? The door is locked!" She tapped again. "John?"

He heard her mutter something; then it was quiet. When he thought it was safe, he again peered around the edge of the counter.

Veda was gone.

Thank you, God.

He rose a fraction—not much—just enough to glance out the front window and see her plump backside hurrying down the street, apparently heading for home.

Releasing a sigh of relief, he sat down flat on the floor. He liked Veda. He really did. But he just couldn't force down another forkful of chicken casserole. At least, not the way Veda fixed it with all that stuff in it. It had been a sad day indeed when Veda accidentally overheard John telling old Mrs. Brandstetter that his favorite dish was chicken casserole. Unfortunately, Mrs. Brandstetter died the next year, and when they buried her, they also buried the only recipe for a decent chicken casserole in the whole town.

He thought about Mae Brandstetter's casserole, and his mouth watered. Though he was quite adept at keeping his living quarters tidy, he'd never mastered the kitchen. His meals were quite inedible—suicide on a plate, his friends were wont to remind him. In order to keep from poisoning himself, he took most of his meals at the Pierson Hotel. Unfortunately, doing so exposed him to the cunning devices of the mothers of Medford. So much so that he'd taken to eating at odd hours. As a matter of fact, he'd missed lunch today.

A noise at the back door caught his attention. Straightening, his heart sank when he saw the door open and Veda Fletcher elbow her way inside.

"John, did you know your front door is locked?"

"Mrs. Fletcher—" His eyes focused on the casserole dish in her hand. Dear God. He would be up half the night. "Door locked? Now how did that happen?"

"Who knows—it's fortunate I came along." She set the bowl on the counter, eyeing him slyly. "Now let me guess: You missed lunch."

"I had a large breakfast—"

"Breakfast! That was hours ago." Beaming, she whisked the lid off the bowl. "Look, John. I brought you one of my chicken casseroles."

She looked so proud of herself, he couldn't think of hurting her feelings.

"Why, that's very nice of you, Mrs. Fletcher."

"No trouble at all. I enjoy doing for people. It's a family trait, you know. The Fletchers are all nurturing people. Why, you remember my niece, Ginger? She's exactly like me—chip off the old block. Just doing for someone all the time. Everyone who knows Ginger says—"

John reached for the dish. "You're right, I did miss lunch." He lifted the lid and sniffed, rolling his eyes with feigned pleasure. "This will certainly hit the spot."

Veda's smile was so genuine, John's guilt lessened at his insincere show of appreciation. If something this simple gave Veda so much pleasure, who was he to complain?

"Thank you again, Mrs. Fletcher."

"Veda. Everyone calls me Veda, John, and you've known me since before your mother died. Why, I feel like you're part of the family." She giggled like a small girl. "And maybe one day you will be. Well, I'll run along now and let you eat. Laundry waiting on the line."

If nothing else, John knew Veda Fletcher was a good housekeeper. Like clockwork, her laundry was on the line by nine o'clock every Monday. She was proud to remind her friends and neighbors that she ironed on Tuesdays, baked on Saturdays, and sat third row from the front at church on Sundays. Likely as not, she would invite Pastor Elrod and his family home for dinner and generally add another family or two as well. Generous to a fault—that was Veda. He couldn't help liking her, even if she did drive him to distraction with her tasteless chicken casseroles and constant hints about her niece, Ginger.

"Oh, I almost forgot. I just received a letter from Ginger." She turned back toward John and wiggled her brows. "She's been planning a visit for some time, you know, and she'll be here any day now. Isn't that wonderful? I can hardly wait for you to meet her. I just know you two will have so much in common."

"Mrs. Fletcher, you know my fiancée is expected any day now. We plan to be married—"

"Oh, I know that's what you plan, but would it hurt for you to just meet my niece? My goodness, John. I'm not exactly asking you to marry Ginger. Well, look. The dear girl has sent a picture in her last letter. Just look at her. Isn't she the prettiest thing you've ever laid eyes on?"

John took the tintype Veda thrust at him. He could tell absolutely nothing about the girl from the blurry image. He wasn't even sure it was a girl.

"She's lovely." He handed the picture back.

Veda cradled the photo in her hands. "She is, isn't she? Such a charming girl. Looks exactly like my sister Prunella looked when she was Ginger's age."

And Jake Pearson's granddaughter was outrageously charming, and Greta George's daughter, and Marly Jenkins's sister. In fact, Freeman Hide's granddaughter was also coming for a visit soon, and John wasn't looking forward to meeting her, either!

"I was talking to poor Ben Grant the other day, and you know his wife isn't getting any better." Veda shook her head sadly. "He can't take care of her and run the blacksmith shop too. He's going to have to find someone to take care of Mary while he's working. I was thinking

Ginger could do that. That way, she could stay here in Medford. Wouldn't that be wonderful?"

Simply ducky. Somehow, in her own seemingly innocent way, Veda was always first to know what was going on in Medford—often before the involved parties did. Granted, everyone knew Veda had a good heart, so her questions were never considered prying, and she was always the first to be at the door if there was a need. There was absolutely no question that Veda Fletcher was a loving, caring woman who, after her husband's death, had devoted herself to serving the town and its citizens. And wasn't that, after all, what people were supposed to do? Take care of one another?

Unfortunately, John was her one blind spot. He and that niece of hers. Veda was determined to get them both to the altar. Together. And soon.

"It would help Ben, I'm sure."

"It would. And Mary is such a dear soul. I'm sure Ginger would be such a blessing. And—" she smiled guilelessly—"her being here for an extended length of time will give you two time to get to know each other." She clapped her birdlike hands together. "I'm so pleased this is working out so well."

"I'm sure you'll enjoy your niece's visit." Should he suggest an earpiece? He was already engaged to another.

Tucking the photo of Ginger into her pocket, she smiled. "I'll introduce you the moment she arrives; you know how unpredictable the stages are. Why, out of the last scheduled four, three haven't come in at all."

John knew that quite well. In fact, Miss Kallahan had been due for the past four weeks and she wasn't here yet. What with the spring rains and muddy roads, there was no telling when the stage could get through.

But Miss Kallahan would come. Her letters had shown her to be a woman of integrity and honesty. He could hardly wait for her arrival so this constant parade of eligible women would cease.

"I'm sure your niece will arrive in good time, Veda. And I'm sure you'll enjoy her visit. If she can help Mary and Ben, then that's wonderful. Now, I have work to do—"

"Eat your lunch," Veda advised with a pat on his arm. "Young men need to keep up their strength."

"Thank you, I will."

"Enjoy."

"Thank you again," John called as Veda headed for the front door.

"Have a good day, John."

"Same to you, Veda."

He waved as he shut the door behind her, then snapped the lock back into place.

Turning, he took a deep breath and faced the chicken casserole.

Chapter Six

Under the cover of darkness, two figures silently emerged from the cave and crept toward a waiting horse. A moment later hoofbeats broke the quiet of the night.

Hope held tightly to Dan's waist, praying that the Lord would guide his efforts. She was still weak from the illness and incredibly tired. She longed for a bath, clean clothing, and a soft bed. Though Dan was most considerate of her needs, there was nothing he could do about clothes and hot water. The best he'd been able to provide was a "spit" bath from rainwater he'd caught in their one cooking pot.

Resting her head against his broad back, she clung to him, dreaming of a steaming tub, pots and pots of hot water, and sweet-smelling lavender soap.

The night seemed endless. Dan promised they would ride down dark lanes, keeping to the side of the road in case they encountered other nocturnal travelers. Hope visualized Big Joe and the others hiding behind every rock and bush, ready to pounce and seize them captive, only this time Dan would be a victim, too. Big Joe would make sure neither she nor Dan got away again. Her hold tightened around Dan's waist.

Her knight in shining armor glanced over his shoulder, the pale moonlight throwing his handsome profile into shadow.

"I know you're getting tired, but if your strength holds up, I want to make as much time as we can."

"Ride as long as you need." He'd been so considerate, so attentive, during her infirmity, she'd be forever grateful. He'd fetched water, kept her fever to a tolerable level, and rarely slept while watching over her. She'd heard him outside the cave tossing in his bedroll. Even in her misery, she was confident he had one ear attuned for danger.

When she'd stir, he was there to see to her every need. At night in the light of the campfire, he read to her from a small Bible he carried in his coat pocket. His responsibility for her weighed heavily on him. She could see it in his eyes and hear it in the timbre of his voice.

"The worst is behind us," she'd whisper, reaching out to take his hand. They had to keep their spirits up if they were to survive the ordeal.

"I pray you're right," he'd answer, and it was easy to tell he was worried.

The horse carried them through the dark night. They passed no one on the road. The infrequent homesteads they encountered lay dark and unthreatening beneath the waning moon.

Hope thought it must be close to dawn. Shadows gradually lifted, and the eastern horizon grew light.

"I'd like to ride until sunup," Dan said over his shoulder.

Hope shivered, puzzled by the effect his calm, reassuring voice induced. Normally she'd be frightened half out of her wits, racing through the night with a man she trusted only by faith. But with Dan, she felt safe, protected, as if no further harm could touch her. "Don't worry about me; I'm fine."

She wasn't fine, but she wasn't going to fret about petty complaints. He didn't have to personally escort her to Medford; he was risking his life by doing so. He could easily put her on a stage and be done with his responsibility.

But Dan Sullivan wasn't one to shirk duty. He was a man of exceptional character. A man any woman would be proud to . . .

She checked her thoughts. The fever had addled her brain. Aunt Thalia would say, "Keep your mind on your business, young lady!" Unfortunately, her business wasn't Dan Sullivan. Her business waited for her in Medford, and she was now more than a month late.

For all she knew, Dan might very well have a lady in Washington awaiting his return. The idea didn't set well with her. In fact, it reminded her of one of Aunt Thalia's awful duck recipes that soured her stomach.

She checked her thoughts a second time. What was she thinking? Riding around the countryside, depending on Dan to look out for her welfare. She'd never depended on anyone except family and God. In spite of the goodness she saw in Dan, she didn't know him—didn't know anything about him. What if he was deliberately misleading her—hoping to gain her confidence and—

What if he had other reasons for befriending her—sinister reasons? She shivered.

"Cold?"

"No, someone just walked over a grave."

"Pardon?"

"Someone just walked over a grave: Aunt Thalia says that's what causes shivers."

"Is that right?" Humor colored his tone.

"That's what my aunt says."

"Then it must be true."

Kidnapped, mistaken for someone else, held captive in a filthy cabin, fed vile food, been deplorably ill . . . and now, riding through the darkness with a man who makes me have thoughts I have no right to think.

I'm weak, Lord! I'm not able to do this!

"You're tired," Dan said, and she wondered if he'd read her thoughts. Heat crept up her neck and covered her cheeks. Oh, she hoped not! It was bad enough to think them!

"We'll stop for the day."

His kindness brought tears to her eyes. "Thank you," she whispered, wondering anew how he could be so attuned to her necessities.

He cut the horse into a thicket and a few moments later lifted Hope down from the saddle. She closed her eyes, trying to absorb his strength, wishing that she had a small portion of it. To the left was a low outcropping where she assumed they would rest for the day. Dan held her for a moment, decidedly a bit too long, then gently set her aside.

"We should be safe here for the day. I'll get a fire going. You're chilled." When he stepped away, she felt as if part of her left with him.

Tears stung her eyes and she swallowed, fighting to stem the rising tide. *Don't cry, Hope!* All he needed was a weepy woman to add to his troubles. Yet teardrops formed in her eyes, and she realized whatever earlier strength she'd boasted of having had vanished with the night. She felt weak and drained.

Dan returned momentarily. Removing the lid from the canteen, he handed it to her, his eyes gentle.

"Thanks." Did he understand what she was feeling? She couldn't meet his gaze for fear of bursting into unmanageable sobs. Right now, she was primed for a pretty good pity party he wouldn't want to attend.

A smile touched the corners of his eyes. "You don't have to be so polite. If you want to scream, tear your hair out, you've earned the right."

She gave him a lame smile, lifting the canteen to take a long swallow. She'd like nothing better than to scream and rail at the injustices she had endured, but no one except Dan would hear, and he certainly didn't deserve to be party to her hysteria.

"Hungry?"

She shook her head. She couldn't remember the last time food interested her.

"Well, no matter how bleak our situation looks right now, a person has to eat. John Jacobs won't take kindly to my depositing a skeleton on his doorstep." He wiped away the one tear that trickled down her cheek with this thumb. The intimate gesture was oddly comforting. "No matter how pretty she might be."

Hope searched somewhere deep within herself and managed to come up with something she hoped resembled a smile. At least he was still optimistic that they'd reach John Jacobs. She wasn't so sure.

"Sorry, I don't mean to be whiny—"

"You're not whiny, Miss Kallahan." He stripped the saddle off the horse and carried it to the outcrop. Her eyes focused on the ridge of impressive muscle that played across his back, shamefully aware that her thoughts should dwell on more fruitful ground. She followed him to the campsite.

"The kidnapping, Big Joe and the gang. It all seems like a bad dream."

"It will be over soon." He straightened, his gaze assessing her soiled appearance. She must look a sight. Her dress was disheveled and dirty, and she'd only half managed to twist her hair into a bun and secure it with the precious few pins she had left.

"Do you like fish?"

She nodded. "I like fish."

"Good, because I spotted a stream a short while back. With any luck, I'll catch our breakfast."

He settled her on a blanket and started a fire. Then he took off in search of the stream. Huddling close to the snapping fire, she watched his tall form disappear into the undergrowth. Goose bumps swelled, and she rubbed her arms, uneasy when he was gone.

Within the hour he returned, whistling and carrying his catch. She smiled at the sight of the large bass. Dan Sullivan's woman would never fear for her next meal.

"Breakfast," he announced with a cocky grin.

"Congratulations."

Squatting, he piled more brush on the fire and grinned up at her. "Dan, you incredible man, you. How did you get so good at catching fish with your hands? she asks."

She blushed at his teasing.

"Well, thank you, Miss Kallahan. I hoped you'd notice my exceptional sporting skills. I got good at catching fish with my hands during the war. Many nights our company would have gone hungry if we hadn't devised our own means of providing food."

"You fought in the war?"

"Yes, ma'am, for way too long." A mask dropped over his features, and she realized she'd touched on a painful subject.

They chatted while he cleaned then skewered the fish and hung it over the flames. They talked briefly about the War between the States and the terrible atrocities it brought upon the people. Kentucky had tried to remain neutral, Dan told her, but that wasn't possible.

"How do you know so much about Kentucky?"

"Had a good friend who lived here."

"Is he here now?"

"He's buried in Lexington."

"I'm sorry," she murmured. "Do you ever feel as if the world is spinning out of control?" She sensed his smile, though he had his back to her.

"Occasionally."

"I never had, until recently. I thought God would keep me safe from all harm."

Lately, God had challenged those thoughts. He never promised there'd be no trials, but somehow she'd just expected her life to be different. Adversity happened to others, not to her. Not until Papa died. Or until she and her sisters split up, and she didn't know when, if ever, she'd see them again. Or until Big Joe took her hostage.

"No one is protected from trouble, Hope. Not on this earth," he said quietly.

They shared the moist, tasty bass, and then Hope slept the day away. She was vaguely aware of Dan keeping watch as he dozed intermittently, but she was too tired to insist that he rest while she guarded their small sanctuary. Toward evening, they finished the last of the fish before Dan doused the fire and saddled the horse.

As twilight faded, they rode on, pausing the second night only long enough to rest the horse and drink from icy cold streams. By the time the sun came up the third morning, although Hope was still reeling with exhaustion, the healing rays were warm on her face, and she thanked God for a new day.

Dan's soft warning jarred her from her lethargic state. "Let me do the talking," he said quietly.

Half asleep, she started at the sound of his voice. "What—what is it?"

"There's a wagon coming."

Her heart raced. Would they be discovered? Why didn't he cut off the road? "Big Joe?"

"No, Joe wouldn't use a wagon. Probably a farmer on his way to town."

A team of sleek black horses came around the bend, and Hope spotted an old man and woman sitting on the spring seat of a short wagon. The woman's pale hair, shot with silver, had come loose from her bonnet. Her body was more square than angular. The old man looked exactly like her—*bookends,* Hope thought, except for the rim of snow white hair protruding wildly from beneath the battered hat he wore low over his lined face. The wagon pulled even with Dan and clattered to a halt.

Smiling, the old man showed a row of uneven, yellow teeth.

"Howdy. You folks are out purty early, ain't ya?"

Dan eased Hope down from the back of the horse. She straightened, working the kinks out of her back. She was grateful for the brief reprieve. The old couple looked harmless enough.

Stepping out of the saddle, Dan walked over to shake hands. "My sister hasn't been well lately. We started out before sunrise to find a doctor, but she's feeling poorly again."

Hope shot Dan a disbelieving look. Sister? Of course. They couldn't announce they were unmarried and traveling together. His returning gaze warned her to go along with the facade.

"We were about to rest a spell when we heard your wagon."

Hope would play along, but she didn't approve of fibs. She could still remember the sting of Papa's hickory switch on the backs of her legs when he'd caught her lying.

Removing his hat, the old man scratched his head.

"Well, our place is up the road aways. You and yore sister are mighty welcome to stop in for a cup of Harriet's coffee."

Hope studied the old woman. Her face was flushed, and she looked as if she'd wallowed in a mudhole in her plain brown cotton dress.

"You shore are!" she invited. "We'd be right proud to have you join us for breakfast."

"Oh no. We couldn't," Hope protested. She shot Dan an anxious look.

"No." Dan smiled. "We don't want to impose—"

"Land sakes! Be no imposition! Got plenty of fresh eggs, and it won't take a minute to whip up a fresh batch of biscuits. Come on now, yore sister looks downright peaked."

Dan glanced back to Hope and she smiled. Lamely, she knew, but it was the best she could do. The thought of a hot meal did sound good.

"I guess we could stop for a minute. Much obliged." Dan reached for the horse's reins. "If you don't mind, would it be all right if my sister rides with you? As I said, she's been feeling poorly. . . ."

"Why, she's welcome as rain. Name's Harriet Bennett. This here's my husband, Luther." She grinned, showing a front tooth chipped clear to the gum. "Just tie your horse on to the back, Mister, then hitch yoreself a ride on the tail."

She jerked a thumb toward the back of the wagon. "Just shove the pig out of the way. She ain't gonna give you no trouble."

"Yes, ma'am." Pig? Hope peered over the side of the wagon. An old sow was standing in the back of the wagon—a very large, very smelly old sow—taking up a full third of the bed. She glanced at Dan, frowning.

He lifted an amused brow. "You heard the woman, Sister—just push the pig out of the way."

Hope climbed aboard the wagon, keeping an eye on the sow.

It eyed her back, snorting.

If they thought she was going to push anything that size out of her way they had another think coming. Scooting to the far side of the bed, she settled back against the sideboard, drawing a deep breath. A pig! She was now riding with two strangers and a pig! She hoped Aunt Thalia never heard about this.

Lord, can it get much worse?

Securing the horse to the back of the wagon, Dan hopped aboard. Luther slapped the reins, and the wagon lurched forward.

"You see ol' Doc Jimster?" Harriet turned to ask above the clattering wheels.

Dan glanced at Hope. "No—the one in Medford."

"Medford!" The old woman turned further in her seat to look at him. "Land sakes! That's a fur piece away." She looked at him as if he, not his sister, needed medical attention.

Dan smiled. "He's family—Sis won't let anyone but Doc—"

"Power," Hope finished. She grinned. "Good ol' Doc Power—worth his weight in gold. Wouldn't see anyone but . . . Doc."

"Well," Harriet frowned. "Ain't goin' nearly as far as Medford, but one more mile along the way is a help, I'd reckon."

Leaning back, Dan met Hope's worried gaze with his own. "Reckon it is, ma'am. We appreciate the ride."

Harriet again turned to look over her shoulder. "Dearie, you look real feverish. You doin' anything for what ails ya?"

Dan answered. "We've been doctoring it, ma'am."

She reached back to give Hope's leg a pat. "We'll have

you in a nice warm kitchen afore too long, drinking one of my hot toddies."

The old man chuckled. "Harriet's hot toddies will either kill ya or cure ya."

"Oh . . ." Hope smiled, preferring the latter. "I'd like that. Without spirits, of course."

The old woman nodded enthusiastically. " 'Course!"

The four looked up as the sound of fast-approaching horses caught their attention. Two men, leaning low over the necks of their animals, galloped full speed around the bend.

The old woman grasped her husband's arm. "Luther!"

About the same time Harriet yelled at her husband, a bullet whizzed past Dan's head. Bolting upright, Hope tried to see what the commotion was all about, but Dan pinned her back down with a hand.

Luther whipped his team of horses to a full run. A second bullet whistled overhead as Dan bent over Hope and pulled out his revolver.

"What's going on?" Hope shouted above the clacking wheels. The old buckboard threatened to break apart as it churned headlong down the road, hitting potholes and deep ruts.

"Stay down!" Dan shouted.

"Hang on!" Luther cracked the whip and the team strained, running harder. The horses barreled down the road, trying to outrun the two men on horseback who were now pursuing them with devilish fervor. "Hold on! We're headin' for th' barn!"

"What's he mean?" Hope grunted, clinging to the side of the wagon. "Heading for the barn—what's going on?"

The pig squealed in protest, rolling wildly about the wagon bed on its fat sides. Hope moved her foot to keep it from being squashed, scooting more to the left.

The old man cackled with glee as he swung the whip over the team's backsides. "Hold on, kiddies!"

Pulling himself upright, Dan leaned close to Harriet's ear. "Who are those people?"

"It's just Lyndon," the old woman shouted. "Nothin' to concern your head about!"

Hope struggled to sit up, but Dan kept pushing her down. "Who are they? Robbers?" That's all she needed—to be taken hostage a second time. John Jacobs would never buy that story!

"It's Lyndon," Dan told Hope.

"Oh." She lay back, trying to hang on. *It's Lyndon. . . .* She frowned. *Who is Lyndon?*

The wagon wheeled around a corner and up a narrow lane. Hope's teeth chattered as the wagon bed bounced over the uneven terrain. Low-hanging branches slapped the wagon, keeping Hope off balance. The riders were closing in, close enough for Hope to get a good look at Lyndon—whichever one he might be.

"Run for th' house," Luther yelled as they shot through the open barn doorway. Sawing on the reins, he stopped the team. Harriet sprang from the wagon seat, motioning to Hope. "Come on!"

Dan lifted Hope from the wagon, and they dashed toward a building that Hope thought faintly resembled a cabin. The boards were nailed haphazardly together, and the roof was fashioned from various pieces of colored tin. Red, blue, yellow—there seemed to be no pattern.

Chickens flapped and darted for cover as Hope's feet hit the porch. Luther followed close on her heels. She could hear him cackling as he shot looks over his shoulder at the pursuers. Hope flew through the front door ahead of Dan and Harriet. Luther waited until the pig cleared the door frame, then slammed the door shut. Leaning against the thick wood, he swiped his brow. "That was close."

Oinking, the pig calmly meandered to a corner and

collapsed, obviously fatigued after her spirited trip across the yard.

A bullet chunked into the side of the cabin, sending splinters of wood flying. Luther grabbed a rifle and ducked behind the front window.

"That crazy Lyndon," he muttered. "The old fool's gonna git hisself shot."

Hope and Dan stood in the middle of the kitchen, looking at each other as Harriet hustled into the bedroom and came back toting a double-barreled shotgun. Kneeling on the opposite side of the window, she hefted the weapon to her shoulder.

A volley of bullets drilled into the front door. Dan and Hope dove for the floor. Crawling beneath the rough-hewn kitchen table, they stayed there.

"Luther?" Dan shouted. "Who is that out there?"

"Oh, it's jest my brother," Luther said, sighting through his rifle. "The thief."

"Thief?"

"Yeah. He stole half our chickens yesterday, the low-down, rotten—"

"Luther," Harriet cautioned, "we got guests."

"If he stole your chickens, why is he shooting at you?" Dan called.

Luther stood up, fired, then ducked down. " 'Cause we got his pig."

"Yep," Harriet crowed. "We got his finest porker this mornin'."

Hope looked at Dan. "A family feud—we're in the middle of a family feud."

"How rotten can our luck get?" he muttered.

Luther poked the rifle out of the open window and fired. A return volley peeled bark off the front of the cabin. The staccato salvos shattered the front window-pane, throwing glass into the room.

"Whooeee, that was close!" Luther chortled, reloading.

"That ol' coot! Thinks he's a good shot. Couldn't hit the broad side of a barn."

"Dan," Hope whispered, scooting closer to him. His arm came around her protectively. "Shouldn't we make a run for it?"

"No—it's too dangerous—" Dan ducked as another round of bullets showered the room. "Let's wait it out."

On her hands and knees Harriet crawled across the floor to the back window. "Jest hold on, young'uns. I'll put that pot of coffee on in a few minutes."

"Harriet?" Dan called.

The old woman glanced over her shoulder. "Yes?"

"How long has this been going on?"

The little woman paused, pondering the question. "Well, now—I reckon for forty year or so. That Lyndon's jest a real pain in the get-a-long. Always has caused trouble. He's had it in for Luther and me since the day he got it in that stubborn head of his that Luther took one of his calves. Wasn't Luther, 'course, but from that moment on, Lyndon jest plain went off his rocker. Started takin' things. So, we jest been takin' 'em back."

Shots rang out, and Harriet sprang to her feet and fired. Ducking, she grinned at Dan. "Me and Luther bested him this week. Yesterday Lyndon and his boys stole six of our ol' scrawny hens ready for the stewpot. This mornin' Luther and me got up real early and stole his best hog—the one he's plannin' to butcher this fall." She poked her head up and fired off another round. "Watch it, Luther. Mary Jane's out to the side. Sneakin' through the blackberry patch."

"Fire a shot over her head, Harriet. Let 'er know we see 'er."

Harriet fired a shot out the window, and the woman running along the back of the lot picked up her skirt tail and ran faster.

Harriet sank to the floor and shoved another round

into the chamber. "Me and Luther's lived here nigh on to forty years—since the day we got hitched. I was fifteen and Luther here was eighteen. Lyndon and Mary Jane tied the knot the next year. They live 'bout three miles down the road. To the south. Real good neighbors 'till Lyndon gets riled."

Hope sent Dan a perplexed glance. If this wasn't a fine kettle of fish! How much time was this delay going to cost them?

Harriet sprang up and squeezed off another round. "Lyndon had an eye for me, you know. He's a couple years older than Luther and thought he might have first claim. Our place was just over the holler, and he'd come by every week or so. He was sweet on me, real sweet, but I didn't cotton to him." Harriet shrugged. "Only had eyes for my Luther."

Hope's gaze traveled to the old man crouched at the window. Love was an odd thing.

"And this feud has been going on ever since?" Dan called from beneath the table.

"Yep. It's jest a cryin' shame." Harriet popped up and blasted another round.

"I'll say," Hope murmured. "I feel like crying myself."

The impasse kept up all morning. Exhausted from traveling the night before and with nothing else to do anyway, Dan and Hope sprawled on the floor and rested while the old couple kept vigil. They awoke by late afternoon. Hope's legs were numb, and he was fit to be tied.

"We've got to do something," Dan muttered. He tried to get up and straighten his long legs. Just then a shot zinged against the house again. Dan dived under the table. Hope grinned, though she found the situation anything but humorous.

"What can we do?" She tried to rub feeling back into her legs. "This could go on all night."

Harriet turned from the window as if she'd just remembered she had guests. "Land sakes, Luther. These young'uns must be half starved. We never did git around to feedin' 'em breakfast."

"Could eat the south end outta a northbound critter myself, Harriet. It's gittin' dark. Lyndon and his bunch'll be headin' home directly." Luther straightened, his eyes narrowing. "Uh-oh."

"What?" Harriet asked from her stance at the back window.

"Mary Jane's got the horse."

"The young'un's horse?"

"Yep—she must think it's ours. She left the saddle though—right thoughtful of her."

"My horse?" Dan whacked his head against the top of the table, wincing. He crawled out, and Hope followed him.

"No need to fret, son. We'll get 'im back," Luther promised. "Boy, my lumbago's killin' me, Harriet. We got any of that salve?"

Harriet came over to stand beside Dan. "We'll get yore horse back—might take a day or two, but we'll get 'im back for you. Don't you worry none 'bout that."

"I'm worried about the saddle. It's a personal keepsake."

"But we can't stay here," Hope protested. John Jacobs was this minute probably worried sick about her whereabouts. Two days' delay here—then another two to three days' ride. They couldn't stay; Dan had to make that clear to Luther. They'd just wanted a cup of coffee and a fresh biscuit!

"Don't you fret yore pretty little head one minute, young'un." Harriet hung the rifle over a peg and stepped to the stove. Pitching in a stick of kindling, she slid the lid over the burner. "Got plenty of room—you ain't put-tin' us out a'tall. Glad to have the company. You and your brother kin stay right here 'til we git yore animal back."

Hope's heart sank. "No . . . really, we can't."

"Why, shore you can." Harriet waved off the courtesy. "Just took fresh sheets off the line yesterday. Luther and yore brother can bunk down in here. Me and you can take th' bedroom."

Hope was about to protest again when Harriet called over her shoulder. "No arguin'. We insist. You don't look none too strong. No way yore gonna make it all the way to Medford feelin' sickly like you do. You jest rest up here a spell afore you move on. Lyndon don't usually keep us pinned down more'n a few days."

"A few days?" Hope mouthed. What happened to one or two?

Dan stepped away from the window. "Ma'am, we wouldn't think of putting Luther out of his bed. We'll stay the night and leave first light in the morning. Hope can sleep on a pallet near the fire, and I'll bunk down in the barn."

"Now that sounds fair, Harriet," Luther said. "These old bones can't hardly take this old floor anymore."

Harriet dragged a heavy skillet out of the oven of the woodstove. "Whatever you say, but I wouldn't be countin' on leavin' in the mornin'." She turned, grin-ning. "Now, how does ham and redeye gravy sound to everyone?"

The old cabin filled with the smell of supper. Hope cut biscuits while Harriet fried thick slices of ham. Hope kept an eye on the sow, praying the meat wasn't one of its relatives.

"Uh-oh," Luther said when he lifted the curtain aside to look out. Darkness had fallen, and a full moon was rising.

Hope had come to dread the phrase "Uh-oh." It invariably meant trouble.

The old woman glanced up. "What's the matter?"

"Lyndon's boys are still here."

"Well, ma's boots—they're gonna make us miss supper." Harriet leaned to peer over her husband's shoulder. "Yes sir, there's little Jim, and John over by the barn. There's Teddie to the right, and Eddie straight out. I'd say the others are farther back in the trees, probably sneakin' around to the back."

Hope glanced up from setting plates on the table. "How many boys does Lyndon have?"

"Oh, eight or so. Then there's four or five of them girls." She tsked. "Real homely, those girls are—though jest as nice as they can be. Real mannerly. He finally got that one, Ethylene, married off last year, but he won't be so lucky with those others. Do you think, Luther?"

"Not likely, though little Merline won't be so bad once she gets a little meat on them bones."

"Luther!" a voice shouted from outside.

"Who is it?" Luther yelled back.

"Teddie."

"What do you want?"

"Our pig."

"What pig?"

"Th' pig you stole from Ma and Pa!"

"Don't know nothin' 'bout yore pig." Luther sat down at the table, his face a mask of determination.

Silence stretched. Luther looked at Harriet and winked. "Do too."

"Do not! You know anything about them chickens Lyndon stole from me?"

Silence.

"No."

"Do too."

The war of words waged on. Hope poured four mugs

of boiled coffee, then wiped her hands on the muslin cloth she'd tied about her waist. Big Joe was after them, and now Lyndon's boys were lying in wait outside. Seemed to her things had gotten worse.

There was a real pig making herself at home in the corner, and those were real bullets imbedded in the cabin wall, and she was so hungry she could eat the walls down. She didn't know about the others, but she was eating.

"Supper's ready!"

Harriet turned from the window. "Why, child, it smells lappin' good. Luther, that young'un's done got supper on the table. Ain't that somethin'?"

"Shore is—real hospitable of you, young'un."

The men washed up while Hope took a pan of biscuits out of the oven.

"Land sakes," Harriet fussed, "I wish you'd let me do that. You not feeling real good and all."

"I'm better, Harriet. Thank you." Hope put two fat biscuits on Dan's plate. He smiled his gratitude, and she longed to give him a hug and tell him it would be over soon. One way or another.

"Why have Luther and his brother fought so long over something so insignificant?" Hope asked as she took her seat.

"Ah, the Bennetts are a hardheaded lot," Harriet explained. "Pride runs real deep."

"But Lyndon is Luther's brother. How can he bear to be at such odds with him? I have two sisters, and we've never had an argument that lasted more than a day. Nothing ever seemed so important that we ceased to be family."

"Well, it ain't a real pleasant situation," Harriet agreed. Luther, Hope noticed, just hung his head at the subject.

Breaking two biscuits apart, Hope ladled gravy over

them. "The Lord says don't be mean to your family, and try your best to love one another—"

Dan broke in quietly. "What Hope means to say is that the Lord instructs families to look past mistakes, forgive misunderstandings, and be slow to take offense and never hold grudges."

Hope pleated her makeshift apron between her fingers. So he knew his Scriptures. He didn't have to be so smart about it. "My Aunt Thalia says if you have family, you're rich. I wouldn't trade my sisters for anything."

Harriet hung her head. "Pride's a powerful enemy, all right. But once ill feelings get started there's no stoppin' them—leastwise not in the Bennett family. Too much water over the dam—too many hurt feelin's."

Luther spread a biscuit with fresh cream butter, his features tight with emotion. "Harriet's right. Lyndon can't be reasoned with. Never could be. Once he's got somethin' in his craw there's no gettin' it out."

They ate the remainder of the meal in silence. When Harriet got up to help with the dishes, Hope motioned her to remain seated.

Pouring Dan another cup of coffee, Hope met his gaze.

"Thanks," he said softly.

"You're welcome."

She liked it when he smiled at her; actually, she liked everything about him.

The pig in the corner grunted and rolled over.

The pig she didn't like.

Luther got up from the table and returned to the window. "Looks like the boys have bedded down for the night."

"Is it safe to sleep with them camped so close by?" Hope scraped leftovers into the dog's bowl.

"Oh sure. Those boys like their sleep. But come daylight, they'll be back at it." Harriet stifled a yawn. "I'll get some extra quilts. The old cabin gets chilly at night."

Harriet returned with an armload of bedding and laid it on the table. "Take what you need for warmth, then use the rest for padding."

"Thank you." Hope smiled. "We'll be comfortable."

Harriet and Luther retired to their room, leaving Dan and Hope to stare at the stack of quilts.

Hope sighed. "Now what?" It wasn't proper for an unmarried couple to sleep in the same room.

"Let's see what morning brings. I don't want to endanger our lives if we don't have to." He handed her a folded quilt.

Hope closed her eyes, weariness overtaking her. "What about the sleeping arrangements? You can't go out to the barn."

"Harriet and Luther are in the next room—we have chaperones. You can sleep on one side of the stove; I'll sleep on the other. We won't be able to see each other."

Hope was too tired to argue. "I don't know why this is happening to us."

"Who would you like it to happen to?"

She could think of several right now. Big Joe at the top of the list. She looked up when Dan took her hands.

When he looked at her like this, all polite and gentlemanly, it was hard to remember that she was trying to reach John Jacobs—the man she was about to marry.

"I know you're worried, but now's the time to put your faith to the test, Hope. I'll get us out of here, but I'm not going to do anything foolish."

She sighed. "Papa said we were to never lose faith, no matter how hopeless the situation seemed—but this seems pretty hopeless. Lyndon's sons are out there just waiting for us to step outside. Harriet and Luther may consider this just harmless fun, but those were real bullets they were firing at us. For all we know, Big Joe, Frog, and

Boris have heard the commotion and have come to investigate—" She blinked back sudden tears. "And Harriet and Luther think we're brother and sister."

She felt anything but "sisterly" toward him.

"Don't you believe God can and will take care of us?"

"I don't know," she said, closing her eyes. She felt like doubting Thomas, but right now her faith was pretty weak. "He can, but—"

Of course she believed God was able; she just wasn't sure she was capable of trusting her life so completely to his care.

Dan blew out the lamp, and Hope lay on her pallet listening to him settle on the other side of the stove. He seemed so confident—so comfortable in his belief. He made her feel so ashamed of her doubts.

Hands tucked beneath her cheek, she lay in the dark, thinking about her life. The old sow snored, its fat sides heaving in and out with exertion.

Exactly what did she believe? Before she could decide, weariness claimed her.

Just before dawn, Dan gently shook her awake.

"The old couple are stirring."

It took Hope a moment to clear the cobwebs from her head. When she did, she got up and quickly folded her quilts. Running her fingers through her hair, she despaired of ever getting the tangles out. They had left the outlaws' cabin so abruptly that Dan failed to bring Anne's valise.

Hope fashioned a careless braid and coiled it at the nape of her neck and secured it. Shaking her skirts in a futile attempt at neatness, she started to the stove to stoke up the fire.

She ducked as a bullet whizzed by her head.

"Luther, they're gonna break every window in the house," Harriet complained, coming out of the bedroom with her gray hair streaming down her back.

"Howdy, young'uns!" Luther greeted as he ducked to one side of the window.

"Howdy." Hope concentrated on dipping water from the stove reservoir for coffee.

They wouldn't be leaving today.

Chapter Seven

THE pig was restless. And Hope had had her fill of dealing with it. Three endless days and she'd had her fill of this senseless feud.

She had used water sparingly, but it was getting dangerously low, and the monotony of the meals was beginning to dim everyone's appetite.

"Can't we leave?" she asked Dan the third morning. She glanced toward Luther and Harriet's closed door. She wouldn't hurt the old couple's feelings for the world, but this was their fight, not hers and Dan's. The Lord knew they had enough problems without taking on more. "I can't stand being cooped up in this tiny room any longer. And if I have to clean up after that pig one more time, we're having pork for supper."

Dan pulled on his boots, his face lined with concern.

"This has gone on long enough. Watch for my signal today. Be ready. When I think it's safe to make a run for it, we'll go."

"Thank goodness." She lifted the curtain to peek out the window. "There's not a soul out there this morning."

"We need a horse."

Hope stepped back to stir a pan of gravy bubbling on the stove. Sunlight streamed through the small window above the cookstove. This morning had been eerily quiet. The usual "I'm here" shots had yet to be fired. Yesterday the only real activity had come from the line of cottonwoods running parallel to the house and then only when Dan had recovered his saddle and put it in the barn. He seemed protective of the saddle, and she remembered that it held special significance for him.

She focused on the gurgling creek running alongside the cabin. If her eyes didn't deceive her, that was watercress growing along the bank. She'd bet Aunt Thalia's best broach that tender mushrooms grew in the shaded areas to the east of the stream and perhaps some poke greens at the edge of the clearing. Her mouth watered at the possibilities. For the past two days they'd eaten nothing but meat and potatoes.

Fresh greens sounded so tempting. The pig oinked and shifted. She turned to give it a sour look. Fresh greens with ham hocks.

Luther emerged from the bedroom and sat down at the table with Dan. Hope could hear Harriet moving around in the other room, pulling the quilt up over the sheets.

She had to get out of the cabin. Just for a moment— one blissful moment—when she could breathe fresh air. She was suffocating from all the closeness.

The men were up at the stove now, pouring themselves coffee. Taking a deep breath, Hope edged toward the back door.

The pig lumbered to its feet and nosed after her. She tried to nudge it away with the tip of her shoe, but the old sow was just as eager for freedom as she was.

Dan turned when he heard the door open.

She smiled. "Just stepping out for a moment."

"Hope—don't be foolish—"

Her words came in a rush. "I'll only be gone a moment. There isn't anyone out back right now—not one shot has been fired this morning."

"You can't be sure there's no one around. I'll go with you—"

"One shot, and I'm back in the house, I promise." She quickly closed the door before he had time to argue.

Bounding off the porch, she glanced both ways for any sign of the other Bennetts. Songbirds chirped overhead, and fat robins hopped around pulling worms from the rocky soil. The pig, obviously with no consideration for her future, shot past and waddled straight for a sturdy-looking pen with a beckoning mudhole. Hope hurried ahead to unlatch the gate.

"Try to clean up a little," she muttered.

Grunting, the old sow settled herself into the mire as Hope quickly swung the gate closed and fastened it with a loop of wire.

Hurrying to the edge of the trees, she quickly gathered greens, keeping one eye on the cabin. Dan would come after her if she stayed out too long, but the idea of fresh greens was just too tempting to pass up.

Using her apron to cradle the tender shoots, Hope poked around in the damp shadows, hoping to find some small, tender morels. She'd barely gathered a handful when she heard a twig snap to her left. She froze, her blood curdling in her chest. *How foolish of me to risk my life for some old greens,* she thought. *Now I've gotten myself into a pickle, and Dan will be upset with me.* He'd have every right to give her a tongue-lashing.

Crouching low in the shadows, she searched the undergrowth for some clue to the stealthy movements that continued a short distance in front of her. Holding her breath, she prayed that an innocent woodland creature was causing the soft rustlings. She'd even welcome a skunk. That would be preferable to a Bennett boy with a shotgun in his hand.

The sounds stopped, and Hope's heart thrummed. A face materialized, not five feet from where she stooped. She strained to make out its features. Blood pounded in her ears. Was it a bear? No, it wasn't an animal, nor was it one of the Bennett boys—it was a girl.

Caught by surprise, the two women stared at each other. It took a moment for Hope to summon the courage to speak. Then her voice came out in a minuscule squeak.

"Hello . . . I'm Hope. Who are you?"

The startled girl didn't answer; she simply stared like a doe caught in a rifle sight. Her elfin features were white with fright, her black dress dirty and unkempt.

"Don't be frightened—I won't hurt you."

The girl's eyes were the color of green grass.

Smiling, Hope extended her hand. "Can you tell me your name?"

"Fawn. Fawn Bennett."

One of Lyndon's children. Luther's niece.

"Lyndon Bennett's daughter?"

"Yes'um." She glanced toward the stand of trees. "I'm the baby—only I ain't no baby no more. I turned thirteen last month—I'm a woman now."

"What are you doing out here, Fawn?"

Her face turned defensive. "Brought my brothers some biscuits and bacon from home. They sent me around back to watch the house whilst they et."

Hope turned to look toward the cabin. No sign of Dan yet. "Your brothers are still out here?"

The girl flashed a quick grin. "Yes'um. My brothers ain't too bright, but they hide real good." She darted a quick look toward the trees, then back to Hope. "You'd better go. They might shoot you."

Startled, Hope started back toward the house, then paused and turned around. "Do you think they'd honestly shoot me?"

The girl thought about it. "Naw. They jest want to skeer you, liken they do Uncle Luther and Aunt Harriet. I best be goin'. They wouldn't want me a jawin' with ya." The young girl turned to leave.

"Wait," Hope whispered. "Can we talk a minute?"

The girl looked doubtful, then gestured for Hope to follow her. A moment later Hope entered a small clearing to the east of the cabin. An abundance of mushrooms grew in the shadows of a fallen tree. She quickly gathered an apron full.

"It's lovely here."

Fawn shrugged. "I like it. Makes me feel close to the Almighty when I'm here."

"Tell me about the feud." Hope set the apron containing mushrooms and greens on the ground, then settled on a rock.

Fawn paced the clearing, apparently uneasy with the arrangement. Her eyes darted back and forth as if she expected her brothers to burst out of the brush any minute. "What about it?"

"Don't you think it's silly? It's senseless for families to be shooting at each other."

The girl turned to look at her. "It's always been this way. Since before any of us young'uns was born."

"How sad. I'm sure it must be hard to live with such hostility."

The girl's shoulders lifted with acceptance. "Every few weeks or so, Pa'll swipe something from Uncle Luther, and Uncle Luther will steal somethin' back. It ain't real pleasant."

"How long does this go on?"

"Until they get back whatever the other took."

Hope couldn't imagine such a dreary existence. "Hasn't anyone thought to settle the problem?" Seemed easy enough to sit down and talk it through, pray for forgiveness—try to respect the other's rights.

Fawn's smile was fleeting. "I'd think so, but Pa won't hear of it. Ma'd like to be friends with Aunt Harriet. She gits real lonely. This fightin' seems ta be the only way they kin talk to one another."

What an interesting thought. "That's too bad."

"Yes'um. Shore nuff is."

"So, you would like to see this end?" Hope said softly.

"Yes'um—real bad. But it don't never seem likely."

Hope was drawn to the girl. For one thing, she seemed the only person in the Bennett family with common sense. For another, she was a lovely waif who seemed at odds with her destiny.

"Then perhaps we can do something about it."

The girl stared at her as if Hope had suddenly grown two heads.

"What kin we do?"

"Does your family believe in God?"

The girl's head bobbed enthusiastically. "Ain't got no church round here, but a preacher comes round once a month and holds a meetin' at somebody's house."

"Well, my papa was a great one for reading the Bible. He had Scripture for every problem."

Fawn's lips curved in a near smile. "Think he'd have one for this?"

Hope nodded. "Most assuredly, if he were alive. He died a few months back."

Fawn paced the clearing, in thought now. The sun ducked behind a cloud, and the wind had a chill that

reminded one it was still early spring. "It'd shore be nice
not to hafta be afraid all the time, to have the two families git along."

Hope longed to give Fawn a reassuring hug, but she
didn't want to frighten her. "Can you read?"

The girl lit with excitement. "Yes'um, I can read real
good-like. Learnt how last year. Mrs. Yodler teached
me."

"Do you think you could talk to your family? Read
the Ten Commandments out loud to them. Be sure both
your brothers and parents understand the commandment
'Thou shalt not steal.' Can you do that?"

She frowned. "I kin try. Where is those commandments in the Bible?"

"In Exodus." Hope wracked her brain. What chapter
was that? Ten? Eighteen? Twenty! "Chapter 20! Do you
have a Bible?"

"Part of one."

Hope hoped it was the Old Testament part. "Good.
And I'll try to reason with your Aunt Harriet and Uncle
Luther. Perhaps together we can reunite your families."

The young girl's features sobered. "Oh no, ma'am. I
cain't light my family. I wouldn't burn 'em or hurt
'em—"

"No, not 'light' them—reunite them—bring them together."

Fawn brightened. "Oh, well now, that'd be real nice."

The girls turned when they heard Dan's voice shouting
for Hope.

Hope jumped up from the rock. "I have to go."

"Yes'um—me too." Fawn hurriedly helped her gather
the greens and mushrooms back into the apron, cringing
as Dan's worried shout filled the small clearing.
"HOPE!"

"Better hurry now. Yore mister sounds a mite put
out."

Patting Fawn's arm, Hope started off. "I'll pray we both have success in making the family see the error of their ways."

"Yes'um—Mrs. Yodler—she's that nice woman who learnt me how to read? She says the Almighty is powerful 'nough to move whole mountains. Is that right?"

Hope nodded. "That's what the Good Book says."

"Then he ought not to have any trouble gettin' Pa and Uncle Luther to stop stealin' each other's chickens and hogs."

Dan's voice again shattered the tranquil morning. "Hope!"

Hope ran from the clearing, carefully cradling the greens and mushrooms in her makeshift sling.

Dan was standing at the doorway with a rifle in his hand. When she bounded onto the porch, his face drained with relief. "Have you lost your mind?"

"No," she said, brushing past him. She dumped the greens and mushrooms on the table.

"You could have been killed!"

"Yes, but I wasn't."

He didn't have to remind her that what she'd done was foolish, but if Fawn could make her family see how silly this feud was, it was worth the risk.

Luther bolted to the door, his eyes scouting the back-yard. "Where's the pig?"

"In the pen—"

The old man shot out the back door and returned a few minutes later dragging the reluctant porker by a rope.

Dan slammed the door behind the muddy entourage and locked it. When his eyes pinned Hope, she got the message. She wasn't to go out again until he gave the signal for escape.

"Luther, for heaven's sake. You're muddying up the kitchen!" Harriet complained.

"Cain't let nothing happen to this hog, Harriet. Lyndon would never forgive me."

Hope ventured a glance at Dan and winced when she saw his stormy features. "I didn't mean to stay so long. I saw these wonderful greens and mushrooms and—"

"Don't leave this cabin again unless I tell you to." He hung the rifle back over the fireplace. "Understand?"

Eyes narrowed, she snapped to attention, saluting him. "Yes, sir, General Sullivan. At your service, sir!"

He turned; he was not amused. "Grow up, Hope. You could have been shot out there."

Grow up? Well! How dare he talk to her like that! Perhaps she had been careless, but nothing had happened.

Harriet resumed her vigil beside Luther at the window, and Hope dumped the mix of greens and mushrooms in the sink and poured a little water into the basin. "You know, Luther, I think this feud would be over if you would stop retaliating. It won't be easy, but if you'll take the first step—apologize to your brother for stealing his pig—then maybe he'll reciprocate and you can put this feud behind you."

"Lyndon steals from me."

"Two wrongs don't make a right." She picked up the cleaned greens and carried them to the stove.

"Hope." Dan's eyes sent her a silent warning. "Luther and Harriet should settle their own problems."

They should, she agreed silently. But obviously they hadn't.

Harriet spent the afternoon sitting next to Luther, knitting. Dan paced the small cabin, occasionally stepping to the back door to look out. Hope held her breath. She could see he was contemplating leaving, and it couldn't come soon enough for her.

Luther praised the tasty greens during supper, and

Hope shot a smug look at Dan. The old couple excused themselves right after the dishes were washed, saying the events of the past few days had plain tuckered them out.

Soon they heard snores coming from the old couple's room. Hope sat cross-legged on her bed pallet, brushing her hair. Harriet had come up with an extra brush for her; at least she could groom her hair now. Once she would have been preoccupied with her looks, but lately she praised God for a comb.

"You're used to dealing with men like Lyndon's sons, aren't you?"

Dan sat at the table sharpening his knife. "I've met a few like them in my time. Hotheaded, single-minded."

"Is that why we haven't tried to get away before now?"

"No, I just don't see any purpose in risking our lives until it's necessary."

"We could have gotten away this morning when the Bennetts were eating breakfast."

"We could have, but that's what they expect us to do. We'll leave soon."

Dan wasn't inclined to open up to her, and that bothered her at times. Sometimes she wondered if he even liked her anymore. He seldom addressed her personally, yet she caught him staring at her when he thought she wasn't watching.

"You've done this a lot, then?"

"Been stranded in a cabin with an old couple, a pig, and a chatterbox?"

She threw the brush at him. "Joined gangs, pretended to be someone you're not, escorted women to fiancés."

He dodged the weapon, smiling at her. "Occasionally."

Occasionally, she silently mimicked. That was his standard answer when he didn't want to address her questions.

"How can you do that? Pretend you're someone else for months at a time?"

"That's one of the reasons I'm retiring. I'm tired of violating my conscience."

"Apparently you've been successful at your work. Can you leave the service so easily?"

"As easily as you can marry a man you've never met."

His mild accusation surprised her. Is that what he thought her marriage to John Jacobs would be—a loveless union between two strangers? It didn't have to be that way . . . she hoped.

"It isn't the same thing."

"Really."

"No—it isn't uncommon for a man, a lonely man, to send for a wife. My sisters are each marrying a fine man: Nicholas Shepherd is a rancher; Eli Messenger, a preacher." She paused, gathering her confidence. "Are you married?"

He shook his head.

"Someone special waiting for you to come home?"

"My dear Miss Kallahan, has anyone ever told you that you talk too much?"

"No, the only thing they've said is 'Grow up, Hope.' "

He glanced up, and she made a face at him.

Returning to his task, he said quietly, "When I leave the service, I'm going to buy a few acres of land in Virginia and farm it. No woman, no prior commitments, no prospects in sight."

"By chance?"

"Nope, by choice."

"You sound as if you don't want commitments. Or a wife."

"I don't, at least not right now. Maybe never."

She got up and put a pan of oil on the stove. "Ever been in love, Dan Sullivan? Really, hopelessly, out-of-your-mind in love?"

"Not in a long time."

Hope didn't know why his admission pleased her—almost made her giddy with relief. Just because he wasn't spoken for didn't mean she could have him. He'd just said he wasn't in the market for a wife.

"But you were once." Hope wasn't going to like this part because she knew the answer before he said it.

"Once. A long time ago."

Dumping kernels of dried corn into the pan, she added a handful of salt and put the lid on the pot. The smell of popped corn promptly scented the air.

"Want to talk about her?"

"No."

"But let's do because we're searching for something in common."

"You might be." He motioned to the sow. "Me and the sow aren't."

He seemed to enjoy teasing her, but she desperately wanted a serious conversation with him. She removed the pan from the burner, drizzled butter over the hot corn, and dumped it into a bowl. Carrying it to the table, she sat down and scooped up a handful. "What's her name?"

For a moment, she thought he wasn't going to answer her. Absently reaching his hand into the bowl, he met her eyes.

"Katie Morris."

"And?"

"And, nothing."

"Oh, no. There was something." She scooted her chair closer. "You loved her madly—out-of-your mind loved her."

"I thought so, at the time."

"But she didn't love you back?" Hope couldn't imagine a woman failing to return his affection. Why, if he loved her—it wouldn't take any effort at all to love him back.

"Katie wasn't ready for marriage or family life. She went off to an eastern women's college. We agreed to write—keep in touch—but after a few months I never heard from her again. Years later I heard that she married a professor."

Hope's handful of popcorn paused at her mouth. "That must have hurt."

He shrugged. "Life hurts sometimes, Hope. You get used to it."

His answers were so simple, so to the point. If only life were that easy.

"I hope to find love with John," she admitted softly.

Laying the knife aside, Dan's eyes met hers over the flickering candle. Goose bumps rose on her arms, and she told herself it was the sound of the wind making her insides feel jittery.

"What about you? Have you ever been in love?"

"Oh . . . no. Maybe puppy love, once. A boy in our church—Milo Evans. Milo was nice and cute, but he married Ellie Thompson last year. They have twins already."

The old clock on the mantel chimed nine. Outside, the wind battered the shutters, but inside, in her heart, sitting with him in this room, snug and warm, the smell of popped corn pleasant in the air, she felt . . . happy. Content.

"My sisters and I didn't want to burden our elderly aunt after our father died," she said, hoping to make him understand why she'd agreed to a mail-order husband. "We prayed a lot over the decision and felt that God was leading us. We did what we felt we had to do."

Of course, she wished she could have met a man and fallen in love, married in the normal manner. But she hadn't. What had Dan just said? Sometimes life hurts?

"There were no men in Michigan?" he asked gently.

"Not where we lived—not suitable men. Dan . . .

I'm sure Mr. Jacobs is a good man." If that's what he was concerned about, she could read him all of Mr. Jacobs's letters—put his mind at ease.

His thoughts, if he had any in particular, didn't register on his face. Pushing the knife back into its sheath, he moved back from the table. "It's late. Time we turned in."

"I guess so." For some reason, she wanted to sit up and talk all night. About nothing, or about everything. The subject wouldn't matter; being with him did.

Reaching for the old Bible in the middle of the table, she opened it to Genesis. "I'm not sleepy yet. You're right. I have been too lax with my studies. I'll get started on memorizing a few verses tonight."

"You're going to start with Genesis?" Dan asked. He glanced at the clock.

She excused the incredulous note in his voice. She didn't intend to memorize the whole thing tonight.

"I'll just read a few chapters—then go back and memorize those three verses a day you advocate."

"Genesis?" he repeated. "Couldn't you start with something simpler—maybe the Beatitudes?"

She thumbed to Genesis 1. "Oh . . . that's all that 'Blessed are' stuff, isn't it?"

"Yes—"

"I think I'll just start with Genesis and work my way right up to that worrisome stuff."

"Revelation?"

She nodded, smoothing the Bible's worn, yellow pages into place. She read to chapter 5, her eyes widening. "My . . . there're an awful lot of 'begets' in here, aren't there?" She glanced at the clock.

When Dan rolled up in his blanket, she was sitting at the table trying to memorize Genesis 1:1-3. Muttering under her breath, she squeezed her eyes shut, whispering,

" 'In the beginning God created the heaven and the earth.' Verse 2: 'And the earth . . .' "

Pause.

"Verse 1: 'In the beginning God created the heaven and the earth.' Verse 2: 'And the earth . . .' "

Pause.

" 'Was without form, and void; and darkness was upon the face of the deep,' " Dan muttered sleepily from the other side of the stove. He pulled his pillow over his head.

"Thank you. 'And the earth . . .' "

Pause.

"Verse 1: 'In the beginning God created the heaven and the earth. . . .' "

"Hope, you have company."

Hope looked up at Dan's soft announcement. It was still so early that the sun was barely visible through the broken windowpane. Luther's intermittent snores resonated from behind his and Harriet's closed door. "Me?"

Parting the curtain a fraction more, Dan said softly. "It's a young girl."

"It must be Fawn, the youngest Bennett girl. I spoke with her yesterday. Maybe she's talked to her parents." Quickly brushing her hair, Hope slipped into one of Harriet's oversized coats and headed for the door.

Dan was waiting for her, arms crossed. Wearing his coat now, he blocked her path. "You're not going out there."

"But she wants to talk to me—she isn't a threat."

"You're not going out there alone."

Hope opened the door a fraction, and the pig squeezed around her. Dan lunged for the animal, but its fat backside was already waddling toward the open pen.

Hurriedly stepping outside, Hope watched the old

porker settle into the mudhole with a satisfied grunt. Dan trailed her onto the porch.

"She won't talk with you here," Hope protested. "You'll only intimidate her. Stay here."

Grasping her shoulders, he turned her toward the stand of cottonwoods. "What do you see over there?"

"The Bennett boys."

"Holding what?"

Hope squinted. "Rifles."

She turned to look at Fawn. The girl must have talked to her parents; otherwise she wouldn't present herself so openly.

Fawn waved, friendly-like. "It's all right, ma'am! My brothers ain't gonna shoot!"

"What do you think?" Hope whispered. She followed Dan's eyes back to the stand of trees. Four of Luther's offspring stood leaning on their rifles, keeping an eye on the exchange.

Dan's voice brooked no nonsense. "I don't trust them. Come back into the house."

Hope continued to study the situation. She didn't trust them, either, but someone had to show a little faith, or the standoff would go on forever.

"I'm going out there."

"Hope," he warned, "you're not to go out there."

Now the Bible says, "Wives, obey your husbands." It doesn't say a thing about women obeying government agents—leastwise not flat out. "Keep an eye on that pig," she murmured. "If anything happens to her, we're sunk."

Right now that old sow was the only thing standing between Luther and Lyndon and all-out war.

Taking a deep breath, Hope walked to the edge of the yard where Fawn was huddled deep in a bedraggled jacket that might once have been red. "Hi."

"Hi," Fawn said as Hope approached. "Need to do some serious jawin'."

"All right." Hope waited for the girl to put her thoughts in order.

"Pa's a knucklehead."

Hope felt a twinge of compassion. "You tried to talk to him about the feud?"

"Yes'um. But he's shore nuff a knucklehead." Fawn shoved her hands deeper into the coat pockets. "He won't listen to nary a word about a truce. Keeps jawin' 'bout 'an eye for an eye' or somethin' like that."

"He won't even talk to his brother?"

"No, ma'am. Says Uncle Luther's an even bigger knucklehead than he is, and he don't want nothin' to do with that Nut Muffin."

"Oh, dear."

The girl brightened. "Did you have any better luck with Uncle Luther?"

"No, your uncle's an even bigger Nut Muffin—won't even hear of a cease-fire." She planned to broach the subject again at breakfast, but her expectation was slim that Luther had changed his mind overnight. "We'll just have to pray about it. Papa always said God would supply our needs."

Fawn stood in the early morning light, tracing irregular patterns in the dew-covered grass with the tip of her scuffed boot. "Got me a plan."

"You do?"

"Yes'um—iffin you'll say it's all right for me to try it."

It wasn't Hope's place to grant her permission to try anything, but she certainly wouldn't stand in the way of progress.

"I'm for peace at almost any cost."

Fawn broke into a wide grin. "Thank ya, ma'am! My plan ort to work—but iffin it shouldn't, I want you to 'splain to the Lord that I done my best."

Smiling, Hope nodded. "I'll tell him. What is this plan?" Would Fawn propose they trick the feuding brothers into meeting—make them sit down and talk about the situation like rational adults? Luther could be stubborn— and Lyndon . . . Her eyes shot to Fawn, who suddenly broke away and was now dashing headlong toward the pigpen. Lightning quick, the young girl released the wire hook and threw open the gate. Waving her arms and yelling at the top of her lungs, she charged the sow. "Soooooeeeee!"

Startled, the old porker shot to its feet, making a bee-line for the exit. Out of the pen it streaked, running faster than Hope thought her four squat legs could carry her.

When the girl and the pig were halfway down the road, Fawn turned to yell over her shoulder. "Don't be mad, ma'am! Now that Pa's got his pig back, there ain't no argument!"

Hope's jaw dropped when she realized that Fawn had outsmarted her!

Bounding off the porch, Dan started after the pig. Shots sounded, and he turned in the middle of the yard and lunged toward Hope.

Speechless, Hope watched the devious girl and the pig hightailing it toward home. Pig snorts gradually faded in the far distance; silence surrounded the barn lot.

"Watch the pig, Dan," Dan mimicked as he came to a skidding halt beside her.

Hope slowly turned around to see the Bennett boys casually lift their rifles again and take aim.

"Ohhh . . . ," she murmured, "we are in so much trouble."

Chapter Eight

JOHN Jacobs glanced out the front window and groaned. There was that nosy Veda crossing the street toward the Mercantile, carrying that infernal casserole basket. He set his jaw. This time, he was going to tell that woman to mind her own business. Whom he chose to marry was his doings, not the town's, and certainly not Veda Fletcher's.

Why, the reason he'd placed that ad in the journal in the first place was so he could court a woman without the whole town knowing about it. As it was, he had had to woo Miss Kallahan by mail, and Megaline Harris, the postmistress, had told everyone in town that he was exchanging letters with some woman in Michigan.

Some woman in Michigan. The very idea of referring to Miss Kallahan as "some woman."

Shouldering her way into the store, Veda set the basket on the counter. No doubt another gastric delight. John mentally cringed at the renewed determination in Veda's eyes.

"Afternoon, John."

"Afternoon, Veda."

"Looks like snow."

"Let's think spring, Veda."

"Think it if you like, but we still get snow this late in the year. I've pulled tender young green onions out of snow many a time. Never took my stove down until first of June—ever."

Lord, forgive me for being so mean to poor Veda, but the woman gets on my nerves worse than chaffed thighs.

But courtesy came first at the Jacobs Mercantile. The customer was always right, and Veda was a good customer—paid her bills on time and didn't complain when a sugar shipment came in late.

"I can't stay long, John. Eudora and I are hanging new curtains this afternoon, but I had to see if you'd had any further news. Don't think I'm nosy, now."

Veda nosy? Never.

"News?"

"Regarding your fiancée."

"No news—I'm expecting her any day now." Even as he defended Hope Kallahan, he knew he was grasping at straws. If Hope were coming, she'd have been here by now. He had to face up to the fact that she'd gotten cold feet and wasn't coming. Dear Lord. How could he face Veda and the town in his despair?

"Oh. That's a pity." John could see it was all she could do to keep from turning handsprings. Veda tried to hide her joy. "Now, John. You wouldn't be trying to fool the town, would you? You've told everyone that Miss Hope Kallahan is arriving any day, but we've not seen hide nor hair of her."

"I haven't told everyone," John corrected.

"You've told me. And Edna and Louise."

Medford has three ways of surefire communication: telegram, tell Veda, or tell Louise.

"Just where is this woman?"

John was wondering the same thing. Where was Hope Kallahan? And why, indeed, hadn't she sent word if she'd been fortuitously delayed?

"I don't know where she is," he admitted.

He'd diligently met each stage that managed to get through. He'd had no further correspondence from Miss Kallahan. She wasn't coming. She'd simply decided she didn't want to marry him. Her letters had sounded as if the arrangement pleased her. But women change their minds.

He could forgive her for changing her mind; what he couldn't tolerate was neglect. Neglecting to inform him of a change in heart was unforgivable.

"Is it possible your fiancée got cold feet?" Veda asked, coyly lifting the cloth on the basket.

John caught a whiff of chicken.

"Miss Kallahan said she was coming. Something undoubtedly has delayed her, but I trust that she is still coming. Now, if you don't mind, Veda, I have an appointment with Edgar."

Veda's brow arched. "The tailor? Your fiancée hasn't even arrived, and you're about to be fitted for a wedding suit?"

"That is precisely what I'm about to do." Jerking his vest coat into place, he stepped around the counter. He'd had just about enough of this inquisition. He wasn't meeting her niece, Ginger, and that was that. "If you'll excuse me."

Veda trailed him out the front door. "My niece, Ginger, arrived on yesterday's stage. Have you seen her yet?"

Only two women got off that stage yesterday. The statuesque young woman with dark hair and ivory porcelain skin who'd turned more than her share of men's heads must have been Freeman Hide's granddaughter. Freeman's whole family was good-looking. Were John not already contracted, he'd be sorely tempted to ask Freeman for introductions.

The other woman was as homely as sin.

"Yes, I did. Lovely young woman."

"You did!" Veda glowed. "Pretty as a picture, isn't she? Didn't I tell you she was a jewel?"

"Yes, ma'am, you did." *At least once a day for the past four months.*

"She's most delicate you know, fragile as china. The long trip from San Francisco wore her out, so she's taken to bed for a few days. Once she's up and around, I'll bring her over to the Mercantile."

Wonderful. She's trying to marry me off to a sickly girl with the constitution of fine china. He stepped off the porch and started across the street.

"John!" Veda hurried after him. "You're going to the box supper, aren't you?"

Box supper? That was a misnomer if there ever was one. It was a man trap. Snares in a basket—albeit bait dressed in an interesting fashion and offered up for auction, but snares nonetheless. The bidder wasn't supposed to know whose box he was bidding on, but one generally had a strong hint.

Every time he attended one of those infernal box suppers, every eligible woman in town dropped clues on which box was hers. The town matchmakers had put him in an impossible situation.

If he dared bid on a certain basket, other women were hurt or angry, and either they or their daughters gave him most unpleasant looks during the course of the long evening.

If he didn't bid, he went without supper.

Enjoying a carefree meal in the comfort of his home above the store wasn't an option for that night. In a town the size of Medford, every absence was noted and unduly speculated upon. He'd tried to get out of going once, and the flood of chicken soup the next day had created such a tizzy for him that he vowed to never try that again.

John picked up his stride, hoping Veda would take the hint. When he glanced over his shoulder, he saw she was still close on his heels. Oliver trotted along behind her.

"You have to eat, John, affianced or not. Just say you'll come to the box supper Friday night. By then, my Ginger will be feeling up to entertaining callers."

He set his jaw and kept walking. "I won't be calling on your niece, Veda."

Veda hurried to keep pace with his long-legged stride. "I'm not talking about calling on her—I know you're not at liberty to do that—not at the moment, but it won't hurt you to be sociable, will it?"

The woman was a bulldog. There'd be no peace until he agreed. "All right, Veda. I'll come."

She paused, grinning. "Now, see. That wasn't so difficult, was it? Ginger's entering a box, you know. I'll make certain you know which one."

John's new suit awaited him. Cut from the finest Italian cloth, the dark blue wool fit him to perfection.

"Excellent job, Edgar."

Edgar was overjoyed with his handiwork. "You're going to make a splendid bridegroom!"

Indeed he was. Examining his mirrored image, he twirled his mustache, wishing anew that Miss Kallahan would get here. Shame to spend all this money and not have it appreciated by the fairer sex.

John toted the apparel back to the Mercantile, smiling

to all he passed. Miss Kallahan was coming, he told himself. When she arrived, she would have a suitable explanation for her tardiness. Pity that Medford's nearest tele-
graph was at Winchester, the other side of the Basin
River. Come to think about it, it was quite easy to see
why she couldn't let him know of her belated arrival.
Nor could he send a telegram to inquire of her whereabouts until the spring rains let up. The river was over its
banks, and the Melhume boys had set the one bridge
linking Medford to Winchester afire two weeks previous.
He brightened, feeling considerably better with that revelation.

The evening of the box supper arrived. Shortly after
seven o'clock that night, John walked into the one-room
schoolhouse that doubled as the community meeting hall.

Everyone who could attend was here tonight. Floralee
Thomas had shoved her teacher's desk to one side, and a
long table had been erected between two sawhorses.
Cloths borrowed from the ladies of the planning committee made a colorful background for the boxed suppers.
His eyes searched for a glimpse of Freeman's granddaughter. Now if the town wanted to play Cupid, why
couldn't Freeman be as eager to introduce his granddaughter as Veda was her niece?

Veda was in charge of the festivities. There was an
intent clear on her face tonight. John sighed. For the
briefest of moments, he wondered which box contained
Freeman's granddaughter's offering, then decided he
didn't want to know. *Temptation, get thee aside.*

He glanced around the room, wishing that Hope were
here so he could introduce her to the doubting Thomases
and end the town's annoying speculation.

Threading his way across the floor, he paused to speak
to his regular customers. He smiled, nodding to the wid-

ows who had taken up court in the long row of chairs lining the east wall. Their particular, odd ceremony puzzled him. Widows separated themselves in such a way that they seemed out of sync with others. The same bizarre ritual occurred at church socials; "Widow's Row" they called it. A woman over forty habitually went there within weeks of her husband's death. Companionship, he'd decided, was the reason. Wasn't it the same sense of aloneness that had led him to place that ad in the journal?

"There you are, John!" Veda sailed across the room, flapping a hand in the air to get his attention.

John whirled and tried to lose himself in the crowd, but Veda had already nailed him. Her shrill voice was drawing attention, the last thing he wanted.

She docked, breathless. Looping her arm through his, she smiled. "There you are. I was worried that you wouldn't come tonight."

John stiffened. "I'm a man of my word, Veda. I said I would be here, and here I am."

"Here you are, and I'm just sick. Ginger is still feeling a little under the weather, and she's asked me to make her apologies for her absence."

John's knees buckled with relief. A reprieve. The good Lord had granted him a reprieve!

"I'm sorry to hear that. I trust your niece will be up and about very soon."

"She will be—I'm having Doc come by in the morning. I'm hoping he will prescribe a tonic for her."

"Yes—a tonic would be just the thing."

Veda straightened when she saw the church elder's wife sailing in their direction. The tall, stout woman resembled a Scandinavian Viking with her shock of steel-colored hair and breastplate of flouncing lace.

"Heavens. Here comes that overbearing Pearl Eddings. She's going to insist that you purchase Cordella's box supper." John winced as Veda painfully tightened her grip on his arm.

"Let me do the talking," she ordered from the corner of her mouth. She smiled as the matronly woman approached. "Good evening, Pearl."

"Veda." Pearl's beady eyes flew over the couple, then landed on John. "Cordella's box is the one with the blue bow."

Stepping in front of John, Veda crossed her arms. "John's affianced, Pearl. He can't be buying your daughter's boxed supper."

Pearl's eyes narrowed, and John edged closer to peer over Veda's shoulder. He'd never seen eyes pulsate this way.

Pearl and Veda faced off.

"He's not married yet, Veda Fletcher."

"He will be, Pearl Eddings."

"And soon," John added, then closed his mouth. He located Cordella standing on the sidelines. The tall, bucktoothed girl wasn't exactly a head turner.

"Hummpt." Pearl leveled a finger at John. "Blue bow. You'll not regret it."

When Pearl departed, Veda patted John's arm. "The very idea of Pearl thinking you'd be interested in Cordella."

"Thank you for coming to my rescue, Veda." Praise God, he was finally getting through to her!

"You're welcome, dear." Veda gave his arm another matronly pat, then absently tidied her hair before merging with the crowd. "Can't imagine what Pearl is thinking," John heard her mumble as she walked away. "Why, you've not even met my Ginger."

Chapter Nine

"DON'T ask questions—run!" Dan caught Hope's hand, and they bolted across the barnyard. Shots rang out. Water flew up from Luther Bennett's rain barrel sitting next to the feed trough.

They ducked into the barn as a hail of bullets riddled the outside walls. Striding toward a stall, Dan seized a horse and quickly threw his saddle on it.

"We can't take Luther's horse! That's stealing!"

"Luther's nephews mean business this time, Hope. I'll send money later. Get on!" Swinging Hope on behind him, he flanked the horse, and it galloped out of the barn. Bullets ricocheted off the trees as Dan rode toward the lane.

"Keep low!"

"I am! Ride faster!"

Lead whined overhead; Hope bent close to Dan's back, hiding her face in his thick shirt.

The Bennett boys stepped from the stand of trees and fired until the bullets were hitting thin air.

The horse galloped for what seemed like miles to Hope before Dan gradually slowed the pace. The horse was lathered, its sides heaving with exertion.

She gradually loosened her grip around Dan's middle, sick with fright when she saw the bright, moist, red stain on her arm. Blood.

"You're hurt!" she cried.

Favoring his left side, he slid off the horse and sank to the ground. The effort brought a fresh surge of red stain to his shirt. "Nothing to worry about . . . it's just a flesh wound."

She slid off and knelt beside him. "We've got to treat it!"

"We have to keep moving." He stood and took a handkerchief from his pocket, folded it into a triangle, and wedged it between his shoulder and shirt. Gaining his bearings, he climbed back on the horse. With his right arm, he hefted her astride.

Throughout the rest of the day, despite Hope's repeated protests, Dan refused to stop; he insisted through clenched teeth that they had to keep moving. By nightfall, he was beyond decision making. Barely conscious, he hung on to the saddle horn with one hand.

The distant rumble of thunder worried Hope. A spring storm was brewing, and she didn't want them to be caught out in it. "We've got to stop," she insisted. *Please, Father. Help us find shelter.*

You can't put God on demand! Papa's voice echoed in Hope's mind. But right now God was her only hope.

They rode on until she spied the mouth of a cave behind a bank of brush. Thunder was closer now, accompanied by sporadic lightning flashes. Dan didn't respond when she pointed to the shelter. Taking the reins out of his hand, she urged the horse through the thicket. Sliding off its back, she tied the animal to a low-hanging limb, then helped Dan off.

"I'm all right—just lost a little blood." His shirt was soaked and his features ashen. He'd lost a lot of blood; she didn't need medical knowledge to know that.

Stepping to the mouth of the cave, she peered inside. Wings fluttered in the black interior. Shuddering, she reached for Dan's arm and helped him through the narrow entrance.

Her strength was quickly overpowered by his weakness. It took all her might to get his considerable bulk through the cramped opening.

"Fire," Dan murmured. "Cold." He was shaking uncontrollably now.

"I'll get one started. Matches—"

"Find two flint stones—strike them together." Removing his coat, he lay down on it.

Once an old Indian had stopped by the parsonage. He'd shown Papa how to start a fire by using two flint stones, repeatedly striking them in a rapid fashion until a spark ignited the ember. But that had been so long ago. Could she remember how to do it?

Rain was falling when she emerged from the cave. Quickly gathering handfuls of small sticks and leaves before they got too wet, she carried them into the cavern. It took awhile to locate the flint stones on the uneven ground, and even longer to get the hang of generating a spark. But after repeated failed attempts, the tinder finally caught. Smoke pillared up.

She sat back on her heels, exhausted. She kept her fears at bay by concentrating on what had to be done. The bleeding must be stopped or Dan would . . . she couldn't voice the thought. *Please, Father. Grant me wisdom in this hour of need. I'm sorry I've been so doubtful lately.*

I'll do better—please don't let Dan die because of my foolishness.

Grow up, Hope. She bit down on her lip until she tasted blood, recalling Dan's gruff admonition. "I'm trying," she whispered. "I'm trying."

The cave was shallow but deep enough for shelter, the ceiling low but high enough for the fire to draw well.

Fighting panic, Hope piled more sticks on the fire. Dan was attempting to shrug out of his shirt when she turned to check on him. His face was pale, his forehead glistening with sweat.

Her heart was drawn to him, and her mind traveled back to less than a week ago when he had cared so diligently for her. If it were possible, she would take part of his pain. "Wait, let me do that."

Her stomach pitched at the sight of the angry wound in his left shoulder. Too weak to argue, he allowed her to peel the last of the bloody fabric away.

"Don't you die on me," she pleaded, her hands shaking as she probed the injury. She checked him front and back. "The bullet went through, so I won't have to dig it out."

Dan grunted. "Do you have the feeling we make a bad team?"

She grinned, laying her head on his good shoulder for a blissful moment. "It would seem our luck isn't the best." Straightening, she wiped the moisture out of her eyes. "Lie still. I need to clean the wound."

He winced. "This is going to hurt, isn't it?"

She didn't have the heart to tell him how much. "I'll need your hat."

His eyes gave her permission to remove it.

She left the cave and returned momentarily with water. Ripping his shirt into pieces, she dipped the cloth into the rainwater, her hand pausing above the injury. "Ready?"

"Be gentle." As painful as the injury was, he was still able to tease. She took small solace in that. "The bullet must have hit something as it went through—it's still bleeding hard."

Touching the cloth to the wound, she recoiled as he sucked in his breath. "Now, Grunt," she chided, trying to disguise her terror, "were you gentle with me when I ran away?"

"No . . . not overly."

"I remember that." How well she remembered how scared she'd been when he'd physically dragged her back to the cabin. He'd not been gentle at all that day.

The water in the hat turned bright red as she continued to cleanse the area.

Catching her arm, he gazed at her. "I was afraid for your life that day. Do you know what would have happened—"

She gently laid her finger across his lips. "Shush, you're making the bleeding worse. I know what you did that day, Dan." She looked away for fear her eyes would reveal more of her feelings than she wanted. "Thank you."

He held tightly to her hand, even when he could have released it.

She shook her head, fear crowding her throat. The wound was bleeding heavily now. "I don't know how to stop the bleeding."

"Cauterize it," he gritted between clenched teeth.

"How?"

"My knife . . . in the fire . . . get the blade red-hot."

"Oh, Dan." She closed her eyes, faint. Could she do such a thing? The pain would be unbearable.

His grip tightened. "Do it, Hope. I'll bleed to death if you don't."

She wouldn't allow him to bleed to death. No matter how vile the cure, she had to do it. Rising, her eyes searched the dim interior. She needed more wood. "I'll be right back."

"Don't take all night," he murmured.

She returned breathless, her hair falling down from its pins. Dropping to her knees, she heaped more sticks on the fire.

"Knife . . . sheath, left side. Hurry, Hope . . ."

"I'm hurrying." Rolling him gently to his right side, she located the knife and removed it. She quickly wiped the blade on a piece of petticoat, then laid it over the flames.

"I can't do this." The mere thought of laying that red-hot brand across his tender flesh made her dizzy.

Rolling to his back, Dan closed his eyes. "Any woman who can make Joe Davidson clean house can do anything."

Smiling between her tears, she reached for the knife. The blade glowed bright red. Closing her eyes, she willed her hands steady.

Dear God, let him lose consciousness. Don't make him go through this pain awake.

"Do it," he whispered. "Now!" Blood gushed from the wound, drenching him and her dress.

Bringing the tip of the blade down, she mashed it to the lesion. Dan's agonized scream as the blade singed the open flesh tore at her heart. The stench of burning flesh filled her nose, and she fought the tide of dizziness that threatened to overcome her. Struggling for breath, she bit her bottom lip until she tasted blood. She sobbed openly now.

When his scream became a low moan, she dared to look down. The wound barely oozed now. With a cry of relief, she flung the knife aside and collapsed on his now unconscious form. "I'm so sorry, darling . . . so sorry."

Her prayer had been answered.

She tended the fire all night, watching Dan sleep, checking every few moments to see if the steady rise and fall of
his chest abated. He would live—the bleeding had
stopped. She'd changed the bandage only twice in an
hour.

From the moment they'd met, she'd caused him nothing but trouble; he'd done nothing but try to help her.
And now he lay near death, his face pale and lifeless, all
because of her. She'd tried to settle a feud that had gone
on for years, and in the process, she'd hurt this wonderful
man.

Blinking back hot tears, she listened to the rain spatter
on the ground outside the cavern, staring at the small fire
that gave off a little warmth. She'd never been more miserable, more alone, in her life. Once her life had been
simple, secure. What had gone wrong? Was God punish-
ing her for ignoring Aunt Thalia's wishes? Thalia hadn't
wanted her or her sisters to be mail-order brides. Why
hadn't they listened—why hadn't she listened? Now, because of her, a man was wounded.

*Why does Dan have to suffer when all he's done is try to
protect me? I don't understand, and I don't know that I've got
enough faith to accept this change in my life without knowing
the reason.*

She threw more wood on the fire, glancing up when
she saw Dan's eyes flicker, then open. He spoke, his voice
thick with pain. "I hope you harbor no thoughts of ever
being a doctor."

Dropping to his side, she threw her arms around his
neck, careful not to disturb the wound. "I know the pain
was awful, but the bleeding's stopped now."

"Careful . . . ," he warned.

She gingerly hugged him to her chest. "I thought you
were never going to wake up."

"What time is it?"

"I'm not sure, somewhere near daybreak, I think."
The night had been the longest of her life.

"Is there any water?"

"It's still raining—I'll catch some in the hat. When it's light, I'll look for a stream."

Outside, she washed the blood from the hat, then caught fresh rainfall and was back within minutes. Cradling his head, she helped him drink, tenderly blotting water that spilled from his mouth.

"Did you get my saddle off the horse?"

"No . . . but I will."

He nodded, licking his dry lips.

"Is the saddle special?"

"Brother gave it to me . . ."

"Sleep," she whispered when his eyes shut with pain. If only there was more she could do.

She moved back to the fire and began to doze, her dreams filled with images of dirty men who stealthily crept toward the mouth of the cave. Animals lured by the scent of blood.

Dan's feverish mumbling brought her out of her confused state.

Though the air was cool, he was sweating profusely. She laid her hand against his forehead. He was so warm. Drawing her coat up to his chin, her mind raced. He was feverish. Infection! She had no means to treat infection. What would Aunt Thalia do? Break the fever—make certain that he drank lots of water.

Stepping out of her petticoat, she used the knife to split it apart. The fabric was soiled, but she'd scrub it in rainwater and use it for fresh bandages and a sling.

When the laundry was drying near the fire, she bathed Dan's hot face, chest, and arms, repeating the process throughout the day as his fever continued to rise.

"Lie still," she whispered as he thrashed about on the bed pallet.

When he shoved her coat aside, Hope patiently drew it back over him, knowing a chill at this point could mean death. Late in the afternoon, she broke sticks from the bushes at the mouth of the cave and wedged them into crevices in the cave wall. She patiently washed more of the petticoat and hung the strips to dry. Unsaddling the horse, she gave it water out of the hat, then lugged the heavy hand-tooled leather saddle into the cave.

When darkness fell, she was able to cleanse Dan's wounds again and apply fresh bandages.

A couple of times he opened his eyes, but she wasn't sure he recognized her. Was she doing enough? Sitting beside him, she studied his features in the firelight. He had a strong face, well defined, ruggedly handsome. He knew what he was about—a man with a purpose in life. What had he told her? He wanted to buy some land in Virginia and farm it. Farming sounded very nice.

Dan Sullivan was exactly the kind of man Aunt Thalia would approve of: a good man, a godly man. Hope had seen his faith, experienced it. In many ways he was making her stronger in her own beliefs. At least he made her stop and think; that was something.

Her thoughts turned to the man she'd promised to marry. Somewhere tonight, he was waiting for her, wondering about her. Poor John. If only she was able to send a note, explain why she hadn't arrived on the stage more than four weeks ago. Did he know about the stagecoach robbery? Had he wired Aunt Thalia and inquired about his intended bride's whereabouts?

Her gaze focused on the man lying beside the fire. *Oh, God, I'm not questioning your wisdom—truly I'm not.*

If only she'd met Dan before—no. Events happened for a reason. Papa had taught her that. But if she was going to start relying on her own faith instead of Papa's, she must trust that God watched over her.

"Grow up, Hope. It's time you took responsibility for

your life," she murmured, getting up to bathe Dan's face again.

Why would she think Dan would even want her after all the trouble she'd caused? At this point he probably prayed for the hour when he could hand her over to another man.

The thought stung. She gently smacked his sleeping form. "How dare you think that. I'd make you a good wife. You'd see, I'd be everything you ever wanted and more."

Outside, darkness covered the earth. A gray drizzle replaced the earlier downpour. Toward daybreak even the drizzle gave way to watery sunshine.

Dan was resting easier now. Hope bathed his face and arms, coaxing him to drink from the hat between parched lips. When he was restless, she soothed him in low tones, reassuring him everything was all right.

She told him stories of when she was young—of the time Papa cut the wrong Christmas tree and brought it home. She and her sisters, Faith and June, had popped corn and made colorful paper chains to hang on the fragrant cedar boughs. But the tree that year was so small Hope had cried. She'd had her heart set on a tall, rather splendid pine that was twice the height of the parsonage ceiling. Papa had dried her eyes and promised that next year they'd either get a taller ceiling or he'd let her have whatever tree she wanted, provided he could get it through the door.

Her thoughts drifted aimlessly. Luther and Harriet. What were they doing tonight? Had they retaliated by stealing something from Lyndon? Were they mad as hatters at Dan and her?

Well, *she* hadn't given the pig back. And she certainly wouldn't have given Fawn permission to let it loose if she'd known what the girl was planning.

Had the world gone mad?

Weren't Christians supposed to be different from unbelievers? Fawn had said her family believed in God, yet Lyndon stole from his own brother. Papa had contended that a Christian wasn't perfect, sinned just as hard as the next person, but a Christian was bothered by the fact and tried harder not to sin. Would Lyndon realize that family was far more important than a pig?

During the long hours in the cave, she read from Dan's Bible. She had part of Genesis memorized, except for all the begets. Dan would be proud of her.

The sun shined warm as Hope moved to the mouth of the cave, her face lifted toward the heavens. Her strength was ebbing; she hadn't slept in two nights, and she didn't think she could go on.

"I can't do this, Lord," she whispered. "I haven't enough faith—I try, try so hard, but I can't hold on to you. You just keep slipping through my fingers. Please strengthen me, Father; grant me powerful faith—like David's faith as he faced Goliath—so I can be of benefit to this injured man."

Resentment swelled within her. Papa had always said to expect the unexpected. She'd gotten on that stage full of hopes and dreams, her thoughts only of John. Her future had seemed rosy and bright. Today she was falling in love with another man and wondering if she or he would live to see another day.

Toward dawn the third day, Hope was startled awake by the horse. Her eyes flew open, and she wondered what had disturbed it. A wild animal?

The horse neighed softly.

Reaching for the rifle, she crept to the mouth of the cave and peered out. Daylight illuminated the small clearing. The horse, definitely upset about something, suddenly reared. Hope heard the rein snap. Seconds later, she heard the animal thrashing off through the underbrush.

Bounding to her feet, she ran outside, foolishly thinking she could somehow catch it. A twig snapped, and she whirled.

A cougar, the size of Aunt Thalia's fainting couch, crouched near the mouth of the cave. Its yellow-eyed gaze held hers captive, its tail slowly twitching.

Dan was in that cave—unprotected, alone.

Helpless.

Swallowing against her rising hysteria, Hope lifted the rifle and took careful aim. She fired twice. When she dared to open her eyes, she saw the tail end of the cat bounding off through the underbrush.

Sinking to her knees, she dropped the gun and stared at the spot where the cougar had been not two minutes ago.

Throwing her head back, she addressed God in a way that would have sent Papa in search of the biggest hickory switch he could find.

"I can't stand anymore of this! Faith! I need faith!"

When she came back into the cave, Dan was sitting up. He glanced at her, his face flushed, his hair tousled, a heavy growth of beard covering his face.

"You look nice."

Cradling his head in his arms, he muttered, "Why are you yelling at God?"

She propped the rifle against the cave wall. "I've tried talking. He isn't listening."

Lying back down, Dan closed his eyes. "Come here."

She moseyed closer, feeling ashamed of herself. Reaching for her hand, he gently pulled her down beside him. Holding her close, he said softly, "God doesn't respond to shouts."

Emotions overcame her, and she broke into tears, sobbing against his good shoulder. It felt so wonderfully good to have someone hold her, someone to help worry for a moment.

"I'm sorry—it's just that you're so sick, and I had to

hurt you so badly, and then there was this big cat that scared off the horse—"

"Cat?" He stopped her, his voice guarded now. "Big cat?"

"Yes—cougar. I shot at it. It's gone."

"That's what woke me—where's the horse?"

"Gone." She cried harder at his frustrated groan. "I'm no good at anything; I'm just a mess."

"No," he said, patting her back tenderly. "You're not a mess."

She cried harder, allowing the fear and frustration to pour from her eyes.

"Think we should pray about this?"

She nodded, snuggling closer to his warmth. He always knew the right thing to do.

In a voice weak in energy but strong in conviction, he softly asked for God's help. "Father, forgive us when we don't rely on you. It's been a rough week, God, and our faith has been tested to the limits. Watch over us, make us ever mindful you're still here running the show."

"And, Father, I'm really sorry I yelled at you," Hope whispered. "I'm just a mess."

Drawing her closer, Dan buried his face in her hair. "He knows you're sorry, but he likes to hear it."

"How did you get so nice?"

"Practice."

She felt his weak grin.

"Well, I'm going to practice harder."

"Go to sleep. Unless I'm mistaken, it's still very early."

Right now, leaving the comfort of his arms was unthinkable, but he needed rest.

"I'll be close by if you need me."

"Hope?"

"Yes?"

"Try to keep out of trouble until I can get over

this . . ." His voice trailed as sleep once again claimed him.

She moved away, settling where she would be close if he needed her. She had plenty to keep her busy—there was always Genesis . . .

The fire burned low. Outside, a new dawn was breaking. Finches chirped in nearby trees; tender shoots of new grass pushed their heads through the damp soil. God's world woke to a new day.

Inside, Bible folded across her chest, Hope slept, feeling safe in God's love for the first time in a long time.

Chapter Ten

By the fourth night Dan was well enough to travel. Hope wasn't convinced that his strength was sufficient for the long walk ahead of them, but the meager rations she'd been able to supply had dwindled to nothing. If they didn't move on, some lone hermit would one day discover their remains in the cave.

"What should we do about the saddle?"

The look on Dan's face confirmed her fears: the beautiful, hand-tooled leather saddle was one of his prized possessions—perhaps his only prized possession.

"My brother made it for me. Gave it to me on my sixteenth birthday." His eyes caressed the worn hide that must have held memories too numerous to count. Days of idyllic youth; months, even years, served in the war. Hope wanted to hold him, cry out at the injustice of it all. He was too weak to carry the saddle, and she didn't have the strength to oblige.

"I'll carry it," she said. She couldn't bear to see it left behind because of her. If it took everything in her, she would carry it.

"You can't carry it. Help me get it on my right shoulder. I'll carry it."

With considerable effort, they got the heavy saddle on his back. Hope hurt just looking at him. "You can't carry that all the way to Medford."

"I'll carry it as far as I can. It's the best we can do."

Was he hoping for a miracle—someone to come along and carry the saddle for him?

Hope wasn't. She was about to give up on miracles. God was putting every obstacle imaginable in front of them, and for what purpose?

"Do you have any idea where we are?" she asked as they started off. Twilight settled over the verdant hillsides, and a warm breeze ruffled bare tree branches. Daffodils pushed their heads up through the ground, and crocuses bloomed by the roadside.

"The map's in my saddlebag."

And the saddlebag was at Luther's. Dan hadn't had time to go back and retrieve it in their hasty getaway.

"So what are we going to do? We have no money, no means to buy either a horse or a map. We don't know where we are or how far we still have to travel."

"We're not more than three or four miles from the Bennetts'. I looked at the map shortly before we met up with Luther and Harriet. Medford is to the east, maybe another thirty miles."

"Thirty miles!" Hope's heart sank. "That's a long way to walk."

"It could be less, Hope. I'm just not sure."

He bent low as the weight of the saddle sapped his strength. Men had it worse than women, Hope decided.

They had to act strong, no matter how they felt. Women, on the other hand, could whine.

"How are you?" she ventured, keeping an eye on his pace.

"Top of the world. How about you?"

"Same."

They traveled by back roads, hoping to go unnoticed. Hope halfway hoped that someone would come along; Dan could put the saddle in the wagon and he could claim it later. It seemed like hours before she heard the welcome sounds of a stream.

"Water."

Dan forged the way through the undergrowth, trampling a path to the water. Throwing the saddle aside, he dropped to the ground and flattened himself to the bank, drinking in the cold, clear water.

Hope quickly joined him. She drank until she had to come up for air. "I've never, ever tasted anything so good." She dunked her face beneath the water and emerged, sputtering.

Dan was sitting up, trying to remove his right boot with his right hand.

"Here." She leaned over and removed it for him. Her eyes located the holes in his socks. The cloth had rubbed away, and blood oozed onto the fabric. "Blisters."

That's all he needed—blisters *and* a gunshot wound.

"I wish I had some butter to rub on them."

He grunted. "If I had butter, it wouldn't go on my feet."

She lay down, rolling to her back. Overhead, stars twinkled in a cloudless sky.

Butter—and hot biscuits. Eggs and ham. Hotcakes and rich maple syrup. They hadn't eaten a decent meal in days. Dan refused to admit it, but he was weak, half starved. The heavy saddle was taking its toll on his energy. How much longer before he was forced to leave it behind?

"I'll carry the saddle for a while."

"You can't lift the saddle, let alone carry it." He lay back, easing his shoulder into a comfortable position.

"I'm hungry," she admitted, more to herself than as a complaint.

"I'll see if I can scare up some game."

"No, tell me what to do, and I'll do it."

"My darling Miss Kallahan. I would let you, but I'd like to eat sometime tonight."

She blushed, recalling the inordinately long waits he'd endured between meals lately. But if he recalled, he'd always eaten; she'd not let him go hungry. Acorns and nuts gathered near the mouth of the cave. She tried running a rabbit down on foot once, but that had consumed all her energy. She wasn't fast or clever enough to best nature.

Toward morning, they finally met a wagon. Hope sat beside Dan on the side of the road; both were too fatigued to go on. Dan had carried the saddle all night; he couldn't walk another step.

Hope sprang up when she spotted a young man who looked no more than fifteen wielding the buckboard. Sawing back on the reins, he brought the wagon to a halt. A goat was tied to the back. "Havin' trouble?" the youth said.

It would take all day to tell him how much trouble they'd had, so Hope came right to the point.

"A cougar spooked our horse, and it ran off. My brother is injured and needs medical care. Can we catch a ride with you to the next town?" When she saw hesitancy in his eyes, she rushed on. "Could you at least haul his saddle in the wagon for us? As soon as my brother's able, he'll be back to get it."

The boy eyed her suspiciously. They must look a

fright—clothes torn and dirty, Dan unshaven, her hair wild as a March hare.

"Muddy Flats is five miles down the road. I spent the night with a friend there, and I'm on my way home to do chores. I'm an hour late; Ma would have my hide if I was to take you all the way back into Muddy Flats and leave those heifers bawling to be milked."

Hope sagged against the wagon. "We really do need your help." Their feet were in bad shape, but they could take it slower, walk the remaining distance to Muddy Flats; but Dan couldn't carry the saddle, and she couldn't bear to see him leave it behind. "If you'll just take the saddle—"

"Ma wouldn't hold for that. Says we ain't to take anything that we don't earn."

"I'm not giving you the saddle; I'm only asking you to keep it for us until we return to claim it."

The boy shook his head. "Cain't. I don't know you folks, and that'd be like taking something that wasn't mine."

Dan slowly got to his feet and walked toward the wagon. The blisters caused his gait to be slow and uneven. Leaning on the wagon's side, he took a deep breath. "Would you make a trade? My saddle for whatever you offer."

"Dan," Hope murmured.

Dan repeated the proposition. "My saddle for whatever you got."

The boy eyed the fine-looking saddle, breaking into a youthful grin. "It's a fine saddle. How 'bout I trade you . . . a goat for it?"

"Yeah—how about that," Dan grumbled.

"Oh, Dan! You can't trade your saddle for a goat." Hope eyed the mangy critter tied to the back of the wagon. It was worse than the pig.

The goat bleated in protest.

Dan turned away. "The goat can walk; the saddle can't."

"It's a deal?" the boy cried.

"It's a deal, Son."

The boy hopped out of the wagon and made a beeline for his prize. Hope hurried along behind him. "We'll be back—will you trade back if we bring money instead of the goat?"

"Money?"

"Twenty-five dollars." It was all the money Hope had to her name, money she'd made sewing and looking after old Mrs. Johnson when she took ill a few years back. The money was in her missing bags, but when she got them back she'd have the money. And she'd use every bit of it to buy Dan's saddle back.

"Twenty-five dollars!" The boy clearly couldn't believe his luck. "I'll trade back for twenty-five dollars!"

Minutes later, the old wagon rumbled away with Dan's saddle lying on the front seat beside the boy. Before he left, Hope got his name.

"Take good care of that saddle!" she yelled as the buckboard rattled off.

"Yes, ma'am! You take good care of my goat!"

Her bottom lip curled with disgust. She'd take care of that goat—but she'd be back for Dan's saddle.

And Clifford Baker had better hand it over.

"How far did he say it was to the next town?"

Walking was easier now that Hope didn't have to worry about Dan and the saddle, but the sun was full up now. Birds flew overhead on their way to breakfast.

"The boy said five miles."

Five miles. It might as well be five hundred. Would she ever see Medford? or John Jacobs? Did she even care any longer? She was beginning to think her intended husband was a curse. As horrible as the past few weeks had been, she still wasn't in any hurry to reach her destination. She was in even less hurry to leave Dan's company. Once they reached Medford, she would never see him again.

"We'll come across a farm before much longer. Maybe we'll find a kind soul who'll offer us a hot meal."

So far, strangers had proved ruinous. She wasn't sure she would accept a meal from a Good Samaritan without serious thought. Still, the idea of a hot meal was delicious to think about. Hotcakes dripping with melted butter, fat sausage patties, cups of cold, spring-cooled milk. She'd taken food for granted in the past, but never again would she be gluttonous without the hurtful knowledge that somewhere, someone was terribly hungry.

Dan pulled the goat behind him, slowing their progress. The animal was stubborn, intent on eating everything she could snatch between steps. They had followed a riverbank for the last hour. The wet hem of Hope's dress slapped against her ankles, but she was barely aware of the discomfort.

Katie Morris, the woman Dan once loved, popped into her mind. Envy only added to her misery. Had Dan looked at Katie the way he had looked at her in the cave during his conscious moments, with helpless masculine vulnerability? Had he held Katie in his arms, whispered his love, and planned a future with her?

Think of more pleasant things, Hope. But there wasn't anything pleasant to think about. She was wet, tired, and hungry, and the goat was getting on her nerves. She couldn't imagine where Dan found the enthusiasm to push ahead when she knew he must be in fierce pain and probably willing to shoot the goat. During the night they milked the animal and drank the warm liquid for sustenance, but Hope's stomach demanded solid food.

"Can't we stop now?"

"Soon—there has to be a family living along the river-bank somewhere."

They walked on until Dan suddenly stopped. The goat plowed into him. Hope plowed into the goat.

Untangling herself from the animal, she pressed closer to Dan, peering around his shoulder. "What is it?" *Please, God. Let it be food and shelter.*

"A cabin."

"A cabin?" She cried out with relief when she spotted a fair-sized dwelling, barn, and outbuilding in a secluded grove. Two mules stood inside a small pen. Her eyes followed Dan's to a garden patch not yet plowed. There was no movement inside the house, no sign of life.

"What do you think?" she whispered.

"I don't know—looks like the place is occupied."

Someone lived here. Food. Warmth. Dry clothing. "Do we take a chance and see if they're friendly?" She held her breath as he studied the situation. His gaze shifted from the barn back to the cabin where a wisp of smoke curled from the chimney.

"We don't have a choice. You need clean clothes and hot food. Maybe we can buy both from whoever lives here."

"How? We have no money."

"I can give a promissory note that my agency will pay for anything we use."

She wanted to wring her hands. "What if no one's there?"

"Then we break down the door and help ourselves. We'll still pay for it later."

How could he be so calm when her heart was racing with anticipation?

She scrambled after him as Dan started down the gentle incline, dragging the goat behind him. She was encouraged when there was no visible sign of interest in their approach.

Red-and-white-checked curtains covered the front windows, but there was no sign of life behind them. Dan hauled the reticent goat up the steps, and Hope followed.

The two exchanged a resigned look, then Dan rapped on the door.

A faint sound penetrated the heavy wood.

"Did you hear that?" Hope whispered.

Dan nodded, then knocked again, harder this time. The faint cry came again.

"Hello?" Dan called, nudging the door open a crack. The old portal groaned on squeaky hinges.

Hope looked around Dan's shoulder, trying to see into the dim interior.

Someone—something, she couldn't make out who or what—was stretched out in a mammoth bed, beckoning them to enter.

Glancing up at Dan, she swallowed. "It wants us to come in."

"Then let's go in."

Hope took a deep breath. No telling what they were getting into this time.

Stepping back, she pointed to the goat. "She goes first."

Chapter Eleven

COME in!" the figure in the bed yelled. "Been waiting for ya!"

Hope entered hesitantly. "Is anything wrong?" she asked.

Dan tied the bleating animal to the porch railing and strode inside.

Nudging her shoulder, Dan whispered, "Don't get involved. We're here for a day's rest; we move out tonight. Whoever this person is or whatever problems he or she is having, we aren't getting involved. Understand?"

"Oh, absolutely," she whispered back. "We're not getting involved."

It was obvious whoever—or whatever—was lying on that bed did have a problem. The cabin's state of disarray, the way the individual's hair looked as if he or she had thrown it in the air and jumped under it—something was wrong, all right.

Dan was right; they couldn't take on one more person's troubles. Every hour they tarried just caused more needless worry for John Jacobs.

Hope's eyes roamed the stale-smelling room. The log home was huge, with massive pieces of hand-hewn furniture crammed about the one enormous room.

"Come closer. Don't be afraid."

Hope crept toward the voice, holding tight to Dan's hand. "Are you ill?"

"Hurt my leg—been praying the Boss would send someone to help." The figure motioned her nearer. "Don't be shy; these old eyes cain't see as good as they once did. Come closer."

Though Hope would have complied, Dan's steely grip restrained her. Clearing his throat, he said, "We're just passing through. We saw your cabin and thought we might impose on your hospitality."

A cackle rent the air, startling Hope. Wide-eyed, she stepped back.

"You're welcome to anything I have, but you'll have to fix it!" the voice crowed. "Pete's sakes—come closer. I cain't see ya."

Wrenching free from Dan, Hope approached the bed. The voice sounded friendly enough. And it sure wasn't Big Joe or Frog trying to trick them. "How long have you been here?" Hope asked.

"Abed? Two days now. I was startin' to think I was a goner for sure."

Hope edged nearer, focusing on the lone figure. The dim light revealed an old woman lying abed, her foot propped up on a stained pillow, her snow-white hair in wild confusion.

"Hello," she said as Hope bent closer. "That's better.

Why, ain't you a pretty little thing. What brings you
clean out this way?"

"Well—"

Dan intervened. "We're on our way to Medford,
ma'am. We'd hoped to be there by now, but we've been
delayed."

A pair of faded molasses-colored eyes looked him up
and down. "You're welcome to stay the night with me.
Hafta sleep on the floor; the bears are a real bother lately,
comin' around at night looking for food. It won't be safe
to sleep outside or in the barn."

Hope turned to look at the floor. Would she ever sleep
in a real bed again?

Dan nodded. "Thank you for your hospitality. We'll be
moving on tonight."

"Tonight! Why, land sakes. A body shouldn't be out
there in the dark. You'll stay the night and strike off early
in the mornin'."

Dan glanced at Hope.

The old woman smiled. She didn't have a tooth in her
mouth. "Glad to have the company. Maybe your wife
will take a look at my wound. Tried to clean it myself,
but ain't had no luck."

"I'd be happy to." Hope located a bucket near the sink
and filled it at the well in back of the house.

Dipping a cup of fresh water from the bucket, Hope
held the old woman's head as she drank thirstily. "Oh
my, that tastes good. I've been makin' my peace with the
Boss," she said, dropping weakly back to the pillow.
"Not many folks come this way. I figured I was about to
be called home."

"How did you hurt your leg?" Hope busied herself
straightening the rumpled sheets. The bedclothes were a
disgrace. They needed a good washing.

"Had a little mishap with the ax."

"You were chopping wood?"

"Choppin' at it. Charlie died last fall. Pneumonie fever, I'd say. My husband was a good man; had enough wood laid up for the whole winter. But now it's gone, and I'm forced to do somethin' about it." She lifted the injured leg, chuckling. "At least Charlie left the old ax sharp."

"Do you have any medicines?" Hope asked. She could cleanse the old woman's leg and apply salve, then properly care for Dan's shoulder.

The woman raised up on a frail arm, her eyes on the sling on Dan's left arm. "Are you feelin' poorly, Son? You're looking a mite peaked."

Before Dan could answer, Hope fielded the question. "We've been walking for days. I apologize for our appearance. We look a sight. I'm Hope, and this is Dan."

"Hope, huh? Well, you're aptly named, young'un. 'Cause that's sure what you've brought me. I'm Letty McGregor. Pleased to meet you. The Boss answered my prayer."

"The Boss?"

"The Big Man—the Almighty. He's my boss—" She paused, her razor-sharp eyes pinning Hope. "Ain't he yours?"

"Oh yes, ma'am," Hope said. "He is." Papa would have switched her good if she'd ever called the Lord "Boss." Just didn't seem proper.

Letty pointed a bony finger at a shelf on the far wall. "See those jars and cups there? They've got herbs and such in them. Bring that biggest jar over here and a bowl to mix in." She glanced at Dan. "Son, would you mind checkin' on my mules? I fear they've not got a drop of water. Haven't been able to tend them since I got hurt. Might have rained, but I ain't heard it."

"Yes, ma'am."

"I'd appreciate that, young fellow. They've been faithful mules."

Hope picked up the big jar of herbs and carried it to the bed, then searched for a bowl in the messy kitchen, jumping back, startled, when her hand encountered a roach.

"You've got a mighty good-lookin' man there," Letty called. "My Charlie was powerful handsome, too."

Yes, Dan was powerful handsome. Any woman would be proud to claim him. But he wasn't hers. "How long were you and Mr. McGregor married?"

"Nigh on to sixty-seven years." Letty lay back on her pillow, staring at the ceiling. "Come from Missouri, you know. I was helpin' Papa farm when Charlie comes along lookin' for work. Papa hired him for room and board and a dollar a month. I was fifteen at the time. The first six dollars Charlie earned, we up and got married." She shook her head, her lined face pale and drawn. Hope suspected she hadn't eaten in two days. "Charlie was a fine man, God rest his soul. Buried out back—you'd see his grave if you was to look."

Hope brought the bowl and a wooden spoon to the bed.

"Take a couple spoonfuls of that powder and add about half as much water." Letty watched Hope's movements. "That's it—now, mix it up real good until it's thick as mud."

Hope wrinkled her nose as the vile smell permeated the area.

Letty chuckled. "Smells like the outhouse, but it works."

When the mixture met the approval of Letty's critical eye, the old woman uncovered her left leg.

Hope stepped back, sucking in a deep breath. The wound was bright red with the beginning of infection.

"It looks bad, but the salve will fix it right up. Spread it on the cut; by morning it'll be workin' on the poison."

Dan returned, carrying a few sticks of wood in his good arm. Hope jumped up to help him.

"You shouldn't be doing this," she scolded, taking the bundle from his arms.

"If you're going to fuss over me, do it by serving me a hot breakfast," he bantered lightly.

They pitched in and got a roaring fire going in the woodstove. Hope set a kettle of fresh water to boil.

"Bless you young'uns' hearts." Letty watched the activity from the bed. "I sure could do with a cup of tea when you get the time."

"Yes, ma'am, hot tea coming right up." Hope eyed the sink piled high with dirty dishes. No one was drinking or eating a morsel until she did something about that.

"There's pork, beef, and deer in the smokehouse, Dan. And there's a hen or two in the chicken coop. There's plenty of eggs out there waitin' to be gathered. You'll find canned goods in the cellar. Land sakes, this couldn't have come at a worse time," Letty complained. "Spring comin' on and I haven't got nary a potato in the ground. Ain't even got the soil tilled. Looks like I'm not gonna be able to now."

"We'll find everything we need, Mrs. McGregor. You just rest." Hope moved about the small kitchen, moving quickly to restore cleanliness and order.

"While you're thinkin' on breakfast, maybe your man will come sit by me—let me have a look at that shoulder."

Dan's eyes darted to the green mass covering Letty's leg, then back to Hope.

"It ain't purty to look at, but this stuff'll fix the problem. Now come over here; let me see why you got that arm in a sling."

"He was shot." Hope pushed Dan toward the chair beside Letty's bed. He sat down, looking as if she'd thrown him before a firing squad.

Letty's brows went up. "Bullet wound, huh? You running from the law?"

"No, ma'am." Dan straightened defensively. "I am the law. I got this wound in the line of duty."

Grunting, the old woman leaned over the side of the bed, peeling the bandage aside. Her eyes assessed the wound. "When Charlie built the house there was a small band of Comanches livin' nearby. They was a mean lot, causing all kinds of trouble. After a while they decided we meant them no harm, even began comin' by for a cup of coffee or a biscuit I'd hand out. They shore loved my strong coffee—said they could hunt for days without tirin' after drinkin' a cup. They're the ones that taught me about herbs and such." Dan winced as her fingers examined the wound. "I trust the Boss for healin', but I believe he helps us by providin' plants and such toward that healin'. Herbs have been all Charlie and I've had through the years." She grunted. "Worked real well till Charlie up and died on me."

Hope watched Letty tend the wounded shoulder, her eyes trying to tease Dan into a better mood.

Letty chuckled. "You two remind me of the way me and Charlie was when we first had eyes for each other. Couldn't git enough lookin'."

"Mrs. McGregor, we're not—," Hope began, compelled to explain the situation, but Dan stopped her.

"Hope would appreciate a bath, if you'd be so kind."

Letty cackled out loud. "And a comb wouldn't be too far amiss. Traveling without nary a thing, are you?" Her sharp-eyed gaze missed little. "Must not afigured on being gone long."

"No, ma'am. We didn't figure on being gone long." Hope quickly averted her gaze for fear of bursting out laughing. Neither had figured on being gone this long, and that was the complete truth.

"We've had to travel slowly because of the wound," Hope admitted, absently patting Dan's back.

"Well, the wound don't look good. You boil some water, and we'll get some hot compresses on it. You're lucky the bullet went clean through."

Hope nodded solemnly. "We have the Boss to thank for that."

"Yes, coulda lost your man. Take that pot there and fill it with water, heat it to a roiling boil. Might as well get more pots goin' so you can wash up before we eat. You'll enjoy your meal more with the tangles out of your hair."

Smiling, Hope wondered if the old woman had any idea what her own hair looked like.

Settling back against the pillow, Letty sighed. "There's a pile of Charlie's shirts in the chest there against the foot of the bed. Might even find a dress or two for you, Hope, and some clean undergarments, if you don't mind wearin' someone else's duds."

Pure joy filled Hope. Clean clothing! "I wouldn't mind at all, thank you!"

"Should be me thankin' you. I'd a-been a goner if the Boss hadn't sent you my way."

Hope carried in buckets of water, refusing Dan's help. Carrying water was something she could do. "You rest that shoulder."

Soon the smallest pot was steaming. Letty still fretted from her bed. "There's muslin in the chest for bandages. Get a poultice on that shoulder; should look better by mornin'."

Hope quickly readied the bandages; then amid vehement protest, she sat Dan down at the table.

He eyed the bandages and hot water. "This is going to hurt."

"Not much."

"I've heard that before."

"Pour some of that hot water in the bowl, dip in the

cloth, and let it cool just enough for him to bear it,"
Letty directed.

Hope followed the old woman's instructions, flinching
each time Dan's face contorted with pain.

"This is for your own good," she whispered.

The muscle in his jaw worked as she alternated hot
compresses. She thought his shoulder looked even angrier
with treatment, but Letty looked satisfied.

"Now, spread the herbs on, heavy-like, and leave off
the bandage until we eat." She watched Hope work, her
birdlike eyes intent on Hope's job. "Those pots hot
enough for bath water?"

Hope glanced toward the stove. "I think so."

"There's a copper tub in the back room, what I call
my bathin' room. There's plenty of soap in there—
nothin' fancy, but it'll get you clean. Towels aplenty."

Hope jumped up to check the pans of boiling water.
The steamy liquid bubbled away. "I'll bathe right after we
eat, Mrs. McGregor."

"Letty, sugar. Call me Letty, and you go on and take
your bath. Won't hurt us to wait breakfast a spell longer,
and you'll feel better. Your man and I can sit and talk
awhile."

Hope glanced at Dan, and he nodded, holding his
smarting shoulder. "Go ahead. I'll keep Mrs. McGregor
company."

Hope smiled, aware that it was the last thing he wanted
to do, but he was a gentleman. She located the oversized
tub, worn smooth by frequent use. A stand containing
soap and towels sat nearby. She quickly filled the tub
with hot water, tempering it with a bucket of cold, then
stripped out of the tattered dress and underclothes. She
sank into the water up to her chin and closed her eyes in
ecstasy.

When she climbed out of the tub and toweled dry half

an hour later, she whispered, "Bless you, Letty. And thank you, Boss."

Letty's dress hung on her slight frame like a feed sack, but it was clean and gloriously dry. Hope began to wonder if she'd ever wear her own clothes again.

Had the stage line shipped her things to John? If so, what must he be thinking? Even when she did reach him, would he accept her story of why she was so late, or would he think she'd been sullied? Her cheeks grew hot at the thought. Big Joe, Frog, and Boris were rude and disgusting louts, but they'd respected her privacy. And Dan . . . Dan had been a perfect gentleman during their times of enforced confinement.

Sullied indeed! *Shame on you, John Jacobs, if you even think such a thing!*

When she returned to the main room, Letty was resting. Dan was dozing by the fire. He glanced up when she entered the room, his gaze appreciatively skimming her fresh-scrubbed appearance. The look spoke more than words ever could. He obviously liked what he saw in a manly, most exciting way. Shivers inundated her. Did he find her beautiful? desirable? Someone he would fall in love with if only she wasn't promised to another man?

She hurried to the stove. "You must be starved. I'll fix us something to eat, then heat water for your bath."

"Your man's already got the water boiling, though I told him not to be movin' about. Needs to keep that poultice on his shoulder," Letty said in a voice thick with sleep.

"He can be stubborn." Hope risked a smile at Dan.

"Aren't you in charge of breakfast?"

"Yes, sir. Coming right up." His sudden gruffness didn't bother her; it meant he was getting better.

Letty opened her eyes. "Charlie hung those hams and smoked beef up high enough the bears can't reach them. You'll need to go with her."

"I can get them, Letty—"

"I'll go with you." Dan reached for the lantern, then preceded Hope out of the cabin. "The smokehouse is behind the barn."

"How do you know where it is?"

"I scouted around while you were taking your bath." He frowned when he saw the goat chewing on the porch railing. "Fool pest."

Hope hurried to catch up. "Think Letty might be a criminal? Maybe she's harboring a band of miscreants on the property?"

He was unaffected by her feisty banter. "You're too trusting, Hope. Never take a stranger at his word, even if it is a kindly old woman bearing food and hot baths."

Hope nodded, sobering. He was far more experienced than she at these matters. Until now, she'd never traveled farther than a few miles from home. She trusted everyone, expecting them to be as honorable as she was. Having met men like Big Joe, Frog, Boris, and yes, even the Bennetts, she was learning that didn't hold true.

His smile made her warm inside. "You've done well. I'm not complaining."

She matched his long strides as they walked toward the smokehouse. "I don't feel as if I've done well. It's as if I've been put to a test and failed."

Dan opened the door to the narrow shed and hung the lantern on a nail. Hope pressed close, straining to see around him. "Be careful . . . there could be a bear in there."

"The only bear you have to worry about is me, Miss Kallahan."

She whacked his back playfully.

"Ouch."

Inside, the smokehouse was dark, the air pungent with smoked meat.

"Even you getting shot was my fault," she reminded him.

Dan paused in the doorway, his right hand catching her upper arm in a gentle motion. His eyes locked with hers, and she thought she might die of love. Oh, dear God. She loved him! How could she have let that happen? "Don't be so hard on yourself. Without you, I would have been in real trouble in that cave—alone, wounded."

Despite her intention to avoid any impropriety, her hand reached out to touch his beard. "You look absolutely disgraceful."

"Yeah?"

A magnetism she was powerless to explain drew her closer. Her gaze focused on his mouth, and she wondered how many women he'd kissed.

"Well, you smell prettier than a woman ought to smell."

The feelings he raised were primitive, and new, and overwhelming. "I look awful. It'll take more than soap and water to repair this damage." She thought about the lemon verbena perfume in her valise and the lovely rose-scented talc Papa had given her one Christmas. She wished she had those things now to please Dan . . . but she shouldn't have such an improper desire. Why weren't her thoughts on John Jacobs?

Was it because she and Dan had been inseparable lately?

Of course she would have mixed feelings. Dan had been good to her; she'd entrusted her life to him. They had formed an indelible bond. Her feelings weren't improper; they were perfectly natural under the circumstances. Once she met John, all thoughts of Dan would recede—except those of profound gratitude.

His eyes skimmed her face, his voice low, deep, and disturbingly masculine. "John Jacobs is a lucky man."

She closed her eyes, about to cry. She wanted to kiss him—longed with every ounce of her will to draw him near, press her lips to his . . .

"Dan—"

He touched a finger to her lips. "I know," he said softly, gently moving her aside. "I'll get that meat now."

She was glad that he still had the sense to distinguish right from wrong. She lost the ability when he was this close. His voice penetrated her confusion.

"What'll it be, Miss Kallahan? Ham or beef?"

"How does ham sound?"

"Sounds good. I saw potatoes and dried peas in the cellar earlier."

Dan appeared a moment later carrying a medium-sized ham and a side of bacon. He pretended to throw the bacon at her.

Hope laughed. "Go ahead."

This time he threw it. The side of pork smacked into her middle.

She threw it back, and he caught it with one arm.

"No fair, I'm injured."

"You're not injured enough to keep you from throwing it at me."

He threw it back.

She faked a throw, and he fell for it. Straightening, he grinned, then staggered backward, catching the bacon before it slammed into his midsection.

The war was on.

Bacon flew back and forth until Hope collapsed in a heap on the ground, breathless with laughter. "Stop! You're going to ruin our breakfast and hurt yourself!"

Dropping the meat, Dan pretended to be in pain. She immediately flew to his side.

He reached down and threw the bacon back at her.

She squealed, running from him as he chased her to the house.

Letty raised herself up on her pillow as a giggling Hope burst through the front door. "Land-o'-the-mighty. Thought you two got lost."

Blood rushed to Hope's cheeks, and she realized how she must look. Cheeks pink, eyes sparkling. Mrs. McGregor would think she had been—no telling what she'd think!

Letty cackled. "Now don't be feeling all guilty. The Boss meant young'uns to fall in love. Charlie and me did our fair share of sparkin', I'll tell you. Now, I could eat a polecat. How about you startin' breakfast?"

Soon the aroma of sizzling ham and potatoes cooking in the oven filled the cabin.

Dan helped Hope set the table. Her cheeks were hot, and she refused to meet his gaze. Hope took a plate over to Letty in bed. As Hope and Dan sat down to eat, Letty prayed from the bed.

"Thank you, Boss, for this good food and for these fine folks who came to rescue me. I'm sure much obliged."

Later, Hope refilled the copper tub and laid a towel and washcloth nearby. Rummaging through the old trunk, she found several pairs of trousers and shirts. She selected a blue shirt and dark pants and laid them beside the tub.

Dan was sitting at the table reading the Bible when she finished. Letty's soft snores filled the old cabin.

"Tub's ready."

"I suppose it would be totally improper to ask that you wash my back?"

"Totally," she agreed. "I'd sooner drown you," she whispered against his ear as she passed him.

"You do smell good," he whispered back.

"You will, too, once you bathe."

"Is that a hint that I smell bad?"

"A strong suggestion."

When he moved to the back room, she reached for the Bible and curled up beside the fire.

She'd finished Genesis when he emerged from the wash room, still drying his hair with a towel. Charlie's trousers were too short in the legs, and the blue shirt was too tight for the width of his shoulders.

"You look breathtaking."

He grinned. "At least I'm clean for the first time in weeks."

Mixing up another batch of herbs, Hope applied the mixture to Dan's wound, then bound the injury in soft white muslin that Letty provided. His dark, damp hair curled over his shoulders and forehead.

Locating a comb, she gently groomed his damp mop. "You need a haircut."

"I'm waiting for you to offer."

She sat down in front of the fire and worked the comb through her matted tangles. Dan sat at the table watching her.

"Dan, I don't feel right about leaving so soon. Letty's virtually helpless. What kind of people are we to just ride off and leave her to fend for herself?"

He sighed, studying his hands. "I know. I was going to talk to you about that. I know you need to reach Medford as quickly as possible, but we can't leave for a while. Letty needs help, someone to look after the animals, plow that garden, lay up a good supply of cordwood."

She wasn't surprised by his answer; she'd been expecting it. It was clear they couldn't leave Letty, not until she was up and about on her own.

"Your shoulder won't permit you to plow and cut wood."

"The mule will do most of the work, and you can help." His eyes met hers. "I'd welcome the company."

She'd welcome his company—more time to be near him. "Of course, and I don't mind the delay. I'll help

Letty with housework, and I can plant a garden—I'm very good at planting. Papa always had a large garden—biggest one in Cold Water."

Dan seemed pleased that she didn't put up an argument. "Letty should be up and around in a few days. By then, my shoulder will be well on the way to mending. Medford should be only a couple of days' ride from here."

Hope nodded, laying the comb aside. "I wonder if Letty shouldn't think about moving closer to a town. What if we hadn't come along?" She looked up when he didn't answer.

"You look almost like you did the first day I saw you," he said softly.

"I hope that's a compliment." She was afraid to have him look closely at her, afraid her love was written so vividly on her face that he would see it.

"It's a compliment," he said quietly. "Hope, if I could . . ." He didn't finish the thought.

Disappointed, she got up to tend the fire. "When we get to Medford, I'm not sure I want people to know what's really happened."

He was so quiet, she wasn't sure he'd heard. Then, "Why not? You're not responsible for anything that's happened."

She shrugged. "I'll tell John, of course, but Aunt Thalia would only be concerned about . . ." She paused, unable to express her anxiety.

"Your reputation? Hope, I'll talk to John. Explain to him that you've been in my custody." His gaze drew hers again and held it. "No one will question your character. I won't allow it."

The days at Letty McGregor's flew by. Dan's shoulder began to heal, and Letty's leg was coming along nicely.

By the end of the week, the old woman moved about the cabin with the assistance of a wooden cane Dan made for her.

The goat ate three shirts and two petticoats off the clothesline, and was now busy at work on the front yard.

Dan hitched a mule to the single plow and turned the garden. Hope raked the rich black soil and planted potatoes, onions, and radishes. At night, the "young'uns" fell onto their quilt pallets, exhausted.

At the end of the week as Dan finished the last bite of egg on Sunday morning, he shoved back from the table. Meeting Hope's expectant look, he announced, "Letty, we hate to leave you, but Hope and I have to go."

Nodding, the old woman looked lonelier than any soul ought to look. "Breaks my heart to see you young'uns go, but of course I understand. You take the other mule," she insisted. "Dandy's fine for plowing, but Cinder's not cut out for harness. He's a good riding mule. He'll get you to Medford."

"Oh, Letty, we can't take your mule," Hope said. "You've done so much for us already."

"Well, I could sure use the goat, if you were a mind to leave it. I'm right partial to the milk, and she could keep the front lawn eat down."

"Letty, you have the goat with my most sincere blessing." Dan swallowed the last of his coffee and stood up.

"I suppose you'll be leavin' today?"

"Yes, we have to be on our way."

"Then you better go to the smokehouse and get another ham. Hope can make sandwiches for the road."

Under Letty's watchful eye, Hope spread bread with golden butter and added thick slices of ham; she filled canteens with fresh water.

When it came time to leave, Dan and Hope stood near Letty, who was seated in a chair, while Dan offered a brief prayer. "Lord, thank you for bringing us to Letty.

Please heal her leg completely, and watch over her. Watch over us also, as we travel. Protect us from harm, and speed us to our destination. Amen."

Letty got up, leaning on her cane. Dan hugged her. "Good-bye, Mrs. McGregor. Thank you, and God bless you."

When he stepped back and it was Hope's turn, she couldn't stop hugging Letty. "I'll think about you every day of my life," Hope said.

Awkwardly thumping Hope on the back, the old woman replied in a voice choked with emotion. "I'll be mentioning you to the Boss, myself, young'un. You take care, now. You hear?"

"Yes, ma'am." Hope wiped her eyes and blew her nose.

"Oh, wait. I've got something for you. You'll be needing a hat." Letty crossed the room and took off a peg a flat straw hat with cloth flowers around the crown.

Hope set it atop her head, then scrambled onto the mule behind Dan.

"Good-bye, Letty!" Hope yelled as Dan nudged the mule's flanks and they trotted off down the lane.

"Bye, young'uns! God speed!"

Hope watched over her shoulder until the cabin and Letty faded from sight. Melancholy assailed her.

"Are you going to cry?" Dan called over his shoulder.

Nodding, she bit her lip.

He covered her hand with his. The gesture touched her deeply. "Don't worry; the worst is over."

Biting her lip harder, she took comfort in the simple statement.

The worst was over.

Nothing else could possibly happen to delay their arrival in Medford.

Chapter Twelve

JOHN ran his index finger around the inside of his collar, looking around to see if anyone had thought to open the windows. It was the second box social in a month. Didn't these women ever give up?

"A little warm under the collar, John?"

John looked up to see Jack Vance sipping a glass of punch. The town barber smiled as if he knew a secret John didn't.

"It's a little warm tonight."

"Oh? Thought it might be the idea of getting hitched." The older man chuckled.

"No." John smiled. "I'm looking forward to that."

"From what I hear, the bride might not be quite so anxious to tie the knot."

"Oh? And who might have formed that opinion?"

"The town. We all think she's not coming."

"Well, the town is wrong. Excuse me, Jack, my cup needs replenishing." John walked away before Jack could respond, but he didn't make the punch bowl before Lawrence Grant stopped him.

"Heard from that bride yet?"

"No, I haven't," John said, determined to be pleasant if it killed him. "How are things at the livery, Larry?"

"Busy, real busy. Got that new buggy in. You still in the market?"

"I'll be over tomorrow to take a look."

First thing tomorrow morning he'd march down to that river and insist Eldon Jacks ferry him across to the other side, where he could wire Thalia Grayson about Hope's whereabouts.

Had Hope even gotten on that blasted stage as planned? He didn't want to alarm the old aunt if Hope had set about on her own adventure, yet if something was amiss, someone neeeded to know. If Mrs. Grayson knew why Hope chose not to honor her commitment to him, would she feel comfortable revealing the reason? It was a troubling predicament, to be sure.

Disappointment beset him. Anyone who had the least consideration for him would have found a way to spare him this embarrassment. Perhaps he'd been wrong about Hope. Could that be? Could he have been so anxious to acquire a wife that he had been taken in by a hard-hearted woman?

Martin Gray clapped John heartily on the shoulder. "John, how's everything at the store?" The Gray family lived five miles outside of town and were among John's best customers.

"Everything is fine. Had a fine winter. New families moving in means good business for me."

"Hear you're about to start your own family."

"I'm hoping to."

"Sort of left at the altar, were ya?"

John bristled. "Who told you that?"

"Well?" Martin laughed apologetically. "Did I get the story wrong?"

"Yes. My intended is a bit late in arriving—"

Martin held up his hand. "Didn't mean to offend, John. Maybe the little lady can't bring herself to leave her family. She got brothers and sisters in Michigan?"

"An aunt." Perhaps that was the reason for her absence. John felt almost faint with relief. Hope didn't want to leave her family—but she could have told him. He was compassionate; he'd understand her hesitancy—but wait. Hope's sisters were leaving, too, also to become mail-order brides.

"Well, there you have it. Women like their families around 'em. Could be she's decided she doesn't want to move clear to Kentucky."

"No . . . I feel confident that she would contact me if that were the case. She's just been delayed."

Martin glanced past John. "Mercy. Who's that pretty young thing?"

John turned to see Freeman Hide's granddaughter standing near the punch bowl, chatting with Jed Lane. Her slender fingers worked a black lace fan back and forth, stirring the humid air. He detected the scent of her perfume even at this distance. His pulse accelerated. By George! Never had he beheld anyone so breathtakingly lovely.

Uncommonly tall, she was dressed in midnight blue lace, her raven black hair piled high atop her head with a delicate lace mantilla falling around her shoulders. The young woman was exquisite.

John approached the punch bowl, searching for a proper introduction. Something neighborly, he told himself, appropriately friendly without being overly solicitous.

"I see your cup has run dry. May I refill it for you?"

Now that was a real conversation stopper, he berated himself.

The lovely young creature turned, and John's knees buckled when confronted with dark-lashed, intelligent eyes the color of thick honey. "Thank you, but I've had quite enough." She gently fanned herself as she gazed at him.

John's tongue whiplashed into a bowknot. For the first time in his life, words failed him. His eyes darted about the room for Freeman. He should be here to make proper introductions.

"Lovely party," he said, absently dipping another cup of punch. The liquid spilled over the sides and onto the white tablecloth. Grabbing for a napkin, he upturned a vase of flowers. Water dribbled off the sides onto his newly polished shoes. When he sprang back, his heel slipped and he grabbed for support. The whole table went down with him in the middle.

The ensuing crash caught every eye and ear in the room. Every woman in attendance rushed to his rescue.

Crawling to his feet, John mopped at the front of his jacket, grinning at the striking beauty. "I'm fine, thank you. Lovely party."

The young woman frowned. "Yes . . . lovely. I'm new in town, and I haven't met many—"

Veda shouldered in with a mop and bucket. The crowd stepped back as the table was set back in place.

John seized the moment. Reaching for the young woman's hand, he turned her toward the front of the room. "Permit me to do the honors. Over there's Mose Foreman. He raises chickens. And Aaron Caldwell sitting in the corner? He's the mayor of Medford, owns two stores on Main Street. Good man, Aaron. And Lynn Baker, the one with the fiddle? He's retired. All he does is fiddle around." John smiled. He wiped at the front of his suit, his mind searching for a new topic of conversation.

"How do you find the weather here?"

"I find it fine," she said. "And you?"

"Spring is my favorite time of the year."

"Mine too. I'm looking forward to investigating the woods surrounding the town. So many lovely wildflowers are starting to bloom."

"You are? Well perhaps—"

John spotted Veda coming back through the crowd, and his smile faded.

The young woman turned to follow his gaze, her eyes searching the room. "Is something wrong?"

"Veda Fletcher." The name was a pox on his lips.

"Who?"

He dropped his voice. "Veda Fletcher, the woman coming toward us in the yellow dress."

She turned. "What about her?"

"I want to avoid her."

"Avoid her?"

"Like a case of hives."

Amusement showed in the woman's smile. "May I ask why?"

"She's intent on introducing me to her niece."

"And you don't want to meet the niece?"

"No."

John's gaze darted to the back door. It was now or never. "Would you care to join me for a stroll in the moonlight?"

John held his breath as she considered the invitation. *Please, a simple walk in the moonlight,* he prayed.

"A breath of air might be nice."

"Come with me." Taking her by the arm, he ushered her quickly out the back door. Several others had taken the opportunity to gain a breath of fresh air and stood talking in small groups around the school yard. At John's direction, they made their way toward a low wall that ran along one side of the school yard.

"It's a beautiful night."

"Yes, it is," he said, taking off his jacket to spread it atop the wall for her to sit on. The air was cooler than inside, and he felt he could breathe again. Moonlight illuminated the young woman's features. Her beauty was almost unearthly.

"Thank you, you're very kind."

"Completely nonthreatening." He smiled.

"But you're threatened by that woman—Veda Fletcher."

Settling beside her on the wall, he drew a deep breath. "Well, Veda is a little intimidating, especially when she's on a mission."

"A mission?"

"Of matrimony."

Her eyes widened. "Veda Fletcher wants to marry you?"

"Not Veda. She wants me to marry her niece."

"Oh . . ." After a moment, she said, "You've met this niece and find her unappealing?"

"No, no, I haven't met Veda's niece. That's what I'm hoping to avoid."

Snapping open her fan, she murmured, "Interesting."

"I know I must sound overly suspicious, but it's the truth. Veda has targeted me for her niece, and I don't intend to oblige her. When I marry, it will be the woman of my own choosing."

"I can imagine your aggravation. One must wonder what sort of woman the niece is if her aunt has to secure a husband for her."

"Yes, that has crossed my mind." John was surprised to discover how much he enjoyed this woman's company. It had been years, if ever, since he'd been this comfortable with a member of the opposite sex. "I fear the niece is exactly like Veda."

"And that would be bad?"

"Well, yes. Veda is a lovely woman, very warm and caring. Unfortunately, she's a hopeless matchmaker, and she makes the worst chicken casserole I've ever tasted. Believe me, I've eaten her casserole enough to make an unbiased judgment."

She smiled. "You can't find it in yourself to tell her you don't like the dish?"

"No! I wouldn't hurt her for the world."

"You're far too nice," she suggested.

"I don't know about that. It's just that Veda is so all-consuming. One can hardly have a thought of his own, much less express it. I worry this compulsion to run everything is a family trait."

The young woman hid the lower half of her face behind her fan, and John had the distinct impression she was laughing as she slid off the wall and took a few steps away from him.

"I'm glad you find it amusing. I assure you, having Veda come into the store every day to arrange my marriage isn't funny."

"Oh, but it is." She turned, dropping the fan from her face. She was smiling. "You see, I am Ginger Gonzales, and I can assure you that I haven't the slightest intentions of trapping you, John Jacobs."

John was struck dumb. This was Veda's niece! This unspeakably lovely creature was the woman with the constitution of fine china?

He'd never felt so foolish in his whole life.

He grappled for something intelligent to say, some graceful way out of his faux pas, but his mind abandoned him. "I—well, I—"

Her smile widened impishly. "Yes, John? Is there something you want to say?"

"I wish I could," he finally managed. He slid off the wall, mortified. He'd managed to insult the most beautiful woman he'd met in his entire life—not only insult and embarrass her but also alienate her from him forever! *Wonderful, John.*

Suddenly her laughter penetrated his fog. She was laughing! The woman was laughing at him! He'd need to be as tough as a twenty-cent steak to get out of this one.

"Miss Gonzales. Is it possible for me to convince you that I'm John Jacobs's evil twin?"

"Umm, how does the real John feel about Aunt Veda?"

"Well," he said, "I'm sorry to say that he doesn't care any more for chicken casserole than I do."

She lowered the fan, flipping it closed with a soft snip. "Frankly, I don't care for Aunt Veda's chicken casseroles either. They're too dry, and every time I eat one, I'm up half the night drinking soda water."

"Soda water?" He hoped his eyes weren't bulging right out of his head. "I have to drink soda water every time I eat one!"

"Well, then, John Jacobs, perhaps we might think about meeting after all." She smiled, a smile so pretty it just about knocked him off his feet. "It seems we have much in common." She cocked an ear toward a mounting commotion inside. "I think they're about to start the bidding for the box dinners. Shall we go in?"

Eternally grateful for her graciously releasing him from utter mortification, John escorted her back inside the school building. He was shaking from the whole experience.

Fred McArthur was trying to get everyone's attention. "Ladies and gentlemen, it's time to get down to what we came here for. Box suppers!"

The crowd clapped and cheered him on.

"You know it's for a good cause, so be generous!"

Veda was helping sort boxes, handing each to Fred as he worked up the crowd, encouraging a wild and furious spate of bidding. As each offering sold, the buyer claimed the box from Veda, passed the money to Fred, then waited for the lady who had prepared the supper to claim it. Depending on whose box supper it was, loud and teasing comments ebbed and flowed from the audience, along with laughter and good-natured jesting.

Since he'd already made a fool of himself, John dispensed with etiquette and looked down at Ginger.

"Which box is yours?"

The fan flipped open again, and she fanned herself, her eyes coy behind the fan. "I can't tell you which box is mine. That would be cheating."

He grinned. Veda had schooled her well.

"Every man in this room knows whose box he's bidding on."

"You don't." Her eyes twinkled merrily behind the fan.

He leaned closer. "Which box, Miss Gonzales?"

"Am I to assume you'd like to spend the evening with me, or is your query merely curiosity?"

He was a little taken aback by her directness, but he liked it. "What if I said I wanted to have supper with you at any cost?"

The fan ceased its movement.

"Then I would say, yellow is my favorite color, and the daisy looks especially inviting."

John's gaze quickly scanned the table. A large woven basket, wrapped in a blue-checked cloth secured with a wide yellow ribbon holding a clutch of daisies to the handle, presided at the end of the table.

"Isn't that a coincidence? I'm rather partial to yellow myself. And I've always had a deep appreciation for daisies."

"Amazing coincidence," she murmured, her gaze capturing his over the open fan she now held to her cheek.

". . . and the red-ribbon box goes to Jefferson Mason. Jeff, better hope Miranda put that supper together."

Laughter rewarded Fred as Veda pushed the yellow-ribboned basket containing Ginger's contribution to the edge of the table. She located John in the crowd and pointed to the offering. Pearl Eddings yelled out.

"No fair, Veda Fletcher!"

"Now here's a fine box. Yellow ribbon, daisies." Fred leaned over to sniff. "And unless my nose is wrong, there's fried chicken in there." He sniffed again. "And chocolate cake."

The crowd laughed. Fred couldn't smell a skunk if it sprayed him.

"Chicken?" John mused softly. "Let me see. Do I want chicken, or should I hold out for a box with roast beef?"

"Fried chicken, best around." Ginger edged closer. "And biscuits and honey, fresh butter, and some of Aunt Veda's special sweet pickles."

Well, Veda could make a mean pickle. John never doubted that.

"Pickles," he swooned, his hand over his heart in mock seriousness. He winked. "And chocolate cake?"

"Apple pie with cheese."

"Ah, a woman with superb taste." He raised his hand. "Five dollars for the yellow-ribboned basket."

"Five dollars from John Jacobs, mercy me! Do I hear five and a quarter?"

"Five and a quarter," someone shouted from the back of the room.

Ginger was watching from the corner of her eye, resting the fan against her cheek.

"Five-fifty," John bid, hoping he had enough money in his pocket.

"Do I hear five seventy-five?" Fred asked expectantly. "I've got five-fifty; do I hear five seventy-five?"

John held his breath.

"Five seventy-five!" someone yelled from the back of the room.

"Six," Ginger urged from behind the fan. "I'll chip in the extra twenty-five cents."

"Seven-fifty!" John yelled, then leaned over to whisper. "Keep your money. I'll pay fifty if I have to."

"Seven-fifty! Sold to John Jacobs for seven dollars and fifty cents! Come claim your supper, John."

John parted his way through the crowd, accepting congratulations as he reached up to take possession of the basket.

Veda looked unforgivably smug. "Enjoy your meal, John."

Handing over the money, he threaded his way back to Ginger. But she wasn't there. His eyes frantically searched the room before he detected a movement toward the back door. Hurrying in that direction, he was relieved to see Ginger casually strolling across the yard to the wall where he'd made such a fool of himself earlier.

He shot out the door and followed her.

"I thought we could picnic out here," Ginger said as he caught up.

"A perfect place," he agreed.

Ginger untied the ribbon and loosened the checked cloth, then spread it across the top of the stone ledge. Handing John the daisies, she opened the basket. The tantalizing aroma of fried chicken wafted upward, and John smiled.

"You are a temptress," he accused.

Ginger laughed, and the charming sound coursed through John's veins like wildfire.

"Biscuits, chicken, Aunt Veda's pickles, baked beans with sorghum, apple pie."

John reached to help extract a round plate. Their hands touched, and he felt as if he'd been hit by lightning.

"And cheese." Their eyes met and held in the moonlight. "A beautiful woman, a warm spring night. Life is good."

"You're a romantic, John Jacobs."

"I like to think so, Miss Gonzales."

Later, they packed the remnants of the meal back into the basket, and John escorted Ginger back into the school building. Excusing herself, Ginger went to gather her things.

"There you are! Yoo-hoo, John!" Veda stood on tiptoe, vying for his attention. "How was the meal?"

Striding toward her, John reached out to take her pudgy hand in his. "Mrs. Fletcher, I owe you my heartfelt apologies."

Veda blushed prettily. "What on earth for?"

"Because you tried to tell me how completely lovely your niece was, and I was reluctant to take your word." He leaned close and whispered into her ear, "Indulgent aunts and parents tend to be a bit prejudiced, you know."

Veda tittered. "I was so pleased when you bid on Ginger's basket," she confessed. "And I didn't even have to tell you which one it was. Could this mean you no longer consider yourself engaged? Have you finally come to your senses and realized Miss Kallahan isn't coming?"

He hadn't thought that far yet, but he supposed he must. And soon. He couldn't go on this way forever. Hope wasn't coming; he'd only been fooling himself. As bad as he hated to admit it, she'd stood him up.

"I'd rather your niece doesn't know anything about my engagement until I think it through."

"Of course, but John—" Veda squeezed his hand affectionately—"I only want the best for you. I know you've thought me pushy and overbearing at times, always on you to meet my niece, and I admit I've been overly anx-

ious. I'm a selfish woman. I want you in the family.
You're a fine man, and my niece couldn't be more
blessed were the two of you to fall in love."

John's gaze located Ginger across the room. She was
chatting with Idella Merriweather, her animated laughter
drifting to him. Three hours ago he would have found
Veda's thoughts ludicrous. At the moment they didn't
seem at all out of place.

"If you don't mind, I would like to walk Ginger and
you home."

"Of course, dear. And you can take your time. It's a
lovely night. I'll be with you in a minute."

Veda zeroed in on Pearl Eddings. "Oh, Pearl!" she war-
bled. "Wait up. I have something to tell you."

Chapter Thirteen

THE old mule, Cinder, was a pest. The cantankerous beast of burden nipped at Dan's dangling legs with its big teeth, making a real nuisance of herself.

"If we didn't need the transportation so badly, I'd shoot this thing!" Dan groused, swatting the critter's rump when she bit him a third time.

Even Hope's newfound positive attitude was flagging. She was beginning to feel as if everything was against her, even the mule. What had her life become? What would Aunt Thalia think if she could see her now—riding a mule, wearing Letty's ridiculous-looking straw hat?

But no matter. She would be in Medford before much longer, and her troubles would be over. By this time next week, she would be serving John Jacobs dinner.

The thought didn't do much to lift her spirits.

She spent the day trying to revel in her final hours of freedom, glorying in the spring flowers blooming along the hillsides, the call of meadowlarks, and the occasional glimpse of a deer through the thick foliage. She sang songs, inviting Dan to join in. To her delight, he did, his rich baritone blending harmoniously with her alto as they rode through the greening countryside.

Hope waved to occasional passersby, though Dan barely noticed them. He seemed preoccupied, deep in thought. Hope wondered if his thoughts included her. At times, she was certain that he was attracted to her; but at others she realized he was a man with a duty and she was only a part of that duty.

Her feelings for Dan had deepened with lightning swiftness. During the idyllic days at Letty's, they had been inseparable, working side by side during the day, talking late into the night over popcorn and sugared tea at the table while Letty snored in her bed.

Yet at other times, they seemed continents apart.

She knew what her problem was—love. But other than the one time at the smokehouse, she'd fought the feeling because there was John to consider.

There was always John.

Her resentment bloomed. What sort of man put an ad for a wife in a journal, anyway? How could she possibly explain to her husband-to-be everything that had happened to her since she'd kissed Aunt Thalia good-bye and boarded the stage in Cold Water?

Had that been almost two months ago? She'd lost track of time.

Would John believe that Dan had been only her protector? Or would he have qualms about her respectability, requesting that she leave? Her spirits lifted at the prospect, then plummeted back to earth. John Jacobs was an honorable man. If he had misgivings about her reputation, she doubted that he would openly voice them.

If God had put these trials upon her to test her faith, then she had most certainly failed. She wasn't even sure God loved her. How could she believe this man she didn't know but was consigned to marry could love her?

"Muddy Flats straight ahead." Dan indicated the silhouette of buildings against the distant horizon.

A few miles back, a passerby had told them the small crossroads settlement had a general store. Letty had insisted that they take fifteen dollars for necessities. Dan assured her the money would be repaid the moment he contacted his commander. When they reached Muddy Flats, they would have to purchase food. The sandwiches would last for one more meal.

"If only there was time to buy a dress that fits me." She lifted the baggy waist of the dress Letty had given her. It was going to be embarrassing to meet John looking like a beggar. "And a bath would be nice."

"We'll see if the town can accommodate your wishes, miss."

"A bath isn't a necessity," she reminded him. "But it sure would be nice."

Dan's hand rested on hers for a brief moment. The artless touch set her heart rate into double time. "We'll make you presentable to meet John. Another couple of hours isn't going to make a difference. You can buy a pretty dress and have a long soak in a hot tub. Come to think about it, a bath sounds good. We'll each have one."

Hope felt like she was going to explode with all the emotions boiling up inside her. "Thank you." She squeezed his waist, and he squeezed her hand back.

Muddy Flats wasn't large, but Hope was happy to see a mercantile, a small livery, a saloon, a blacksmith, and a boardinghouse that promised bathing facilities.

"We might even stay the night," Dan decided as they rode the mule down Main Street. "Probably do you good to sleep in your own bed, stay in your own room for the

185

first time in weeks. We can start out early in the morning, be in Medford by noon. What would you say to that?"

"Sleep in a clean bed with real sheets? I'd say yes!"

"I'll leave you at the Mercantile. You pick out a pretty dress and buy some matching shoes. I want John Jacobs's bride to be the talk of the town."

She did too; she just wished she wasn't that bride. She poked her foot out and studied her once-fashionable foot attire. During the weeks since she'd left Michigan, she'd plowed through wet grass, forded streams, and walked untold miles. Her shoes weren't a pretty sight.

"What will you do while I shop?"

"I'm going to sell this ornery critter. Or bury it." He jumped when the mule turned, trying to take a chunk out of his leg. He boxed the animal's ears. "Either way, Lucifer, here, and I are parting company."

Dan stopped the animal in front of the Mercantile, and Hope slid off the mule's back. "Stay out of trouble." He winked at her.

"I'll try." It was her heart, not her feet, that needed to stay out of trouble.

She felt like a street urchin as she opened the door to the Mercantile and stepped inside.

"Afternoon!" A short, round older man behind the counter greeted her, his gaze sweeping her appearance.

"I need a new dress," she explained.

The clerk's mouth turned up in a half smile. "That right? Right pert hat you've got there."

"Well," she admitted, "it keeps the sun off, thank you."

"I see that. Hiram Burk, clerk, at your service."

"Hope Kallahan, battered traveler, at yours." She extended a soiled hand and they shook.

"I suppose you'd like to look at some ready-mades?"

"Yes, and shoes. Comfortable ones—inexpensive, comfortable ones. I don't have much money."

She had no idea what a mule would bring. Not much, she ventured to guess, and they would need all they could get to buy a horse to replace it. She needed to be thrifty, even though they also had Letty's fifteen dollars.

"Dresses to the right, bonnets three aisles back. You'll find everything you need."

Hope easily located the rack of ready-made gowns. Most were too large for her, but she eventually decided on a pink-and-white calico. Browsing through the rack of bonnets, she found a pretty white one; then she selected a few simple undergarments and carried them to the counter.

"How much?" she asked, anxiously watching the clerk tally the apparel.

"Well, let's see." The old gentleman figured on a piece of brown paper, his pencil flying. "Three dollars."

"Three?" She worried her teeth on her lower lip. "Dan and I both need comfortable walking shoes."

"Three dollars includes two pairs of shoes," he said with a friendly smile. "I'd throw in a brush and comb for three and a quarter." He leaned forward slightly. "Got some fine bathing facilities up at the boardinghouse."

"Thank you," Hope said, heartened by his generosity. As Papa would say, the world needed more men like Hiram Burk. "You're so very kind."

"The Lord's been good to me; I like to pass it on." Straightening, he picked up his duster and tidied the counter. "Looks to me like you've had a time of it. You slip off one of those shoes and I'll see if I can match the size. Meanwhile, there's some finely milled soap, sweetest smelling thing this side of heaven, right over there near the window. You pick out a bar, and I'll sell it to you for a penny."

Hope unlaced her shoes and handed them over the

counter, then went to see about the soap. She smelled each and every bar before she selected one that smelled like the roses that vined along Aunt Thalia's backyard fence.

"Now let's see, little lady. Think these will fit?" Mr. Burk held a sturdy brown pair of shoes aloft for her inspection.

"They look as if they might."

Sitting on a stool Mr. Burk provided, Hope slipped her feet into the shoes and stood up, testing their length.

"They look mighty fetching on you."

"They're perfect." She sat down and pulled them off.

"Don't you want to wear them? I could wrap up this old pair—"

"No, I won't wear them until I have a bath," Hope said.

Mr. Burk smiled, nodding with understanding. "Just what my wife, Beulah, would say."

Reaching for her parcels, Hope smiled. Sometimes a person just knew when she was in the presence of angels. This was one of those times. "God bless you, Mr. Burk."

The old clerk looked almost angelic. "It's mighty nice to be of service. You send your man in, and I'll fix him up too."

Hope didn't bother to correct Mr. Burk's assumption that Dan was her husband. She rather fancied the idea herself.

Hurrying out of the store, she anticipated the hot bath, rose-scented soap, shampoo for her hair, clean, new clothes, and a night's rest in a real bed with clean sheets and feather pillows.

Not looking where she was going, she ran smack into a tall man just exiting the mouth of the alley. She opened her mouth to apologize.

"I'm so—no!" She shrieked as Joe Davidson's filthy hand clamped over her mouth.

"Thought ya could escape Big Joe, huh? Well, think again, missy."

Hope's heart hammered wildly in her chest as the outlaw hooked an arm around her waist and hauled her into the alleyway. Her packages scattered. Struggling, she pawed at his hand, but Big Joe's grip was far superior. He stifled her cries by stuffing a dirty bandanna into her mouth.

"Now, hush up!"

Manhandling her onto a waiting horse, he stepped into the saddle, digging his spurs into the horse's flanks.

The gelding burst from the alleyway and headed east.

Dan emerged from the boardinghouse and strode toward the Mercantile, whistling.

Stepping onto the porch, he cupped his hands, peeking through the store window. His gaze swept the empty store, and he frowned. A moment later he entered through the front door.

The portly man behind the counter glanced up. "Can I help you?"

Dan's eyes scanned the empty aisles. "I'm looking for a woman. Dark hair, wearing a yellow dress, silly hat?"

"Mrs. Kallahan! You must be the mister."

Dan smiled. "Is she still here?"

"No, she left a moment ago—you must have passed her on the way in." The friendly clerk stepped to the front window and looked out. "Now that's odd. She couldn't have gone far."

Dan joined him to look out. "I didn't pass her on the way over. I'd have noticed that."

The clerk walked outside, and Dan followed him. The two men stood on the porch, their eyes searching the street.

"I think she was heading over to the boardinghouse. Said something about wanting a bath."

Dan suddenly bounded off the porch and started running.

"Mister! Hey, mister!" the clerk called. "I'm sure she's all right—"

Dan dodged the packages spilled in the dirt—a dress box, a pair of brown shoes. A small bar of feminine-looking soap.

"Hope!" He ran faster, his breath coming in bursts, his eyes searching the sidewalks and walkways.

"Did anyone see anything?" he shouted as a crowd started to form.

Serious expressions stared back. Not a man, woman, or child indicated they'd seen anything peculiar.

His eyes swung to an old-timer dozing in a chair propped against the saloon wall on the opposite side of the street. Dan sprinted across the road.

"Did you see a young woman come out of the Mercantile a few minutes ago?"

The old man cracked a sleepy eye, peering up at him. "Eh?"

"A young, pretty woman. Coming out of the store—just a few minutes ago."

"Young woman?"

"Yes."

"Pretty?"

"Tall, slim, dark hair, wearing a silly straw hat."

"Oh, that woman." The old fellow stroked his bristling jaw. "Yes, sir, I did see that little filly. Wearing a dirty yeller dress, leastwise it looked yeller—could have been white. Can't even say it wasn't faded brown; could even have been coffee-colored—knew a woman once who had a coffee-colored dress. It was real pretty. Or it could have been—"

Dan cut him off. "Where did she go?"

"Rode out of town."

"Rode out?" Dan whirled to look down the road.

"Yep. On th' back of a horse . . . with a big ol' fella."

Dan grabbed the front of the old-timer's vest. "How long ago?"

The old man showed surprising strength. He struggled to break Dan's grip. "Now hold on, you young whipper-snapper—"

Relaxing the clench, Dan stepped back. He swiped a hand over his face. "This is important. What did the man look like?"

Frowning, the old man shook his head. "Big—tall, hat pulled low. Beard. Ridin' a big gelding. That one's trouble, I tell you. Why any woman would want to—"

"Joe Davidson," Dan muttered. "Which way did he go?"

"Thataway." The man pointed up the street. "If you want to catch him, you better lasso yourself a cyclone, Sonny. That feller was in a powerful big hurry."

Leaping off the porch, Dan sprang aboard a big roan standing at the saloon hitching post.

A cowpoke just coming out from the watering hole threw his arms in the air, yelling, "Hey! That's my horse!"

"I'll return it later!" Wheeling the mare, Dan spurred the animal's flanks and galloped out of town.

Chapter Fourteen

*W*ELL. *This is getting out of hand, Lord! Is there a particular lesson you want me to learn from this insanity?*

Hope huddled beside the fire, glaring at her captors— Big Joe, Boris, and Frog. Why hadn't she been more cautious? In her eagerness for clean clothing and a hot bath, she had been careless, thinking only of herself. Now once again, an oafish lout and his two similarly oafish sidekicks were holding her prisoner. If there was a lesson to be learned, she didn't have the slightest notion what it was.

She had no idea where they were. They had ridden for what seemed like hours. Dan would be hunting for her, trying to determine who had taken her, and where—or at least she hoped he would. He'd have a fair idea of who was responsible for the nefarious act, but how would he find her? They could have taken her anywhere.

Lord, I don't know how you'll work it, but guide Dan's steps—lead him to me, Father. "God, please be here," she murmured.

Lo, I am with you always, the wind seemed to whisper.

Big Joe, Frog, and Boris sat around the campfire, bandannas tucked into their collars, slurping pork and beans from tin bowls.

"Want some?" Boris asked when he caught her staring.

She shook her head, averting her gaze. "No."

"Still snooty, huh? Well, good. Jest more for me." The bandit leaned over and dipped his bowl back into the iron pot hung over the fire.

Their manners were still atrocious. They'd forgotten everything she'd taught them.

Boris grinned as if he'd read her thought. "Aw, she don't like our ettin' skills, gentlemen." He winked at the others. "We're jest a bunch of heathens—but right fine-lookin' ones, right, Joe?"

Big Joe nodded. "Right fine." He belched, loud enough to wake the dead.

Boris sopped up stew broth with a cold biscuit. "Ain't changin' the way I eat for her again. Iffin it's good enough for Ma, it's good enough for Miss Snooty here."

"Animals," Hope murmured.

Big Joe glanced up. "What was that?"

"I said you are like animals, eating like pigs, dripping broth down your front, slurping, burping. I've met pigs with better behavior."

At least the Bennett pig didn't have slop dripping off its chin.

"She ain't happy with us," Big Joe said, falling over Boris's shoulder to sob mock tears. "Don't that jest break yore hearts, boys?"

"Aw, let up on her, Joe. Cain't you see she's what she is, and she ain't gonna change?"

Heads pivoted to stare at Frog.

Boris swallowed, his Adam's apple bobbing. "What'd ya mean, 'let up on her'? You goin' soft on us, Frog?"

"No. But you do et like a pig, Boris. You got drippin's on yore face. Wipe 'em off."

Boris took a swipe at his mouth with his shirtsleeve. Big Joe leaned over to swat him. "You don't hafta do what she says!"

Hope looked away. *Where are you, Dan? Please hurry. Please, Lord, give him wisdom and a strong sense of direction.*

The men went back to eating. Big Joe crammed a wad of biscuit into his mouth, talking to Boris at the same time. Crumbs flew in Boris's face and sprayed out on the front of the outlaw's chest.

"Et with some manners, Joe!" hollered Frog.

Big Joe scowled as he whirled to face Frog.

Frog looked down at his plate, refusing to meet Joe's glare. "Don't jaw with yore mouth full—it ain't appetizin'."

The ruffian gestured to Hope with his spoon, slinging beans. "You sidin' with her? She's a troublemaker. Has been from the minute we took her off that stage. Nothin' but trouble. And now, she's gonna be more trouble until we git rid of her, which we gotta do right off. She can identify ever' last one of us, and don't you fergit it, Frog."

"No I can't," Hope said. "I mean, I won't, if that's what you're worried about. If you'll let me go, I'll lose my memory—I won't be able to identity myself, let alone you, I promise."

Big Joe scooped up another bite. "Like I'm gonna believe that."

"I won't," she contended. "And Dan—" Realizing

she'd just given them Grunt's real name, she bit her tongue.

"Dan?" Big Joe's eyes narrowed. "You talkin' about that low-down, connivin', yeller-bellied dog, Grunt?"

"No, I don't know why I said Dan—I meant—"

"Dan, huh? So that's the polecat's name. Well, you kin jest tell *Dan* for me that when he shows up to git you— which I figure he's tryin' his best to do right now—we'll have a little present waitin' for 'im." He patted the Colt revolver at his side.

"He isn't looking for me; he couldn't care less what happens to me. He's happy as a tick at a dog fair that I'm your problem now and not his. I'm nothing but a head-ache, honest. And mean, real mean-spirited."

She prayed Dan didn't feel that way about her, but if they thought for a moment that Dan cared about her welfare, she would endanger him more.

Big Joe scoffed. "Mean? You ain't mean, little missy. I've met women meaner than a scalded cat."

Her temper flared, and she struggled against the ropes binding her wrists. "You untie these ropes and I'll show you mean, Mr. Davidson."

"Ooowee. You scarin' the puddin' right outta me."

"What are we gonna do with her?" Boris grunted. "Her and her highfalutin ways are gettin' on my nerves."

"Gonna git rid of her, and the sooner the better."

"No!" Hope cried.

"Wadda ya mean, no. You ain't talkin', I am. Now pipe down." Big Joe rammed another wad of bread into his mouth.

"Maybe that ain't so smart, Joe." Frog set his bowl aside.

"What're you talkin' about, Frog?" Joe said, talking with his mouth full.

"We're jest wanted for robbery. I don't hold with no killin'."

"Too bad. I'm still not convinced Ferry ain't her pa. Maybe he had that newspaper article planted so's to catch us."

Not my father, Hope mouthed in astonishment. And no ransom money.

Didn't he get it?

The three men tossed their bowls in a pile and swigged down the last of their coffee. Hope watched the appalling exhibition, wondering what would happen to her. She hoped Dan was trying frantically to find her. He'd have seen her scattered parcels and put two and two together. Any moment, he would come bursting into camp and save her.

But what if he didn't? What if he didn't have an inkling who had taken her or in what direction they had ridden? Joe said they had to do away with her and soon.

How soon?

She focused on Frog, who was quiet now. Of the three outlaws, Frog seemed the most—what? Certainly not intelligent, but perhaps the one most open to suggestion. He sat beside the fire, staring into the flames, apparently removing himself from the fray. In an odd way, her heart went out to him. Perhaps it was the innate sympathy one felt for a weaker brother. Had anyone ever told Frog about God and his love? "The rain falls on the just and unjust," Papa used to say. It was hard to convince herself that God loved Joe and Boris and Frog as much as he loved her. But his Word said that he did.

Could it be that simple? If these men knew someone cared about them, really cared about them, would they change?

Warming to the thought, her mind ricocheted in lightning fashion. If these men—Boris, Frog, and Big Joe—were to experience God's saving grace, their lives would change forever. And if their lives changed, it would be because of God's unending love.

What if she told them about God's mercy? She, Hope Kallahan, daughter of Thomas Kallahan, preacher. What harm could it do? They couldn't get any madder at her; they were already furious. She'd not witnessed before; Papa was the preacher in the family, not her. But Papa was dead, and she was here. Poor manners or unpardonable belching wouldn't put off God.

Straightening, Hope squared her shoulders. God loves these numbskulls—she was going to tell them so.

She shrank back. How should she start? She could see Papa with the Bible in his hand, preaching, urging sinners to repent. But she didn't have a calling, and she sure wasn't Papa with his solid convictions and impeccable Scripture knowledge. She made a real mess of things when she tried to quote anything. Why, she was barely an adequate talker. How could she be a witness for God?

Ye have not chosen me, but I have chosen you, that ye should bring forth fruit, and that your fruit should remain. . . .

Oh, Lord! Why me? She pondered the problem.

. . . Whatsoever ye shall ask the Father in my name, he will give to you. These things I command you, that ye love one another. She couldn't believe she was remembering the Scriptures—though she still would be hard-pressed to cite chapter and verse. Drawing a deep breath, she muttered, "Why do you steal?"

The men looked up. Big Joe's eyes tapered into venomous slits. "I told you to pipe down."

Clearing her throat, she continued, willing authority into her voice. "As soon as you tell me why you steal."

" 'Cause we want to."

"Why?"

"Why?"

"Why."

"We steal, Miss Snooty," Boris said, " 'cause . . .

well, 'cause. . . ." He glanced at Joe. "Tell her why we steal, Big Joe."

"We steal 'cause we feel like it," Big Joe said. He elbowed Boris, laughing. "We like to take other folks' things, ain't that right?"

Boris nodded emphatically. "That's right."

Hope noticed Frog wasn't joining in the conversation.

"You take other people's things, live in filthy cabins, wear foul-smelling clothes, eat out of dirty dishes, sleep on the hard ground, forsake the love of family and home because you like it?"

Big Joe nodded. "We like it."

"That's nuts," she said. "Your life could be so different."

The men exchanged glances, then went back to talking among themselves.

"Hey!"

Their eyes shot back to her.

"Did you hear what I said?"

"We heered; we jest ain't interested in anythin' you got to say."

"Don't you want to be different?"

They swapped another set of impatient looks.

"Wadda you mean, different?" Frog finally said. "Like we'd ought to hit banks instead of stages? Different like that?"

"No, nothing like that."

Frog was the only one who took the censure to heart. In a while, he snorted. "What? Workin' for wages, havin' somebody tell us what to do all the time?"

"Quit eggin' her on, Frog," Joe snapped. "She's trying to confuse us with talk about livin' different. Ain't no way we can live different. We are what we are."

"Wrong."

Joe rewarded her with an acid look. "Don't say 'wrong.'"

"But you are wrong. There's a better way to live, and you're not too old, or too mean, or too set in your ways to change. Not even you, Joe."

Frog seemed uncomfortable with the subject. "I agree with Joe. You oughtta stop talking."

"All right. Can I read?"

"Read?" Joe shook his head as if she was trying him beyond his limits. "Yore a nuisance, ya know that? You ain't got nothin' to read."

"I have a Bible. It's in my pocket."

"Good for you. Now shut up." He leaned back, tipping his hat over his eyes.

"OK, I won't read. Can I recite out loud?"

"Recite all you want. Just don't bother me." Boris chuckled, getting up to move around. Frog sat by the fire, whittling on a piece of wood.

"For God so loved the world, that he gave his only begotten Son, that whosoever believeth in him should not perish, but have everlasting life." Hope sighed, proud of herself. All that Bible reading was paying off. "John 3:16."

Big Joe and Boris acted as if they hadn't heard. Frog looked up, catching Hope's eye. "My ma read that to me once."

Hope quelled her fear. The Lord was with her; she could feel it. "Do you understand what it means, Frog?"

He shook his head. "Not really."

"It means that God loved you so much that he allowed his Son, Jesus Christ, to die a most shocking death on a cross. For your sins, and my sins, and Joe's sins, and Boris's sins. Christ was buried and rose on the third day. Before he left this earth, he promised that he would prepare a place in heaven for those who believed in his name, and someday he will return for his children. He wants you to be his child."

A strained silence fell over the camp. Overhead, a full

moon rose higher. A lone coyote called to its mate. The men stood around the fire cradling cups of coffee in their hands.

"He gonna build a bigger fire, give us better blankets, better food?" Joe scoffed.

"He can, if you ask. He's not in the business of catering to our whims, but he has the ability to move a mountain, if he wants to."

"That's the stupidest thing I ever heered. Move a mountain—no one can do that. And why would God's Son die for me? I ain't even met the man." Boris kicked dirt into the fire.

"That I can't say. I certainly wouldn't. I can only tell you, he did die for your sins, and mine. That's the joy of his love. No one asked him to die; he did it because he loved us. And we have no way of saving ourselves but through him."

"That's jest stupid," Joe pronounced. "I'm going ta bed."

Hope looked at Frog, who refused to meet her eyes now. Was she reaching him?

"Guess I'll turn in too," Frog said. He walked past Hope, pausing in front of her. He dropped his voice. "Iffin I was to git that book . . . the Bible. Where would I find that stuff yore yammerin' about?"

"You can have this one."

"Cain't read," he whispered gruffly.

"You can have someone read it to you."

Nodding, he glanced over his shoulder. "You jest keep the Bible for now, and don't go tellin' Joe 'bout this."

"Don't worry." Hope's eyes traced Frog's. "He wouldn't listen if I did."

Later, she lay gazing up at the moon. Was Frog thinking about the plan of salvation? She prayed that God would open the outlaw's eyes and his heart.

Oh, Dan, maybe there is a reason why we've been thrown together. God loves Frog so much he sent someone to tell him so.

Somewhere, Dan was under the same sky, searching for her. She closed her eyes, trying to remember his smell, the way his eyes lit when he smiled. Hot tears burned behind her lids. Would she ever see him again?

"Miss Kallahan?"

Hope wasn't sure she heard her name spoken, but she opened her eyes. Frog was leaning over her. Her heart sprang to her throat.

"What is it?"

Kneeling beside her, he lay a hand across her mouth. "Don't wake the others. I need to talk to you."

She nodded, her eyes making a silent promise.

Untying her hands, he helped her up. She nearly cried out from relief. Flexing her fingers, she tried to revive the circulation.

"Come with me."

He led her away from the fire where the other men's snores clogged the chilly night air.

They sat down on a carpet of moss beneath an oak tree. Moonlight streamed through the branches, illuminating the setting. Frog suddenly got back up and started to pace.

"I want to know what you was talkin' about earlier."

"John 3:16?"

"Yeah," he said. "Was it the truth, or are you jest tryin' to pull our legs?"

"It's the truth. I was talking about the power of Jesus Christ to save us—each of us—from the consequences of our sin."

"He cain't do nothin' 'bout me. I'm too far gone . . . he cain't help me."

"Oh, Frog. I know it sounds like wishful thinking. We've all sinned and fallen short of God's glory. But when we confess our sins and ask for forgiveness, the Lord is swift to pardon us. But we—you and I—have to surrender our life to the Almighty. He'll settle for nothing less."

"Surrender?" Frog shook his head. "I ain't never surrendered to no one."

"Well, it isn't easy," she granted. "To die to our own will is hard. But once we do, the Lord can come into our heart and bless us in such a mighty way we can only fall on our knees and thank him for his unbelievable love."

She smiled, aware that she was talking to herself as well as to Frog. "I struggle with placing my whole trust in the Lord. To trust him with my life, and my thoughts, and my future—most of all my future—is difficult."

Exceptionally hard. She had to work at it every day; but it was getting easier. She still didn't understand why God would choose to place her in the path of Big Joe and his gang, or why she met Dan after she agreed to marry John. Or why she'd gotten so sick, and Dan had been shot and had to surrender his fine, leather-tooled saddle for a mangy old goat. Why Letty wanted to trade that old mean mule for that scruffy old goat that'd eat the clothes off a person's back if they'd let it. She couldn't explain any of those things; she just chalked it up to the fact that God in his infinite wisdom knew what he was doing.

"You see, Frog, we have a choice, a simple choice, actually. We choose to live for Jesus Christ or for Satan. Has anyone ever told you about God's love for you?"

Frog nodded, sheepish now. "Ma tried; it jest never got through my thick noggin."

"God loves you. He loves you more than I can ever make you understand." She pressed Dan's Bible into his hands. "I know you can't read this, but hold it close to your heart and talk to God. He can hear our deepest needs. We don't have to see words to apply them to our hearts. We only have to know that they're there and believe them."

Nodding, Frog said quietly, "Thank you, ma'am. I'm gonna think real hard on this."

"How long has it been since you've seen your papa?"

Tears welled in his eyes. "A long time."

"God's your heavenly Father. Our heavenly Father. He'll listen and understand your problems just as your earthly father would. Even more so. And he'll remember those sins no more. You can't hide from God, Frog. There's nowhere to go; he's with us every moment. Once you've confessed your sins and asked Jesus to come into your heart, no one can ever separate you from his wondrous love."

Frog glanced toward Big Joe, whose snores were lifting the bedroll.

"Nobody?"

"Nobody."

Hope leaned closer. "Nobody."

He looked at her, his eyes dark with need. "It sounds mighty simple."

"It is simple. Living for him is harder, but the Scriptures are there to guide us. We may step away, but he doesn't."

He pressed the Bible to his heart, then squeezed her hand.

"We gotta git back. It'd be real hard on you if Joe was to catch us talkin'."

"Frog?"

"Yes, ma'am?"

"I'll pray for you every night."

"Yes, ma'am—I'm much obliged."

They crept back to camp. Hope held up her wrists, and Frog secured them with the rope. He obviously took pains, making sure the cord wasn't too tight. His touch was gentle.

"Thank ya again, ma'am," he whispered. "I won't let them hurt ya."

"Thank you, Frog. God bless you."

The rain falls on the just and unjust, she thought as she watched him walk away. Her eyes shifted to Big Joe and Boris, where funny-sounding whistles were coming from their gaping mouths. *He also takes care of fools and children.*

How did a man turn to crime and violence when his mama prayed for his salvation every night? She guessed she just might ask God that when she met him. But she hoped that tonight, God might have answered Frog's mama's prayers.

Thank you, Father. We all fall into the category of fools and children, don't we?

Somehow, through his grace, the terror of this long day had turned into a blessing.

"You're right as usual, Papa," she murmured as she huddled beneath a thin blanket to stave off the chill wind. "God is good."

Chapter Fifteen

DARKNESS was closing in as Dan topped a rise, drawing the heavily lathered roan to a halt. In the distance, a tuft of campfire smoke spiraled toward the early evening sky.

Clicking his tongue, he nudged the horse down a steep incline. With the edge of the forest as cover, he rode the fringe of the pines until he picked up a set of new tracks. He urged the horse up a steep bluff, then slowed as the aroma of side pork, beans, and coffee reached him. He studied the terrain.

Up ahead, a line of cedars stretched across the rugged landscape. The thick, prickly growth provided what he needed. Minutes later, he stepped out of the saddle, letting the horse graze as he squatted behind the cover. And waited.

One hour. Two hours. One by one, the men rolled into their blankets for the night. Dan kept his eyes on Hope, who was lying at the edge of the campfire, her wrists bound tightly behind her back. When the camp settled down, Dan began to carefully plan his approach. Then a movement caught his eye. Frog! He was untying Hope's wrists. Leading her away from the camp. If he dared touch her. . . . Dan felt his blood begin to boil.

Frog led Hope to a spot under an oak tree. They seemed to be talking, from what Dan could make out in the moonlight. Frog was pacing. After a while, Frog led Hope back to camp, retied her wrists, and settled down on his bedroll. What had that been about? Relief flooded Dan; Frog hadn't hurt her.

A little longer; wait until the camp is quiet again before you make your approach.

Big Joe's snores overrode the crackling fire as Dan crept toward the sleeping encampment.

Creeping silently around the sleeping forms, he made his way to Hope. Slipping his hand over her mouth, he pulled her upright. Predictably, her eyes popped wide open. When her eyes registered recognition, he removed his hand and cut the rawhide cord binding her wrists.

He pressed his mouth close to her ear. "Move quickly."

Every rustle of clothing, every footfall sounded like a gunshot as they crawled out of the circle of firelight and disappeared into the shadows. When they were in the clear, Hope threw herself into his arms.

"I knew you would come," she whispered, throwing her arms around his neck. "I don't know how you found me, but I prayed that you would."

"You don't think you could get away from me that easily, do you?"

Her hold on him tightened. "I didn't want to get away from you at all."

Dan held her close, smoothing her hair. "Are you all right?"

"I'm fine. They didn't hurt me." She stepped back, grinning. "Frog accepted the Lord—at least I think he has!"

Dan frowned. "Frog?"

"Frog—our Frog. I think that he's accepted Jesus!"

"Our Frog?"

"It's true, Dan. Frog is thinking about things of the Lord. It's nothing short of a miracle. I'm so thankful God brought me here to witness to him. It's been a real blessing."

"Our Frog?" Dan repeated.

"Our Frog. For the first time I know, really know, what Papa meant when he said leading a person to Christ is the most exciting thing in the world."

Dan chuckled, pulling her closer.

"What?"

"You're amazing, you know that? You're the only woman I know who could get herself kidnapped twice and consider it a blessing."

She laughed. "Well, not the kidnapping, but the conversion is, and I want to experience it again. And again, and again. Now what?"

Dan drew a deep breath. "I have to arrest Joe and Frog and Boris, Hope."

Her face fell. "Do you have to arrest Frog?"

"He's part of the gang. I was sent to do a job, and I'm bound by duty to finish it. I haven't been able to find out where the gang gets its information, but the Davidson gang has stolen their last payroll."

She glanced at the sleeping camp. He was right; Frog was a part of the gang, but how she prayed that tonight he had felt the touch of God's hand. "All right . . . I'll help. Tell me what to do."

"You aren't to do anything. It's too dangerous. With

any luck, I'll have them arrested before they know what's happening. Stay here and keep quiet. I can handle this. All right?"

She bit her lower lip. "I—"

Dan finished the thought for her. "Will do as I'm told, Dan. Thank you." Bending down, he kissed her.

She looked up, eyes wide.

"All right?"

Reaching out, she hurriedly drew him back into an embrace.

"All right?" she whispered.

"More than all right." He kissed her once more, lightly, then set her aside. He was about to walk off when she reached out again and latched on to his arm. When he saw the look in her eye he mentally groaned.

"I really want to help."

"No. You'll only be in the way."

"I won't get in the way, I promise. It's only fair that you let me help; I have a stake in seeing Big Joe and Boris behind bars. I wish Frog didn't have to be, but with God's help he'll serve his time and come out a new man." Her eyes plaintively beseeched him. "Please, Dan, let me help."

She smiled, blinking violet-colored eyes at him prettily. "Please?"

"All right, but you're to do what I say, when I say it."

"I promise." She wiggled closer, her eyes bright with excitement. "What's our plan?"

Dan's eyes scanned the sleeping outlaws. "Do you know anything about a gun?"

"Only that you point it and pull the trigger."

"That should work."

"I don't want to shoot anyone. Not even Big Joe, although the thought is tempting."

Dan quickly outlined what he wanted to do, and they crept back into the clearing.

Moving silently, they approached the sleeping men. Big Joe had his back to the fire. Frog lay facing it. Boris angled on his right side, his head burrowed under a matted blanket. Moving on hands and knees, Dan reached out and struck Boris behind his left ear, rendering him unconscious without a sound. Unbuckling the outlaw's holster, Dan pitched the gun to Hope.

Hope remained at the edge of the firelight, gripping the gun in both hands as Dan crept to Big Joe.

"Hey, Davidson."

Big Joe woke with a start, his eyes unfocused. Spotting Dan, he sprang to his feet with a snarl.

Dan pinned the rifle on him. "Guess who. You're under arrest."

Big Joe's gaze swept the campsite. Swallowing, Hope steadied the gun, her eyes locked with the outlaw's.

Joe's eyes switched to an unconscious Boris. On the opposite side of the fire, Frog began to stir.

"Don't anybody move," Dan warned, loud enough for Frog to hear. "Frog, get over here."

Eyes on Hope, Frog got slowly to his feet and moved toward Dan.

Handing Frog a strip of rawhide he'd taken off the saddlebags, Dan motioned to Joe. "Tie his hands, Frog, and do it right."

Frog's eyes flew to Joe's. Joe snarled, "Take him, Frog. I'll back ya up!"

Dan calmly leveled the rifle at Frog. "Tie Joe's hands. It will go easier on you."

Emotions warred on Frog's face. Finally, the outlaw reluctantly wound the rope around Joe's wrists.

"Polecat," the leader hissed. "Turncoat."

"Shut up, Joe."

Dan glanced toward Hope. "Come over here. Easy now."

Hope skirted the fire, staying clear of the two outlaws. When she reached Dan, he handed her a strip of leather.

"Tie Frog's hands."

Nodding, she handed Dan the gun. "I'm sorry," she apologized to Frog a moment later. "I wish I didn't have to do this."

He refused to look at her. "We do what we gotta do."

She secured the knot, then leaned closer to whisper, "You've got a new friend watching over you now. Put your trust in his hands."

"Yes, ma'am. I'm tryin' real hard to do that."

Giving his bound wrists a supportive squeeze, she stepped back to Dan and reclaimed the gun.

Dan quickly secured Boris's hands as the outlaw groaned, regaining consciousness. He set him on his feet. Lining the outlaws in front of the fire, he glanced at Hope. "Good job."

Sinking to the ground, she let the gun fall out of her hand. Burying her face in her hands, she asked in a shaky voice, "What now?"

"Now?" Dan came over to sit down beside her. "We wait for dawn."

As the eastern sky brightened, Dan instructed the three outlaws at gunpoint to mount their waiting horses. Pulling Hope onto his horse behind him, they started back to Muddy Flats.

The strange ensemble rode into town by late afternoon. A storm was brewing; dark clouds scudded overhead, and the wind whipped dust across Main Street.

When Dan marched the three prisoners into the one-room jail, he found the sheriff reared back in his chair, boots propped on the desk, sawing logs.

Leaning close, Dan rapped smartly. "You got company."

Sheriff Ettes's boots thumped to the floor. The portly,

balding man blinked up at them sleepily. "Yes, sir. What can I do for you?"

Dan nodded toward the outlaws. "I need you to keep these men for me until I come back."

The sheriff eyed the scruffy-looking bunch. "The Davidson gang?"

Big Joe smirked. "That's right, Sheriff, the Davidson gang." He stepped closer. "Boo!"

The old man frowned. "Well, well. Big Joe Davidson, not an ornerier polecat around. Someone finally caught up with you, huh?"

Joe's eyes narrowed. "No one caught me, Sheriff. This here is Grunt Lawson. He's tryin' to pull a fast one on ya. Used to ride with us, but all of a sudden, him and his woman decided they wanted more than their fair share, so they're tryin' to pull a slick one on ya, Sheriff."

The sheriff turned to look at Dan. "You don't say?"

"I'm Dan Sullivan, and I work for the government. These men are under arrest. I need you to keep them for me until I deliver Miss Kallahan to Medford."

"He's lyin'. He's Grunt Lawson; been our lookout on the last four robberies."

Dan shot Joe a quelling look. "Davidson, pipe down."

"He's lyin', Sheriff. Don't fall for it."

"Well, this is easy enough to settle." The lawman turned back to Dan. "Let's see your credentials, Son."

Dan's hand went to his pocket. "Right here . . ." He looked up sheepishly. "In my saddlebags."

Hope mentally groaned. And the saddlebags were with the Bennetts.

"Joe Davidson, you stop this lying!" She struck out, smacking Joe in the middle of his chest. The outlaw staggered, fixing her with a sullen look.

The sheriff's gaze swung from the three bound men to Dan. Then to Hope.

"Frog," Hope said. "Tell the sheriff the truth."

Frog opened his mouth to speak, but Big Joe's look silenced him.

Dan frowned. "Now look, Sheriff. I'm—"

"Just hold on," the sheriff interrupted. He turned to assess Hope, his eyes skimming her mangy appearance. "What do you have to say for yourself, young lady?"

"He is Dan Sullivan, Sheriff. He's a government agent sent to infiltrate the Davidson gang and learn how they're able to know what stages to—"

"A government agent?" The sheriff frowned. "In Muddy Flats?"

"In Washington," Dan said.

"Then what are you doin' here?"

"I'm trying to get Miss Kallahan to her fiancé."

The sheriff turned back to give Hope another once-over. His eyes fixed on her stringy hair and filthy dress.

"I'm getting married." Hope smiled lamely.

"And I'm trying to deliver her to her future husband—in Medford," Dan added.

Sheriff Ettes frowned. "Thought you said you were working for the government."

"I am; I'm also trying to get Miss Kallahan to Medford to meet her fiancé!"

Big Joe snickered. "A likely tale. He's makin' a fool of you, Sheriff. We ain't done nothin'. He's jest sore 'cause he thinks we cheated him outta wages."

"Wages, huh?" The lawman stroked his chin.

Boris nodded. "He's lyin', Sheriff. Grunt's a sorehead."

"You big oaf!" Hope reached out to smack Boris; Dan caught her arm.

"This is bunk! I work for the government, and these men are under arrest. I demand that you house them until I can transport them back to Washington on federal charges."

The sheriff's brows lifted. "You demand, huh?"

"That's right. I demand."

Heaving himself to his feet, the sheriff fished a ring of keys off a hook just above the desk.

Dan sent Hope a satisfied glance.

"Put your pistol on the desk," he told Dan. "You're all in jail until I can sort this out."

"Jail!" Hope exclaimed. "You can't—"

"Sheriff—," Dan protested.

"I can, and I am, little lady," the sheriff said emphatically, gesturing toward the cells with his gun. "Now git! All of you."

Dan laid his rifle on the desk, motioning for Hope to do the same with her pistol. She did, scowling at Joe.

Sheriff Ettes herded the three outlaws into one cell and Dan and Hope into the other.

"Look, Sheriff, wire Frank Talsman in the Department of Justice. He'll verify who I am," Dan called as the cell door slammed shut and the lock turned.

"Can't until the river goes down."

"River goes down—what?" Dan winced as a clap of thunder shook the jail.

"It's outta banks—with all this rain we ain't been able to cross it for days."

"Good grief—how long will it take to go down?" Hope said.

"Don't know. Depends how much new rain this storm dumps on us." Another thunderous boom rattled the windowpane. "River's predicted to go down by mornin', but who knows? Could be days. But soon as she lets up, I'll wire Washington."

Sinking onto the cot, Hope stared glumly through the bars. "It won't stop. It'll rain cats and dogs, and we'll have to build an ark to get out of here."

"You folks just make yourself at home," the sheriff said. "I'll have the missus round up some grub. Every last one of you looks as if you could use a square meal."

Dan rattled the bars. "You can't leave Miss Kallahan in here!"

The old man swung the key back over the hook. "Now, Son, I suppose that I can do pretty well what I want. The little lady chose the company she's keepin'. Shouldn't be too much of a strain to endure it awhile longer until we can get this thing straightened out."

The sheriff walked back to his desk and sat down. In a few moments, he was dozing again.

"Well, well. Look at the big government man and his woman now," Big Joe taunted from the other cell. "How do you like them fixin's?"

"Cut it out, Joe!" Frog bowed his head, staring at his boots. "Miss Kallahan don't deserve to be in here with th' likes of us, and you know it."

"Shut your trap." Big Joe started pacing his cell like a caged animal. Boris sat on the floor, his back to the iron barrier.

Frog edged closer to the bars, his eyes on Hope. "It's not right. You don't belong in here. Don't you worry. The sheriff will have you out in no time atall."

"Shut up, Frog," Joe repeated.

Hope sat on the narrow bunk, looking at Dan. "Do you think the sheriff will send a wire?"

"I don't know." Dan sat down beside her. "Hope, I'm sorry."

"It's not your fault. The sheriff's just doing his duty. When he wires your commander, everything will be fine . . ."

Her voice trailed off. "What?"

"Nothing. I just hope Frank's in town."

She shot off the cot. "He might be gone?"

"No—I don't know! He's in and out—I can't recall his saying anything about leaving, but that's been months ago. This job was supposed to take two weeks—three at the most."

"Wish the missus would get here with the grub," Boris complained. "Hope she brings corn bread—I love corn bread."

Frog sank to a bunk, closing his eyes. Big Joe kicked his foot. "What are you doin', Judas?"

"Praying," Frog murmured, refusing to look up.

Dan glanced at Hope and she smiled. "Didn't I tell you he'd changed? It's a miracle."

"Well, we need another one," Dan said softly. "And soon."

She slipped her hand into his. "Thank you for rescuing me," she said softly.

"I should have been with you. It wouldn't have happened a second time—"

"But it did, and I'm all right. We'll be fine. The Lord will deliver us."

Leaning back against the wall, Dan stared at the stained ceiling. "I don't know—I'm beginning to wonder. I'm supposed to be in charge of this, arrest the Davidson gang, and get you safely to Medford. Every day there's a new problem."

"Don't blame yourself. You've only tried to help me."

Pulling her to him, he whispered, "I will get you there, Hope. I give you my word."

Hope smiled, burying her face in his chest. "I'm not worried."

"Try to get some rest," he said, holding her tighter. Streaks of lightning lit the cell, followed by thunderous booms. Rain pelted the sides of the jail.

"The river will be down in the morning, and the sheriff will wire Franklin. We'll be out of here by noon."

"Breakfast," the sheriff called out. Unlocking the cell door, he handed Dan a tray of food. "Eat up! The missus went to a lot of trouble to cook for you."

Joe eyed the food piteously. "Slop."

"Eat it anyway."

Hope was on her feet in a flash. "Is the river down enough to cross it?"

"Don't know; ain't checked yet. Soon as I get you fed, I'll go have a look."

Hope sank back to the cot.

The day dragged by. Afternoon came, and there was still no sign of the sheriff. Dan alternately paced the small cell and kept Hope company. Frog sat on a bunk, praying.

Big Joe complained about the food and the lack of room.

Boris slept.

The sun was an orange glow when Sheriff Ettes finally returned. "Evenin', folks. Trust you've had a fine day?"

Dan straightened from where he leaned against the wall. "Did you contact Washington?"

"Yes, sir, shore did. God's lookin' after you. It's a miracle, but last night's rain didn't interfere with gettin' across the river—"

"Did you reach Franklin?"

"Yep. And you're clear." The sheriff pinned Joe with a stern look. "Now, Big Joe," he began patiently, "you ought not to lie like that. You've caused me a whole heap of trouble."

Big Joe sat down on his cot, a scowl on his face.

The door to Dan and Hope's cell swung open. "Son, you and the little lady are free to go. Sorry about the mix-up, but no self-respectin' federal man would let his credentials out of his possession."

"There's a story behind that, Sheriff." Dan settled his hat on his head and reached for Hope's hand. "I have to deliver Miss Kallahan to Medford. I'll be back in a day."

"Guess you been after these three a long time, huh?"

"A long time."

Frog slipped off his cot. "Can I talk to Miss Kallahan a minute afore she leaves?"

"No you cain't," Big Joe growled.

"Sheriff?" Frog frowned. "It's real important."

Sheriff Ettes glanced at Dan. Dan shrugged.

"Well," the sheriff said, scratching his chin, "I suppose I could let you, but not alone."

"Frog!" Big Joe was on his feet, staring down the other prisoner. "You keep yore mouth shut!"

Frog ignored him. "That's all right, Sheriff. I kin say what I got to say in front of ya."

The sheriff opened the cell and motioned him out.

"What is it you want to say?" Hope asked as they walked to the desk.

"Judas!" Joe yelled. "Yellow-bellied coward!"

The outlaw cleared his throat, hanging his head. "I jest want to say thank you for talkin' to me the other night. I've never felt so free, though I know I'm going to spend the next several years in jail."

Hope smiled. "I'm happy for you. Knowing Jesus Christ is liberating. I'll pray for you every day."

"Well, I need to clear my conscience," he said, lifting his eyes to meet hers.

"About what?"

"You want to know where the money is," Frog said softly, glancing at Joe.

"Turncoat!"

Dan straightened. "The army payrolls? Can you tell me?"

"There's a cave not far from the cabin."

"Frog!" Joe bellowed.

Dan frowned. "Three miles or so, off to the right?"

"Yes."

"Dan, that's where we stayed the first—" Dan stopped Hope.

"The money is buried toward the back. Big Joe and me hid it there."

"We were right on top of it!" Hope exclaimed.

"You were there?" Frog asked.

"The night Dan took me from the cabin. I was sick, and we took refuge in the cave."

They ignored Big Joe's rantings from the other cell.

A roguish smile played about Frog's mouth. "Big Joe don't like it, but I don't care. That's where the money is, almost all of it. Spent a few dollars on grub, but the rest is there."

Dan stuck out his hand. "Thank you."

"Ain't nothin'. Miss Kallahan said I had to turn my sins over to God, and I figure I might as well turn Joe's over too, 'cause there's not much chance he ever will. The good Lord's forgiven me, but I still got things to settle. This is the first one."

"God bless you," Dan murmured.

Tears swelled to the outlaw's eyes. "He has already."

The sheriff shoved his hat to the back of his head. "Well, Frog, guess you're gettin' a little cramped in that cell?"

"It's tighter than Grannie's corset in here!" Big Joe shouted. "Move me to the empty one! Git me away from that dirty, low-down double-crosser!"

"Nope, the empty cell goes to this gentleman." Sheriff winked at Frog. "Liars never win."

Chapter Sixteen

Sheriff Ettes insisted that Hope and Dan stay the night. He rounded up new clothes and arranged for hot baths and two rooms at the hotel.

"Can't meet your new husband looking like that!" the old law officer teased.

Hope stared at her image in the mirror over the washstand. She hardly recognized herself anymore. Gone was the young, naive girl who got on the stage in Michigan. The likeness she saw reflected was a woman's—a woman who had survived adversity and a crisis of faith. She'd changed inside, a good change, a change more to her liking.

Leading Frog to an acceptance of Jesus Christ as his Savior had brought a renewal of her own commitment and a revelation of what she needed to do to deepen her own spirituality. It would require a great deal more Bible study and prayer, but she was ready now. Ready to rely on her own faith, not Papa's.

And somewhere along the way to her spiritual awakening, she'd fallen in love. She sank onto the edge of the bed she'd recently vacated.

Dan Sullivan.

Hope sighed. They'd been through so much together, and she couldn't imagine life without him. They'd overcome fear and misfortune, put up with a temperamental goat, a vile-smelling pig, a hungry cougar, inept outlaws, and a sweet, helpless old woman, managing to laugh in spite of it all.

Oddly enough, the times they'd been drawn together by danger or illness had been the best. Times when there had been no one to depend upon but God and themselves.

Hope smiled. Dan Sullivan was a man to be reckoned with. He'd gone from a dangerous outlaw to a dear friend tenderly protective of her. He'd literally snatched her from the jaws of death, not once but twice. Three times, if she counted this last kidnapping.

Dan. From outlaw to tough undercover government agent. A rugged man with protective instincts, a man who respected her commitment to another man but whose kiss evoked such a myriad of feelings and emotions that it made her head spin.

But their time together was coming to an end. In a few moments she would be on her way to Medford to become wife to John Jacobs. The certainty of it caused an ache in her heart.

A knock on the door roused Hope from her reflections. When she opened the door, she found Dan, freshly shaved and dressed in clean clothes that fit his sturdy frame. Love overflowed in her heart.

"Hungry?"

"Famished," she said, tossing her hairbrush on the bed.

The light touch of his hand in the center of her back was like a brand, his brand, on her heart. She savored every moment of his company as if it were the last, because soon it would be, and she didn't want to waste a single minute. One day, when she was an old woman, she would tell her grandchildren about her great adventure on her way to marry their grandfather, and she would tell them about Dan Sullivan, a man she had deeply and irrevocably loved with all of her heart.

No, she couldn't tell them about Dan, but she would tell them about how important it was to follow the heart in matters of love. But she couldn't follow her heart; she must fulfill a promise, a covenant to marry a man she didn't even know.

When Dan and Hope arrived in the hotel dining room, the other guests looked up in expectation. Judging by the curiosity on their faces, they'd heard about the kidnapping, the rescue, the arrest, and the Davidson gang now securely locked away in Sheriff Ettes's jail.

Hope wasn't inclined to share what had actually happened, and Dan couldn't reveal any facts. Once the gang was transported to Washington, Dan would still have an obligation to fulfill. Big Joe, Frog, and Boris would be held for trial, and Dan would be called to testify, so any inquiries were now passed over with polite apologies.

Hope realized they lingered over breakfast far longer than was fashionable. Neither seemed eager to leave. The accidental touches and the lingering conversation only prolonged the inevitable.

"I should have wired John," Hope said, as Dan saddled their horse. "Let him know I'll be arriving today."

"Ettes tells me that someone will have to take the wire across the river and deliver it to John. By the time he gets it, you'll be there."

"Yes . . . I suppose." She sighed. "What if he doesn't

want me?" She'd never considered that possibility. She brightened. What if after all this trouble to get there, he'd changed his mind? Her hopes rocketed. She would be free to marry anyone she chose!

Dan's hands paused on the cinch. "He's figured out you've run into problems getting there. Maybe he's been in touch with your aunt, sent her a telegram."

She frowned. "Oh, I hope not. Aunt Thalia would be worried sick if she were to learn that I hadn't reached Medford. She must be fretting as it is, wondering why I haven't written."

"You can write her a long letter when you reach Medford and tell her all about your trials and your new husband."

"Yes. She'll enjoy that." Aunt Thalia might enjoy it, but Hope sure didn't relish the prospect.

All the way to Medford, Hope wished that things were different. But she could wish all she wanted, and nothing would change.

Why, oh why, God, did I answer that ad?

Dan would buy that piece of land in Virginia he loved. She liked Virginia—well, she'd never actually been there, but she knew she could love it. She'd love anywhere Dan resided.

They rode in silence, Medford drawing ever closer. Should she be telling Dan the things that were in her heart? It would only make their parting more difficult.

Did he have anything he wanted to tell her?

God, if he does, let him find the courage to speak.

When Dan finally drew the horse to a halt on a small rise, she was so deep in her thoughts she didn't realize the journey was over.

"Why have you stopped?"

"There's the Basin River. Medford's on the other side. It looks as if there's a ferry to take you across."

"Yes, I see it."

Her heart ached. How could she say good-bye to the man she loved so much it hurt? Should she beg him not to leave, throw herself on his mercy?

She'd die. There was no doubt about it; she was going to expire if she had to leave him.

"Ready?" he asked quietly.

"Ready."

He urged the horse down the slope and hailed the boatman. Hope waited as the two men talked, her heart heavy as Dan negotiated their passage.

"He'll take us," Dan said when he returned.

She couldn't look at him. "You don't have to come with me. I can make it on my own now."

"I want to go with you, Hope."

She lifted her head. Their eyes held, unspoken words clouding their gazes.

"I want to speak to John, explain what's happened."

"No, that won't be necessary." She would explain and trust that he understood. If he didn't, then she couldn't marry him. Marriage was built on trust and respect. Anything less was unacceptable.

He helped her off the horse, and Hope, Dan, and the boatman stepped onto the small flatboat a short while later.

"So, you're going to Medford," the boatman said.

"Yes." Hope smiled, trying to get a glimpse of her new home. She spotted a few buildings and a hotel sign. The town looked small.

"Nice place. Nice people."

"So I've heard."

The closer they got to shore, the more anxious she became. She was doing the right thing. She had to believe that if God had brought her this far, he meant for her to be with John. She'd prayed, recommitting the problem into God's hands. She had to accept his answer, though it most certainly wasn't hers.

No, her heart cried. *I love Dan!*

She had to face the truth. She had made her commitment to John and she had to honor it, no matter how strongly she felt about Dan. John would be good to her; God wouldn't throw her to the lions, would he?

The boat bumped into the shore, and Dan reached out to steady her. His touch was confident, unlike her chaotic reservations.

The boatman lent a hand as she disembarked. Dan followed with the horse. They walked several yards to the edge of the road and stood looking at the hill that led into Medford.

"Are you uneasy?"

She glanced up, willing him to stop her from going. "Yes."

"Why? John will understand, Hope."

"I'll . . . I'll explain why I'm so late, and yes, he'll understand. I've decided to tell him everything that's happened. After that, if he still wants me, then . . . I suppose we'll begin to build our life together."

A muscle worked tightly in Dan's jaw. "I don't want it to end this way. Let me go with you."

Yes, yes, her heart cried. *Go with me, never leave me again.* "No, there's no need. You've done so much already."

She tried to memorize everything about him. The way he wore his hat, the way his eyes softened to a rich cinnamon when he looked at her, the way his hair fell in soft waves around his shoulders.

"I'll . . . miss you."

"Miss you, too." She longed to reach out, take his hand and never let it go.

The silence stretched.

Drawing a deep breath, she willed herself not to cry. "I wish I could thank you for everything, but there aren't enough words to express my gratitude." Pausing, she took another breath, swallowing against the tight knot that suddenly crowded her throat. "Truth is, I wish—"

"I know," he said gruffly. "I wish it too."

She blinked back hot tears, biting down hard on her lower lip. "I know I shouldn't say it, but I love you more than I could ever love John Jacobs."

There, she'd said it. The admission that haunted her day and night. She could never love any other man the way she loved Dan.

"Hope—"

"Well . . . I'd best be going. Happiness is only a few feet away." She tried to laugh to lighten the mood, but it didn't come out right.

He nodded. "If you ever need anything . . ."

"Thanks. You too. Anything."

Walk away, Hope. Now, while you still can.

"Well, I'll be going now."

She started off, refusing to look back. Tears rolled down her cheeks, blinding her vision.

Don't let me go, Dan. Please. Don't let me go.

Turning around, she called over her shoulder, "I'm trying hard to grow up, Dan Sullivan! But it's not easy!"

"You're doing a fine job, Hope Kallahan," he called back.

She could feel his eyes on her as she walked up the long hill leading to town.

Medford was just as John had described it. A small, friendly town. Folks smiled as Hope stepped onto the wooden porch and tried to glimpse through the plateglass window the man she was about to marry. A tall, rather ordinary-looking man with a handlebar mustache stood behind the counter, handing a wrapped package to a customer.

John Jacobs, future husband and father of her children.

She waited until the customer left before going inside. A bell over the door sounded as she entered the Mercantile. The store was roomy, well stocked, and smelled of coffee and spices.

John's back was to her. Smiling, he turned from replacing a jar of candies on the shelf.

"Afterno—" His greeting died, his jaw dropping when he recognized her. "Oh . . . oh, my goodness."

Summoning a timid smile, Hope said softly, "Hello, Mr. Jacobs."

"Hope Kallahan?"

"John." She drew a long, suffering breath. "I know I'm late, but I can explain."

"Late?" His eyes darted to the back of the store. "Yes—yes, you are . . . quite late. Uh, I'd given up—"

"I know you must have thought I wasn't coming," she apologized, approaching the counter.

Dear God, let me be able to do this. I trust your will for my life, but this is so very hard.

John backed off as if an apparition was about to confront him.

"I understand your consternation," she said, worried that he might faint. The color had drained from his angular features. "I was so afraid you'd think horrible things of me, but I can explain. You see, I was kidnapped off the coach—"

"Believe me, I . . . I had no way of knowing . . . what with the river up, and I couldn't wire . . ."

"Oh, I know. I wouldn't blame you for thinking that I'd decided not to come, but things got very complicated." She smoothed her skirts, trying not to cry. *Lord, I don't want to do this; I want to be with Dan.* "It was impossible to send a wire—though I thought about it, thought about it a lot, actually. But I couldn't; I was kidnapped three times."

John was apparently having a hard time grasping the explanation. "Three times?"

She nodded. "I know it sounds absurd. You see, I'm not Thomas Ferry's daughter." She edged closer to the counter as he continued to back away. "Luckily, there was this handsome undercover agent who knew I wasn't the senator's daughter, and so in order to rescue me from this horrible gang, he had to kidnap me. Then I got terribly sick, he got shot; then we had to carry his favorite saddle until he just couldn't tote it another mile. Do you know, we swapped that perfectly good saddle—Dan's prized possession—for a goat. Well. That goat ate everything in sight." Rolling her eyes, she continued.

"We walked for days, well, actually it seemed more like weeks, off and on. Oh—did I say we stopped to have breakfast with an old couple, and they were fighting with kin over this stolen pig, and we nearly got shot ourselves—well, Dan did get shot when we tried to escape—but I think I've already said that, haven't I?"

John nodded mutely.

"Well, I had to nurse Dan back to health because he came down with a fever. Just when he got to feeling better and we were on our way to Medford again, we stopped to help an old woman who'd hurt her leg with an ax. She was chopping wood when she shouldn't have been. We intended to leave right away, but we couldn't—Letty was down in bed and couldn't see after the farm, so don't you see, we had to stay on for a few days. By the time we got to Muddy Flats, we were wearing clothes way too big for us—why, we both looked like roosters wearing socks—we were riding that awful old mule, Cinder. Well, the moment we thought we were safe again, who should show up but that horrible Joe Davidson! Lo and behold, he kidnapped me again. Can you believe it?" She circled her ear with a finger, frowning. "Nutty as a squirrel, that one.

"Fortunately, Grunt—who's really Dan, the government agent—rescued me again, bless his heart. And this time he arrested the gang and put them behind bars where they belong. Big Joe, Boris, and Frog are this moment in Muddy Flats awaiting Dan's return. He'll have to transport them back to Washington because they're his prisoners—federal prisoners, you understand. The only good thing about all of this is that Frog made a commitment to Christ, which makes the whole ridiculous episode worthwhile, I guess. And so, here I am. Finally." She pasted on a brave grin. "Ready to get married."

John opened his mouth, but nothing came out.

"I know," she soothed. "It sounds like a dime novel, doesn't it? But I swear—no, I don't swear anymore because the past few weeks have taught me a valuable lesson. I depended on Papa's faith, not mine. I'll not be doing that again, thank you very much. I was too lax with my beliefs—actually I didn't know what I believed until now—but I know I believe in the Lord and his teachings. Did you know I can recite two chapters of Genesis by heart—almost?"

John shook his head lamely.

"Well, I can, and all because of Dan—and the Lord, of course. You know—Grunt?" She smiled lamely. "He's just wonderful . . . but I think I might have said that."

Hope glanced up as a beautiful dark-haired young woman emerged from the back room wiping her hands on her apron. "John, you'll need to put flour on the next order—" She paused, smiling. "Good afternoon."

Hope nodded. "Hello."

The young woman joined John behind the counter. "I don't believe we've met. Of course, I've not met everyone who comes to Medford to shop." Smiling, she extended her hand. "I'm Ginger Jacobs. Veda Fletcher's niece."

Hope's smile gradually faded. "Jacobs?"

"Yes, John's wife." She glanced up at her husband adoringly. "We married a week ago."

"A week ago?"

John's face turned cherry red. He was having trouble meeting Hope's apprehensive gaze.

"Ginger, uh—," John began.

Hope let the words sink in slowly, gloriously.

John was married. John was married? John was married!

Praise God! John was married!

Hope stuck her hand out. "Hope Kallahan. I'm so glad to meet you, Mrs. Jacobs."

Ginger's eyes widened. "Oh, dear—you're Hope?"

"I'm so sorry," John said. "I thought—" He cleared his throat. "Well, after weeks passed, and you hadn't arrived, I assumed—"

"Just what anyone would assume! That I'd changed my mind and wasn't coming. I'm not angry!"

The realization that she was free—free to marry anyone she chose—left her giddy. And the man she wanted to marry most in the world was about to get away.

"It's a long story. I'll write you both a letter and explain it all, soon, but right now I really have something I must do—congratulations! I hope you'll both be very happy."

She whirled, leaving the young couple staring after her as she ran out the door and back down the hill.

Running as if her life depended on it, Hope prayed. *Please, God, don't let Dan be gone. I know I don't deserve your mercy the way I've been acting and thinking, but please, don't take Dan away from me.*

Suddenly, events of the past few weeks became clear to her: She'd been accusing God of deserting her, blaming him for all her troubles, doubting that he loved her, when in fact he was only trying to help her!

When she got sick and Dan nursed her back to health

231

in the cave, God had removed them from Big Joe's path long enough to convince the outlaw they'd gotten away. When Dan got shot, God tucked them safely in another cave where the Bennetts couldn't find them. If it weren't for that old goat they swapped for Dan's beautiful saddle, they couldn't have traded with Letty for the mule—

She came to a skidding halt in the road, thunderstruck by the enormity of the revelation.

If she hadn't been kidnapped, then she would have reached Medford and married John. John would have missed the love of his life, and she, most certainly, would have missed hers.

But best of all, if she hadn't met Frog, she couldn't have told him that God loves him—truly loves him.

Dear God! Can you ever forgive me for being such a dunderhead?

By the time she reached the boat landing, she had a stitch in her side and her hair had come loose from the pins.

Dan was standing beside his horse as she ran toward him.

"Dan!" she shouted.

Dropping the reins, he ran toward her. His boots covered the uneven ground in long, impatient strides. "Hope?"

She raced toward him, her breath coming in painful gasps. It took an eternity to reach him.

Catching her in midstride, he held her tightly, the shelter of his arms firm and strong. "What's wrong? What's happened?"

Hugging his neck, she laughed with pure joy. "Nothing. Absolutely nothing! For the first time in weeks, everything is fine!"

He let her slide to the ground, still holding on to her. "Where's John?"

"With his wife."

"With his—what?"

"John is married."

His eyes anxiously searched hers. "Married? But—"

"I know. It's crazy, but so is everything else that's happened lately! Her name is Ginger, and she's the most beautiful woman I've ever seen. She and John got married last week, and I just know that God's going to shine on their union." She hugged him so tightly he stepped backward, swaying with the force. "Oh, Dan, they look as if they absolutely adore each other."

Dan stiffened. "Wait a minute. Jacobs is married? How could he do that? He's engaged to you."

She laughed. This protective side of him thrilled her. "It's all right. I'll be forever grateful that he did! He thought I wasn't coming—and why wouldn't he?"

"You're not upset?"

"No. Relieved. Ever so much relieved."

Dan took a deep breath, then pulled her back into his arms and held her as if he'd never let her go. "That's good, because I was coming after you."

"You were?" Her heart sang. The Lord was just pouring out blessings! Dan Sullivan was coming after her!

His arms tightened possessively around her waist. "You bet I was. I'm not about to let another man have you, even if you had given your word. I tried—I prayed about it, and God and I came to an understanding. We agreed I had too much time invested in you to let you go. We belong to each other. Until we're old and gray and have fifteen grandchildren."

"Fifteen!"

Picking her up, he threw her up in the air, catching her about the waist, laughing and kissing her. "I was on my way to get you when you came flying back down the hill."

"Rescuing me again?" She grinned down at him.

"No, loving you." The devotion in his eyes overwhelmed her. "If John could make you happy, then maybe you might have made me go away—but I doubt it. I love you, Hope. I have from the first moment I set eyes on you."

"John couldn't make me happy," she said softly.

"No?"

"Not the way you can. You make me happy. I've known that for weeks, and I didn't know how I could ever marry John when I loved you so much." She tilted her head to one side. "Well, I'm a free woman, Mr. Sullivan. Will you marry me?"

Aunt Thalia wouldn't approve of her boldness, but then, what Aunt Thalia didn't know couldn't hurt her.

Dan grinned, his eyes dancing with laughter. "You're asking me to permanently hook up with a woman with your kind of luck?"

She sobered. "I know that you don't want any commitments, but I'll try real hard to make you happy, and I would never break your heart like Katie Morris did. And ordinarily, my luck isn't that bad. It brought us together, didn't it?"

"No," he said softly, tilting her face up to meet his. "God brought us together. Haven't you figured it out yet? It was his plan all along."

She nodded, breathless from his nearness. "I know—I have so much to tell you." Later, she would tell him of her revelation and of how God had been working in her life all the while she'd been yelling at him.

Brushing a tendril of loose hair away from her face, he smiled down at her. "How do you feel about moving to Virginia?"

She nodded solemnly. "I'd feel real good about it. Thank you."

"Then I guess we ought to get married just about as quick as we can find a preacher."

"Muddy Flats!" they chorused.

"Let's hurry before trouble can find us again." Hope hooked her arm into Dan's, and they set off for the ferry.

"Dan?"

"Yes?"

"How far is Virginia from Michigan?"

"A long way. Why?"

She held on to his arm tightly, afraid he might get away. She'd been through too much to get him; she wasn't about to lose him now. "I want to see my sisters, Faith and June. Faith's in Texas, and June will be living in Seattle, but we could all travel to Aunt Thalia's for Christmas. Would that be impossible?"

She longed to show off her handsome government agent and meet Faith's and June's new husbands, share her exciting adventure. Why, Faith and June wouldn't believe what she'd gone through to get her husband!

"My love, we can go anywhere you want." He bent over to kiss her. "A Kallahan Christmas family reunion. I like the idea." When she would have walked on, he caught her back to him, and they tarried in the middle of the road exchanging long kisses.

Three horses galloped out of Medford and blew past them on their way down the hill. Jerking apart, Dan started to yell at the inconsiderate horsemen when Hope quickly slapped a hand over his mouth.

"Mhdidhgy?"

Shaking her head, she pointed to the fleeing riders. The lead horseman had a chicken coop wedged between him and the saddle horn. Feathers flew as they galloped toward town.

"More trouble," they murmured.

Dan and Hope swapped a silent look, then locked hands and bolted off in the opposite direction.

"Is this what our life is going to be like?" Hope puffed as they raced down the hill to the ferry. It didn't matter, but she'd just like to be prepared for disasters on a daily basis.

"I hope not!"

Their feet flew over the ground in record fashion.

Throwing her arms in the air, Hope couldn't contain herself any longer. She shouted and whooped, making a powerful noise. She was going to marry the man she loved! "I love you, Dan Sullivan!"

"I love you, Hope Kallahan!"

The boatman looked up, waving.

And somewhere above, their heavenly Father smiled down and said, "I love you, too."

A Note to Readers

Dear Reader,

I hope you've had as much fun with the Kallahan sisters—Faith, June, and Hope—as I have had writing about them.

When God called me to write Christian romances, I reacted with trepidation. Maybe I felt I wasn't worthy enough to minister through the written word; there are certainly others more qualified. Also, I'm a person who resists change, even though I believe that God will uphold his children wherever he puts them, if only they will follow him. A Scripture verse that means a lot to me is Matthew 8:26, where Jesus calms the storm: "And he saith unto them, Why are ye fearful, O ye of little faith? Then he arose, and rebuked the winds and the sea; and there was a great calm."

I'm happy to say my earlier trepidation quickly vanished, replaced with absolute certainty of God's will. I'm thankful that God heard the desires of my heart. Writing Brides of the West has been an unparalleled blessing for me. What joy I've found in "letting go and letting God" do his work! Today I write with a smile and a song in my heart for my Savior, honoring the Lord Jesus Christ. How blessed can one person be?

I thank you so very much for accepting Brides of the West in such an overwhelming manner. If you haven't read *Faith* or *June* yet, I hope you will put them on your "must read" list.

In his name,
Lori Copeland

About the Author

 Lori Copeland has published more than fifty romance novels and has won numerous awards for her books. Publishing with HeartQuest allows her the freedom to write stories that express her love of God and her personal convictions.

Lori lives with her wonderful husband, Lance, in Springfield, Missouri. She has three incredibly handsome grown sons, three absolutely gorgeous daughters-in-law, and three exceptionally bright grandchildren—but then, she freely admits to being partial when it comes to her family. Lori enjoys reading biographies, attending book discussion groups, participating in morning water-aerobic exercises at the local YMCA, and she is presently trying very hard to learn to play bridge. She loves to travel and is always thrilled to meet her readers.

When asked what one thing Lori would like others to know about her, she readily says, "I'm not perfect, just forgiven by the grace of God." Christianity to Lori means peace, joy, and the knowledge that she has a Friend, a Savior, who never leaves her side. Through her books, she hopes to share this wondrous assurance with others.

Lori welcomes letters written to her in care of Tyndale House Author Relations, P.O. Box 80, Wheaton, IL 60189-0080.

HeartQuest Books by Lori Copeland

Faith—Book 1 in the exciting new series Brides of the West, which follows three sisters as they become mail-order brides. Faith leaves her Michigan home for a husband on a Texas ranch in a lighthearted story that reminds readers of the importance of growing in their faith. Nicholas did not know what to expect from his mail-order bride. What he found in Faith changed his life forever.

June—The second book in Lori Copeland's historical romance series about three sisters who become mail-order brides. June leaves her home in Michigan to become the mail-order bride of a preacher in Washington State. A lighthearted, easy-to-read story that teaches the important theme of God's faithfulness even during times when we don't know what his plan or purposes are.

With This Ring—A quartet of charming stories about four very special weddings. Stories by Lori Copeland, Dianna Crawford, Ginny Aiken, and Catherine Palmer. "Something Old"—How will Anna Marie ever honor her parents' wishes and the traditions of her fiancé's immigrant family without alienating anyone? "Something New"—An arranged marriage awaits Rachel in San Francisco. But her discovery on the voyage from the Old Country threatens to change everything. "Something Borrowed"— Emma's prayers are answered when she inherits a ranch. More than land is at stake, however, when a former bounty hunter disputes her claim. And "Something Blue"—Stranded in a strange land, Astrid dreams of returning to her native Norway. The key to her future lies in her most prized possession. Or does it?

Heartwarming Anthologies from HeartQuest

A Bouquet of Love—An arrangement of four beautiful novellas about friendship and love. Stories by Ginny Aiken, Ranee McCollum, Jeri Odell, and Debra White Smith.

A Victorian Christmas Cottage—Four novellas centering around hearth and home at Christmastime. Stories by Catherine Palmer, Jeri Odell, Debra White Smith, and Peggy Stoks.

A Victorian Christmas Tea—Four novellas about life and love at Christmastime. Stories by Catherine Palmer, Dianna Crawford, Peggy Stoks, and Katherine Chute.

A Victorian Christmas Quilt—A patchwork of four novellas about love and joy at Christmastime. Stories by Catherine Palmer, Ginny Aiken, Peggy Stoks, and Debra White Smith.

Reunited—Four stories about reuniting friends, old memories, and new romance. Includes favorite recipes from the authors. Stories by Judy Baer, Jan Duffy, Jeri Odell, and Peggy Stoks.

With This Ring—A quartet of charming stories about four very special weddings. Stories by Lori Copeland, Dianna Crawford, Ginny Aiken, and Catherine Palmer.